The Editor

VINCENT O'SULLIVAN is a novelist, poet, and biographer and until recently was Professor of English at Victoria University of Wellington. He is the editor of *The Oxford Book of New Zealand Poetry*, *The Oxford Book of New Zealand Short Stories*, *The Selected Letters of Katherine Mansfield*, *Poems of Katherine Mansfield*, and, with Margaret Scott, the five-volume edition of *The Collected Letters of Katherine Mansfield*.

W. W. NORTON & COMPANY, INC.
Also Publishes

THE NORTON ANTHOLOGY OF AFRICAN AMERICAN LITERATURE
edited by Henry Louis Gates Jr. and Nellie Y. McKay et al.

THE NORTON ANTHOLOGY OF AMERICAN LITERATURE
edited by Nina Baym et al.

THE NORTON ANTHOLOGY OF CHILDREN'S LITERATURE
edited by Jack Zipes et al.

THE NORTON ANTHOLOGY OF CONTEMPORARY FICTION
edited by R. V. Cassill and Joyce Carol Oates

THE NORTON ANTHOLOGY OF ENGLISH LITERATURE
edited by M. H. Abrams and Stephen Greenblatt et al.

THE NORTON ANTHOLOGY OF LITERATURE BY WOMEN
edited by Sandra M. Gilbert and Susan Gubar

THE NORTON ANTHOLOGY OF MODERN AND CONTEMPORARY POETRY
edited by Jahan Ramazani, Richard Ellmann, and Robert O'Clair

THE NORTON ANTHOLOGY OF POETRY
edited by Margaret Ferguson, Mary Jo Salter, and Jon Stallworthy

THE NORTON ANTHOLOGY OF SHORT FICTION
edited by R. V. Cassill and Richard Bausch

THE NORTON ANTHOLOGY OF THEORY AND CRITICISM
edited by Vincent B. Leitch et al.

THE NORTON ANTHOLOGY OF WORLD LITERATURE
edited by Sarah Lawall et al.

THE NORTON FACSIMILE OF THE FIRST FOLIO OF SHAKESPEARE
prepared by Charlton Hinman

THE NORTON INTRODUCTION TO LITERATURE
edited by Alison Booth, J. Paul Hunter, and Kelly J. Mays

THE NORTON INTRODUCTION TO THE SHORT NOVEL
edited by Jerome Beaty

THE NORTON READER
edited by Linda H. Peterson and John C. Brereton

THE NORTON SAMPLER
edited by Thomas Cooley

THE NORTON SHAKESPEARE, BASED ON THE OXFORD EDITION
edited by Stephen Greenblatt et al.

For a complete list of Norton Critical Editions, visit
www.wwnorton.com/college/english/nce_home.htm

A NORTON CRITICAL EDITION

KATHERINE MANSFIELD'S SELECTED STORIES

THE TEXTS OF THE STORIES

KATHERINE MANSFIELD: FROM HER LETTERS

CRITICISM

Selected and Edited by

VINCENT O'SULLIVAN

VICTORIA UNIVERSITY OF WELLINGTON

W. W. NORTON & COMPANY

New York • London

W. W. Norton & Company has been independent since its founding in 1923, when William Warder Norton and Mary D. Herter Norton first published lectures delivered at the People's Institute, the adult education division of New York City's Cooper Union. The Nortons soon expanded their program beyond the Institute, publishing books by celebrated academics from America and abroad. By mid-century, the two major pillars of Norton's publishing program—trade books and college texts—were firmly established. In the 1950s, the Norton family transferred control of the company to its employees, and today—with a staff of four hundred and a comparable number of trade, college, and professional titles published each year—W. W. Norton & Company stands as the largest and oldest publishing house owned wholly by its employees.

Printed in the United States of America.
First Edition.

The text of this book is composed in Fairfield Medium
with the display set in Bernhard Modern.
Composition by PennSet, Inc.
Manufacturing by the Maple-Vail Book Group.
Book design by Antonina Krass.
Production manager: Benjamin Reynolds.

Library of Congress Cataloging-in-Publication Data
Mansfield, Katherine, 1888–1923.
[Selections. 2005]
Katherine Mansfield's selected stories : the texts of the stories, Katherine Mansfield—from her letters, criticism / selected and edited by Vincent O'Sullivan.
p. cm. — (A Norton critical edition)
Includes bibliographical references.
ISBN 0–393–92533–1
1. New Zealand—Social life and customs—Fiction. 2. Europe—Social life and customs—Fiction. 3. Mansfield, Katherine, 1888–1923—Criticism and interpretation. 4. Mansfield, Katherine, 1888–1923—Correspondence. 5. Authors, New Zealand—20th century—Correspondence. I. O'Sullivan, Vincent. II. Title. III. Series.

PR9639.3.M258A6 2005
823'.912—dc22

2005051295

W. W. Norton & Company, Inc., 500 Fifth Avenue, New York, N.Y. 10110-0017
www.wwnorton.com

W. W. Norton & Company Ltd., Castle House,
75/76 Wells Street, London W1T 3QT

1 2 3 4 5 6 7 8 9 0

Contents

Katherine Mansfield: From Her Letters

Criticism

Preface

All but the first four of the stories in this selection were written within a period of ten years. Katherine Mansfield developed quickly as a writer, and from 1918 until a few months before her death in February 1923, she wrote with the urgency of a woman who knew the time available to her was limited. She wrote also for the money she needed to treat her tuberculosis, and as she so insisted, what she achieved fell short of what she had hoped. Yet in the two short volumes published toward the end of her life—she would not have counted her earlier collection of German stories in 1911—she brought unique elements of style and perception to modern fiction.

The fact that she was what her English contemporaries regarded as "colonial," and that she wrote only short stories, meant that what she brought to her own art form and to modernism was often regarded as both marginal and minor. There was a handful of fellow writers, like Elizabeth Bowen and Rebecca West, and a small number of academics, who made larger claims for her. They responded at once to her technically original narratives, as they did to her vivid and intense perceptions. There were others, like Frank O'Connor, who felt uncomfortable even as they admired. But it was not until the profound changes in critical methods in the second half of the twentieth century that Mansfield received extended and detailed attention. The combined forces of feminist and postcolonial studies, in particular, have brought more expansive and more probing readings of her work. Her growing inclusion in university and college courses has meant a fresh and widening readership, although her appeal to general readers is such that her books have been continuously in print in the eighty years since her death.

Almost all of Mansfield's stories first appeared in magazines and periodicals, before either she, or after her death her husband, the critic John Middleton Murry, arranged them in collections. Two of her longer stories—"Je Ne Parle Pas Français" and "Prelude"—came out first in small editions from the private presses of friends, before they were included in *Bliss* in 1920. Other stories she revised, usually only in small matters of wording or punctuation, in that earlier volume, then again in *The Garden Party* in 1922. Some that she preferred not to publish, and ones that were left unfinished, her husband brought together soon after her death.

The texts in this Norton Critical Edition reproduce the versions that Mansfield herself revised or selected. "An Indiscreet Journey," a story that for personal reasons she chose not to publish, and a few others, written shortly before her death, or early in her career, are taken from the posthumous collections. Any small variances from these follow the emendations of Antony Alpers's splendidly edited *The Stories of Katherine Mansfield* (Oxford University Press, 1984). The Oxford volume, together with his *Life of Katherine Mansfield* (Penguin Books, 1982), confirms Alpers's preeminence among Mansfield scholars.

The extracts included from Mansfield's letters are those in which she wrote—as she did only rarely—about the craft of writing, or about how she herself considered her work. The critical material reprinted suggests something of the changing emphases in how one reads this author who, as was recently observed in the *New York Times Book Review*, now seems "the most emblematic woman writer of her time."[1]

I am pleased to say how indebted I am to Helen O'Sullivan, how grateful to Christiane Mortelier and Angela Smith, and how obliged to the Stout Research Centre at Victoria University, Wellington.

1. Patricia Hampl, "Whistling in the Dark," review of *The Notebooks of Katherine Mansfield*, ed. Margaret Scott, *New York Times Book Review*, 16 March 2003, p. 12.

The Texts of
KATHERINE MANSFIELD'S SELECTED STORIES

The Tiredness of Rosabel (1908)†

At the corner of Oxford Circus Rosabel bought a bunch of violets, and that was practically the reason why she had so little tea—for a scone and a boiled egg and a cup of cocoa at Lyons[1] are not ample sufficiency after a hard day's work in a millinery establishment. As she swung on to the step of the Atlas 'bus,[2] grabbed her skirt with one hand, and clung to the railing with the other, Rosabel thought she would have sacrificed her soul for a good dinner—roast duck and green peas, chestnut stuffing, pudding with brandy sauce—something hot and strong and filling. She sat down next to a girl very much her own age who was reading 'Anna Lombard'[3] in a cheap, paper-covered edition, and the rain had tear-spattered the pages. Rosabel looked out of the windows; the street was blurred and misty, but light striking on the panes turned their dullness to opal and silver and the jeweller's shops, seen through this, were fairy palaces. Her feet were horribly wet and she knew the bottom of her skirt and petticoat would be coated with black, greasy mud. There was a sickening smell of warm humanity—it seemed to be oozing out of everybody in the 'bus—and everybody had the same expression, sitting so still, staring in front of them. How many times had she read these advertisements—'Sapolio Saves Time, Saves Labor'—'Heinz's Tomato Sauce'—and the inane, annoying dialogue between doctor and judge concerning the superlative merits of 'Lamplough's Pyretic Saline'.[4] She glanced at the book which the girl read so earnestly, mouthing the words in a way that Rosabel detested, licking her first finger and thumb each time that she turned the page. She could not see very clearly; it was something about a hot, voluptuous night, a band playing, and a girl with lovely, white shoulders. Oh, heavens! Rosabel stirred suddenly and unfastened the two top buttons of her coat—she felt almost stifled. Through her half-closed eyes the whole row of people on the opposite seat seemed to resolve into one fatuous, staring face—and this was her corner. She stumbled a little on her way out and lurched against the girl next her. 'I beg your pardon,' said Rosabel, but the girl did not even look up. Rosabel saw that she was smiling as she read.

† First published after Mansfield's death, in *Something Childish and Other Stories* (1924). The manuscript is dated before Mansfield's return to London in July 1908, although Antony Alpers, in *The Stories of Katherine Mansfield* (Oxford University Press, 1984), p. 546, notes difficulties with this dating.

1. Lyons Corner Houses: a chain of modestly priced tearooms. Oxford Circus: a circular junction of roads in central London.
2. A British make of bus.
3. *Anna Lombard* (1901), a novel by Victoria Cross.
4. A salt solution for reducing fever. Sapolio: a domestic cleaner.

Westbourne Grove[5] looked as she had always imagined Venice to look at night, mysterious, dark; even the hansoms were like gondolas dodging up and down, and the lights trailing luridly—tongues of flame licking the wet street—magic fish swimming in the Grand Canal. She was more than glad to reach Richmond Road, but from the corner of the street until she came to No. 26 she thought of those four flights of stairs. Oh, why four flights! It was really criminal to expect people to live so high up. Every house ought to have a lift, something simple and inexpensive, or else an electric staircase like the one at Earl's Court[6]—but four flights! When she stood in the hall and saw the first flight ahead of her and the stuffed albatross head on the landing, glimmering ghostlike in the light of the little gas jet, she almost cried. Well, they had to be faced; it was very like bicycling up a steep hill, but there was not the satisfaction of flying down the other side. . . .

Her own room at last! She closed the door, lit the gas, took off her hat and coat, skirt, blouse; unhooked her old flannel dressing gown from behind the door, pulled it on, then unlaced her boots—on consideration her stockings were not wet enough to change. She went over to the washstand; the jug had not been filled again today, there was just enough water to soak the sponge, and the enamel was coming off the basin—that was the second time she had scratched her chin.

It was just seven o'clock. If she pulled the blind up and put out the gas, it was much more restful—Rosabel did not want to read. So she knelt down on the floor, pillowing her arms on the windowsill . . . just one little sheet of glass between her and the great, wet world outside!

She began to think of all that had happened during the day. Would she ever forget that awful woman in the gray mackintosh[7] who had wanted a trimmed motor cap—'something purple with something rosy each side'—or the girl who had tried on every hat in the shop and then said she would 'call in to-morrow and decide definitely'. Rosabel could not help smiling; the excuse was worn so thin.

But there had been one other—a girl with beautiful red hair and a white skin and eyes the color of that green ribbon shot with gold they had got from Paris last week. Rosabel had seen her electric brougham at the door; a man had come in with her, quite a young man, and so well dressed.

5. A residential area near Paddington Station where Mansfield stayed in a student hostel on her return to London in August 1908. The hostel overlooked the Grand Union Canal, in an area known as "Little Venice."
6. Another central London area.
7. A full-length waterproof coat.

'What is it exactly that I want, Harry?' she said, as Rosabel took the pins out of her hat, untied her veil, and gave her a hand mirror.

'You must have a black hat,' he answered, 'a black hat with a feather that goes right round it and then round your neck and ties in a bow under your chin, and the ends tuck into your belt—a decent-sized feather.'

The girl glanced at Rosabel laughingly: 'Have you any hats like that?'

They had been very hard to please; Harry would demand the impossible, and Rosabel was almost in despair. Then she remembered the big, untouched box upstairs.

'Oh, one moment madam,' she had said; 'I think perhaps I can show you something that will please you better.' She had run up, breathlessly, cut the cords, scattered the tissue paper, and yes, there was the very hat—rather large, soft, with a great, curled feather, and a black velvet rose, nothing else. They had been charmed. The girl had put it on and then handed it to Rosabel.

'Let me see how it looks on you,' she said, frowning a little, very serious indeed.

Rosabel turned to the mirror and placed it on her brown hair, then faced them.

'Oh, Harry, isn't it adorable!' the girl cried. 'I must have that!' She smiled again at Rosabel. 'It suits you, beautifully.'

A sudden ridiculous feeling of anger had seized Rosabel. She longed to throw the lovely, perishable thing in the girl's face, and bent over the hat, flushing.

'It's exquisitely finished off inside, madam,' she said. The girl swept out to her brougham, and left Harry to pay and bring the box with him.

'I shall go straight home and put it on before I come out to lunch with you,' Rosabel heard her say.

The man leant over her as she made out the bill; then, as he counted the money into her hand—'Ever been painted?' he said. 'No,' said Rosabel shortly, realizing swiftly the change in his voice, the slight tinge of insolence, of familiarity.

'Oh, well, you ought to be,' said Harry. 'You've got such a damned pretty little figure.'

Rosabel did not pay the slightest attention.

How handsome he had been! She had thought of no one else all day; his face fascinated her; she could see clearly his fine, straight eyebrows, and his hair grew back from his forehead with just the slightest suspicion of crisp curl; his laughing, disdainful mouth. She saw again his slim hands counting the money into hers. . . . Rosabel suddenly pushed the hair back from her face; her forehead was hot . . . if those slim hands could rest one moment! The luck of that girl!

Suppose they changed places. Rosabel would drive home with him. Of course they were in love with each other, but not engaged—very nearly—and she would say: 'I won't be one moment.' He would wait in the brougham while her maid took the hat box up the stairs, following Rosabel. Then the great white and pink bedroom with roses everywhere in dull silver vases. She would sit down before the mirror, and the little French maid would fasten her hat and find her a thin, fine veil and another pair of white suède gloves—a button had come off the ones she had worn that morning.

She had scented her furs and gloves and handkerchief, taken a big muff and run downstairs. The butler opened the door, Harry was waiting, they drove away together. . . . *That* was life, thought Rosabel! On the way to the Carlton they stopped at Gerard's.[8] Harry bought her great sprays of Parma violets, filled her hands with them.

'Oh, they are sweet,' she said, holding them against her face.

'It is as you always should be,' said Harry, 'with your hands full of violets.'

(Rosabel realized that her knees were getting stiff; she sat down on the floor and leant her head against the wall.) Oh, that lunch! The table, covered with flowers; a band hidden behind a grove of palms playing music that fired her blood like wine; the soup, and oysters, and pigeons, and creamed potatoes, and champagne, of course, and afterwards coffee and cigarettes. She would lean over the table fingering her glass with one hand, talking with that charming gaiety which Harry so appreciated. Afterwards a matinée, something that gripped them both, and then tea at the 'Cottage'.

'Sugar? Milk? Cream?' The little homely questions seemed to suggest a joyous intimacy. And then home again in the dusk, and the scent of the Parma violets seemed to drench the air with their sweetness.

'I'll call for you at nine,' he said as he left her.

The fire had been lighted in her boudoir, the curtains drawn; there were a great pile of letters waiting her—invitations for the Opera, dinners, balls, a week-end on the river, a motor tour—she glanced through them listlessly as she went upstairs to dress. A fire in her bedroom too, and her beautiful, shining dress spread on the bed—white tulle over silver, silver shoes, silver scarf, a little silver fan. Rosabel knew that she was the most famous woman at the ball that night; men paid her homage, a foreign prince desired to be

8. An expensive restaurant. The Carlton: a fashionable hotel in London.

presented to this English wonder. Yes, it was a voluptuous night, a band playing, and *her* lovely white shoulders. . . .

But she became very tired. Harry took her home, and came in with her for just one moment. The fire was out in the drawing room but the sleepy maid waited for her in her boudoir. She took off her cloak, dismissed the servant, and went over to the fireplace, and stood peeling off her gloves; the firelight shone on her hair. Harry came across the room and caught her in his arms: 'Rosabel, Rosabel, Rosabel!' . . . Oh the haven of those arms, and she was very tired!

(The real Rosabel, the girl crouched on the floor in the dark, laughed aloud, and put her hand up to her hot mouth.)

Of course they rode in the park next morning, the engagement had been announced in the Court Circular,[9] all the world knew, all the world was shaking hands with her. . . .

They were married shortly afterward at St George's, Hanover Square,[1] and motored down to Harry's old ancestral home for the honeymoon; the peasants in the village curtseyed to them as they passed; under the folds of the rug he pressed her hands convulsively. And that night she wore again her white and silver frock. She was tired after the journey and went upstairs to bed—quite early. . . .

The real Rosabel got up from the floor and undressed slowly, folding her clothes over the back of a chair. She slipped over her head her coarse, calico nightdress, and took the pins out of her hair—the soft, brown flood of it fell round her, warmly. Then she blew out the candle and groped her way into bed, pulling the blankets and grimy 'honeycomb'[2] quilt closely round her neck, cuddling down in the darkness. . . .

So she slept and dreamed, and smiled in her sleep, and once threw out her arm to feel for something which was not there, dreaming still.

And the night passed. Presently the cold fingers of dawn closed over her uncovered hand; gray light flooded the dull room. Rosabel shivered, drew a little gasping breath, sat up. And because her heritage was that tragic optimism which is all too often the only inheritance of Youth, still half asleep, she smiled, with a little nervous tremor round her mouth.

9. A daily report on the activities of the royal family, with details of diplomatic appointments and fashionable marriages and engagements, published in the *Times*.
1. A church known for celebrity weddings.
2. A quilt made up of hexagonal sections reminiscent of a honeycomb pattern.

At "Lehmann's" (1910)†

Certainly Sabina did not find life slow. She was on the trot from early morning until late at night. At five o'clock she tumbled out of bed, buttoned on her clothes, wearing a long-sleeved alpaca pinafore over her black frock, and groped her way downstairs into the kitchen.

Anna, the cook, had grown so fat during the summer that she adored her bed because she did not have to wear her corsets there, but could spread as much as she liked, roll about under the great mattress, calling upon Jesus and Holy Mary and Blessed Anthony[1] himself that her life was not fit for a pig in a cellar.

Sabina was new to her work. Pink colour still flew in her cheeks; there was a little dimple on the left side of her mouth that even when she was most serious, most absorbed, popped out and gave her away. And Anna blessed that dimple. It meant an extra half-hour in bed for her; it made Sabina light the fire, turn out the kitchen and wash endless cups and saucers that had been left over from the evening before. Hans, the scullery boy, did not come until seven. He was the son of the butcher—a mean, undersized child very much like one of his father's sausages, Sabina thought. His red face was covered with pimples, and his nails indescribably filthy. When Herr Lehmann himself told Hans to get a hairpin and clean them he said they were stained from birth because his mother had always got so inky doing the accounts—and Sabina believed him and pitied him.

Winter had come very early to Mindelbau.[2] By the end of October the streets were banked waist-high with snow, and the greater number of the 'Cure Guests', sick unto death of cold water and herbs, had departed in nothing approaching peace. So the large salon was shut at Lehmann's and the breakfast-room was all the accommodation the café afforded. Here the floor had to be washed over, the tables rubbed, coffee-cups set out, each with its little china platter of sugar, and newspapers and magazines hung on their hooks along the walls before Herr Lehmann appeared at seven-thirty and opened business.

† First published in the *New Age*, 7 July 1910, and collected in *In a German Pension* (1911). Like most of the satirical stories in that collection, it drew on Mansfield's time in Worishofen, Bavaria, Germany, for most of 1909. She would not allow the German stories to be reprinted when pressure was put on her to do so during World War One and again after the success of her collection *Bliss*, at the end of 1920. As she wrote to John Middleton Murry, 4 February 1920, "I cannot have 'The German Pension' reprinted under any circumstances. It is far too *immature*, and I don't even acknowledge it today. I mean I don't 'hold' by it. I can't go foisting that kind of stuff on the public. *It's not good enough* * * * It's positively *juvenile*, and besides that, it's not what I mean; it's a lie." *The Collected Letters of Katherine Mansfield*, vol. 3, 1993, p. 206.

1. St. Anthony of Padua, an Italian saint much implored by those in ill health.
2. A village close to Worishofen, Bavaria, an area famous for the various forms of "water-cure" in its baths.

As a rule his wife served in the shop leading into the café, but she had chosen the quiet season to have a baby, and, a big woman at the best of times, she had grown so enormous in the process that her husband told her she looked unappetising, and had better remain upstairs and sew.

Sabina took on the extra work without any thought of extra pay. She loved to stand behind the counter, cutting up slices of Anna's marvellous chocolate-spotted confections, or doing up packets of sugar almonds in pink and blue striped bags.

'You'll get varicose veins, like me,' said Anna. 'That's what the Frau's got, too. No wonder the baby doesn't come! All her swelling's got into her legs.' And Hans was immensely interested.

During the morning business was comparatively slack. Sabina answered the shop bell, attended to a few customers who drank a liqueur to warm their stomachs before the midday meal, and ran upstairs now and again to ask the Frau if she wanted anything. But in the afternoon six or seven choice spirits played cards, and everybody who was anybody drank tea or coffee.

'Sabina . . . Sabina. . . .'

She flew from one table to the other, counting out handfuls of small change, giving orders to Anna through the 'slide', helping the men with their heavy coats, always with that magical child air about her, that delightful sense of perpetually attending a party.

'How is the Frau Lehmann?' the women would whisper.

'She feels rather low, but as well as can be expected,' Sabina would answer, nodding confidentially.

Frau Lehmann's bad time was approaching. Anna and her friends referred to it as her 'journey to Rome', and Sabina longed to ask questions, yet, being ashamed of her ignorance, was silent, trying to puzzle it out for herself. She knew practically nothing except that the Frau had a baby inside her, which had to come out—very painful indeed. One could not have one without a husband—that also she realised. But what had the man got to do with it? So she wondered as she sat mending tea towels in the evening, head bent over her work, light shining on her brown curls. Birth—what was it? wondered Sabina. Death—such a simple thing. She had a little picture of her dead grandmother dressed in a black silk frock, tired hands clasping the crucifix that dragged between her flattened breasts, mouth curiously tight, yet almost secretly smiling. But the grandmother had been born once—that was the important fact.

As she sat there one evening, thinking, the Young Man entered the café, and called for a glass of port wine. Sabina rose slowly. The long day and the hot room made her feel a little languid, but as she poured out the wine she felt the Young Man's eyes fixed on her, looked down at him and dimpled.

'It's cold out,' she said, corking the bottle.

The Young Man ran his hands through his snow-powdered hair and laughed.

'I wouldn't call it exactly tropical,' he said. 'But you're very snug in here—look as though you've been asleep.'

Very languid felt Sabina in the hot room, and the Young Man's voice was strong and deep. She thought she had never seen anybody who looked so strong—as though he could take up the table in one hand—and his restless gaze wandering over her face and figure gave her a curious thrill deep in her body, half pleasure, half pain. . . . She wanted to stand there, close beside him, while he drank his wine. A little silence followed. Then he took a book out of his pocket, and Sabina went back to her sewing. Sitting there in the corner, she listened to the sound of the leaves being turned and the loud ticking of the clock that hung over the gilt mirror. She wanted to look at him again—there was a something about him, in his deep voice, even in the way his clothes fitted. From the room above she heard the heavy, dragging sound of Frau Lehmann's footsteps, and again the old thoughts worried Sabina. If she herself should one day look like that—feel like that! Yet it would be very sweet to have a little baby to dress and jump up and down.

'Fräulein—what's your name—what are you smiling at?' called the Young Man.

She blushed and looked up, hands quiet in her lap, looked across the empty tables and shook her head.

'Come here, and I'll show you a picture,' he commanded.

She went and stood beside him. He opened the book, and Sabina saw a coloured sketch of a naked girl sitting on the edge of a great, crumpled bed, a man's opera hat on the back of her head.

He put his hand over the body, leaving only the face exposed, then scrutinised Sabina closely.

'Well?'

'What do you mean?' she asked, knowing perfectly well.

'Why, it might be your own photograph—the face, I mean—that's as far as I can judge.'

'But the hair's done differently,' said Sabina, laughing. She threw back her head, and the laughter bubbled in her round, white throat.

'It's a rather nice picture, don't you think?' he asked. But she was looking at a curious ring he wore on the hand that covered the girl's body, and only nodded.

'Ever seen anything like it before?'

'Oh, there's plenty of those funny ones in the illustrated papers.'

'How would you like to have your picture taken that way?'

'Me? I'd never let anybody see it. Besides, I haven't got a hat like that!'

'That's easily remedied.'

Again a little silence, broken by Anna throwing up the slide.

Sabina ran into the kitchen.

'Here, take this milk and egg up to the Frau,' said Anna. 'Who've you got in there?'

'Got such a funny man! I think he's a little gone here,' tapping her forehead.

Upstairs in the ugly room the Frau sat sewing, a black shawl round her shoulders, her feet encased in red woollen slippers. The girl put the milk on a table by her, then stood, polishing a spoon on her apron.

'Nothing else?'

'Na,' said the Frau, heaving up in her chair. 'Where's my man?'

'He's playing cards over at Luitpold's. Do you want him?'

'Dear heaven, leave him alone. I'm nothing. I don't matter. . . . And the whole day waiting here.'

Her hand shook as she wiped the rim of the glass with her fat finger.

'Shall I help you to bed?'

'You go downstairs, leave me alone. Tell Anna not to let Hans grub the sugar—give him one on the ear.'

'Ugly—ugly—ugly,' muttered Sabina returning to the café where the Young Man stood coat-buttoned, ready for departure.

'I'll come again to-morrow,' said he. 'Don't twist your hair back so tightly; it will lose all its curl.'

'Well, you are a funny one,' she said. 'Good-night.'

By the time Sabina was ready for bed Anna was snoring. She brushed out her long hair and gathered it in her hands. . . . Perhaps it would be a pity if it lost all its curl. Then she looked down at her straight chemise, and drawing it off, sat down on the side of the bed.

'I wish,' she whispered, smiling sleepily, 'there was a great big looking-glass in this room.'

Lying down in the darkness, she hugged her little body.

'I wouldn't be the Frau for one hundred marks—not for a thousand marks. To look like that.'

And, half-dreaming, she imagined herself heaving up in her chair with the port wine bottle in her hand as the Young Man entered the café.

Cold and dark the next morning. Sabina woke, tired, feeling as though something heavy had been pressing under her heart all night. There was a sound of footsteps shuffling along the passage. Herr Lehmann! She must have overslept herself. Yes, he was rattling the door-handle.

'One moment, one moment,' she called, dragging on her stockings.

'Bina, tell Anna to go to the Frau—but quickly. I must ride for the nurse.'

'Yes, yes!' she cried. 'Has it come?'

But he had gone, and she ran over to Anna and shook her by the shoulder.

'The Frau—the baby—Herr Lehmann for the nurse,' she stuttered.

'Name of God!' said Anna, flinging herself out of bed.

No complaints to-day. Importance—enthusiasm in Anna's whole bearing.

'You run downstairs and light the oven. Put on a pan of water'—speaking to an imaginary sufferer as she fastened her blouse—'Yes, yes, I know—we must be worse before we are better—I'm coming—patience.'

It was dark all that day. Lights were turned on immediately the café opened, and business was very brisk. Anna, turned out of the Frau's room by the nurse, refused to work, and sat in a corner nursing herself, listening to sounds overhead. Hans was more sympathetic than Sabina. He also forsook work, and stood by the window, picking his nose.

'But why must I do everything?' said Sabina, washing glasses. 'I can't help the Frau; she oughtn't to take such a time about it.'

'Listen,' said Anna, 'they've moved her into the back bedroom above here, so as not to disturb the people. That was a groan—that one!'

'Two small beers,' shouted Herr Lehmann through the slide.

'One moment, one moment.'

At eight o'clock the café was deserted. Sabina sat down in the corner without her sewing. Nothing seemed to have happened to the Frau. A doctor had come—that was all.

'Ach,' said Sabina. 'I think no more of it. I listen no more. Ach, I would like to go away—I hate this talk. I will not hear it. No, it is too much.' She leaned both elbows on the table—cupped her face in her hands and pouted.

But the outer door suddenly opening, she sprang to her feet and laughed. It was the Young Man again. He ordered more port, and brought no book this time.

'Don't go and sit miles away,' he grumbled. 'I want to be amused. And here, take my coat. Can't you dry it somewhere?—snowing again.'

'There's a warm place—the ladies' cloak-room,' she said. 'I'll take it in there—just by the kitchen.'

She felt better, and quite happy again.

'I'll come with you,' he said. 'I'll see where you put it.'

And that did not seem at all extraordinary. She laughed and beckoned to him.

'In here,' she cried. 'Feel how warm. I'll put more wood on that oven. It doesn't matter, they're all busy upstairs.'

She knelt down on the floor, and thrust the wood into the oven, laughing at her own wicked extravagance.

The Frau was forgotten, the stupid day was forgotten. Here was someone beside her laughing, too. They were together in the little warm room stealing Herr Lehmann's wood. It seemed the most exciting adventure in the world. She wanted to go on laughing—or burst out crying—or—or—catch hold of the Young Man.

'What a fire,' she shrieked, stretching out her hands.

'Here's a hand; pull up,' said the Young Man. 'There, now, you'll catch it to-morrow.'

They stood opposite to each other, hands still clinging. And again that strange tremor thrilled Sabina.

'Look here,' he said roughly, 'are you a child, or are you playing at being one?'

'I—I—'

Laughter ceased. She looked up at him once, then down at the floor, and began breathing like a frightened little animal.

He pulled her closer still and kissed her mouth. 'Na, what are you doing—what are you doing?' she whispered.

He let go her hands, he placed his on her breasts, and the room seemed to swim round Sabina. Suddenly, from the room above, a frightful, tearing shriek.

She wrenched herself away, tightened herself, drew herself up.

'Who did that—who made that noise?'

In the silence the thin wailing of a baby.

'Achk!' shrieked Sabina, rushing from the room.

Frau Brechenmacher Attends a Wedding (1910)†

Getting ready was a terrible business. After supper Frau Brechenmacher packed four of the five babies to bed, allowing Rosa to stay with her and help to polish the buttons of Herr Brechenmacher's uniform. Then she ran over his best shirt with a hot iron, polished his boots, and put a stitch or two into his black satin necktie.

'Rosa,' she said, 'fetch my dress and hang it in front of the stove to get the creases out. Now, mind, you must look after the children and not sit up later than half-past eight, and not touch the lamp—you know what will happen if you do.'

'Yes, mamma,' said Rosa, who was nine and felt old enough to

† First published in the *New Age*, 21 July 1910, then collected in *In a German Pension* (1911).

manage a thousand lamps. 'But let me stay up—the "Bub" may wake and want some milk.'

'Half-past eight!' said the Frau. 'I'll make the father tell you, too.'

Rosa drew down both corners of her mouth.

'But . . . but . . .'

'Here comes the father. You go into the bedroom and fetch my blue silk handkerchief. You can wear my black shawl while I'm out—there now!'

Rosa dragged it off her mother's shoulders and wound it carefully round her own, tying the two ends in a knot at the back. After all, she reflected, if she had to go to bed at half-past eight she would keep the shawl on. Which resolution comforted her absolutely.

'Now, then, where are my clothes?' cried Herr Brechenmacher, hanging his empty letter-bag behind the door and stamping the snow out of his boots. 'Nothing ready, of course, and everybody at the wedding by this time. I heard the music as I passed. What are you doing? You're not dressed. You can't go like that.'

'Here they are—all ready for you on the table, and some warm water in the tin basin. Dip your head in. Rosa, give your father the towel. Everything ready except the trousers. I haven't had time to shorten them. You must tuck the ends into your boots until we get there.'

'Nu,' said the Herr, 'there isn't room to turn. I want the light. You go and dress in the passage.'

Dressing in the dark was nothing to Frau Brechenmacher. She hooked her skirt and bodice, fastened her handkerchief round her neck with a beautiful brooch that had four medals to the Virgin dangling from it, and then drew on her cloak and hood.

'Here, come and fasten this buckle,' called Herr Brechenmacher. He stood in the kitchen puffing himself out, the buttons on his blue uniform shining with an enthusiasm which nothing but official buttons could possibly possess. 'How do I look?'

'Wonderful,' replied the little Frau, straining at the waist buckle and giving him a little pull here, a little tug there. 'Rosa, come and look at your father.'

Herr Brechenmacher strode up and down the kitchen, was helped on with his coat, then waited while the Frau lighted the lantern.

'Now, then—finished at last! Come along.'

'The lamp, Rosa,' warned the Frau, slamming the front door behind them.

Snow had not fallen all day; the frozen ground was slippery as an ice-pond. She had not been out of the house for weeks past, and the day had so flurried her that she felt muddled and stupid—felt that Rosa had pushed her out of the house and her man was running away from her.

'Wait, wait!' she cried.

'No. I'll get my feet damp—you hurry.'

It was easier when they came into the village. There were fences to cling to, and leading from the railway station to the Gasthaus[1] a little path of cinders had been strewn for the benefit of the wedding guests.

The Gasthaus was very festive. Lights shone out from every window, wreaths of fir twigs hung from the ledges. Branches decorated the front doors, which swung open, and in the hall the landlord voiced his superiority by bullying the waitresses, who ran about continually with glasses of beer, trays of cups and saucers, and bottles of wine.

'Up the stairs—up the stairs!' boomed the landlord. 'Leave your coats on the landing.'

Herr Brechenmacher, completely overawed by this grand manner, so far forgot his rights as a husband as to beg his wife's pardon for jostling her against the banisters in his efforts to get ahead of everybody else.

Herr Brechenmacher's colleagues greeted him with acclamation as he entered the door of the Festsaal,[2] and the Frau straightened her brooch and folded her hands, assuming the air of dignity becoming to the wife of a postman and the mother of five children. Beautiful indeed was the Festsaal. Three long tables were grouped at one end, the remainder of the floor space cleared for dancing. Oil lamps, hanging from the ceiling, shed a warm, bright light on the walls decorated with paper flowers and garlands; shed a warmer, brighter light on the red faces of the guests in their best clothes.

At the head of the centre table sat the bride and bridegroom, she in a white dress trimmed with stripes and bows of coloured ribbon, giving her the appearance of an iced cake all ready to be cut and served in neat little pieces to the bridegroom beside her, who wore a suit of white clothes much too large for him and a white silk tie that rose half way up his collar. Grouped about them, with a fine regard for dignity and precedence, sat their parents and relations; and perched on a stool at the bride's right hand a little girl in a crumpled muslin dress with a wreath of forget-me-nots hanging over one ear. Everybody was laughing and talking, shaking hands, clinking glasses, stamping on the floor—a stench of beer and perspiration filled the air.

1. Guesthouse.
2. Banqueting room.

Frau Brechenmacher, following her man down the room after greeting the bridal party, knew that she was going to enjoy herself. She seemed to fill out and become rosy and warm as she sniffed that familiar, festive smell. Somebody pulled at her skirt, and, looking down, she saw Frau Rupp, the butcher's wife, who pulled out an empty chair and begged her to sit beside her.

'Fritz will get you some beer,' she said. 'My dear, your skirt is open at the back. We could not help laughing as you walked up the room with the white tape of your petticoat showing!'

'But how frightful!' said Frau Brechenmacher, collapsing into her chair and biting her lip.

'Na, it's over now,' said Frau Rupp, stretching her fat hands over the table and regarding her three mourning rings with intense enjoyment; 'but one must be careful, especially at a wedding.'

'And such a wedding as this,' cried Frau Ledermann, who sat on the other side of Frau Brechenmacher. 'Fancy Theresa bringing that child with her. It's her own child, you know, my dear and it's going to live with them. That's what I call a sin against the Church for a free-born child to attend its own mother's wedding.'

The three women sat and stared at the bride, who remained very still, with a little vacant smile on her lips, only her eyes shifting uneasily from side to side.

'Beer they've given it, too,' whispered Frau Rupp, 'and white wine and an ice. It never did have a stomach; she ought to have left it at home.'

Frau Brechenmacher turned round and looked towards the bride's mother. She never took her eyes off her daughter, but wrinkled her brown forehead like an old monkey, and nodded now and again very solemnly. Her hands shook as she raised her beer mug, and when she had drunk she spat on the floor and savagely wiped her mouth with her sleeve. Then the music started and she followed Theresa with her eyes, looking suspiciously at each man who danced with her.

'Cheer up, old woman,' shouted her husband, digging her in the ribs; 'this isn't Theresa's funeral.' He winked at the guests, who broke into loud laughter.

'I *am* cheerful,' mumbled the old woman, and beat upon the table with her fist, keeping time to the music, proving she was not out of the festivities.

'She can't forget how wild Theresa has been,' said Frau Ledermann. 'Who could—with the child there? I heard that last Sunday evening Theresa had hysterics and said that she would not marry this man. They had to get the priest to her.'

'Where is the other one?' asked Frau Brechenmacher. 'Why didn't he marry her?'

The woman shrugged her shoulders.

'Gone—disappeared. He was a traveller, and only stayed at their house two nights. He was selling shirt buttons—I bought some myself, and they were beautiful shirt buttons—but what a pig of a fellow! I can't think what he saw in such a plain girl—but you never know. Her mother says she's been like fire ever since she was sixteen!'

Frau Brechenmacher looked down at her beer and blew a little hole in the froth.

'That's not how a wedding should be,' she said; 'it's not religion to love two men.'

'Nice time she'll have with this one,' Frau Rupp exclaimed. 'He was lodging with me last summer and I had to get rid of him. He never changed his clothes once in two months, and when I spoke to him of the smell in his room he told me he was sure it floated up from the shop. Ah, every wife has her cross. Isn't that true, my dear?'

Frau Brechenmacher saw her husband among his colleagues at the next table. He was drinking far too much, she knew—gesticulating wildly, the saliva spluttering out of his mouth as he talked.

'Yes,' she assented, 'that's true. Girls have a lot to learn.'

Wedged in between these two fat old women, the Frau had no hope of being asked to dance. She watched the couples going round and round; she forgot her five babies and her man and felt almost like a girl again. The music sounded sad and sweet. Her roughened hands clasped and unclasped themselves in the folds of her skirt. While the music went on she was afraid to look anybody in the face, and she smiled with a little nervous tremor round the mouth.

'But, my God,' Frau Rupp cried, 'they've given that child of Theresa's a piece of sausage. It's to keep her quiet. There's going to be a presentation now—your man has to speak.'

Frau Brechenmacher sat up stiffly. The music ceased, and the dancers took their places again at the tables.

Herr Brechenmacher alone remained standing—he held in his hands a big silver coffee-pot. Everybody laughed at his speech, except the Frau; everybody roared at his grimaces, and at the way he carried the coffee-pot to the bridal pair, as if it were a baby he was holding.

She lifted the lid, peeped in, then shut it down with a little scream and sat biting her lips. The bridegroom wrenched the pot away from her and drew forth a baby's bottle and two little cradles holding china dolls. As he dandled these treasures before Theresa the hot room seemed to heave and sway with laughter.

Frau Brechenmacher did not think it funny. She stared round at the laughing faces, and suddenly they all seemed strange to her. She wanted to go home and never come out again. She imagined that all these people were laughing at her, more people than there were in the room even—all laughing at her because they were so much stronger than she was.

They walked home in silence. Herr Brechenmacher strode ahead, she stumbled after him. White and forsaken lay the road from the railway station to their house—a cold rush of wind blew her hood from her face, and suddenly she remembered how they had come home together the first night. Now they had five babies and twice as much money; *but—*

'Na, what is it all for?' she muttered, and not until she had reached home, and prepared a little supper of meat and bread for her man did she stop asking herself that silly question.

Herr Brechenmacher broke the bread into his plate, smeared it round with his fork, and chewed greedily.

'Good?' she asked, leaning her arms on the table and pillowing her breast against them.

'But fine!'

He took a piece of the crumb, wiped it round his plate edge, and held it up to her mouth. She shook her head.

'Not hungry,' she said.

'But it is one of the best pieces, and full of the fat.'

He cleared the plate; then pulled off his boots and flung them into a corner.

'Not much of a wedding,' he said, stretching out his feet and wriggling his toes in the worsted socks.

'N—no,' she replied, taking up the discarded boots and placing them on the oven to dry.

Herr Brechenmacher yawned and stretched himself, and then looked up at her, grinning.

'Remember the night that we came home? You were an innocent one, you were.'

'Get along! Such a time ago I forget.' Well she remembered.

'Such a clout on the ear as you gave me. . . . But I soon taught you.'

'Oh, don't start talking. You've too much beer. Come to bed.'

He tilted back in his chair, chuckling with laughter.

'That's not what you said to me that night. God, the trouble you gave me!'

But the little Frau seized the candle and went into the next room. The children were all soundly sleeping. She stripped the mattress off the baby's bed to see if he was still dry, then began unfastening her blouse and skirt.

'Always the same,' she said—'all over the world the same; but, God in heaven—but *stupid*.'

Then even the memory of the wedding faded quite. She lay down on the bed and put her arm across her face like a child who expected to be hurt as Herr Brechenmacher lurched in.

The Swing of the Pendulum (1911)†

The landlady knocked at the door.

'Come in,' said Viola.

'There is a letter for you,' said the landlady, 'a special letter'—she held the green envelope in a corner of her dingy apron.

'Thanks.' Viola, kneeling on the floor poking at the little dusty stove, stretched out her hand. 'Any answer?'

'No; the messenger has gone.'

'Oh, all right!' She did not look the landlady in the face; she was ashamed of not having paid her rent, and wondered grimly, without any hope, if the woman would begin to bluster again.

'About this money owing to me—' said the landlady.

'Oh, the Lord—off she goes!' thought Viola, turning her back on the woman and making a grimace at the stove.

'It's settle—or it's go!' The landlady raised her voice; she began to bawl. 'I'm a lady, I am, and a respectable woman, I'll have you know. I'll have no lice in my house, sneaking their way into the furniture and eating up everything. It's cash—or out you go before twelve o'clock tomorrow.'

Viola felt rather than saw the woman's gesture. She shot out her arm in a stupid, helpless way, as though a dirty pigeon had suddenly flown at her face. 'Filthy old beast! Ugh! And the smell of her—like stale cheese and damp washing.'

'Very well!' she answered shortly; 'it's cash down or I leave tomorrow. All right: don't shout.'

It was extraordinary—always before this woman came near her she trembled in her shoes—even the sound of those flat feet stumping up the stairs made her feel sick, but once they were face to face she felt immensely calm and indifferent, and could not understand why she even worried about money, nor why she sneaked out of the house on tiptoe, not even daring to shut the door after her in case the landlady should hear and shout something terrible, nor why she spent nights pacing up and down her room—drawing up sharply before the mirror and saying to a tragic reflection: 'Money, money, money!' When she was alone her poverty was like a

† First published in *In a German Pension* (1911).

huge dream-mountain on which her feet were fast rooted—aching with the ache of the size of the thing—but if it came to a definite action, with no time for imaginings, her dream-mountain dwindled into a beastly 'hold-your-nose' affair, to be passed by as quickly as possible, with anger and a strong sense of superiority.

The landlady bounced out of the room, banging the door, so that it shook and rattled as though it had listened to the conversation and fully sympathised with the old hag.

Squatting on her heels, Viola opened the letter. It was from Casimir:

'I shall be with you at three o'clock this afternoon—and must be off again this evening. All news when we meet. I hope you are happier than I.—Casimir.'

'Huh! how kind!' she sneered; 'how condescending. Too good of you, really!' She sprang to her feet, crumbling the letter in her hands. 'And how are you to know that I shall stick here awaiting your pleasure until three o'clock this afternoon?' But she knew she would; her rage was only half sincere. She longed to see Casimir, for she was confident that this time she would make him understand the situation. . . . 'For, as it is, it's intolerable—intolerable!' she muttered.

It was ten o'clock in the morning of a grey day curiously lighted by pale flashes of sunshine. Searched by these flashes her room looked tumbled and grimed. She pulled down the window-blinds—but they gave a persistent, whitish glare which was just as bad. The only thing of life in the room was a jar of hyacinths given her by the landlady's daughter: it stood on the table exuding a sickly perfume from its plump petals; there were even rich buds unfolding, and the leaves shone like oil.

Viola went over to the washstand, poured some water into the enamel basin, and sponged her face and neck. She dipped her face into the water, opened her eyes, and shook her head from side to side—it was exhilarating. She did it three times. 'I suppose I could drown myself if I stayed under long enough,' she thought. 'I wonder how long it takes to become unconscious? . . . Often read of women drowning in a bucket. I wonder if any air enters by the ears—if the basin would have to be as deep as a bucket?' She experimented—gripped the washstand with both hands and slowly sank her head into the water, when again there was a knock on the door. Not the landlady this time—it must be Casimir. With her face and hair dripping, with her petticoat bodice unbuttoned, she ran and opened it.

A strange man stood against the lintel—seeing her, he opened his eyes very wide and smiled delightfully. 'Excuse me—does Fräulein Schäfer live here?'

'No; never heard of her.' His smile was so infectious, she wanted to smile too—and the water had made her feel so fresh and rosy.

The strange man appeared overwhelmed with astonishment. 'She doesn't?' he cried. 'She is out, you mean!'

'No, she's not living here,' answered Viola.

'But—pardon—one moment.' He moved from the door lintel, standing squarely in front of her. He unbuttoned his greatcoat and drew a slip of paper from the breast pocket, smoothing it in his gloved fingers before handing it to her.

'Yes, that's the address, right enough, but there must be a mistake in the number. So many lodging-houses in this street, you know, and so big.'

Drops of water fell from her hair on to the paper. She burst out laughing. 'Oh, *how* dreadful I must look—one moment!' She ran back to the washstand and caught up a towel. The door was still open. . . . After all, there was nothing more to be said. Why on earth had she asked him to wait a moment? She folded the towel round her shoulders, and returned to the door, suddenly grave. 'I'm sorry; I know no such name,' in a sharp voice.

Said the strange man: 'Sorry, too. Have you been living here long?'

'Er—yes—a long time.' She began to close the door slowly.

'Well—good-morning, thanks so much. Hope I haven't been a bother.'

'Good-morning.'

She heard him walk down the passage and then pause—lighting a cigarette. Yes—a faint scent of delicious cigarette smoke penetrated her room. She sniffed at it, smiling again. Well, that had been a fascinating interlude! He looked so amazingly happy: his heavy clothes and big buttoned gloves; his beautifully brushed hair . . . and that smile. . . . 'Jolly' was the word—just a well-fed boy with the world for his playground. People like that did one good—one felt 'made over' at the sight of them. *Sane* they were—so sane and solid. You could depend on them never having one mad impulse from the day they were born until the day they died. And Life was in league with them—jumped them on her knee—quite rightly, too. At that moment she noticed Casimir's letter, crumpled up on the floor—the smile faded. Staring at the letter she began braiding her hair—a dull feeling of rage crept through her—she seemed to be braiding it into her brain, and binding it, tightly, above her head. . . . Of course that had been the mistake all along. What had? Oh,

Casimir's frightful seriousness. If she had been happy when they first met she never would have looked at him—but they had been like two patients in the same hospital ward—each finding comfort in the sickness of the other—sweet foundation for a love episode! Misfortune had knocked their heads together: they had looked at each other, stunned with the conflict and sympathised . . . . 'I wish I could step outside the whole affair and just judge it—then I'd find a way out. I certainly was in love with Casimir. . . . Oh, be sincere for once.' She flopped down on the bed and hid her face in the pillow. 'I was not in love. I wanted somebody to look after me—and keep me until my work began to sell—and he kept bothers with other men away. And what would have happened if he hadn't come along? I would have spent my wretched little pittance, and then—Yes, that was what decided me, thinking about that "then". He was the only solution. And I believed in him then. I thought his work had only to be recognised once, and he'd roll in wealth. I thought perhaps we might be poor for a month—but he said, if only he could have me, the stimulus. . . . Funny, if it wasn't so damned tragic! Exactly the contrary has happened—he hasn't had a thing published for months—neither have I—but then I didn't expect to. Yes, the truth is, I'm hard and bitter, and I have neither faith nor love for unsuccessful men. I always end by despising them as I despise Casimir. I suppose it's the savage pride of the female who likes to think the man to whom she has given herself must be a very great chief indeed. But to stew in this disgusting house while Casimir scours the land in the hope of finding one editorial open door—it's humiliating. It's changed my whole nature. I wasn't born for poverty—I only flower among really jolly people, and people who never are worried.'

The figure of the strange man rose before her—would not be dismissed. 'That was the man for me, after all is said and done—a man without a care—who'd give me everything I want and with whom I'd always feel that sense of life and of being in touch with the world. I never wanted to fight—it was thrust on me. Really, there's a fount of happiness in me, that is drying up, little by little, in this hateful existence. I'll be dead if this goes on—and'—she stirred in the bed and flung out her arms—'I want passion, and love, and adventure—I yearn for them. Why should I stay here and rot?—I am rotting!' she cried, comforting herself with the sound of her breaking voice. 'But if I tell Casimir all this when he comes this afternoon, and he says, "Go"—as he certainly will—that's another thing I loathe about him,—he's under my thumb—what should I do then—where should I go to?' There was nowhere. 'I don't want to work—or carve out my own path. I want ease and any amount of nursing in the lap of luxury. There is only one thing I'm fitted for, and that is to be a great courtesan.' But she did not know how to go about it. She was frightened to go into the streets—she heard of such awful things happening to those women—men with diseases—or men who didn't pay—besides, the idea of a strange man every night—no, that was out of the question. 'If I'd the clothes I would go to a really good hotel and find some wealthy man . . . like the strange man this morning. He would be ideal. Oh, if I only had his address—I am sure I would fascinate him. I'd keep him laughing all day—I'd make him give me unlimited money. . . .' At the thought she grew warm and soft. She began to dream of a wonderful house, and of presses full of clothes and of perfumes. She saw herself stepping into carriages—looking at the strange man with a mysterious, voluptuous glance—she practised the glance, lying on the bed—and never another worry, just drugged with happiness. That was the life for her. Well, the thing to do was to let Casimir go on his wild-goose chase that evening, and while he was away—what? Also—please to remember—there was the rent to be paid before twelve next morning, and she hadn't the money for a square meal. At the thought of food she felt a sharp twinge in her stomach, a sensation as though there were a hand in her stomach, squeezing it dry. She was terribly hungry—all Casimir's fault—and that man had lived on the fat of the land ever since he was born. He looked as though he could order a magnificent dinner. Oh, why hadn't she played her cards better?—he'd been sent by Providence—and she'd snubbed him. 'If I had that time over again, I'd be safe by now.' And instead of the ordinary man who had spoken with her at the door her mind created a brilliant, laughing image, who would treat her like a queen. . . . 'There's only one thing I could not stand—that he should be coarse or vulgar. Well, he wasn't—he was obviously a man of the world—and the way he apologised . . . I have enough faith in my own power and beauty to know I could make a man treat me just as I wanted to be treated.' . . . It floated into her dreams—that sweet scent of cigarette smoke. And then she remembered that she had heard nobody go down the stone stairs. Was it possible that the strange man was still there? . . . The thought was too absurd—Life didn't play tricks like that—and yet—she was quite conscious of his nearness. Very quietly she got up, unhooked from the back of the door a long white gown, buttoned it on—smiling slyly. She did not know what was going to happen. She only thought: 'Oh, what fun!' and that they were playing a delicious game—this strange man and she. Very gently she turned the door-handle, screwing up her face and biting her lip as the lock snapped back. Of course, there he was—leaning against the banister rail. He wheeled round as she slipped into the passage.

'Da,' she muttered, folding her gown tightly around her, 'I must go downstairs and fetch some wood. Brr! the cold!'

'There isn't any wood,' volunteered the strange man. She gave a little cry of astonishment, and then tossed her head.

'You, again,' she said scornfully, conscious the while of his merry eye, and the fresh, strong smell of his healthy body.

'The landlady shouted out there was no wood left. I just saw her go out to buy some.'

'Story—story!' she longed to cry. He came quite close to her, stood over her and whispered:

'Aren't you going to ask me to finish my cigarette in your room?'

She nodded. 'You may if you want to!'

In that moment together in the passage a miracle had happened. Her room was quite changed—it was full of sweet light and the scent of hyacinth flowers. Even the furniture appeared different—exciting. Quick as a flash she remembered childish parties when they had played charades, and one side had left the room and come in again to act a word—just what she was doing now. The strange man went over to the stove and sat down in her arm-chair. She did not want him to talk or come near her—it was enough to see him in the room, so secure and happy. How hungry she had been for the nearness of someone like that—who knew nothing at all about her—and made no demands—but just lived. Viola ran over to the table and put her arms round the jar of hyacinths.

'Beautiful! Beautiful!' she cried—burying her head in the flowers—and sniffing greedily at the scent. Over the leaves she looked at the man and laughed.

'You are a funny little thing,' said he lazily.

'Why? Because I love flowers?'

'I'd far rather you loved other things,' said the strange man slowly. She broke off a little pink petal and smiled at it.

'Let me send you some flowers,' said the strange man. 'I'll send you a roomful if you'd like them.'

His voice frightened her slightly. 'Oh no, thanks—this one is quite enough for me.'

'No, it isn't'—in a teasing voice.

'What a stupid remark!' thought Viola, and looking at him again he did not seem quite so jolly. She noticed that his eyes were set too closely together—and they were too small. Horrible thought, that he should prove stupid.

'What do you do all day?' she asked hastily.

'Nothing.'

'Nothing at all?'

'Why should I do anything?'

'Oh, don't imagine for one moment that I condemn such wisdom—only it sounds too good to be true!'

'What's that?'—he craned forward. 'What sounds too good to be true?' Yes—there was no denying it—he looked silly.

'I suppose the searching after Fräulein Schäfer doesn't occupy all your days.'

'Oh no'—he smiled broadly—'that's very good! By Jove! no, I drive a good bit—are you keen on horses?'

She nodded. 'Love them.'

'You must come driving with me—I've got a fine pair of greys. Will you?'

'Pretty I'd look perched behind greys in my one and only hat,' thought she. Aloud: 'I'd love to.' Her easy acceptance pleased him.

'How about to-morrow?' he suggested. 'Suppose you have lunch with me to-morrow and I take you driving.'

After all—this was just a game. 'Yes, I'm not busy to-morrow,' she said.

A little pause—then the strange man patted his leg. 'Why don't you come and sit down?' he said.

She pretended not to see and swung on to the table. 'Oh, I'm all right here.'

'No, you're not'—again the teasing voice. 'Come and sit on my knee.'

'Oh no,' said Viola very heartily, suddenly busy with her hair.

'Why not?'

'I don't want to.'

'Oh, come along'—impatiently.

She shook her head from side to side. 'I wouldn't dream of such a thing.'

At that he got up and came over to her. 'Funny little puss cat!' He put up one hand to touch her hair.

'Don't,' she said—and slipped off the table. 'I—I think it's time you went now.' She was quite frightened now—thinking only: 'This man must be got rid of as quickly as possible.'

'Oh, but you don't want me to go?'

'Yes, I do—I'm very busy.'

'Busy. What does the pussy cat do all day?'

'Lots and lots of things!' She wanted to push him out of the room and slam the door on him—idiot—fool—cruel disappointment.

'What's she frowning for?' he asked. 'Is she worried about anything?' Suddenly serious: 'I say—you know, are you in any financial difficulty? Do you want money? I'll give it to you if you like!'

'Money! Steady on the brake—don't lose your head!'—so she spoke to herself.

'I'll give you two hundred marks if you'll kiss me.'

'Oh, boo! What a condition! And I don't want to kiss you—I don't like kissing. Please go!'

'Yes—you do!—yes, you do.' He caught hold of her arms above the elbows. She struggled, and was quite amazed to realise how angry she felt.

'Let me go—immediately!' she cried—and he slipped one arm round her body, and drew her towards him—like a bar of iron across her back—that arm.

'Leave me alone! I tell you. Don't be mean! I didn't want this to happen when you came into my room. How dare you?'

'Well, kiss me and I'll go!'

It was too idiotic—dodging that stupid, smiling face.

'I won't kiss you!—you brute!—I won't!' Somehow she slipped out of his arms and ran to the wall—stood back against it—breathing quickly.

'Get out!' she stammered. 'Go on now, clear out!'

At that moment, when he was not touching her, she quite enjoyed herself. She thrilled at her own angry voice. 'To think I should talk to a man like that!' An angry flush spread over his face—his lips curled back, showing his teeth—just like a dog, thought Viola. He made a rush at her, and held her against the wall—pressed upon her with all the weight of his body. This time she could not get free.

'I won't kiss you. I won't. Stop doing that! Ugh! You're like a dog—you ought to find lovers round lamp-posts—you beast—you fiend!'

He did not answer. With an expression of the most absurd determination he pressed ever more heavily upon her. He did not even look at her—but rapped out in a sharp voice: 'Keep quiet—keep quiet.'

'Gar-r! Why are men so strong?' She began to cry. 'Go away—I don't want you, you dirty creature. I want to murder you. Oh, my God! if I had a knife.'

'Don't be silly—come and be good!' He dragged her towards the bed.

'Do you suppose I'm a light woman?' she snarled, and swooping over she fastened her teeth in his glove.

'Ach! don't do that—you are hurting me!'

She did not let go, but her heart said, 'Thank the Lord I thought of this.'

'Stop this minute—you vixen—you bitch.' He threw her away from him. She saw with joy that his eyes were full of tears. 'You've really hurt me,' he said in a choking voice.

'Of course I have. I meant to. That's nothing to what I'll do if you touch me again.'

The strange man picked up his hat. 'No thanks,' he said grimly. 'But I'll not forget this—I'll go to your landlady.'

'Pooh!' She shrugged her shoulders and laughed. 'I'll tell her you forced your way in here and tried to assault me. Who will she believe?—with your bitten hand. You go and find your Schäfers.'

A sensation of glorious, intoxicating happiness flooded Viola. She rolled her eyes at him. 'If you don't go away this moment I'll bite you again,' she said, and the absurd words started her laughing. Even when the door was closed, hearing him descending the stairs, she laughed, and danced about the room.

What a morning! Oh, chalk it up. That was her first fight, and she'd won—she'd conquered that beast—all by herself. Her hands were still trembling. She pulled up the sleeve of her gown—great red marks on her arms. 'My ribs will be blue. I'll be blue all over,' she reflected. 'If only that beloved Casimir could have seen us.' And the feeling of rage and disgust against Casimir had totally disappeared. How could the poor darling help not having any money? It was her fault as much as his, and he, just like her, was apart from the world, fighting it, just as she had done. If only three o'clock would come. She saw herself running towards him and putting her arms round his neck. 'My blessed one! Of course we are bound to win. Do you love me still? Oh, I have been horrible lately.'

The Woman at the Store (1912)†

All that day the heat was terrible. The wind blew close to the ground—it rooted among the tussock grass—slithered along the road, so that the white pumice dust swirled in our faces—settled and sifted over us and was like a dry-skin itching for growth on our bodies. The horses stumbled along, coughing and chuffing. The pack horse was sick—with a big, open sore rubbed under the belly. Now and again she stopped short, threw back her head, looked at us as though she were going to cry, and whinnied. Hundreds of larks shrilled—the sky was slate colour, and the sound of the larks reminded me of slate pencils scraping over its surface. There was nothing to be seen but wave after wave of tussock grass—patched with purple orchids and manuka[1] bushes covered with thick spider webs.

Jo rode ahead. He wore a blue galatea[2] shirt, corduroy trousers and riding boots. A white handkerchief, spotted with red—it looked

† Published in *Rhythm* (spring 1912). The story drew much of its detail from a camping trip Mansfield took through the center of the North Island, New Zealand, in the summer of 1907. Her notebook kept during the trip was published as *The Urewera Notebook*, ed. I. A. Gordon (Oxford: Oxford University Press, 1978). The story was not reprinted during Mansfield's lifetime, but appeared in *Something Childish and Other Stories* (1924).

1. A common bush or small tree with small delicate flowers.
2. Made from a blue-striped cotton material.

as though his nose had been bleeding on it—knotted round his throat. Wisps of white hair straggled from under his wideawake[3]—his moustache and eyebrows were called white—he slouched in the saddle—grunting. Not once that day had he sung 'I don't care, for don't you see, my wife's mother was in front of me!' . . . It was the first day we had been without it for a month, and now there seemed something uncanny in his silence. Hin rode beside me—white as a clown, his black eyes glittered, and he kept shooting out his tongue and moistening his lips. He was dressed in a Jaeger vest—a pair of blue duck[4] trousers, fastened round the waist with a plaited leather belt. We had hardly spoken since dawn. At noon we had lunched off fly biscuits and apricots by the side of a swampy creek.

'My stomach feels like the crop of a hen,' said Jo. 'Now then, Hin, you're the bright boy of the party—where's this 'ere store you kep' on talking about. "Oh, yes," you says, "I know a fine store, with a paddock for the horses an' a creek runnin' through, owned by a friend of mine who'll give yer a bottle of whisky before 'e shakes hands with yer." I'd like ter see that place—merely as a matter of curiosity—not that I'd ever doubt yer word—as yer know very well—*but*. . . .'

Hin laughed. 'Don't forget there's a woman too, Jo, with blue eyes and yellow hair, who'll promise you something else before she shakes hands with you. Put that in your pipe and smoke it.'

'The heat's making you balmy,[5] said Jo. But he dug his knees into his horse. We shambled on. I half fell asleep, and had a sort of uneasy dream that the horses were not moving forward at all—then that I was on a rocking-horse, and my old mother was scolding me for raising such a fearful dust from the drawing-room carpet. 'You've entirely worn off the pattern of the carpet,' I heard her saying, and she gave the reins a tug. I snivelled and woke to find Hin leaning over me, maliciously smiling.

'That was a case of all but,' said he, 'I just caught you. What's up, been bye-bye?'

'No!' I raised my head. 'Thank the Lord we're arriving somewhere.'

We were on the brow of the hill, and below us there was a whare[6] roofed in with corrugated iron. It stood in a garden, rather far back from the road—a big paddock opposite, and a creek and a clump of young willow trees. A thin line of blue smoke stood up straight from the chimney of the whare, and as I looked, a woman came out, fol-

3. A hat with a wide brim and low flat crown.
4. A strong cotton cloth used for workmen's clothes. *Jaeger*: the proprietary name of an all-wool cloth, and a garment made from it.
5. Very probably a misprint for "barmy," meaning "foolish."
6. Originally a Maori house or building, then, after European settlement, more broadly used for a makeshift dwelling or shack.

lowed by a child and a sheep dog—the woman carrying what appeared to me a black stick. She made frantic gestures at us. The horses put on a final spurt, Jo took off his wideawake, shouted, threw out his chest, and began singing, 'I don't care, for don't you see. . . .' The sun pushed through the pale clouds and shed a vivid light over the scene. It gleamed on the woman's yellow hair, over her flapping pinafore and the rifle she was carrying. The child hid behind her, and the yellow dog, a mangy beast, scuttled back into the whare, his tail between his legs. We drew rein and dismounted.

'Hallo,' screamed the woman. 'I thought you was three 'awks. My kid comes runnin' in ter me. "Mumma," says she, "there's three brown things comin' over the 'ill," says she. An' I comes out smart, I can tell yer. They'll be 'awks, I says to her. Oh, the 'awks about 'ere, yer wouldn't believe.'

The 'kid' gave us the benefit of one eye from behind the woman's pinafore—then retired again.

'Where's your old man,' asked Hin.

The woman blinked rapidly, screwing up her face.

'Away shearin'. Bin away a month. I suppose yer not goin' to stop, are yer? There's a storm comin' up.'

'You bet we are,' said Jo. 'So you're on your lonely, missis?'

She stood, pleating the frills of her pinafore, and glancing from one to the other of us, like a hungry bird. I smiled at the thought of how Hin had pulled Jo's leg about her. Certainly her eyes were blue, and what hair she had was yellow, but ugly. She was a figure of fun. Looking at her, you felt there was nothing but sticks and wires under that pinafore—her front teeth were knocked out, she had red pulpy hands, and she wore on her feet a pair of dirty 'Bluchers'.[7]

'I'll go and turn out the horses,' said Hin. 'Got any embrocation?[8] Poi's rubbed herself to hell!'

'Arf a mo!' The woman stood silent a moment, her nostrils expanding as she breathed. Then she shouted violently, 'I'd rather you didn't stop—you *can't* and there's the end of it. I don't let out that paddock any more. You'll have to go on; I ain't got nothing!'

'Well, I'm blest!' said Jo, heavily. He pulled me aside. 'Gone a bit off 'er dot,' he whispered, 'too much alone, *you know*,' very significantly. 'Turn the sympathetic tap on 'er, she'll come round all right.'

But there was no need—she had come round by herself.

'Stop if yer like!' she muttered, shrugging her shoulders. To me—'I'll give yer the embrocation if yer come along.'

'Right-o, I'll take it down to them.' We walked together up the

7. Leather half-boots.
8. A liquid for rubbing on sprains and sore joints.

garden path. It was planted on both sides with cabbages. They smelled like stale dishwater. Of flowers there were double poppies and sweet-williams. One little patch was divided off by pawa[9] shells—presumably it belonged to the child—for she ran from her mother and began to grub in it with a broken clothes peg. The yellow dog lay across the doorstep, biting fleas; the woman kicked him away.

'Gar-r, get away, you beast . . . the place ain't tidy. I 'aven't 'ad time ter fix things to-day—been ironing. Come right in.'

It was a large room, the walls plastered with old pages of English periodicals. Queen Victoria's Jubilee[1] appeared to be the most recent number—a table with an ironing board and wash tub on it—some wooden forms—a black horsehair sofa, and some broken cane chairs pushed against the walls. The mantelpiece above the stove was draped in pink paper, further ornamented with dried grasses and ferns and a coloured print of Richard Seddon.[2] There were four doors—one, judging from the smell, let into the 'Store', one on to the 'back yard', through the third I saw the bedroom. Flies buzzed in circles round the ceiling, and treacle papers and bundles of dried clover were pinned to the window curtains. I was alone in the room—she had gone into the store for the embrocation. I heard her stamping about and muttering to herself: 'I got some, now where did I put that bottle? . . . It's behind the pickles . . . no, it ain't.' I cleared a place on the table and sat there, swinging my legs. Down in the paddock I could hear Jo singing and the sound of hammer strokes as Hin drove in the tent poles. It was sunset. There is no twilight to our New Zealand days, but a curious half-hour when everything appears grotesque—it frightens—as though the savage spirit of the country walked abroad and sneered at what it saw. Sitting alone in the hideous room I grew afraid. The woman next door was a long time finding that stuff. What was she doing in there? Once I thought I heard her bang her hands down on the counter, and once she half moaned, turning it into a cough and clearing her throat. I wanted to shout 'Buck up,' but I kept silent.

'Good Lord, what a life!' I thought. 'Imagine being here day in, day out, with that rat of a child and a mangy dog. Imagine bothering about ironing—*mad*, of course she's mad! Wonder how long she's been here—wonder if I could get her to talk.'

At that moment she poked her head round the door.

9. A large shellfish, usually spelled *paua*, closely related to the abalone, with an attractive iridescent inner shell.
1. Victoria was Queen of Great Britain and Ireland from 1837 to 1901. In 1897 the Jubilee of her sixty years as monarch was widely celebrated.
2. Richard Seddon (1845–1906), the prime minister of New Zealand from 1893 to 1906, a man of strong liberal principles and a close friend of Mansfield's father.

'Wot was it yer wanted,' she asked.

'Embrocation.'

'Oh, I forgot. I got it, it was in front of the pickle jars.'

She handed me the bottle.

'My, you do look tired, you do! Shall I knock yer up a few scones for supper? There's some tongue in the store, too, and I'll cook yer a cabbage if you fancy it.'

'Right-o.' I smiled at her. 'Come down to the paddock and bring the kid for tea.'

She shook her head, pursing up her mouth.

'Oh no. I don't fancy it. I'll send the kid down with the things and a billy of milk. Shall I knock up a few extry scones to take with you ter-morrow?'

'Thanks.'

She came and stood by the door.

'How old is the kid?'

'Six—come next Christmas. I 'ad a bit of trouble with 'er one way an' another. I 'adn't any milk till a month after she was born and she sickened like a cow.'

'She's not like you—takes after her father?' Just as the woman had shouted her refusal at us before, she shouted at me then.

'No, she don't; she's the dead spit of me. Any fool could see that. Come on in now, Els, you stop messing in the dirt.'

I met Jo climbing over the paddock fence.

'What's the old bitch got in the store?' he asked.

'Don't know—didn't look.'

'Well, of all the fools. Hin's slanging you. What have you been doing all the time?'

'She couldn't find this stuff. Oh, my shakes, you are smart!'

Jo had washed, combed his wet hair in a line across his forehead, and buttoned a coat over his shirt. He grinned.

Hin snatched the embrocation from me. I went to the end of the paddock where the willows grew and bathed in the creek. The water was clear and soft as oil. Along the edges held by the grass and rushes, white foam tumbled and bubbled. I lay in the water and looked up at the trees that were still a moment, then quivered lightly, and again were still. The air smelt of rain. I forgot about the woman and the kid until I came back to the tent. Hin lay by the fire, watching the billy boil.

I asked where Jo was and if the kid had brought our supper.

'Pooh,' said Hin, rolling over and looking up at the sky. 'Didn't you see how Jo had been tittivating—he said to me before he went up to the whare, "Dang it! she'll look better by night light—at any rate, my buck, she's female flesh!" '

'You had Jo about her looks—you had me, too.'

'No—look here. I can't make it out. It's four years since I came past this way, and I stopped here two days. The husband was a pal of mine once, down the West Coast—a fine, big chap, with a voice on him like a trombone. She'd been barmaid down the Coast—as pretty as a wax doll. The coach used to come this way then once a fortnight, that was before they opened the railway up Napier[3] way, and she had no end of a time! Told me once in a confidential moment that she knew one hundred and twenty-five different ways of kissing!'

'Oh, go on, Hin! She isn't the same woman!'

'Course she is. . . . I can't make it out. What I think is the old man's cleared out and left her: that's all my eye about shearing. Sweet life! The only people who come through now are Maoris and sundowners!'[4]

Through the dark we saw the gleam of the kid's pinafore. She trailed over to us with a basket in her hand, the milk billy in the other. I unpacked the basket, the child standing by.

'Come over here,' said Hin, snapping his fingers at her.

She went, the lamp from the inside of the tent cast a bright light over her. A mean, undersized brat, with whitish hair, and weak eyes. She stood, legs wide apart and her stomach protruding.

'What do you do all day?' asked Hin.

She scraped out one ear with her little finger, looked at the result and said—'Draw.'

'Huh! What do you draw?—leave your ears alone.'

'Pictures.'

'What on?'

'Bits of butter paper an' a pencil of my Mumma's.'

'Boh! What a lot of words at one time!' Hin rolled his eyes at her. 'Baa-lambs and moo-cows?'

'No, everything. I'll draw all of you when you're gone, and your horses and the tent, and that one'—she pointed to me—'with no clothes on in the creek. I looked at her where she wouldn't see me from.'

'Thanks very much! How ripping of you,' said Hin. 'Where's Dad?'

The kid pouted. 'I won't tell you because I don't like yer face!' She started operations on the other ear.

'Here,' I said. 'Take the basket, get along home and tell the other man supper's ready.'

'I don't want to.'

'I'll give you a box on the ear if you don't,' said Hin, savagely.

3. A port on the east coast of the North Island.
4. Itinerants or tramps.

'Hie! I'll tell Mumma. I'll tell Mumma'—the kid fled.

We ate until we were full and had arrived at the smoke stage before Jo came back, very flushed and jaunty, a whisky bottle in his hand.

' 'Ave a drink—you two!' he shouted, carrying off matters with a high hand. ' 'Ere, shove along the cups.'

'One hundred and twenty-five different ways,' I murmured to Hin.

'What's that? Oh! stow it!' said Jo. 'Why 'ave you always got your knife into me. You gas like a kid at a Sunday School beano.[5] She wants us to go up there to-night, and have a comfortable chat. I'—he waved his hand airily—'I got 'er round.'

'Trust you for that,' laughed Hin. 'But did she tell you where the old man's got to?'

Jo looked up. 'Shearing! You 'eard 'er, you fool!'

The woman had fixed up the room, even to a light bouquet of sweet-williams on the table. She and I sat one side of the table, Jo and Hin the other. An oil lamp was set between us, the whisky bottle and glasses, and a jug of water. The kid knelt against one of the forms, drawing on butter paper. I wondered, grimly, if she was attempting the creek episode. But Jo had been right about night time. The woman's hair was tumbled—two red spots burned in her cheeks—her eyes shone—and we knew that they were kissing feet under the table. She had changed the blue pinafore for a white calico dressing jacket and a black skirt—the kid was decorated to the extent of a blue sateen hair ribbon. In the stifling room with the flies buzzing against the ceiling and dropping on to the table—we got slowly drunk.

'Now listen to me,' shouted the woman, banging her fist on the table. 'It's six years since I was married, and four miscarriages. I says to 'im, I says, what do you think I'm doin' up 'ere? If you was back at the Coast, I'd 'ave you lynched for child murder. Over and over I tells 'im—you've broken my spirit and spoiled my looks, and wot for—that's wot I'm driving at.' She clutched her head with her hands and stared round at us. Speaking rapidly, 'Oh, some days—an' months of them I 'ear them two words knockin' inside me all the time—"Wot for," but sometimes I'll be cooking the spuds an' I lifts the lid off to give 'em a prong and I 'ears, quite sudden again, "Wot for." Oh! I don't mean only the spuds and the kid—I mean—I mean,' she hiccoughed—'you know what I mean, Mr Jo.'

'I know,' said Jo, scratching his head.

'Trouble with me is,' she leaned across the table, 'he left me too much alone. When the coach stopped coming, sometimes he'd go

5. Party.

away days, sometimes he'd go away weeks, and leave me ter look after the store. Back 'e'd come—pleased as Punch.[6] "Oh, 'allo," 'e'd say. "Ow are you gettin' on. Come and give us a kiss." Sometimes I'd turn a bit nasty, and then 'e'd go off again, and if I took it all right, 'e'd wait till 'e could twist me round 'is finger, then 'e'd say, "Well, so long, I'm off," and do you think I could keep 'im?—not me!'

'Mumma,' bleated the kid, 'I made a picture of them on the 'ill, an' you an' me, an' the dog down below.'

'Shut your mouth,' said the woman.

A vivid flash of lightning played over the room—we heard the mutter of thunder.

'Good thing that's broke loose,' said Jo. 'I've 'ad it in me 'ead for three days.'

'Where's your old man now?' asked Hin slowly.

The woman blubbered and dropped her head on to the table. 'Hin, 'e's gone shearin' and left me alone again,' she wailed.

' 'Ere, look out for the glasses,' said Jo. 'Cheer-o, 'ave another drop. No good cryin' over spilt 'usbands! You Hin, you blasted cuckoo!'

'Mr Jo,' said the woman, drying her eyes on her jacket frill, 'you're a gent, an' if I was a secret woman, I'd place any confidence in your 'ands. I don't mind if I do 'ave a glass on that.'

Every moment the lightning grew more vivid and the thunder sounded nearer. Hin and I were silent—the kid never moved from her bench. She poked her tongue out and blew on it as she drew.

'It's the loneliness,' said the woman, addressing Jo—he made sheep's eyes at her—and bein' shut up 'ere like a broody 'en.' He reached his hand across the table and held hers, and though the position looked most uncomfortable when they wanted to pass the water and whisky, their hands stuck together as though glued. I pushed back my chair and went over to the kid, who immediately sat flat down on her artistic achievements and made a face at me.

'You're not to look,' said she.

'Oh, come on, don't be so nasty!' Hin came over to us, and we were just drunk enough to wheedle the kid into showing us. And those drawings of hers were extraordinary and repulsively vulgar. The creations of a lunatic with a lunatic's cleverness. There was no doubt about it, the kid's mind was diseased. While she showed them to us, she worked herself up into a mad excitement, laughing and trembling, and shooting out her arms.

'Mumma,' she yelled. 'Now I'm going to draw them what you told me I never was to—now I am.'

6. The exuberant grotesque figure in the traditional English Punch and Judy puppet show.

The woman rushed from the table and beat the child's head with the flat of her hand.

'I'll smack you with yer clothes turned up if yer dare say that again,' she bawled.

Jo was too drunk to notice, but Hin caught her by the arm. The kid did not utter a cry. She drifted over to the window and began picking flies from the treacle paper.[7]

We returned to the table—Hin and I sitting one side, the woman and Jo, touching shoulders, the other. We listened to the thunder, saying stupidly, 'That was a near one,' 'There it goes again,' and Jo, with a heavy hit, 'Now we're off,' 'Steady on the brake,' until rain began to fall, sharp as cannon shot on the iron roof.

'You'd better doss here for the night,' said the woman.

'That's right,' assented Jo, evidently in the know about this move.

'Bring up yer things from the tent. You two can doss in the store along with the kid—she's used to sleep in there and won't mind you.'

'O, Mumma, I never did,' interrupted the kid.

'Shut yer lies! An' Mr Jo can 'ave this room.'

It sounded a ridiculous arrangement, but it was useless to attempt to cross them, they were too far gone. While the woman sketched the plan of action, Jo sat, abnormally solemn and red, his eyes bulging, and pulled at his moustache.

'Give us a lantern,' said Hin. 'I'll go down to the paddock.' We two went together. Rain whipped in our faces, the land was as light as though a bush fire was raging—we behaved like two children let loose in the thick of an adventure—laughed and shouted to each other, and came back to the whare to find the kid already bedded in the counter of the store. The woman brought us a lamp. Jo took his bundle from Hin, the door was shut.

'Good-night all,' shouted Jo.

Hin and I sat on two sacks of potatoes. For the life of us we could not stop laughing. Strings of onions and half-hams dangled from the ceiling—wherever we looked there were advertisements for 'Camp Coffee' and tinned meats. We pointed at them, tried to read them aloud—overcome with laughter and hiccoughs. The kid in the counter stared at us. She threw off her blanket and scrambled to the floor where she stood in her grey flannel night gown, rubbing one leg against the other. We paid no attention to her.

'Wot are you laughing at,' she said, uneasily.

'You!' shouted Hin, 'the red tribe of you, my child.'

She flew into a rage and beat herself with her hands. 'I won't be

7. Strips of paper were spread with treacle to attract and catch flies.

laughed at, you curs—you.' He swooped down upon the child and swung her on to the counter.'

'Go to sleep, Miss Smarty—or make a drawing—here's a pencil—you can use Mumma's account book.'

Through the rain we heard Jo creak over the boarding of the next room—the sound of a door being opened—then shut to.

'It's the loneliness,' whispered Hin.

'One hundred and twenty-five different ways—alas! my poor brother!'

The kid tore out a page and flung it at me.

'There you are,' she said. 'Now I done it ter spite Mumma for shutting me up 'ere with you two. I done the one she told me I never ought to. I done the one she told me she'd shoot me if I did. Don't care! Don't care!'

The kid had drawn the picture of the woman shooting at a man with a rook rifle and then digging a hole to bury him in.

She jumped off the counter and squirmed about on the floor biting her nails.

Hin and I sat till dawn with the drawing beside us. The rain ceased, the little kid fell asleep, breathing loudly. We got up, stole out of the whare, down into the paddock. White clouds floated over a pink sky—a chill wind blew; the air smelled of wet grass. Just as we swung into the saddle, Jo came out of the whare—he motioned to us to ride on.

'I'll pick you up later,' he shouted.

A bend in the road, and the whole place disappeared.

How Pearl Button Was Kidnapped (1912)†

Pearl Button swung on the little gate in front of the House of Boxes. It was the early afternoon of a sunshiny day with little winds playing hide-and-seek in it. They blew Pearl Button's pinafore frill into her mouth and they blew the street dust all over the House of Boxes. Pearl watched it—like a cloud—like when mother peppered her fish and the top of the pepper-pot came off. She swung on the little gate, all alone, and she sang a small song. Two big women came walking down the street. One was dressed in red and the other was dressed in yellow and green. They had pink handkerchiefs over their heads, and both of them carried a big flax basket of ferns. They had no shoes and stockings on and they came walking along, slowly, because they were so fat, and talking to each

† Published under the pseudonym "Lili Heron" in *Rhythm* (September 1912) and collected in *Something Childish and Other Stories* (1924). "How Pearl Button Was Kidnapped" is Mansfield's only story with a Maori background.

other and always smiling. Pearl stopped swinging and when they saw her they stopped walking. They looked and looked at her and then they talked to each other waving their arms and clapping their hands together. Pearl began to laugh. The two women came up to her, keeping close to the hedge and looking in a frightened way towards the House of Boxes. 'Hallo, little girl!' said one. Pearl said, 'Hallo!' 'You all alone by yourself?' Pearl nodded. 'Where's your mother?' 'In the kitching, ironing-because-its-Tuesday.' The women smiled at her and Pearl smiled back. 'Oh,' she said, 'haven't you got very white teeth indeed! Do it again.' The dark women laughed and again they talked to each other with funny words and wavings of the hands. 'What's your name?' they asked her. 'Pearl Button.' 'You coming with us, Pearl Button? We got beautiful things to show you,' whispered one of the women. So Pearl got down from the gate and she slipped out into the road. And she walked between the two dark women down the windy road, taking little running steps to keep up and wondering what they had in their House of Boxes.

They walked a long way. 'You tired?' asked one of the women, bending down to Pearl. Pearl shook her head. They walked much further. 'You not tired?' asked the other woman. And Pearl shook her head again, but tears shook from her eyes at the same time and her lips trembled. One of the women gave over her flax basket of ferns and caught Pearl Button up in her arms and walked with Pearl Button's head against her shoulder and her dusty little legs dangling. She was softer than a bed and she had a nice smell—a smell that made you bury your head and breathe and breathe it. . . . They set Pearl Button down in a long room full of other people the same colour as they were—and all these people came close to her and looked at her, nodding and laughing and throwing up their eyes. The woman who had carried Pearl took off her hair ribbon and shook her curls loose. There was a cry from the other women and they crowded close and some of them ran a finger through Pearl's yellow curls, very gently, and one of them, a young one, lifted all Pearl's hair and kissed the back of her little white neck. Pearl felt shy but happy at the same time. There were some men on the floor, smoking, with rugs and feather mats round their shoulders. One of them made a funny face at her and he pulled a great big peach out of his pocket and set it on the floor, and flicked it with his finger as though it were a marble. It rolled right over to her. Pearl picked it up. 'Please can I eat it?' she asked. At that they all laughed and clapped their hands and the man with the funny face made another at her and pulled a pear out of his pocket and sent it bobbling over the floor. Pearl laughed. The women sat on the floor and Pearl sat down too. The floor was very dusty. She carefully pulled up her pinafore and dress and sat on her petticoat as she had been taught to sit in dusty places, and she ate the fruit, the juice running all down her front. 'Oh,' she said, in a very frightened voice to one of the women, 'I've spilt all the juice!' 'That doesn't matter at all,' said the woman, patting her cheek. A man came into the room with a long whip in his hand. He shouted something. They all got up, shouting, laughing, wrapping themselves up in rugs and blankets and feather mats. Pearl was carried again, this time into a great cart, and she sat on the lap of one of her women with the driver beside her. It was a green cart with a red pony and a black pony. It went very fast out of the town. The driver stood up and waved the whip round his head. Pearl peered over the shoulder of her woman. Other carts were behind like a procession. She waved at them. Then the country came. First fields of short grass with sheep on them and little bushes of white flowers and pink briar rose baskets—then big trees on both sides of the road—and nothing to be seen except big trees. Pearl tried to look through them but it was quite dark. Birds were singing. She nestled closer in the big lap. The woman was warm as a cat and she moved up and down when she breathed, just like purring. Pearl played with a green ornament round her neck and the woman took the little hand and kissed each of her fingers and then turned it over and kissed the dimples. Pearl had never been happy like this before. On the top of a big hill they stopped. The driving man turned to Pearl and said 'Look, look!' and pointed with his whip. And down at the bottom of the hill was something perfectly different—a great big piece of blue water was creeping over the land. She screamed and clutched at the big woman. 'What is it, what is it?' 'Why,' said the woman, 'it's the sea.' 'Will it hurt us—is it coming?' 'Ai-e, no, it doesn't come to us. It's very beautiful. You look again.' Pearl looked. 'You're sure it can't come,' she said. 'Ai-e, no. It stays in its place,' said the big woman. Waves with white tops came leaping over the blue. Pearl watched them break on a long piece of land covered with garden-path shells. They drove round a corner. There were some little houses down close to the sea, with wood fences round them and gardens inside. They comforted her. Pink and red and blue washing hung over the fences and as they came near more people came out and five yellow dogs with long thin tails. All the people were fat and laughing, with little naked babies holding on to them or rolling about in the gardens like puppies. Pearl was lifted down and taken into a tiny house with only one room and a veranda. There was a girl there with two pieces of black hair down to her feet. She was setting the dinner on the floor. 'It *is* a funny place,' said Pearl, watching the pretty girl while the woman unbuttoned her little drawers for her. She was very hungry. She ate meat and vegetables and fruit and the woman gave her milk out of a green cup. And it was quite silent except for the sea outside and the laughs of the two women watching her. 'Haven't you got any Houses in Boxes?' she said. 'Don't you all live in a row? Don't the men go to offices? Aren't there any nasty things?'

They took off her shoes and stockings, her pinafore and dress. She walked about in her petticoat and then she walked outside with the grass pushing between her toes. The two women came out with different sorts of baskets. They took her hands. Over a little paddock, through a fence, and then on warm sand with brown grass in it they went down to the sea. Pearl held back when the sand grew wet, but the women coaxed. 'Nothing to hurt, very beautiful. You come.' They dug in the sand and found some shells which they threw into the baskets. The sand was wet as mud pies. Pearl forgot her fright and began digging too. She got hot and wet and suddenly over her feet broke a little line of foam. 'Oo, oo!' she shrieked, dabbling with her feet, 'Lovely, lovely!' She paddled in the shallow water. It was warm. She made a cup of her hands and caught some of it. But it stopped being blue in her hands. She was so excited that she rushed over to her woman and flung her little thin arms round the woman's neck, hugging her, kissing. . . . Suddenly the girl gave a frightful scream. The woman raised herself and Pearl slipped down on the sand and looked towards the land. Little men in blue coats—little blue men came running, running towards her with shouts and whistlings—a crowd of little blue men to carry her back to the House of Boxes.

Ole Underwood (1912)†

Down the windy hill stalked Ole Underwood. He carried a black umbrella in one hand, in the other a red and white spotted handkerchief knotted into a lump. He wore a black peaked cap like a pilot; gold rings gleamed in his ears and his little eyes snapped like two sparks. Like two sparks they glowed in the smoulder of his bearded face. On one side of the hill grew a forest of pines from the road right down to the sea. On the other side short tufted grass and little bushes of white manuka flower. The pine-trees roared like waves in their topmost branches, their stems creaked like the timber of ships; in the windy air flew the white manuka flower. Ah—k! shouted Ole Underwood, shaking his umbrella at the wind bearing

† Published in *Rhythm* (January 1913) and collected in *Something Childish and Other Stories* (1924). As Antony Alpers notes in *The Stories of Katherine Mansfield* (1984), p. 552, "Ole Underwood's original, a familiar sight in Wellington, is said to have been brought before Mr Harold Beachamp, JP, on a vagrancy charge. The setting is authentic windy Wellington, with its prison on the hill above the harbor." "JP" is "Justice of the Peace," a role that allows one to adjudicate minor civil offenses.

down upon him, beating him, half strangling him with his black cape. Ah—k! shouted the wind a hundred times as loud, and filled his mouth and nostrils with dust. Something inside Ole Underwood's breast beat like a hammer. One two—one two—never stopping, never changing. He couldn't do anything. It wasn't loud. No, it didn't make a noise—only a thud. One, two—one, two—like someone beating on an iron in a prison—someone in a secret place—bang—bang—bang—trying to get free. Do what he would, fumble at his coat, throw his arms about, spit, swear, he couldn't stop the noise. Stop! Stop! Stop! Stop! Ole Underwood began to shuffle and run.

Away below the sea heaving against the stone walls, and the little town just out of its reach close packed together, the better to face the grey water. And up on the other side of the hill the prison with high red walls. Over all bulged the grey sky with black web-like clouds streaming.

Ole Underwood slackened his pace as he neared the town, and when he came to the first house he flourished his umbrella like a herald's staff and threw out his chest, his head glancing quickly from right to left. They were ugly little houses leading into the town, built of wood—two windows and a door, a stumpy veranda and a green mat of grass before. Under one veranda yellow hens huddled out of the wind. Shoo! shouted Ole Underwood, and laughed to see them fly, and laughed again at the woman who came to the door and shook a red, soapy fist at him. A little girl stood in another yard untwisting some rags from a clothes line. When she saw Ole Underwood she let the clothes prop fall and rushed screaming to the door, beating it, screaming 'Mum-ma—Mum-ma!' That started the hammer in Ole Underwood's heart. Mum-ma—Mum-ma! He saw an old face with a trembling chin and grey hair nodding out of the window as they dragged him past. Mum-ma—Mum-ma! He looked up at the big red prison perched on the hill and he pulled a face as if he wanted to cry. At the corner in front of the pub some carts were pulled up, and some men sat in the porch of the pub drinking and talking. Ole Underwood wanted a drink. He slouched into the bar. It was half full of old and young men in big coats and top boots with stock whips in their hands. Behind the counter a big girl with red hair pulled the beer handles and cheeked the men. Ole Underwood sneaked to one side, like a cat. Nobody looked at him, only the men looked at each other, one or two of them nudged. The girl nodded and winked at the fellow she was serving. He took some money out of his knotted handkerchief and slipped it on to the counter. His hand shook. He didn't speak. The girl took no notice; she served everybody, went on with her talk, and then as if by accident shoved a mug towards him. A great big jar of red pinks stood on the bar counter. Ole Underwood stared at them as he drank and frowned at them. Red—red—red—red! beat the hammer. It was very warm in the bar and quiet as a pond, except for the talk and the girl. She kept on laughing. Ha! ha! That was what the men liked to see, for she threw back her head and her great breasts lifted and shook to her laughter. In one corner sat a stranger. He pointed at Ole Underwood. 'Cracked!' said one of the men. 'When he was a young fellow, thirty years ago, a man 'ere done in 'is woman, an' 'e foun' out an' killed 'er. Got twenty year in quod[1] up on the 'ill. Came out cracked'. 'Oo done 'er in?' asked the man. 'Dunno. 'E don' no, nor nobody. 'E was a sailor till 'e marrid 'er. Cracked!' The man spat and smeared the spittle in the floor, shrugging his shoulders. ' 'E's 'armless enough.' Ole Underwood heard; he did not turn, but he shot out an old claw and crushed up the red pinks. 'Uh-Uh! You ole beast! Uh! You ole swine!' screamed the girl, leaning across the counter and banging him with a tin jug. 'Get art! Get art! Don' you never come 'ere no more!' Somebody kicked him: he scuttled like a rat.

He walked past the Chinamen's shops. The fruit and vegetables were all piled up against the windows. Bits of wooden cases, straw, and old newspapers were strewn over the pavement. A woman flounced out of a shop and slushed a pail of slops over his feet. He peered in at the windows, at the Chinamen sitting in little groups on old barrels playing cards. They made him smile. He looked and looked, pressing his face against the glass and sniggering. They sat still with their long pigtails bound round their heads and their faces yellow as lemons. Some of them had knives in their belts and one old man sat by himself on the floor plaiting his long crooked toes together. The Chinamen didn't mind Ole Underwood. When they saw him they nodded. He went to the door of a shop and cautiously opened it. In rushed the wind with him, scattering the cards. 'Ya-Ya! Ya-Ya!' screamed the Chinamen, and Ole Underwood rushed off, the hammer beating quick and hard. Ya-Ya! He turned a corner out of sight. He thought he heard one of the Chinks after him and he slipped into a timber-yard. There he lay panting. . . . Close by him, under another stack there was a heap of yellow shavings. As he watched them they moved and a little grey cat unfolded herself and came out waving her tail. She trod delicately over to Ole Underwood and rubbed against his sleeve. The hammer in Ole Underwood's heart beat madly. It pounded up into his throat, and then it seemed to half stop and beat very, very faintly. 'Kit! Kit! Kit!' That was what she used to call the little cat he brought her off the ship. Kit! Kit! Kit! and stoop down with the saucer in her hands. 'Ah! my

1. In prison.

God!—my Lord!' Ole Underwood sat up and took the kitten in his arms and rocked to and fro, crushing it against his face. It was warm and soft, and it mewed faintly. He buried his eyes in its fur. My God! My Lord! He tucked the little cat in his coat and stole out of the wood-yard, and slouched down toward the wharves. As he came near the sea, Ole Underwood's nostrils expanded. The mad wind smelled of tar and ropes and slime and salt. He crossed the railway line, he crept behind the wharf-sheds and along a little cinder path that threaded through a patch of rank fennel to some stone drain pipes carrying the sewage into the sea. And he stared up at the wharves and at the ships with flags flying and suddenly the old, old lust swept over Ole Underwood. 'I will! I will! I will!' he muttered. He tore the little cat out of his coat and swung it by its tail and flung it out to the sewer opening. The hammer beat loud and strong. He tossed his head, he was young again. He walked on to the wharves, past the wool-bales, past the loungers and the loafers to the extreme end of the wharves. The sea sucked against the wharf-poles as though it drank something from the land. One ship was loading wool. He heard a crane rattle and the shriek of a whistle. So he came to the little ship lying by herself with a bit of plank for a gangway and no sign of anybody—anybody at all. Ole Underwood looked once back at the town, at the prison perched like a red bird, at the black, webby clouds trailing. Then he went up the gangway and on to the slippery deck. He grinned, and rolled in his walk, carrying high in his hand the red and white handkerchief. His ship! Mine! Mine! Mine! beat the hammer. There was a door latched open on the lee-side, labelled 'State-room'. He peered in. A man lay sleeping on a bunk——his bunk——a great big man in a seaman's coat with a long fair beard and hair on the red pillow. And looking down upon him from the wall there shone her picture—his woman's picture—smiling and smiling at the big sleeping man.

Millie (1913)†

Millie stood leaning against the verandah until the men were out of sight. When they were far down the road Willie Cox turned round on his horse and waved. But she didn't wave back. She nodded her head a little and made a grimace. Not a bad young fellow, Willie Cox, but a bit too free and easy for her taste. Oh, my word! it was hot. Enough to fry your hair! Millie put her handkerchief over her

† Published in the *Blue Review* (June 1913) and collected in *Something Childish and Other Stories* (1924). "Millie" was the last of Mansfield's stories of colonial violence.

head and shaded her eyes with her hand. In the distance along the dusty road she could see the horses—like brown spots dancing up and down, and when she looked away from them and over the burnt paddocks she could see them still—just before her eyes, jumping like mosquitoes. It was half-past two in the afternoon. The sun hung in the faded blue sky like a burning mirror, and away beyond the paddocks the blue mountains quivered and leapt like sea. Sid wouldn't be back until half-past ten. He had ridden over to the township with four of the boys to help hunt down the young fellow who'd murdered Mr Williamson. Such a dreadful thing! And Mrs Williamson left all alone with all those kids. Funny! she couldn't think of Mr Williamson being dead! He was such a one for a joke. Always having a lark. Willie Cox said they found him in the barn, shot bang through the head, and the young English 'johnny' who'd been on the station[1] learning farming—disappeared. Funny! she wouldn't think of anyone shooting Mr Williamson, and him so popular and all. My word! when they caught that young man! Well—you couldn't be sorry for a young fellow like that. As Sid said, if he wasn't strung up where would they all be? A man like that doesn't stop at one go. There was blood all over the barn. And Willie Cox said he was that knocked out he picked a cigarette up out of the blood and smoked it. My word! he must have been half dotty.

Millie went back into the kitchen. She put some ashes on the stove and sprinkled them with water. Languidly, the sweat pouring down her face, and dropping off her nose and chin, she cleared away the dinner, and going into the bedroom, stared at herself in the fly-specked mirror, and wiped her face and neck with a towel. She didn't know what was the matter with herself that afternoon. She could have had a good cry—just for nothing—and then change her blouse and have a good cup of tea. Yes, she felt like that! She flopped down on the side of the bed and stared at the coloured print on the wall opposite, 'Garden Party at Windsor Castle'.[2] In the foreground emerald lawns planted with immense oak trees, and in their grateful shade, a muddle of ladies and gentlemen and parasols and little tables. The background was filled with the towers of Windsor Castle, flying three Union Jacks, and in the middle of the picture the old Queen, like a tea cosy with a head on top of it. 'I wonder if it really looked like that.' Millie stared at the flowery ladies, who simpered back at her. 'I wouldn't care for that sort of thing. Too much side. What with the Queen an' one thing an' another.' Over the packing case dressing-table there was a large photograph of her and Sid, taken on their wedding day. Nice picture

1. A sheep station was usually a large grazing property with its homestead and farm buildings. Johnny: a term for a recent arrival in the country.
2. A royal residence at Windsor, close to London.

that—if you *do* like. She was sitting down in a basket chair, in her cream cashmere and satin ribbons, and Sid, standing with one hand on her shoulder, looking at her bouquet. And behind them there were some fern trees, and a waterfall, and Mount Cook[3] in the distance, covered with snow. She had almost forgotten her wedding day; time did pass so, and if you hadn't any one to talk things over with, they soon dropped out of your mind. 'I wunner why we never had no kids. . . .' She shrugged her shoulders——gave it up. 'Well, *I've* never missed them. I wouldn't be surprised if Sid had, though. He's softer than me.'

And then she sat, quiet, thinking of nothing at all, her red swollen hands rolled in her apron, her feet stuck out in front of her, her little head with the thick screw of dark hair, dropped on her chest. 'Tick-tick' went the kitchen clock, the ashes clinked in the grate, and the venetian blind knocked against the kitchen window. Quite suddenly Millie felt frightened. A queer trembling started inside her—in her stomach—and then spread all over to her knees and hands. 'There's somebody about.' She tiptoed to the door and peered into the kitchen. Nobody there; the verandah doors were closed, the blinds were down, and in the dusky light the white face of the clock shone, and the furniture seemed to bulge and breathe . . . and listen, too. The clock—the ashes—and the venetian—and then again—something else—like steps in the back yard. 'Go an' see what it is, Millie Evans.' She started to the back door, opened it, and at the same moment someone ducked behind the wood pile. 'Who's that,' she cried in a loud, bold voice. 'Come out o' that. I seen yer. I know where you are. I got my gun. Come out from behind of that wood stack.' She was not frightened any more. She was furiously angry. Her heart banged like a drum. 'I'll teach you to play tricks with a woman,' she yelled, and she took a gun from the kitchen corner, and dashed down the verandah steps, across the glaring yard to the other side of the wood stack. A young man lay there, on his stomach, one arm across his face. 'Get up! You're shamming!' Still holding the gun she kicked him in the shoulders. He gave no sign. 'Oh, my God, I believe he's dead.' She knelt down, seized hold of him, and turned him over on his back. He rolled like a sack. She crouched back on her haunches, staring, her lips and nostrils fluttered with horror.

He was not much more than a boy, with fair hair, and a growth of fair down on his lips and chin. His eyes were open, rolled up, showing the whites, and his face was patched with dust caked with sweat. He wore a cotton shirt and trousers with sandshoes on his

3. Now known by its Maori name Aorangi; at over 12,000 feet, it is the highest peak in New Zealand.

feet. One of the trousers stuck to his leg with a patch of dark blood. 'I *can't*,' said Millie, and then, 'You've got to.' She bent over and felt his heart. 'Wait a minute,' she stammered, 'wait a minute,' and she ran into the house for brandy and a pail of water. 'What are you going to do, Millie Evans? Oh, I don't know. I never seen anyone in a dead faint before.' She knelt down, put her arm under the boy's head and poured some brandy between his lips. It spilled down both sides of his mouth. She dipped a corner of her apron in the water and wiped his face, and his hair and his throat, with fingers that trembled. Under the dust and sweat his face gleamed, white as her apron, and thin, and puckered in little lines. A strange dreadful feeling gripped Millie Evans' bosom—some seed that had never flourished there, unfolded, and struck deep roots and burst into painful leaf. 'Are yer coming round? Feeling all right again?' The boy breathed sharply, half choked, his eyelids quivered, and he moved his head from side to side. 'You're better,' said Millie, smoothing his hair. 'Feeling fine now again, ain't you?' The pain in her bosom half suffocated her. 'It's no good you crying, Millie Evans. You got to keep your head.' Quite suddenly he sat up and leaned against the wood pile, away from her, staring on the ground. 'There now!' cried Millie Evans, in a strange, shaking voice. The boy turned and looked at her, still not speaking, but his eyes were so full of pain and terror that she had to shut her teeth and clench her hand to stop from crying. After a long pause he said in the little voice of a child talking in his sleep, 'I'm hungry.' His lips quivered. She scrambled to her feet and stood over him. 'You come right into the house and have a set down meal,' she said. 'Can you walk?' 'Yes,' he whispered, and swaying he followed her across the glaring yard to the verandah. At the bottom step he paused, looking at her again. 'I'm not coming in,' he said. He sat on the verandah step in the little pool of shade that lay round the house. Millie watched him. 'When did yer last 'ave anythink to eat?' He shook his head. She cut a chunk off the greasy corned beef and a round of bread plastered with butter; but when she brought it he was standing up, glancing round him, and paid no attention to the plate of food. 'When are they coming back?' he stammered.

At that moment she knew. She stood, holding the plate, staring. He was Harrison. He was the English johnny who'd killed Mr Williamson. 'I know who you are,' she said, very slowly, 'yer can't fox me. That's who you are. I must have been blind in me two eyes not to 'ave known from the first.' He made a movement with his hands as though that was all nothing. 'When are they coming back?' And she meant to say, 'Any minute. They're on their way now.' Instead she said to the dreadful, frightened face, 'Not till 'arf past ten.' He sat down, leaning against one of the verandah poles.

His face broke up into little quivers. He shut his eyes and tears streamed down his cheeks. 'Nothing but a kid. An' all them fellows after 'im. 'E don't stand any more of a chance than a kid would.' 'Try a bit of beef,' said Millie. 'It's the food you want. Something to steady your stomach.' She moved across the verandah and sat down beside him, the plate on her knees. ' 'Ere—try a bit.' She broke the bread and butter into little pieces, and she thought, 'They won't ketch 'im. Not if I can 'elp it. Men is all beasts. I don' care wot 'e's done, or wot 'e 'asn't done. See 'im through, Millie Evans. 'E's nothink but a sick kid.'

Millie lay on her back, her eyes wide open, listening. Sid turned over, hunched the quilt round his shoulders, muttered 'Good night, ole girl.' She heard Willie Cox and the other chap drop their clothes on to the kitchen floor, and then their voices, and Willie Cox saying, 'Lie down, Gumboil. Lie down, yer little devil,' to his dog. The house dropped quiet. She lay and listened. Little pulses tapped in her body, listening, too. It was hot. She was frightened to move because of Sid. ' 'E must get off. 'E must. I don' care anythink about justice an' all the rot they've bin spouting to-night,' she thought, savagely. ' 'Ow are yer to know what anythink's like till yer *do* know. It's all rot.' She strained to the silence. He ought to be moving. . . . Before there was a sound from outside Willie Cox's Gumboil got up and padded sharply across the kitchen floor and sniffed at the back door. Terror started up in Millie. 'What's that dog doing? Uh! What a fool that young fellow is with a dog 'anging about. Why don't 'e lie down an' sleep.' The dog stopped, but she knew it was listening. Suddenly, with a sound that made her cry out in horror the dog started barking and rushing to and fro. 'What's that? What's up?' Sid flung out of bed. 'It ain't nothink. It's only Gumboil. Sid, Sid.' She clurched his arm, but he shook her off. My Christ, there's somethink up. My God.' Sid flung into his trousers. Willie Cox opened the back door. Gumboil in a fury darted out into the yard, round the corner of the house. 'Sid, there's someone in the paddock,' roared the other chap. 'What's it—what's that?' Sid dashed out on to the front verandah. 'Here, Millie, take the lantin. Willie, some skunk's got 'old of one of the 'orses.' The three men bolted out of the house and at the same moment Millie saw Harrison dash across the paddock on Sid's horse and down the road. 'Millie, bring that blasted lantin.' She ran in her bare feet, her nightdress flicking her legs. They were after him in a flash. And at the sight of Harrison in the distance, and the three men hot after, a strange mad joy smothered everything else. She rushed into the road—she laughed and shrieked and danced in the dust, jigging the lantern. 'A—ah! Arter 'im, Sid! A—a—a—h! ketch 'im, Willie. Go it! Go it! A—ah, Sid! Shoot 'im down. Shoot 'im!'

Bains Turcs (1913)†

'Third storey—to the left, Madame,' said the cashier, handing me a pink ticket. 'One moment—I will ring for the elevator.' Her black satin skirt swished across the scarlet and gold hall, and she stood among the artificial palms, her white neck and powdered face topped with masses of gleaming orange hair—like an over-ripe fungus bursting from a thick, black stem. She rang and rang. 'A thousand pardons, Madame. It is disgraceful. A new attendant. He leaves this week.' With her fingers on the bell she peered into the cage as though she expected to see him, lying on the floor, like a dead bird. 'It is disgraceful!' There appeared from nowhere a tiny figure disguised in a peaked cap and dirty white cotton gloves. 'Here you are!' she scolded. 'Where have you been? What have you been doing?' For answer the figure hid its face behind one of the white cotton gloves and sneezed twice. 'Ugh! Disgusting! Take Madame to the third storey!' The midget stepped aside, bowed, entered after me and clashed the gates to. We ascended, very slowly, to an accompaniment of sneezes and prolonged, half whistling sniffs. I asked the top of the patent leather cap: 'Have you a cold?' 'It is the air, Madame,' replied the creature, speaking through its nose with a restrained air of great relish, 'one is never dry here. Third floor—*if* you please,' sneezing over my ten-centime tip.

I walked along a tiled corridor decorated with advertisements for lingerie and bust improvers—was allotted a tiny cabin and a blue print chemise and told to undress and find the Warm Room as soon as possible. Through the matchboard walls and from the corridor sounded cries and laughter and snatches of conversation. 'Are you ready?' 'Are you coming out now?' 'Wait till you see me!' 'Berthe—Berthe!' 'One moment! One moment! Immediately!' I undressed quickly and carelessly, feeling like one of a troupe of little schoolgirls let loose in a swimming bath.

The Warm Room was not large. It had terra cotta painted walls with a fringe of peacocks, and a glass roof, through which one could see the sky, pale and unreal as a photographer's background screen. Some round tables strewn with shabby fashion journals, a marble basin in the centre of the room, filled with yellow lilies, and on the long, towel enveloped chairs, a number of ladies, apparently languid as the flowers. . . . I lay back with a cloth over my head, and the air, smelling of jungles and circuses and damp washing made me begin to dream. . . . Yes, it might have been very fascinating to

† The third in a set of "Epilogues," "Bains Turcs" was published in the *Blue Review* (July 1913) and collected in *Something Childish and Other Stories* (1924). The title means "Turkish Baths."

have married an explorer . . . and lived in a jungle, as long as he didn't shoot anything or take anything captive. I detest performing beasts. Oh . . . those circuses at home . . . the tent in the paddock and the children swarming over the fence to stare at the waggons and at the clown making up with his glass stuck on the waggon wheel—and the steam organ playing the *Honeysuckle and the Bee* much too fast . . . over and over. . . . I know what this air reminds me of—a game of follow my leader among the clothes hung out to dry. . . .

The door opened. Two tall blonde women in red and white check gowns came in and took the chairs opposite mine. One of them carried a box of mandarins wrapped in silver paper and the other a manicure set. They were very stout, with gay, bold faces, and quantities of exquisite whipped fair hair.

Before sitting down they glanced round the room, looked the other women up and down, turned to each other, grimaced, whispered something, and one of them said, offering the box, 'Have a mandarin?' At that they started laughing—they lay back and shook, and each time they caught sight of each other broke out afresh. 'Ah, that was too good,' cried one, wiping her eyes very carefully, just at the corners. 'You and I, coming in here, quite serious, you know, very correct—and looking round the room—and—and as a result of our *careful* inspection—I offer you a mandarin. No, it's too funny. I must remember that. It's good enough for a music hall. Have a mandarin?' 'But I cannot imagine,' said the other, 'why women look so hideous in Turkish baths—like beef steaks in chemises. Is it the women—or is it the air? Look at that one, for instance—the skinny one, reading a book and sweating at the moustache—and those two over in the corner, discussing whether or not they ought to tell their non-existent babies how babies come—and . . . Heavens! Look at this one coming in. Take the box, dear. Have all the mandarins.'

The newcomer was a short stout little woman with flat, white feet and a black mackintosh cap[1] over her hair. She walked up and down the room, swinging her arms, in affected unconcern, glanced contemptuously at the laughing women and rang the bell for the attendant. It was answered immediately by 'Berthe', half naked and sprinkled with soapsuds. 'Well, what is it, Madame. I've no time. . . .' 'Please bring me a hand towel,' said the Mackintosh Cap, in German. 'Pardon? I do not understand. Do you speak French?' 'Non,' said the Mackintosh Cap. 'Ber—the!' shrieked one of the blonde women, 'have a mandarin. Oh, mon Dieu, I shall die of laughing.' The Mackintosh Cap went through a pantomime of finding herself wet and rubbing herself dry. '*Verstehen Sie.*' 'Mais non,

1. A bathing cap made from rubberized cloth.

Madame,'[2] said Berthe, watching with round eyes that snapped with laughter, and she left the Mackintosh Cap, winked at the blonde women, came over, felt them as though they had been a pair of prize poultry, said 'You are doing very well,' and disappeared again. The Mackintosh Cap sat down on the edge of a chair, snatched a fashion journal, smacked over the crackling pages and pretended to read and the blonde women leaned back eating the mandarins and throwing the peelings into the lily basin. A scent of fruit, fresh and penetrating, hung on the air. I looked round at the other women. Yes, they were hideous, lying back, red and moist, with dull eyes and lank hair, the only little energy they had vented in shocked prudery at the behaviour of the two blondes. Suddenly I discovered Mackintosh Cap staring at me over the top of her fashion journal, so intently that I took flight and went into the hot room. But in vain! Mackintosh Cap followed after and planted herself in front of me.

'I know,' she said, confident and confiding, 'that you can speak German. I saw it in your face just now. Wasn't that a scandal about the attendant refusing me a towel? I shall speak to the management about that and I shall get my husband to write them a letter this evening. Things always come better from a man, don't they? No,' she said, rubbing her yellowish arms, 'I've never been in such a scandalous place—and four francs fifty to pay! Naturally, I shall not give a tip. You wouldn't, would you? Not after that scandal about a hand towel. . . . I've a great mind to complain about those women as well. Those two that keep on laughing and eating. Do you know who they are?' She shook her head. 'They're not respectable women—you can tell at a glance. At least I can, any married woman can. They're nothing but a couple of street women. I've never been so insulted in my life. Laughing at me, mind you! The great big fat pigs like that! And I haven't sweated at all properly, just because of them. I got so angry that the sweat turned in instead of out; it does in excitement, you know, sometimes, and now instead of losing my cold, I wouldn't be surprised if I brought on a fever.'

I walked round the hot room in misery pursued by the Mackintosh Cap until the two blonde women came in, and seeing her, burst into another fit of laughter. To my rage and disgust Mackintosh Cap sidled up to me, smiled meaningly, and drew down her mouth. 'I don't care,' she said, in her hideous German voice. 'I shouldn't lower myself by paying any attention to a couple of street women. If my husband knew he'd never get over it. Dreadfully particular he is. We've been married six years. We come from Salzburg. It's a nice town. Four children I have living, and it was really to get

2. You understand. [German] But no, Madame. [French]

over the shock of the fifth that we came here. The fifth,' she whispered, padding after me, 'was born, a fine healthy child, and it never breathed! Well, after nine months, a woman can't help being disappointed, can she?'

I moved towards the vapour room. 'Are you going in there?' she said. 'I wouldn't if I were you. Those two have gone in. They may think you want to strike up an acquaintance with them. You never know, women like that.' At that moment they came out, wrapping themselves in the rough gowns, and passing Mackintosh Cap like disdainful queens. 'Are you going to take your chemise off in the vapour room?' asked she. 'Don't mind me, you know. Woman is woman, and besides, if you'd rather, I won't look at you. I know—I used to be like that. I wouldn't mind betting,' she went on savagely, 'those filthy women had a good look at each other. Pooh! women like that. You can't shock them. And don't they look dreadful. Bold and all that false hair. That manicure box one of them had was fitted up with gold. Well, I don't suppose it was real, but I think it was disgusting to bring it. One might at least cut one's nails in private, don't you think? I *cannot* see,' she said, 'what men see in such women. No, a husband and children and a home to look after, that's what a woman needs. That's what my husband says. Fancy one of these hussies peeling potatoes or choosing the meat! Are you going already?'

I flew to find Berthe and all the time I was soaped and smacked and sprayed and thrown in a cold water tank I could not get out of my mind the ugly, wretched figure of the little German with a good husband and four children railing against the two fresh beauties who had never peeled potatoes nor chosen the right meat. In the anteroom I saw them once again. They were dressed in blue. One was pinning on a bunch of violets, the other buttoning a pair of ivory suède gloves. In their charming feathered hats and furs they stood talking. 'Yes, there they are,' said a voice at my elbow. And Mackintosh Cap, transformed, in a blue and white check blouse and crochet collar, with the little waist and large hips of the German woman and a terrible bird nest, which Salzburg doubtless called *Reise Hut*[3] on her head. 'How do you suppose they can afford clothes like that? The horrible, low creatures. No, they're enough to make a young girl think twice.' And as the two walked out of the anteroom, Mackintosh Cap stared after them, her sallow face all mouth and eyes, like the face of a hungry child before a forbidden table.

3. A traveling hat.

The Little Governess (1915)†

Oh dear, how she wished that it wasn't night-time. She'd have much rather travelled by day, much much rather. But the lady at the Governess Bureau had said: 'You had better take an evening boat and then if you get into a compartment for "Ladies Only" in the train you will be far safer than sleeping in a foreign hotel. Don't go out of the carriage; don't walk about the corridors and *be sure* to lock the lavatory door if you go there. The train arrives at Munich at eight o'clock, and Frau Arnholdt says that the Hotel Grünewald is only one minute away. A porter can take you there. She will arrive at six the same evening, so you will have a nice quiet day to rest after the journey and rub up your German. And when you want anything to eat I would advise you to pop into the nearest baker's and get a bun and some coffee. You haven't been abroad before, have you?' 'No.' 'Well, I always tell my girls that it's better to mistrust people at first rather than trust them, and it's safer to suspect people of evil intentions rather than good ones. . . . It sounds rather hard but we've got to be women of the world, haven't we?'

It had been nice in the Ladies' Cabin. The stewardess was so kind and changed her money for her and tucked up her feet. She lay on one of the hard pink-sprigged couches and watched the other passengers, friendly and natural, pinning their hats to the bolsters, taking off their boots and skirts, opening dressing-cases and arranging mysterious rustling little packages, tying their heads up in veils before lying down. *Thud, thud, thud*, went the steady screw of the steamer. The stewardess pulled a green shade over the light and sat down by the stove, her skirt turned back over her knees, a long piece of knitting on her lap. On a shelf above her head there was a water-bottle with a tight bunch of flowers stuck in it. 'I like travelling very much,' thought the little governess. She smiled and yielded to the warm rocking.

But when the boat stopped and she went up on deck, her dress-basket in one hand, her rug and umbrella in the other, a cold, strange wind flew under her hat. She looked up at the masts and spars of the ship black against a green glittering sky and down to the dark landing stage where strange muffled figures lounged, waiting; she moved forward with the sleepy flock, all knowing where to go to and what to do except her, and she felt afraid. Just a little—just enough to wish—oh, to wish that it was daytime and that one of those women who had smiled at her in the glass, when they both did their hair in the Ladies' Cabin, was somewhere near now. 'Tick-

† Published under the pseudonym "Matilda Berry" in installments in *Signature* (18 October and 1 November 1915) and collected in *Bliss and Other Stories* (1920).

ets, please. Show your tickets. Have your tickets ready.' She went down the gangway balancing herself carefully on her heels. Then a man in a black leather cap came forward and touched her on the arm. 'Where for, Miss?' He spoke English—he must be a guard or a stationmaster with a cap like that. She had scarcely answered when he pounced on her dress-basket. 'This way,' he shouted, in a rude, determined voice, and elbowing his way he strode past the people. 'But I don't want a porter.' What a horrible man! 'I don't want a porter. I want to carry it myself.' She had to run to keep up with him, and her anger, far stronger than she, ran before her and snatched the bag out of the wretch's hand. He paid no attention at all, but swung on down the long dark platform, and across a railway line. 'He is a robber.' She was sure he was a robber as she stepped between the silvery rails and felt the cinders crunch under her shoes. On the other side—oh, thank goodness!—there was a train with Munich written on it. The man stopped by the huge lighted carriages. 'Second class?' asked the insolent voice. 'Yes, a Ladies' compartment.' She was quite out of breath. She opened her little purse to find something small enough to give this horrible man while he tossed her dress-basket into the rack of an empty carriage that had a ticket, *Dames Seules*,[1] gummed on the window. She got into the train and handed him twenty centimes. 'What's this?' shouted the man, glaring at the money and then at her, holding it up to his nose, sniffing at it as though he had never in his life seen, much less held, such a sum. 'It's a franc. You know that, don't you? It's a franc. That's my fare!' A franc! Did he imagine that she was going to give him a franc for playing a trick like that just because she was a girl and travelling alone at night? Never, never! She squeezed her purse in her hand and simply did not see him—she looked at a view of St Malo on the wall opposite and simply did not hear him. 'Ah, no. Ah, no. Four sous. You make a mistake. Here, take it. It's a franc I want.' He leapt on to the step of the train and threw the money on to her lap. Trembling with terror she screwed herself tight, tight, and put out an icy hand and took the money—stowed it away in her hand. 'That's all you're going to get,' she said. For a minute or two she felt his sharp eyes pricking her all over, while he nodded slowly, pulling down his mouth: 'Ve-ry well. *Trrrès bien*.' He shrugged his shoulders and disappeared into the dark. Oh, the relief! How simply terrible that had been! As she stood up to feel if the dress-basket was firm she caught sight of herself in the mirror, quite white, with big round eyes. She untied her 'motor veil'[2]

1. "Unaccompanied Women" in its traveling context; the phrase also came to be associated with Mansfield's favorite theme of single or lonely women.
2. In the early days of motoring, women often wore a special veil as protection against wind and dust.

and unbuttoned her green cape. 'But it's all over now,' she said to the mirror face, feeling in some way that it was more frightened than she.

People began to assemble on the platform. They stood together in little groups talking; a strange light from the station lamps painted their faces almost green. A little boy in red clattered up with a huge tea wagon and leaned against it, whistling and flicking his boots with a serviette. A woman in a black alpaca apron pushed a barrow with pillows for hire. Dreamy and vacant she looked—like a woman wheeling a perambulator—up and down, up and down—with a sleeping baby inside it. Wreaths of white smoke floated up from somewhere and hung below the roof like misty vines. 'How strange it all is,' thought the little governess, 'and the middle of the night, too.' She looked out from her safe corner, frightened no longer but proud that she had not given that franc. 'I can look after myself—of course I can. The great thing is not to—' Suddenly from the corridor there came a stamping of feet and men's voices, high and broken with snatches of loud laughter. They were coming her way. The little governess shrank into her corner as four young men in bowler hats passed, staring through the door and window. One of them, bursting with the joke, pointed to the notice *Dames Seules* and the four bent down the better to see the one little girl in the corner. Oh dear, they were in the carriage next door. She heard them tramping about and then a sudden hush followed by a tall thin fellow with a tiny black moustache who flung her door open. 'If mademoiselle cares to come in with us,' he said, in French. She saw the others crowding behind him, peeping under his arm and over his shoulder, and she sat very straight and still. 'If mademoiselle will do us the honour,' mocked the tall man. One of them could be quiet no longer; his laughter went off in a loud crack. 'Mademoiselle is serious,' persisted the young man, bowing and grimacing. He took off his hat with a flourish, and she was alone again.

'*En voiture. En voi-ture!*'[3] Some one ran up and down beside the train. 'I wish it wasn't night-time. I wish there was another woman in the carriage. I'm frightened of the men next door.' The little governess looked out to see her porter coming back again—the same man making for her carriage with his arms full of luggage. But—but what *was* he doing? He put his thumb nail under the label *Dames Seules* and tore it right off and then stood aside squinting at her while an old man wrapped in a plaid cape climbed up the high step. 'But this is a ladies' compartment.' 'Oh, no, Mademoiselle, you make a mistake. No, no, I assure you. Merci, Monsieur.' '*En*

3. Into the carriage. Into the carriage!

voi-turre!' A shrill whistle. The porter stepped off triumphant and the train started. For a moment or two big tears brimmed her eyes and through them she saw the old man unwinding a scarf from his neck and untying the flaps of his Jaeger cap. He looked very old. Ninety at least. He had a white moustache and big gold-rimmed spectacles with little blue eyes behind them and pink wrinkled cheeks. A nice face—and charming the way he bent forward and said in halting French: 'Do I disturb you, Mademoiselle? Would you rather I took all these things out of the rack and found another carriage?' What! that old man have to move all those heavy things just because she. . . . 'No, it's quite all right. You don't disturb me at all.' 'Ah, a thousand thanks.' He sat down opposite her and unbuttoned the cape of his enormous coat and flung it off his shoulders.

The train seemed glad to have left the station. With a long leap it sprang into the dark. She rubbed a place in the window with her glove but she could see nothing—just a tree outspread like a black fan or a scatter of lights, or the line of a hill, solemn and huge. In the carriage next door the young men started singing '*Un, deux, trois*.' They sang the same song over and over at the tops of their voices.

'I never could have dared to go to sleep if I had been alone,' she decided. '*I couldn't* have put my feet up or even taken off my hat.' The singing gave her a queer little tremble in her stomach and, hugging herself to stop it, with her arms crossed under her cape, she felt really glad to have the old man in the carriage with her. Careful to see that he was not looking she peeped at him through her long lashes. He sat extremely upright, the chest thrown out, the chin well in, knees pressed together, reading a German paper. That was why he spoke French so funnily. He was a German. Something in the army, she supposed—a Colonel or a General—once, of course, not now; he was too old for that now. How spick and a span he looked for an old man. He wore a pearl pin stuck in his black tie and a ring with a dark red stone on his little finger; the tip of a white silk handkerchief showed in the pocket of his double-breasted jacket. Somehow, altogether, he was really nice to look at. Most old men were so horrid. She couldn't bear them doddery—or they had a disgusting cough or something. But not having a beard—that made all the difference—and then his cheeks were so pink and his moustache so very white. Down went the German paper and the old man leaned forward with the same delightful courtesy: 'Do you speak German, Mademoiselle?' '*Ja, ein wenig, mehr als Franzosisch,*'[4] said the little governess, blushing a deep pink colour that spread slowly over her cheeks and made her blue eyes

4. Yes, a little, more than I speak French.

look almost black. 'Ach, so!' The old man bowed graciously. 'Then perhaps you would care to look at some illustrated papers.' He slipped a rubber band from a little roll of them and handed them across. 'Thank you very much.' She was very fond of looking at pictures, but first she would take off her hat and gloves. So she stood up, unpinned the brown straw and put it neatly in the rack beside the dress-basket, stripped off her brown kid gloves, paired them in a tight roll and put them in the crown of the hat for safety, and then sat down again, more comfortably this time, her feet crossed, the papers on her lap. How kindly the old man in the corner watched her bare little hand turning over the big white pages, watched her lips moving as she pronounced the long words to herself, rested upon her hair that fairly blazed under the light. Alas! how tragic for a little governess to possess hair that made one think of tangerines and marigolds, of apricots and tortoiseshell cats and champagne! Perhaps that was what the old man was thinking as he gazed and gazed, and that not even the dark ugly clothes could disguise her soft beauty. Perhaps the flush that licked his cheeks and lips was a flush of rage that anyone so young and tender should have to travel alone and unprotected through the night. Who knows he was not murmuring in his sentimental German fashion: '*Ja, es ist eine Tragœdie!* Would to God I were the child's grandpapa!'

'Thank you very much. They were very interesting.' She smiled prettily handing back the papers. 'But you speak German extremely well,' said the old man. 'You have been in Germany before, of course?' 'Oh no, this is the first time'—a little pause, then—'this is the first time that I have ever been abroad at all.' 'Really! I am surprised. You gave me the impression, if I may say so, that you were accustomed to travelling.' 'Oh, well—I have been about a good deal in England, and to Scotland, once.' 'So. I myself have been in England once, but I could not learn English.' He raised one hand and shook his head, laughing. 'No, it was too difficult for me. . . . "Owdo-you-do. Please vich is ze vay to Leicestaire Squaare."'[5] She laughed too. 'Foreigners always say. . . .' They had quite a little talk about it. 'But you will like Munich,' said the old man. 'Munich is a wonderful city. Museums, pictures, galleries, fine buildings and shops, concerts, theatres, restaurants—all are in Munich. I have travelled all over Europe many, many times in my life, but it is always to Munich that I return. You will enjoy yourself there.' 'I am not going to *stay* in Munich,' said the little governess, and she added shyly, 'I am going to a post as governess to a doctor's family in Augsburg.' Ah, that was it. Augsburg he knew. Augsburg—well—

5. Leicester Square, in the center of London's theater and gallery area.

was not beautiful. A solid manufacturing town. But if Germany was new to her he hoped she would find something interesting there too. 'I am sure I shall.' 'But what a pity not to see Munich before you go. You ought to take a little holiday on your way'—he smiled—'and store up some pleasant memories.' 'I am afraid I could not do *that*,' said the little governess, shaking her head, suddenly important and serious. 'And also, if one is alone. . . .' He quite understood. He bowed, serious too. They were silent after that. The train shattered on, baring its dark, flaming breast to the hills and to the valleys. It was warm in the carriage. She seemed to lean against the dark rushing and to be carried away and away. Little sounds made themselves heard; steps in the corridor, doors opening and shutting—a murmur of voices—whistling. . . . Then the window was pricked with long needles of rain. . . . But it did not matter . . . it was outside . . . and she had her umbrella . . . she pouted, sighed, opened and shut her hands once and fell fast asleep.

'Pardon! Pardon!' The sliding back of the carriage door woke her with a start. What had happened? Some one had come in and gone out again. The old man sat in his corner, more upright than ever, his hands in the pockets of his coat, frowning heavily. 'Ha! ha! ha!' came from the carriage next door. Still half asleep, she put her hands to her hair to make sure it wasn't a dream. 'Disgraceful!' muttered the old man more to himself than to her. 'Common, vulgar fellows! I am afraid they disturbed you, gracious Fräulein, blundering in here like that.' No, not really. She was just going to wake up, and she took out her silver watch to look at the time. Half-past four. A cold blue light filled the window panes. Now when she rubbed a place she could see bright patches of fields, a clump of white houses like mushrooms, a road 'like a picture' with poplar trees on either side, a thread of river. How pretty it was! How pretty and how different! Even those pink clouds in the sky looked foreign. It was cold, but she pretended that it was far colder and rubbed her hands together and shivered, pulling at the collar of her coat because she was so happy.

The train began to slow down. The engine gave a long shrill whistle. They were coming to a town. Taller houses, pink and yellow, glided by, fast asleep behind their green eyelids, and guarded by the poplar trees that quivered in the blue air as if on tiptoe, listening. In one house a woman opened the shutters, flung a red and white mattress across the window frame and stood staring at the train. A pale woman with black hair and a white woollen shawl over her shoulders. More women appeared at the doors and at the windows of the sleeping houses. There came a flock of sheep. The shepherd wore a blue blouse and pointed wooden shoes. Look! look what flowers—and by the railway station too! Standard roses like bridesmaids' bouquets, white geraniums, waxy pink ones that you would *never* see out of a greenhouse at home. Slower and slower. A man with a watering-can was spraying the platform. 'A-a-a-ah!' Somebody came running and waving his arms. A huge fat woman waddled through the glass doors of the station with a tray of strawberries. Oh, she was thirsty! She was very thirsty! 'A-a-a-ah!' The same somebody ran back again. The train stopped.

The old man pulled his coat round him and got up, smiling at her. He murmured something she didn't quite catch, but she smiled back at him as he left the carriage. While he was away the little governess looked at herself again in the glass, shook and patted herself with the precise practical care of a girl who is old enough to travel by herself and has nobody else to assure her that she is 'quite all right behind'. Thirsty and thirsty! The air tasted of water. She let down the window and the fat woman with the strawberries passed as if on purpose; holding up the tray to her. '*Nein, danke*,' said the little governess, looking at the big berries on their gleaming leaves. '*Wie viel*?'[6] she asked as the fat woman moved away. 'Two marks fifty, Fräulein.' 'Good gracious!' She came in from the window and sat down in the corner, very sobered for a minute. Half a crown! 'H-o-o-o-o-e-e-e!' shrieked the train, gathering itself together to be off again. She hoped the old man wouldn't be left behind. Oh, it was daylight—everything was lovely if only she hadn't been so thirsty. Where *was* the old man—oh, here he was—she dimpled at him as though he were an old accepted friend as he closed the door and, turning, took from under his cape a basket of the strawberries. 'If Fräulein would honour me by accepting these. . . .' 'What for me?' But she drew back and raised her hands as though he were about to put a wild little kitten on her lap.

'Certainly, for you,' said the old man. 'For myself it is twenty years since I was brave enough to eat strawberries.' 'Oh, thank you very much. *Danke bestens*,' she stammered, '*sie sind so sehr schön!*'[7] 'Eat them and see,' said the old man looking pleased and friendly. 'You won't have even one?' 'No, no, no.' Timidly and charmingly her hand hovered. They were so big and juicy she had to take two bites to them—the juice ran all down her fingers—and it was while she munched the berries that she first thought of the old man as a grandfather. What a perfect grandfather he would make! Just like one out of a book!

The sun came out, the pink clouds in the sky, the strawberry

6. No, thank you. How much does it cost?
7. Thank you so much, you are so very kind!

clouds were eaten by the blue. 'Are they good?' asked the old man. 'As good as they look?'

When she had eaten them she felt she had known him for years. She told him about Frau Arnholdt and how she had got the place. Did he know the Hotel Grünewald? Frau Arnholdt would not arrive until the evening. He listened, listened until he knew as much about the affair as she did, until he said—not looking at her—but smoothing the palms of his brown suède gloves together: 'I wonder if you would let me show you a little of Munich to-day. Nothing much—but just perhaps a picture gallery and the Englischer Garten.[8] It seems such a pity that you should have to spend the day at the hotel, and also a little uncomfortable . . . in a strange place. *Nicht wahr*?[9] You would be back there by the early afternoon or whenever you wish, of course, and you would give an old man a great deal of pleasure.'

It was not until long after she had said 'Yes'—because the moment she had said it and he had thanked her he began telling her about his travels in Turkey and attar of roses—that she wondered whether she had done wrong. After all, she really did not know him. But he was so old and he had been so very kind—not to mention the strawberries. . . . And she couldn't have explained the reason why she said 'No,' and it was her *last* day in a way, her last day to really enjoy herself in. 'Was I wrong? Was I?' A drop of sunlight fell into her hands and lay there, warm and quivering. 'If I might accompany you as far as the hotel,' he suggested, 'and call for you again at about ten o'clock.' He took out his pocket-book and handed her a card. 'Herr Regierungsrat. . . .' He had a title![1] Well, it was *bound* to be all right! So after that the little governess gave herself up to the excitement of being really abroad, to looking out and reading the foreign advertisement signs, to being told about the places they came to—having her attention and enjoyment looked after by the charming old grandfather—until they reached Munich and the Hauptbahnhof.[2] 'Porter! Porter!' He found her a porter, disposed of his own luggage in a few words, guided her through the bewildering crowd out of the station down the clean white steps into the white road to the hotel. He explained who she was to the manager as though all this had been bound to happen, and then for one moment her little hand lost itself in the big brown suède ones. 'I will call for you at ten o'clock.' He was gone.

'This way, Fräulein,' said a waiter, who had been dodging behind the manager's back, all eyes and ears for the strange couple. She

8. The English Garden, a large park in the center of Munich.
9. Isn't that so?
1. The title of a senior government official.
2. Main railway station.

followed him up two flights of stairs into a dark bedroom. He dashed down her dress-basket and pulled up a clattering, dusty blind. Ugh! what an ugly, cold room—what enormous furniture! Fancy spending the day in here! 'Is this the room Frau Arnholdt ordered?' asked the little governess. The waiter had a curious way of staring as if there was something *funny* about her. He pursed up his lips about to whistle, and then changed his mind. '*Gewiss*,' he said. Well, why didn't he go? Why did he stare so? '*Gehen Sie*,' said the little governess, with frigid English simplicity. His little eyes, like currants, nearly popped out of his doughy cheeks. '*Gehen Sie sofort*,'[3] she repeated icily. At the door he turned. 'And the gentleman,' said he, 'shall I show the gentleman upstairs when he comes?'

Over the white streets big white clouds fringed with silver—and sunshine everywhere. Fat, fat coachmen driving fat cabs; funny women with little round hats cleaning the tramway lines; people laughing and pushing against one another; trees on both sides of the streets and everywhere you looked almost, immense fountains; a noise of laughing from the footpaths or the middle of the streets or the open windows. And beside her, more beautifully brushed than ever, with a rolled umbrella in one hand and yellow gloves instead of brown ones, her grandfather who had asked her to spend the day. She wanted to run, she wanted to hang on his arm, she wanted to cry every minute, 'Oh, I am so frightfully happy!' He guided her across the roads, stood still while she 'looked', and his kind eyes beamed on her and he said 'just whatever you wish'. She ate two white sausages and two little rolls of fresh bread at eleven o'clock in the morning and she drank some beer, which he told her wasn't intoxicating, wasn't at all like English beer, out of a glass like a flower vase. And then they took a cab and really she must have seen thousands and thousands of wonderful classical pictures in about a quarter of an hour! 'I shall have to think them over when I am alone.' . . . But when they came out of the picture gallery it was raining. The grandfather unfurled his umbrella and held it over the little governess. They started to walk to the restaurant for lunch. She, very close beside him so that he should have some of the umbrella, too. 'It goes easier,' he remarked in a detached way, 'if you take my arm, Fräulein. And besides it is the custom in Germany.' So she took his arm and walked beside him while he pointed out the famous statues, so interested that he quite forgot to put down the umbrella even when the rain was long over.

After lunch they went to a café to hear a gipsy band, but she did not like that at all. Ugh! such horrible men were there with heads

3. Certainly. Go away. Go away at once!

like eggs and cuts on their faces, so she turned her chair and cupped her burning cheeks in her hands and watched her old friend instead. . . . Then they went to the Englischer Garten.

'I wonder what the time is,' asked the little governess. 'My watch has stopped. I forgot to wind it in the train last night. We've seen such a lot of things that I feel it must be quite late.' 'Late!' He stopped in front of her laughing and shaking his head in a way she had begun to know. 'Then you have not really enjoyed yourself. Late! Why, we have not had any ice cream yet!' 'Oh, but I have enjoyed myself,' she cried, distressed, 'more than I can possibly say. It has been wonderful! Only Frau Arnholdt is to be at the hotel at six and I ought to be there by five.' 'So you shall. After the ice cream I shall put you into a cab and you can go there comfortably.' She was happy again. The chocolate ice cream melted—melted in little sips a long way down. The shadows of the trees danced on the table cloths, and she sat with her back safely turned to the ornamental clock that pointed to twenty-five minutes to seven. 'Really and truly,' said the little governess earnestly, 'this has been the happiest day of my life. I've never even imagined such a day.' In spite of the ice cream her grateful baby heart glowed with love for the fairy grandfather.

So they walked out of the garden down a long alley. The day was nearly over. 'You see those big buildings opposite,' said the old man. 'The third storey—that is where I live. I and the old housekeeper who looks after me.' She was very interested. 'Now just before I find a cab for you, will you come and see my little "home" and let me give you a bottle of the attar of roses I told you about in the train? For remembrance?' She would love to. 'I've never seen a bachelor's flat in my life,' laughed the little governess.

The passage was quite dark. 'Ah, I suppose my old woman has gone out to buy me a chicken. One moment.' He opened a door and stood aside for her to pass, a little shy but curious, into a strange room. She did not know quite what to say. It wasn't pretty. In a way it was very ugly—but neat, and, she supposed, comfortable for such an old man. 'Well, what do you think of it?' He knelt down and took from a cupboard a round tray with two pink glasses and a tall pink bottle. 'Two little bedrooms beyond,' he said gaily, 'and a kitchen. It's enough, eh?' 'Oh, quite enough.' 'And if ever you should be in Munich and care to spend a day or two—why there is always a little nest—a wing of a chicken, and a salad, and an old man delighted to be your host once more and many many times, dear little Fräulein!' He took the stopper out of the bottle and poured some wine into the two pink glasses. His hand shook and the wine spilled over the tray. It was very quiet in the room. She said: 'I think I ought to go now.' 'But you will have a tiny glass of wine with me—

just one before you go?' said the old man. 'No, really no. I never drink wine. I—I have promised never to touch wine or anything like that.' And though he pleaded and though she felt dreadfully rude, especially when he seemed to take it to heart so, she was quite determined. 'No, *really*, please.' 'Well, will you just sit down on the sofa for five minutes and let me drink your health?' The little governess sat down on the edge of the red velvet couch and he sat down beside her and drank her health at a gulp. 'Have you really been happy to-day?' asked the old man, turning round, so close beside her that she felt his knee twitching against hers. Before she could answer he held her hands. 'And are you going to give me one little kiss before you go?' he asked, drawing her closer still.

It was a dream! It wasn't true! It wasn't the same old man at all. Ah, how horrible! The little governess stared at him in terror. 'No, no, no!' she stammered, struggling out of his hands. 'One little kiss. A kiss. What is it? Just a kiss, dear little Fräulein. A kiss.' He pushed his face forward, his lips smiling broadly; and how his little blue eyes gleamed behind the spectacles! 'Never—never. How can you!' She sprang up, but he was too quick and he held her against the wall, pressed against her his hard old body and his twitching knee and, though she shook her head from side to side, distracted, kissed her on the mouth. On the mouth! Where not a soul who wasn't a near relation had ever kissed her before. . . .

She ran, ran down the street until she found a broad road with tram lines and a policeman standing in the middle like a clockwork doll. 'I want to get a tram to the Hauptbahnhof,' sobbed the little governess. 'Fräulein?' She wrung her hands at him. 'The Hauptbahnhof. There—there's one now,' and while he watched very much surprised, the little girl with her hat on one side, crying without a handkerchief, sprang on to the tram—not seeing the conductor's eyebrows, nor hearing the *hochwohlgebildete Dame*[4] talking her over with a scandalized friend. She rocked herself and cried out loud and said 'Ah, ah!' pressing her hands to her mouth. 'She has been to the dentist,' shrilled a fat old woman, too stupid to be uncharitable. '*Na, sagen Sie 'mal*,[5] what toothache! The child hasn't one left in her mouth.' While the tram swung and jangled through a world full of old men with twitching knees.

When the little governess reached the hall of the Hotel Grünewald the same waiter who had come into her room in the morning was standing by a table, polishing a tray of glasses. The sight of the little governess seemed to fill him out with some inexplicable impor-

4. Highly cultivated woman.
5. Now, just tell me.

tant content. He was ready for her question; his answer came pat and suave. 'Yes, Fräulein, the lady has been here. I told her that you had arrived and gone out again immediately with a gentleman. She asked me when you were coming back again—but of course I could not say. And then she went to the manager.' He took up a glass from the table, held it up to the light, looked at it with one eye closed, and started polishing it with a corner of his apron. '. . . ?' 'Pardon, Fräulein? Ach, no, Fräulein. The manager could tell her nothing—nothing.' He shook his head and smiled at the brilliant glass. 'Where is the lady now?' asked the little governess, shuddering so violently that she had to hold her handkerchief up to her mouth. 'How should I know?' cried the waiter, and as he swooped past her to pounce upon a new arrival his heart beat so hard against his ribs that he nearly chuckled aloud. 'That's it! that's it!' he thought. 'That will show her.' And as he swung the new arrival's box on to his shoulders—hoop!—as though he were a giant and the box a feather, he minced over again the little governess's words, '*Gehen Sie. Gehen Sie sofort*.[6] Shall I! Shall I!' he shouted to himself.

An Indiscreet Journey (1915)†

She is like St. Anne.[1] Yes, the concierge[2] is the image of St Anne, with that black cloth over her head, the wisps of grey hair hanging, and the tiny smoking lamp in her hand. Really very beautiful, I thought, smiling at St Anne, who said severely: 'Six o'clock. You have only just got time. There is a bowl of milk on the writing table.' I jumped out of my pyjamas and into a basin of cold water like any English lady in any French novel. The concierge, persuaded that I was on my way to prison cells and death by bayonets, opened the shutters and the cold clear light came through. A little steamer hooted on the river; a cart with two horses at a gallop flung past. The rapid swirling water; the tall black trees on the far side, grouped together like negroes conversing. Sinister, very, I thought, as I buttoned on my age-old Burberry.[3] (That Burberry was very significant. It did not belong to me. I had borrowed it from a friend. My eye lighted upon it hanging in her little dark hall. The very thing! The perfect and adequate disguise—an old Burberry. Lions

6. Go away at once.

† Published in *Something Childish and Other Stories* (1924). The probable reason for its not appearing in Mansfield's lifetime was that it was a semi-fictional account of her brief liaison with the French novelist Francis Carco (1886–1959) and her visit to him in the military zone at Gray, near Dijon, in February 1915. The likely date for the story is 1915.

1. The mother of the Virgin Mary.
2. The caretaker of a small hotel or apartment building who lives on the premises.
3. A lightweight belted raincoat, usually beige in color.

have been faced in a Burberry. Ladies have been rescued from open boats in mountainous seas wrapped in nothing else. An old Burberry seems to me the sign and the token of the undisputed venerable traveller, I decided, leaving my purple peg-top with the real seal collar and cuffs in exchange.)

'You will never get there,' said the concierge, watching me turn up the collar. 'Never! Never!' I ran down the echoing stairs—strange they sounded, like a piano flicked by a sleepy housemaid—and on to the Quai. 'Why so fast, *ma mignonne*?' said a lovely little boy in coloured socks, dancing in front of the electric lotus buds that curve over the entrance to the Métro.[4] Alas! there was not even time to blow him a kiss. When I arrived at the big station I had only four minutes to spare, and the platform entrance was crowded and packed with soldiers, their yellow papers in one hand and big untidy bundles. The Commissaire of Police[5] stood on one side, a Nameless Official on the other. Will he let me pass? Will he? He was an old man with a fat swollen face covered with big warts. Horn-rimmed spectacles squatted on his nose. Trembling, I made an effort. I conjured up my sweetest early-morning smile and handed it with the papers. But the delicate thing fluttered against the horn spectacles and fell. Nevertheless, he let me pass, and I ran, ran in and out among the soldiers and up the high steps into the yellow-painted carriage.

'Does one go direct to X?' I asked the collector who dug at my ticket with a pair of forceps and handed it back again. 'No, Mademoiselle, you must change at X. Y. Z.'

'At—?'

'X. Y. Z.'

Again I had not heard. 'At what time do we arrive there if you please?'

'One o'clock.' But that was no good to me. I hadn't a watch. Oh, well—later.

Ah! the train had begun to move. The train was on my side. It swung out of the station, and soon we were passing the vegetable gardens, passing the tall blind houses to let, passing the servants beating carpets. Up already and walking in the fields, rosy from the rivers and the red-fringed pools, the sun lighted upon the swinging train and stroked my muff and told me to take off that Burberry. I was not alone in the carriage. An old woman sat opposite, her skirt turned back over her knees, a bonnet of black lace on her head. In her fat hands, adorned with a wedding and two mourning rings, she held a letter. Slowly, slowly she sipped a sentence, and then looked

4. The underground railway in Paris. *Ma mignonne*: my sweet one.
5. Police captain in the United States, Police superintendent in Britain.

up and out of the window, her lips trembling a little, and then another sentence, and again the old face turned to the light, tasting it. . . . Two soldiers leaned out of the window, their heads nearly touching—one of them was whistling, the other had his coat fastened with some rusty safety-pins. And now there were soldiers everywhere working on the railway line, leaning against trucks or standing hands on hips, eyes fixed on the train as though they expected at least one camera at every window. And now we were passing big wooden sheds like rigged-up dancing halls or seaside pavilions, each flying a flag. In and out of them walked the Red Cross men; the wounded sat against the walls sunning themselves. At all the bridges, the crossings, the stations, a *petit soldat*,[6] all boots and bayonet. Forlorn and desolate he looked,—like a little comic picture waiting for the joke to be written underneath. Is there really such a thing as war? Are all these laughing voices really going to the war? These dark woods lighted so mysteriously by the white stems of the birch and the ash—these watery fields with the big birds flying over—these rivers green and blue in the light—have battles been fought in places like these?

What beautiful cemeteries we are passing! They flash gay in the sun. They seem to be full of cornflowers and poppies and daisies. How can there be so many flowers at this time of the year? But they are not flowers at all. They are bunches of ribbons tied on to the soldiers' graves.

I glanced up and caught the old woman's eye. She smiled and folded the letter. 'It is from my son—the first we have had since October. I am taking it to my daughter-in-law.'

'. . . . . ?'

'Yes, very good,' said the old woman, shaking down her skirt and putting her arm through the handle of her basket. 'He wants me to send him some handkerchieves and a piece of stout string.'

What is the name of the station where I have to change? Perhaps I shall never know. I got up and leaned my arms across the window rail, my feet crossed. One cheek burned as in infancy on the way to the sea-side. When the war is over I shall have a barge and drift along these rivers with a white cat and a pot of mignonette to bear me company.

Down the side of the hill filed the troops, winking red and blue in the light. Far away, but plainly to be seen, some more flew by on bicycles. But really, *ma France adorée*, this uniform is ridiculous. Your soldiers are stamped upon your bosom like bright irreverent transfers.

6. A "little soldier," meaning here the rank of private.

The train slowed down, stopped. . . . Everybody was getting out except me. A big boy, his sabots[7] tied to his back with a piece of string, the inside of his tin wine cup stained a lovely impossible pink, looked very friendly. Does one change here perhaps for X? Another whose képi[8] had come out of a wet paper cracker swung my suit-case to earth. What darlings soldiers are! 'Merci bien, Monsieur, vous êtes tout à fait aimable. . . .'[9] 'Not this way,' said a bayonet. 'Nor this,' said another. So I followed the crowd. 'Your passport, Mademoiselle. . . .' *'We, Sir Edward Grey . . .'*[1] I ran through the muddy square and into the buffet.

A green room with a stove jutting out and tables on each side. On the counter, beautiful with coloured bottles, a woman leans, her breasts in her folded arms. Through an open door I can see a kitchen, and the cook in a white coat breaking eggs into a bowl and tossing the shells into a corner. The blue and red coats of the men who are eating hang upon the walls. Their short swords and belts are piled upon chairs. Heavens! what a noise. The sunny air seemed all broken up and trembling with it. A little boy, very pale, swung from table to table, taking the orders, and poured me out a glass of purple coffee. *Ssssh*, came from the eggs. They were in a pan. The woman rushed from behind the counter and began to help the boy. *Toute de suite, tout' suite!*[2] she chirruped to the loud impatient voices. There came a clatter of plates and the pop-pop of corks being drawn.

Suddenly in the doorway I saw someone with a pail of fish—brown speckled fish, like the fish one sees in a glass case, swimming through forests of beautiful pressed sea-weed. He was an old man in a tattered jacket, standing humbly, waiting for someone to attend to him. A thin beard fell over his chest, his eyes under the tufted eyebrows were bent on the pail he carried. He looked as though he had escaped from some holy picture, and was entreating the soldiers' pardon for being there at all. . . .

But what could I have done? I could not arrive at X with two fishes hanging on a straw; and I am sure it is a penal offence in France to throw fish out of railway-carriage windows, I thought, miserably climbing into a smaller, shabbier train. Perhaps I might have taken them to—*ah, mon Dieu*[3]—I had forgotten the name of my uncle and aunt again! Buffard, Buffon—what was it? Again I read the unfamiliar letter in the familiar handwriting.

7. Clogs.
8. A peaked flat-topped military hat.
9. Thank you, sir, you are so kind.
1. Sir Edward Grey (1862–1933), British foreign secretary whose name appeared on the authorization of passports.
2. Quickly, get a move on!
3. My God.

'My dear niece,

'Now that the weather is more settled, your uncle and I would be charmed if you would pay us a little visit. Telegraph me when you are coming. I shall meet you outside the station if I am free. Otherwise our good friend, Madame Grinçon, who lives in the little toll-house by the bridge, *juste en face de la gare*, will conduct you to our home. *Je vous embrasse bien tendrement*,[4] JULIE BOIFFARD.'

A visiting card was enclosed: *M. Paul Boiffard*.

Boiffard—of course that was the name. *Ma tante Julie et mon oncle Paul*[5]—suddenly they were there with me, more real, more solid than any relations I had ever known. I saw *tante Julie* bridling, with the soup-tureen in her hands, and *oncle Paul* sitting at the table, with a red and white napkin tied round his neck. Boiffard—Boiffard—I must remember the name. Supposing the Commissaire Militaire[6] should ask me who the relations were I was going to and I muddled the name—Oh, how fatal! Buffard—no, Boiffard. And then for the first time, folding Aunt Julie's letter, I saw scrawled in a corner of the empty back page: *Venez vite, vite.*[7] Strange impulsive woman! My heart began to beat. . . .

'Ah, we are not far off now,' said the lady opposite. 'You are going to X, Mademoiselle?'

'Oui, Madame.'

'I also. . . . You have been there before?'

'No, Madame. This is the first time.'

'Really, it is a strange time for a visit.'

I smiled faintly, and tried to keep my eyes off her hat. She was quite an ordinary little woman, but she wore a black velvet toque, with an incredibly surprised looking sea-gull camped on the very top of it. Its round eyes, fixed on me so inquiringly, were almost too much to bear. I had a dreadful impulse to shoo it away, or to lean forward and inform her of its presence. . . .

'*Excusez-moi, madame*, but perhaps you have not remarked there is an *espèce de* sea-gull *couché sur votre chapeau.*'[8]

Could the bird be there on purpose? I must not laugh. . . . I must not laugh. Had she ever looked at herself in a glass with that bird on her head?

'It is very difficult to get into X at present, to pass the station,' she said, and she shook her head with the sea-gull at me. 'Ah, such an affair. One must sign one's name and state one's business.'

'Really, is it as bad as all that?'

4. Exactly opposite the station. I embrace you most tenderly.
5. My aunt Julie and my uncle Paul.
6. Military superintendent.
7. Come quickly, quickly.
8. Excuse me, Madame, . . . there is a kind of seagull nested on your hat.

'But naturally. You see the whole place is in the hands of the military, and'—she shrugged—'they have to be strict. Many people do not get beyond the station at all. They arrive. They are put in the waiting-room, and there they remain.'

Did I or did I not detect in her voice a strange, insulting relish?

'I suppose such strictness is absolutely necessary,' I said coldly, stroking my muff.

'Necessary,' she cried. 'I should think so. Why, *mademoiselle*, you cannot imagine what it would be like otherwise! You know what women are like about soldiers'—she raised a final hand—'mad, completely mad. But—' and she gave a little laugh of triumph—'they could not get into X. *Mon Dieu*, no! There is no question about that.'

'I don't suppose they even try,' said I.

'Don't you?' said the sea-gull.

Madame said nothing for a moment. 'Of course the authorities are very hard on the men. It means instant imprisonment, and then—off to the firing-line without a word.'

'What are *you* going to X for?' said the sea-gull. 'What on earth are *you* doing here?'

'Are you making a long stay in X, *mademoiselle*?'

She had won, she had won. I was terrified. A lamp-post swam past the train with the fatal name upon it. I could hardly breathe—the train had stopped. I smiled gaily at Madame and danced down the steps to the platform. . . .

It was a hot little room completely furnished with two colonels seated at two tables. They were large grey-whiskered men with a touch of burnt red on their cheeks. Sumptuous and omnipotent they looked. One smoked what ladies love to call a heavy Egyptian cigarette, with a long creamy ash, the other toyed with a gilded pen. Their heads rolled on their tight collars, like big over-ripe fruits. I had a terrible feeling, as I handed my passport and ticket, that a soldier would step forward and tell me to kneel. I would have knelt without question.

'What's this?' said God I., querulously. He did not like my passport at all. The very sight of it seemed to annoy him. He waved a dissenting hand at it, with a '*Non, je ne peux pas manger ça*'[9] air.

'But it won't do. It won't do at all, you know. Look,—read for yourself,' and he glanced with extreme distaste at my photograph, and then with even greater distaste his pebble eyes looked at me.

'Of course the photograph is deplorable,' I said, scarcely breathing with terror, 'but it has been viséd and viséd.'

He raised his big bulk and went over to God II.

9. No, I'm not able to eat that.

'Courage!' I said to my muff and held it firmly, 'Courage!'

God II. held up a finger to me, and I produced Aunt Julie's letter and her card. But he did not seem to feel the slightest interest in her. He stamped my passport idly, scribbled a word on my ticket, and I was on the platform again.

'That way—you pass out that way.'

Terribly pale, with a faint smile on his lips, his hand at salute, stood the little corporal. I gave no sign, I am sure I gave no sign. He stepped behind me.

'And then follow me as though you do not see me,' I heard him half whisper, half sing.

How fast he went, through the slippery mud toward a bridge. He had a postman's bag on his back, a paper parcel and the *Matin*[1] in his hand. We seemed to dodge through a maze of policemen, and I could not keep up at all with the little corporal who began to whistle. From the toll-house 'our good friend, Madame Grinçon', her hands wrapped in a shawl, watched our coming, and against the toll-house there leaned a tiny faded cab. *Montez vite, vite!*[2] said the little corporal, hurling my suit-case, the postman's bag, the paper parcel and the *Matin* on to the floor.

'A-ie! A-ie! Do not be so mad. Do not ride yourself. You will be seen,' wailed 'our good friend, Madame Grinçon'.

'Ah, je m'en f . . . .'[3] said the little corporal.

The driver jerked into activity. He lashed the bony horse and away we flew, both doors, which were the complete sides of the cab, flapping and banging

'Bon jour, mon amie.'

'Bon jour, mon ami,'

And then he swooped down and clutched at the banging doors. They would not keep shut. They were fools of doors.

'Lean back, let me do it!' I cried. 'Policemen are as thick as violets everywhere.'

At the barracks the horse reared up and stopped. A crowd of laughing faces blotted the window.

'Prends ça, mon vieux,'[4] said the little corporal, handing the paper parcel.

'It's all right,' called someone.

We waved, we were off again. By a river, down a strange white street, with little houses on either side, gay in the late sunlight.

'Jump out as soon as he stops again. The door will be open. Run

1. Meaning "*Morning*," a daily newspaper.
2. Get in, quickly, quickly!
3. I couldn't care less.
4. Take this, old chap.

straight inside. I will follow. The man is already paid. I know you will like the house. It is quite white, and the room is white, too, and the people are——'

'White as snow.'

We looked at each other. We began to laugh. 'Now,' said the little corporal.

Out I flew and in at the door. There stood, presumably, my aunt Julie. There in the background hovered, I supposed, my uncle Paul.

'Bon jour, madame!' 'Bon jour, monsieur!'

'It is all right, you are safe,' said my aunt Julie. Heavens, how I loved her! And she opened the door of the white room and shut it upon us. Down went the suit-case, the postman's bag, the *Matin*. I threw my passport up into the air, and the little corporal caught it.

What an extraordinary thing. We had been there to lunch and to dinner each day; but now in the dusk and alone I could not find it. I clop-clopped in my borrowed *sabots* through the greasy mud, right to the end of the village, and there was not a sign of it. I could not even remember what it looked like, or if there was a name painted on the outside, or any bottles or tables showing at the window. Already the village houses were sealed for the night behind big wooden shutters. Strange and mysterious they looked in the ragged drifting light and thin rain, like a company of beggars perched on the hill-side, their bosoms full of rich unlawful gold. There was nobody about but the soldiers. A group of wounded stood under a lamp-post, petting a mangy, shivering dog. Up the street came four big boys singing:

Dodo, mon homme, fais vit' dodo . . .[5]

and swung off down the hill to their sheds behind the railway station. They seemed to take the last breath of the day with them. I began to walk slowly back.

'It must have been one of these houses. I remember it stood far back from the road—and there were no steps, not even a porch—one seemed to walk right through the window.' And then quite suddenly the waiting-boy came out of just such a place. He saw me and grinned cheerfully, and began to whistle through his teeth.

'Bon soir, mon petit.'

'Bon soir, madame.' And he followed me up the café to our special table, right at the far end by the window, and marked by a bunch of violets that I had left in a glass there yesterday.

'You are two?' asked the waiting-boy, flicking the table with a red

5. "Dodo, my man, come quickly, Dodo." A line from a popular song of the period, "Idylle Rouge" ("Red Idylle"), by Georges Picquet.

and white cloth. His long swinging steps echoed over the bare floor. He disappeared into the kitchen and came back to light the lamp that hung from the ceiling under a spreading shade, like a haymaker's hat. Warm light shone on the empty place that was really a barn, set out with dilapidated tables and chairs. Into the middle of the room a black stove jutted. At one side of it there was a table with a row of bottles on it, behind which Madame sat and took the money and made entries in a red book. Opposite her desk a door led into the kitchen. The walls were covered with a creamy paper patterned all over with green and swollen trees—hundreds and hundreds of trees reared their mushroom heads to the ceiling. I began to wonder who had chosen the paper and why. Did Madame think it was beautiful, or that it was a gay and lovely thing to eat one's dinner at all seasons in the middle of a forest. . . . On either side of the clock there hung a picture: one, a young gentleman in black tights wooing a pear-shaped lady in yellow over the back of a garden seat, *Premier Rencontre*; two, the black and yellow in amorous confusion. *Triomphe d'Amour*.[6]

The clock ticked to a soothing lilt, *C'est ça, C'est ça*.[7] In the kitchen the waiting-boy was washing up. I heard the ghostly chatter of the dishes.

And years passed. Perhaps the war is long since over—there is no village outside at all—the streets are quiet under the grass. I have an idea this is the sort of thing one will do on the very last day of all—sit in an empty café and listen to a clock ticking until——.

Madame came through the kitchen door, nodded to me and took her seat behind the table, her plump hands folded on the red book. *Ping* went the door. A handful of soldiers came in, took off their coats and began to play cards, chaffing and poking fun at the pretty waiting-boy, who threw up his little round head, rubbed his thick fringe out of his eyes and cheeked them back in his broken voice. Sometimes his voice boomed up from his throat, deep and harsh, and then in the middle of a sentence it broke and scattered in a funny squeaking. He seemed to enjoy it himself. You would not have been surprised if he had walked into the kitchen on his hands and brought back your dinner turning a catherine-wheel.

Ping went the door again. Two more men came in. They sat at the table nearest Madame, and she leaned to them with a birdlike movement, her head on one side. Oh, they had a grievance! The Lieutenant was a fool—nosing about—springing out at them—and they'd only been sewing on buttons. Yes, that was all—sewing on buttons, and up comes this young spark. 'Now then, what are you up to?' They mimicked the idiotic voice. Madame drew down her

6. Love's Triumph. *Premier Rencontre*: First Meeting.
7. 'That's it, that's it.' An imitative sound to suggest the ticking of the clock.

mouth, nodding sympathy. The waiting-boy served them with glasses. He took a bottle of some orange-coloured stuff and put it on the table-edge. A shout from the card-players made him turn sharply, and crash! over went the bottle, spilling on the table, the floor—smash! to tinkling atoms. An amazed silence. Through it the drip-drip of the wine from the table on to the floor. It looked very strange dropping so slowly, as though the table were crying. Then there came a roar from the card-players. 'You'll catch it, my lad! That's the style! Now you've done it! . . . Sept, huit, neuf.' They started playing again. The waiting-boy never said a word. He stood, his head bent, his hands spread out, and then he knelt and gathered up the glass, piece by piece, and soaked the wine up with a cloth. Only when Madame cried cheerfully, 'You wait until *he* finds out,' did he raise his head.

'He can't say anything, if I pay for it,' he muttered, his face jerking, and he marched off into the kitchen with the soaking cloth.

'*Il pleure de colère*,'[8] said Madame delightedly, patting her hair with her plump hands.

The café slowly filled. It grew very warm. Blue smoke mounted from the tables and hung about the haymaker's hat in misty wreaths. There was a suffocating smell of onion soup and boots and damp cloth. In the din the door sounded again. It opened to let in a weed of a fellow, who stood with his back against it, one hand shading his eyes.

'Hullo! you've got the bandage off?'

'How does it feel, *mon vieux*?'[9]

'Let's have a look at them.'

But he made no reply. He shrugged and walked unsteadily to a table, sat down and leant against the wall. Slowly his hand fell. In his white face his eyes showed, pink as a rabbit's. They brimmed and spilled, brimmed and spilled. He dragged a white cloth out of his pocket and wiped them.

'It's the smoke,' said someone. 'It's the smoke tickles them up for you.'

His comrades watched him a bit, watched his eyes fill again, again brim over. The water ran down his face, off his chin on to the table. He rubbed the place with his coat-sleeve, and then, as though forgetful, went on rubbing, rubbing with his hand across the table, staring in front of him.[1] And then he started shaking his head to the movement of his hand. He gave a loud strange groan and dragged out the cloth again.

8. He's crying with rage.
9. My old friend.
1. Mansfield was among the first to describe the effects of chlorine gas, which the Germans first used in combat in April 1915.

'*Huit, neuf, dix,*' said the card-players.

'*P'tit*, some more bread.'

'Two coffees.'

'*Un Picon!*'

The waiting-boy, quite recovered, but with scarlet cheeks, ran to and fro. A tremendous quarrel flared up among the card-players, raged for two minutes, and died in flickering laughter. 'Ooof!' groaned the man with the eyes, rocking and mopping. But nobody paid any attention to him except Madame. She made a little grimace at her two soldiers.

'*Mais vous savez, c'est un peu dégoûtant, ça,*'[2] she said severely.

'*Ah, oui, Madame,*' answered the soldiers, watching her bent head and pretty hands, as she arranged for the hundredth time a frill of lace on her lifted bosom.

'*V'là monsieur!*'[3] cawed the waiting-boy over his shoulder to me. For some silly reason I pretended not to hear, and I leaned over the table smelling the violets, until the little corporal's hand closed over mine.

'Shall we have *un peu de charcuterie*[4] to begin with?' he asked tenderly.

'In England,' said the blue-eyed soldier, 'you drink whiskey with your meals. *N'est-ce pas, mademoiselle*? A little glass of whiskey neat before eating. Whiskey and soda with your *bifteks*, and after, more whiskey with hot water and lemon.'

'Is it true, that?' asked his great friend who sat opposite, a big red-faced chap with a black beard and large moist eyes and hair that looked as though it had been cut with a sewing-machine.

'Well, not quite true,' said I.

'*Si, si,*' cried the blue-eyed soldier. 'I ought to know. I'm in business. English travellers come to my place, and it's always the same thing.'

'Bah, I can't stand whiskey,' said the little corporal. 'It's too disgusting the morning after. Do you remember, *ma fille*, the whiskey in that little bar at Montmartre?'

'*Souvenir tendre,*'[5] sighed Blackbeard, putting two fingers in the breast of his coat and letting his head fall. He was very drunk.

'But I know something that you've never tasted,' said the blue-eyed soldier pointing a finger at me; 'something really good,' *Cluck* he went with his tongue. '*É-pa-tant!*[6] And the curious thing is that you'd hardly know it from whiskey except that it's'—he felt with his

2. But you know, it's a little disgusting, that.
3. There you are, sir.
4. A little pork something?
5. Happy memory.
6. Astonishing!

hand for the word—'finer, sweeter perhaps, not so sharp, and it leaves you feeling gay as a rabbit next morning.'

'What is it called?'

'Mirabelle!'[7] He rolled the word round his mouth, under his tongue. 'Ah-ha, that's the stuff.'

'I could eat another mushroom,' said Blackbeard. 'I would like another mushroom very much. I am sure I could eat another mushroom if Mademoiselle gave it to me out of her hand.'

'You ought to try it,' said the blue-eyed soldier, leaning both hands on the table and speaking so seriously that I began to wonder how much more sober he was than Blackbeard. 'You ought to try it, and to-night. I would like you to tell me if you don't think it's like whiskey.'

'Perhaps they've got it here,' said the little corporal, and he called the waiting-boy. '*P'tit!*'

'*Non, monsieur*,' said the boy, who never stopped smiling. He served us with dessert plates painted with blue parrots and horned beetles.

'What is the name for this in English?' said Blackbeard, pointing. I told him 'Parrot'.

'Ah, *mon Dieu*! . . . Pair-rot.' He put his arms round his plate. 'I love you, *ma petite* pair-rot. You are sweet, you are blonde, you are English. You do not know the difference between whiskey and mirabelle.'

The little corporal and I looked at each other, laughing. He squeezed up his eyes when he laughed, so that you saw nothing but the long curly lashes.

'Well, I know a place where they do keep it,' said the blue-eyed soldier. '*Café des Amis*. We'll go there—I'll pay—I'll pay for the whole lot of us.' His gesture embraced thousands of pounds.

But with a loud whirring noise the clock on the wall struck half-past eight; and no soldier is allowed in a café after eight o'clock at night.

'It is fast,' said the blue-eyed soldier. The little corporal's watch said the same. So did the immense turnip that Blackbeard produced, and carefully deposited on the head of one of the horned beetles.

'Ah, well, we'll take the risk,' said the blue-eyed soldier, and he thrust his arms into his immense cardboard coat. 'It's worth it,' he said. 'It's worth it. You just wait.'

Outside, stars shone between wispy clouds, and the moon fluttered like a candle flame over a pointed spire. The shadows of the dark plume-like trees waved on the white houses. Not a soul to be

7. An alcoholic drink made from yellow plums.

seen. No sound to be heard but the *Hsh! Hsh!* of a far-away train, like a big beast shuffling in its sleep.

'You are cold,' whispered the little corporal. 'You are cold, *ma fille*.'

'No, really not.'

'But you are trembling.'

'Yes, but I'm not cold.'

'What are the women like in England?' asked Blackbeard. 'After the war is over I shall go to England. I shall find a little English woman and marry her—and her pair-rot.' He gave a loud choking laugh.

'Fool!' said the blue-eyed soldier, shaking him; and he leant over to me. 'It is only after the second glass that you really taste it,' he whispered. 'The second little glass and then—ah!—then you know.'

Café des Amis gleamed in the moonlight. We glanced quickly up and down the road. We ran up the four wooden steps, and opened the ringing glass door into a low room lighted with a hanging lamp, where about ten people were dining. They were seated on two benches at a narrow table.

'Soldiers!' screamed a woman, leaping up from behind a white soup-tureen—a scrag of a woman in a black shawl. 'Soldiers! At this hour! Look at that clock, look at it.' And she pointed to the clock with the dripping ladle.

'It's fast,' said the blue-eyed soldier. 'It's fast, madame. And don't make so much noise, I beg of you. We will drink and we will go.'

'Will you?' she cried, running round the table and planting herself in front of us. 'That's just what you won't do. Coming into an honest woman's house this hour of the night—making a scene—getting the police after you. Ah, no! Ah, no! It's a disgrace, that's what it is.'

'Sh!' said the little corporal, holding up his hand. Dead silence. In the silence we heard steps passing.

'The police,' whispered Blackbeard, winking at a pretty girl with rings in her ears, who smiled back at him, saucy. 'Sh!'

The faces lifted, listening. 'How beautiful they are!' I thought. 'They are like a family party having supper in the New Testament. . . .' The steps died away.

'Serve you very well right if you had been caught,' scolded the angry woman. 'I'm sorry on your account that the police didn't come. You deserve it—you deserve it.'

'A little glass of mirabelle and we will go,' persisted the blue-eyed soldier.

Still scolding and muttering she took four glasses from the cupboard and a big bottle. 'But you're not going to drink in here. Don't you believe it.' The little corporal ran into the kitchen. 'Not there! Not there! Idiot!' she cried. 'Can't you see there's a window there, and a wall opposite where the police come every evening to. . . .'

'Sh!' Another scare.

'You are mad and you will end in prison,—all four of you,' said the woman. She flounced out of the room. We tiptoed after her into a dark smelling scullery, full of pans of greasy water, of salad leaves and meat-bones.

'There now,' she said, putting down the glasses. 'Drink and go!'

'Ah, at last!' The blue-eyed soldier's happy voice trickled through the dark. 'What do you think? Isn't it just as I said? Hasn't it got a taste of excellent—*ex-cellent* whiskey?'

The Wind Blows (1915)†

Suddenly—dreadfully—she wakes up. What has happened? Something dreadful has happened. No—nothing has happened. It is only the wind shaking the house, rattling the windows, banging a piece of iron on the roof and making her bed tremble. Leaves flutter past the window, up and away; down in the avenue a whole newspaper wags in the air like a lost kite and falls, spiked on a pine tree. It is cold. Summer is over—it is autumn—everything is ugly. The carts rattle by, swinging from side to side; two Chinamen lollop along under their wooden yokes with the straining vegetable baskets—their pigtails and blue blouses fly out in the wind. A white dog on three legs yelps past the gate. It is all over! What is? Oh, everything! And she begins to plait her hair with shaking fingers, not daring to look in the glass. Mother is talking to grandmother in the hall.

'A perfect idiot! Imagine leaving anything out on the line in weather like this. . . . Now my best little Teneriffe-work[1] teacloth is simply in ribbons. *What* is that extraordinary smell? It's the porridge burning. Oh, heavens—this wind!'

She has a music lesson at ten o'clock. At the thought the minor movement of the Beethoven begins to play in her head, the trills long and terrible like little rolling drums. . . . Marie Swainson runs into the garden next door to pick the 'chrysanths' before they are ruined. Her skirt flies up above her waist; she tries to beat it down, to tuck it between her legs while she stoops, but it is no use—up it flies. All the trees and bushes beat about her. She picks as quickly as she can, but she is quite distracted. She doesn't mind what she does—she pulls the plants up by the roots and bends and twists them, stamping her foot and swearing.

† Published as "Autumns: II," under the pseudonym Matilda Berry, in the *Signature* (4 October 1915), then in a revised form and under its present title in the *Athenaeum* (27 August 1920), before being included in *Bliss and Other Stories* (1920).

1. A kind of lacework from Teneriffe, the largest of the Canary Islands, in the Atlantic.

'For heaven's sake keep the front door shut! Go round to the back,' shouts someone. And then she hears Bogey:

'Mother, you're wanted on the telephone. Telephone, Mother. It's the butcher.'

How hideous life is—revolting, simply revolting. . . . And now her hat-elastic's snapped. Of course it would. She'll wear her old tam[2] and slip out the back way. But Mother has seen.

'Matilda. Matilda. Come back im-me-diately! What on earth have you got on your head? It looks like a tea cosy. And why have you got that mane of hair on your forehead.'

'I can't come back, Mother. I'll be late for my lesson.'

'Come back immediately!'

She won't. She won't. She hates Mother. 'Go to hell,' she shouts, running down the road.

In waves, in clouds, in big round whirls the dust comes stinging, and with it little bits of straw and chaff and manure. There is a loud roaring sound from the trees in the gardens, and standing at the bottom of the road outside Mr Bullen's gate she can hear the sea sob: 'Ah! . . . Ah! . . . Ah-h!' But Mr Bullen's drawing-room is as quiet as a cave. The windows are closed, the blinds half pulled, and she is not late. The-girl-before-her has just started playing MacDowell's[3] 'To an Iceberg'. Mr Bullen looks over at her and half smiles.

'Sit down,' he says. 'Sit over there in the sofa corner, little lady.'

How funny he is. He doesn't exactly laugh at you . . . but there is just something. . . . Oh, how peaceful it is here. She likes this room. It smells of art serge[4] and stale smoke and chrysanthemums . . . there is a big vase of them on the mantelpiece behind the pale photograph of Rubinstein[5] . . . *à mon ami Robert Bullen*. . . . Over the black glittering piano hangs 'Solitude'[6]—a dark tragic woman draped in white, sitting on a rock, her knees crossed, her chin on her hands.

'No, no!' says Mr Bullen, and he leans over the other girl, puts his arms over her shoulders and plays the passage for her. The stupid—she's blushing! How ridiculous!

Now the-girl-before-her has gone; the front door slams. Mr Bullen comes back and walks up and down, very softly, waiting for her. What an extraordinary thing. Her fingers tremble so that she can't undo the knot in the music satchel. It's the wind. . . . And her heart beats so hard she feels it must lift her blouse up and down. Mr Bullen does

2. Tam-o'-shanter, a round woolen cap of Scottish origin.
3. Edward MacDowell (1861–1908), an American composer.
4. A twilled woolen fabric.
5. Anton Rubinstein (1829–1894), a Russian composer and pianist.
6. A much reproduced painting exhibited in 1890 by Frederic, Lord Leighton.

not say a word. The shabby red piano seat is long enough for two people to sit side by side. Mr Bullen sits down by her.

'Shall I begin with scales,' she asks, squeezing her hands together. 'I had some arpeggios, too.'

But he does not answer. She doesn't believe he even hears . . . and then suddenly his fresh hand with the ring on it reaches over and opens Beethoven.

'Let's have a little of the old master,' he says.

But why does he speak so kindly—so awfully kindly—and as though they had known each other for years and years and knew everything about each other.

He turns the page slowly. She watches his hand—it is a very nice hand and always looks as though it had just been washed.

'Here we are,' says Mr Bullen.

Oh, that kind voice—Oh, that minor movement. Here come the little drums. . . .

'Shall I take the repeat?'

'Yes, dear child.'

His voice is far, far too kind. The crotchets and quavers are dancing up and down the stave like little black boys on a fence. Why is he so . . . She will not cry—she has nothing to cry about. . . .

'What is it, dear child?'

Mr Bullen takes her hands. His shoulder is there—just by her head. She leans on it ever so little, her cheek against the springy tweed.

'Life is so dreadful,' she murmurs, but she does not feel it's dreadful at all. He says something about 'waiting' and 'marking time' and 'that rare thing, a woman', but she does not hear. It is so comfortable . . . for ever. . . .

Suddenly the door opens and in pops Marie Swainson, hours before her time.

'Take the allegretto a little faster,' says Mr Bullen, and gets up and begins to walk up and down again.

'Sit in the sofa corner, little lady,' he says to Marie.

The wind, the wind. It's frightening to be here in her room by herself. The bed, the mirror, the white jug and basin gleam like the sky outside. It's the bed that is frightening. There it lies, sound asleep. . . . Does Mother imagine for one moment that she is going to darn all those stockings knotted up on the quilt like a coil of snakes? She's not. No, Mother. I do not see why I should. . . . The wind—the wind! There's a funny smell of soot blowing down the chimney. Hasn't anyone written poems to the wind? . . . 'I bring fresh flowers to the leaves and showers.'[7] . . . What nonsense.

7. Percy Bysshe Shelley, "I bring fresh showers for the thirsting flowers," *The Cloud*, line 1.

'Is that you, Bogey?'

'Come for a walk round the esplanade, Matilda. I can't stand this any longer.'

'Right-o. I'll put on my ulster.[8] Isn't it an awful day!' Bogey's ulster is just like hers. Hooking the collar she looks at herself in the glass. Her face is white, they have the same excited eyes and hot lips. Ah, they know those two in the glass. Good-bye, dears; we shall be back soon.

'This is better, isn't it?'

'Hook on,' says Bogey.

They cannot walk fast enough. Their heads bent, their legs just touching, they stride like one eager person through the town, down the asphalt zigzag where the fennel grows wild and on to the esplanade. It is dusky—just getting dusky. The wind is so strong that they have to fight their way through it, rocking like two old drunkards. All the poor little pohutukawas[9] on the esplanade are bent to the ground.

'Come on! Come on! Let's get near.'

Over by the breakwater the sea is very high. They pull off their hats and her hair blows across her mouth, tasting of salt. The sea is so high that the waves do not break at all; they thump against the rough stone wall and suck up the weedy, dripping steps. A fine spray skims from the water right across the esplanade. They are covered with drops; the inside of her mouth tastes wet and cold.

Bogey's voice is breaking. When he speaks he rushes up and down the scale. It's funny—it makes you laugh—and yet it just suits the day. The wind carries their voices—away fly the sentences like the narrow ribbons.

'Quicker! Quicker!'

It is getting very dark. In the harbour the coal hulks show two lights—one high on a mast, and one from the stern.

'Look, Bogey. Look over there.'

A big black steamer with a long loop of smoke streaming, with the portholes lighted, with lights everywhere, is putting out to sea. The wind does not stop her; she cuts through the waves, making for the open gate between the pointed rocks that leads to. . . . It's the light that makes her look so awfully beautiful and mysterious. . . . *They* are on board leaning over the rail arm in arm.

'. . . Who are they?'

'. . . Brother and sister.'

'Look, Bogey, there's the town. Doesn't it look small? There's the post office clock chiming for the last time. There's the esplanade where we walked that windy day. Do you remember? I cried at my

8. A long loose overcoat with a belt at the back.
9. Native evergreen trees whose spectacular red blossoms appear in December.

music lesson that day—how many years ago! Good-bye, little island, good-bye. . . .'

Now the dark stretches a wing over the tumbling water. They can't see those two any more. Good-bye, good-bye. Don't forget. . . . But the ship is gone, now.

The wind—the wind.

Prelude (1917)†

I

There was not an inch of room for Lottie and Kezia in the buggy. When Pat swung them on top of the luggage they wobbled; the grandmother's lap was full and Linda Burnell could not possibly have held a lump of a child on hers for any distance. Isabel, very superior, was perched beside the new handy-man on the driver's seat. Hold-alls, bags and boxes were piled upon the floor. 'These are absolute necessities that I will not let out of my sight for one instant,' said Linda Burnell, her voice trembling with fatigue and excitement.

Lottie and Kezia stood on the patch of lawn just inside the gate all ready for the fray in their coats with brass anchor buttons and little round caps with battleship ribbons. Hand in hand, they stared with round solemn eyes first at the absolute necessities and then at their mother.

'We shall simply have to leave them. That is all. We shall simply have to cast them off,' said Linda Burnell. A strange little laugh flew from her lips; she leaned back against the buttoned leather cushions and shut her eyes, her lips trembling with laughter. Happily at that moment Mrs Samuel Josephs, who had been watching the scene from behind her drawing-room blind, waddled down the garden path.

'Why nod leave the chudren with be for the afterdoon, Brs Burnell? They could go on the dray with the storeban when he comes in the eveding. Those thigs on the path have to go, dod't they?'

'Yes, everything outside the house is supposed to go,' said Linda Burnell, and she waved a white hand at the tables and chairs standing on their heads on the front lawn. How absurd they looked! Either they ought to be the other way up, or Lottie and Kezia ought to stand on their heads, too. And she longed to say: 'Stand on your

† First published as a sixty-four-page book by Virginia and Leonard Woolf at their hand-set Hogarth Press in 1918, then collected in *Bliss and Other Stories* (1920). "Prelude" was fashioned during the summer of 1917 from the much longer *The Aloe*, which Mansfield had worked on in 1915–16. A comparative edition of *The Aloe* with "Prelude," ed. Vincent O'Sullivan, was published by Port Nicholson Press (1982).

heads, children, and wait for the storeman.' It seemed to her that would be so exquisitely funny that she could not attend to Mrs Samuel Josephs.

The fat creaking body leaned across the gate, and the big jelly of a face smiled. 'Dod't you worry, Brs Burnell. Loddie and Kezia can have tea with by chudren in the dursery, and I'll see theb on the dray afterwards.'

The grandmother considered. 'Yes, it really is quite the best plan. We are very obliged to you, Mrs Samuel Josephs. Children, say "thank you" to Mrs Samuel Josephs.'

Two subdued chirrups: 'Thank you, Mrs Samuel Josephs.'

'And be good little girls, and—come closer—they advanced, 'don't forget to tell Mrs Samuel Josephs when you want to. . . .'

'No, granma.'

'Dod't worry, Brs Burnell.'

At the last moment Kezia let go Lottie's hand and darted towards the buggy.

'I want to kiss my granma good-bye again.'

But she was too late. The buggy rolled off up the road, Isabel bursting with pride, her nose turned up at all the world, Linda Burnell prostrated, and the grandmother rummaging among the very curious oddments she had put in her black silk reticule at the last moment, for something to give her daughter. The buggy twinkled away in the sunlight and fine golden dust up the hill and over. Kezia bit her lip, but Lottie, carefully finding her handkerchief first, set up a wail.

'Mother! Granma!'

Mrs Samuel Josephs, like a huge warm black silk tea cosy, enveloped her.

'It's all right, by dear. Be a brave child. You come and blay in the dursery!'

She put her arm round weeping Lottie and led her away. Kezia followed, making a face at Mrs Samuel Josephs' placket, which was undone as usual, with two long pink corset laces hanging out of it. . . .

Lottie's weeping died down as she mounted the stairs, but the sight of her at the nursery door with swollen eyes and a blob of a nose gave great satisfaction to the S. J.'s, who sat on two benches before a long table covered with American cloth and set out with immense plates of bread and dripping and two brown jugs that faintly steamed.

'Hullo! You've been crying!'

'Ooh! Your eyes have gone right in.'

'Doesn't her nose look funny.'

'You're all red-and-patchy.'

Lottie was quite a success. She felt it and swelled, smiling timidly.

'Go and sit by Zaidee, ducky,' said Mrs Samuel Josephs, 'and Kezia, you sid ad the end by Boses.'

Moses grinned and gave her a nip as she sat down; but she pretended not to notice. She did hate boys.

'Which will you have?' asked Stanley, leaning across the table very politely, and smiling at her. 'Which will you have to begin with—strawberries and cream or bread and dripping?'

'Strawberries and cream, please,' said she.

'Ah-h-h-h.' How they all laughed and beat the table with their teaspoons. Wasn't that a take in! Wasn't it now! Didn't he fox her! Good old Stan!

'Ma! She thought it was real.'

Even Mrs Samuel Josephs, pouring out the milk and water, could not help smiling. 'You bustn't tease theb on their last day,' she wheezed.

But Kezia bit a big piece out of her bread and dripping, and then stood the piece up on her plate. With the bite out it made a dear little sort of a gate. Pooh! She didn't care! A tear rolled down her cheek, but she wasn't crying. She couldn't have cried in front of those awful Samuel Josephs. She sat with her head bent, and as the tear dripped slowly down, she caught it with a neat little whisk of her tongue and ate it before any of them had seen.

II

After tea Kezia wandered back to their own house. Slowly she walked up the back steps, and through the scullery into the kitchen. Nothing was left in it but a lump of gritty yellow soap in one corner of the kitchen window sill and a piece of flannel stained with a blue bag in another. The fireplace was choked up with rubbish. She poked among it but found nothing except a hair-tidy with a heart painted on it that had belonged to the servant girl. Even that she left lying, and she trailed through the narrow passage into the drawing-room. The Venetian blind was pulled down but not drawn close. Long pencil rays of sunlight shone through and the wavy shadow of a bush outside danced on the gold lines. Now it was still, now it began to flutter again, and now it came almost as far as her feet. Zoom! Zoom! a blue-bottle knocked against the ceiling; the carpet-tacks had little bits of red fluff sticking to them.

The dining-room window had a square of coloured glass at each corner. One was blue and one was yellow. Kezia bent down to have one more look at a blue lawn with blue arum lilies growing at the gate, and then at a yellow lawn with yellow lilies and a yellow fence. As she looked a little Chinese Lottie came out on to the lawn and began to dust the tables and chairs with a corner of her pinafore. Was that really Lottie? Kezia was not quite sure until she had looked through the ordinary window.

Upstairs in her father's and mother's room she found a pill box black and shiny outside and red in, holding a blob of cotton wool.

'I could keep a bird's egg in that,' she decided.

In the servant girl's room there was a stay-button stuck in a crack of the floor, and in another crack some beads and a long needle. She knew there was nothing in her grandmother's room; she had watched her pack. She went over to the window and leaned against it, pressing her hands against the pane.

Kezia liked to stand so before the window. She liked the feeling of the cold shining glass against her hot palms, and she liked to watch the funny white tops that came on her fingers when she pressed them hard against the pane. As she stood there, the day flickered out and dark came. With the dark crept the wind snuffling and howling. The windows of the empty house shook, a creaking came from the walls and floors, a piece of loose iron on the roof banged forlornly. Kezia was suddenly quite, quite still, with wide open eyes and knees pressed together. She was frightened. She wanted to call Lottie and to go on calling all the while she ran downstairs and out of the house. But IT was just behind her, waiting at the door, at the head of the stairs, at the bottom of the stairs, hiding in the passage, ready to dart out at the back door. But Lottie was at the back door, too.

'Kezia!' she called cheerfully. 'The storeman's here. Everything is on the dray and three horses, Kezia. Mrs Samuel Josephs has given us a big shawl to wear round us, and she says to button up your coat. She won't come out because of asthma.'

Lottie was very important.

'Now then, you kids,' called the storeman. He hooked his big thumbs under their arms and up they swung. Lottie arranged the shawl 'most beautifully' and the storeman tucked up their feet in a piece of old blanket.

'Lift up. Easy does it.'

They might have been a couple of young ponies. The storeman felt over the cords holding his load, unhooked the brakechain from the wheel, and whistling, he swung up beside them.

'Keep close to me,' said Lottie, 'because otherwise you pull the shawl away from my side, Kezia.'

But Kezia edged up to the storeman. He towered beside her big as a giant and he smelled of nuts and new wooden boxes.

III

It was the first time that Lottie and Kezia had ever been out so late. Everything looked different—the painted wooden houses far smaller than they did by day, the gardens far bigger and wilder. Bright stars speckled the sky and the moon hung over the harbour dabbling the waves with gold. They could see the lighthouse shining on Quarantine Island,[1] and the green lights on the old coal hulks.

'There comes the Picton[2] boat,' said the storeman, pointing to a little steamer all hung with bright beads.

But when they reached the top of the hill and began to go down the other side the harbour disappeared, and although they were still in the town they were quite lost. Other carts rattled past. Everybody knew the storeman.

'Night, Fred.'

'Night O,' he shouted.

Kezia liked very much to hear him. Whenever a cart appeared in the distance she looked up and waited for his voice. He was an old friend; and she and her grandmother had often been to his place to buy grapes. The storeman lived alone in a cottage that had a glasshouse against one wall built by himself. All the glasshouse was spanned and arched over with one beautiful vine. He took her brown basket from her, lined it with three large leaves, and then he felt in his belt for a little horn knife, reached up and snapped off a big blue cluster and laid it on the leaves so tenderly that Kezia held her breath to watch. He was a very big man. He wore brown velvet trousers, and he had a long brown beard. But he never wore a collar, not even on Sunday. The back of his neck was burnt bright red.

'Where are we now?' Every few minutes one of the children asked him the question.

'Why, this is Hawk Street, or Charlotte Crescent.'

'Of course it is,' Lottie pricked up her ears at the last name; she always felt that Charlotte Crescent belonged specially to her. Very few people had streets with the same name as theirs.

'Look, Kezia, there is Charlotte Crescent. Doesn't it look different?' Now everything familiar was left behind. Now the big dray rattled into unknown country, along new roads with high clay banks on either side, up steep, steep hills, down into bushy valleys, through wide shallow rivers. Further and further. Lottie's head wagged; she drooped, she slipped half into Kezia's lap and lay there. But Kezia could not open her eyes wide enough. The wind blew and she shivered; but her cheeks and ears burned.

1. The name given locally to Somes Island, now Matiu Island, in the middle of Wellington harbor.
2. A port at the top of the South Island of New Zealand.

'Do stars ever blow about?' she asked.

'Not to notice,' said the storeman.

'We've got a nuncle and a naunt living near our new house,' said Kezia. 'They have got two children, Pip, the eldest is called, and the youngest's name is Rags. He's got a ram. He has to feed it with a nenamuel teapot and a glove top over the spout. He's going to show us. What is the difference between a ram and a sheep?'

'Well, a ram has horns and runs for you.'

Kezia considered. 'I don't want to see it frightfully,' she said. 'I hate rushing animals like dogs and parrots. I often dream that animals rush at me—even camels—and while they are rushing, their heads swell e-enormous.'

The storeman said nothing. Kezia peered up at him, screwing up her eyes. Then she put her finger out and stroked his sleeve; it felt hairy. 'Are we near?' she asked.

'Not far off, now,' answered the storeman. 'Getting tired?'

'Well, I'm not an atom bit sleepy,' said Kezia. 'But my eyes keep curling up in such a funny sort of way.' She gave a long sigh, and to stop her eyes from curling she shut them. . . . When she opened them again they were clanking through a drive that cut through the garden like a whip lash, looping suddenly an island of green, and behind the island, but out of sight until you came upon it, was the house. It was long and low built, with a pillared verandah and balcony all the way round. The soft white bulk of it lay stretched upon the green garden like a sleeping beast. And now one and now another of the windows leaped into light. Someone was walking through the empty rooms carrying a lamp. From a window downstairs the light of a fire flickered. A strange beautiful excitement seemed to stream from the house in quivering ripples.

'Where are we?' said Lottie, sitting up. Her reefer[3] cap was all on one side and on her cheek there was the print of an anchor button she had pressed against while sleeping. Tenderly the storeman lifted her, set her cap straight, and pulled down her crumpled clothes. She stood blinking on the lowest verandah step watching Kezia who seemed to come flying through the air to her feet.

'Ooh!' cried Kezia, flinging up her arms. The grandmother came out of the dark hall carrying a little lamp. She was smiling.

'You found your way in the dark?' said she.

'Perfectly well.'

But Lottie staggered on the lowest verandah step like a bird fallen out of the nest. If she stood still for a moment she fell asleep, if she leaned against anything her eyes closed. She could not walk another step.

3. A casual term for midshipman.

'Kezia,' said the grandmother, 'can I trust you to carry the lamp?'

'Yes, my granma.'

The old woman bent down and gave the bright breathing thing into her hands and then she caught up drunken Lottie. 'This way.'

Through a square hall filled with bales and hundreds of parrots (but the parrots were only on the wall-paper) down a narrow passage where the parrots persisted in flying past Kezia with her lamp.

'Be very quiet,' warned the grandmother, putting down Lottie and opening the dining-room door. 'Poor little mother has got such a headache.'

Linda Burnell, in a long cane chair, with her feet on a hassock, and a plaid over her knees, lay before a crackling fire. Burnell and Beryl sat at the table in the middle of the room eating a dish of fried chops and drinking tea out of a brown china teapot. Over the back of her mother's chair leaned Isabel. She had a comb in her fingers and in a gentle absorbed fashion she was combing the curls from her mother's forehead. Outside the pool of lamp and firelight the room stretched dark and bare to the hollow windows.

'Are those the children?' But Linda did not really care; she did not even open her eyes to see.

'Put down the lamp, Kezia,' said Aunt Beryl, 'or we shall have the house on fire before we are out of the packing cases. More tea, Stanley?'

'Well, you might just give me five-eighths of a cup,' said Burnell, leaning across the table. 'Have another chop, Beryl. Tip-top meat, isn't it? Not too lean and not too fat.' He turned to his wife. 'You're sure you won't change your mind, Linda darling?'

'The very thought of it is enough.' She raised one eyebrow in the way she had. The grandmother brought the children bread and milk and they sat up to the table, flushed and sleepy behind the wavy steam.

'I had meat for my supper,' said Isabel, still combing gently.

'I had a whole chop for my supper, the bone and all and Worcester Sauce. Didn't I, father?'

'Oh, don't boast, Isabel,' said Aunt Beryl.

Isabel looked astounded. 'I wasn't boasting, was I, Mummy? I never thought of boasting. I thought they would like to know. I only meant to tell them.'

'Very well. That's enough,' said Burnell. He pushed back his plate, took a tooth-pick out of his pocket and began picking his strong white teeth.

'You might see that Fred has a bite of something in the kitchen before he goes, will you, mother?'

'Yes, Stanley.' The old woman turned to go.

'Oh, hold on half a jiffy. I suppose nobody knows where my slippers were put? I suppose I shall not be able to get at them for a month or two—what?'

'Yes,' came from Linda. 'In the top of the canvas hold-all marked "urgent necessities".'

'Well you might get them for me will you, mother?'

'Yes, Stanley.'

Burnell got up, stretched himself, and going over to the fire he turned his back to it and lifted up his coat tails.

'By Jove, this is a pretty pickle. Eh, Beryl?'

Beryl, sipping tea, her elbows on the table, smiled over the cup at him. She wore an unfamiliar pink pinafore; the sleeves of her blouse were rolled up to her shoulders showing her lovely freckled arms, and she had let her hair fall down her back in a long pig-tail.

'How long do you think it will take to get straight—couple of weeks—eh?' he chaffed.

'Good heavens, no,' said Beryl airily. 'The worst is over already. The servant girl and I have simply slaved all day, and ever since mother came she has worked like a horse, too. We have never sat down for a moment. We have had a day.'

Stanley scented a rebuke.

'Well, I suppose you did not expect me to rush away from the office and nail carpets—did you?'

'Certainly not,' laughed Beryl. She put down her cup and ran out of the dining-room.

'What the hell does she expect us to do?' asked Stanley. 'Sit down and fan herself with a palm leaf fan while I have a gang of professionals to do the job? By Jove, if she can't do a hand's turn occasionally without shouting about it in return for. . . .'

And he gloomed as the chops began to fight the tea in his sensitive stomach. But Linda put up a hand and dragged him down to the side of her long chair.

'This is a wretched time for you, old boy,' she said. Her cheeks were very white but she smiled and curled her fingers into the big red hand she held. Burnell became quiet. Suddenly he began to whistle 'Pure as a lily, joyous and free'—a good sign.

'Think you're going to like it?' he asked.

'I don't want to tell you, but I think I ought to, mother,' said Isabel. 'Kezia is drinking tea out of Aunt Beryl's cup.'

IV

They were taken off to bed by the grandmother. She went first with a candle; the stairs rang to their climbing feet. Isabel and Lottie lay in a room to themselves, Kezia curled in her grandmother's soft bed.

'Aren't there going to be any sheets, my granma?'

'No, not to-night.'

'It's tickly,' said Kezia, 'but it's like Indians.' She dragged her grandmother down to her and kissed her under the chin. 'Come to bed soon and be my Indian brave.'

'What a silly you are,' said the old woman, tucking her in as she loved to be tucked.

'Aren't you going to leave me a candle?'

'No. Sh-h. Go to sleep.'

'Well, can I have the door left open?'

She rolled herself up into a round but she did not go to sleep. From all over the house came the sound of steps. The house itself creaked and popped. Loud whispering voices came from downstairs. Once she heard Aunt Beryl's rush of high laughter, and once she heard a loud trumpeting from Burnell blowing his nose. Outside the window hundreds of black cats with yellow eyes sat in the sky watching her—but she was not frightened. Lottie was saying to Isabel:

'I'm going to say my prayers in bed to-night.'

'No you can't, Lottie.' Isabel was very firm. 'God only excuses you saying your prayers in bed if you've got a temperature.' So Lottie yielded:

Gentle Jesus meek anmile,
Look pon a little chile.
Pity me, simple Lizzie
Suffer me to come to thee.[4]

And then they lay down back to back, their little behinds just touching, and fell asleep.

Standing in a pool of moonlight Beryl Fairfield undressed herself. She was tired, but she pretended to be more tired than she really was—letting her clothes fall, pushing back with a languid gesture her warm, heavy hair.

'Oh, how tired I am—very tired.'

She shut her eyes a moment, but her lips smiled. Her breath rose and fell in her breast like two fanning wings. The window was wide open; it was warm, and somewhere out there in the garden a young man, dark and slender, with mocking eyes, tip-toed among the bushes, and gathered the flowers into a big bouquet, and slipped under her window and held it up to her. She saw herself bending forward. He thrust his head among the bright waxy flowers, sly and laughing. 'No, no,' said Beryl. She turned from the window and dropped her nightgown over her head.

4. The child's inaccurate version of a 1742 hymn by Charles Wesley.

'How frightfully unreasonable Stanley is sometimes,' she thought, buttoning. And then, as she lay down, there came the old thought, the cruel thought—ah, if only she had money of her own.

A young man, immensely rich, has just arrived from England. He meets her quite by chance. . . . The new governor is unmarried. . . . There is a ball at Government house.[5] . . . Who is that exquisite creature in *eau de nil*[6] satin? Beryl Fairfield. . . .

'The thing that pleases me,' said Stanley, leaning against the side of the bed and giving himself a good scratch on his shoulders and back before turning in, 'is that I've got the place dirt cheap, Linda. I was talking about it to little Wally Bell to-day and he said he simply could not understand why they had accepted my figure. You see land about here is bound to become more and more valuable . . . in about ten years' time . . . of course we shall have to go very slow and cut down expenses as fine as possible. Not asleep—are you?'

'No, dear, I've heard every word,' said Linda. He sprang into bed, leaned over her and blew out the candle.

'Good night, Mr Business Man,' said she, and she took hold of his head by the ears and gave him a quick kiss. Her faint far-away voice seemed to come from a deep well.

'Good night, darling.' He slipped his arm under her neck and drew her to him.

'Yes, clasp me,' said the faint voice from the deep well.

Pat the handy man sprawled in his little room behind the kitchen. His sponge-bag, coat and trousers hung from the door-peg like a hanged man. From the edge of the blanket his twisted toes protruded, and on the floor beside him there was an empty cane bird-cage. He looked like a comic picture.

'Honk, honk,' came from the servant girl. She had adenoids.

Last to go to bed was the grandmother.

'What. Not asleep yet?'

'No, I'm waiting for you,' said Kezia. The old woman sighed and lay down beside her. Kezia thrust her head under the grandmother's arm and gave a little squeak. But the old woman only pressed her faintly, and sighed again, took out her teeth, and put them in a glass of water beside her on the floor.

In the garden some tiny owls, perched on the branches of a lace-bark tree, called: 'More pork; more pork.'[7] And far away in the bush there sounded a harsh rapid chatter: 'Ha-ha-ha . . . Ha-ha-ha.'

5. The residence of the governor general, the British monarch's representative in New Zealand.
6. Water of the Nile, a pale greenish color.
7. Morepork, a small brown native owl so called because of its distinctive call.

V

Dawn came sharp and chill with red clouds on a faint green sky and drops of water on every leaf and blade. A breeze blew over the garden, dropping dew and dropping petals, shivered over the drenched paddocks, and was lost in the sombre bush. In the sky some tiny stars floated for a moment and then they were gone—they were dissolved like bubbles. And plain to be heard in the early quiet was the sound of the creek in the paddock running over the brown stones, running in and out of the sandy hollows, hiding under clumps of dark berry bushes, spilling into a swamp of yellow water flowers and cresses.

And then at the first beam of sun the birds began. Big cheeky birds, starlings and mynahs, whistled on the lawns, the little birds, the goldfinches and linnets and fantails flicked from bough to bough. A lovely kingfisher perched on the paddock fence preening his rich beauty, and a *tui* sang his three notes and laughed and sang them again.

'How loud the birds are,' said Linda in her dream. She was walking with her father through a green paddock sprinkled with daisies. Suddenly he bent down and parted the grasses and showed her a tiny ball of fluff just at her feet. 'Oh, Papa, the darling.' She made a cup of her hands and caught the tiny bird and stroked its head with her finger. It was quite tame. But a funny thing happened. As she stroked it began to swell, it ruffled and pouched, it grew bigger and bigger and its round eyes seemed to smile knowingly at her. Now her arms were hardly wide enough to hold it and she dropped it into her apron. It had become a baby with a big naked head and a gaping bird-mouth, opening and shutting. Her father broke into a loud clattering laugh and she woke to see Burnell standing by the windows rattling the Venetian blind up to the very top.

'Hullo,' he said. 'Didn't wake you, did I? Nothing much wrong with the weather this morning.'

He was enormously pleased. Weather like this set a final seal on his bargain. He felt, somehow, that he had bought the lovely day, too—got it chucked in dirt cheap with the house and ground. He dashed off to his bath and Linda turned over and raised herself on one elbow to see the room by daylight. All the furniture had found a place—all the old paraphernalia—as she expressed it. Even the photographs were on the mantelpiece and the medicine bottles on the shelf above the wash-stand. Her clothes lay across a chair—her outdoor things, a purple cape and a round hat with a plume in it. Looking at them she wished that she was going away from this house, too. And she saw herself driving away from them all in a little buggy, driving away from everybody and not even waving.

Back came Stanley girt with a towel, glowing and slapping his thighs. He pitched the wet towel on top of her hat and cape, and standing firm in the exact centre of a square of sunlight he began to do his exercises. Deep breathing, bending and squatting like a frog and shooting out his legs. He was so delighted with his firm, obedient body that he hit himself on the chest and gave a loud 'Ah.' But this amazing vigour seemed to set him worlds away from Linda. She lay on the white tumbled bed and watched him as if from the clouds.

'Oh, damn! Oh, blast!' said Stanley, who had butted into a crisp white shirt only to find that some idiot had fastened the neck-band and he was caught. He stalked over to Linda waving his arms.

'You look like a big fat turkey,' said she.

'Fat. I like that,' said Stanley. 'I haven't a square inch of fat on me. Feel that.'

'It's rock—it's iron,' mocked she.

'You'd be surprised,' said Stanley, as though this were intensely interesting, 'at the number of chaps at the club who have got a corporation.[8] Young chaps, you know—men of my age.' He began parting his bushy ginger hair, his blue eyes fixed and round in the glass, his knees bent, because the dressing table was always—confound it—a bit too low for him. 'Little Wally Bell, for instance,' and he straightened, describing upon himself an enormous curve with the hairbrush. 'I must say I've a perfect horror. . . .'

'My dear, don't worry. You'll never be fat. You are far too energetic.'

'Yes, yes, I suppose that's true,' said he, comforted for the hundredth time, and taking a pearl pen-knife out of his pocket he began to pare his nails.

'Breakfast, Stanley.' Beryl was at the door. 'Oh, Linda, mother says you are not to get up yet.' She popped her head in at the door. She had a big piece of syringa[9] stuck through her hair.

'Everything we left on the verandah last night is simply sopping this morning. You should see poor dear mother wringing out the tables and the chairs. However, there is no harm done—' this with the faintest glance at Stanley.

'Have you told Pat to have the buggy round in time? It's a good six and a half miles to the office.'

'I can imagine what this early start for the office will be like,' thought Linda. 'It will be very high pressure indeed.'

'Pat, Pat.' She heard the servant girl calling. But Pat was evidently hard to find; the silly voice went baa-baaing through the garden.

8. A euphemism for being overweight.
9. A shrub with fragrant blossoms.

Linda did not rest again until the final slam of the front door told her that Stanley was really gone.

Later she heard her children playing in the garden. Lottie's stolid, compact little voice cried: 'Ke—zia. Isa—bel.' She was always getting lost or losing people only to find them again, to her great surprise, round the next tree or the next corner. 'Oh, there you are after all.' They had been turned out after breakfast and told not to come back to the house until they were called. Isabel wheeled a neat pramload of prim dolls and Lottie was allowed for a great treat to walk beside her holding the doll's parasol over the face of the wax one.

'Where are you going to, Kezia?' asked Isabel, who longed to find some light and menial duty that Kezia might perform and so be roped in under her government.

'Oh, just away,' said Kezia. . . .

Then she did not hear them any more. What a glare there was in the room. She hated blinds pulled up to the top at any time, but in the morning it was intolerable. She turned over to the wall and idly, with one finger, she traced a poppy on the wall-paper with a leaf and a stem and a fat bursting bud. In the quiet, and under her tracing finger, the poppy seemed to come alive. She could feel the sticky, silky petals, the stem, hairy like a gooseberry skin, the rough leaf and the tight glazed bud. Things had a habit of coming alive like that. Not only large substantial things like furniture but curtains and the patterns of stuffs and the fringes of quilts and cushions. How often she had seen the tassel fringe of her quilt change into a funny procession of dancers with priests attending. . . . For there were some tassels that did not dance at all but walked stately, bent forward as if praying or chanting. How often the medicine bottles had turned into a row of little men with brown top-hats on; and the washstand jug had a way of sitting in the basin like a fat bird in a round nest.

'I dreamed about birds last night,' thought Linda. What was it? She had forgotten. But the strangest part of this coming alive of things was what they did. They listened, they seemed to swell out with some mysterious important content, and when they were full she felt that they smiled. But it was not for her, only, their sly secret smile; they were members of a secret society and they smiled among themselves. Sometimes, when she had fallen asleep in the daytime, she woke and could not lift a finger, could not even turn her eyes to left or right because THEY were there; sometimes when she went out of a room and left it empty, she knew as she clicked the door to that THEY were filling it. And there were times in the evenings when she was upstairs, perhaps, and everybody else was down, when she could hardly escape from them. Then she could not hurry, she could not hum a tune; if she tried to say ever so carelessly—'Bother that old thimble'—THEY were not deceived. THEY knew how frightened she was; THEY saw how she turned her head away as she passed the mirror. What Linda always felt was that THEY wanted something of her, and she knew that if she gave herself up and was quiet, more than quiet, silent, motionless, something would really happen.

'It's very quiet now,' she thought. She opened her eyes wide, and she heard the silence spinning its soft endless web. How lightly she breathed; she scarcely had to breathe at all.

Yes, everything had come alive down to the minutest, tiniest particle, and she did not feel her bed, she floated, held up in the air. Only she seemed to be listening with her wide open watchful eyes, waiting for someone to come who just did not come, watching for something to happen that just did not happen.

VI

In the kitchen at the long deal table under the two windows old Mrs Fairfield was washing the breakfast dishes. The kitchen window looked out on to a big grass patch that led down to the vegetable garden and the rhubarb beds. On one side the grass patch was bordered by the scullery and wash-house and over this whitewashed lean-to there grew a knotted vine. She had noticed yesterday that a few tiny corkscrew tendrils had come right through some cracks in the scullery ceiling and all the windows of the lean-to had a thick frill of ruffled green.

'I am very fond of a grape vine,' declared Mrs Fairfield, 'but I do not think that the grapes will ripen here. It takes Australian sun.' And she remembered how Beryl when she was a baby had been picking some white grapes from the vine on the back verandah of their Tasmanian house and she had been stung on the leg by a huge red ant. She saw Beryl in a little plaid dress with red ribbon tie-ups on the shoulders screaming so dreadfully that half the street rushed in. And how the child's leg had swelled! 'T—t—t—t!' Mrs Fairfield caught her breath remembering. 'Poor child, how terrifying it was.' And she set her lips tight and went over to the stove for some more hot water. The water frothed up in the big soapy bowl with pink and blue bubbles on top of the foam. Old Mrs Fairfield's arms were bare to the elbow and stained a bright pink. She wore a grey foulard dress patterned with large purple pansies, a white linen apron and a high cap shaped like a jelly mould of white muslin. At her throat there was a silver crescent moon with five little owls seated on it, and round her neck she wore a watch-guard made of black beads.

It was hard to believe that she had not been in that kitchen for years; she was so much a part of it. She put the crocks away with a sure, precise touch, moving leisurely and ample from the stove to the dresser, looking into the pantry and the larder as though there were not an unfamiliar corner. When she had finished, everything in the kitchen had become part of a series of patterns. She stood in the middle of the room wiping her hands on a check cloth; a smile beamed on her lips; she thought it looked very nice, very satisfactory.

'Mother! Mother! Are you there?' called Beryl.

'Yes, dear. Do you want me?'

'No. I'm coming,' and Beryl rushed in, very flushed, dragging with her two big pictures.

'Mother, whatever can I do with these awful hideous Chinese paintings that Chung Wah gave Stanley when he went bankrupt? It's absurd to say that they are valuable, because they were hanging in Chung Wah's fruit shop for months before. I can't make out why Stanley wants them kept. I'm sure he thinks them just as hideous as we do, but it's because of the frames,' she said spitefully. 'I suppose he thinks the frames might fetch something some day or other.'

'Why don't you hang them in the passage?' suggested Mrs Fairfield; 'they would not be much seen there.'

'I can't. There is no room. I've hung all the photographs of his office there before and after building, and the signed photos of his business friends, and that awful enlargement of Isabel lying on the mat in her singlet.' Her angry glance swept the placid kitchen. 'I know what I'll do. I'll hang them here. I will tell Stanley they got a little damp in the moving so I have put them in here for the time being.'

She dragged a chair forward, jumped on it, took a hammer and a big nail out of her pinafore pocket and banged away.

'There! That is enough! Hand me the picture, mother.'

'One moment, child.' Her mother was wiping over the carved ebony frame.

'Oh, mother, really you need not dust them. It would take years to dust all those little holes.' And she frowned at the top of her mother's head and bit her lip with impatience. Mother's deliberate way of doing things was simply maddening. It was old age, she supposed, loftily.

At last the two pictures were hung side by side. She jumped off the chair, stowing away the little hammer.

'They don't look so bad there, do they?' said she. 'And at any rate nobody need gaze at them except Pat and the servant girl—have I got a spider's web on my face, mother? I've been poking into that cupboard under the stairs and now something keeps tickling my nose.'

But before Mrs Fairfield had time to look Beryl had turned away. Someone tapped on the window: Linda was there, nodding and smiling. They heard the latch of the scullery door lift and she came in. She had no hat on; her hair stood up on her head in curling rings and she was wrapped up in an old cashmere shawl.

'I'm so hungry,' said Linda: 'where can I get something to eat, mother? This is the first time I've been in the kitchen. It says "mother" all over; everything is in pairs.'

'I will make you some tea,' said Mrs Fairfield, spreading a clean napkin over a corner of the table, 'and Beryl can have a cup with you.'

'Beryl, do you want half my gingerbread?' Linda waved the knife at her. 'Beryl, do you like the house now that we are here?'

'Oh yes, I like the house immensely and the garden is beautiful, but it feels very far away from everything to me. I can't imagine people coming out from town to see us in that dreadful jolting bus, and I am sure there is not anyone here to come and call. Of course it does not matter to you because——'

'But there's the buggy,' said Linda. 'Pat can drive you into town whenever you like.'

That was a consolation, certainly, but there was something at the back of Beryl's mind, something she did not even put into words for herself.

'Oh, well, at any rate it won't kill us,' she said dryly, putting down her empty cup and standing up and stretching. 'I am going to hang curtains.' And she ran away singing:

> How many thousand birds I see
> That sing aloud from every tree . . .

'. . . birds I see That sing aloud from every tree. . . .' But when she reached the dining-room she stopped singing, her face changed; it became gloomy and sullen.

'One may as well rot here as anywhere else,' she muttered savagely, digging the stiff brass safety-pins into the red serge curtains.

The two left in the kitchen were quiet for a little. Linda leaned her cheek on her fingers and watched her mother. She thought her mother looked wonderfully beautiful with her back to the leafy window. There was something comforting in the sight of her that Linda felt she could never do without. She needed the sweet smell of her flesh, and the soft feel of her cheeks and her arms and shoulders still softer. She loved the way her hair curled, silver at her forehead, lighter at her neck, and bright brown still in the big coil under the muslin cap. Exquisite were her mother's hands, and the two rings she wore seemed to melt into her creamy skin. And she was always so fresh, so delicious. The old woman could bear nothing but linen next to her body and she bathed in cold water winter and summer.

'Isn't there anything for me to do?' asked Linda.

'No, darling. I wish you would go into the garden and give an eye to your children; but that I know you will not do.'

'Of course I will, but you know Isabel is much more grown up than any of us.'

'Yes, but Kezia is not,' said Mrs Fairfield.

'Oh, Kezia has been tossed by a bull hours ago,' said Linda, winding herself up in her shawl again.

But no, Kezia had seen a bull through a hole in a knot of wood in the paling that separated the tennis lawn from the paddock. But she had not liked the bull frightfully, so she had walked away back through the orchard, up the grassy slope, along the path by the lace bark tree and so into the spread tangled garden. She did not believe that she would ever not get lost in this garden. Twice she had found her way back to the big iron gates they had driven through the night before, and then had turned to walk up the drive that led to the house, but there were so many little paths on either side. On one side they all led into a tangle of tall dark trees and strange bushes with flat velvet leaves and feathery cream flowers that buzzed with flies when you shook them—this was the frightening side, and no garden at all. The little paths here were wet and clayey with tree roots spanned across them like the marks of big fowls' feet.

But on the other side of the drive there was a high box border and the paths had box edges and all of them led into a deeper and deeper tangle of flowers. The camellias were in bloom, white and crimson and pink and white striped with flashing leaves. You could not see a leaf on the syringa bushes for the white clusters. The roses were in flower—gentlemen's button-hole roses, little white ones, but far too full of insects to hold under anyone's nose, pink monthly roses with a ring of fallen petals round the bushes, cabbage roses on thick stalks, moss roses, always in bud, pink smooth beauties opening curl on curl, red ones so dark they seemed to turn black as they fell, and a certain exquisite cream kind with a slender red stem and bright scarlet leaves.

There were clumps of fairy bells, and all kinds of geraniums, and there were little trees of verbena and bluish lavender bushes and a bed of pelargoniums with velvet eyes and leaves like moths' wings. There was a bed of nothing but mignonette and another of nothing but pansies—borders of double and single daisies and all kinds of little tufty plants she had never seen before.

The red-hot pokers were taller than she; the Japanese sunflowers grew in a tiny jungle. She sat down on one of the box borders. By pressing hard at first it made a nice seat. But how dusty it was inside! Kezia bent down to look and sneezed and rubbed her nose.

And then she found herself at the top of the rolling grassy slope that led down to the orchard. . . . She looked down at the slope a moment; then she lay down on her back, gave a squeak and rolled over and over into the thick flowery orchard grass. As she lay waiting for things to stop spinning, she decided to go up to the house and ask the servant girl for an empty match-box. She wanted to make a surprise for the grandmother. . . . First she would put a leaf inside with a big violet lying on it, then she would put a very small white picotee,[1] perhaps, on each side of the violet, and then she would sprinkle some lavender on the top, but not to cover their heads.

She often made these surprises for the grandmother, and they were always most successful.

'Do you want a match, my granny?'

'Why, yes, child, I believe a match is just what I'm looking for.'

The grandmother slowly opened the box and came upon the picture inside.

'Good gracious, child! How you astonished me!'

'I can make her one every day here,' she thought, scrambling up the grass on her slippery shoes.

But on her way back to the house she came to that island that lay in the middle of the drive, dividing the drive into two arms that met in front of the house. The island was made of grass banked up high. Nothing grew on the top except one huge plant with thick, grey-green, thorny leaves, and out of the middle there sprang up a tall stout stem. Some of the leaves of the plant were so old that they curled up in the air no longer; they turned back, they were split and broken; some of them lay flat and withered on the ground.

Whatever could it be? She had never seen anything like it before. She stood and stared. And then she saw her mother coming down the path.

'Mother, what is it?' asked Kezia.

Linda looked up at the fat swelling plant with its cruel leaves and fleshy stem. High above them, as though becalmed in the air, and yet holding so fast to the earth it grew from, it might have had claws instead of roots. The curving leaves seemed to be hiding something; the blind stem cut into the air as if no wind could ever shake it.

'That is an aloe, Kezia,' said her mother.

'Does it ever have any flowers?'

1. A kind of small carnation.

'Yes, Kezia,' and Linda smiled down at her, and half shut her eyes. 'Once every hundred years.'

VII

On his way home from the office Stanley Burnell stopped the buggy at the Bodega,[2] got out and bought a large bottle of oysters. At the Chinaman's shop next door he bought a pineapple in the pink of condition, and noticing a basket of fresh black cherries he told John to put him a pound of those as well. The oysters and the pine he stowed away in the box under the front seat, but the cherries he kept in his hand.

Pat, the handy-man, leapt off the box and tucked him up again in the brown rug.

'Lift yer feet, Mr Burnell, while I give yer a fold under,' said he.

'Right! Right! First-rate!' said Stanley. 'You can make straight for home now.'

Pat gave the grey mare a touch and the buggy sprang forward.

'I believe this man is a first-rate chap,' thought Stanley. He liked the look of him sitting up there in his neat brown coat and brown bowler.[3] He liked the way Pat had tucked him in, and he liked his eyes. There was nothing servile about him—and if there was one thing he hated more than another it was servility. And he looked as if he was pleased with his job, happy and contented already.

The grey mare went very well; Burnell was impatient to be out of the town. He wanted to be home. Ah, it was splendid to live in the country—to get right out of that hole of a town once the office was closed; and this drive in the fresh warm air, knowing all the while that his own house was at the other end, with its garden and paddocks, its three tip-top cows and enough fowls and ducks to keep them in poultry, was splendid too.

As they left the town finally and bowled away up the deserted road his heart beat hard for joy. He rooted in the bag and began to eat the cherries, three or four at a time, chucking the stones over the side of the buggy. They were delicious, so plump and cold, without a spot or a bruise on them.

Look at those two, now—black one side and white the other—perfect! A perfect little pair of Siamese twins. And he stuck them in his button-hole. . . . By Jove, he wouldn't mind giving that chap up there a handful—but no, better not. Better wait until he had been with him a bit longer.

He began to plan what he would do with his Saturday afternoons and his Sundays. He wouldn't go to the club for lunch on Saturday.

2. Wine cellar (Spanish), but used here as the name of a general store.
3. A hard felt hat with a round dome-shaped crown.

No, cut away from the office as soon as possible and get them to give him a couple of slices of cold meat and half a lettuce when he got home. And then he'd get a few chaps out from town to play tennis in the afternoon. Not too many—three at most. Beryl was a good player, too. . . . He stretched out his right arm and slowly bent it, feeling the muscle. . . . A bath, a good rub-down, a cigar on the verandah after dinner. . . .

On Sunday morning they would go to church—children and all. Which reminded him that he must hire a pew, in the sun if possible and well forward so as to be out of the draught from the door. In fancy he heard himself intoning extremely well: 'When thou did overcome the *Sharp*ness of Death Thou didst open the *King*dom of Heaven to *all* Believers.'[4] And he saw the neat brass-edged card on the corner of the pew—Mr Stanley Burnell and family. . . . The rest of the day he'd loaf about with Linda. . . . Now they were walking about the garden; she was on his arm, and he was explaining to her at length what he intended doing at the office the week following. He heard her saying: 'My dear, I think that is most wise.' . . . Talking things over with Linda was a wonderful help even though they were apt to drift away from the point.

Hang it all! They weren't getting along very fast. Pat had put the brake on again. Ugh! What a brute of a thing it was. He could feel it in the pit of his stomach.

A sort of panic overtook Burnell whenever he approached near home. Before he was well inside the gate he would shout to anyone within sight: 'Is everything all right?' And then he did not believe it was until he heard Linda say: 'Hullo! Are you home again?' That was the worst of living in the country—it took the deuce of a long time to get back. . . . But now they weren't far off. They were on the top of the last hill; it was a gentle slope all the way now and not more than half a mile.

Pat trailed the whip over the mare's back and he coaxed her: 'Goop now. Goop now.'

It wanted a few minutes to sunset. Everything stood motionless bathed in bright, metallic light and from the paddocks on either side there streamed the milky scent of ripe grass. The iron gates were open. They dashed through and up the drive and round the island, stopping at the exact middle of the verandah.

'Did she satisfy yer, Sir?' said Pat, getting off the box and grinning at his master.

'Very well indeed, Pat,' said Stanley.

4. From the translation of the Latin hymn "Te Deum Laudamus," "We Praise Thee, God," line 17, *The Anglican Book of Common Prayer*.

Linda came out of the glass door; her voice rang in the shadowy quiet. 'Hullo! Are you home again?'

At the sound of her his heart beat so hard that he could hardly stop himself dashing up the steps and catching her in his arms.

'Yes, I'm home again. Is everything all right?'

Pat began to lead the buggy round to the side gate that opened into the courtyard.

'Here, half a moment,' said Burnell. 'Hand me those two parcels.' And he said to Linda, 'I've brought you back a bottle of oysters and a pineapple,' as though he had brought her back all the harvest of the earth.

They went into the hall; Linda carried the oysters in one hand and the pineapple in the other. Burnell shut the glass door, threw his hat down, put his arms round her and strained her to him, kissing the top of her head, her ears, her lips, her eyes.

'Oh, dear! Oh, dear!' said she. 'Wait a moment. Let me put down these silly things,' and she put the bottle of oysters and the pine on a little carved chair. 'What have you got in your buttonhole—cherries?' She took them out and hung them over his ear.

'Don't do that, darling. They are for you.'

So she took them off his ear again. 'You don't mind if I save them. They'd spoil my appetite for dinner. Come and see your children. They are having tea.'

The lamp was lighted on the nursery table. Mrs Fairfield was cutting and spreading bread and butter. The three little girls sat up to table wearing large bibs embroidered with their names. They wiped their mouths as their father came in ready to be kissed. The windows were open; a jar of wild flowers stood on the mantelpiece, and the lamp made a big soft bubble of light on the ceiling.

'You seem pretty snug, mother,' said Burnell, blinking at the light. Isabel and Lottie sat one on either side of the table, Kezia at the bottom—the place at the top was empty.

'That's where my boy ought to sit,' thought Stanley. He tightened his arm round Linda's shoulder. By God, he was a perfect fool to feel as happy as this!

'We are, Stanley. We are very snug,' said Mrs Fairfield, cutting Kezia's bread into fingers.

'Like it better than town—eh, children?' asked Burnell.

'Oh, yes,' said the three little girls, and Isabel added as an afterthought: 'Thank you very much indeed, father dear.'

'Come upstairs,' said Linda. 'I'll bring your slippers.'

But the stairs were too narrow for them to go up arm in arm. It was quite dark in the room. He heard her ring tapping on the marble mantelpiece as she felt for the matches.

'I've got some, darling. I'll light the candles.'

But instead he came up behind her and again he put his arms round her and pressed her head into his shoulder.

'I'm so confoundedly happy,' he said.

'Are you?' She turned and put her hands on his breast and looked up at him.

'I don't know what has come over me,' he protested.

It was quite dark outside now and heavy dew was falling. When Linda shut the window the cold dew touched her finger tips. Far away a dog barked. 'I believe there is going to be a moon,' she said.

At the words, and with the cold wet dew on her fingers, she felt as though the moon had risen—that she was being strangely discovered in a flood of cold light. She shivered; she came away from the window and sat down upon the box ottoman beside Stanley.

In the dining-room, by the flicker of a wood fire, Beryl sat on a hassock playing the guitar. She had bathed and changed all her clothes. Now she wore a white muslin dress with black spots on it and in her hair she had pinned a black silk rose.

> Nature has gone to her rest, love,
>   See, we are alone.
> Give me your hand to press, love,
>   Lightly within my own.[5]

She played and sang half to herself, for she was watching herself playing and singing. The firelight gleamed on her shoes, on the ruddy belly of the guitar, and on her white fingers. . . .

'If I were outside the window and looked in and saw myself I really would be rather struck,' thought she. Still more softly she played the accompaniment—not singing now but listening.

. . . 'The first time that I ever saw you, little girl—oh, you had no idea that you were not alone—you were sitting with your little feet upon a hassock, playing the guitar. God, I can never forget. . . .' Beryl flung up her head and began to sing again:

> Even the moon is aweary . . .

But there came a loud bang at the door. The servant girl's crimson face popped through.

'Please, Miss Beryl, I've got to come and lay.'

'Certainly, Alice,' said Beryl, in a voice of ice. She put the guitar in a corner. Alice lunged in with a heavy black iron tray.

5. From a sentimental Victorian ballad.

'Well, I have had a job with that oving,' said she. 'I can't get nothing to brown.'

'Really!' said Beryl.

But no, she could not stand that fool of a girl. She ran into the dark drawing-room and began walking up and down. . . . Oh, she was restless, restless. There was a mirror over the mantel. She leaned her arms along and looked at her pale shadow in it. How beautiful she looked, but there was nobody to see, nobody.

'Why must you suffer so?' said the face in the mirror. 'You were not made for suffering. . . . Smile!'

Beryl smiled, and really her smile *was* so adorable that she smiled again—but this time because she could not help it.

VIII

'Good morning, Mrs Jones.'

'Oh, good morning, Mrs Smith. I'm so glad to see you. Have you brought your children?'

'Yes, I've brought both my twins. I have had another baby since I saw you last, but she came so suddenly that I haven't had time to make her any clothes, yet. So I left her. . . . How is your husband?'

'Oh, he is very well, thank you. At least he had a nawful cold but Queen Victoria—she's my godmother, you know—sent him a case of pineapples and that cured it im-mediately. Is that your new servant?'

'Yes, her name's Gwen. I've only had her two days. Oh, Gwen, this is my friend, Mrs Smith.'

'Good morning, Mrs Smith. Dinner won't be ready for about ten minutes.'

'I don't think you ought to introduce me to the servant. I think I ought to just begin talking to her.'

'Well, she's more of a lady-help than a servant and you do introduce lady-helps, I know, because Mrs Samuel Josephs had one.'

'Oh, well, it doesn't matter,' said the servant, carelessly, beating up a chocolate custard with half a broken clothes peg. The dinner was baking beautifully on a concrete step. She began to lay the cloth on a pink garden seat. In front of each person she put two geranium leaf plates, a pine needle fork and a twig knife. There were three daisy heads on a laurel leaf for poached eggs, some slices of fuchsia petal cold beef, some lovely little rissoles made of earth and water and dandelion seeds, and the chocolate custard which she had decided to serve in the pawa shell she had cooked it in.

'You needn't trouble about my children,' said Mrs Smith graciously. 'If you'll just take this bottle and fill it at the tap—I mean at the dairy.'

'Oh, all right,' said Gwen, and she whispered to Mrs Jones: 'Shall I go and ask Alice for a little bit of real milk?'

But someone called from the front of the house and the luncheon party melted away, leaving the charming table, leaving the rissoles and the poached eggs to the ants and to an old snail who pushed his quivering horns over the edge of the garden seat and began to nibble a geranium plate.

'Come round to the front, children. Pip and Rags have come.'

The Trout boys were the cousins Kezia had mentioned to the storeman. They lived about a mile away in a house called Monkey Tree Cottage. Pip was tall for his age, with lank black hair and a white face, but Rags was very small and so thin that when he was undressed his shoulder blades stuck out like two little wings. They had a mongrel dog with pale blue eyes and a long tail turned up at the end who followed them everywhere; he was called Snooker. They spent half their time combing and brushing Snooker and dosing him with various awful mixtures concocted by Pip, and kept secretly by him in a broken jug covered with an old kettle lid. Even faithful little Rags was not allowed to know the full secret of these mixtures. . . . Take some carbolic tooth powder and a pinch of sulphur powdered up fine, and perhaps a bit of starch to stiffen up Snooker's coat. . . . But that was not all; Rags privately thought that the rest was gun-powder. . . . And he never was allowed to help with the mixing because of the danger. . . . 'Why if a spot of this flew in your eye, you would be blinded for life,' Pip would say, stirring the mixture with an iron spoon. 'And there's always the chance—just the chance, mind you—of it exploding if you whack it hard enough. . . . Two spoons of this in a kerosene tin will be enough to kill thousands of fleas.' But Snooker spent all his spare time biting and snuffling, and he stank abominably.

'It's because he is such a grand fighting dog,' Pip would say. 'All fighting dogs smell.'

The Trout boys had often spent the day with the Burnells in town, but now that they lived in this fine house and boncer garden they were inclined to be very friendly. Besides, both of them liked playing with girls—Pip, because he could fox them so, and because Lottie was so easily frightened, and Rags for a shameful reason. He adored dolls. How he would look at a doll as it lay asleep, speaking in a whisper and smiling timidly, and what a treat it was to him to be allowed to hold one. . . .

'Curve your arms round her. Don't keep them stiff like that. You'll drop her,' Isabel would say sternly.

Now they were standing on the verandah and holding back Snooker who wanted to go into the house but wasn't allowed to because Aunt Linda hated decent dogs.

'We came over in the bus with Mum,' they said, 'and we're going to spend the afternoon with you. We brought over a batch of our gingerbread for Aunt Linda. Our Minnie made it. It's all over nuts.'

'I skinned the almonds,' said Pip. 'I just stuck my hand into a saucepan of boiling water and grabbed them out and gave them a kind of pinch and the nuts flew out of the skins, some of them as high as the ceiling. Didn't they, Rags?'

Rags nodded. 'When they make cakes at our place,' said Pip, 'we always stay in the kitchen, Rags and me, and I get the bowl and he gets the spoon and the egg beater. Sponge cake's best. It's all frothy stuff, then.'

He ran down the verandah steps to the lawn, planted his hands on the grass, bent forward, and just did not stand on his head.

'That lawn's all bumpy,' he said. 'You have to have a flat place for standing on your head. I can walk round the monkey tree on my head at our place. Can't I, Rags?'

'Nearly,' said Rags faintly.

'Stand on your head on the verandah. That's quite flat,' said Kezia.

'No, smarty,' said Pip. 'You have to do it on something soft. Because if you give a jerk and fall over, something in your neck goes click, and it breaks off. Dad told me.'

'Oh, do let's play something,' said Kezia.

'Very well,' said Isabel quickly, 'we'll play hospitals. I will be the nurse and Pip can be the doctor and you and Lottie and Rags can be the sick people.'

Lottie didn't want to play that, because last time Pip had squeezed something down her throat and it hurt awfully.

'Pooh,' scoffed Pip. 'It was only the juice out of a bit of mandarin peel.'

'Well, let's play ladies,' said Isabel. 'Pip can be the father and you can be all our dear little children.'

'I hate playing ladies,' said Kezia. 'You always make us go to church hand in hand and come home and go to bed.'

Suddenly Pip took a filthy handkerchief out of his pocket. 'Snooker! Here, sir,' he called. But Snooker, as usual, tried to sneak away, his tail between his legs. Pip leapt on top of him, and pressed him between his knees.

'Keep his head firm, Rags,' he said, and he tied the handkerchief round Snooker's head with a funny knot sticking up at the top.

'Whatever is that for?' asked Lottie.

'It's to train his ears to grow more close to his head—see?' said Pip. 'All fighting dogs have ears that lie back. But Snooker's ears are a bit too soft.'

'I know,' said Kezia. 'They are always turning inside out. I hate that.'

Snooker lay down, made one feeble effort with his paw to get the handkerchief off, but finding he could not, trailed after the children, shivering with misery.

IX

Pat came swinging along; in his hand he held a little tomahawk that winked in the sun.

'Come with me,' he said to the children, 'and I'll show you how the kings of Ireland chop the head off a duck.'

They drew back—they didn't believe him, and besides, the Trout boys had never seen Pat before.

'Come on now,' he coaxed, smiling and holding out his hand to Kezia.

'Is it a real duck's head? One from the paddock?'

'It is,' said Pat. She put her hand in his hard dry one, and he stuck the tomahawk in his belt and held out the other to Rags. He loved little children.

'I'd better keep hold of Snooker's head if there's going to be any blood about,' said Pip, 'because the sight of blood makes him awfully wild.' He ran ahead dragging Snooker by the handkerchief.

'Do you think we ought to go?' whispered Isabel. 'We haven't asked or anything. Have we?'

At the bottom of the orchard a gate was set in the paling fence. On the other side a steep bank led down to a bridge that spanned the creek, and once up the bank on the other side you were on the fringe of the paddocks. A little old stable in the first paddock had been turned into a fowl house. The fowls had strayed far away across the paddock down to a dumping ground, in a hollow, but the ducks kept close to that part of the creek that flowed under the bridge.

Tall bushes overhung the stream with red leaves and yellow flowers and clusters of blackberries. At some places the stream was wide and shallow, but at others it tumbled into deep little pools with foam at the edges and quivering bubbles. It was in these pools that the big white ducks had made themselves at home, swimming and guzzling along the weedy banks.

Up and down they swam, preening their dazzling breasts, and other ducks with the same dazzling breasts and yellow bills swam upside down with them.

'There is the little Irish navy,' said Pat, 'and look at the old admiral there with the green neck and the grand little flagstaff on his tail.'

He pulled a handful of grain from his pocket and began to walk towards the fowl-house, lazy, his straw hat with the broken crown pulled over his eyes.

'Lid. Lid—lid—lid—lid——' he called.

'Qua. Qua—qua—qua—qua——' answered the ducks, making for land, and flapping and scrambling up the bank they streamed after him in a long waddling line. He coaxed them, pretending to throw the grain, shaking it in his hands and calling to them until they swept round him in a white ring.

From far away the fowls heard the clamour and they too came running across the paddock, their heads thrust forward, their wings spread, turning in their feet in the silly way fowls run and scolding as they came.

Then Pat scattered the grain and the greedy ducks began to gobble. Quickly he stooped, seized two, one under each arm, and strode across to the children. Their darting heads and round eyes frightened the children—all except Pip.

'Come on, sillies,' he cried, 'they can't bite. They haven't any teeth. They've only got those two little holes in their beaks for breathing through.'

'Will you hold one while I finish with the other?' asked Pat. Pip let go of Snooker. 'Won't I? Won't I? Give us one. I don't mind how much he kicks.'

He nearly sobbed with delight when Pat gave the white lump into his arms.

There was an old stump beside the door of the fowl-house. Pat grabbed the duck by the legs, laid it flat across the stump, and almost at the same moment down came the little tomahawk and the duck's head flew off the stump. Up the blood spurted over the white feathers and over his hand.

When the children saw the blood they were frightened no longer. They crowded round him and began to scream. Even Isabel leaped about crying: 'The blood! The blood!' Pip forgot all about his duck. He simply threw it away from him and shouted, 'I saw it. I saw it,' and jumped round the wood block.

Rags, with cheeks as white as paper, ran up to the little head, put out a finger as if he wanted to touch it, shrank back again and then again put out a finger. He was shivering all over.

Even Lottie, frightened little Lottie, began to laugh and pointed at the duck and shrieked: 'Look, Kezia, look.'

'Watch it!' shouted Pat. He put down the body and it began to waddle—with only a long spurt of blood where the head had been; it began to pad away without a sound towards the steep bank that led to the stream. . . . That was the crowning wonder.

'Do you see that? Do you see that?' yelled Pip. He ran among the little girls tugging at their pinafores.

'It's like a little engine. It's like a funny little railway engine,' squealed Isabel.

But Kezia suddenly rushed at Pat and flung her arms round his legs and butted her head as hard as she could against his knees.

'Put head back! Put head back!' she screamed.

When he stooped to move her she would not let go or take her head away. She held on as hard as she could and sobbed: 'Head back! Head back!' until it sounded like a loud strange hiccup.

'It's stopped. It's tumbled over. It's dead,' said Pip.

Pat dragged Kezia up into his arms. Her sun-bonnet had fallen back, but she would not let him look at her face. No, she pressed her face into a bone in his shoulder and clasped her arms round his neck.

The children stopped screaming as suddenly as they had begun. They stood round the dead duck. Rags was not frightened of the head any more. He knelt down and stroked it, now.

'I don't think the head is quite dead yet,' he said. 'Do you think it would keep alive if I gave it something to drink?'

But Pip got very cross: 'Bah! You baby.' He whistled to Snooker and went off.

When Isabel went up to Lottie, Lottie snatched away.

'What are you always touching me for, Isabel?'

'There now,' said Pat to Kezia. 'There's the grand little girl.'

She put up her hands and touched his ears. She felt something. Slowly she raised her quivering face and looked. Pat wore little round gold ear-rings. She never knew that men wore ear-rings. She was very much surprised.

'Do they come on and off?' she asked huskily.

X

Up in the house, in the warm tidy kitchen, Alice, the servant girl, was getting the afternoon tea. She was 'dressed'. She had on a black stuff dress that smelt under the arms, a white apron like a large sheet of paper, and a lace bow pinned on to her hair with two jetty pins. Also her comfortable carpet slippers were changed for a pair of black leather ones that pinched her corn on her little toe something dreadful. . . .

It was warm in the kitchen. A blow-fly buzzed, a fan of whity steam came out of the kettle, and the lid kept up a rattling jig as the water bubbled. The clock ticked in the warm air, slow and deliberate, like the click of an old woman's knitting needle, and sometimes—for no reason at all, for there wasn't any breeze—the blind swung out and back, tapping the window.

Alice was making water-cress sandwiches. She had a lump of

butter on the table, a barracouta loaf, and the cresses[6] tumbled in a white cloth.

But propped against the butter dish there was a dirty, greasy little book, half unstitched, with curled edges, and while she mashed the butter she read:

'To dream of black-beetles drawing a hearse is bad. Signifies death of one you hold near or dear, either father, husband, brother, son, or intended. If beetles crawl backwards as you watch them it means death from fire or from great height such as flight of stairs, scaffolding, etc.

'Spiders. To dream of spiders creeping over you is good. Signifies large sum of money in near future. Should party be in family way an easy confinement may be expected. But care should be taken in sixth month to avoid eating of probable present of shell fish. . . .'

How many thousand birds I see.

Oh, life. There was Miss Beryl. Alice dropped the knife and slipped the *Dream Book* under the butter dish. But she hadn't time to hide it quite, for Beryl ran into the kitchen and up to the table, and the first thing her eye lighted on were those greasy edges. Alice saw Miss Beryl's meaning little smile and the way she raised her eyebrows and screwed up her eyes as though she were not quite sure what that could be. She decided to answer if Miss Beryl should ask her: 'Nothing as belongs to you, Miss.' But she knew Miss Beryl would not ask her.

Alice was a mild creature in reality, but she had the most marvellous retorts ready for questions that she knew would never be put to her. The composing of them and the turning of them over and over in her mind comforted her just as much as if they'd been expressed. Really, they kept her alive in places where she'd been that chivvied[7] she'd been afraid to go to bed at night with a box of matches on the chair in case she bit the tops off in her sleep, as you might say.

'Oh, Alice,' said Miss Beryl. 'There's one extra to tea, so heat a plate of yesterday's scones, please. And put on the Victoria sandwich as well as the coffee cake. And don't forget to put little doyleys under the plates—will you? You did yesterday, you know, and the tea looked so ugly and common. And, Alice, don't put that dreadful old pink and green cosy on the afternoon teapot again. That is only for the mornings. Really, I think it ought to be kept for the

6. Plants with edible, pungent leaves. Barracouta: a long, narrow loaf of bread, named after the fish it vaguely resembles.
7. Told repeatedly to do something.

kitchen—it's so shabby, and quite smelly. Put on the Japanese one. You quite understand, don't you?'

Miss Beryl had finished.

That sing aloud from every tree . . .

she sang as she left the kitchen, very pleased with her firm handling of Alice.

Oh, Alice was wild. She wasn't one to mind being told, but there was something in the way Miss Beryl had of speaking to her that she couldn't stand. Oh, that she couldn't. It made her curl up inside, as you might say, and she fair trembled. But what Alice really hated Miss Beryl for was that she made her feel low. She talked to Alice in a special voice as though she wasn't quite all there; and she never lost her temper with her—never. Even when Alice dropped anything or forgot anything important Miss Beryl seemed to have expected it to happen.

'If you please, Mrs Burnell,' said an imaginary Alice, as she buttered the scones, 'I'd rather not take my orders from Miss Beryl. I may be only a common servant girl as doesn't know how to play the guitar, but. . . .'

This last thrust pleased her so much that she quite recovered her temper.

'The only thing to do,' she heard, as she opened the dining-room door, 'is to cut the sleeves out entirely and just have a broad band of black velvet over the shoulders instead. . . .'

XI

The white duck did not look as if it had ever had a head when Alice placed it in front of Stanley Burnell that night. It lay, in beautifully basted resignation, on a blue dish—its legs tied together with a piece of string and a wreath of little balls of stuffing round it.

It was hard to say which of the two, Alice or the duck, looked the better basted; they were both such a rich colour and they both had the same air of gloss and strain. But Alice was fiery red and the duck a Spanish mahogany.

Burnell ran his eye along the edge of the carving knife. He prided himself very much upon his carving, upon making a first-class job of it. He hated seeing a woman carve; they were always too slow and they never seemed to care what the meat looked like afterwards. Now he did; he took a real pride in cutting delicate shaves of cold beef, little wads of mutton, just the right thickness, and in dividing a chicken or a duck with nice precision. . . .

'Is this the first of the home products?' he asked, knowing perfectly well that it was.

'Yes, the butcher did not come. We have found out that he only calls twice a week.'

But there was no need to apologise. It was a superb bird. It wasn't meat at all, but a kind of very superior jelly. 'My father would say,' said Burnell, 'this must have been one of those birds whose mother played to it in infancy upon the German flute. And the sweet strains of the dulcet instrument acted with such effect upon the infant mind. . . . Have some more, Beryl? You and I are the only ones in this house with a real feeling for food. I'm perfectly willing to state, in a court of law, if necessary, that I love good food.'

Tea was served in the drawing-room, and Beryl, who for some reason had been very charming to Stanley ever since he came home, suggested a game of crib.[8] They sat at a little table near one of the open windows. Mrs Fairfield disappeared, and Linda lay in a rocking-chair, her arms above her head, rocking to and fro.

'You don't want the light—do you, Linda?' said Beryl. She moved the tall lamp so that she sat under its soft light.

How remote they looked, those two, from where Linda sat and rocked. The green table, the polished cards, Stanley's big hands and Beryl's tiny ones, all seemed to be part of one mysterious movement. Stanley himself, big and solid, in his dark suit, took his ease, and Beryl tossed her bright head and pouted. Round her throat she wore an unfamiliar velvet ribbon. It changed her, somehow—altered the shape of her face—but it was charming, Linda decided. The room smelled of lilies; there were two big jars of arums in the fire-place.

'Fifteen two—fifteen four—and a pair is six and a run of three is nine,' said Stanley, so deliberately, he might have been counting sheep.

'I've nothing but two pairs,' said Beryl, exaggerating her woe because she knew how he loved winning.

The cribbage pegs were like two little people going up the road together, turning round the sharp corner, and coming down the road again. They were pursuing each other. They did not so much want to get ahead as to keep near enough to talk—to keep near, perhaps that was all.

But no, there was always one who was impatient and hopped away as the other came up, and would not listen. Perhaps the white peg was frightened of the red one, or perhaps he was cruel and would not give the red one a chance to speak. . . .

In the front of her dress Beryl wore a bunch of pansies, and once when the little pegs were side by side, she bent over and the pansies dropped out and covered them.

8. Cribbage, a card game for two players, with the score kept by pegs on a small board.

'What a shame,' said she, picking up the pansies. 'Just as they had a chance to fly into each other's arms.'

'Farewell, my girl,' laughed Stanley, and away the red peg hopped.

The drawing-room was long and narrow with glass doors that gave on to the verandah. It had a cream paper with a pattern of gilt roses, and the furniture, which had belonged to old Mrs Fairfield, was dark and plain. A little piano stood against the wall with yellow pleated silk let into the carved front. Above it hung an oil painting by Beryl of a large cluster of surprised looking clematis. Each flower was the size of a small saucer, with a centre like an astonished eye fringed in black. But the room was not finished yet. Stanley had set his heart on a Chesterfield[9] and two decent chairs. Linda liked it best as it was. . . .

Two big moths flew in through the window and round and round the circle of lamplight.

'Fly away before it is too late. Fly out again.'

Round and round they flew; they seemed to bring the silence and the moonlight in with them on their silent wings. . . .

'I've two kings,' said Stanley. 'Any good?'

'Quite good,' said Beryl.

Linda stopped rocking and got up. Stanley looked across. 'Anything the matter, darling?'

'No, nothing. I'm going to find mother.'

She went out of the room and standing at the foot of the stairs she called, but her mother's voice answered her from the verandah.

The moon that Lottie and Kezia had seen from the storeman's wagon was full, and the house, the garden, the old woman and Linda—all were bathed in dazzling light.

'I have been looking at the aloe,' said Mrs Fairfield. 'I believe it is going to flower this year. Look at the top there. Are those buds, or is it only an effect of light?'

As they stood on the steps, the high grassy bank on which the aloe rested rose up like a wave, and the aloe seemed to ride upon it like a ship with the oars lifted. Bright moonlight hung upon the lifted oars like water, and on the green wave glittered the dew.

'Do you feel it, too,' said Linda, and she spoke to her mother with the special voice that women use at night to each other as though they spoke in their sleep or from some hollow cave—'Don't you feel that it is coming towards us?'

She dreamed that she was caught up out of the cold water into the ship with the lifted oars and the budding mast. Now the oars fell striking quickly, quickly. They rowed far away over the top of the garden trees, the paddocks and the dark bush beyond. Ah,

9. A sofa with padded arms.

she heard herself cry: 'Faster! Faster!' to those who were rowing.

How much more real this dream was than that they should go back to the house where the sleeping children lay and where Stanley and Beryl played cribbage.

'I believe those are buds,' said she. 'Let us go down into the garden, mother. I like that aloe. I like it more than anything here. And I am sure I shall remember it long after I've forgotten all the other things.'

She put her hand on her mother's arm and they walked down the steps, round the island and on to the main drive that led to the front gates.

Looking at it from below she could see the long sharp thorns that edged the aloe leaves, and at the sight of them her heart grew hard. . . . She particularly liked the long sharp thorns. . . . Nobody would dare to come near the ship or to follow after.

'Not even my Newfoundland dog,' thought she, 'that I'm so fond of in the daytime.'

For she really was fond of him; she loved and admired and respected him tremendously. Oh, better than anyone else in the world. She knew him through and through. He was the soul of truth and decency, and for all his practical experience he was awfully simple, easily pleased and easily hurt. . . .

If only he wouldn't jump at her so, and bark so loudly, and watch her with such eager, loving eyes. He was too strong for her; she had always hated things that rush at her, from a child. There were times when he was frightening—really frightening. When she just had not screamed at the top of her voice: 'You are killing me.' And at those times she had longed to say the most coarse, hateful things. . . .

'You know I'm very delicate. You know as well as I do that my heart is affected, and the doctor has told you I may die any moment. I have had three great lumps of children already. . . .'

Yes, yes, it was true. Linda snatched her hand from mother's arm. For all her love and respect and admiration she hated him. And how tender he always was after times like those, how submissive, how thoughtful. He would do anything for her; he longed to serve her. . . . Linda heard herself saying in a weak voice:

'Stanley, would you light a candle?'

And she heard his joyful voice answer: 'Of course I will, my darling,' and he leapt out of bed as though he were going to leap at the moon for her.

It had never been so plain to her as it was at this moment. There were all her feelings for him, sharp and defined, one as true as the other. And there was this other, this hatred, just as real as the rest. She could have done her feelings up in little packets and given them to Stanley. She longed to hand him that last one, for a surprise. She could see his eyes as he opened that. . . .

She hugged her folded arms and began to laugh silently. How absurd life was—it was laughable, simply laughable. And why this mania of hers to keep alive at all? For it really was a mania, she thought, mocking and laughing.

'What am I guarding myself for so preciously? I shall go on having children and Stanley will go on making money and the children and the gardens will grow bigger and bigger, with whole fleets of aloes in them for me to choose from.'

She had been walking with her head bent, looking at nothing. Now she looked up and about her. They were standing by the red and white camellia trees. Beautiful were the rich dark leaves spangled with light and the round flowers that perch among them like red and white birds. Linda pulled a piece of verbena and crumpled it, and held her hands to her mother.

'Delicious,' said the old woman. 'Are you cold, child? Are you trembling? Yes, your hands are cold. We had better go back to the house.'

'What have you been thinking about?' said Linda. 'Tell me.'

'I haven't really been thinking of anything. I wondered as we passed the orchard what the fruit trees were like and whether we should be able to make much jam this autumn. There are splendid healthy currant bushes in the vegetable garden. I noticed them today. I should like to see those pantry shelves thoroughly well stocked with our own jam. . . .'

XII

'My Darling Nan,

Don't think me a piggy wig because I haven't written before. I haven't had a moment, dear, and even now I feel so exhausted that I can hardly hold a pen.

Well, the dreadful deed is done. We have actually left the giddy whirl of town, and I can't see how we shall ever go back again, for my brother-in-law has bought this house "lock, stock and barrel", to use his own words.

In a way, of course, it is an awful relief, for he has been threatening to take a place in the country ever since I've lived with them—and I must say the house and garden are awfully nice—a million times better than that awful cubby-hole in town.

But buried, my dear. Buried isn't the word.

We have got neighbours, but they are only farmers—big louts of boys who seem to be milking all day, and two dreadful females with rabbit teeth who brought us some scones when we were moving and said they would be pleased to help. But my sister who lives a mile away doesn't know a soul here, so I am sure we never shall. It's pretty certain nobody will ever come out from town to see us, because though there is a bus it's an awful old rattling thing with black leather sides that any decent person would rather die than ride in for six miles.

Such is life. It's a sad ending for poor little B. I'll get to be a most awful frump in a year or two and come and see you in a mackintosh and a sailor hat tied on with a white china silk motor veil. So pretty.

Stanley says that now we are settled—for after the most awful week of my life we really are settled—he is going to bring out a couple of men from the club on Saturday afternoons for tennis. In fact, two are promised as a great treat to-day. But, my dear, if you could see Stanley's men from the club . . . rather fattish, the type who look frightfully indecent without waistcoats—always with toes that turn in rather—so conspicuous when you are walking about a court in white shoes. And they are pulling up their trousers every minute—don't you know—and whacking at imaginary things with their rackets.

I used to play with them at the club last summer, and I am sure you will know the type when I tell you that after I'd been there about three times they all called me Miss Beryl. It's a weary world. Of course mother simply loves the place, but then I suppose when I am mother's age I shall be content to sit in the sun and shell peas into a basin. But I'm not—not—not.

What Linda thinks about the whole affair, per usual, I haven't the slightest idea. Mysterious as ever. . . .

My dear, you know that white satin dress of mine. I have taken the sleeves out entirely, put bands of black velvet across the shoulders and two big red poppies off my dear sister's *chapeau*. It is a great success, though when I shall wear it I do not know.'

Beryl sat writing this letter at a little table in her room. In a way, of course, it was all perfectly true, but in another way it was all the greatest rubbish and she didn't believe a word of it. No, that wasn't true. She felt all those things, but she didn't really feel them like that.

It was her other self who had written that letter. It not only bored, it rather disgusted her real self.

'Flippant and silly,' said her real self. Yet she knew that she'd send it and she'd always write that kind of twaddle to Nan Pym. In fact, it was a very mild example of the kind of letter she generally wrote.

Beryl leaned her elbows on the table and read it through again. The voice of the letter seemed to come up to her from the page. It was faint already, like a voice heard over the telephone, high, gushing, with something bitter in the sound. Oh, she detested it to-day.

'You've always got so much animation,' said Nan Pym. 'That's why men are so keen on you.' And she had added, rather mournfully, for men were not at all keen on Nan, who was a solid kind of girl, with fat hips and a high colour—'I can't understand how you can keep it up. But it is your nature, I suppose.'

What rot. What nonsense. It wasn't her nature at all. Good heavens, if she had ever been her real self with Nan Pym, Nannie would have jumped out of the window with surprise. . . . My dear, you know that white satin of mine. . . . Beryl slammed the letter-case to.

She jumped up and half unconsciously, half consciously she drifted over to the looking-glass.

There stood a slim girl in white—a white serge skirt, a white silk blouse, and a leather belt drawn in very tightly at her tiny waist.

Her face was heart-shaped, wide at the brows and with a pointed chin—but not too pointed. Her eyes, her eyes were perhaps her best feature; they were such a strange uncommon colour—greeny blue with little gold points in them.

She had fine black eyebrows and long lashes—so long, that when they lay on her cheeks you positively caught the light in them, someone or other had told her.

Her mouth was rather large. Too large? No, not really. Her underlip protruded a little; she had a way of sucking it in that somebody else had told her was awfully fascinating.

Her nose was her least satisfactory feature. Not that it was really ugly. But it was not half as fine as Linda's. Linda really had a perfect little nose. Hers spread rather—not badly. And in all probability she exaggerated the spreadiness of it just because it was her nose, and she was so awfully critical of herself. She pinched it with a thumb and first finger and made a little face. . . .

Lovely, lovely hair. And such a mass of it. It had the colour of fresh fallen leaves, brown and red with a glint of yellow. When she did it in a long plait she felt it on her backbone like a long snake. She loved to feel the weight of it dragging her head back, and she loved to feel it loose, covering her bare arms. 'Yes, my dear, there is no doubt about it, you really are a lovely little thing.'

At the words her bosom lifted; she took a long breath of delight, half closing her eyes.

But even as she looked the smile faded from her lips and eyes. Oh God, there she was, back again, playing the same old game. False—false as ever. False as when she'd written to Nan Pym. False even when she was alone with herself, now.

What had that creature in the glass to do with her, and why was she staring? She dropped down to one side of her bed and buried her face in her arms.

'Oh,' she cried, 'I am so miserable—so frightfully miserable. I know that I'm silly and spiteful and vain; I'm always acting a part.

I'm never my real self for a moment.' And plainly, plainly, she saw her false self running up and down the stairs, laughing a special trilling laugh if they had visitors, standing under the lamp if a man came to dinner, so that he should see the light on her hair, pouting and pretending to be a little girl when she was asked to play the guitar. Why? She even kept it up for Stanley's benefit. Only last night when he was reading the paper her false self had stood beside him and leaned against his shoulder on purpose. Hadn't she put her hand over his, pointing out something so that he should see how white her hand was beside his brown one.

How despicable! Despicable! Her heart was cold with rage. 'It's marvellous how you keep it up,' said she to the false self. But then it was only because she was so miserable—so miserable. If she had been happy and leading her own life, her false life would cease to be. She saw the real Beryl—a shadow . . . a shadow. Faint and unsubstantial she shone. What was there of her except the radiance? And for what tiny moments she was really she. Beryl could almost remember every one of them. At those times she had felt: 'Life is rich and mysterious and good, and I am rich and mysterious and good, too.' Shall I ever be that Beryl for ever? Shall I? How can I? And was there ever a time when I did not have a false self? . . . But just as she had got that far she heard the sound of little steps running along the passage; the door handle rattled. Kezia came in.

'Aunt Beryl, mother says will you please come down? Father is home with a man and lunch is ready.'

Botheration! How she had crumpled her skirt, kneeling in that idiotic way.

'Very well, Kezia.' She went over to the dressing table and powdered her nose.

Kezia crossed too, and unscrewed a little pot of cream and sniffed it. Under her arm she carried a very dirty calico[1] cat.

When Aunt Beryl ran out of the room she sat the cat up on the dressing table and stuck the top of the cream jar over its ear.

'Now look at yourself,' said she sternly.

The calico cat was so overcome by the sight that it toppled over backwards and bumped and bumped on to the floor. And the top of the cream jar flew through the air and rolled like a penny in a round on the linoleum—and did not break.

But for Kezia it had broken the moment it flew through the air, and she picked it up, hot all over, and put it back on the dressing table.

Then she tip-toed away, far too quickly and airily. . . .

1. A toy cat made from calico—plain, unbleached cotton—cloth.

A Dill Pickle (1917)†

And then, after six years, she saw him again. He was seated at one of those little bamboo tables decorated with a Japanese vase of paper daffodils. There was a tall plate of fruit in front of him, and very carefully, in a way she recognized immediately as his 'special' way, he was peeling an orange.

He must have felt that shock of recognition in her for he looked up and met her eyes. Incredible! He didn't know her! She smiled; he frowned. She came towards him. He closed his eyes an instant, but opening them his face lit up as though he had struck a match in a dark room. He laid down the orange and pushed back his chair, and she took her little warm hand out of her muff and gave it to him.

'Vera!' he exclaimed. 'How strange. Really, for a moment I didn't know you. Won't you sit down? You've had lunch? Won't you have some coffee?'

She hesitated, but of course she meant to.

'Yes, I'd like some coffee.' And she sat down opposite him.

'You've changed. You've changed very much,' he said, staring at her with that eager, lighted look. 'You look so well. I've never seen you look so well before.'

'Really?' She raised her veil and unbuttoned her high fur collar. 'I don't feel very well. I can't bear this weather, you know.'

'Ah, no. You hate the cold. . . .'

'Loathe it.' She shuddered. 'And the worst of it is that the older one grows. . . .'

He interrupted her. 'Excuse me,' and tapped on the table for the waitress. 'Please bring some coffee and cream.' To her: 'You are sure you won't eat anything? Some fruit, perhaps. The fruit here is very good.'

'No, thanks. Nothing.'

'Then that's settled.' And smiling just a hint too broadly he took up the orange again. 'You were saying—the older one grows—'

'The colder,' she laughed. But she was thinking how well she remembered that trick of his—the trick of interrupting her—and of how it used to exasperate her six years ago. She used to feel then as though he, quite suddenly, in the middle of what she was saying, put his hand over her lips, turned from her, attended to something different, and then took his hand away, and with just the same slightly too broad smile, gave her his attention again. . . . Now we are ready. That is settled.

† Published in the *New Age* (4 October 1917), then revised for *Bliss and Other Stories* (1920).

'The colder!' He echoed her words, laughing too. 'Ah, ah. You still say the same things. And there is another thing about you that is not changed at all—your beautiful voice—your beautiful way of speaking.' Now he was very grave; he leaned towards her, and she smelled the warm, stinging scent of the orange peel. 'You have only to say one word and I would know your voice among all other voices. I don't know what it is—I've often wondered—that makes your voice such a—haunting memory. . . . Do you remember that first afternoon we spent together at Kew Gardens?[1] You were so surprised because I did not know the names of any flowers. I am still just as ignorant for all your telling me. But whenever it is very fine and warm, and I see some bright colours—it's awfully strange—I hear your voice saying: "Geranium, marigold and verbena." And I feel those three words are all I recall of some forgotten, heavenly language. . . . You remember that afternoon?'

'Oh, yes, very well.' She drew a long, soft breath, as though the paper daffodils between them were almost too sweet to bear. Yet, what had remained in her mind of that particular afternoon was an absurd scene over the tea table. A great many people taking tea in a Chinese pagoda,[2] and he behaving like a maniac about the wasps—waving them away, flapping at them with his straw hat, serious and infuriated out of all proportion to the occasion. How delighted the sniggering tea drinkers had been. And how she had suffered.

But now, as he spoke, that memory faded. His was the truer. Yes, it had been a wonderful afternoon, full of geranium and marigold and verbena, and—warm sunshine. Her thoughts lingered over the last two words as though she sang them.

In the warmth, as it were, another memory unfolded. She saw herself sitting on a lawn. He lay beside her, and suddenly, after a long silence, he rolled over and put his head in her lap.

'I wish,' he said, in a low troubled voice, 'I wish that I had taken poison and were about to die—here now!'

At that moment a little girl in a white dress, holding a long, dripping water lily, dodged from behind a bush, stared at them, and dodged back again. But he did not see. She leaned over him.

'Ah, why do you say that? I could not say that.'

But he gave a kind of soft moan, and taking her hand he held it to his cheek.

'Because I know I am going to love you too much—far too much. And I shall suffer so terribly, Vera, because you never, never will love me.'

He was certainly far better looking now than he had been then.

1. The Royal Botanic Gardens at Kew, in Richmond, London.
2. The gardens include a tiered Buddhist temple.

He had lost all that dreamy vagueness and indecision. Now he had the air of a man who has found his place in life, and fills it with a confidence and an assurance which was, to say the least, impressive. He must have made money, too. His clothes were admirable, and at that moment he pulled a Russian cigarette case out of his pocket.

'Won't you smoke?'

'Yes, I will.' She hovered over them. 'They look very good.'

'I think they are. I get them made for me by a little man in St. James's Street.[3] I don't smoke very much. I'm not like you—but when I do, they must be delicious, very fresh cigarettes. Smoking isn't a habit with me; it's a luxury—like perfume. Are you still so fond of perfumes? Ah, when I was in Russia. . . .'

She broke in: 'You've really been to Russia?'

'Oh, yes. I was there for over a year. Have you forgotten how we used to talk of going there?'

'No, I've not forgotten.'

He gave a strange half laugh and leaned back in his chair. 'Isn't it curious. I have really carried out all those journeys that we planned. Yes, I have been to all those places that we talked of, and stayed in them long enough to—as you used to say, "air oneself" in them. In fact, I have spent the last three years of my life travelling all the time. Spain, Corsica, Siberia, Russia, Egypt. The only country left is China, and I mean to go there, too, when the war is over.'

As he spoke, so lightly, tapping the end of his cigarette against the ash-tray, she felt the strange beast that had slumbered so long within her bosom stir, stretch itself, yawn, prick up its ears, and suddenly bound to its feet, and fix its longing, hungry stare upon those far away places. But all she said was, smiling gently: 'How I envy you.'

He accepted that. 'It has been,' he said, 'very wonderful—especially Russia. Russia was all that we had imagined, and far, far more. I even spent some days on a river boat on the Volga.[4] Do you remember that boatman's song that you used to play?'

'Yes.' It began to play in her mind as she spoke.

'Do you ever play it now?'

'No, I've no piano.'

He was amazed at that. 'But what has become of your beautiful piano?'

She made a little grimace. 'Sold. Ages ago.'

'But you were so fond of music,' he wondered.

'I've no time for it now,' said she.

3. A street in the fashionable West End of London.
4. The longest river in Europe, flowing from northwest Russia to the Caspian Sea.

He let it go at that. 'That river life,' he went on, 'is something quite special. After a day or two you cannot realize that you have ever known another. And it is not necessary to know the language—the life of the boat creates a bond between you and the people that's more than sufficient. You eat with them, pass the day with them, and in the evening there is that endless singing.'

She shivered, hearing the boatman's song break out again loud and tragic, and seeing the boat floating on the darkening river with melancholy trees on either side. . . . 'Yes, I should like that,' said she, stroking her muff.

'You'd like almost everything about Russian life,' he said warmly. 'It's so informal, so impulsive, so free without question. And then the peasants are so splendid. They are such human beings—yes, that is it. Even the man who drives your carriage has—has some real part in what is happening. I remember the evening a party of us, two friends of mine and the wife of one of them, went for a picnic by the Black Sea. We took supper and champagne and ate and drank on the grass. And while we were eating the coachman came up. "Have a dill pickle," he said. He wanted to share with us. That seemed to me so right, so—you know what I mean?'

And she seemed at that moment to be sitting on the grass beside the mysteriously Black Sea, black as velvet, and rippling against the banks in silent, velvet waves. She saw the carriage drawn up to one side of the road, and the little group on the grass, their faces and hands white in the moonlight. She saw the pale dress of the woman outspread and her folded parasol, lying on the grass like a huge pearl crochet hook. Apart from them, with his supper in a cloth on his knees, sat the coachman. 'Have a dill pickle,' said he, and although she was not certain what a dill pickle was, she saw the greenish glass jar with a red chili like a parrot's beak glimmering through. She sucked in her cheeks; the dill pickle was terribly sour. . . .

'Yes, I know perfectly what you mean,' she said.

In the pause that followed they looked at each other. In the past when they had looked at each other like that they had felt such a boundless understanding between them that their souls had, as it were, put their arms round each other and dropped into the same sea, content to be drowned, like mournful lovers. But now, the surprising thing was that it was he who held back. He who said:

'What a marvellous listener you are. When you look at me with those wild eyes I feel that I could tell you things that I would never breathe to another human being.'

Was there just a hint of mockery in his voice or was it her fancy? She could not be sure.

'Before I met you,' he said, 'I had never spoken of myself to anybody. How well I remember one night, the night that I brought you the little Christmas tree, telling you all about my childhood. And of how I was so miserable that I ran away and lived under a cart in our yard for two days without being discovered. And you listened, and your eyes shone, and I felt that you had even made the little Christmas tree listen too, as in a fairy story.'

But of that evening she had remembered a little pot of caviare. It had cost seven and sixpence. He could not get over it. Think of it—a tiny jar like that costing seven and sixpence. While she ate it he watched her, delighted and shocked.

'No, really, that *is* eating money. You could not get seven shillings into a little pot that size. Only think of the profit they must make. . . .' And he had begun some immensely complicated calculations. . . . But now good-bye to the caviare. The Christmas tree was on the table, and the little boy lay under the cart with his head pillowed on the yard dog.

'The dog was called Bosun,' she cried delightedly.

But he did not follow. 'Which dog? Had you a dog? I don't remember a dog at all.'

'No, no. I mean the yard dog when you were a little boy.' He laughed and snapped the cigarette case to.

'Was he? Do you know I had forgotten that. It seems such ages ago. I cannot believe that it is only six years. After I had recognized you to-day—I had to take such a leap—I had to take a leap over my whole life to get back to that time. I was such a kid then.' He drummed on the table. 'I've often thought how I must have bored you. And now I understand so perfectly why you wrote to me as you did—although at the time that letter nearly finished my life. I found it again the other day, and I couldn't help laughing as I read it. It was so clever—such a true picture of me.' He glanced up. 'You're not going?'

She had buttoned her collar again and drawn down her veil.

'Yes, I am afraid I must,' she said, and managed a smile. Now she knew that he had been mocking.

'Ah, no, please,' he pleaded. 'Don't go just for a moment,' and he caught up one of her gloves from the table and clutched at it as if that would hold her. 'I see so few people to talk to nowadays, that I have turned into a sort of barbarian,' he said. 'Have I said something to hurt you?'

'Not a bit,' she lied. But as she watched him draw her glove through his fingers, gently, gently, her anger really did die down, and besides, at the moment he looked more like himself of six years ago. . . .

'What I really wanted then,' he said softly, 'was to be a sort of carpet—to make myself into a sort of carpet for you to walk on so that you need not be hurt by the sharp stones and the mud that you hated so. It was nothing more positive than that—nothing more selfish. Only I did desire, eventually, to turn into a magic carpet and carry you away to all those lands you longed to see.'

As he spoke she lifted her head as though she drank something; the strange beast in her bosom began to purr. . . .

'I felt that you were more lonely than anybody else in the world,' he went on, 'and yet, perhaps, that you were the only person in the world who was really, truly alive. Born out of your time,' he murmured, stroking the glove, 'fated.'

Ah, God! What had she done! How had she dared to throw away her happiness like this. This was the only man who had ever understood her. Was it too late? Could it be too late? *She* was that glove that he held in his fingers. . . .

'And then the fact that you had no friends and never had made friends with people. How I understood that, for neither had I. Is it just the same now?'

'Yes,' she breathed. 'Just the same. I am as alone as ever.'

'So am I,' he laughed gently, 'just the same.'

Suddenly with a quick gesture he handed her back the glove and scraped his chair on the floor. 'But what seemed to me so mysterious then is perfectly plain to me now. And to you, too, of course. . . . It simply was that we were such egoists, so self-engrossed, so wrapped up in ourselves that we hadn't a corner in our hearts for anybody else. Do you know,' he cried, naive and hearty, and dreadfully like another side of that old self again, 'I began studying a Mind System[5] when I was in Russia, and I found that we were not peculiar at all. It's quite a well known form of. . . .'

She had gone. He sat there, thunder-struck, astounded beyond words. . . . And then he asked the waitress for his bill.

'But the cream has not been touched,' he said. 'Please do not charge me for it.'

Je ne Parle Pas Français (1918)†

I do not know why I have such a fancy for this little café. It's dirty and sad, sad. It's not as if it had anything to distinguish it from a hundred others—it hasn't; or as if the same strange types came here every day, whom one could watch from one's corner and

5. A system of personal psychology.

† Written early in 1918 and first published in a small, privately printed edition from the Heron Press, Hampstead, hand-set by Mansfield's brother-in-law, Richard Murry. Her full text was expurgated, at the insistence of her publisher, before the story was included in *Bliss and Other Stories* (1920). This Norton Critical Edition gives Mansfield's original text.

recognise and more or less (with a strong accent on the less) get the hang of.

But pray don't imagine that those brackets are a confession of my humility before the mystery of the human soul. Not at all; I don't believe in the human soul. I never have. I believe that people are like portmanteaux—packed with certain things, started going, thrown about, tossed away, dumped down, lost and found, half emptied suddenly, or squeezed fatter than ever, until finally the Ultimate Porter swings them on to the Ultimate Train and away they rattle. . . .

Not but what these portmanteaux can be very fascinating. Oh, but very! I see myself standing in front of them, don't you know, like a Customs official.

'Have you anything to declare? Any wines, spirits, cigars, perfumes, silks?'

And the moment of hesitation as to whether I am going to be fooled just before I chalk that squiggle, and then the other moment of hesitation just after, as to whether I have been, are perhaps the two most thrilling instants in life. Yes, they are, to me.

But before I started that long and rather far-fetched and not frightfully original digression, what I meant to say quite simply was that there are no portmanteaux to be examined here because the clientele of this café, ladies and gentlemen, does not sit down. No, it stands at the counter, and it consists of a handful of workmen who come up from the river, all powdered over with white flour, lime or something, and a few soldiers, bringing with them thin, dark girls with silver rings in their ears and market baskets on their arms.

Madame is thin and dark, too, with white cheeks and white hands. In certain lights she looks quite transparent, shining out of her black shawl with an extraordinary effect. When she is not serving she sits on a stool with her face turned, always, to the window. Her dark-ringed eyes search among and follow after the people passing, but not as if she was looking for somebody. Perhaps, fifteen years ago, she was; but now the pose has become a habit. You can tell from her air of fatigue and hopelessness that she must have given them up for the last ten years, at least. . . .

And then there is the waiter. Not pathetic—decidedly not comic. Never making one of those perfectly insignificant remarks which amaze you so coming from a waiter (as though the poor wretch were a sort of cross between a coffee-pot and a wine bottle and not expected to hold so much as a drop of anything else). He is grey, flat-footed and withered, with long, brittle nails that set your nerves on edge while he scrapes up your two sous. When he is not smearing over the table or flicking at a dead fly or two, he stands with one hand on the back of a chair, in his far too long apron, and over his other arm the three-cornered dip of dirty napkin, waiting to be photographed in connection with some wretched murder. 'Interior of Café where Body was Found.' You've seen him hundreds of times.

Do you believe that every place has its hour of the day when it really does come alive? That's not exactly what I mean. It's more like this. There does seem to be a moment when you realize that, quite by accident, you happen to have come on to the stage at exactly the moment you were expected. Everything is arranged for you—waiting for you. Ah, master of the situation! You fill with important breath. And at the same time you smile, secretly, slyly, because Life seems to be opposed to granting you these entrances, seems indeed to be engaged in snatching them from you and making them impossible, keeping you in the wings until it is too late, in fact. . . . Just for once you've beaten the old hag.

I enjoyed one of these moments the first time I ever came in here. That's why I keep coming back, I suppose. Revisiting the scene of my triumph, or the scene of the crime where I had the old bitch by the throat for once and did what I pleased with her.

Query: Why am I so bitter against Life? And why do I see her as a rag-picker on the American cinema, shuffling along wrapped in a filthy shawl with her old claws crooked over a stick?

Answer: The direct result of the American cinema acting upon a weak mind.

Anyhow, the 'short winter afternoon was drawing to a close', as they say, and I was drifting along, either going home or not going home, when I found myself in here, walking over to this seat in the corner.

I hung up my English overcoat and grey felt hat on that same peg behind me, and after I had allowed the waiter time for at least twenty photographers to snap their fill of him, I ordered a coffee.

He poured me out a glass of the familiar, purplish stuff with a green wandering light playing over it, and shuffled off, and I sat pressing my hands against the glass because it was bitterly cold outside.

Suddenly I realized that quite apart from myself, I was smiling. Slowly I raised my head and saw myself in the mirror opposite. Yes, there I sat, leaning on the table, smiling my deep, sly smile, the glass of coffee with its vague plume of steam before me and beside it the ring of white saucer with two pieces of sugar.

I opened my eyes very wide. There I had been for all eternity, as it were, and now at last I was coming to life. . . .

It was very quiet in the café. Outside, one could just see through the dusk that it had begun to snow. One could just see the shapes of horses and carts and people, soft and white, moving through the feathery air. The waiter disappeared and reappeared with an armful of straw. He strewed it over the floor from the door to the counter and round about the stove with humble, almost adoring gestures. One would not have been surprised if the door had opened and the Virgin Mary had come in, riding upon an ass, her meek hands folded over her big belly. . . .

That's rather nice, don't you think, that bit about the Virgin? It comes from the pen so gently; it has such a 'dying fall'. I thought so at the time and decided to make a note of it. One never knows when a little tag like that may come in useful to round off a paragraph. So, taking care to move as little as possible because the 'spell' was still unbroken (you know that?), I reached over to the next table for a writing pad.

No paper or envelopes, of course. Only a morsel of pink blotting-paper, incredibly soft and limp and almost moist, like the tongue of a little dead kitten, which I've never felt.

I sat—but always underneath, in this state of expectation, rolling the little dead kitten's tongue round my finger and rolling the soft phrase round my mind while my eyes took in the girls' names and dirty jokes and drawings of bottles and cups that would not sit in the saucers, scattered over the writing pad.

They are always the same, you know. The girls always have the same names, the cups never sit in the saucers; all the hearts are stuck and tied up with ribbons.

But then, quite suddenly, at the bottom of the page, written in green ink, I fell on to that stupid, stale little phrase: *Je ne parle pas français*.

There! it had come—the moment—the *geste!*[1] And although I was so ready, it caught me, it tumbled me over; I was simply overwhelmed. And the physical feeling was so curious, so particular. It was as if all of me, except my head and arms, all of me that was under the table, had simply dissolved, melted, turned into water. Just my head remained and two sticks of arms pressing on to the table. But, ah! the agony of that moment! How can I describe it? I didn't think of anything. I didn't even cry out to myself. Just for one moment I was not. I was Agony, Agony, Agony.

Then it passed, and the very second after I was thinking: 'Good God! Am I capable of feeling as strongly as that? But I was absolutely unconscious! I hadn't a phrase to meet it with! I was overcome! I was swept off my feet! I didn't even try, in the dimmest way, to put it down!'

And up I puffed and puffed, blowing off finally with: 'After all I

1. Gesture. *Je ne parle pas français*: I don't speak French.

must be first-rate. No second-rate mind could have experienced such an intensity of feeling so . . . purely.'

The waiter has touched a spill at the red stove and lighted a bubble of gas under a spreading shade. It is no use looking out of the window, Madame; it is quite dark now. Your white hands hover over your dark shawl. They are like two birds that have come home to roost. They are restless, restless. . . . You tuck them, finally, under your warm little armpits.

Now the waiter has taken a long pole and clashed the curtains together. 'All gone', as children say.

And besides, I've no patience with people who can't let go of things, who will follow after and cry out. When a thing's gone, it's gone. It's over and done with. Let it go then! Ignore it, and comfort yourself, if you do want comforting, with the thought that you never do recover the same thing that you lose. It's always a new thing. The moment it leaves you it's changed. Why, that's even true of a hat you chase after; and I don't mean superficially—I mean profoundly speaking. . . . I have made it a rule of my life never to regret and never to look back. Regret is an appalling waste of energy, and no one who intends to be a writer can afford to indulge in it. You can't get it into shape; you can't build on it; it's only good for wallowing in. Looking back, of course, is equally fatal to Art. It's keeping yourself poor. Art can't and won't stand poverty.

Je ne parle pas français. Je ne parle pas français. All the while I wrote that last page my other self has been chasing up and down out in the dark there. It left me just when I began to analyse my grand moment, dashed off distracted, like a lost dog who thinks at last, at last, he hears the familiar step again.

'Mouse! Mouse! Where are you? Are you near? Is that you leaning from the high window and stretching out your arms for the wings of the shutters? Are you this soft bundle moving towards me through the feathery snow? Are you this little girl pressing through the swing-doors of the restaurant? Is that your dark shadow bending forward in the cab? Where are you? Where are you? Which way must I turn? Which way shall I run? And every moment I stand here hesitating you are farther away again. Mouse! Mouse!'

Now the poor dog has come back into the café, his tail between his legs, quite exhausted.

'It was a . . . false . . . alarm. She's nowhere . . . to . . . be seen.'

'Lie down then! Lie down! Lie down!'

My name is Raoul Duquette. I am twenty-six years old and a Parisian, a true Parisian. About my family—it really doesn't matter.

I have no family; I don't want any. I never think about my childhood. I've forgotten it.

In fact, there's only one memory that stands out at all. That is rather interesting because it seems to me now so very significant as regards myself from the literary point of view. It is this.

When I was about ten our laundress was an African woman, very big, very dark, with a check handkerchief over her frizzy hair. When she came to our house she always took particular notice of me, and after the clothes had been taken out of the basket she would lift me up into it and give me a rock while I held tight to the handles and screamed for joy and fright. I was tiny for my age, and pale, with a lovely little half-open mouth—I feel sure of that.

One day when I was standing at the door, watching her go, she turned round and beckoned to me, nodding and smiling in a strange secret way. I never thought of not following. She took me into a little outhouse at the end of the passage, caught me up in her arms and began kissing me. Ah, those kisses! Especially those kisses inside my ears that nearly deafened me.

And then with a soft growl she tore open her bodice and put me to her. When she set me down she took from her pocket a little round fried cake covered with sugar and I reeled along the passage back to our door.

As this performance was repeated once a week it is no wonder that I remember it so vividly. Besides, from that very first afternoon, my childhood was, to put it prettily, 'kissed away'. I became very languid, very caressing, and greedy beyond measure. And so quickened, so sharpened, I seemed to understand everybody and be able to do what I liked with everybody.

I suppose I was in a state of more or less physical excitement, and that was what appealed to them. For all Parisians are more than half—oh, well, enough of that. And enough of my childhood, too. Bury it under a laundry basket instead of a shower of roses and *passons outre*.[2]

I date myself from the moment that I became the tenant of a small bachelor flat on the fifth floor of a tall, not too shabby house, in a street that might or might not be discreet. Very useful, that. . . . There I emerged, came out into the light and put out my two horns with a study and a bedroom and a kitchen on my back. And real furniture planted in the rooms. In the bedroom a wardrobe with a long glass, a big bed covered with a yellow puffed-up quilt, a bed table with a marbled top and a toilet set sprinkled with tiny ap-

2. Let us move on to something else.

ples. In my study—English writing table with drawers, writing chair with leather cushions, books, arm-chair, side table with paper-knife and lamp on it and some nude studies on the walls. I didn't use the kitchen except to throw old papers into.

Ah, I can see myself that first evening, after the furniture men had gone and I'd managed to get rid of my atrocious old concierge—walking about on tip-toe, arranging and standing in front of the glass with my hands in my pockets and saying to that radiant vision: 'I am a young man who has his own flat. I write for two newspapers. I am going in for serious literature. I am starting a career. The book that I shall bring out will simply stagger the critics. I am going to write about things that have never been touched before. I am going to make a name for myself as a writer about the submerged world. But not as others have done before me. Oh, no! Very naively, with a sort of tender humour and from the inside, as though it were all quite simple, quite natural. I see my way quite perfectly. Nobody has ever done it as I shall do it because none of the others have lived my experiences. I'm rich—I'm rich.'

All the same I had no more money than I have now. It's extraordinary how one can live without money. . . . I have quantities of good clothes, silk underwear, two evening suits, four pairs of patent leather boots with light uppers, all sorts of little things, like gloves and powder boxes and a manicure set, perfumes, very good soap, and nothing is paid for. If I find myself in need of right-down cash—well, there's always an African laundress and an outhouse, and I am very frank and *bon enfant*[3] about plenty of sugar on the little fried cake afterwards. . . .

And here I should like to put something on record. Not from any strutting conceit, but rather with a mild sense of wonder. I've never yet made the first advances to any woman. It isn't as though I've known only one class of woman—not by any means. But from little prostitutes and kept women and elderly widows and shop girls and wives of respectable men, and even advanced modern literary ladies at the most select dinners and soirées (I've been there), I've met invariably with not only the same readiness, but with the same positive invitation. It surprised me at first. I used to look across the table and think 'Is that very distinguished young lady, discussing *le Kipling*[4] with the gentleman with the brown beard, really pressing my foot?' And I was never really certain until I had pressed hers.

Curious, isn't it? Why should I be able to have any woman I want? I don't look at all like a maiden's dream. . . .

3. An expression meaning "a good fellow," used here to suggest direct, up front.
4. Rudyard Kipling (1865–1936), poet, short-story writer, and novelist; his work was often set in India, where he was born.

I am little and light with an olive skin, black eyes with long lashes, black silky hair cut short, tiny square teeth that show when I smile. My hands are supple and small. A woman in a bread shop once said to me: 'You have the hands for making fine little pastries.' I confess, without my clothes I am rather charming. Plump, almost like a girl, with smooth shoulders, and I wear a thin gold bracelet above my left elbow.

But, wait! Isn't it strange I should have written all that about my body and so on? It's the result of my bad life, my submerged life. I am like a little woman in a café who has to introduce herself with a handful of photographs. 'Me in my chemise,[5] coming out of an eggshell. . . . Me upside down in a swing, with a frilly behind like a cauliflower. . . .' You know the things.

If you think what I've written is merely superficial and impudent and cheap you're wrong. I'll admit it does sound so, but then it is not all. If it were, how could I have experienced what I did when I read that stale little phrase written in green ink, in the writing-pad? That proves there's more in me and that I really am important, doesn't it? Anything a fraction less than that moment of anguish I might have put on. But no! That was real.

'Waiter, a whisky.'

I hate whisky. Every time I take it into my mouth my stomach rises against it, and the stuff they keep here is sure to be particularly vile. I only ordered it because I am going to write about an Englishman. We French are incredibly old-fashioned and out of date still in some ways. I wonder I didn't ask him at the same time for a pair of tweed knickerbockers, a pipe, some long teeth and a set of ginger whiskers.

'Thanks, *mon vieux*.[6] You haven't got perhaps a set of ginger whiskers?'

'No, monsieur,' he answers sadly. 'We don't sell American drinks.'

And having smeared a corner of the table he goes back to have another couple of dozen taken by artificial light.

Ugh! The smell of it! And the sickly sensation when one's throat contracts.

'It's bad stuff to get drunk on,' says Dick Harmon, turning his little glass in his fingers and smiling his slow, dreaming smile. So he gets drunk on it slowly and dreamily and at a certain moment begins to sing very low, very low, about a man who walks up and down trying to find a place where he can get some dinner.

Ah! how I loved that song, and how I loved the way he sang it, slowly, slowly, in a dark, soft voice

5. A loose-fitting undergarment.
6. Old man (affectionately).

There was a man
Walked up and down
To get a dinner in the town . . .[7]

It seemed to hold, in its gravity and muffled measure, all those tall grey buildings, those fogs, those endless streets, those sharp shadows of policemen that mean England.

And then—the subject! The lean, starved creature walking up and down with every house barred against him because he had no 'home'. How extraordinarily English that is. . . . I remember that it ended where he did at last 'find a place' and ordered a little cake of fish, but when he asked for bread the waiter cried contemptuously, in a loud voice: 'We don't serve bread with one fish ball.'

What more do you want? How profound those songs are! There is the whole psychology of a people; and how un-French—how un-French!

'Once more, Deeck, once more!' I would plead, clasping my hands and making a pretty mouth at him. He was perfectly content to sing it for ever.

There again. Even with Dick. It was he who made the first advances.

I met him at an evening party given by the editor of a new review. It was a very select, very fashionable affair. One or two of the older men were there and the ladies were extremely *comme il faut*.[8] They sat on cubist[9] sofas in full evening dress and allowed us to hand them thimbles of cherry brandy and to talk to them about their poetry. For, as far as I can remember, they were all poetesses.

It was impossible not to notice Dick. He was the only Englishman present, and instead of circulating gracefully round the room as we all did, he stayed in one place leaning against the wall, his hands in his pockets, that dreamy half smile on his lips, and replying in excellent French in his low, soft voice to anybody who spoke to him.

'Who is he?'

'An Englishman. From London. A writer. And he is making a special study of modern French literature.'

That was enough for me. My little book, *False Coins*, had just been published. I was a young, serious writer who was making a special study of modern English literature.

But I really had not time to fling my line before he said, giving himself a soft shake, coming right out of the water after the bait,

7. A traditional music-hall song.
8. Correct in behavior.
9. A fashionable style in painting and design, emphasizing simple geometric shapes.

as it were: 'Won't you come and see me at my hotel? Come about five o'clock and we can have a talk before going out to dinner.'

'Enchanted!'

I was so deeply, deeply flattered that I had to leave him then and there to preen and preen myself before the cubist sofas. What a catch! An Englishman, reserved, serious, making a special study of French literature. . . .

That same night a copy of *False Coins* with a carefully cordial inscription was posted off, and a day or two later we did dine together and spent the evening talking.

Talking—but not only of literature. I discovered to my relief that it wasn't necessary to keep to the tendency of the modern novel, the need of a new form, or the reason why our young men appeared to be just missing it. Now and again, as if by accident, I threw in a card that seemed to have nothing to do with the game, just to see how he'd take it. But each time he gathered it into his hands with his dreamy look and smile unchanged. Perhaps he murmured: 'That's very curious.' But not as if it were curious at all.

That calm acceptance went to my head at last. It fascinated me. It led me on and on till I threw every card that I possessed at him and sat back and watched him arrange them in his hand.

'Very curious and interesting. . . .'

By that time we were both fairly drunk, and he began to sing his song very soft, very low, about the man who walked up and down seeking his dinner.

But I was quite breathless at the thought of what I had done. I had shown somebody both sides of my life. Told him everything as sincerely and truthfully as I could. Taken immense pains to explain things about my submerged life that really were disgusting and never could possibly see the light of literary day. On the whole I had made myself out far worse than I was—more boastful, more cynical, more calculating.

And there sat the man I had confided in, singing to himself and smiling. . . . It moved me so that real tears came into my eyes. I saw them glittering on my long silky lashes—so charming.

After that I took Dick about with me everywhere, and he came to my flat, and sat in the arm-chair, very indolent, playing with the paper-knife. I cannot think why his indolence and dreaminess always gave me the impression he had been to sea. And all his leisurely slow ways seemed to be allowing for the movement of the ship. This impression was so strong that often when we were together and he got up and left a little woman just when she did not expect him to get up and leave her, but quite the contrary, I would explain: 'He can't help it, Baby. He has to go back to his ship.' And I believed it far more than she did.

All the while we were together Dick never went with a woman. I sometimes wondered whether he wasn't completely innocent. Why didn't I ask him? Because I never did ask him anything about himself. But late one night he took out his pocket-book and a photograph dropped out of it. I picked it up and glanced at it before I gave it to him. It was of a woman. Not quite young. Dark, handsome, wild-looking, but so full in every line of a kind of haggard pride that even if Dick had not stretched out so quickly I wouldn't have looked longer.

'Out of my sight, you little perfumed fox-terrier of a Frenchman,' said she. (In my very worst moments my nose reminds me of a fox-terrier's.)

'That is my Mother,' said Dick, putting up the pocket-book.

But if he had not been Dick I should have been tempted to cross myself, just for fun.

This is how we parted. As we stood outside his hotel one night waiting for the concierge to release the catch of the outer door, he said, looking up at the sky: 'I hope it will be fine to-morrow. I am leaving for England in the morning.'

'You're not serious.'

'Perfectly. I have to get back. I've some work to do that I can't manage here.'

'But—but have you made all your preparations?'

'Preparations?' He almost grinned. 'I've none to make.'

'But—*enfin*,[1] Dick, England is not the other side of the boulevard.'

'It isn't much farther off,' said he. 'Only a few hours, you know.' The door cracked open.

'Ah, I wish I'd known at the beginning of the evening!'

I felt hurt. I felt as a woman must feel when a man takes out his watch and remembers an appointment that cannot possibly concern her, except that its claim is the stronger. 'Why didn't you tell me?'

He put out his hand and stood, lightly swaying upon the step as though the whole hotel were his ship, and the anchor weighed.

'I forgot. Truly I did. But you'll write, won't you? Good night, old chap. I'll be over again one of these days.'

And then I stood on the shore alone, more like a little fox-terrier than ever. . . .

1. Finally.

'But after all it was you who whistled to me, you who asked me to come! What a spectacle I've cut wagging my tail and leaping round you, only to be left like this while the boat sails off in its slow, dreamy way. . . . Curse these English! No, this is too insolent altogether. Who do you imagine I am? A little paid guide to the night pleasures of Paris? . . . No, monsieur. I am a young writer, very serious, and extremely interested in modern English literature. And I have been insulted—insulted.'

Two days after came a long, charming letter from him, written in French that was a shade too French, but saying how he missed me and counted on our friendship, on keeping in touch.

I read it standing in front of the (unpaid for) wardrobe mirror. It was early morning. I wore a blue kimono embroidered with white birds and my hair was still wet; it lay on my forehead, wet and gleaming.

'Portrait of Madame Butterfly,' said I, 'on hearing of the arrival of *ce cher Pinkerton*.'[2]

According to the books I should have felt immensely relieved and delighted. '. . . Going over to the window he drew apart the curtains and looked out at the Paris trees, just breaking into buds and green. . . . Dick! Dick! My English friend!'

I didn't. I merely felt a little sick. Having been up for my first ride in an aeroplane I didn't want to go up again, just now.

That passed, and months after, in the winter, Dick wrote that he was coming back to Paris to stay indefinitely. Would I take rooms for him? He was bringing a woman friend with him.

Of course I would. Away the little fox-terrier flew. It happened most usefully, too; for I owed much money at the hotel where I took my meals, and two English people requiring rooms for an indefinite time was an excellent sum on account.

Perhaps I did rather wonder, as I stood in the larger of the two rooms with Madame, saying 'Admirable,' what the woman friend would be like, but only vaguely. Either she would be very severe, flat back and front, or she would be tall, fair, dressed in mignonette[3] green, name—Daisy, and smelling of rather sweetish lavender water.

You see, by this time, according to my rule of not looking back, I had almost forgotten Dick. I even got the tune of his song about the unfortunate man a little bit wrong when I tried to hum it. . . .

2. *Madame Butterfly*, the 1904 opera by Giacomo Puccini (1858–1924) on the love of a Japanese geisha for an American naval officer, "this dear Pinkerton," to whom Duquette refers.
3. A plant with small fragrant green flowers.

I very nearly did not turn up at the station after all. I had arranged to, and had, in fact, dressed with particular care for the occasion. For I intended to take a new line with Dick this time. No more confidences and tears on eyelashes. No, thank you!

'Since you left Paris,' said I, knotting my black silver-spotted tie in the (also unpaid for) mirror over the mantelpiece, 'I have been very successful, you know. I have two more books in preparation, and then I have written a serial story, *Wrong Doors*, which is just on the point of publication and will bring me in a lot of money. And then my little book of poems,' I cried, seizing the clothes-brush and brushing the velvet collar of my new indigo-blue overcoat, 'my little book—*Left Umbrellas*—really did create,' and I laughed and waved the brush, 'an immense sensation!'

It was impossible not to believe this of the person who surveyed himself finally, from top to toe, drawing on his soft grey gloves. He was looking the part; he was the part.

That gave me an idea. I took out my notebook, and still in full view, jotted down a note or two. . . . How can one look the part and not be the part? Or be the part and not look it? Isn't looking—being? Or being—looking? At any rate who is to say that it is not? . . .

This seemed to me extraordinarily profound at the time, and quite new. But I confess that something did whisper as, smiling, I put up the notebook: 'You—literary? you look as though you've taken down a bet on a racecourse!' But I didn't listen. I went out, shutting the door of the flat with a soft, quick pull so as not to warn the concierge of my departure, and ran down the stairs quick as a rabbit for the same reason.

But ah! the old spider. She was too quick for me. She let me run down the last little ladder of the web and then she pounced. 'One moment. One little moment, Monsieur,' she whispered, odiously confidential. 'Come in. Come in.' And she beckoned with a dripping soup ladle. I went to the door, but that was not good enough. Right inside and the door shut before she would speak.

There are two ways of managing your concierge if you haven't any money. One is—to take the high hand, make her your enemy, bluster, refuse to discuss anything; the other is—to keep in with her, butter her up to the two knots of the black rag tying up her jaws, pretend to confide in her, and rely on her to arrange with the gas man and to put off the landlord.

I had tried the second. But both are equally detestable and unsuccessful. At any rate whichever you're trying is the worse, the impossible one.

It was the landlord this time. . . . Imitation of the landlord by the concierge threatening to toss me out. . . . Imitation of the concierge by the concierge taming the wild bull. . . . Imitation of the landlord rampant again, breathing in the concierge's face. I was the concierge. No, it was too nauseous. And all the while the black pot on the gas ring bubbling away, stewing out the hearts and livers of every tenant in the place.

'Ah!' I cried, staring at the clock on the mantelpiece, and then, realizing that it didn't go, striking my forehead as though the idea had nothing to do with it. 'Madame, I have a very important appointment with the director of my newspaper at nine-thirty. Perhaps to-morrow I shall be able to give you. . . .'

Out, out. And down the métro and squeezed into a full carriage. The more the better. Everybody was one bolster the more between me and the concierge. I was radiant.

'Ah! pardon, Monsieur!' said the tall charming creature in black with a big full bosom and a great bunch of violets dropping from it. As the train swayed it thrust the bouquet right into my eyes. 'Ah! pardon, Monsieur!'

But I looked up at her, smiling mischievously.

'There is nothing I love more, Madame, than flowers on a balcony.'

At the very moment of speaking I caught sight of the huge man in a fur coat against whom my charmer was leaning. He poked his head over her shoulder and he went white to the nose; in fact his nose stood out a sort of cheese green.

'What was that you said to my wife?'

Gare Saint Lazare[4] saved me. But you'll own that even as the author of *False Coins, Wrong Doors, Left Umbrellas*, and two in preparation, it was not too easy to go on my triumphant way.

At length, after countless trains had steamed into my mind, and countless Dick Harmons had come rolling towards me, the real train came. The little knot of us waiting at the barrier moved up close, craned forward, and broke into cries as though we were some kind of many-headed monster, and Paris behind us nothing but a great trap we had set to catch these sleepy innocents.

Into the trap they walked and were snatched and taken off to be devoured. Where was my prey?

'Good God!' My smile and my lifted hand fell together. For one terrible moment I thought this was the woman of the photograph, Dick's mother, walking towards me in Dick's coat and hat. In the effort—and you saw what an effort it was—to smile, his lips curled in

4. One of the major railway stations in Paris.

just the same way and he made for me, haggard and wild and proud.

What had happened? What could have changed him like this? Should I mention it?

I waited for him and was even conscious of venturing a fox-terrier wag or two to see if he could possibly respond, in the way I said: 'Good evening, Dick! How are you, old chap? All right?'

'All right. All right.' He almost gasped. 'You've got the rooms?'

Twenty times, good God! I saw it all. Light broke on the dark waters and my sailor hadn't been drowned. I almost turned a somersault with amusement.

It was nervousness, of course. It was embarrassment. It was the famous English seriousness. What fun I was going to have! I could have hugged him.

'Yes, I've got the rooms,' I nearly shouted. 'But where is Madame?'

'She's been looking after the luggage,' he panted. 'Here she comes, now.'

Not this baby walking beside the old porter as though he were her nurse and had just lifted her out of her ugly perambulator while he trundled the boxes on it.

'And she's not Madame,' said Dick, drawling suddenly.

At that moment she caught sight of him and hailed him with her minute muff. She broke away from her nurse and ran up and said something, very quick, in English; but he replied in French: 'Oh, very well. I'll manage.'

But before he turned to the porter he indicated me with a vague wave and muttered something. We were introduced. She held out her hand in that strange boyish way Englishwomen do, and standing very straight in front of me with her chin raised and making—she too—the effort of her life to control her preposterous excitement, she said, wringing my hand (I'm sure she didn't know it was mine), *Je ne parle pas français*.

'But I'm sure you do,' I answered, so tender, so reassuring, I might have been a dentist about to draw her first little milk tooth.

'Of course she does.' Dick swerved back to us. 'Here, can't we get a cab or taxi or something? We don't want to stay in this cursed station all night. Do we?'

This was so rude that it took me a moment to recover; and he must have noticed, for he flung his arm round my shoulder in the old way, saying: 'Ah, forgive me, old chap. But we've had such a loathsome, hideous journey. We've taken years to come. Haven't we?' To her. But she did not answer. She bent her head and began stroking her grey muff; she walked beside us stroking her grey muff all the way.

'Have I been wrong?' thought I. 'Is this simply a case of frenzied impatience on their part? Are they merely "in need of a bed", as we say? Have they been suffering agonies on the journey? Sitting, perhaps, very close and warm under the same travelling rug?' and so on and so on while the driver strapped on the boxes. That done—

'Look here, Dick. I go home by métro. Here is the address of your hotel. Everything is arranged. Come and see me as soon as you can.'

Upon my life I thought he was going to faint. He went white to the lips.

'But you're coming back with us,' he cried. 'I thought it was all settled. Of course you're coming back. You're not going to leave us.'

No, I gave it up. It was too difficult, too English for me.

'Certainly, certainly. Delighted. I only thought, perhaps. . . .'

'You must come!' said Dick to the little fox-terrier. And again he made that big awkward turn towards her.

'Get in, Mouse.'

And Mouse got in the black hole and sat stroking Mouse II and not saying a word.

Away we jolted and rattled like three little dice that life had decided to have a fling with.

I had insisted on taking the flap seat facing them because I would not have missed for anything those occasional flashing glimpses I had as we broke through the white circles of lamplight.

They revealed Dick, sitting far back in his corner, his coat collar turned up, his hands thrust in his pockets, and his broad dark hat shading him as if it were a part of him—a sort of wing he hid under. They showed her, sitting up very straight, her lovely little face more like a drawing than a real face—every line was so full of meaning and so sharp cut against the swimming dark.

For Mouse was beautiful. She was exquisite, but so fragile and fine that each time I looked at her it was as if for the first time. She came upon you with the same kind of shock that you feel when you have been drinking tea out of a thin innocent cup and suddenly, at the bottom, you see a tiny creature, half butterfly, half woman, bowing to you with her hands in her sleeves.

As far as I could make out she had dark hair and blue or black eyes. Her long lashes and the two little feathers traced above were most important.

She wore a long dark cloak such as one sees in old-fashioned pictures of Englishwomen abroad. Where her arms came out of it there was grey fur—fur round her neck, too, and her close-fitting cap was furry.

'Carrying out the mouse idea,' I decided.

Ah, but how intriguing it was—how intriguing! Their excitement came nearer and nearer to me, while I ran out to meet it, bathed in it, flung myself far out of my depth, until at last I was as hard put to it to keep control as they.

But what I wanted to do was to behave in the most extraordinary fashion—like a clown. To start singing, with large extravagant gestures, to point out of the window and cry: 'We are now passing, ladies and gentlemen, one of the sights for which *notre Paris* is justly famous'; to jump out of the taxi while it was going, climb over the roof and dive in by another door; to hang out of the window and look for the hotel through the wrong end of a broken telescope, which was also a peculiarly ear-splitting trumpet.

I watched myself do all this, you understand, and even managed to applaud in a private way by putting my gloved hands gently together, while I said to Mouse: 'And is this your first visit to Paris?'

'Yes, I've not been here before.'

'Ah, then you have a great deal to see.'

And I was just going to touch lightly upon the objects of interest and the museums when we wrenched to a stop.

Do you know—it's very absurd—but as I pushed open the door for them and followed up the stairs to the bureau on the landing I felt somehow that this hotel was mine.

There was a vase of flowers on the window sill of the bureau and I even went so far as to re-arrange a bud or two and to stand off and note the effect while the manageress welcomed them. And when she turned to me and handed me the keys (the *garçon* was hauling up the boxes) and said: 'Monsieur Duquette will show you your rooms'—I had a longing to tap Dick on the arm with a key and say, very confidentially: 'Look here, old chap. As a friend of mine I'll be only too willing to make a slight reduction. . . .'

Up and up we climbed. Round and round. Past an occasional pair of boots (why is it one never sees an attractive pair of boots outside a door?). Higher and higher.

'I'm afraid they're rather high up,' I murmured idiotically. 'But I chose them because. . . .'

They so obviously did not care why I chose them that I went no further. They accepted everything. They did not expect anything to be different. This was just part of what they were going through—that was how I analysed it.

'Arrived at last.' I ran from one side of the passage to the other, turning on the lights, explaining.

'This one I thought for you, Dick. The other is larger and it has a little dressing-room in the alcove.'

My 'proprietary' eye noted the clean towels and covers, and the bed linen embroidered in red cotton. I thought them rather charming rooms, sloping, full of angles, just the sort of rooms one would expect to find if one had not been to Paris before.

Dick dashed his hat down on the bed.

'Oughtn't I to help that chap with the boxes?' he asked—nobody.

'Yes, you ought,' replied Mouse, 'they're dreadfully heavy.'

And she turned to me with the first glimmer of a smile: 'Books, you know.' Oh, he darted such a strange look at her before he rushed out. And he not only helped, he must have torn the box off the *garçon*'s back, for he staggered back, carrying one, dumped it down and then fetched in the other.

'That's yours, Dick,' said she.

'Well, you don't mind it standing here for the present, do you?' he asked, breathless, breathing hard (the box must have been tremendously heavy). He pulled out a handful of money. 'I suppose I ought to pay this chap.'

The *garçon*, standing by, seemed to think so too.

'And will you require anything further, Monsieur?'

'No! No!' said Dick impatiently.

But at that Mouse stepped forward. She said, too deliberately, not looking at Dick, with her quaint clipped English accent: 'Yes, I'd like some tea. Tea for three.'

And suddenly she raised her muff as though her hands were clasped inside it, and she was telling the pale, sweaty *garçon* by that action that she was at the end of her resources, that she cried out to him to save her with 'Tea. Immediately!'

This seemed to me so amazingly in the picture, so exactly the gesture and cry that one would expect (though I couldn't have imagined it) to be wrung out of an Englishwoman faced with a great crisis, that I was almost tempted to hold up my hand and protest.

'No! No! Enough. Enough. Let us leave off there. At the word—tea. For really, really, you've filled your greediest subscriber so full that he will burst if he has to swallow another word.'

It even pulled Dick up. Like someone who has been unconscious for a long long time he turned slowly to Mouse and slowly looked at her with his tired, haggard eyes, and murmured with the echo of his dreamy voice: 'Yes. That's a good idea.' And then: 'You must be tired, Mouse. Sit down.'

She sat down in a chair with lace tabs on the arms; he leaned against the bed, and I established myself on a straight-backed chair, crossed my legs and brushed some imaginary dust off the knees of my trousers. (The Parisian at his ease.)

There came a tiny pause. Then he said: 'Won't you take off your coat, Mouse?'

'No, thanks. Not just now.'

Were they going to ask me? Or should I hold up my hand and call out in a baby voice: 'It's my turn to be asked.'

No, I shouldn't. They didn't ask me.

The pause became a silence. A real silence.

'. . . Come, my Parisian fox-terrier! Amuse these sad English! It's no wonder they are such a nation for dogs.'

But, after all—why should I? It was not my 'job', as they would say. Nevertheless, I made a vivacious little bound at Mouse.

'What a pity it is that you did not arrive by daylight. There is such a charming view from these two windows. You know, the hotel is on a corner and each window looks down an immensely long, straight street.'

'Yes,' said she.

'Not that that sounds very charming,' I laughed. 'But there is so much animation—so many absurd little boys on bicycles and people hanging out of windows and—oh, well, you'll see for yourself in the morning. . . . Very amusing. Very animated.'

'Oh, yes,' said she.

If the pale, sweaty *garçon* had not come in at that moment, carrying the tea-tray high on one hand as if the cups were cannonballs and he a heavy weight lifter on the cinema. . . .

He managed to lower it on to a round table.

'Bring the table over here,' said Mouse. The waiter seemed to be the only person she cared to speak to. She took her hands out of her muff, drew off her gloves and flung back the old-fashioned cape.

'Do you take milk and sugar?'

'No milk, thank you, and no sugar.'

I went over for mine like a little gentleman. She poured out another cup.

'That's for Dick.'

And the faithful fox-terrier carried it across to him and laid it at his feet, as it were.

'Oh, thanks,' said Dick.

And then I went back to my chair and she sank back in hers.

But Dick was off again. He stared wildly at the cup of tea for a moment, glanced round him, put it down on the bed-table, caught up his hat and stammered at full gallop: 'Oh, by the way, do you mind posting a letter for me? I want to get it off by to-night's post. I must. It's very urgent. . . .' Feeling her eyes on him, he flung: 'It's to my mother.' To me: 'I won't be long. I've got everything I want. But it must go off to-night. You don't mind? It . . . it won't take any time.'

'Of course I'll post it. Delighted.'

'Won't you drink your tea first?' suggested Mouse softly.

. . . Tea? Tea? Yes, of course. Tea. . . . A cup of tea on the bed-table. . . . In his racing dream he flashed the brightest, most charming smile at his little hostess.

'No, thanks. Not just now.'

And still hoping it would not be any trouble to me he went out of the room and closed the door, and we heard him cross the passage.

I scalded myself with mine in my hurry to take the cup back to the table and to say as I stood there: 'You must forgive me if I am impertinent . . . if I am too frank. But Dick hasn't tried to disguise it—has he? There is something the matter. Can I help?'

(Soft music. Mouse gets up, walks the stage for a moment or so before she returns to her chair and pours him out, oh, such a brimming, such a burning cup that the tears come into the friend's eyes while he sips—while he drains it to the bitter dregs. . . .)

I had time to do all this before she replied. First she looked in the teapot, filled it with hot water, and stirred it with a spoon.

'Yes, there is something the matter. No, I'm afraid you can't help, thank you.' Again I got that glimmer of a smile. 'I'm awfully sorry. I must be horrid for you.'

Horrid, indeed! Ah, why couldn't I tell her that it was months and months since I had been so entertained?

'But you are suffering,' I ventured softly, as though that was what I could not bear to see.

She didn't deny it. She nodded and bit her under-lip and I thought I saw her chin tremble.

'And there is really nothing I can do?' More softly still.

She shook her head, pushed back the table and jumped up.

'Oh, it will be all right soon,' she breathed, walking over to the dressing-table and standing with her back towards me. 'It will be all right. It can't go on like this.'

'But of course it can't.' I agreed, wondering whether it would look heartless if I lit a cigarette; I had a sudden longing to smoke.

In some way she saw my hand move to my breast pocket, half draw out my cigarette case and put it back again, for the next thing she said was: 'Matches . . . in . . . candlestick. I noticed them.'

And I heard from her voice that she was crying.

'Ah! thank you. Yes. Yes. I've found them.' I lighted my cigarette and walked up and down, smoking.

It was so quiet it might have been two o'clock in the morning. It was so quiet you heard the boards creak and pop as one does in a house in the country. I smoked the whole cigarette and stabbed the end into my saucer before Mouse turned round and came back to the table.

'Isn't Dick being rather a long time?'

'You are very tired. I expect you want to go to bed,' I said kindly. (And pray don't mind me if you do, said my mind.)

'But isn't he being a very long time?' she insisted.

I shrugged. 'He is, rather.'

Then I saw she looked at me strangely. She was listening.

'He's been gone ages,' she said, and she went with little light steps to the door, opened it, and crossed the passage into his room.

I waited. I listened too, now. I couldn't have borne to miss a word. She had left the door open. I stole across the room and looked after her. Dick's door was open, too. But—there wasn't a word to miss.

You know I had the mad idea that they were kissing in that quiet room—a long comfortable kiss. One of those kisses that not only puts one's grief to bed, but nurses it and warms it and tucks it up and keeps it fast enfolded until it is sleeping sound. Ah! how good that is.

It was over at last. I heard some one move and tip-toed away.

It was Mouse. She came back. She felt her way into the room carrying the letter for me. But it wasn't in an envelope; it was just a sheet of paper and she held it by the corner as though it was still wet.

Her head was bent so low—so tucked in her furry collar that I hadn't a notion—until she let the paper fall and almost fell herself on to the floor by the side of the bed, leaned her cheek against it, flung out her hands as though the last of her poor little weapons was gone and now she let herself be carried away, washed out into the deep water.

Flash! went my mind. Dick has shot himself, and then a succession of flashes while I rushed in, saw the body, head unharmed, small blue hole over temple, roused hotel, arranged funeral, attended funeral, closed cab, new morning coat. . . .

I stooped down and picked up the paper and would you believe it—so ingrained is my Parisian sense of *comme il faut*[5]—I murmured 'pardon' before I read it.

'Mouse, my little Mouse,

It's not good. It's impossible. I can't see it through. Oh, I do love you. I do love you, Mouse, but I can't hurt her. People have been

5. What is appropriate.

hurting her all her life. I simply dare not give her this final blow. You see, though she's stronger than both of us, she's so frail and proud. It would kill her—kill her, Mouse. And, oh God, I can't kill my mother! Not even for you. Not even for us. You do see that—don't you.

It all seemed so possible when we talked and planned, but the very moment the train started it was all over. I felt her drag me back to her—calling. I can hear her now as I write. And she's alone and she doesn't know. A man would have to be a devil to tell her and I'm not a devil, Mouse. She mustn't know. Oh, Mouse, somewhere, somewhere in you don't you agree? It's all so unspeakably awful that I don't know if I want to go or not. Do I? Or is Mother just dragging me? I don't know. My head is too tired. Mouse, Mouse—what will you do? But I can't think of that, either. I dare not. I'd break down. And I must not break down. All I've got to do is—just to tell you this and go. I couldn't have gone off without telling you. You'd have been frightened. And you must not be frightened. You won't—will you? I can't bear—but no more of that. And don't write. I should not have the courage to answer your letters and the sight of your spidery handwriting———

Forgive me. Don't love me any more. Yes. Love me. Love me. Dick.'

What do you think of that? Wasn't that a rare find? My relief at his not having shot himself was mixed with a wonderful sense of elation. I was even—more than even with my 'that's very curious and interesting' Englishman. . . .

She wept so strangely. With her eyes shut, with her face quite calm except for the quivering eyelids. The tears pearled down her cheeks and she let them fall.

But feeling my glance upon her she opened her eyes and saw me holding the letter.

'You've read it?'

Her voice was quite calm, but it was not her voice any more. It was like the voice you might imagine coming out of a tiny, cold sea-shell swept high and dry at last by the salt tide. . . .

I nodded, quite overcome, you understand, and laid the letter down.

'It's incredible! incredible!' I whispered.

At that she got up from the floor, walked over to the wash-stand, dipped her handkerchief into the jug and sponged her eyes, saying: 'Oh, no. It's not incredible at all.' And still pressing the wet ball to her eyes she came back to me, to her chair with the lace tabs, and sank into it.

'I knew all along, of course,' said the cold, salty little voice. 'From the very moment that we started. I felt it all through me, but I still went on hoping—' and here she took the handkerchief down and gave me a final glimmer—'as one so stupidly does, you know.'

'As one does.'

Silence.

'But what will you do? You'll go back? You'll see him?'

That made her sit right up and stare across at me.

'What an extraordinary idea!' she said, more coldly than ever. 'Of course I shall not dream of seeing him. As for going back—that is quite out of the question. I can't go back.'

'But. . . .'

'It's impossible. For one thing all my friends think I am married.'

I put out my hand—'Ah, my poor little friend.'

But she shrank away. (False move.)

Of course there was one question that had been at the back of my mind all this time. I hated it.

'Have you any money?'

'Yes, I have twenty pounds—here,' and she put her hand on her breast. I bowed. It was a great deal more than I had expected.

'And what are your plans?'

Yes, I know. My question was the most clumsy, the most idiotic one I could have put. She had been so tame, so confiding, letting me, at any rate spiritually speaking, hold her tiny quivering body in one hand and stroke her furry head—and now, I'd thrown her away. Oh, I could have kicked myself.

She stood up. 'I have no plans. But—it's very late. You must go now, please.'

How could I get her back? I wanted her back, I swear I was not acting then.

'Do feel that I am your friend,' I cried. 'You will let me come to-morrow, early? You will let me look after you a little—take care of you a little? You'll use me just as you think fit?'

I succeeded. She came out of her hole . . . timid . . . but she came out.

'Yes, you're very kind. Yes. Do come to-morrow. I shall be glad. It makes things rather difficult because—' and again I clasped her boyish hand—'*je ne parle pas français.*'

Not until I was half-way down the boulevard did it come over me—the full force of it.

Why, they were suffering . . . those two . . . really suffering. I have seen two people suffer as I don't suppose I ever shall again. . . . And. . . . 'Good-night, my little cat,' said I, impudently, to the fattish old prostitute picking her way home through the slush. . . . I didn't give her time to reply.

Of course you know what to expect. You anticipate, fully, what I am going to write. It wouldn't be me, otherwise.

I never went near the place again.

Yes, I still owe that considerable amount for lunches and dinners, but that's beside the mark. It's vulgar to mention it in the same breath with the fact that I never saw Mouse again.

Naturally, I intended to. Started out—got to the door—wrote and tore up letters—did all those things. But I simply could not make the final effort.

Even now I don't fully understand why. Of course I knew that I couldn't have kept it up. That had a great deal to do with it. But you would have thought, putting it at its lowest, curiosity couldn't have kept my fox-terrier nose away. . . .

Je ne parle pas français. That was her swan song for me.

But how she makes me break my rule. Oh, you've seen for yourself, but I could give you countless examples.

. . . Evenings, when I sit in some gloomy café, and an automatic piano starts playing a 'mouse' tune (there are dozens of tunes that evoke just her) I begin to dream things like . . . .

A little house on the edge of the sea, somewhere far, far away. A girl outside in a frock rather like Red Indian women wear, hailing a light, bare-foot boy who runs up from the beach.

'What have you got?'

'A fish.' I smile and give it to her.

. . . The same girl, the same boy, different costumes—sitting at an open window, eating fruit and leaning out and laughing.

'All the wild strawberries are for you, Mouse. I won't touch one.'

. . . A wet night. They are going home together under an umbrella. They stop on the door to press their wet cheeks together.

And so on and so on until some dirty old gallant comes up to my table and sits opposite and begins to grimace and yap. Until I hear myself saying: 'But I've got the little girl for you, *mon vieux*. So little . . . so tiny. And a virgin.' I kiss the tips of my fingers—'A virgin'—and lay them upon my heart. 'I give you my word of honour as a gentleman, a writer, serious, young, and extremely interested in modern English literature.'

I must go. I must go. I reach down my coat and hat. Madame knows me. 'You haven't dined yet?' she smiles.

'No, not yet, Madame.'

I'd rather like to dine with her. Even to sleep with her afterwards. Would she be pale like that all over?

But no. She'd have large moles. They go with that kind of skin. And I can't bear them. They remind me somehow, disgustingly, of mushrooms.

Bliss (1918)†

Although Bertha Young was thirty she still had moments like this when she wanted to run instead of walk, to take dancing steps on and off the pavement, to bowl a hoop, to throw something up in the air and catch it again, or to stand still and laugh at—nothing—at nothing, simply.

What can you do if you are thirty and, turning the corner of your own street, you are overcome, suddenly, by a feeling of bliss—absolute bliss!—as though you'd suddenly swallowed a bright piece of that late afternoon sun and it burned in your bosom, sending out a little shower of sparks into every particle, into every finger and toe? . . .

Oh, is there no way you can express it without being 'drunk and disorderly'? How idiotic civilization is! Why be given a body if you have to keep it shut up in a case like a rare, rare fiddle?

'No, that about the fiddle is not quite what I mean,' she thought, running up the steps and feeling in her bag for the key—she'd forgotten it, as usual—and rattling the letter-box. 'It's not what I mean, because—Thank you, Mary'—she went into the hall. 'Is Nurse back?'

'Yes, M'm.'

'And has the fruit come?'

'Yes, M'm. Everything's come.'

'Bring the fruit up to the dining-room, will you? I'll arrange it before I go upstairs.'

It was dusky in the dining-room and quite chilly. But all the same Bertha threw off her coat; she could not bear the tight clasp of it another moment, and the cold air fell on her arms.

But in her bosom there was still that bright glowing place—that shower of little sparks coming from it. It was almost unbearable. She hardly dared to breathe for fear of fanning it higher, and yet she breathed deeply, deeply. She hardly dared to look into the cold mirror—but she did look, and it gave her back a woman, radiant, with smiling, trembling lips, with big, dark eyes and an air of listening, waiting for something . . . divine to happen . . . that she knew must happen . . . infallibly.

Mary brought in the fruit on a tray and with it a glass bowl, and a blue dish, very lovely, with a strange sheen on it as though it had been dipped in milk.

'Shall I turn on the light, M'm?'

'No, thank you. I can see quite well.'

† First published in the *English Review* (August 1918) and then in *Bliss and Other Stories* (1920).

There were tangerines and apples stained with strawberry pink. Some yellow pears, smooth as silk; some white grapes covered with a silver bloom and a big cluster of purple ones. These last she had bought to tone in with the new dining-room carpet. Yes, that did sound rather far-fetched and absurd, but it was really why she had bought them. She had thought in the shop: 'I must have some purple ones to bring the carpet up to the table.' And it had seemed quite sense at the time.

When she had finished with them and had made two pyramids of these bright round shapes, she stood away from the table to get the effect—and it really was most curious. For the dark table seemed to melt into the dusky light and the glass dish and the blue bowl to float in the air. This, of course in her present mood, was so incredibly beautiful. . . . She began to laugh.

'No, no. I'm getting hysterical.' And she seized her bag and coat and ran upstairs to the nursery.

Nurse sat at a low table giving Little B her supper after her bath. The baby had on a white flannel gown and a blue woollen jacket, and her dark, fine hair was brushed up into a funny little peak. She looked up when she saw her mother and began to jump.

'Now, my lovey, eat it up like a good girl,' said Nurse, setting her lips in a way that Bertha knew, and that meant she had come into the nursery at another wrong moment.

'Has she been good, Nanny?'

'She's been a little sweet all the afternoon,' whispered Nanny. 'We went to the park and I sat down on a chair and took her out of the pram and a big dog came along and put its head on my knee and she clutched its ear, tugged it. Oh, you should have seen her.'

Bertha wanted to ask if it wasn't rather dangerous to let her clutch at a strange dog's ear. But she did not dare to. She stood watching them, her hands by her side, like the poor little girl in front of the rich little girl with the doll.

The baby looked up at her again, stared, and then smiled so charmingly that Bertha couldn't help crying:

'Oh, Nanny, do let me finish giving her her supper while you put the bath things away.'

'Well, M'm, she oughtn't to be changed hands while she's eating,' said Nanny, still whispering. 'It unsettles her; it's very likely to upset her.'

How absurd it was. Why have a baby if it has to be kept—not in a case like a rare, rare fiddle—but in another woman's arms?

'Oh, I must!' said she.

Very offended, Nanny handed her over.

'Now, don't excite her after her supper. You know you do, M'm. And I have such a time with her after!'

Thank heaven! Nanny went out of the room with the bath towels.

'Now I've got you to myself, my little precious,' said Bertha, as the baby leaned against her.

She ate delightfully, holding up her lips for the spoon and then waving her hands. Sometimes she wouldn't let the spoon go; and sometimes, just as Bertha had filled it, she waved it away to the four winds.

When the soup was finished Bertha turned round to the fire.

'You're nice—you're very nice!" said she, kissing her warm baby. 'I'm fond of you. I like you.'

And, indeed, she loved Little B so much—her neck as she bent forward, her exquisite toes as they shone transparent in the firelight—that all her feeling of bliss came back again, and again she didn't know how to express it—what to do with it.

'You're wanted on the telephone,' said Nanny, coming back in triumph and seizing *her* Little B.

Down she flew. It was Harry.

'Oh, is that you, Ber? Look here. I'll be late. I'll take a taxi and come along as quickly as I can, but get dinner put back ten minutes—will you? All right?'

'Yes, perfectly. Oh, Harry!'

'Yes?'

What had she to say? She'd nothing to say. She only wanted to get in touch with him for a moment. She couldn't absurdly cry: 'Hasn't it been a divine day!'

'What is it?' rapped out the little voice.

'Nothing. *Entendu*,'[1] said Bertha, and hung up the receiver, thinking how more than idiotic civilization was.

They had people coming to dinner. The Norman Knights—a very sound couple—he was about to start a theatre, and she was awfully keen on interior decoration, a young man, Eddie Warren, who had just published a little book of poems and whom everybody was asking to dine, and a 'find' of Bertha's called Pearl Fulton. What Miss Fulton did, Bertha didn't know. They had met at the club and Bertha had fallen in love with her, as she always did fall in love with beautiful women who had something strange about them.

The provoking thing was that, though they had been about together and met a number of times and really talked, Bertha couldn't yet make her out. Up to a certain point Miss Fulton was rarely, wonderfully frank, but the certain point was there, and beyond that she would not go.

1. Agreed.

Was there anything beyond it? Harry said 'No.' Voted her dullish, and 'cold like all blond women, with a touch, perhaps, of anæmia of the brain.' But Bertha wouldn't agree with him; not yet, at any rate.

'No, the way she has of sitting with her head a little on one side, and smiling, has something behind it, Harry, and I must find out what that something is.'

'Most likely it's a good stomach,' answered Harry.

He made a point of catching Bertha's heels with replies of that kind . . . 'liver frozen, my dear girl', or 'pure flatulence', or 'kidney disease', . . . and so on. For some strange reason Bertha liked this, and almost admired it in him very much.

She went into the drawing-room and lighted the fire; then, picking up the cushions, one by one, that Mary had disposed so carefully, she threw them back on to the chairs and the couches. That made all the difference; the room came alive at once. As she was about to throw the last one she surprised herself by suddenly hugging it to her, passionately, passionately. But it did not put out the fire in her bosom. Oh, on the contrary!

The windows of the drawing-room opened on to a balcony overlooking the garden. At the far end, against the wall, there was a tall, slender pear tree in fullest, richest bloom; it stood perfect, as though becalmed against the jade-green sky. Bertha couldn't help feeling, even from this distance, that it had not a single bud or a faded petal. Down below, in the garden beds, the red and yellow tulips, heavy with flowers, seemed to lean upon the dusk. A grey cat, dragging its belly, crept across the lawn, and a black one, its shadow, trailed after. The sight of them, so intent and so quick, gave Bertha a curious shiver.

'What creepy things cats are!' she stammered, and she turned away from the window and began walking up and down. . . .

How strong the jonquils smelled in the warm room. Too strong? Oh, no. And yet, as though overcome, she flung down on a couch and pressed her hands to her eyes.

'I'm too happy—too happy!' she murmured.

And she seemed to see on her eyelids the lovely pear tree with its wide open blossoms as a symbol of her own life.

Really—really—she had everything. She was young. Harry and she were as much in love as ever, and they got on together splendidly and were really good pals. She had an adorable baby. They didn't have to worry about money. They had this absolutely satisfactory house and garden. And friends—modern, thrilling friends, writers and painters and poets or people keen on social questions—just the kind of friends they wanted. And then there were books, and there was music, and she had found a wonderful little dress-maker, and they were going abroad in the summer, and their new cook made the most superb omelettes. . . .

'I'm absurd. Absurd!' She sat up; but she felt quite dizzy, quite drunk. It must have been the spring.

Yes, it was the spring. Now she was so tired she could not drag herself upstairs to dress.

A white dress, a string of jade beads, green shoes and stockings. It wasn't 'intentional'. She had thought of this scheme hours before she stood at the drawing-room window.

Her petals rustled softly into the hall, and she kissed Mrs Norman Knight, who was taking off the most amusing orange coat with a procession of black monkeys round the hem and up the fronts.

'. . . Why! Why! Why is the middle-class so stodgy—so utterly without a sense of humour! My dear, it's only by a fluke that I am here at all—Norman being the protective fluke. For my darling monkeys so upset the train that it rose to a man and simply ate me with its eyes. Didn't laugh—wasn't amused—that I should have loved. No, just stared—and bored me through and through.'

'But the cream of it was,' said Norman, pressing a large tortoise-shell-rimmed monocle into his eye, 'you don't mind me telling this, Face, do you?' (In their home and among their friends they called each other Face and Mug.) 'The cream of it was when she, being full fed, turned to the woman beside her and said: "Haven't you ever seen a monkey before?" '

'Oh, yes!' Mrs Norman Knight joined in the laughter. 'Wasn't that too absolutely creamy?'

And a funnier thing still was that now her coat was off she did look like a very intelligent monkey—who had even made that yellow silk dress out of scraped banana skins. And her amber ear-rings; they were like little dangling nuts.

'This is a sad, sad fall!' said Mug, pausing in front of Little B's perambulator. 'When the perambulator comes into the hall—' and he waved the rest of the quotation away.

The bell rang. It was lean, pale Eddie Warren (as usual) in a state of acute distress.

'It *is* the right house, *isn't* it?' he pleaded.

'Oh, I think so—I hope so,' said Bertha brightly.

'I have had such a *dreadful* experience with a taxi-man; he was *most* sinister. I couldn't get him to *stop*. The *more* I knocked and called the *faster* he went. And *in* the moonlight this *bizarre* figure with the *flattened* head *crouching* over the *lit-tle* wheel. . . .'

He shuddered, taking off an immense white silk scarf. Bertha noticed that his socks were white, too—most charming.

'But how dreadful!' she cried.

'Yes, it really was,' said Eddie, following her into the drawing-room. 'I saw myself *driving* through Eternity in a *timeless* taxi.'

He knew the Norman Knights. In fact, he was going to write a play for N. K. when the theatre scheme came off.

'Well, Warren, how's the play?' said Norman Knight, dropping his monocle and giving his eye a moment in which to rise to the surface before it was screwed down again.

And Mrs Norman Knight: 'Oh, Mr Warren, what happy socks?'

'I *am* so glad you like them,' said he, staring at his feet. 'They seem to have got so *much* whiter since the moon rose.' And he turned his lean sorrowful young face to Bertha. 'There *is* a moon, you know.'

She wanted to cry: 'I am sure there is—often—often!'

He really was a most attractive person. But so was Face, crouched before the fire in her banana skins, and so was Mug, smoking a cigarette and saying as he flicked the ash: 'Why doth the bridegroom tarry?'[2]

'There he is, now.'

Bang went the front door open and shut. Harry shouted: 'Hullo, you people. Down in five minutes.' And they heard him swarm up the stairs. Bertha couldn't help smiling; she knew how he loved doing things at high pressure. What, after all, did an extra five minutes matter? But he would pretend to himself that they mattered beyond measure. And then he would make a great point of coming into the drawing-room, extravagantly cool and collected.

Harry had such a zest for life. Oh, how she appreciated it in him. And his passion for fighting—for seeking in everything that came up against him another test of his power and of his courage—that, too, she understood. Even when it made him just occasionally, to other people, who didn't know him well, a little ridiculous perhaps. . . . For there were moments when he rushed into battle where no battle was. . . . She talked and laughed and positively forgot until he had come in (just as she had imagined) that Pearl Fulton had not turned up.

'I wonder if Miss Fulton has forgotten?'

'I expect so,' said Harry. 'Is she on the 'phone?'

'Ah! There's a taxi, now.' And Bertha smiled with that little air of proprietorship that she always assumed while her women finds were new and mysterious. 'She lives in taxis.'

'She'll run to fat if she does,' said Harry coolly, ringing the bell for dinner. 'Frightful danger for blond women.'

'Harry—don't,' warned Bertha, laughing up at him.

2. "While the bridegroom tarried, they all slumbered and slept" (Matt. 25.5).

Came another tiny moment, while they waited, laughing and talking, just a trifle too much at their ease, a trifle too unaware. And then Miss Fulton, all in silver, with a silver fillet[3] binding her pale blond hair, came in smiling, her head a little on one side.

'Am I late?'

'No, not at all,' said Bertha. 'Come along.' And she took her arm and they moved into the dining-room.

What was there in the touch of that cool arm that could fan—fan—start blazing—blazing—the fire of bliss that Bertha did not know what to do with?

Miss Fulton did not look at her; but then she seldom did look at people directly. Her heavy eyelids lay upon her eyes and the strange half smile came and went upon her lips as though she lived by listening rather than seeing. But Bertha knew, suddenly, as if the longest, most intimate look had passed between them—as if they had said to each other: 'You, too?'—that Pearl Fulton, stirring the beautiful red soup in the grey plate, was feeling just what she was feeling.

And the others? Face and Mug, Eddie and Harry, their spoons rising and falling—dabbing their lips with their napkins, crumbling bread, fiddling with the forks and glasses and talking.

'I met her at the Alpha[4] show—the weirdest little person. She'd not only cut off her hair, but she seemed to have taken a dreadfully good snip off her legs and arms and her neck and her poor little nose as well.'

'Isn't she very *liée*[5] with Michael Oat?'

'The man who wrote *Love in False Teeth*?'

'He wants to write a play for me. One act. One man. Decides to commit suicide. Gives all the reasons why he should and why he shouldn't. And just as he has made up his mind either to do it or not to do it—curtain. Not half a bad idea.'

'What's he going to call it—"Stomach Trouble"?'

'I *think* I've come across the *same* idea in a lit-tle French review, *quite* unknown in England.'

No, they didn't share it. They were dears—dears—and she loved having them there, at her table, and giving them delicious food and wine. In fact, she longed to tell them how delightful they were, and what a decorative group they made, how they seemed to set one another off and how they reminded her of a play by Tchekof![6]

Harry was enjoying his dinner. It was part of his—well, not his

3. A band or ribbon.
4. A satirical reference to the Omega Workshops, which Virginia Woolf's sister Vanessa Bell had helped establish to promote contemporary interior design and furniture.
5. Involved with.
6. Anton Chekhov (1860–1904), Russian playwright and short-story writer.

nature, exactly, and certainly not his pose—his—something or other—to talk about food and to glory in his 'shameless passion for the white flesh of the lobster' and 'the green of pistachio ices—green and cold like the eyelids of Egyptian dancers'.

When he looked up at her and said: 'Bertha, this is a very admirable *soufflée*!' she almost could have wept with child-like pleasure.

Oh, why did she feel so tender towards the whole world to-night? Everything was good—was right. All that happened seemed to fill again her brimming cup of bliss.

And still, in the back of her mind, there was the pear tree. It would be silver now, in the light of poor dear Eddie's moon, silver as Miss Fulton, who sat there turning a tangerine in her slender fingers that were so pale a light seemed to come from them.

What she simply couldn't make out—what was miraculous—was how she should have guessed Miss Fulton's mood so exactly and so instantly. For she never doubted for a moment that she was right, and yet what had she to go on? Less than nothing.

'I believe this does happen very, very rarely between women. Never between men,' thought Bertha. 'But while I am making the coffee in the drawing-room perhaps she will "give a sign".'

What she meant by that she did not know, and what would happen after that she could not imagine.

While she thought like this she saw herself talking and laughing. She had to talk because of her desire to laugh.

'I must laugh or die.'

But when she noticed Face's funny little habit of tucking something down the front of her bodice—as if she kept a tiny, secret hoard of nuts there, too—Bertha had to dig her nails into her hands—so as not to laugh too much.

It was over at last. And: 'Come and see my new coffee machine,' said Bertha.

'We only have a new coffee machine once a fortnight,' said Harry. Face took her arm this time; Miss Fulton bent her head and followed after.

The fire had died down in the drawing-room to a red, flickering 'nest of baby phœnixes', said Face.

'Don't turn up the light for a moment. It is so lovely.' And down she crouched by the fire again. She was always cold . . . 'without her little red flannel jacket, of course,' thought Bertha.

At that moment Miss Fulton 'gave the sign'.

'Have you a garden?' said the cool, sleepy voice.

This was so exquisite on her part that all Bertha could do was to obey. She crossed the room, pulled the curtains apart, and opened those long windows.

'There!' she breathed.

And the two women stood side by side looking at the slender, flowering tree. Although it was so still it seemed, like the flame of a candle, to stretch up, to point, to quiver in the bright air, to grow taller and taller as they gazed—almost to touch the rim of the round, silver moon.

How long did they stand there? Both, as it were, caught in that circle of unearthly light, understanding each other perfectly, creatures of another world, and wondering what they were to do in this one with all this blissful treasure that burned in their bosoms and dropped, in silver flowers, from their hair and hands?

For ever—for a moment? And did Miss Fulton murmur: 'Yes. Just *that*.' Or did Bertha dream it?

Then the light was snapped on and Face made the coffee and Harry said: 'My dear Mrs Knight, don't ask me about my baby. I never see her. I shan't feel the slightest interest in her until she has a lover,' and Mug took his eye out of the conservatory for a moment and then put it under glass again and Eddie Warren drank his coffee and set down the cup with a face of anguish as though he had drunk and seen the spider.[7]

'What I want to do is to give the young men a show. I believe London is simply teeming with first-chop, unwritten plays. What I want to say to 'em is: "Here's the theatre. Fire ahead." '

'You know, my dear, I am going to decorate a room for the Jacob Nathans. Oh, I am so tempted to do a fried-fish scheme, with the backs of the chairs shaped like frying pans and lovely chip potatoes embroidered all over the curtains.'

'The trouble with our young writing men is that they are still too romantic. You can't put out to sea without being seasick and wanting a basin. Well, why won't they have the courage of those basins?'

'A *dreadful* poem about a *girl* who was *violated* by a beggar *without* a nose in a lit-tle wood. . . .'

Miss Fulton sank into the lowest, deepest chair and Harry handed round the cigarettes.

From the way he stood in front of her shaking the silver box and saying abruptly: 'Egyptian? Turkish? Virginian? They're all mixed up,' Bertha realized that she not only bored him; he really disliked her. And she decided from the way Miss Fulton said: 'No, thank you, I won't smoke,' that she felt it, too, and was hurt.

'Oh, Harry, don't dislike her. You are quite wrong about her. She's wonderful, wonderful. And, besides, how can you feel so differently about someone who means so much to me. I shall try to tell you

7. "I have drunk, and seen the spider," from Shakespeare, *The Winter's Tale* 2.1.47—based on the belief that a spider in one's cup would not poison one unless observed.

when we are in bed to-night what has been happening. What she and I have shared.'

At those last words something strange and almost terrifying darted into Bertha's mind. And this something blind and smiling whispered to her: 'Soon these people will go. The house will be quiet—quiet. The lights will be out. And you and he will be alone together in the dark room—the warm bed. . . .'

She jumped up from her chair and ran over to the piano.

'What a pity someone does not play!' she cried. 'What a pity somebody does not play.'

For the first time in her life Bertha Young desired her husband.

Oh, she'd loved him—she'd been in love with him, of course, in every other way, but just not in that way. And, equally, of course, she'd understood that he was different. They'd discussed it so often. It had worried her dreadfully at first to find that she was so cold, but after a time it had not seemed to matter. They were so frank with each other—such good pals. That was the best of being modern.

But now—ardently! ardently! The word ached in her ardent body! Was this what that feeling of bliss had been leading up to? But then, then—

'My dear,' said Mrs Norman Knight, 'you know our shame. We are the victims of time and train. We live in Hampstead.[8] It's been so nice.'

'I'll come with you into the hall,' said Bertha. 'I loved having you. But you must not miss the last train. That's so awful, isn't it?'

'Have a whisky, Knight, before you go?' called Harry.

'No, thanks, old chap.'

Bertha squeezed his hand for that as she shook it.

'Good night, good-bye,' she cried from the top step, feeling that this self of hers was taking leave of them for ever.

When she got back into the drawing-room the others were on the move.

'. . . Then you can come part of the way in my taxi.'

'I shall be *so* thankful *not* to have to face *another* drive *alone* after my *dreadful* experience.'

'You can get a taxi at the rank just at the end of the street. You won't have to walk more than a few yards.'

'That's a comfort. I'll go and put on my coat.'

Miss Fulton moved towards the hall and Bertha was following when Harry almost pushed past.

'Let me help you.'

8. A residential suburb of north London, favored by writers and artists.

Bertha knew that he was repenting his rudeness—she let him go. What a boy he was in some ways—so impulsive—so—simple.

And Eddie and she were left by the fire.

'I *wonder* if you have seen Bilks' *new* poem called *Table d'Hôte*[9],' said Eddie softly. 'It's *so* wonderful. In the last Anthology. Have you got a copy? I'd *so* like to *show* it to you. It begins with an *incredibly* beautiful line: "Why Must it Always be Tomato Soup?" '

'Yes,' said Bertha. And she moved noiselessly to a table opposite the drawing-room door and Eddie glided noiselessly after her. She picked up the little book and gave it to him; they had not made a sound.

While he looked it up she turned her head towards the hall. And she saw . . . Harry with Miss Fulton's coat in his arms and Miss Fulton with her back turned to him and her head bent. He tossed the coat away, put his hands on her shoulders and turned her violently to him. His lips said: 'I adore you,' and Miss Fulton laid her moonbeam fingers on his cheeks and smiled her sleepy smile. Harry's nostrils quivered; his lips curled back in a hideous grin while he whispered: 'To-morrow,' and with her eyelids Miss Fulton said: 'Yes.'

'Here it is,' said Eddie. ' "Why Must it Always be Tomato Soup?" It's so *deeply* true, don't you feel? Tomato soup is so *dreadfully* eternal.'

'If you prefer,' said Harry's voice, very loud, from the hall, 'I can phone you a cab to come to the door.'

'Oh, no. It's not necessary,' said Miss Fulton, and she came up to Bertha and gave her the slender fingers to hold.

'Good-bye. Thank you so much.'

'Good-bye,' said Bertha.

Miss Fulton held her hand a moment longer.

'Your lovely pear tree!' she murmured.

And then she was gone, with Eddie following, like the black cat following the grey cat.

'I'll shut up shop,' said Harry, extravagantly cool and collected.

'Your lovely pear tree—pear tree—pear tree!'

Bertha simply ran over to the long windows.

'Oh, what is going to happen now?' she cried.

But the pear tree was as lovely as ever and as full of flower and as still.

Psychology (1919)†

When she opened the door and saw him standing there she was more pleased than ever before, and he, too, as he followed her into the studio, seemed very very happy to have come.

9. A phrase used for the set menu in a restaurant.
† First published in *Bliss and Other Stories* (1920).

'Not busy?'

'No. Just going to have tea.'

'And you are not expecting anybody?'

'Nobody at all.'

'Ah! That's good.'

He laid aside his coat and hat gently, lingeringly, as though he had time and to spare for everything, or as though he were taking leave of them for ever, and came over to the fire and held out his hands to the quick, leaping flame.

Just for a moment both of them stood silent in that leaping light. Still, as it were, they tasted on their smiling lips the sweet shock of their greeting. Their secret selves whispered:

'Why should we speak? Isn't this enough?'

'More than enough. I never realized until this moment. . . .'

'How good it is just to be with you. . . .'

'Like this. . . .'

'It's more than enough.'

But suddenly he turned and looked at her and she moved quickly away.

'Have a cigarette? I'll put the kettle on. Are you longing for tea?'

'No. Not longing.'

'Well, I am.'

'Oh, you.' He thumped the Armenian cushion and flung on to the *sommier*.[1] 'You are a perfect little Chinee.'

'Yes, I am,' she laughed. 'I long for tea as strong men long for wine.'

She lighted the lamp under its broad orange shade, pulled the curtains and drew up the tea table. Two birds sang in the kettle; the fire fluttered. He sat up clasping his knees. It was delightful—this business of having tea—and she always had delicious things to eat—little sharp sandwiches, short sweet almond fingers, and a dark, rich cake tasting of rum—but it was an interruption. He wanted it over, the table pushed away, their two chairs drawn up to the light, and the moment came when he took out his pipe, filled it, and said, pressing the tobacco tight into the bowl: 'I have been thinking over what you said last time and it seems to me. . . .'

Yes, that was what he waited for and so did she. Yes, while she shook the teapot hot and dry over the spirit flame she saw those other two, him, leaning back, taking his ease among the cushions, and her, curled up *en escargot*[2] in the blue shell arm-chair. The picture was so clear and so minute it might have been painted on the blue teapot lid. And yet she couldn't hurry. She could almost have

1. A divan bed.
2. Like a snail.

cried: 'Give me time.' She must have time in which to grow calm. She wanted time in which to free herself from all these familiar things with which she lived so vividly. For all these gay things round her were part of her—her offspring—and they knew it and made the largest, most vehement claims. But now they must go. They must be swept away, shooed away—like children, sent up the shadowy stairs, packed into bed and commanded to go to sleep—at once—without a murmur!

For the special thrilling quality of their friendship was in their complete surrender. Like two open cities in the midst of some vast plain their two minds lay open to each other. And it wasn't as if he rode into hers like a conqueror, armed to the eyebrows and seeing nothing but a gay silken flutter—nor did she enter his like a queen walking soft on petals. No, they were eager, serious travellers, absorbed in understanding what was to be seen and discovering what was hidden—making the most of this extraordinary absolute chance which made it possible for him to be utterly truthful to her and for her to be utterly sincere with him.

And the best of it was they were both of them old enough to enjoy their adventure to the full without any stupid emotional complication. Passion would have ruined everything; they quite saw that. Besides, all that sort of thing was over and done with for both of them—he was thirty-one, she was thirty—they had had their experiences, and very rich and varied they had been, but now was the time for harvest—harvest. Weren't his novels to be very big novels indeed? And her plays. Who else had her exquisite sense of real English Comedy? . . .

Carefully she cut the cake into thick little wads and he reached across for a piece.

'Do realize how good it is,' she implored. 'Eat it imaginatively. Roll your eyes if you can and taste it on the breath. It's not a sandwich from the hatter's bag—it's the kind of cake that might have been mentioned in the Book of Genesis. . . . And God said: "Let there be cake. And there was cake. And God saw that it was good."[3]

'You needn't entreat me,' said he. 'Really you needn't. It's a queer thing but I always do notice what I eat here and never anywhere else. I suppose it comes of living alone so long and always reading while I feed . . . my habit of looking upon food as just food . . . something that's there, at certain times . . . to be devoured . . . to be . . . not there.' He laughed. 'That shocks you. Doesn't it?'

'To the bone,' said she.

'But—look here—' He pushed away his cup and began to speak

3. A parody of "And God said, Let there be light: and there was light. And God saw the light, that it was good" (Genesis 1.3–4).

very fast. 'I simply haven't got any external life at all. I don't know the names of things a bit—trees and so on—and I never notice places or furniture or what people look like. One room is just like another to me—a place to sit and read or talk in—except,' and here he paused, smiled in a strange naive way, and said, 'except this studio.' He looked round him and then at her; he laughed in his astonishment and pleasure. He was like a man who wakes up in a train to find that he has arrived, already, at the journey's end.

'Here's another queer thing. If I shut my eyes I can see this place down to every detail—every detail. . . . Now I come to think of it—I've never realized this consciously before. Often when I am away from here I revisit it in spirit—wander about among your red chairs, stare at the bowl of fruit on the black table—and just touch, very lightly, that marvel of a sleeping boy's head.'

He looked at it as he spoke. It stood on the corner of the mantelpiece; the head to one side down-drooping, the lips parted, as though in his sleep the little boy listened to some sweet sound. . . .

'I love that little boy,' he murmured. And then they both were silent.

A new silence came between them. Nothing in the least like the satisfactory pause that had followed their greetings—the 'Well, here we are together again, and there's no reason why we shouldn't go on from just where we left off last time.' That silence could be contained in the circle of warm, delightful fire and lamplight. How many times hadn't they flung something into it just for the fun of watching the ripples break on the easy shores. But into this unfamiliar pool the head of the little boy sleeping his timeless sleep dropped—and the ripples flowed away, away—boundlessly far—into deep glittering darkness.

And then both of them broke it. She said: 'I must make up the fire,' and he said: 'I have been trying a new. . . .' Both of them escaped. She made up the fire and put the table back, the blue chair was wheeled forward, she curled up and he lay back among the cushions. Quickly! Quickly! They must stop it from happening again.

'Well, I read the book you left last time.'

'Oh, what do you think of it?'

They were off and all was as usual. But was it? Weren't they just a little too quick, too prompt with their replies, too ready to take each other up? Was this really anything more than a wonderfully good imitation of other occasions? His heart beat; her cheek burned and the stupid thing was she could not discover where exactly they were or what exactly was happening. She hadn't time to glance back. And just as she had got so far it happened again. They faltered, wavered, broke down, were silent. Again they were conscious of the boundless, questioning dark. Again, there they were—two hunters, bending over their fire, but hearing suddenly from the jungle beyond a shake of wind and a loud, questioning cry. . . .

She lifted her head. 'It's raining,' she murmured. And her voice was like his when he had said: 'I love that little boy.'

Well. Why didn't they just give way to it—yield—and see what will happen then? But no. Vague and troubled though they were, they knew enough to realize their precious friendship was in danger. She was the one who would be destroyed—not they—and they'd be no party to that.

He got up, knocked out his pipe, ran his hand through his hair and said: 'I have been wondering very much lately whether the novel of the future will be a psychological novel or not. How sure are you that psychology *qua* psychology has got anything to do with literature at all?'

'Do you mean you feel there's quite a chance that the mysterious non-existent creatures—the young writers of to-day—are trying simply to jump the psycho-analyst's claim?'

'Yes, I do. And I think it's because this generation is just wise enough to know that it is sick and to realize that its only chance of recovery is by going into its symptoms—making an exhaustive study of them—tracking them down—trying to get at the root of the trouble.'

'But oh,' she wailed. 'What a dreadfully dismal outlook.'

'Not at all,' said he. 'Look here. . . .' On the talk went. And now it seemed they really had succeeded. She turned in her chair to look at him while she answered. Her smile said: 'We have won.' And he smiled back, confident: 'Absolutely.'

But the smile undid them. It lasted too long; it became a grin. They saw themselves as two little grinning puppets jigging away in nothingness.

'What have we been talking about?' thought he. He was so utterly bored he almost groaned.

'What a spectacle we have made of ourselves,' thought she. And she saw him laboriously—oh, laboriously—laying out the grounds and herself running after, putting here a tree and there a flowery shrub and here a handful of glittering fish in a pool. They were silent this time from sheer dismay.

The clock struck six merry little pings and the fire made a soft flutter. What fools they were—heavy, stodgy, elderly—with positively upholstered minds.

And now the silence put a spell upon them like solemn music. It was anguish—anguish for her to bear it and he would die—he'd die if it were broken. . . . And yet he longed to break it. Not by speech. At any rate not by their ordinary maddening chatter. There was another way for them to speak to each other, and in the new way he wanted to murmur: 'Do you feel this too? Do you understand it at all?'

Instead, to his horror, he heard himself say: 'I must be off; I'm meeting Brand at six.'

What devil made him say that instead of the other? She jumped —simply jumped out of her chair, and he heard her crying: 'You must rush, then. He's so punctual. Why didn't you say so before?'

'You've hurt me; you've hurt me! We've failed!' said her secret self while she handed him his hat and stick, smiling gaily. She wouldn't give him a moment for another word, but ran along the passage and opened the big outer door.

Could they leave each other like this? How could they? He stood on the step and she just inside holding the door. It was not raining now.

'You've hurt me—hurt me,' said her heart. 'Why don't you go? No, don't go. Stay. No—go!' And she looked out upon the night.

She saw the beautiful fall of the steps, the dark garden ringed with glittering ivy, on the other side of the road the huge bare willows and above them the sky big and bright with stars. But of course he would see nothing of all this. He was superior to it all. He—with his wonderful 'spiritual' vision!

She was right. He did see nothing at all. Misery! He'd missed it. It was too late to do anything now. Was it too late? Yes, it was. A cold snatch of hateful wind blew into the garden. Curse life! He heard her cry 'au revoir' and the door slammed.

Running back into the studio she behaved so strangely. She ran up and down lifting her arms and crying: 'Oh! Oh! How stupid! How imbecile! How stupid!' And then she flung herself down on the *sommier* thinking of nothing—just lying there in her rage. All was over. What was over? Oh—something was. And she'd never see him again—never. After a long long time (or perhaps ten minutes) had passed in that black gulf her bell rang a sharp quick jingle. It was he, of course. And equally, of course, she oughtn't to have paid the slightest attention to it but just let it go on ringing and ringing. She flew to answer.

On the doorstep there stood an elderly virgin, a pathetic creature who simply idolized her (heaven knows why) and had this habit of turning up and ringing the bell and then saying, when she opened the door: 'My dear, send me away!' She never did. As a rule she asked her in and let her admire everything and accepted the bunch of slightly soiled looking flowers—more than graciously. But today. . . .

'Oh, I am so sorry,' she cried. 'But I've got someone with me. We are working on some wood-cuts. I'm hopelessly busy all evening.'

'It doesn't matter. It doesn't matter at all, darling,' said the good friend. 'I was just passing and I thought I'd leave you some violets.' She fumbled down among the ribs of a large old umbrella. 'I put them down here. Such a good place to keep flowers out of the wind. Here they are,' she said, shaking out a little dead bunch.

For a moment she did not take the violets. But while she stood just inside, holding the door, a strange thing happened. . . . Again she saw the beautiful fall of the steps, the dark garden ringed with glittering ivy, the willows, the big bright sky. Again she felt the silence that was like a question. But this time she did not hesitate. She moved forward. Very softly and gently, as though fearful of making a ripple in that boundless pool of quiet she put her arms round her friend.

'My dear,' murmured her happy friend, quite overcome by this gratitude. 'They are really nothing. Just the simplest little thrippenny bunch.'

But as she spoke she was enfolded—more tenderly, more beautifully embraced, held by such a sweet pressure and for so long that the poor dear's mind positively reeled and she just had the strength to quaver: 'Then you really don't mind me too much?'

'Good night, my friend,' whispered the other. 'Come again soon.'

'Oh, I will. I will.'

This time she walked back to the studio slowly, and standing in the middle of the room with half-shut eyes she felt so light, so rested, as if she had woken up out of a childish sleep. Even the act of breathing was a joy. . . .

The *sommier* was very untidy. All the cushions 'like furious mountains' as she said; she put them in order before going over to the writing-table.

'I have been thinking over our talk about the psychological novel,' she dashed off, 'it really is intensely interesting.' . . . And so on and so on.

At the end she wrote: 'Good night, my friend. Come again soon.'

Pictures (1919)†

Eight o'clock in the morning. Miss Ada Moss lay in a black iron bedstead, staring up at the ceiling. Her room, a Bloomsbury top-

† First appeared as a dialogue, "The Common Round," in the *New Age* (31 May 1917), then in its present form in *Art and Letters* (Autumn 1919). It was collected in *Bliss and Other Stories* (1920). "Pictures" drew on Mansfield's experience as an extra in films.

floor back, smelled of soot and face powder and the paper of fried potatoes she brought in for supper the night before.

'Oh, dear,' thought Miss Moss, 'I am cold. I wonder why it is that I always wake up so cold in the mornings now. My knees and feet and my back—especially my back; it's like a sheet of ice. And I always was such a one for being warm in the old days. It's not as if I was skinny—I'm just the same full figure that I used to be. No, it's because I don't have a good hot dinner in the evenings.'

A pageant of Good Hot Dinners passed across the ceiling, each of them accompanied by a bottle of Nourishing Stout. . . .

'Even if I were to get up now,' she thought, 'and have a sensible substantial breakfast. . . .' A pageant of Sensible Substantial Breakfasts followed the dinners across the ceiling, shepherded by an enormous, white, uncut ham. Miss Moss shuddered and disappeared under the bedclothes. Suddenly, in bounced the landlady.

'There's a letter for you, Miss Moss.'

'Oh,' said Miss Moss, far too friendly, 'thank you very much, Mrs Pine. It's very good of you, I'm sure, to take the trouble.'

'No trouble at all,' said the landlady. 'I thought perhaps it was the letter you'd been expecting.'

'Why,' said Miss Moss brightly, 'yes, perhaps it is.' She put her head on one side and smiled vaguely at the letter. 'I shouldn't be surprised.'

The landlady's eyes popped. 'Well, I should, Miss Moss,' said she, 'and that's how it is. And I'll trouble you to open it, if you please. Many is the lady in my place as would have done it for you and have been within her rights. For things can't go on like this, Miss Moss, no indeed they can't. What with week in and week out and first you've got it and then you haven't, and then it's another letter lost in the post or another manager down at Brighton but will be back on Tuesday for certain—I'm fair sick and tired and I won't stand it no more. Why should I, Miss Moss, I ask you, at a time like this, with prices flying up in the air and my poor dear lad in France? My sister Eliza was only saying to me yesterday—"Minnie," she says, "you're too soft-hearted. You could have let that room time and time again," says she, "and if people won't look after themselves in times like these, nobody else will," she says. "She may have had a College eddication and sung in West End concerts," says she, "but if your Lizzie says what's true," she says, "and she's washing her own wovens and drying them on the towel rail, it's easy to see where the finger's pointing. And it's high time you had done with it," says she.'

Miss Moss gave no sign of having heard this. She sat up in bed, tore open her letter and read:

'Dear Madam,

Yours to hand. Am not producing at present, but have filed photo for future ref.

Yours truly,
BACKWASH FILM CO.'

This letter seemed to afford her peculiar satisfaction; she read it through twice before replying to the landlady.

'Well, Mrs Pine, I think you'll be sorry for what you said. This is from a manager, asking me to be there with evening dress at ten o'clock next Saturday morning.'

But the landlady was too quick for her. She pounced, secured the letter.

'Oh, is it! Is it indeed!' she cried.

'Give me back that letter. Give it back to me at once, you bad, wicked woman,' cried Miss Moss, who could not get out of bed because her nightdress was slit down the back. 'Give me back my private letter.' The landlady began slowly backing out of the room, holding the letter to her buttoned bodice.

'So it's come to this, has it?' said she. 'Well, Miss Moss, if I don't get my rent at eight o'clock to-night, we'll see who's a bad, wicked woman—that's all.' Here she nodded, mysteriously. 'And I'll keep this letter.' Here her voice rose. 'It will be a pretty little bit of evidence!' And here it fell, sepulchral, '*My lady.*'

The door banged and Miss Moss was alone. She flung off the bed clothes, and sitting by the side of the bed, furious and shivering, she stared at her fat white legs with their great knots of greeny-blue veins.

'Cockroach! That's what she is. She's a cockroach!' said Miss Moss. 'I could have her up for snatching my letter—I'm sure I could.' Still keeping on her nightdress she began to drag on her clothes.

'Oh, if I could only pay that woman, I'd give her a piece of my mind that she wouldn't forget. I'd tell her off proper.' She went over to her chest of drawers for a safety-pin, and seeing herself in the glass she gave a vague smile and shook her head. 'Well, old girl,' she murmured, 'you're up against it this time, and no mistake.' But the person in the glass made an ugly face at her.

'You silly thing,' scolded Miss Moss. 'Now what's the good of crying: you'll only make your nose red. No, you get dressed and go out and try your luck—that's what you've got to do.'

She unhooked her vanity bag from the bedpost, rooted in it, shook it, turned it inside out.

'I'll have a nice cup of tea at an A B C[1] to settle me before I go

1. The ABC (Aerated Bread Company) was a chain of tearooms with low prices.

anywhere,' she decided. 'I've got one and thrippence—yes, just one and three.'

Ten minutes later, a stout lady in blue serge, with a bunch of artificial 'parmas'[2] at her bosom, a black hat covered with purple pansies, white gloves, boots with white uppers, and a vanity bag containing one and three, sang in a low contralto voice:

Sweet-heart, remember when days are forlorn
It al-ways is dar-kest before the dawn.

But the person in the glass made a face at her, and Miss Moss went out. There were grey crabs all the way down the street slopping water over grey stone steps. With his strange, hawking cry and the jangle of the cans the milk boy went his rounds. Outside Brittweiler's Swiss House he made a splash, and an old brown cat without a tail appeared from nowhere, and began greedily and silently drinking up the spill. It gave Miss Moss a queer feeling to watch—a sinking—as you might say.

But when she came to the A B C she found the door propped open; a man went in and out carrying trays of rolls, and there was nobody inside except a waitress doing her hair and the cashier unlocking the cash-boxes. She stood in the middle of the floor but neither of them saw her.

'My boy came home last night,[3] sang the waitress.

'Oh, I say—how topping for you!' gurgled the cashier.

'Yes, wasn't it,' sang the waitress. 'He brought me a sweet little brooch. Look, it's got "Dieppe"[4] written on it.'

The cashier ran across to look and put her arm round the waitress' neck.

'Oh, I say—how topping for you.'

'Yes, isn't it,' said the waitress. 'O-oh, he is brahn. "Hullo," I said, "hullo, old mahogany." '

'Oh, I say,' gurgled the cashier, running back into her cage and nearly bumping into Miss Moss on the way. 'You are a *treat*!' Then the man with the rolls came in again, swerving past her.

'Can I have a cup of tea, Miss?' she asked.

But the waitress went on doing her hair. 'Oh,' she sang, 'we're not *open* yet.' She turned round and waved her comb at the cashier.

'*Are* we, dear?'

'Oh, no,' said the cashier. Miss Moss went out.

'I'll go to Charing Cross.[5] Yes, that's what I'll do,' she decided. 'But I won't have a cup of tea. No, I'll have a coffee. There's more

2. Parma violets.
3. That is, home from active service in World War One (1914–18).
4. A port on the northern coast of France.
5. A major railway station in the center of London.

of a tonic in coffee. . . . Cheeky, those girls are! Her boy came home last night; he brought her a brooch with "Dieppe" written on it.' She began to cross the road. . . .

'Look out, Fattie; don't go to sleep!' yelled a taxi driver. She pretended not to hear.

'No, I won't go to Charing Cross,' she decided. 'I'll go straight to Kig and Kadgit. They're open at nine. If I get there early Mr Kadgit may have something by the morning's post. . . . I'm very glad you turned up so early, Miss Moss. I've just heard from a manager who wants a lady to play. . . . I think you'll just suit him. I'll give you a card to go and see him. It's three pounds a week and all found. If I were you I'd hop round as fast as I could. Lucky you turned up so early. . . .'

But there was nobody at Kig and Kadgit's except the charwoman wiping over the 'lino' in the passage.

'Nobody here yet, Miss,' said the char.

'Oh, isn't Mr Kadgit here?' said Miss Moss, trying to dodge the pail and brush. 'Well, I'll just wait a moment, if I may.'

'You can't wait in the waiting-room, Miss. I 'aven't done it yet. Mr Kadgit's never 'ere before 'leven-thirty Saturdays. Sometimes 'e don't come at all.' And the char began crawling towards her.

'Dear me—how silly of me,' said Miss Moss. 'I forgot it was Saturday.'

'Mind your feet, *please*, Miss,' said the char. And Miss Moss was outside again.

That was one thing about Beit and Bithems; it was lively. You walked into the waiting-room, into a great buzz of conversation, and there was everybody; you knew almost everybody. The early ones sat on chairs and the later ones sat on the early ones' laps, while the gentlemen leaned negligently against the walls or preened themselves in front of the admiring ladies.

'Hello,' said Miss Moss, very gay. 'Here we are again!'

And young Mr Clayton, playing the banjo on his walking-stick, sang: 'Waiting for the Robert E. Lee.'[6]

'Mr Bithem here yet?' asked Miss Moss, taking out an old dead powder puff and powdering her nose mauve.

'Oh, yes, dear,' cried the chorus. 'He's been here for ages. We've all been waiting here for more than an hour.'

'Dear me!' said Miss Moss. 'Anything doing, do you think?'

'Oh, a few jobs going for South Africa,' said young Mr Clayton. 'Hundred and fifty a week for two years, you know.'

'Oh!' cried the chorus. 'You *are* weird, Mr Clayton. Isn't he a

6. A popular song by Lewis F. Muir, with words by L. Wolfe Gilbert, referring to a steamboat named after Robert E. Lee (1807–1870), an eminent Confederate general in the American Civil War.

cure?[7] Isn't he a *scream*, dear? Oh, Mr Clayton, you do make me laugh. Isn't he a *comic*?'

A dark, mournful girl touched Miss Moss on the arm.

'I just missed a lovely job yesterday,' she said. 'Six weeks in the provinces and then the West End. The manager said I would have got it for certain if only I'd been robust enough. He said if my figure had been fuller, the part was made for me.' She stared at Miss Moss, and the dirty dark red rose under the brim of her hat looked, somehow, as though it shared the blow with her, and was crushed, too.

'Oh, dear, that was hard lines,' said Miss Moss trying to appear indifferent. 'What was it—if I may ask?'

But the dark, mournful girl saw through her and a gleam of spite came into her heavy eyes.

'Oh, no good to you, my dear,' said she. 'He wanted someone young, you know—a dark Spanish type—my style, but more figure, that was all.'

The inner door opened and Mr Bithem appeared in his shirt sleeves. He kept one hand on the door ready to whisk back again, and held up the other.

'Look here, ladies—' and then he paused, grinned his famous grin before he said—'*and bhoys*.' The waiting-room laughed so loudly at this that he had to hold both hands up. 'It's no good waiting this morning. Come back Monday; I'm expecting several calls on Monday.'

Miss Moss made a desperate rush forward. 'Mr Bithem, I wonder if you've heard from. . . .'

'Now let me see,' said Mr Bithem slowly, staring; he had only seen Miss Moss four times a week for the past—how many weeks? 'Now, who are you?'

'Miss Ada Moss.'

'Oh, yes, yes; of course, my dear. Not yet, my dear. Now I had a call for twenty-eight ladies to-day, but they had to be young and able to hop it a bit—see? And I had another call for sixteen—but they had to know something about sand-dancing. Look here, my dear, I'm up to the eyebrows this morning. Come back on Monday week; it's no good coming before that.' He gave her a whole grin to herself and patted her fat back. 'Hearts of oak, dear lady,' said Mr Bithem, 'hearts of oak!'

At the North-East Film Company the crowd was all the way up the stairs. Miss Moss found herself next to a fair little baby thing about thirty in a white lace hat with cherries round it.

'What a crowd!' said she. 'Anything special on?'

'*Didn't* you know, dear?' said the baby, opening her immense pale eyes. 'There was a call at nine-thirty for *attractive* girls. We've all

7. A laugh, an amusing character.

been waiting for *hours*. Have you played for this company before?' Miss Moss put her head on one side. 'No, I don't think I have.'

'They're a lovely company to play for,' said the baby. 'A friend of mine has a friend who gets thirty pounds a day. . . . Have you *arcted* much for the *fil*-lums?'

'Well, I'm not an actress by profession,' confessed Miss Moss. 'I'm a contralto singer. But things have been so bad lately that I've been doing a little.'

'It's *like* that, isn't it, dear?' said the baby.

'I had a splendid education at the College of Music,' said Miss Moss, 'and I got my silver medal for singing. I've often sung at West End concerts. But I thought, for a change, I'd try my luck. . . .'

'Yes, it's *like* that, isn't it, dear?' said the baby.

At the moment a beautiful typist appeared at the top of the stairs.

'Are you all waiting for the North-East call?'

'Yes!' cried the chorus.

'Well, it's off. I've just had a phone through.'

'But look here! What about our expenses?' shouted a voice.

The typist looked down at them, and she couldn't help laughing.

'Oh, you weren't to have been *paid*. The North-East never *pay* their crowds.'

There was only a little round window at the Bitter Orange Company. No waiting-room—nobody at all except a girl, who came to the window when Miss Moss knocked, and said: 'Well?'

'Can I see the producer, please?' said Miss Moss pleasantly. The girl leaned on the window-bar, half shut her eyes and seemed to go to sleep for a moment. Miss Moss smiled at her. The girl not only frowned; she seemed to smell something vaguely unpleasant; she sniffed. Suddenly she moved away, came back with a paper and thrust it at Miss Moss.

'Fill up the form!' said she. And banged the window down.

'Can you aviate—high-dive—drive a car—buck-jump—shoot?' read Miss Moss. She walked along the street asking herself those questions. There was a high, cold wind blowing; it tugged at her, slapped her face, jeered; it knew she could not answer them. In the Square Gardens she found a little wire basket to drop the form into. And then she sat down on one of the benches to powder her nose. But the person in the pocket mirror made a hideous face at her, and that was too much for Miss Moss; she had a good cry. It cheered her wonderfully.

'Well, that's over,' she sighed. 'It's one comfort to be off my feet. And my nose will soon get cool in the air. . . . It's very nice in here. Look at the sparrows. Cheep. Cheep. How close they come. I expect somebody feeds them. No, I've nothing for you, you cheeky little things. . . .' She looked away from them. What was the big building opposite—the Café de Madrid? My goodness, what a smack that little child came down! Poor little mite! Never mind—up again. . . . By eight o'clock to-night . . . Café de Madrid. 'I could just go in and sit there and have a coffee, that's all,' thought Miss Moss: 'It's such a place for artists too. I might just have a stroke of luck. . . . A dark handsome gentleman in a fur coat comes in with a friend, and sits at my table, perhaps. "No, old chap, I've searched London for a contralto and I can't find a soul. You see, the music is difficult; have a look at it." ' And Miss Moss heard herself saying: "Excuse me, I happen to be a contralto, and I have sung that part many times." . . . "Extraordinary! Come back to my studio and I'll try your voice now." . . . Ten pounds a week. . . . Why should I feel nervous? It's not nervousness. Why shouldn't I go to the Café de Madrid? I'm a respectable woman—I'm a contralto singer. And I'm only trembling because I've had nothing to eat to-day. . . . 'A nice little piece of evidence, *my lady*.' . . . Very well, Mrs Pine. Café de Madrid. They have concerts there in the evenings. . . . "Why don't they begin?" "The contralto has not arrived." . . . "Excuse me, I happen to be a contralto; I have sung that music many times." '

It was almost dark in the café. Men, palms, red plush seats, white marble tables, waiters in aprons, Miss Moss walked through them all. Hardly had she sat down when a very stout gentleman wearing a very small hat that floated on the top of his head like a little yacht flopped into the chair opposite hers.

'Good evening!' said he.

Miss Moss said, in her cheerful way: 'Good evening!'

'Fine evening,' said the stout gentleman.

'Yes, very fine. Quite a treat, isn't it?' said she.

He crooked a sausage finger at the waiter—'Bring me a large whisky'—and turned to Miss Moss. 'What's yours?'

'Well, I think I'll take a brandy if it's all the same.'

Five minutes later the stout gentleman leaned across the table and blew a puff of cigar smoke full in her face.

'That's a tempting bit o' ribbon!' said he.

Miss Moss blushed until a pulse at the top of her head that she never had felt before pounded away.

'I always was one for pink,' said she.

The stout gentleman considered her, drumming with her fingers on the table.

'I like 'em firm and well covered,' said he.

Miss Moss, to her surprise, gave a loud snigger.

Five minutes later the stout gentleman heaved himself up. 'Well, am I goin' your way, or are you comin' mine?' he asked.

'I'll come with you, if it's all the same,' said Miss Moss. And she sailed after the little yacht out of the café.

The Man without a Temperament (1920)†

He stood at the hall door turning the ring, turning the heavy signet ring upon his little finger while his glance travelled coolly, deliberately, over the round tables and basket-chairs scattered about the glassed-in verandah. He pursed his lips—he might have been going to whistle—but he did not whistle—only turned the ring—turned the ring on his pink, freshly washed hands.

Over in the corner sat The Two Topknots, drinking a decoction they always drank at this hour—something whitish, greyish, in glasses, with little husks floating on the top—and rooting in a tin full of paper shavings for pieces of speckled biscuit, which they broke, dropped into the glasses and fished for with spoons. Their two coils of knitting, like two snakes, slumbered beside the tray.

The American Woman sat where she always sat against the glass wall, in the shadow of a great creeping thing with wide open purple eyes that pressed—that flattened itself against the glass, hungrily watching her. And she knoo it was there—she knoo it was looking at her just that way. She played up to it; she gave herself little airs. Sometimes she even pointed at it, crying: 'Isn't that the most terrible thing you've ever seen! Isn't that ghoulish!' It was on the other side of the verandah, after all . . . and besides it couldn't touch her, could it, Klaymongso?[1] She was an American Woman, wasn't she Klaymongso, and she'd just go right away to her Consul. Klaymongso, curled in her lap, with her torn antique brocade bag, a grubby handkerchief, and a pile of letters from home on top of him, sneezed for reply.

The other tables were empty. A glance passed between the American and the Topknots. She gave a foreign little shrug; they waved an understanding biscuit. But he saw nothing. Now he was still, now from his eyes you saw he listened. 'Hoo-e-zip-zoo-oo!' sounded the lift. The iron cage clanged open. Light dragging steps sounded across the hall, coming towards him. A hand, like a leaf, fell on his shoulder. A soft voice said: 'Let's go and sit over there—where we can see the drive. The trees are so lovely.' And he moved forward with the hand still on his shoulder, and the light, dragging steps beside his. He pulled out a chair and she sank into it, slowly, leaning her head against the back, her arms falling along the sides.

'Won't you bring the other up closer? It's such miles away.' But he did not move.

'Where's your shawl?' he asked.

† First published in *Art and Letters* (Spring 1920), then included in *Bliss and Other Stories* (1920).

1. Presumably the dog was named after Georges Clemenceau (1841–1929), premier of France early in the century and again from 1917 to 1920.

'Oh!' She gave a little groan of dismay. 'How silly I am, I've left it upstairs on the bed. Never mind. Please don't go for it. I shan't want it, I know I shan't.'

'You'd better have it.' And he turned and swiftly crossed the verandah into the dim hall with its scarlet plush and gilt furniture—conjuror's furniture—its Notice of Services at the English Church, its green baize board with the unclaimed letters climbing the black lattice, huge 'Presentation' clock that struck the hours at the half-hours, bundles of sticks and umbrellas and sunshades in the clasp of a brown wooden bear, past the two crippled palms, two ancient beggars at the foot of the staircase, up the marble stairs three at a time, past the life-size group on the landing of two stout peasant children with their marble pinnies full of marble grapes, and along the corridor, with its piled-up wreckage of old tin boxes, leather trunks, canvas hold-alls, to their room.

The servant girl was in their room, singing loudly while she emptied soapy water into a pail. The windows were open wide, the shutters put back, and the light glared in. She had thrown the carpets and the big white pillows over the balcony rails; the nets were looped up from the beds; on the writing table there stood a pan of fluff and match-ends. When she saw him her small impudent eyes snapped and her singing changed to humming. But he gave no sign. His eyes searched the glaring room. Where the devil was the shawl!

'*Vous desirez, Monsieur*?'[2] mocked the servant girl.

No answer. He had seen it. He strode across the room, grabbed the grey cobweb and went out, banging the door. The servant girl's voice at its loudest and shrillest followed him along the corridor.

'Oh, there you are. What happened? What kept you? The tea's here, you see. I've just sent Antonio off for the hot water. Isn't it extraordinary? I must have told him about it sixty times at least, and still he doesn't bring it. Thank you. That's very nice. One does just feel the air when one bends forward.'

'Thanks.' He took his tea and sat down in the other chair. 'No, nothing to eat.'

'Oh do! Just one, you had so little at lunch and it's hours before dinner.'

Her shawl dropped off as she bent forward to hand him the biscuits. He took one and put it in his saucer.

'Oh, those trees along the drive,' she cried, 'I could look at them for ever. They are like the most exquisite huge ferns. And you see that one with the grey-silver bark and the clusters of cream coloured flowers, I pulled down a head of them yesterday to smell

2. You want something, sir?

and the scent'—she shut her eyes at the memory and her voice thinned away, faint, airy—was like freshly ground nutmegs.' A little pause. She turned to him and smiled. 'You do know what nutmegs smell like—do you, Robert?'

And he smiled back at her. 'Now how am I going to prove to you that I do?'

Back came Antonio with not only the hot water—with letters on a salver and three rolls of paper.

'Oh, the post! Oh, how lovely! Oh, Robert, they mustn't be all for you! Have they just come, Antonio?' Her thin hands flew up and hovered over the letters that Antonio offered her, bending forward.

'Just this moment, Signora,' grinned Antonio. 'I took-a them from the postman myself. I made-a the postman give them for me.'

'Noble Antonio!' laughed she. 'There—those are mine, Robert; the rest are yours.'

Antonio wheeled sharply, stiffened, the grin went out of his face. His striped linen jacket and his flat gleaming fringe made him look like a wooden doll.

Mr. Salesby put the letters into his pocket; the papers lay on the table. He turned the ring, turned the signet ring on his little finger and stared in front of him, blinking, vacant.

But she—with her teacup in one hand, the sheets of thin paper in the other, her head tilted back, her lips open, a brush of bright colour on her cheek-bones, sipped, sipped, drank . . . drank. . . .

'From Lottie,' came her soft murmur. 'Poor dear . . . such trouble . . . left foot. She thought . . . neuritis . . . Doctor Blyth . . . flat foot . . . massage. So many robins this year . . . maid most satisfactory . . . Indian Colonel . . . every grain of rice separate . . . very heavy fall of snow.' And her wide lighted eyes looked up from the letter. 'Snow, Robert! Think of it!' And she touched the little dark violets pinned on her thin bosom and went back to the letter.

. . . Snow. Snow in London. Millie with the early morning cup of tea. 'There's been a terrible fall of snow in the night, Sir.' 'Oh, has there, Millie?' The curtains ring apart, letting in the pale, reluctant light. He raises himself in the bed; he catches a glimpse of the solid houses opposite framed in white, of their window boxes full of great sprays of white coral. . . . In the bathroom—overlooking the back garden. Snow—heavy snow over everything. The lawn is covered with a wavy pattern of cat's paws; there is a thick, thick icing on the garden table; the withered pods of the laburnum tree are white tassels; only here and there in the ivy is a dark leaf showing. . . . Warming his back at the dining-room fire, the paper drying over a chair. Millie with the bacon. 'Oh, if you please, Sir, there's two little boys come as will do the steps and front for a shilling, shall I let them?' . . . And then flying lightly, lightly down the stairs—Jinnie. 'Oh, Robert, isn't it wonderful! Oh, what a pity it has to melt. Where's the pussy-wee?' 'I'll get him from Millie' . . . 'Millie, you might just hand me up the kitten if you've got him down there.' 'Very good, Sir.' He feels the little beating heart under his hand. 'Come on, old chap, your Missus wants you.' 'Oh, Robert, do show him the snow—his first snow. Shall I open the window and give him a little piece on his paw to hold? . . .'

'Well, that's very satisfactory on the whole—very. Poor Lottie! Darling Anne! How I only wish I could send them something of this,' she cried, waving her letters at the brilliant, dazzling garden. 'More tea, Robert? Robert dear, more tea?'

'No, thanks, no. It was very good,' he drawled.

'Well mine wasn't. Mine was just like chopped hay. Oh, here comes the Honeymoon Couple.'

Half striding, half running, carrying a basket between them and rods and lines, they came up the drive, up the shallow steps.

'My! have you been out fishing?' cried the American Woman.

They were out of breath, they panted: 'Yes, yes, we have been out in a little boat all day. We have caught seven. Four are good to eat. But three we shall give away. To the children.'

Mrs Salesby turned her chair to look; the Topknots laid the snakes down. They were a very dark young couple—black hair, olive skin, brilliant eyes and teeth. He was dressed 'English fashion' in a flannel jacket, white trousers and shoes. Round his neck he wore a silk scarf; his head, with his hair brushed back, was bare. And he kept mopping his forehead, rubbing his hands with a brilliant handkerchief. Her white skirt had a patch of wet; her neck and throat were stained a deep pink. When she lifted her arms big half-hoops of perspiration showed under her arm-pits; her hair clung in wet curls to her cheeks. She looked as though her young husband had been dipping her in the sea, and fishing her out again to dry in the sun and then—in with her again—all day.

'Would Klaymongso like a fish?' they cried. Their laughing voices charged with excitement beat against the glassed-in verandah like birds, and a strange saltish smell came from the basket.

'You will sleep well to-night,' said a Topknot, picking her ear with a knitting needle while the other Topknot smiled and nodded.

The Honeymoon Couple looked at each other. A great wave seemed to go over them. They gasped, gulped, staggered a little and then came up laughing—laughing.

'We cannot go upstairs, we are too tired. We must have tea just as we are. Here—coffee. No—tea. No—coffee. Tea—coffee, Antonio!' Mrs Salesby turned.

'Robert! Robert!' Where was he? He wasn't there. Oh, there he was at the other end of the verandah, with his back turned, smoking a cigarette. 'Robert, shall we go for our little turn?'

'Right.' He stumped the cigarette into an ashtray and sauntered over, his eyes on the ground. 'Will you be warm enough?'

'Oh, quite.'

'Sure?'

'Well,' she put her hand on his arm, 'perhaps'—and gave his arm the faintest pressure—'it's not upstairs, it's only in the hall—perhaps you'd get me my cape. Hanging up.'

He came back with it and she bent her small head while he dropped it on her shoulders. Then, very stiff, he offered her his arm. She bowed sweetly to the people on the verandah while he just covered a yawn, and they went down the steps together.

'*Vous avez voo ça!*'[3] said the American Woman.

'He is not a man,' said the Two Topknots, 'he is an ox. I say to my sister in the morning and at night when we are in bed, I tell her—*No* man is he, but an ox!'

Wheeling, tumbling, swooping, the laughter of the Honeymoon Couple dashed against the glass of the verandah.

The sun was still high. Every leaf, every flower in the garden lay open, motionless, as if exhausted, and a sweet, rich, rank smell filled the quivering air. Out of the thick, fleshy leaves of a cactus there rose an aloe stem loaded with pale flowers that looked as though they had been cut out of butter; light flashed upon the lifted spears of the palms; over a bed of scarlet waxen flowers some big black insects 'zoomed-zoomed'; a great gaudy creeper, orange splashed with jet, sprawled against a wall.

'I don't need my cape after all,' said she. 'It's really too warm.' So he took it off and carried it over his arm. 'Let us go down this path here. I feel so well to-day—marvellously better. Good heavens—look at those children! And to think it's November!'

In a corner of the garden there were two brimming tubs of water. Three little girls, having thoughtfully taken off their drawers and hung them on a bush, their skirts clasped to their waists, were standing in the tubs and tramping up and down. They screamed, their hair fell over their faces, they splashed one another. But suddenly, the smallest, who had a tub to herself, glanced up and saw who was looking. For a moment she seemed overcome with terror, then clumsily she struggled and strained out of her tub, and still holding her clothes above her waist. 'The Englishman! The Englishman!' she shrieked and fled away to hide. Shrieking and screaming, the other two followed her. In a moment they were

3. "Vous avez vu ça!" Did you see that!

gone; in a moment there was nothing but the two brimming tubs and their little drawers on the bush.

'How—very—extraordinary!' said she. 'What made them so frightened? Surely they were much too young to. . . .' She looked up at him. She thought he looked pale—but wonderfully handsome with that great tropical tree behind him with its long, spiked thorns.

For a moment he did not answer. Then he met her glance, and smiling his slow smile, '*Très* rum!'[4] said he.

Très rum! Oh, she felt quite faint. Oh, why should she love him so much just because he said a thing like that. *Très* rum! That was Robert all over. Nobody else but Robert could ever say such a thing. To be so wonderful, so brilliant, so learned, and then to say in that queer, boyish voice. . . . She could have wept.

'You know you're very absurd, sometimes,' said she.

'I am,' he answered. And they walked on.

But she was tired. She had had enough. She did not want to walk any more.

'Leave me here and go for a little constitutional,[5] won't you? I'll be in one of these long chairs. What a good thing you've got my cape; you won't have to go upstairs for a rug. Thank you, Robert, I shall look at that delicious heliotrope. . . . You won't be gone long?'

'No—no. You don't mind being left?'

'Silly! I want you to go. I can't expect you to drag after your invalid wife every minute. . . . How long will you be?'

He took out his watch. 'It's just after half-past four. I'll be back at a quarter past five.'

'Back at a quarter past five,' she repeated, and she lay still in the long chair and folded her hands.

He turned away. Suddenly he was back again. 'Look here, would you like my watch?' And he dangled it before her.

'Oh!' She caught her breath. 'Very, very much.' And she clasped the watch, the watch, watch, the darling watch in her fingers. 'Now go quickly.'

The gates of the Pension Villa Excelsior were open wide, jammed open against some bold geraniums. Stooping a little, staring straight ahead, walking swiftly, he passed through them and began climbing the hill that wound behind the town like a great rope looping the villas together. The dust lay thick. A carriage came bowling along driving towards the Excelsior. In it sat the General and the Countess; they had been for his daily airing. Mr Salesby stepped to one side but the dust beat up, thick, white, stifling like wool. The Countess just had time to nudge the General.

4. 'Very rum!' *Rum* is a dated British expression for odd, peculiar.
5. A walk taken regularly to maintain health.

'There he goes,' she said spitefully.

But the General gave a loud caw and refused to look.

'It is the Englishman,' said the driver, turning round and smiling. And the Countess threw up her hands and nodded so amiably that he spat with satisfaction and gave the stumbling horse a cut.

On—on—past the finest villas in the town, magnificent places, palaces, worth coming any distance to see, past the public gardens with the carved grottoes and statues and stone animals drinking at the fountain, into a poorer quarter. Here the road ran narrow and foul between high lean houses, the ground floors of which were scooped and hollowed into stables and carpenters' shops. At a fountain ahead of him two old hags were beating linen. As he passed them they squatted back on their haunches, stared, and then their 'A-hak-kak-kak!' with the slap, slap, of the stone on the linen sounded after him.

He reached the top of the hill; he turned a corner and the town was hidden. Down he looked into a deep valley with a dried up river bed at the bottom. This side and that was covered with small dilapidated houses that had broken stone verandahs where the fruit lay drying, tomato canes in the garden, and from the gates to the doors a trellis of vines. The late sunlight, deep, golden, lay in the cup of the valley; there was a smell of charcoal in the air. In the gardens the men were cutting grapes. He watched a man standing in the greenish shade, raising up, holding a black cluster in one hand, taking the knife from his belt, cutting, laying the bunch in a flat boat-shaped basket. The man worked leisurely, silently, taking hundreds of years over the job. On the hedges on the other side of the road there were grapes small as berries, growing wild, growing among the stones. He leaned against a wall, filled his pipe, put a match to it. . . .

Leaned across a gate, turned up the collar of his mackintosh. It was going to rain. It didn't matter, he was prepared for it. You didn't expect anything else in November. He looked over the bare field. From the corner by the gate there came the smell of swedes, a great stack of them, wet, rank coloured. Two men passed walking towards the straggling village. 'Good day!' 'Good day!' By Jove! he had to hurry if he was going to catch that train home. Over the gate, across a field, over the stile, into the lane, swinging along in the drifting rain and dusk. . . . Just home in time for a bath and then a change before supper. . . . In the drawing-room; Jinnie is sitting pretty nearly in the fire. 'Oh, Robert, I didn't hear you come in. Did you have a good time? How nice you smell! A present?' 'Some bits of blackberry I picked for you. Pretty colour.' 'Oh, lovely, Robert! Dennis and Beaty are coming to supper.' Supper—cold beef, potatoes in their jackets, claret, household bread. They are gay—everybody's laughing. 'Oh, we all know Robert,' says Dennis, breathing on his eyeglasses and polishing them. 'By the way, Dennis, I picked up a very jolly little edition of. . . .'

A clock struck. He wheeled sharply. What time was it. Five? A quarter past? Back, back the way he came. As he passed through the gates he saw her on the look-out. She got up, waved and slowly she came to meet him, dragging the heavy cape. In her hand she carried a spray of heliotrope.

'You're late,' she cried gaily. 'You're three minutes late. Here's your watch, it's been very good while you were away. Did you have a nice time? Was it lovely? Tell me. Where did you go?'

'I say—put this *on*,' he said taking the cape from her.

'Yes, I will. Yes, it's getting chilly. Shall we go up to our room?'

When they reached the lift she was coughing. He frowned.

'It's nothing. I haven't been out too late. Don't be cross.' She sat down on one of the red plush chairs while he rang and rang, and then, getting no answer, kept his finger on the bell.

'Oh, Robert, do you think you ought to?'

'Ought to what?'

The door of the *salon* opened. 'What is that? Who is making that noise?' sounded from within. Klaymongso began to yelp. 'Caw! Caw! Caw!' came from the General. A Topknot darted out with one hand to her ear, opened the staff door, 'Mr Queet! Mr Queet!' she bawled. That brought the manager up at a run.

'Is that you ringing the bell, Mr Salesby? Do you want the lift? Very good, Sir. I'll take you up myself. Antonio wouldn't have been a minute, he was just taking off his apron—' And having ushered them in, the oily manager went to the door of the *salon*. 'Very sorry you should have been troubled, ladies and gentlemen.' Salesby stood in the cage, sucking in his cheeks, staring at the ceiling and turning the ring, turning the signet ring on his little finger. . . .

Arrived in their room he went swiftly over to the washstand, shook the bottle, poured her out a dose and brought it across.

'Sit down. Drink it. And don't talk.' And he stood over her while she obeyed. Then he took the glass, rinsed it and put it back in its case. 'Would you like a cushion?'

'No, I'm quite all right. Come over here. Sit down by me just a minute, will you, Robert? Ah, that's very nice.' She turned and thrust the piece of heliotrope in the lapel of his coat. 'That,' she said, 'is most becoming.' And then she leaned her head against his shoulder, and he put his arm round her.

'Robert—' her voice like a sigh—like a breath.

'Yes—'

They sat there for a long while. The sky flamed, paled; the two white beds were like two ships. . . . At last he heard the servant girl running along the corridor with the hot water cans, and gently he released her and turned on the light.

'Oh, what time is it? Oh, what a heavenly evening. Oh, Robert, I was thinking while you were away this afternoon. . . .'

They were the last couple to enter the dining-room. The Countess was there with her lorgnette[6] and her fan, the General was there with his special chair and the air cushion and the small rug over his knees. The American Woman was there showing Klaymongso a copy of the *Saturday Evening Post*. . . . 'We're having a feast of reason and a flow of soul.'[7] The Two Topknots were there feeling over the peaches and the pears in their dish of fruit, and putting aside all they considered unripe or overripe to show to the manager, and the Honeymoon Couple leaned across the table, whispering, trying not to burst out laughing.

Mr Queet, in everyday clothes and white canvas shoes, served the soup, and Antonio, in full evening dress, handed it round.

'No,' said the American Woman, 'take it away, Antonio. We can't eat soup. We can't eat anything mushy, can we, Klaymongso?'

'Take them back and fill them to the rim!' said the Topknots, and they turned and watched while Antonio delivered the message.

'What is it? Rice? Is it cooked?' The Countess peered through her lorgnette. 'Mr Queet, the General can have some of this soup if it is cooked.'

'Very good, Countess.'

The Honeymoon Couple had their fish instead.

'Give me that one. That's the one I caught. No it's not. Yes, it is. No it's not. Well, it's looking at me with its eye so it must be. Tee! Hee! Hee!' Their feet were locked together under the table.

'Robert, you're not eating again. Is anything the matter?'

'No. Off food, that's all.'

'Oh, what a bother. There are eggs and spinach coming. You don't like spinach, do you. I must tell them in future. . . .'

An egg and mashed potatoes for the General.

'Mr Queet! Mr Queet!'

'Yes, Countess.'

'The General's egg's too hard again.'

'Caw! Caw! Caw!'

'Very sorry, Countess. Shall I have you another cooked, General?'

. . . They are the first to leave the dining-room. She rises, gathering her shawl and he stands aside, waiting for her to pass, turning

6. A pair of glasses held by a long handle on one side.
7. "The Feast of Reason and the Flow of Soul," Alexander Pope, *Imitation of Horace*, Satire 1, Book 2 (1733), line 128.

the ring, turning the signet ring on his little finger. In the hall Mr Queet hovers. 'I thought you might not want to wait for the lift. Antonio's just serving the finger bowls. And I'm sorry the bell won't ring, it's out of order. I can't think what's happened.'

'Oh, I do hope. . . .' from her.

'Get in,' says he.

Mr Queet steps after them and slams the door. . . .

. . . 'Robert, do you mind if I go to bed very soon? Won't you go down to the *salon* or out into the garden? Or perhaps you might smoke a cigar on the balcony. It's lovely out there. And I like cigar smoke. I always did. But if you'd rather. . . .'

'No, I'll sit here.'

He takes a chair and sits on the balcony. He hears her moving about in the room, lightly, lightly, moving and rustling. Then she comes over to him. 'Good night, Robert.'

'Good night.' He takes her hand and kisses the palm. 'Don't catch cold.'

The sky is the colour of jade. There are a great many stars; an enormous white moon hangs over the garden. Far away lightning flutters—flutters like a wing—flutters like a broken bird that tries to fly and sinks again and again struggles.

The lights from the *salon* shine across the garden path and there is the sound of a piano. And once the American Woman, opening the French window to let Klaymongso into the garden, cries: 'Have you seen this moon?' But nobody answers.

He gets very cold sitting there, staring at the balcony rail. Finally he comes inside. The moon—the room is painted white with moonlight. The light trembles in the mirrors; the two beds seem to float. She is asleep. He sees her through the nets, half sitting, banked up with pillows, her white hands crossed on the sheet. Her white cheeks, her fair hair pressed against the pillow, are silvered over. He undresses quickly, stealthily and gets into bed. Lying there, his hands clasped behind his head. . . .

. . . In his study. Late summer. The virginia creeper just on the turn. . . .

'Well, my dear chap, that's the whole story. That's the long and the short of it. If she can't cut away for the next two years and give a decent climate a chance she don't stand a dog's—h'm—show. Better be frank about these things.' 'Oh, certainly. . . .' 'And hang it all, old man, what's to prevent you going with her? It isn't as though you've got a regular job like us wage earners. You can do what you do wherever you are—' 'Two years.' 'Yes, I should give it two years.

You'll have no trouble about letting this house you know. As a matter of fact. . . .'

. . . He is with her. 'Robert, the awful thing is—I suppose it's my illness—I simply feel I could not go alone. You see—you're everything. You're bread and wine, Robert, bread and wine. Oh, my darling—what am I saying? Of course I could, of course I won't take you away. . . .'

He hears her stirring. Does she want something?

'Boogles?'

Good Lord! She is talking in her sleep. They haven't used that name for years.

'Boogles. Are you awake?'

'Yes, do you want anything?'

'Oh, I'm going to be a bother. I'm so sorry. Do you mind? There's a wretched mosquito inside my net—I can hear him singing. Would you catch him? I don't want to move because of my heart.'

'No, don't move. Stay where you are.' He switches on the light, lifts the net. 'Where is the little beggar? Have you spotted him?'

'Yes, there, over by the corner. Oh, I do feel such a fiend to have dragged you out of bed. Do you mind dreadfully?'

'No, of course not.' For a moment he hovers in his blue and white pyjamas. Then, 'got him,' he said.

'Oh, good. Was he a juicy one?'

'Beastly.' He went over to the washstand and dipped his fingers in water. 'Are you all right now? Shall I switch off the light?'

'Yes, please. No. Boogles! Come back here a moment. Sit down by me. Give me your hand.' She turns his signet ring. 'Why weren't you asleep? Boogles, listen. Come closer. I sometimes wonder—do you mind awfully being out here with me?'

He bends down. He kisses her. He tucks her in, he smoothes the pillow.

'Rot!' he whispers.

Revelations (1920)†

From eight o'clock in the morning until about half-past eleven Monica Tyrell suffered from her nerves, and suffered so terribly that these hours were—agonizing, simply. It was not as though she could control them. 'Perhaps if I were ten years younger. . . .' she would say. For now that she was thirty-three she had a queer little

† Published in the *Athenaeum* (11 June 1920), then collected in *Bliss and Other Stories* (1920).

way of referring to her age on all occasions, of looking at her friends with grave, childish eyes and saying: 'Yes, I remember how twenty years ago. . . .' or of drawing Ralph's attention to the girls—real girls—with lovely youthful arms and throats and swift hesitating movements who sat near them in restaurants. 'Perhaps if I were ten years younger. . . .'

'Why don't you get Marie to sit outside your door and absolutely forbid anybody to come near your room until you ring your bell?'

'Oh, if it were as simple as that!' She threw her little gloves down and pressed her eyelids with her fingers in the way he knew so well. 'But in the first place I'd be so conscious of Marie sitting there, Marie shaking her finger at Rudd and Mrs Moon, Marie as a kind of cross between a wardress and a nurse for mental cases! And then, there's the post. One can't get over the fact that the post comes, and once it has come, who—who—could wait until eleven for the letters?'

His eyes grew bright; he quickly, lightly clasped her. '*My* letters, darling?'

'Perhaps,' she drawled, softly, and she drew her hand over his reddish hair, smiling too, but thinking: 'Heavens! What a stupid thing to say!'

But this morning she had been awakened by one great slam of the front door. Bang. The flat shook. What was it? She jerked up in bed, clutching the eiderdown; her heart beat. What could it be? Then she heard voices in the passage. Marie knocked, and, as the door opened, with a sharp tearing rip out flew the blind and the curtains, stiffening, flapping, jerking. The tassel of the blind knocked—knocked against the window. 'Eh-h, *voilà!*' cried Marie, setting down the tray and running. '*C'est le vent, Madame. C'est un vent insupportable.*'[1]

Up rolled the blind; the window went up with a jerk; a whitey-greyish light filled the room. Monica caught a glimpse of a huge pale sky and a cloud like a torn shirt dragging across before she hid her eyes with her sleeve.

'Marie! the curtains! Quick, the curtains!' Monica fell back into the bed and then 'Ring-ting-a-ping-ping, ring-ting-a-ping-ping.' It was the telephone. The limit of her suffering was reached; she grew quite calm. 'Go and see, Marie.'

'It is Monsieur. To know if Madame will lunch at Princes' at one-thirty to-day.' Yes, it was Monsieur himself. Yes, he had asked that the message be given to Madame immediately. Instead of replying, Monica put her cup down and asked Marie in a small wondering voice what time it was. It was half-past nine. She lay still and half

1. There we are! It's the wind, Madame. It's a dreadful wind.

closed her eyes. 'Tell Monsieur I cannot come,' she said gently. But as the door shut, anger—anger suddenly gripped her close, close, violent, half strangling her. How dared he? How dared Ralph do such a thing when he knew how agonizing her nerves were in the morning! Hadn't she explained and described and even—though lightly, of course; she couldn't say such a thing directly—given him to understand that this was the one unforgivable thing.

And then to choose this frightful windy morning. Did he think it was just a fad of hers, a little feminine folly to be laughed at and tossed aside? Why, only last night she had said: 'Ah, but you must take me seriously, too.' And he had replied: 'My darling, you'll not believe me, but I know you infinitely better than you know yourself. Every delicate thought and feeling I bow to, I treasure. Yes, laugh! I love the way your lip lifts'—and he had leaned across the table—'I don't care who sees that I adore all of you. I'd be with you on a mountain-top and have all the searchlights of the world play upon us.'

'Heavens!' Monica almost clutched her head. Was it possible he had really said that? How incredible men were! And she had loved him—how could she have loved a man who talked like that. What had she been doing ever since that dinner party months ago, when he had seen her home and asked if he might come and 'see again that slow Arabian smile'?[2] Oh, what nonsense—what utter nonsense—and yet she remembered at the time a strange deep thrill unlike anything she had ever felt before.

'Coal! Coal! Coal! Old iron! Old iron! Old iron!' sounded from below. It was all over. Understand her? He had understood nothing. That ringing her up on a windy morning was immensely significant. Would he understand that? She could almost have laughed. 'You rang me up when the person who understood me simply couldn't have.' It was the end. And when Marie said: 'Monsieur replied he would be in the vestibule in case Madame changed her mind,' Monica said: 'No, not verbena, Marie. Carnations. Two handfuls.'

A wild white morning, a tearing, rocking wind. Monica sat down before the mirror. She was pale. The maid combed back her dark hair—combed it all back—and her face was like a mask, with pointed eyelids and dark red lips. As she stared at herself in the blueish shadowy glass she suddenly felt—oh, the strangest, most tremendous excitement filling her slowly, slowly, until she wanted to fling out her arms, to laugh, to scatter everything, to shock Marie, to cry: 'I'm free. I'm free. I'm free as the wind.' And now all this vibrating, trembling, exciting, flying world was hers. It was her kingdom. No, no, she belonged to nobody but Life.

2. "Arabian" presumably suggested exotic, fascinating.

'That will do, Marie,' she stammered. 'My hat, my coat, my bag. And now get me a taxi.' Where was she going? Oh, anywhere. She could not stand this silent flat, noiseless Marie, this ghostly, quiet, feminine interior. She must be out; she must be driving quickly—anywhere, anywhere.

'The taxi is there, Madame.' As she pressed open the big outer doors of the flats the wild wind caught her and floated her across the pavement. Where to? She got in, and smiling radiantly at the cross, cold-looking driver, she told him to take her to her hairdresser's. What would she have done without her hairdresser? Whenever Monica had nowhere else to go to or nothing on earth to do she drove there. She might just have her hair waved, and by that time she'd have thought out a plan. The cross, cold driver drove at a tremendous pace, and she let herself be hurled from side to side. She wished he would go faster and faster. Oh, to be free of Princes' at one-thirty, of being the tiny kitten in the swansdown basket, of being the Arabian, and the grave, delighted child and the little wild creature. . . . 'Never again,' she cried aloud, clenching her small fist. But the cab had stopped, and the driver was standing holding the door open for her.

The hairdresser's shop was warm and glittering. It smelled of soap and burnt paper and wallflower brilliantine. There was Madame behind the counter, round, fat, white, her head like a powder-puff rolling on a black satin pin-cushion. Monica always had the feeling that they loved her in this shop and understood her—the real her—far better than many of her friends did. She was her real self here, and she and Madame had often talked—quite strangely—together. Then there was George who did her hair, young, dark, slender George. She was really fond of him.

But to-day—how curious! Madame hardly greeted her. Her face was whiter than ever, but rims of bright red showed round her blue bead eyes, and even the rings on her pudgy fingers did not flash. They were cold, dead, like chips of glass. When she called through the wall-telephone to George there was a note in her voice that had never been there before. But Monica would not believe this. No, she refused to. It was just her imagination. She sniffed greedily the warm, scented air, and passed behind the velvet curtain into the small cubicle.

Her hat and jacket were off and hanging from the peg, and still George did not come. This was the first time he had ever not been there to hold the chair for her, to take her hat and hang up her bag, dangling it in his fingers as though it were something he'd never seen before—something fairy. And how quiet the shop was! There was not a sound even from Madame. Only the wind blew, shaking the old house; the wind hooted, and the portraits of Ladies of the

Pompadour Period[3] looked down and smiled, cunning and sly. Monica wished she hadn't come. Oh, what a mistake to have come! Fatal. Fatal. Where was George? If he didn't appear the next moment she would go away. She took off the white kimono. She didn't want to look at herself any more. When she opened a big pot of cream on the glass shelf her fingers trembled. There was a tugging feeling at her heart as though her happiness—her marvellous happiness—were trying to get free.

'I'll go. I'll not stay.' She took down her hat. But just at that moment steps sounded, and, looking in the mirror, she saw George bowing in the doorway. How queerly he smiled! It was the mirror of course. She turned round quickly. His lips curled back in a sort of grin, and—wasn't he unshaved?—he looked almost green in the face.

'Very sorry to have kept you waiting,' he mumbled, sliding, gliding forward.

Oh, no, she wasn't going to stay. 'I'm afraid,' she began. But he had lighted the gas and laid the tongs across, and was holding out the kimono.

'It's a wind,' he said. Monica submitted. She smelled his fresh young fingers pinning the jacket under her chin. 'Yes, there is a wind,' said she, sinking back into the chair. And silence fell. George took out the pins in his expert way. Her hair tumbled back, but he didn't hold it as he usually did, as though to feel how fine and soft and heavy it was. He didn't say it 'was in a lovely condition.' He let it fall, and, taking a brush out of a drawer, he coughed faintly, cleared his throat and said dully: 'Yes, it's a pretty strong one, I should say it was.'

She had no reply to make. The brush fell on her hair. Oh, oh, how mournful, how mournful! It fell quick and light, it fell like leaves; and then it fell heavy, tugging like the tugging at her heart. 'That's enough,' she cried, shaking herself free.

'Did I do it too much?' asked George. He crouched over the tongs. 'I'm sorry.' There came the smell of burnt paper—the smell she loved—and he swung the hot tongs round in his hand, staring before him. 'I shouldn't be surprised if it rained.' He took up a piece of her hair, when—she couldn't bear it any longer—she stopped him. She looked at him; she saw herself looking at him in the white kimono like a nun. 'Is there something the matter here? Has something happened?' But George gave a half shrug and a grimace. 'Oh, no, Madame. Just a little occurrence.' And he took up the piece of hair again. But, oh, she wasn't deceived. That was it. Something

3. Madame de Pompadour (1721–1764), a French noblewoman and mistress of King Louis XV.

awful had happened. The silence—really, the silence seemed to come drifting down like flakes of snow. She shivered. It was cold in the little cubicle, all cold and glittering. The nickel taps and jets and sprays looked somehow almost malignant. The wind rattled the window-frame; a piece of iron banged, and the young man went on changing the tongs, crouching over her. Oh, how terrifying Life was, thought Monica. How dreadful. It is the loneliness which is so appalling. We whirl along like leaves, and nobody knows—nobody cares where we fall, in what black river we float away. The tugging feeling seemed to rise into her throat. It ached, ached; she longed to cry. 'That will do,' she whispered. 'Give me the pins.' As he stood beside her, so submissive, so silent, she nearly dropped her arms and sobbed. She couldn't bear any more. Like a wooden man the gay young George still slid, glided, handed her her hat and veil, took the note, and brought back the change. She stuffed it into her bag. Where was she going now?

George took a brush. 'There is a little powder on your coat,' he murmured. He brushed it away. And then suddenly he raised himself and, looking at Monica, gave a strange wave with the brush and said: 'The truth is, Madame, since you are an old customer—my little daughter died this morning. A first child'—and then his white face crumpled like paper, and he turned his back on her and began brushing the cotton kimono. 'Oh, oh,' Monica began to cry. She ran out of the shop into the taxi. The driver, looking furious, swung off the seat and slammed the door again. 'Where to?'

'Princes',' she sobbed. And all the way there she saw nothing but a tiny wax doll with a feather of gold hair, lying meek, its tiny hands and feet crossed. And then just before she came to Princes' she saw a flower shop full of white flowers. Oh, what a perfect thought. Lilies-of-the-valley, and white pansies, double white violets and white velvet ribbon. . . . From an unknown friend. . . . From one who understands. . . . For a Little Girl. . . . She tapped against the window, but the driver did not hear; and, anyway, they were at Princes' already.

The Escape (1920)†

It was his fault, wholly and solely his fault, that they had missed the train. What if the idiotic hotel people had refused to produce the bill? Wasn't that simply because he hadn't impressed upon the waiter at lunch that they must have it by two o'clock? Any other

† Published in the *Athenaeum* (9 July 1920) and collected in *Bliss and Other Stories* (1920).

man would have sat there and refused to move until they handed it over. But no! His exquisite belief in human nature had allowed him to get up and expect one of those idiots to bring it to their room. . . . And then, when the *voiture* did arrive, while they were still (Oh, Heavens!) waiting for change, why hadn't he seen to the arrangement of the boxes so that they could, at least, have started the moment the money had come? Had he expected her to go outside, to stand under the awning in the heat and point with her parasol? Very amusing picture of English domestic life. Even when the driver had been told how fast he had to drive he had paid no attention whatsoever—just smiled. 'Oh,' she groaned, 'if she'd been a driver she couldn't have stopped smiling herself at the absurd, ridiculous way he was urged to hurry.' And she sat back and imitated his voice: '*Allez, vite, vite*'[1] and begged the driver's pardon for troubling him. . . .

And then the station—unforgettable—with the sight of the jaunty little train shuffling away and those hideous children waving from the windows. 'Oh, why am I made to bear these things? Why am I exposed to them? . . .' The glare, the flies, while they waited, and he and the stationmaster put their heads together over the time-table, trying to find this other train, which, of course, they wouldn't catch. The people who'd gathered round, and the woman who'd held up that baby with that awful, awful head. . . . 'Oh, to care as I care—to feel as I feel, and never to be saved anything—never to know for one moment what it was to . . . to. . . .'

Her voice had changed. It was shaking now—crying now. She fumbled with her bag, and produced from its little maw a scented handkerchief. She put up her veil and, as though she were doing it for somebody else, pitifully, as though she were saying to somebody else: 'I know, my darling,' she pressed the handkerchief to her eyes.

The little bag, with its shiny, silvery jaws open, lay on her lap. He could see her powder-puff, her rouge stick, a bundle of letters, a phial of tiny black pills like seeds, a broken cigarette, a mirror, white ivory tablets with lists on them that had been heavily scored through. He thought: 'In Egypt she would be buried with those things.'

They had left the last of the houses, those small straggling houses with bits of broken pot flung among the flower-beds and half-naked hens scratching round the doorsteps. Now they were mounting a long steep road that wound round the hill and over into the next bay. The horses stumbled, pulling hard. Every five minutes, every two minutes the driver trailed the whip across them. His stout back was solid as wood; there were boils on his reddish neck, and he wore a new, a shining new straw hat. . . .

1. Go on, quickly, quickly.

There was a little wind, just enough wind to blow to satin the new leaves on the fruit trees, to stroke the fine grass, to turn to silver the smoky olives—just enough wind to start in front of the carriage a whirling, twirling snatch of dust that settled on their clothes like the finest ash. When she took out her powder-puff the powder came flying over them both.

'Oh, the dust,' she breathed, 'the disgusting, revolting dust.' And she put down her veil and lay back as if overcome.

'Why don't you put up your parasol?' he suggested. It was on the front seat, and he leaned forward to hand it to her. At that she suddenly sat upright and blazed again.

'Please leave my parasol alone! I don't want my parasol! And anyone who was not utterly insensitive would know that I'm far, far too exhausted to hold up a parasol. And with a wind like this tugging at it. . . . Put it down at once,' she flashed, and then snatched the parasol from him, tossed it into the crumpled hood behind, and subsided, panting.

Another bend of the road, and down the hill there came a troop of little children, shrieking and giggling, little girls with sun-bleached hair, little boys in faded soldiers' caps. In their hands they carried flowers—any kind of flowers—grabbed by the head, and these they offered, running beside the carriage. Lilac, faded lilac, greeny-white snowballs, one arum lily, a handful of hyacinths. They thrust the flowers and their impish faces into the carriage; one even threw into her lap a bunch of marigolds. Poor little mice! He had his hand in his trouser pocket before her. 'For Heaven's sake don't give them anything. Oh, how typical of you! Horrid little monkeys! Now they'll follow us all the way. Don't encourage them; you *would* encourage beggars'; and she hurled the bunch out of the carriage with, 'Well, do it when I'm not there, please.'

He saw the queer shock on the children's faces. They stopped running, lagged behind, and then they began to shout something, and went on shouting until the carriage had rounded yet another bend.

'Oh, how many more are there before the top of the hill is reached? The horses haven't trotted once. Surely it isn't necessary for them to walk the whole way.'

'We shall be there in a minute now,' he said, and took out his cigarette-case. At that she turned round towards him. She clasped her hands and held them against her breast; her dark eyes looked immense, imploring, behind her veil; her nostrils quivered, she bit her lip, and her head shook with a little nervous spasm. But when she spoke, her voice was quite weak and very, very calm.

'I want to ask you something. I want to beg something of you,' she said. 'I've asked you hundreds and hundreds of times before, but you've forgotten. It's such a little thing, but if you knew what it meant to me. . . .' She pressed her hands together. 'But you can't know. No human creature could know and be so cruel.' And then, slowly, deliberately, gazing at him with those huge, sombre eyes: 'I beg and implore you for the last time that when we are driving together you won't smoke. If you could imagine,' she said, 'the anguish I suffer when that smoke comes floating across my face. . . .'

'Very well,' he said. 'I won't. I forgot.' And he put the case back.

'Oh, no,' said she, and almost began to laugh, and put the back of her hand across her eyes. 'You couldn't have forgotten. Not that.'

The wind came, blowing stronger. They were at the top of the hill. 'Hoy-yip-yip-yip,' cried the driver. They swung down the road that fell into a small valley, skirted the sea coast at the bottom of it, and then coiled over a gentle ridge on the other side. Now there were houses again, blue-shuttered against the heat, with bright burning gardens, with geranium carpets flung over the pinkish walls. The coast-line was dark; on the edge of the sea a white silky fringe just stirred. The carriage swung down the hill, bumped, shook. 'Yi-ip,' shouted the driver. She clutched the sides of the seat, she closed her eyes, and he knew she felt this was happening on purpose; this swinging and bumping, this was all done—and he was responsible for it, somehow—to spite her because she had asked if they couldn't go a little faster. But just as they reached the bottom of the valley there was one tremendous lurch. The carriage nearly overturned, and he saw her eyes blaze at him, and she positively hissed, 'I suppose you are enjoying this?'

They went on. They reached the bottom of the valley. Suddenly she stood up. '*Cocher! Cocher! Arrêtez-vous!*'[2] She turned round and looked into the crumpled hood behind. 'I knew it,' she exclaimed. 'I knew it. I heard it fall, and so did you, at that last bump.'

'What? Where?'

'My parasol. It's gone. The parasol that belonged to my mother. The parasol that I prize more than—more than. . . .' She was simply beside herself. The driver turned round, his gay, broad face smiling.

'I, too, heard something,' said he, simply and gaily. 'But I thought as Monsieur and Madame said nothing. . . .'

'There. You hear that. Then you must have heard it too. So *that* accounts for the extraordinary smile on your face. . . .'

'Look here,' he said, 'it can't be gone. If it fell out it will be there still. Stay where you are. I'll fetch it.'

But she saw through that. Oh, how she saw through it! 'No, thank you.' And she bent her spiteful, smiling eyes upon him, re-

2. Driver! Driver! Stop!

gardless of the driver. 'I'll go myself. I'll walk back and find it, and trust you not to follow. For'—knowing the driver did not understand, she spoke softly, gently—'if I don't escape from you for a minute I shall go mad.'

She stepped out of the carriage. 'My bag.' He handed it to her.

'Madame prefers. . . .'

But the driver had already swung down from his seat, and was seated on the parapet reading a small newspaper. The horses stood with hanging heads. It was still. The man in the carriage stretched himself out, folded his arms. He felt the sun beat on his knees. His head was sunk on his breast. 'Hish, hish,' sounded from the sea. The wind sighed in the valley and was quiet. He felt himself, lying there, a hollow man, a parched, withered man, as it were, of ashes. And the sea sounded, 'Hish, hish.'

It was then that he saw the tree, that he was conscious of its presence just inside a garden gate. It was an immense tree with a round, thick silver stem and a great arc of copper leaves that gave back the light and yet were sombre. There was something beyond the tree—a whiteness, a softness, an opaque mass, half-hidden—with delicate pillars. As he looked at the tree he felt his breathing die away and he became part of the silence. It seemed to grow, it seemed to expand in the quivering heat until the great carved leaves hid the sky, and yet it was motionless. Then from within its depths or from beyond there came the sound of a woman's voice. A woman was singing. The warm untroubled voice floated upon the air, and it was all part of the silence as he was part of it. Suddenly, as the voice rose, soft, dreaming, gentle, he knew that it would come floating to him from the hidden leaves and his peace was shattered. What was happening to him? Something stirred in his breast. Something dark, something unbearable and dreadful pushed in his bosom, and like a great weed it floated, rocked . . . it was warm, stifling. He tried to struggle to tear at it, and at the same moment—all was over. Deep, deep, he sank into the silence, staring at the tree and waiting for the voice that came floating, falling, until he felt himself enfolded.

In the shaking corridor of the train. It was night. The train rushed and roared through the dark. He held on with both hands to the brass rail. The door of their carriage was open.

'Do not disturb yourself, Monsieur. He will come in and sit down when he wants to. He likes—he likes—it is his habit. . . . *Oui, Madame, je suis un peu souffrante. . . . Mes nerfs,*[3] Oh, but my hus-

3. Yes, Madame, I am a little unwell. My nerves.

band is never so happy as when he is travelling. He likes roughing it. . . . My husband. . . . My husband. . . .'

The voices murmured, murmured. They were never still. But so great was his heavenly happiness as he stood there he wished he might live for ever.

The Young Girl (1920)†

In her blue dress, with her cheeks lightly flushed, her blue, blue eyes, and her gold curls pinned up as though for the first time—pinned up to be out of the way for her flight—Mrs Raddick's daughter might have just dropped from this radiant heaven. Mrs Raddick's timid, faintly astonished, but deeply admiring glance looked as if she believed it, too; but the daughter didn't appear any too pleased—why should she?—to have alighted on the steps of the Casino. Indeed, she was bored—bored as though Heaven had been full of casinos with snuffy old saints for *croupiers*[1] and crowns to play with.

'You don't mind taking Hennie?' said Mrs Raddick. 'Sure you don't? There's the car, and you'll have tea and we'll be back here on this step—right here—in an hour. You see, I want her to go in. She's not been before, and it's worth seeing. I feel it wouldn't be fair to her.'

'Oh, shut up, mother,' said she wearily. 'Come along. Don't talk so much. And your bag's open; you'll be losing all your money again.'

'I'm sorry, darling,' said Mrs Raddick.

'Oh, *do* come in! I want to make money,' said the impatient voice. 'It's all jolly well for you—but I'm broke!'

'Here—take fifty francs, darling, take a hundred!' I saw Mrs Raddick pressing notes into her hand as they passed through the swing doors.

Hennie and I stood on the steps a minute, watching the people. He had a very broad, delighted smile.

'I say,' he cried, 'there's an English bulldog. Are they allowed to take dogs in there?'

'No, they're not.'

'He's a ripping chap, isn't he? I wish I had one. They're such fun. They frighten people so, and they're never fierce with their—the people they belong to.' Suddenly he squeezed my arm. 'I say, *do* look at that old woman. Who is she? Why does she look like that? Is she a gambler?'

† Published in the *Athenaeum* (29 October 1920) and collected in *The Garden Party and Other Stories* (1922).

1. Persons in charge of the gambling tables in a casino.

The ancient, withered creature, wearing a green satin dress, a black velvet cloak and a white hat with purple feathers, jerked slowly, slowly up the steps as though she were being drawn up on wires. She stared in front of her, she was laughing and nodding and cackling to herself; her claws clutched round what looked like a dirty boot-bag.

But just at that moment there was Mrs Raddick again with—*her*—and another lady hovering in the background. Mrs Raddick rushed at me. She was brightly flushed, gay, a different creature. She was like a woman who is saying 'good-bye' to her friends on the station platform, with not a minute to spare before the train starts.

'Oh, you're here, still. Isn't that lucky! You've not gone. Isn't that fine! I've had the most dreadful time with—her,' and she waved to her daughter, who stood absolutely still, disdainful, looking down, twiddling her foot on the step, miles away. 'They won't let her in. I swore she was twenty-one. But they won't believe me. I showed the man my purse; I didn't dare to do more. But it was no use. He simply scoffed. . . . And now I've just met Mrs MacEwen from New York, and she just won thirteen thousand in the *Salle Privée*[2]—and she wants me to go back with her while the luck lasts. Of course I can't leave—her. But if you'd—'

At that 'she' looked up; she simply withered her mother. 'Why can't you leave me?' she said furiously. 'What utter rot! How dare you make a scene like this? This is the last time I'll come out with you. You really are too awful for words.' She looked her mother up and down. 'Calm yourself,' she said superbly.

Mrs Raddick was desperate, just desperate. She was 'wild' to go back with Mrs MacEwen, but at the same time. . . .

I seized my courage. 'Would you—do you care to come to tea with—us?'

'Yes, yes, she'll be delighted. That's just what I wanted, isn't it darling? Mrs MacEwen . . . I'll be back here in an hour . . . or less . . . I'll—'

Mrs R. dashed up the steps. I saw her bag was open again.

So we three were left. But really it wasn't my fault. Hennie looked crushed to the earth, too. When the car was there she wrapped her dark coat round her—to escape contamination. Even her little feet looked as though they scorned to carry her down the steps to us.

'I am so awfully sorry,' I murmured as the car started.

'Oh, I don't *mind*,' said she. 'I don't *want* to look twenty-one. Who would—if they were seventeen! It's—and she gave a faint shudder—'the stupidity I loathe, and being stared at by fat old men. Beasts!'

2. "Private room," a term used in a casino for an area reserved for those risking high stakes.

Hennie gave her a quick look and then peered out of the window.

We drew up before an immense palace of pink-and-white marble with orange-trees outside the doors in gold-and-black tubs.

'Would you care to go in?' I suggested.

She hesitated, glanced, bit her lip, and resigned herself. 'Oh well, there seems nowhere else,' said she. 'Get out, Hennie.'

I went first—to find the table, of course—she followed. But the worst of it was having her little brother, who was only twelve, with us. That was the last, final straw—having that child, trailing at her heels.

There was one table. It had pink carnations and pink plates with little blue tea-napkins for sails.

'Shall we sit here?'

She put her hand wearily on the back of a white wicker chair.

'We may as well. Why not?' said she.

Hennie squeezed past her and wriggled on to a stool at the end. He felt awfully out of it. She didn't even take her gloves off. She lowered her eyes and drummed on the table. When a faint violin sounded she winced and bit her lip again. Silence.

The waitress appeared. I hardly dared to ask her. 'Tea—coffee? China tea—or iced tea with lemon?'

Really she didn't mind. It was all the same to her. She didn't really want anything. Hennie whispered, 'Chocolate!'

But just as the waitress turned away she cried out carelessly, 'Oh, you may as well bring me a chocolate, too.'

While we waited she took out a little, gold powder-box with a mirror in the lid, shook the poor little puff as though she loathed it, and dabbed her lovely nose.

'Hennie,' she said, 'take those flowers away.' She pointed with her puff to the carnations, and I heard her murmur, 'I can't bear flowers on a table.' They had evidently been giving her intense pain, for she positively closed her eyes as I moved them away.

The waitress came back with the chocolate and the tea. She put the big, frothing cups before them and pushed across my clear glass. Hennie buried his nose, emerged, with, for one dreadful moment, a little trembling blob of cream on the tip. But he hastily wiped it off like a little gentleman. I wondered if I should dare draw her attention to her cup. She didn't notice it—didn't see it—until suddenly, quite by chance, she took a sip. I watched anxiously; she faintly shuddered.

'Dreadfully sweet!' said she.

A tiny boy with a head like a raisin and a chocolate body came round with a tray of pastries—row upon row of little freaks, little inspirations, little melting dreams. He offered them to her. 'Oh, I'm not at all hungry. Take them away.'

He offered them to Hennie. Hennie gave me a swift look—it must have been satisfactory—for he took a chocolate cream, a coffee éclair, a meringue stuffed with chestnut and a tiny horn filled with fresh strawberries. She could hardly bear to watch him. But just as the boy swerved away she held up her plate.

'Oh well, give me *one*,' said she.

The silver tongs dropped one, two, three—and a cherry tartlet. 'I don't know why you're giving me all these,' she said, and nearly smiled. 'I shan't eat them; I couldn't!'

I felt much more comfortable. I sipped my tea, leaned back, and even asked if I might smoke. At that she paused, the fork in her hand, opened her eyes and really did smile. 'Of course,' said she. 'I always expect people to.'

But at that moment a tragedy happened to Hennie. He speared his pastry horn too hard, and it flew in two, and one half spilled on the table. Ghastly affair! He turned crimson. Even his ears flared, and one ashamed hand crept across the table to take what was left of the body away.

'You *utter* little beast!' said she.

Good heavens! I had to fly to the rescue. I cried hastily, 'Will you be abroad long?'

But she had already forgotten Hennie. I was forgotten, too. She was trying to remember something. . . . She was miles away.

'I—don't—know,' she said slowly, from that far place.

'I suppose you prefer it to London. It's more—more——'

When I didn't go on she came back and looked at me, very puzzled. 'More——?'

'*Enfin*[3]—gayer,' I cried, waving my cigarette.

But that took a whole cake to consider. Even then, 'Oh well, that depends!' was all she could safely say.

Hennie had finished. He was still very warm.

I seized the butterfly list off the table. 'I say—what about an ice, Hennie? What about tangerine and ginger? No, something cooler. What about a fresh pineapple cream?'

Hennie strongly approved. The waitress had her eye on us. The order was taken when she looked up from her crumbs.

'Did you say tangerine and ginger? I like ginger. You can bring me one.' And then quickly, 'I wish that orchestra wouldn't play things from the year One. We were dancing to that all last Christmas. It's too sickening!'

But it was a charming air. Now that I noticed it, it warmed me.

'I think this is rather a nice place, don't you, Hennie?' I said.

3. In a word.

Hennie said: 'Ripping!' He meant to say it very low, but it came out very high in a kind of squeak.

Nice? This place? Nice? For the first time she stared about her, trying to see what there was. . . . She blinked; her lovely eyes wondered. A very good-looking elderly man stared back at her through a monocle on a black ribbon. But him she simply couldn't see. There was a hole in the air where he was. She looked through and through him.

Finally the little flat spoons lay still on the glass plates. Hennie looked rather exhausted, but she pulled on her white gloves again. She had some trouble with her diamond wrist-watch; it got in her way. She tugged at it—tried to break the stupid little thing—it wouldn't break. Finally, she had to drag her glove over. I saw, after that, she couldn't stand this place a moment longer, and, indeed, she jumped up and turned away while I went through the vulgar act of paying for the tea.

And then we were outside again. It had grown dusky. The sky was sprinkled with small stars; the big lamps glowed. While we waited for the car to come up she stood on the step, just as before, twiddling her foot, looking down.

Hennie bounded forward to open the door and she got in and sank back with—oh—such a sigh!

'Tell him,' she gasped, 'to drive as fast as he can.'

Hennie grinned at his friend the chauffeur. *'Allie veet!'*[4] said he. Then he composed himself and sat on the small seat facing us.

The gold powder-box came out again. Again the poor little puff was shaken; again there was that swift, deadly-secret glance between her and the mirror.

We tore through the black-and-gold town like a pair of scissors tearing through brocade. Hennie had great difficulty not to look as though he were hanging on to something.

And when we reached the Casino, of course Mrs Raddick wasn't there. There wasn't a sign of her on the steps—not a sign.

'Will you stay in the car while I go and look?'

But no—she wouldn't do that. Good heavens, no! Hennie could stay. She couldn't bear sitting in a car. She'd wait on the steps.

'But I scarcely like to leave you,' I murmured. 'I'd very much rather not leave you here.'

At that she threw back her coat; she turned and faced me; her lips parted. 'Good heavens—why! I—I don't mind it a bit. I—I like waiting.' And suddenly her cheeks crimsoned, her eyes grew dark—for a moment I thought she was going to cry. 'L—let me, please,' she stammered, in a warm, eager voice. 'I like it. I love waiting!

4. "Allez vite," drive quickly.

Really—really I do! I'm always waiting—in all kinds of places. . . .'

Her dark coat fell open, and her white throat—all her soft young body in the blue dress—was like a flower that is just emerging from its dark bud.

The Stranger (1920)†

It seemed to the little crowd on the wharf that she was never going to move again. There she lay, immense, motionless on the grey crinkled water, a loop of smoke above her, an immense flock of gulls screaming and diving after the galley droppings at the stern. You could just see little couples parading—little flies walking up and down the dish on the grey crinkled tablecloth. Other flies clustered and swarmed at the edge. Now there was a gleam of white on the lower deck—the cook's apron or the stewardess perhaps. Now a tiny black spider raced up the ladder on to the bridge.

In the front of the crowd a strong-looking, middle-aged man, dressed very well, very snugly in a grey overcoat, grey silk scarf, thick gloves and dark felt hat, marched up and down, twirling his folded umbrella. He seemed to be the leader of the little crowd on the wharf and at the same time to keep them together. He was something between the sheep-dog and the shepherd.

But what a fool—what a fool he had been not to bring any glasses! There wasn't a pair of glasses between the whole lot of them.

'Curious thing, Mr Scott, that none of us thought of glasses. We might have been able to stir 'em up a bit. We might have managed a little signalling. *Don't hesitate to land. Natives harmless.* Or: *A welcome awaits you. All is forgiven.* What? Eh?'

Mr Hammond's quick, eager glance, so nervous and yet so friendly and confiding, took in everybody on the wharf, roped in even those old chaps lounging against the gangways. They knew, every man-jack of them, that Mrs Hammond was on that boat, and he was so tremendously excited it never entered his head not to believe that this marvellous fact meant something to them too. It warmed his heart towards them. They were, he decided, as decent a crowd of people—Those old chaps over by the gangways, too—fine, solid old chaps. What chests—by Jove! And he squared his own, plunged his thick-gloved hands into his pockets, rocked from heel to toe.

'Yes, my wife's been in Europe for the last ten months. On a visit

† Published in the *London Mercury* (January 1921) and collected in *The Garden Party and Other Stories*. The story, set in Auckland, is based on an incident in Mansfield's parents' lives.

to our eldest girl, who was married last year. I brought her up here, as far as Auckland, myself. So I thought I'd better come and fetch her back. Yes, yes, yes.' The shrewd grey eyes narrowed again and searched anxiously, quickly, the motionless liner. Again his overcoat was unbuttoned. Out came the thin, butter-yellow watch again, and for the twentieth—fiftieth—hundredth time he made the calculation.

'Let me see, now. It was two fifteen when the doctor's launch went off. Two fifteen. It is now exactly twenty-eight minutes past four. That is to say, the doctor's been gone two hours and thirteen minutes. Two hours and thirteen minutes! Whee-ooh!' He gave a queer little half-whistle and snapped his watch to again. 'But I think we should have been told if there was anything up—don't you, Mr Gaven?'

'Oh, yes, Mr Hammond! I don't think there's anything to—anything to worry about,' said Mr Gaven, knocking out his pipe against the heel of his shoe. 'At the same time—'

'Quite so! Quite so!' cried Mr Hammond. 'Dashed annoying!' He paced quickly up and down and came back again to his stand between Mr and Mrs Scott and Mr Gaven. 'It's getting quite dark, too,' and he waved his folded umbrella as though the dusk at least might have had the decency to keep off for a bit. But the dusk came slowly, spreading like a slow stain over the water. Little Jean Scott dragged at her mother's hand.

'I wan' my tea, mammy!' she wailed.

'I expect you do,' said Mr Hammond. 'I expect all these ladies want their tea.' And his kind, flushed, almost pitiful glance roped them all in again. He wondered whether Janey was having a final cup of tea in the saloon out there. He hoped so; he thought not. It would be just like her not to leave the deck. In that case perhaps the deck steward would bring her up a cup. If he'd been there he'd have got it for her—somehow. And for a moment he was on deck, standing over her, watching her little hand fold round the cup in the way she had, while she drank the only cup of tea to be got on board. . . . But now he was back here, and the Lord only knew when that cursed Captain would stop hanging about in the stream. He took another turn, up and down, up and down. He walked as far as the cab-stand to make sure his driver hadn't disappeared; back he swerved again to the little flock huddled in the shelter of the banana crates. Little Jean Scott was still wanting her tea. Poor little beggar! He wished he had a bit of chocolate on him.

'Here, Jean!' he said. 'Like a lift up?' And easily, gently, he swung the little girl on to a higher barrel. The movement of holding her, steadying her, relieved him wonderfully, lightened his heart.

'Hold on,' he said, keeping an arm round her.

'Oh, don't worry about *Jean*, Mr Hammond!' said Mrs Scott.

'That's all right, Mrs. Scott. No trouble. It's a pleasure. Jean's a little pal of mine, aren't you, Jean?'

'Yes, Mr Hammond,' said Jean, and she ran her finger down the dent of his felt hat.

But suddenly she caught him by the ear and gave a loud scream. 'Lo-ok, Mr Hammond! She's moving! Look, she's coming in!'

By Jove! So she was. At last! She was slowly, slowly turning round. A bell sounded far over the water and a great spout of steam gushed into the air. The gulls rose; they fluttered away like bits of white paper. And whether that deep throbbing was her engines or his heart Mr Hammond couldn't say. He had to nerve himself to bear it, whatever it was. At that moment old Captain Johnson, the harbour-master, came striding down the wharf, a leather portfolio under his arm.

'Jean'll be all right,' said Mr Scott. 'I'll hold her.' He was just in time. Mr Hammond had forgotten about Jean. He sprang away to greet old Captain Johnson.

'Well, Captain,' the eager, nervous voice rang out again, 'you've taken pity on us at last.'

'It's no good blaming me, Mr Hammond,' wheezed old Captain Johnson, staring at the liner. 'You got Mrs Hammond on board, ain't yer?'

'Yes, yes!' said Hammond, and he kept by the harbour-master's side. 'Mrs Hammond's there. Hul-lo! We shan't be long now!'

With her telephone ring-ringing, the thrum of her screw filling the air, the big liner bore down on them, cutting sharp through the dark water so that big white shavings curled to either side. Hammond and the harbour-master kept in front of the rest. Hammond took off his hat; he raked the decks—they were crammed with passengers; he waved his hat and bawled a loud, strange 'Hul-lo!' across the water, and then turned round and burst out laughing and said something—nothing—to old Captain Johnson.

'Seen her?' asked the harbour-master.

'No, not yet. Steady—wait a bit!' And suddenly, between two great clumsy idiots—'Get out of the way there!' he signed with his umbrella—he saw a hand raised—a white glove shaking a handkerchief. Another moment, and—thank God, thank God!—there she was. There was Janey. There was Mrs Hammond, yes, yes, yes—standing by the rail and smiling and nodding and waving her handkerchief.

'Well, that's first class—first class! Well, well, well!' He positively stamped. Like lightning he drew out his cigar-case and offered it to old Captain Johnson. 'Have a cigar, Captain! They're pretty good. Have a couple! Here'—and he pressed all the cigars in the case on the harbour-master—'I've a couple of boxes up at the hotel.'

'Thenks, Mr Hammond!' wheezed old Captain Johnson.

Hammond stuffed the cigar-case back. His hands were shaking, but he'd got hold of himself again. He was able to face Janey. There she was, leaning on the rail, talking to some woman and at the same time watching him, ready for him. It struck him, as the gulf of water closed, how small she looked on that huge ship. His heart was wrung with such a spasm that he could have cried out. How little she looked to have come all that long way and back by herself! Just like her, though. Just like Janey. She had the courage of a ——— And now the crew had come forward and parted the passengers; they had lowered the rails for the gangways.

The voices on shore and the voices on board flew to greet each other.

'All well?'

'All well.'

'How's mother?'

'Much better.'

'Hello, Jean!'

'Hillo, Aun' Emily!'

'Had a good voyage?'

'Splendid!'

'Shan't be long now!'

'Not long now.'

The engines stopped. Slowly she edged to the wharf-side.

'Make way there—make way—make way!' And the wharf hands brought the heavy gangways along at a sweeping run. Hammond signed to Janey to stay where she was. The old harbour-master stepped forward; he followed. As to 'ladies first', or any rot like that, it never entered his head.

'After you, Captain!' he cried genially. And, treading on the old man's heels, he strode up the gangway on to the deck in a bee-line to Janey, and Janey was clasped in his arms.

'Well, well, well! Yes, yes! Here we are at last!' he stammered. It was all he could say. And Janey emerged, and her cool little voice—the only voice in the world for him—said,

'Well, darling! Have you been waiting long?'

No; not long. Or, at any rate, it didn't matter. It was over now. But the point was, he had a cab waiting at the end of the wharf. Was she ready to go off? Was her luggage ready? In that case they could cut off sharp with her cabin luggage and let the rest go hang until to-morrow. He bent over her and she looked up with her familiar half-smile. She was just the same. Not a day changed. Just as he'd always known her. She laid her small hand on his sleeve.

'How are the children, John?' she asked.

(Hang the children!) 'Perfectly well. Never better in their lives.'

'Haven't they sent me letters?'

'Yes, yes—of course! I've left them at the hotel for you to digest later on.'

'We can't go quite so fast,' said she. 'I've got people to say good-bye to—and then there's the Captain.' As his face fell she gave his arm a small understanding squeeze. 'If the Captain comes off the bridge I want you to thank him for having looked after your wife so beautifully.' Well, he'd got her. If she wanted another ten minutes—As he gave way she was surrounded. The whole first-class seemed to want to say good-bye to Janey.

'Good-bye, *dear* Mrs Hammond! And next time you're in Sydney I'll *expect* you.'

'Darling Mrs Hammond! You won't forget to write to me, will you?'

'Well, Mrs Hammond, what this boat would have been without you!'

It was as plain as a pikestaff that she was by far the most popular woman on board. And she took it all—just as usual. Absolutely composed. Just her little self—just Janey all over; standing there with her veil thrown back. Hammond never noticed what his wife had on. It was all the same to him whatever she wore. But to-day he did notice that she wore a black 'costume'—didn't they call it?—with white frills, trimmings he supposed they were, at the neck and sleeves. All this while Janey handed him round.

'John, dear!' And then: 'I want to introduce you to—'

Finally they did escape, and she led the way to her state-room. To follow Janey down the passage that she knew so well—that was so strange to him; to part the green curtains after her and to step into the cabin that had been hers gave him exquisite happiness. But—confound it!—the stewardess was there on the floor, strapping up the rugs.

'That's the last, Mrs Hammond,' said the stewardess, rising and pulling down her cuffs.

He was introduced again, and then Janey and the stewardess disappeared into the passage. He heard whisperings. She was getting the tipping business over, he supposed. He sat down on the striped sofa and took his hat off. There were the rugs she had taken with her; they looked good as new. All her luggage looked fresh, perfect. The labels were written in her beautiful little clear hand—'Mrs. John Hammond'.

'Mrs John Hammond!' He gave a long sigh of content and leaned back, crossing his arms. The strain was over. He felt he could have sat there for ever sighing his relief—the relief at being rid of that horrible tug, pull, grip on his heart. The danger was over. That was the feeling. They were on dry land again.

But at that moment Janey's head came round the corner.

'Darling—do you mind? I just want to go and say good-bye to the doctor.'

Hammond started up. 'I'll come with you.'

'No, no!' she said. 'Don't bother. I'd rather not. I'll not be a minute.'

And before he could answer she was gone. He had half a mind to run after her; but instead he sat down again.

Would she really not be long? What was the time now? Out came the watch; he stared at nothing. That was rather queer of Janey, wasn't it? Why couldn't she have told the stewardess to say good-bye for her? Why did she have to go chasing after the ship's doctor? She could have sent a note from the hotel even if the affair had been urgent. Urgent? Did it—could it mean that she had been ill on the voyage—she was keeping something from him? That was it! He seized his hat. He was going off to find that fellow and to wring the truth out of him at all costs. He thought he'd noticed just something. She was just a touch too calm—too steady. From the very first moment———.

The curtains rang. Janey was back. He jumped to his feet.

'Janey, have you been ill on this voyage? You have!'

'Ill?' Her airy little voice mocked him. She stepped over the rugs, came up close, touched his breast, and looked up at him.

'Darling,' she said, 'don't frighten me. Of course I haven't! Whatever makes you think I have? Do I look ill?'

But Hammond didn't see her. He only felt that she was looking at him and that there was no need to worry about anything. She was here to look after things. It was all right. Everything was.

The gentle pressure of her hand was so calming that he put his over hers to hold it there. And she said:

'Stand still. I want to look at you. I haven't seen you yet. You've had your beard beautifully trimmed, and you look—younger, I think, and decidedly thinner! Bachelor life agrees with you.'

'Agrees with me!' He groaned for love and caught her close again. And again, as always, he had the feeling he was holding something that never was quite his—his. Something too delicate, too precious, that would fly away once he let go.

'For God's sake let's get off to the hotel so that we can be by ourselves!' And he rang the bell hard for some one to look sharp with the luggage.

Walking down the wharf together she took his arm. He had her on his arm again. And the difference it made to get into the cab after Janey—to throw the red-and-yellow striped blanket round them both—to tell the driver to hurry because neither of them had had any tea. No more going without his tea or pouring out his own. She was back. He turned to her, squeezed her hand, and said gently, teasingly, in the 'special' voice he had for her: 'Glad to be home again, dearie?' She smiled; she didn't even bother to answer, but gently she drew his hand away as they came to the lighted streets.

'We've got the best room in the hotel,' he said. 'I wouldn't be put off with another. And I asked the chambermaid to put in a bit of a fire in case you felt chilly. She's a nice, attentive girl. And I thought now we were here we wouldn't bother to go home to-morrow, but spend the day looking round and leave the morning after. Does that suit you? There's no hurry, is there? The children will have you soon enough. . . . I thought a day's sight-seeing might make a nice break in your journey—eh, Janey?'

'Have you taken the tickets for the day after?' she asked.

'I should think I have!' He unbuttoned his overcoat and took out his bulging pocket-book. 'Here we are! I reserved a first-class carriage to Napier. There it is——"Mr *and* Mrs John Hammond". I thought we might as well do ourselves comfortably, and we don't want other people butting in, do we? But if you'd like to stop here a bit longer—?'

'Oh, no!' said Janey quickly. 'Not for the world! The day after tomorrow, then. And the children—'

But they had reached the hotel. The manager was standing in the broad, brilliantly-lighted porch. He came down to greet them. A porter ran from the hall for their boxes.

'Well, Mr Arnold, here's Mrs Hammond at last!'

The manager led them through the hall himself and pressed the elevator-bell. Hammond knew there were business pals of his sitting at the little hall tables having a drink before dinner. But he wasn't going to risk interruption; he looked neither to the right nor the left. They could think what they pleased. If they didn't understand, the more fools they—and he stepped out of the lift, unlocked the door of their room, and shepherded Janey in. The door shut. Now, at last, they were alone together. He turned up the light. The curtains were drawn; the fire blazed. He flung his hat on to the huge bed and went towards her.

But—would you believe it!—again they were interrupted. This time it was the porter with the luggage. He made two journeys of it, leaving the door open in between, taking his time, whistling through his teeth in the corridor. Hammond paced up and down the room, tearing off his gloves, tearing off his scarf. Finally he flung his overcoat on to the bedside.

At last the fool was gone. The door clicked. Now they *were* alone. Said Hammond: 'I feel I'll never have you to myself again. These cursed people! Janey'—and he bent his flushed, eager gaze upon her—'let's have dinner up here. If we go down to the restaurant we'll be interrupted, and then there's the confounded music' (the music he'd praised so highly, applauded so loudly last night!). 'We shan't be able to hear each other speak. Let's have something up here in front of the fire. It's too late for tea. I'll order a little supper, shall I? How does the idea strike you?'

'Do, darling!' said Janey. 'And while you're away—the children's letters—'

'Oh, later on will do!' said Hammond.

'But then we'd get it over,' said Janey. 'And I'd first have time to—'

'Oh, I needn't go down!' explained Hammond. 'I'll just ring and give the order . . . you don't want to send me away, do you?'

Janey shook her head and smiled.

'But you're thinking of something else. You're worrying about something,' said Hammond. 'What is it? Come and sit here—come and sit on my knee before the fire.'

'I'll just unpin my hat,' said Janey, and she went over to the dressing-table. 'A-ah!' She gave a little cry.

'What is it?'

'Nothing, darling. I've just found the children's letters. That's all right! They will keep. No hurry now!' She turned to him, clasping them. She tucked them into her frilled blouse. She cried quickly, gaily: 'Oh, how typical this dressing-table is of you!'

'Why? What's the matter with it?' said Hammond.

'If it were floating in eternity I should say "John!" ' laughed Janey, staring at the big bottle of hair tonic, the wicker bottle of eau-de-Cologne, the two hair-brushes, and a dozen new collars tied with pink tape. 'Is this all your luggage?'

'Hang my luggage!' said Hammond; but all the same he liked being laughed at by Janey. 'Let's talk. Let's get down to things. Tell me'—and as Janey perched on his knees he leaned back and drew her into the deep, ugly chair—'tell me you're really glad to be back, Janey.'

'Yes, darling, I am glad,' she said.

But just as when he embraced her he felt she would fly away, so Hammond never knew—never knew for dead certain that she was as glad as he was. How could he know? Would he ever know? Would he always have this craving—this pang like hunger, somehow, to make Janey so much part of him that there wasn't any of her to escape? He wanted to blot out everybody, everything. He wished now he'd turned off the light. That might have brought her nearer. And now those letters from the children rustled in her blouse. He could have chucked them into the fire.

'Janey,' he whispered.

'Yes, dear?' She lay on his breast, but so lightly, so remotely. Their breathing rose and fell together.

'Janey!'

'What is it?'

'Turn to me,' he whispered. A slow, deep flush flowed into his forehead. 'Kiss me, Janey! You kiss me!'

It seemed to him there was a tiny pause—but long enough for him to suffer torture—before her lips touched his, firmly, lightly—kissing them as she always kissed him, as though the kiss—how could he describe it?—confirmed what they were saying, signed the contract. But that wasn't what he wanted; that wasn't at all what he thirsted for. He felt suddenly, horribly tired.

'If you knew,' he said, opening his eyes, 'what it's been like—waiting to-day. I thought the boat never would come in. There we were, hanging about. What kept you so long?'

She made no answer. She was looking away from him at the fire. The flames hurried—hurried over the coals, flickered, fell.

'Not asleep, are you?' said Hammond, and he jumped her up and down.

'No,' she said. And then: 'Don't do that, dear. No, I was thinking. As a matter of fact,' she said, 'one of the passengers died last night—a man. That's what held us up. We brought him in—I mean, he wasn't buried at sea. So, of course, the ship's doctor and the shore doctor—'

'What was it?' asked Hammond uneasily. He hated to hear of death. He hated this to have happened. It was, in some queer way, as though he and Janey had met a funeral on their way to the hotel.

'Oh, it wasn't anything in the least infectious!' said Janey. She was speaking scarcely above her breath. 'It was *heart*.' A pause. 'Poor fellow!' she said. 'Quite young.' And she watched the fire flicker and fall. 'He died in my arms,' said Janey.

The blow was so sudden that Hammond thought he would faint. He couldn't move; he couldn't breathe. He felt all his strength flowing—flowing into the big dark chair, and the big dark chair held him fast, gripped him, forced him to bear it.

'What?' he said dully. 'What's that you say?'

'The end was quite peaceful,' said the small voice. 'He just'—and Hammond saw her lift her gentle hand—'breathed his life away at the end.' And her hand fell.

'Who—else was there?' Hammond managed to ask.

'Nobody. I was alone with him.'

Ah, my God, what was she saying! What was she doing to him! This would kill him! And all the while she spoke:

'I saw the change coming and I sent the steward for the doctor, but the doctor was too late. He couldn't have done anything, anyway.'

'But—why *you*, why *you*?' moaned Hammond.

At that Janey turned quickly, quickly searched his face.

'You don't *mind*, John, do you?' she asked. 'You don't—It's nothing to do with you and me.'

Somehow or other he managed to shake some sort of smile at her. Somehow or other he stammered: 'No—go—on, go on! I want you to tell me.'

'But, John darling—'

'Tell me, Janey!'

'There's nothing to tell,' she said, wondering. 'He was one of the first-class passengers. I saw he was very ill when he came on board. . . . But he seemed to be so much better until yesterday. He had a severe attack in the afternoon—excitement—nervousness, I think, about arriving. And after that he never recovered.'

'But why didn't the stewardess—'

'Oh, my dear—the stewardess!' said Janey. 'What would he have felt? And besides . . . he might have wanted to leave a message . . . to—'

'Didn't he?' muttered Hammond. 'Didn't he say anything?'

'No, darling, not a word!' She shook her head softly. 'All the time I was with him he was too weak . . . he was too weak even to move a finger. . . .'

Janey was silent. But her words, so light, so soft, so chill, seemed to hover in the air, to rain into his breast like snow.

The fire had gone red. Now it fell in with a sharp sound and the room was colder. Cold crept up his arms. The room was huge, immense, glittering. It filled his whole world. There was the great blind bed, with his coat flung across it like some headless man saying his prayers. There was the luggage, ready to be carried away again, anywhere, tossed into trains, carted on to boats.

. . . 'He was too weak. He was too weak to move a finger.' And yet he died in Janey's arms. She—who'd never—never once in all these years—never on one single solitary occasion——

No; he mustn't think of it. Madness lay in thinking of it. No, he wouldn't face it. He couldn't stand it. It was too much to bear!

And now Janey touched his tie with her fingers. She pinched the edges of the tie together.

'You're not—sorry I told you, John darling? It hasn't made you sad? It hasn't spoilt our evening—our being alone together?'

But at that he had to hide his face. He put his face into her bosom and his arms enfolded her.

Spoilt their evening! Spoilt their being alone together! They would never be alone together again.

Miss Brill (1920)†

Although it was so brilliantly fine—the blue sky powdered with gold and great spots of light like white wine splashed over the Jardins Publiques—Miss Brill was glad that she had decided on her fur. The air was motionless, but when you opened your mouth there was just a faint chill, like a chill from a glass of iced water before you sip, and now and again a leaf came drifting—from nowhere, from the sky. Miss Brill put up her hand and touched her fur. Dear little thing! It was nice to feel it again. She had taken it out of its box that afternoon, shaken out the moth-powder, given it a good brush, and rubbed the life back into the dim little eyes. 'What has been happening to me?' said the sad little eyes. Oh, how sweet it was to see them snap at her again from the red eiderdown! . . . But the nose, which was of some black composition, wasn't at all firm. It must have had a knock, somehow. Never mind—a little dab of black sealing-wax when the time came—when it was absolutely necessary. . . . Little rogue! Yes, she really felt like that about it. Little rogue biting its tail just by her left ear. She could have taken it off and laid it on her lap and stroked it. She felt a tingling in her hands and arms, but that came from walking, she supposed. And when she breathed, something light and sad—no, not sad, exactly—something gentle seemed to move in her bosom.

There were a number of people out this afternoon, far more than last Sunday. And the band sounded louder and gayer. That was because the Season had begun. For although the band played all the year round on Sundays, out of season it was never the same. It was like some one playing with only the family to listen; it didn't care how it played if there weren't any strangers present. Wasn't the conductor wearing a new coat, too? She was sure it was new. He scraped with his foot and flapped his arms like a rooster about to crow, and the bandsmen sitting in the green rotunda blew out their cheeks and glared at the music. Now there came a little 'flutey' bit—very pretty!—a little chain of bright drops. She was sure it would be repeated. It was; she lifted her head and smiled.

Only two people shared her 'special' seat: a fine old man in a velvet coat, his hands clasped over a huge carved walking-stick, and a big old woman, sitting upright, with a roll of knitting on her embroidered apron. They did not speak. This was disappointing, for Miss Brill always looked forward to the conversation. She had be-

† Published in the *Athenaeum*, 26 November 1920, and collected in *The Garden Party and Other Stories* (1922).

come really quite expert, she thought, at listening as though she didn't listen, at sitting in other people's lives just for a minute while they talked round her.

She glanced, sideways, at the old couple. Perhaps they would go soon. Last Sunday, too, hadn't been as interesting as usual. An Englishman and his wife, he wearing a dreadful Panama hat and she button boots. And she'd gone on the whole time about how she ought to wear spectacles; she knew she needed them; but that it was no good getting any; they'd be sure to break and they'd never keep on. And he'd been so patient. He'd suggested everything—gold rims, the kind that curved round your ears, little pads inside the bridge. No, nothing would please her. 'They'll always be sliding down my nose!' Miss Brill had wanted to shake her.

The old people sat on the bench, still as statues. Never mind, there was always the crowd to watch. To and fro, in front of the flower-beds and the band rotunda, the couples and groups paraded, stopped to talk, to greet, to buy a handful of flowers from the old beggar who had his tray fixed to the railings. Little children ran among them, swooping and laughing; little boys with big white silk bows under their chins, little girls, little French dolls, dressed up in velvet and lace. And sometimes a tiny staggerer came suddenly rocking into the open from under the trees, stopped, stared, as suddenly sat down 'flop', until its small high-stepping mother, like a young hen, rushed scolding to its rescue. Other people sat on the benches and green chairs, but they were nearly always the same, Sunday after Sunday, and—Miss Brill had often noticed—there was something funny about nearly all of them. They were odd, silent, nearly all old, and from the way they stared they looked as though they'd just come from dark little rooms or even—even cupboards!

Behind the rotunda the slender trees with yellow leaves down drooping, and through them just a line of sea, and beyond the blue sky with gold-veined clouds.

Tum-tum-tum tiddle-um! tiddle-um! tum tiddley-um tum ta! blew the band.

Two young girls in red came by and two young soldiers in blue met them, and they laughed and paired and went off arm-in-arm. Two peasant women with funny straw hats passed, gravely, leading beautiful smoke-coloured donkeys. A cold, pale nun hurried by. A beautiful woman came along and dropped her bunch of violets, and a little boy ran after to hand them to her, and she took them and threw them away as if they'd been poisoned. Dear me! Miss Brill didn't know whether to admire that or not! And now an ermine toque[1] and a gentleman in grey met just in front of her. He was tall,

1. A small brimless hat. Ermine: the white winter fur of the stoat.

stiff, dignified, and she was wearing the ermine toque she'd bought when her hair was yellow. Now everything, her hair, her face, even her eyes, was the same colour as the shabby ermine, and her hand, in its cleaned glove, lifted to dab her lips, was a tiny yellowish paw. Oh, she was so pleased to see him—delighted! She rather thought they were going to meet that afternoon. She described where she'd been—everywhere, here, there, along by the sea. The day was so charming—didn't he agree? And wouldn't he, perhaps? . . . But he shook his head, lighted a cigarette, slowly breathed a great deep puff into her face, and, even while she was still talking and laughing, flicked the match away and walked on. The ermine toque was alone; she smiled more brightly than ever. But even the band seemed to know what she was feeling and played more softly, played tenderly, and the drum beat, 'The Brute! The Brute!' over and over. What would she do? What was going to happen now? But as Miss Brill wondered, the ermine toque turned, raised her hand as though she'd seen some one else, much nicer, just over there, and pattered away. And the band changed again and played more quickly, more gaily than ever, and the old couple on Miss Brill's seat got up and marched away, and such a funny old man with long whiskers hobbled along in time to the music and was nearly knocked over by four girls walking abreast.

Oh, how fascinating it was! How she enjoyed it! How she loved sitting here, watching it all! It was like a play. It was exactly like a play. Who could believe the sky at the back wasn't painted? But it wasn't till a little brown dog trotted on solemn and then slowly trotted off, like a little 'theatre' dog, a little dog that had been drugged, that Miss Brill discovered what it was that made it so exciting. They were all on the stage. They weren't only the audience, not only looking on; they were acting. Even she had a part and came every Sunday. No doubt somebody would have noticed if she hadn't been there; she was part of the performance after all. How strange she'd never thought of it like that before! And yet it explained why she made such a point of starting from home at just the same time each week—so as not to be late for the performance—and it also explained why she had quite a queer, shy feeling at telling her English pupils how she spent her Sunday afternoons. No wonder! Miss Brill nearly laughed out loud. She was on the stage. She thought of the old invalid gentleman to whom she read the newspaper four afternoons a week while he slept in the garden. She had got quite used to the frail head on the cotton pillow, the hollowed eyes, the open mouth and the high pinched nose. If he'd been dead she mightn't have noticed for weeks; she wouldn't have minded. But suddenly he knew he was having the paper read to him by an actress! 'An actress!' The old head lifted; two points of light quivered in the old eyes. 'An actress—are ye?' And Miss Brill smoothed the newspaper as though it were the manuscript of her part and said gently: 'Yes, I have been an actress for a long time.'

The band had been having a rest. Now they started again. And what they played was warm, sunny, yet there was just a faint chill—a something what was it?—not sadness—no, not sadness—a something that made you want to sing. The tune lifted, lifted, the light shone; and it seemed to Miss Brill that in another moment all of them, all the whole company, would begin singing. The young ones, the laughing ones who were moving together, they would begin, and the men's voices, very resolute and brave, would join them. And then she too, she too, and the others on the benches—they would come in with a kind of accompaniment—something low, that scarcely rose or fell, something so beautiful—moving. . . . And Miss Brill's eyes filled with tears and she looked smiling at all the other members of the company. Yes, we understand, we understand, she thought—though what they understood she didn't know.

Just at that moment a boy and a girl came and sat down where the old couple had been. They were beautifully dressed; they were in love. The hero and heroine, of course, just arrived from his father's yacht. And still soundlessly singing, still with that trembling smile, Miss Brill prepared to listen.

'No, not now,' said the girl. 'Not here, I can't.'

'But why? Because of that stupid old thing at the end there?' asked the boy. 'Why does she come here at all—who wants her? Why doesn't she keep her silly old mug at home?'

'It's her fu-fur which is so funny,' giggled the girl. 'It's exactly like a fried whiting[2].'

'Ah, be off with you!' said the boy in an angry whisper. Then: 'Tell me, ma petite chèrie—'

'No, not here,' said the girl. 'Not *yet*.'

On her way home she usually bought a slice of honey-cake at the baker's. It was her Sunday treat. Sometimes there was an almond in her slice, sometimes not. It made a great difference. If there was an almond it was like carrying home a tiny present—a surprise—something that might very well not have been there. She hurried on the almond Sundays and struck the match for the kettle in quite a dashing way.

But to-day she passed the baker's by, climbed the stairs, went into the little dark room—her room like a cupboard—and sat down on the red eiderdown. She sat there for a long time. The box that the fur came out of was on the bed. She unclasped the necklet

2. A narrow-bodied fish of the cod family.

quickly; quickly, without looking, laid it inside. But when she put the lid on she thought she heard something crying.

Poison (1920)†

The post was very late. When we came back from our walk after lunch it still had not arrived.

'*Pas encore, Madame*,'[1] sang Annette, scurrying back to her cooking.

We carried our parcels into the dining-room. The table was laid. As always, the sight of the table laid for two—for two people only—and yet so finished, so perfect, there was no possible room for a third, gave me a queer, quick thrill as though I'd been struck by that silver lightning that quivered over the white cloth, the brilliant glasses, the shallow bowl of freesias.

'Blow the old postman! Whatever can have happened to him?' said Beatrice. 'Put those things down, dearest.'

'Where would you like them. . . ?'

She raised her head; she smiled her sweet, teasing smile.

'Anywhere—Silly.'

But I knew only too well that there was no such place for her, and I would have stood holding the squat liqueur bottle and the sweets for months, for years, rather than risk giving another tiny shock to her exquisite sense of order.

'Here—I'll take them.' She plumped them down on the table with her long gloves and a basket of figs. 'The Luncheon Table. Short story by—by—' She took my arm. 'Let's go on to the terrace—' and I felt her shiver. '*Ça sent*,' she said faintly, '*de la cuisine*. . . .'[2]

I had noticed lately—we had been living in the south for two months—that when she wished to speak of food, or the climate, or, playfully, of her love for me, she always dropped into French.

We perched on the balustrade under the awning. Beatrice leaned over gazing down—down to the white road with its guard of cactus spears. The beauty of her ear, just her ear, the marvel of it was so great that I could have turned from regarding it to all that sweep of glittering sea below and stammered: 'You know—her ear! She has ears that are simply the most. . . .'

She was dressed in white, with pearls round her throat and lilies-of-the-valley tucked into her belt. On the third finger of her left hand she wore one pearl ring—no wedding ring.

† Written in 1920, and published after Mansfield's death, in *Something Childish and Other Stories* (1924).

1. Not yet, Madam.
2. There's the smell of cooking.

'Why should I, *mon ami*? Why should we pretend? Who could possibly care?'

And of course I agreed, though privately, in the depths of my heart, I would have given my soul to have stood beside her in a large, yes, a large, fashionable church, crammed with people, with old reverend clergymen, with *The Voice that breathed o'er Eden*,[3] with palms and the smell of scent, knowing there was a red carpet and confetti outside, and somewhere, a wedding-cake and champagne and a satin shoe to throw after the carriage—if I could have slipped our wedding-ring on to her finger.

Not because I cared for such horrible shows, but because I felt it might possibly perhaps lessen this ghastly feeling of absolute freedom, *her* absolute freedom, of course.

Oh, God! What torture happiness was—what anguish! I looked up at the villa, at the windows of our room hidden so mysteriously behind the green straw blinds. Was it possible that she ever came moving through the green light and smiling that secret smile, that languid, brilliant smile that was just for me? She put her arm round my neck; the other hand softly, terribly, brushed back my hair.

'Who are you?' Who was she? She was—Woman.

. . . On the first warm evening in Spring, when lights shone like pearls through the lilac air and voices murmured in the fresh-flowering gardens, it was she who sang in the tall house with the tulle curtains. As one drove in the moonlight through the foreign city hers was the shadow that fell across the quivering gold of the shutters. When the lamp was lighted, in the new-born stillness her steps passed your door. And she looked out into the autumn twilight, pale in her furs, as the automobile swept by. . . .

In fact, to put it shortly, I was twenty-four at the time. And when she lay on her back, with the pearls slipped under her chin, and sighed 'I'm thirsty, dearest. *Donne-moi un orange*,'[4] I would gladly, willingly, have dived for an orange into the jaws of a crocodile—if crocodiles ate oranges.

> 'Had I two little feathery wings
> And were a little feathery bird . . .'[5]

sang Beatrice.

I seized her hand. 'You wouldn't fly away?'

'Not far. Not further than the bottom of the road.'

'Why on earth there?'

She quoted: 'He cometh not, she said. . . .'[6]

3. From the hymn by John Keble, "Holy Matrimony," 1857.
4. Give me an orange.
5. Samuel Taylor Coleridge, "Something Childish, but Very Natural," 1799, ll. 1–2.
6. Alfred Tennyson, "Mariana," 1830, has the refrain:
    She only said, "The day is dreary,
    He cometh not, she said."

'Who? The silly old postman? But you're not expecting a letter.'

'No, but it's maddening all the same. Ah!' Suddenly she laughed and leaned against me. 'There he is—look—like a blue beetle.'

And we pressed our cheeks together and watched the blue beetle beginning to climb.

'Dearest,' breathed Beatrice. And the word seemed to linger in the air, to throb in the air like the note of a violin.

'What is it?'

'I don't know,' she laughed softly. 'A wave of—a wave of affection, I suppose.'

I put my arm round her. 'Then you wouldn't fly away?'

And she said rapidly and softly: 'No! No! Not for worlds. Not really. I love this place. I've loved being here. I could stay here for years, I believe. I've never been so happy as I have these last two months, and you've been so perfect to me, dearest, in every way.'

This was such bliss—it was so extraordinary, so unprecedented, to hear her talk like this that I had to try to laugh it off.

'Don't! You sound as if you were saying good-bye.'

'Oh, nonsense, nonsense. You mustn't say such things even in fun!' She slid her little hand under my white jacket and clutched my shoulder. 'You've been happy, haven't you?'

'Happy? Happy? O, God—if you knew what I feel at this moment. . . . Happy! My Wonder! My Joy!'

I dropped off the balustrade and embraced her, lifting her up in my arms. And while I held her lifted I pressed my face in her breast and muttered: 'You *are* mine?' And for the first time in all the desperate months I'd known her, even counting the last month of—surely—Heaven—I believed her absolutely when she answered:

'Yes, I am yours.'

The creak of the gate and the postman's steps on the gravel drew us apart. I was dizzy for the moment. I simply stood there, smiling, I felt rather stupidly. Beatrice walked over to the cane chairs.

'You go—go for the letters,' said she.

I—well—I almost reeled away. But I was too late. Annette came running. '*Pas de lettres*,[7] said she.

My reckless smile in reply as she handed me the paper must have surprised her. I was wild with joy. I threw the paper up into the air and sang out:

'No letters, darling!' as I came over to where the beloved woman was lying in the long chair.

For a moment she did not reply. Then she said slowly as she tore

7. No letters.

off the newspaper wrapper: 'The world forgetting, *by* the world forgot.'[8]

There are times when a cigarette is just the very one thing that will carry you over the moment. It is more than a confederate, even; it is a secret, perfect little friend who knows all about it and understands absolutely. While you smoke you look down at it—smile or frown, as the occasion demands; you inhale deeply and expel the smoke in a slow fan. This was one of those moments. I walked over to the magnolia and breathed my fill of it. Then I came back and leaned over her shoulder. But quickly she tossed the paper away on to the stone.

'There's nothing in it,' said she. 'Nothing. There's only some poison trial. Either some man did or didn't murder his wife, and twenty thousand people have sat in court every day and two million words have been wired all over the world after each proceeding.'

'Silly world!' said I, flinging into another chair. I wanted to forget the paper, to return, but cautiously, of course, to that moment before the postman came. But when she answered I knew from her voice the moment was over for now. Never mind. I was content to wait—five hundred years, if need be—now that I knew.

'Not so very silly,' said Beatrice. 'After all it isn't only morbid curiosity on the part of the twenty thousand.'

'What is it, darling?' Heavens knows I didn't care.

'Guilt!' she cried. 'Guilt! Didn't you realise that? They're fascinated like sick people are fascinated by anything—any scrap of news about their own case. The man in the dock may be innocent enough, but the people in court are nearly all of them poisoners. Haven't you ever thought'—she was pale with excitement—'of the amount of poisoning that goes on: It's the exception to find married people who don't poison each other—married people and lovers. Oh,' she cried, 'the number of cups of tea, glasses of wine, cups of coffee that are just tainted. The number I've had myself, and drunk, either knowing or not knowing—and risked it. The only reason why so many couples'—she laughed—'*survive*, is because the one is frightened of giving the other the fatal dose. That dose takes nerve! But it's bound to come sooner or later. There's no going back once the first little dose has been given. It's the beginning of the end, really—don't you agree? Don't you see what I mean?'

She didn't wait for me to answer. She unpinned the lilies-of-the-valley and lay back, drawing them across her eyes.

'Both my husbands poisoned me,' said Beatrice. 'My first husband gave me a huge dose almost immediately, but my second was

8. Alexander Pope, "Eloisa to Abelard," 1717, l. 208.

really an artist in his way. Just a tiny pinch, now and again, cleverly disguised—Oh, so cleverly!—until one morning I woke up and in every single particle of me, to the ends of my fingers and toes, there was a tiny grain. I was just in time. . . .'

I hated to hear her mention her husbands so calmly, especially to-day. It hurt. I was going to speak, but suddenly she cried mournfully:

'Why! Why should it have happened to me? What have I done? Why have I been all my life singled out by. . . . It's a conspiracy.'

I tried to tell her it was because she was too perfect for this horrible world—too exquisite, too fine. It frightened people. I made a little joke.

'But I—I haven't tried to poison you.'

Beatrice gave a queer small laugh and bit the end of a lily stem.

'You!' said she. 'You wouldn't hurt a fly!'

Strange. That hurt, though. Most horribly.

Just then Annette ran out with our *apéritifs*. Beatrice leaned forward and took a glass from the tray and handed it to me. I noticed the gleam of the pearl on what I called her pearl finger. How could I be hurt at what she said?

'And you,' I said, taking the glass, 'you've never poisoned anybody.'

That gave me an idea; I tried to explain. 'You—you do just the opposite. What is the name for one like you who, instead of poisoning people, fills them—everybody, the postman, the man who drives us, our boatman, the flower-seller, me—with new life, with something of her own radiance, her beauty, her—'

Dreamily she smiled; dreamily she looked at me.

'What are you thinking of—my lovely darling?'

'I was wondering,' she said, 'whether, after lunch, you'd go down to the post-office and ask for the afternoon letters. Would you mind, dearest? Not that I'm expecting one—but—I just thought, perhaps—it's silly not to have the letters if they're there. Isn't it? Silly to wait till to-morrow.' She twirled the stem of the glass in her fingers. Her beautiful head was bent. But I lifted my glass and drank, sipped rather—sipped slowly, deliberately, looking at that dark head and thinking of—postmen and blue beetles and farewells that were not farewells and. . . .

Good God! Was it fancy? No, it wasn't fancy. The drink tasted chill, bitter, *queer*.

The Daughters of the Late Colonel (1920)†

I

The week after was one of the busiest weeks of their lives. Even when they went to bed it was only their bodies that lay down and rested; their minds went on, thinking things out, talking things over, wondering, deciding, trying to remember where. . . .

Constantia lay like a statue, her hands by her sides, her feet just overlapping each other, the sheet up to her chin. She stared at the ceiling.

'Do you think father would mind if we gave his top-hat to the porter?'

'The porter?' snapped Josephine. 'Why ever the porter? What a very extraordinary idea!'

'Because,' said Constantia slowly, 'he must often have to go to funerals. And I noticed at—at the cemetery that he only had a bowler.' She paused. 'I thought then how very much he'd appreciate a top-hat. We ought to give him a present, too. He was always very nice to father.'

'But,' cried Josephine, flouncing on her pillow and staring across the dark at Constantia, 'father's head!' And suddenly, for one awful moment, she nearly giggled. Not, of course, that she felt in the least like giggling. It must have been habit. Years ago, when they had stayed awake at night talking, their beds had simply heaved. And now the porter's head, disappearing, popped out, like a candle, under father's hat. . . . The giggle mounted, mounted; she clenched her hands; she fought it down; she frowned fiercely at the dark and said 'Remember' terribly sternly.

'We can decide to-morrow,' she said.

Constantia had noticed nothing; she sighed.

'Do you think we ought to have our dressing-gowns dyed as well?'

'Black?' almost shrieked Josephine.

'Well, what else?' said Constantia. 'I was thinking—it doesn't seem quite sincere, in a way, to wear black out of doors and when we're fully dressed, and then when we're at home—'

'But nobody sees us,' said Josephine. She gave the bedclothes such a twitch that both her feet came uncovered, and she had to creep up the pillows to get them well under again.

'Kate does,' said Constantia. 'And the postman very well might.'

Josephine thought of her dark-red slippers, which matched her dressing-gown, and of Constantia's favourite indefinite green ones which went with hers. Black! Two black dressing-gowns and two

† Written in late 1920, published in the *London Mercury* (May 1921), and then collected in *The Garden Party and Other Stories* (1922).

pairs of black woolly slippers, creeping off to the bath-room like black cats.

'I don't think it's absolutely necessary,' said she.

Silence. Then Constantia said, 'We shall have to post the papers with the notice in them to-morrow to catch the Ceylon mail. . . . How many letters have we had up till now?'

'Twenty-three.'

Josephine had replied to them all, and twenty-three times when she came to 'We miss our dear father so much' she had broken down and had to use her handkerchief, and on some of them even to soak up a very light-blue tear with an edge of blotting-paper. Strange! She couldn't have put it on—but twenty-three times. Even now, though, when she said over to herself sadly 'We miss our dear father *so* much,' she could have cried if she'd wanted to.

'Have you got enough stamps?' came from Constantia.

'Oh, how can I tell?' said Josephine crossly. 'What's the good of asking me that now?'

'I was just wondering,' said Constantia mildly.

Silence again. There came a little rustle, a scurry, a hop.

'A mouse,' said Constantia.

'It can't be a mouse because there aren't any crumbs,' said Josephine.

'But it doesn't know there aren't,' said Constantia.

A spasm of pity squeezed her heart. Poor little thing! She wished she'd left a tiny piece of biscuit on the dressing-table. It was awful to think of it not finding anything. What would it do?

'I can't think how they manage to live at all,' she said slowly.

'Who?' demanded Josephine.

And Constantia said more loudly than she meant to, 'Mice.'

Josephine was furious. 'Oh, what nonsense, Con!' she said. 'What have mice got to do with it? You're asleep.'

'I don't think I am,' said Constantia. She shut her eyes to make sure. She was.

Josephine arched her spine, pulled up her knees, folded her arms so that her fists came under her ears, and pressed her cheek hard against the pillow.

II

Another thing which complicated matters was they had Nurse Andrews staying on with them that week. It was their own fault; they had asked her. It was Josephine's idea. On the morning—well, on the last morning, when the doctor had gone, Josephine had said to Constantia, 'Don't you think it would be rather nice if we asked Nurse Andrews to stay on for a week as our guest?'

'Very nice,' said Constantia.

'I thought,' went on Josephine quickly, 'I should just say this afternoon, after I've paid her, "My sister and I would be very pleased, after all you've done for us, Nurse Andrews, if you would stay on for a week as our guest." I'd have to put that in about being our guest in case—

'Oh, but she could hardly expect to be paid!' cried Constantia.

'One never knows,' said Josephine sagely.

Nurse Andrews had, of course, jumped at the idea. But it was a bother. It meant they had to have regular sit-down meals at the proper times, whereas if they'd been alone they could just have asked Kate if she wouldn't have minded bringing them a tray wherever they were. And meal-times now that the strain was over were rather a trial.

Nurse Andrews was simply fearful about butter. Really they couldn't help feeling that about butter, at least, she took advantage of their kindness. And she had that maddening habit of asking for just an inch more bread to finish what she had on her plate, and then, at the last mouthful, absent-mindedly—of course it wasn't absent-mindedly—taking another helping. Josephine got very red when this happened, and she fastened her small, bead-like eyes on the tablecloth as if she saw a minute strange insect creeping through the web of it. But Constantia's long, pale face lengthened and set, and she gazed away—away—far over the desert, to where that line of camels unwound like a thread of wool. . . .

'When I was with Lady Tukes,' said Nurse Andrews, 'she had such a dainty little contray-vance for the buttah. It was a silvah Cupid balanced on the—on the bordah of a glass dish, holding a tayny fork. And when you wanted some buttah you simply pressed his foot and he bent down and speared you a piece. It was quite a gayme.'

Josephine could hardly bear that. But 'I think those things are very extravagant' was all she said.

'But whey?' asked Nurse Andrews, beaming through her eyeglasses. 'No one, surely, would take more buttah than one wanted—would one?'

'Ring, Con,' cried Josephine. She couldn't trust herself to reply.

And proud young Kate, the enchanted princess, came in to see what the old tabbies wanted now. She snatched away their plates of mock something or other and slapped down a white, terrified blancmange.

'Jam, please, Kate,' said Josephine kindly.

Kate knelt and burst open the sideboard, lifted the lid of the jam-pot, saw it was empty, put it on the table, and stalked off.

'I'm afraid,' said Nurse Andrews a moment later, 'there isn't any.'

'Oh, what a bother!' said Josephine. She bit her lip. 'What had we better do?'

Constantia looked dubious. 'We can't disturb Kate again,' she said softly.

Nurse Andrews waited, smiling at them both. Her eyes wandered, spying at everything behind her eye-glasses. Constantia in despair went back to her camels. Josephine frowned heavily—concentrated. If it hadn't been for this idiotic woman she and Con would, of course, have eaten their blancmange without. Suddenly the idea came.

'I know,' she said. 'Marmalade. There's some marmalade in the sideboard. Get it, Con.'

'I hope,' laughed Nurse Andrews, and her laugh was like a spoon tinkling against a medicine-glass—'I hope it's not very bittah marmalayde.'

III

But, after all, it was not long now, and then she'd be gone for good. And there was no getting over the fact that she had been very kind to father. She had nursed him day and night at the end. Indeed, both Constantia and Josephine felt privately she had rather overdone the not leaving him at the very last. For when they had gone in to say good-bye Nurse Andrews had sat beside his bed the whole time, holding his wrist and pretending to look at her watch. It couldn't have been necessary. It was so tactless, too. Supposing father had wanted to say something—something private to them. Not that he had. Oh, far from it! He lay there, purple, a dark, angry purple in the face, and never even looked at them when they came in. Then, as they were standing there, wondering what to do, he had suddenly opened one eye. Oh, what a difference it would have made, what a difference to their memory of him, how much easier to tell people about it, if he had only opened both! But no—one eye only. It glared at them a moment and then . . . went out.

IV

It had made it very awkward for them when Mr Farolles, of St John's, called the same afternoon.

'The end was quite peaceful, I trust?' were the first words he said as he glided towards them through the dark drawing-room.

'Quite,' said Josephine faintly. They both hung their heads. Both of them felt certain that eye wasn't at all a peaceful eye.

'Won't you sit down?' said Josephine.

'Thank you, Miss Pinner,' said Mr Farolles gratefully. He folded his coat-tails and began to lower himself into father's arm-chair, but just as he touched it he almost sprang up and slid into the next chair instead.

He coughed. Josephine clasped her hands; Constantia looked vague.

'I want you to feel, Miss Pinner,' said Mr Farolles, 'and you, Miss Constantia, that I'm trying to be helpful. I want to be helpful to you both, if you will let me. These are the times,' said Mr Farolles, very simply and earnestly, 'when God means us to be helpful to one another.'

'Thank you very much, Mr Farolles,' said Josephine and Constantia.

'Not at all,' said Mr Farolles gently. He drew his kid gloves through his fingers and leaned forward. 'And if either of you would like a little Communion, either or both of you, here *and* now, you have only to tell me. A little Communion is often very help—a great comfort,' he added tenderly.

But the idea of a little Communion terrified them. What! In the drawing-room by themselves—with no—no altar or anything! The piano would be much too high, thought Constantia, and Mr Farolles could not possibly lean over it with the chalice. And Kate would be sure to come bursting in and interrupt them, thought Josephine. And supposing the bell rang in the middle? It might be somebody important—about their mourning. Would they get up reverently and go out, or would they have to wait . . . in torture?

'Perhaps you will send round a note by your good Kate if you would care for it later,' said Mr Farolles.

'Oh yes, thank you very much!' they both said.

Mr Farolles got up and took his black straw hat from the round table.

'And about the funeral,' he said softly. 'I may arrange that—as your dear father's old friend and yours, Miss Pinner—and Miss Constantia?'

Josephine and Constantia got up too.

'I should like it to be quite simple,' said Josephine firmly, 'and not too expensive. At the same time, I should like—'

'A good one that will last,' thought dreamy Constantia, as if Josephine were buying a nightgown. But of course Josephine didn't say that. 'One suitable to our father's position.' She was very nervous.

'I'll run round to our good friend Mr Knight,' said Mr Farolles soothingly. 'I will ask him to come and see you. I am sure you will find him very helpful indeed.'

V

Well, at any rate, all that part of it was over, though neither of them could possibly believe that father was never coming back. Josephine had had a moment of absolute terror at the cemetery, while the coffin was lowered, to think that she and Constantia had done this thing without asking his permission. What would father say when he found out? For he was bound to find out sooner or later. He always did. 'Buried. You two girls had me *buried*!' She heard his stick thumping. Oh, what would they say? What possible excuse could they make? It sounded such an appallingly heartless thing to do. Such a wicked advantage to take of a person because he happened to be helpless at the moment. The other people seemed to treat it all as a matter of course. They were strangers; they couldn't be expected to understand that father was the very last person for such a thing to happen to. No, the entire blame for it all would fall on her and Constantia. And the expense, she thought, stepping into the tight-buttoned cab. When she had to show him the bills. What would he say then?

She heard him absolutely roaring, 'And do you expect me to pay for this gimcrack excursion of yours?'

'Oh,' groaned poor Josephine aloud, 'we shouldn't have done it, Con!'

And Constantia, pale as a lemon in all that blackness, said in a frightened whisper, 'Done what, Jug?'

'Let them bu-bury father like that,' said Josephine, breaking down and crying into her new, queer-smelling mourning handkerchief.

'But what else could we have done?' asked Constantia wonderingly. 'We couldn't have kept him, Jug—we couldn't have kept him unburied. At any rate, not in a flat that size.'

Josephine blew her nose; the cab was dreadfully stuffy.

'I don't know,' she said forlornly. 'It is all so dreadful. I feel we ought to have tried to, just for a time at least. To make perfectly sure. One thing's certain'—and her tears sprang out again—'father will never forgive us for this—never!'

VI

Father would never forgive them. That was what they felt more than ever when, two mornings later, they went into his room to go through his things. They had discussed it quite calmly. It was even down on Josephine's list of things to be done. *Go through father's things and settle about them.* But that was a very different matter from saying after breakfast:

'Well, are you ready, Con?'

'Yes, Jug—when you are.'

'Then I think we'd better get it over.'

It was dark in the hall. It had been a rule for years never to disturb father in the morning, whatever happened. And now they were going to open the door without knocking even. . . . Constantia's eyes were enormous at the idea; Josephine felt weak in the knees.

'You—you go first,' she gasped, pushing Constantia.

But Constantia said, as she always had said on those occasions, 'No, Jug, that's not fair. You're eldest.'

Josephine was just going to say—what at other times she wouldn't have owned to for the world—what she kept for her very last weapon, 'But you're tallest,' when they noticed that the kitchen door was open, and there stood Kate. . . .

'Very stiff,' said Josephine, grasping the door-handle and doing her best to turn it. As if anything ever deceived Kate!

It couldn't be helped. That girl was. . . . Then the door was shut behind them, but—but they weren't in father's room at all. They might have suddenly walked through the wall by mistake into a different flat altogether. Was the door just behind them? They were too frightened to look. Josephine knew that if it was it was holding itself tight shut; Constantia felt that, like the doors in dreams, it hadn't any handle at all. It was the coldness which made it so awful. Or the whiteness—which? Everything was covered. The blinds were down, a cloth hung over the mirror, a sheet hid the bed; a huge fan of white paper filled the fire-place. Constantia timidly put out her hand; she almost expected a snowflake to fall. Josephine felt a queer tingling in her nose, as if her nose was freezing. Then a cab klop-klopped over the cobbles below, and the quiet seemed to shake into little pieces.

'I had better pull up a blind,' said Josephine bravely.

'Yes, it might be a good idea,' whispered Constantia.

They only gave the blind a touch, but it flew up and the cord flew after, rolling round the blind-stick, and the little tassel tapped as if trying to get free. That was too much for Constantia.

'Don't you think—don't you think we might put it off for another day?' she whispered.

'Why?' snapped Josephine, feeling, as usual, much better now that she knew for certain that Constantia was terrified. 'It's got to be done. But I do wish you wouldn't whisper, Con.'

'I didn't know I was whispering,' whispered Constantia.

'And why do you keep on staring at the bed?' said Josephine, raising her voice almost defiantly. 'There's nothing *on* the bed.'

'Oh, Jug, don't say so!' said poor Connie. 'At any rate, not so loudly.'

Josephine felt herself that she had gone too far. She took a wide swerve over to the chest of drawers, put out her hand, but quickly drew it back again.

'Connie!' she gasped, and she wheeled round and leaned with her back against the chest of drawers.

'Oh, Jug—what?'

Josephine could only glare. She had the most extraordinary feeling that she had just escaped something simply awful. But how could she explain to Constantia that father was in the chest of drawers? He was in the top drawer with his handkerchiefs and neck-ties, or in the next with his shirts and pyjamas, or in the lowest of all with his suits. He was watching there, hidden away—just behind the door-handle—ready to spring.

She pulled a funny old-fashioned face at Constantia, just as she used to in the old days when she was going to cry.

'I can't open,' she nearly wailed.

'No, don't, Jug,' whispered Constantia earnestly. 'It's much better not to. Don't let's open anything. At any rate, not for a long time.'

'But—but it seems so weak,' said Josephine, breaking down.

'But why not be weak for once, Jug?' argued Constantia, whispering quite fiercely. 'If it is weak.' And her pale stare flew from the locked writing-table—so safe—to the huge glittering wardrobe, and she began to breathe in a queer, panting way. 'Why shouldn't we be weak for once in our lives, Jug? It's quite excusable. Let's be weak—be weak, Jug. It's much nicer to be weak than to be strong.'

And then she did one of those amazingly bold things that she'd done about twice before in their lives; she marched over to the wardrobe, turned the key, and took it out of the lock. Took it out of the lock and held it up to Josephine, showing Josephine by her extraordinary smile that she knew what she'd done, she'd risked deliberately father being in there among his overcoats.

If the huge wardrobe had lurched forward, had crashed down on Constantia, Josephine wouldn't have been surprised. On the contrary, she would have thought it the only suitable thing to happen. But nothing happened. Only the room seemed quieter than ever, and bigger flakes of cold air fell on Josephine's shoulders and knees. She began to shiver.

'Come, Jug,' said Constantia, still with that awful callous smile, and Josephine followed just as she had that last time, when Constantia had pushed Benny into the Round Pond.

VII

But the strain told on them when they were back in the dining-room. They sat down, very shaky, and looked at each other.

'I don't feel I can settle to anything,' said Josephine, 'until I've had something. Do you think we could ask Kate for two cups of hot water?'

'I really don't see why we shouldn't,' said Constantia carefully. She was quite normal again. 'I won't ring. I'll go to the kitchen door and ask her.'

'Yes, do,' said Josephine, sinking down into a chair. 'Tell her, just two cups, Con, nothing else—on a tray.'

'She needn't even put the jug on, need she?' said Constantia, as though Kate might very well complain if the jug had been there.

'Oh no, certainly not! The jug's not at all necessary. She can pour it direct out of the kettle,' cried Josephine, feeling that would be a labour-saving indeed.

Their cold lips quivered at the greenish brims. Josephine curved her small red hands round the cup; Constantia sat up and blew on the wavy steam, making it flutter from one side to the other.

'Speaking of Benny,' said Josephine.

And though Benny hadn't been mentioned Constantia immediately looked as though he had.

'He'll expect us to send him something of father's, of course. But it's so difficult to know what to send to Ceylon.'

'You mean things get unstuck so on the voyage,' murmured Constantia.

'No, lost,' said Josephine sharply. 'You know there's no post. Only runners.'

Both paused to watch a black man in white linen drawers running through the pale fields for dear life, with a large brown-paper parcel in his hands. Josephine's black man was tiny; he scurried along glistening like an ant. But there was something blind and tireless about Constantia's tall, thin fellow, which made him, she decided, a very unpleasant person indeed. . . . On the verandah, dressed all in white and wearing a cork helmet, stood Benny. His right hand shook up and down, as father's did when he was impatient. And behind him, not in the least interested, sat Hilda, the unknown sister-in-law. She swung in a cane rocker and flicked over the leaves of the *Tatler*.[1]

'I think his watch would be the most suitable present,' said Josephine.

Constantia looked up; she seemed surprised.

'Oh, would you trust a gold watch to a native?'

'But of course I'd disguise it,' said Josephine. 'No one would know it was a watch.' She liked the idea of having to make a parcel such a curious shape that no one could possibly guess what it was.

1. A fashionable illustrated periodical.

She even thought for a moment of hiding the watch in a narrow cardboard corset-box that she'd kept by her for a long time, waiting for it to come in for something. It was such beautiful firm cardboard. But, no, it wouldn't be appropriate for this occasion. It had lettering on it: *Medium Women's* 28. *Extra Firm Busks.*[2] It would be almost too much of a surprise for Benny to open that and find father's watch inside.

'And of course it isn't as though it would be going—ticking, I mean,' said Constantia, who was still thinking of the native love of jewellery. 'At least,' she added, 'it would be very strange if after all that time it was.'

VIII

Josephine made no reply. She had flown off on one of her tangents. She had suddenly thought of Cyril. Wasn't it more usual for the only grandson to have the watch? And then dear Cyril was so appreciative, and a gold watch meant so much to a young man. Benny, in all probability, had quite got out of the habit of watches; men so seldom wore waistcoats in those hot climates. Whereas Cyril in London wore them from year's end to year's end. And it would be so nice for her and Constantia, when he came to tea, to know it was there. 'I see you've got on grandfather's watch, Cyril.' It would be somehow so satisfactory.

Dear boy! What a blow his sweet, sympathetic little note had been! Of course they quite understood; but it was most unfortunate.

'It would have been such a point, having him,' said Josephine.

'And he would have enjoyed it so,' said Constantia, not thinking what she was saying.

However, as soon as he got back he was coming to tea with his aunties. Cyril to tea was one of their rare treats.

'Now, Cyril, you mustn't be frightened of our cakes. Your Auntie Con and I bought them at Buszard's this morning. We know what a man's appetite is. So don't be ashamed of making a good tea.'

Josephine cut recklessly into the rich dark cake that stood for her winter gloves or the soling and heeling of Constantia's only respectable shoes. But Cyril was most unmanlike in appetite.

'I say, Aunt Josephine, I simply can't. I've only just had lunch, you know.'

'Oh, Cyril, that can't be true! It's after four,' cried Josephine. Constantia sat with her knife poised over the chocolate-roll.

'It is, all the same,' said Cyril. 'I had to meet a man at Victoria, and he kept me hanging about till . . . there was only time to get

2. Steel or whalebone strips to stiffen corsets.

lunch and to come on here. And he gave me—phew'—Cyril put his hand to his forehead—'a terrific blow-out,' he said.

It was disappointing—today of all days. But still he couldn't be expected to know.

'But you'll have a meringue, won't you, Cyril?' said Aunt Josephine. 'These meringues were bought specially for you. Your dear father was so fond of them. We were sure you are, too.'

'I *am*, Aunt Josephine,' cried Cyril ardently. 'Do you mind if I take half to begin with?'

'Not at all, dear boy; but we mustn't let you off with that.'

'Is your dear father still so fond of meringues?' asked Auntie Con gently. She winced faintly as she broke through the shell of hers.

'Well, I don't quite know, Auntie Con,' said Cyril breezily.

At that they both looked up.

'Don't know?' almost snapped Josephine. 'Don't know a thing like that about your own father, Cyril?'

'Surely,' said Auntie Con softly.

Cyril tried to laugh it off. 'Oh, well,' he said, 'it's such a long time since—' He faltered. He stopped. Their faces were too much for him.

'Even *so*,' said Josephine.

And Auntie Con looked.

Cyril put down his teacup. 'Wait a bit,' he cried. 'Wait a bit, Aunt Josephine. What am I thinking of?'

He looked up. They were beginning to brighten. Cyril slapped his knee.

'Of course,' he said, 'it was meringues. How could I have forgotten? Yes, Aunt Josephine, you're perfectly right. Father's most frightfully keen on meringues.'

They didn't only beam. Aunt Josephine went scarlet with pleasure; Auntie Con gave a deep, deep sigh.

'And now, Cyril, you must come and see father,' said Josephine. 'He knows you were coming to-day.'

'Right,' said Cyril, very firmly and heartily. He got up from his chair; suddenly he glanced at the clock.

'I say, Auntie Con, isn't your clock a bit slow? I've got to meet a man at—at Paddington just after five. I'm afraid I shan't be able to stay very long with grandfather.'

'Oh, he won't expect you to stay *very* long!' said Aunt Josephine.

Constantia was still gazing at the clock. She couldn't make up her mind if it was fast or slow. It was one or the other, she felt almost certain of that. At any rate, it had been.

Cyril still lingered. 'Aren't you coming along, Auntie Con?'

'Of course,' said Josephine, 'we shall all go. Come on, Con.'

IX

They knocked at the door, and Cyril followed his aunts into grandfather's hot, sweetish room.

'Come on,' said Grandfather Pinner. 'Don't hang about. What is it? What've you been up to?'

He was sitting in front of a roaring fire, clasping his stick. He had a thick rug over his knees. On his lap there lay a beautiful pale yellow silk handkerchief.

'It's Cyril, father,' said Josephine shyly. And she took Cyril's hand and led him forward.

'Good afternoon, grandfather,' said Cyril, trying to take his hand out of Aunt Josephine's. Grandfather Pinner shot his eyes at Cyril in the way he was famous for. Where was Auntie Con? She stood on the other side of Aunt Josephine; her long arms hung down in front of her; her hands were clasped. She never took her eyes off grandfather.

'Well,' said Grandfather Pinner, beginning to thump, 'What have you got to tell me?'

What had he, what had he got to tell him? Cyril felt himself smiling like a perfect imbecile. The room was stifling, too.

But Aunt Josephine came to his rescue. She cried brightly, 'Cyril says his father is still very fond of meringues, father dear.'

'Eh?' said Grandfather Pinner, curving his hand like a purple meringue-shell over one ear.

Josephine repeated, 'Cyril says his father is still very fond of meringues.'

'Can't hear,' said old Colonel Pinner. And he waved Josephine away with his stick, then pointed with his stick to Cyril. 'Tell me what she's trying to say,' he said.

(My God!) 'Must I?' said Cyril, blushing and staring at Aunt Josephine.

'Do, dear,' she smiled. 'It will please him so much.'

'Come on, out with it!' cried Colonel Pinner testily, beginning to thump again.

And Cyril leaned forward and yelled, 'Father's still very fond of meringues.'

At that Grandfather Pinner jumped as though he had been shot.

'Don't shout!' he cried. 'What's the matter with the boy? *Meringues!* What about 'em?'

'Oh, Aunt Josephine, must we go on?' groaned Cyril desperately.

'It's quite all right, dear boy,' said Aunt Josephine, as though he and she were at the dentist's together. 'He'll understand in a minute.' And she whispered to Cyril, 'He's getting a bit deaf, you know.' Then she leaned forward and really bawled at Grandfather

Pinner, 'Cyril only wanted to tell you, father dear, that *his* father is still very fond of meringues.'

Colonel Pinner heard that time, heard and brooded, looking Cyril up and down.

'What an esstrordinary thing!' said old Grandfather Pinner. 'What an esstrordinary thing to come all this way here to tell me!'

And Cyril felt it *was*.

'Yes, I shall send Cyril the watch,' said Josephine.

'That would be very nice,' said Constantia. 'I seem to remember last time he came there was some little trouble about the time.'

X

They were interrupted by Kate bursting through the door in her usual fashion, as though she had discovered some secret panel in the wall.

'Fried or boiled?' asked the bold voice.

Fried or boiled? Josephine and Constantia were quite bewildered for the moment. They could hardly take it in.

'Fried or boiled what, Kate?' asked Josephine, trying to begin to concentrate.

Kate gave a loud sniff. 'Fish.'

'Well, why didn't you say so immediately?' Josephine reproached her gently. 'How could you expect us to understand, Kate? There are a great many things in this world, you know, which are fried or boiled.' And after such a display of courage she said quite brightly to Constantia, 'Which do you prefer, Con?'

'I think it might be nice to have it fried,' said Constantia. 'On the other hand, of course boiled fish is very nice. I think I prefer both equally well. . . . Unless you. . . . In that case—'

'I shall fry it,' said Kate, and she bounced back, leaving their door open and slamming the door of her kitchen.

Josephine gazed at Constantia; she raised her pale eyebrows until they rippled away into her pale hair. She got up. She said in a very lofty, imposing way, 'Do you mind following me into the drawing-room, Constantia? I've something of great importance to discuss with you.'

For it was always to the drawing-room they retired when they wanted to talk over Kate.

Josephine closed the door meaningly. 'Sit down, Constantia,' she said, still very grand. She might have been receiving Constantia for the first time. And Con looked round vaguely for a chair, as though she felt indeed quite a stranger.

'Now the question is,' said Josephine, bending forward, 'whether we shall keep her or not.'

'That is the question,' agreed Constantia.

'And this time,' said Josephine firmly, 'we must come to a definite decision.'

Constantia looked for a moment as though she might begin going over all the other times, but she pulled herself together and said, 'Yes, Jug.'

'You see, Con,' explained Josephine, 'everything is so changed now.' Constantia looked up quickly. 'I mean,' went on Josephine, 'we're not dependent on Kate as we were.' And she blushed faintly. 'There's not father to cook for.'

'That is perfectly true,' agreed Constantia. 'Father certainly doesn't want any cooking now whatever else—'

Josephine broke in sharply, 'You're not sleepy, are you, Con?'

'Sleepy, Jug?' Constantia was wide-eyed.

'Well, concentrate more,' said Josephine sharply, and she returned to the subject. 'What it comes to is, if we did'—and this she barely breathed, glancing at the door—'give Kate notice'—she raised her voice again—'we could manage our own food.'

'Why not?' cried Constantia. She couldn't help smiling. The idea was so exciting. She clasped her hands. 'What should we live on, Jug?'

'Oh, eggs in various forms!' said Jug, lofty again. 'And, besides, there are all the cooked foods.'

'But I've always heard,' said Constantia, 'they are considered so very expensive.'

'Not if one buys them in moderation,' said Josephine. But she tore herself away from this fascinating bypath and dragged Constantia after her.

'What we've got to decide now, however, is whether we really do trust Kate or not.'

Constantia leaned back. Her flat little laugh flew from her lips.

'Isn't it curious, Jug,' said she, 'that just on this one subject I've never been able to quite make up my mind?'

XI

She never had. The whole difficulty was to prove anything. How did one prove things, how could one? Suppose Kate had stood in front of her and deliberately made a face. Mightn't she very well have been in pain? Wasn't it impossible, at any rate, to ask Kate if she was making a face at her? If Kate answered 'No'—and of course she would say 'No'—what a position! How undignified! Then again Constantia suspected, she was almost certain that Kate went to her chest of drawers when she and Josephine were out, not to take things but to spy. Many times she had come back to find her amethyst cross in the most unlikely places, under her lace ties or on top of her evening Bertha.[3] More than once she had laid a trap for Kate. She had arranged things in a special order and then called Josephine to witness.

'You see, Jug?'

'Quite, Con.'

'Now we shall be able to tell.'

But, oh dear, when she did go to look, she was as far off from a proof as ever! If anything was displaced, it might so very well have happened as she closed the drawer; a jolt might have done it so easily.

'You come, Jug, and decide. I really can't. It's too difficult.'

But after a pause and a long glare Josephine would sigh, 'Now you've put the doubt into my mind, Con, I'm sure I can't tell myself.'

'Well, we can't postpone it again,' said Josephine. 'If we postpone it this time—'

XII

But at that moment in the street below a barrel-organ struck up. Josephine and Constantia sprang to their feet together.

'Run, Con,' said Josephine. 'Run quickly. There's sixpence on the—'

Then they remembered. It didn't matter. They would never have to stop the organ-grinder again. Never again would she and Constantia be told to make that monkey take his noise somewhere else. Never would sound that loud, strange bellow when father thought they were not hurrying enough. The organ-grinder might play there all day and the stick would not thump.

It never will thump again,
It never will thump again,

played the barrel-organ.

What was Constantia thinking? She had such a strange smile; she looked different. She couldn't be going to cry.

'Jug, Jug,' said Constantia softly, pressing her hands together. 'Do you know what day it is? It's Saturday. It's a week to-day, a whole week.'

A week since father died,
A week since father died,

cried the barrel-organ. And Josephine, too, forgot to be practical and sensible; she smiled faintly, strangely. On the Indian carpet

3. A deep collar attached to a low-cut evening dress.

there fell a square of sunlight, pale red; it came and went and came—and stayed, deepened—until it shone almost golden.

'The sun's out,' said Josephine, as though it really mattered.

A perfect fountain of bubbling notes shook from the barrel-organ, round, bright notes, carelessly scattered.

Constantia lifted her big, cold hands as if to catch them, and then her hands fell again. She walked over to the mantelpiece to her favourite Buddha. And the stone and gilt image, whose smile always gave her such a queer feeling, almost a pain and yet a pleasant pain, seemed to-day to be more than smiling. He knew something; he had a secret. 'I know something that you don't know,' said her Buddha. Oh, what was it, what could it be? And yet she had always felt there was . . . something.

The sunlight pressed through the windows, thieved its way in, flashed its light over the furniture and the photographs. Josephine watched it. When it came to mother's photograph, the enlargement over the piano, it lingered as though puzzled to find so little remained of mother, except the ear-rings shaped like tiny pagodas and a black feather boa. Why did the photographs of dead people always fade so? wondered Josephine. As soon as a person was dead their photograph died too. But, of course, this one of mother was very old. It was thirty-five years old. Josephine remembered standing on a chair and pointing out that feather boa to Constantia and telling her that it was a snake that had killed their mother in Ceylon. . . . Would everything have been different if mother hadn't died? She didn't see why. Aunt Florence had lived with them until they had left school, and they had moved three times and had their yearly holiday and . . . and there'd been changes of servants, of course.

Some little sparrows, young sparrows they sounded, chirped on the window-ledge. *Yeep—eyeep—yeep.* But Josephine felt they were not sparrows, not on the window-ledge. It was inside her, that queer little crying noise. *Yeep—eyeep—yeep.* Ah, what was it crying, so weak and forlorn?

If mother had lived, might they have married? But there had been nobody for them to marry. There had been father's Anglo-Indian friends before he quarrelled with them. But after that she and Constantia never met a single man except clergymen. How did one meet men? Or even if they'd met them, how could they have got to know men well enough to be more than strangers? One read of people having adventures, being followed, and so on. But nobody had ever followed Constantia and her. Oh yes, there had been one year at Eastbourne a mysterious man at their boarding-house who had put a note on the jug of hot water outside their bedroom door! But by the time Connie had found it the steam had made the writing too faint to read; they couldn't even make out to which of them it was addressed. And he had left next day. And that was all. The rest had been looking after father, and at the same time keeping out of father's way. But now? But now? The thieving sun touched Josephine gently. She lifted her face. She was drawn over to the window by gentle beams. . . .

Until the barrel-organ stopped playing Constantia stayed before the Buddha, wondering, but not as usual, not vaguely. This time her wonder was like longing. She remembered the times she had come in here, crept out of bed in her nightgown when the moon was full, and lain on the floor with her arms outstretched, as though she was crucified. Why? The big, pale moon had made her do it. The horrible dancing figures on the carved screen had leered at her and she hadn't minded. She remembered too how, whenever they were at the seaside, she had gone off by herself and got as close to the sea as she could, and sung something, something she had made up, while she gazed all over that restless water. There had been this other life, running out, bringing things home in bags, getting things on approval, discussing them with Jug, and taking them back to get more things on approval, and arranging father's trays and trying not to annoy father. But it all seemed to have happened in a kind of tunnel. It wasn't real. It was only when she came out of the tunnel into the moonlight or by the sea or into a thunderstorm that she really felt herself. What did it mean? What was it she was always wanting? What did it all lead to? Now? Now?

She turned away from the Buddha with one of her vague gestures. She went over to where Josephine was standing. She wanted to say something to Josephine, something frightfully important, about—about the future and what. . . .

'Don't you think perhaps—' she began.

But Josephine interrupted her. 'I was wondering if now—' she murmured. They stopped; they waited for each other.

'Go on, Con,' said Josephine.

'No, no, Jug; after you,' said Constantia.

'No, say what you were going to say. You began,' said Josephine.

'I . . . I'd rather hear what you were going to say first,' said Constantia.

'Don't be absurd, Con.'

'Really, Jug.'

'Connie!'

'Oh, *Jug*!'

A pause. Then Constantia said faintly, 'I can't say what I was going to say, Jug, because I've forgotten what it was . . . that I was going to say.'

Josephine was silent for a moment. She stared at a big cloud where the sun had been. Then she replied shortly, 'I've forgotten too.'

Life of Ma Parker (1920)†

When the literary gentleman, whose flat old Ma Parker cleaned every Tuesday, opened the door to her that morning, he asked after her grandson. Ma Parker stood on the doormat inside the dark little hall, and she stretched out her hand to help her gentleman shut the door before she replied. 'We buried 'im yesterday, sir,' she said quietly.

'Oh, dear me! I'm sorry to hear that,' said the literary gentleman in a shocked tone. He was in the middle of his breakfast. He wore a very shabby dressing-gown and carried a crumpled newspaper in one hand. But he felt awkward. He could hardly go back to the warm sitting-room without saying something—something more. Then because these people set such store by funerals he said kindly, 'I hope the funeral went off all right.'

'Beg parding, sir?' said old Ma Parker huskily.

Poor old bird! She did look dashed. 'I hope the funeral was a—a—success,' said he. Ma Parker gave no answer. She bent her head and hobbled off to the kitchen, clasping the old fish bag that held her cleaning things and an apron and a pair of felt shoes. The literary gentleman raised his eyebrows and went back to his breakfast.

'Overcome, I suppose,' he said aloud, helping himself to the marmalade.

Ma Parker drew the two jetty spears out of her toque[1] and hung it behind the door. She unhooked her worn jacket and hung that up too. Then she tied her apron and sat down to take off her boots. To take off her boots or to put them on was an agony to her, but it had been an agony for years. In fact, she was so accustomed to the pain that her face was drawn and screwed up ready for the twinge before she'd so much as untied the laces. That over, she sat back with a sigh and softly rubbed her knees. . . .

'Gran! Gran!' Her little grandson stood on her lap in his button boots. He'd just come in from playing in the street.

'Look what a state you've made your gran's skirt into—you wicked boy!'

But he put his arms round her neck and rubbed his cheek against hers.

'Gran, gi' us a penny!' he coaxed.

'Be off with you; Gran ain't got no pennies.'

'Yes, you 'ave.'

† First published in the *Athenaeum* (26 February 1921) and collected in *The Garden Party and Other Stories* (1922).

1. A small brimless hat.

'No, I ain't.'

'Yes, you 'ave. Gi' us one!'

Already she was feeling for the old, squashed, black leather purse.

'Well, what'll you give your gran?'

He gave a shy little laugh and pressed closer. She felt his eyelid quivering against her cheek. 'I ain't got nothing,' he murmured. . . .

The old woman sprang up, seized the iron kettle off the gas stove and took it over to the sink. The noise of the water drumming in the kettle deadened her pain, it seemed. She filled the pail, too, and the washing-up bowl.

It would take a whole book to describe the state of that kitchen. During the week the literary gentleman 'did' for himself. That is to say, he emptied the tea leaves now and again into a jam jar set aside for that purpose, and if he ran out of clean forks he wiped over one or two on the roller towel. Otherwise, as he explained to his friends, his 'system' was quite simple, and he couldn't understand why people made all this fuss about housekeeping.

'You simply dirty everything you've got, get a hag in once a week to clean up, and the thing's done.'

The result looked like a gigantic dustbin. Even the floor was littered with toast crusts, envelopes, cigarette ends. But Ma Parker bore him no grudge. She pitied the poor young gentleman for having no one to look after him. Out of the smudgy little window you could see an immense expanse of sad-looking sky, and whenever there were clouds they looked very worn, old clouds, frayed at the edges, with holes in them, or dark stains like tea.

While the water was heating, Ma Parker began sweeping the floor. 'Yes,' she thought, as the broom knocked, 'what with one thing and another I've had my share. I've had a hard life.'

Even the neighbours said that of her. Many a time, hobbling home with her fish bag she heard them, waiting at the corner, or leaning over the area railings, say among themselves, 'She's had a hard life, has Ma Parker.' And it was so true she wasn't in the least proud of it. It was just as if you were to say she lived in the basement-back at Number 27. A hard life! . . .

At sixteen she'd left Stratford and come up to London as kitching-maid. Yes, she was born in Stratford-on-Avon. Shakespeare, sir? No, people were always arsking her about him. But she'd never heard his name until she saw it on the theatres.

Nothing remained of Stratford except that 'sitting in the fire-place of a evening you could see the stars through the chimley,' and 'Mother always 'ad 'er side of bacon 'anging from the ceiling.' And there was something—a bush, there was—at the front door, that smelt ever so nice. But the bush was very vague. She'd only remembered it once or twice in the hospital, when she'd been taken bad.

That was a dreadful place—her first place. She was never allowed out. She never went upstairs except for prayers morning and evening. It was a fair cellar. And the cook was a cruel woman. She used to snatch away her letters from home before she'd read them, and throw them in the range because they made her dreamy. . . . And the beedles! Would you believe it?—until she came to London she'd never seen a black beedle. Here Ma always gave a little laugh, as though—not to have seen a black beedle! Well! It was as if to say you'd never seen your own feet.

When that family was sold up she went as 'help' to a doctor's house, and after two years there, on the run from morning till night, she married her husband. He was a baker.

'A baker, Mrs Parker!' the literary gentleman would say. For occasionally he laid aside his tomes and lent an ear, at least, to this product called Life. 'It must be rather nice to be married to a baker!'

Mrs Parker didn't look so sure.

'Such a clean trade,' said the gentleman.

Mrs Parker didn't look convinced.

'And didn't you like handing the new loaves to the customers?'

'Well, sir,' said Mrs Parker, 'I wasn't in the shop above a great deal. We had thirteen little ones and buried seven of them. If it wasn't the 'ospital it was the infirmary, you might say!'

'You might, *indeed*, Mrs Parker!' said the gentleman, shuddering, and taking up his pen again.

Yes, seven had gone, and while the six were still small her husband was taken ill with consumption. It was flour on the lungs, the doctor told her at the time. . . . Her husband sat up in bed with his shirt pulled over his head, and the doctor's finger drew a circle on his back.

'Now, if we were to cut him open *here*, Mrs Parker,' said the doctor, 'you'd find his lungs chock-a-block with white powder. Breathe, my good fellow!' And Mrs Parker never knew for certain whether she saw or whether she fancied she saw a great fan of white dust come out of her poor dear husband's lips. . . .

But the struggle she'd had to bring up those six little children and keep herself to herself. Terrible it had been! Then, just when they were old enough to go to school her husband's sister came to stop with them to help things along, and she hadn't been there more than two months when she fell down a flight of steps and hurt her spine. And for five years Ma Parker had another baby—

and such a one for crying!—to look after. Then young Maudie went wrong and took her sister Alice with her; the two boys emigrimated, and young Jim went to India with the army, and Ethel, the youngest, married a good-for-nothing little waiter who died of ulcers the year little Lennie was born. And now little Lennie—my grandson. . . .

The piles of dirty cups, dirty dishes, were washed and dried. The ink-black knives were cleaned with a piece of potato and finished off with a piece of cork. The table was scrubbed, and the dresser and the sink that had sardine tails swimming in it. . . .

He'd never been a strong child—never from the first. He'd been one of those fair babies that everybody took for a girl. Silvery fair curls he had, blue eyes, and a little freckle like a diamond on one side of his nose. The trouble she and Ethel had had to rear that child! The things out of the newspapers they tried him with! Every Sunday morning Ethel would read aloud while Ma Parker did her washing.

'Dear Sir,—Just a line to let you know my little Myrtil was laid out for dead. . . . After four bottils . . . gained 8 lbs. in 9 weeks, *and is still putting it on.*'

And then the egg-cup of ink would come off the dresser and the letter would be written, and Ma would buy a postal order on her way to work next morning. But it was no use. Nothing made little Lennie put it on. Taking him to the cemetery, even, never gave him a colour; a nice shake-up in the bus never improved his appetite.

But he was gran's boy from the first. . . .

'Whose boy are you?' said old Ma Parker, straightening up from the stove and going over to the smudgy window. And a little voice, so warm, so close, it half stifled her—it seemed to be in her breast under her heart—laughed out, and said, 'I'm gran's boy!'

At that moment there was a sound of steps, and the literary gentleman appeared, dressed for walking.

'Oh, Mrs Parker, I'm going out.'

'Very good, sir.'

'And you'll find your half-crown in the tray of the inkstand.'

'Thank you, sir.'

'Oh, by the way, Mrs Parker,' said the literary gentleman quickly, 'you didn't throw away any cocoa last time you were here—did you?'

'No, sir.'

'*Very* strange. I could have sworn I left a teaspoonful of cocoa in the tin.' He broke off. He said softly and firmly, 'You'll always tell me when you throw things away—won't you, Mrs Parker?' And he walked off very well pleased with himself, convinced, in fact, he'd shown Mrs Parker that under his apparent carelessness he was as vigilant as a woman.

The door banged. She took her brushes and cloths into the bedroom. But when she began to make the bed, smoothing, tucking, patting, the thought of little Lennie was unbearable. Why did he have to suffer so? That's what she couldn't understand. Why should a little angel child have to arsk for his breath and fight for it? There was no sense in making a child suffer like that.

. . . From Lennie's little box of a chest there came a sound as though something was boiling. There was a great lump of something bubbling in his chest that he couldn't get rid of. When he coughed the sweat sprang out on his head; his eyes bulged, his hands waved, and the great lump bubbled as a potato knocks in a saucepan. But what was more awful than all was when he didn't cough he sat against the pillow and never spoke or answered, or even made as if he heard. Only he looked offended.

'It's not your poor old gran's doing it, my lovey,' said old Ma Parker, patting back the damp hair from his little scarlet ears. But Lennie moved his head and edged away. Dreadfully offended with her he looked—and solemn. He bent his head and looked at her sideways as though he couldn't have believed it of his gran.

But at the last . . . Ma Parker threw the counterpane[2] over the bed. No, she simply couldn't think about it. It was too much—she'd had too much in her life to bear. She'd borne it up till now, she'd kept herself to herself, and never once had she been seen to cry. Never by a living soul. Not even her own children had seen Ma break down. She'd kept a proud face always. But now! Lennie gone—what had she? She had nothing. He was all she'd got from life, and now he was took too. Why must it all have happened to me? she wondered. 'What have I done?' said old Ma Parker. 'What have I done?'

As she said those words she suddenly let fall her brush. She found herself in the kitchen. Her misery was so terrible that she pinned on her hat, put on her jacket and walked out of the flat like a person in a dream. She did not know what she was doing. She was like a person so dazed by the horror of what has happened that he walks away—anywhere, as though by walking away he could escape. . . .

It was cold in the street. There was a wind like ice. People went flitting by, very fast; the men walked like scissors; the women trod like cats. And nobody knew—nobody cared. Even if she broke

2. A quilt or bedspread.

down, if at last, after all these years, she were to cry, she'd find herself in the lock-up as like as not.

But at the thought of crying it was as though little Lennie leapt in his gran's arms. Ah, that's what she want to do, my dove. Gran wants to cry. If she could only cry now, cry for a long time, over everything, beginning with her first place and the cruel cook, going on to the doctor's, and then the seven little ones, death of her husband, the children's leaving her, and all the years of misery that led up to Lennie. But to have a proper cry over all these things would take a long time. All the same, the time for it had come. She must do it. She couldn't put it off any longer; she couldn't wait any more. . . . Where could she go?

'She's had a hard life, has Ma Parker.' Yes, a hard life, indeed! Her chin began to tremble; there was no time to lose. But where? Where?

She couldn't go home; Ethel was there. It would frighten Ethel out of her life. She couldn't sit on a bench anywhere; people would come arsking her questions. She couldn't possibly go back to the gentleman's flat; she had no right to cry in strangers' houses. If she sat on some steps a policeman would speak to her.

Oh, wasn't there anywhere where she could hide and keep herself to herself and stay as long as she liked, not disturbing anybody, and nobody worrying her? Wasn't there anywhere in the world where she could have her cry out—at last?

Ma Parker stood, looking up and down. The icy wind blew out her apron into a balloon. And now it began to rain. There was nowhere.

Her First Ball (1921)†

Exactly when the ball began Leila would have found it hard to say. Perhaps her first real partner was the cab. It did not matter that she shared the cab with the Sheridan girls and their brother. She sat back in her own little corner of it, and the bolster on which her hand rested felt like the sleeve of an unknown young man's dress suit; and away they bowled, past waltzing lamp-posts and houses and fences and trees.

'Have you really never been to a ball before, Leila? But, my child, how too weird'—cried the Sheridan girls.

'Our nearest neighbour was fifteen miles,' said Leila softly, gently opening and shutting her fan.

† Published in the *Sphere* (28 November 1921) and collected in *The Garden Party and Other Stories* (1922).

Oh, dear, how hard it was to be indifferent like the others! She tried not to smile too much; she tried not to care. But every single thing was so new and exciting. . . . Meg's tuberoses,[1] Jose's long loop of amber, Laura's little dark head, pushing above her white fur like a flower through snow. She would remember for ever. It even gave her a pang to see her cousin Laurie throw away the wisps of tissue paper he pulled from the fastenings of his new gloves. She would like to have kept those wisps as a keepsake, as a remembrance. Laurie leaned forward and put his hand on Laura's knee.

'Look here, darling,' he said. 'The third and the ninth as usual. Twig?'

Oh, how marvellous to have a brother! In her excitement Leila felt that if there had been time, if it hadn't been impossible, she couldn't have helped crying because she was an only child, and no brother had ever said 'Twig?' to her; no sister would ever say, as Meg said to Jose that moment, 'I've never known your hair go up more successfully than it has to-night!'

But, of course, there was no time. They were at the drill hall already; there were cabs in front of them and cabs behind. The road was bright on either side with moving fan-like lights, and on the pavement gay couples seemed to float through the air; little satin shoes chased each other like birds.

'Hold on to me, Leila; you'll get lost,' said Laura.

'Come on, girls, let's make a dash for it,' said Laurie.

Leila put two fingers on Laura's pink velvet cloak, and they were somehow lifted past the big golden lantern, carried along the passage, and pushed into the little room marked 'Ladies'. Here the crowd was so great there was hardly space to take off their things; the noise was deafening. Two benches on either side were stacked high with wraps. Two old women in white aprons ran up and down tossing fresh armfuls. And everybody was pressing forward trying to get at the little dressing-table and mirror at the far end.

A great quivering jet of gas lighted the ladies' room. It couldn't wait; it was dancing already. When the door opened again and there came a burst of tuning from the drill hall, it leaped almost to the ceiling.

Dark girls, fair girls were patting their hair, tying ribbons again, tucking handkerchiefs down the fronts of their bodices, smoothing marble-white gloves. And because they were all laughing it seemed to Leila that they were all lovely.

'Aren't there any invisible hair-pins?' cried a voice. 'How most extraordinary! I can't see a single invisible hair-pin.'

'Powder my back, there's a darling,' cried some one else.

1. Heavily scented white waxy flowers.

'But I must have a needle and cotton. I've torn simply miles and miles of the frill,' wailed a third.

Then, 'Pass them along, pass them along!' The straw basket of programmes was tossed from arm to arm. Darling little pink-and-silver programmes, with pink pencils and fluffy tassels. Leila's fingers shook as she took one out of the basket. She wanted to ask some one, 'Am I meant to have one too?' but she had just time to read: 'Waltz 3. *Two, Two in a Canoe*. Polka 4. *Making the Feathers Fly*,' when Meg cried, 'Ready, Leila?' and they pressed their way through the crush in the passage towards the big double doors of the drill hall.

Dancing had not begun yet, but the band had stopped tuning, and the noise was so great it seemed that when it did begin to play it would never be heard. Leila, pressing close to Meg, looking over Meg's shoulder, felt that even the little quivering coloured flags strung across the ceiling were talking. She quite forgot to be shy; she forgot how in the middle of dressing she had sat down on the bed with one shoe off and one shoe on and begged her mother to ring up her cousins and say she couldn't go after all. And the rush of longing she had had to be sitting on the verandah of their forsaken up-country home, listening to the baby owls crying 'More pork' in the moonlight, was changed to a rush of joy so sweet that it was hard to bear alone. She clutched her fan, and, gazing at the gleaming, golden floor, the azaleas, the lanterns, the stage at one end with its red carpet and gilt chairs and the band in a corner, she thought breathlessly, 'How heavenly; how simply heavenly!'

All the girls stood grouped together at one side of the doors, the men at the other, and the chaperones in dark dresses, smiling rather foolishly, walked with little careful steps over the polished floor towards the stage.

'This is my little country cousin Leila. Be nice to her. Find her partners; she's under my wing,' said Meg, going up to one girl after another.

Strange faces smiled at Leila—sweetly, vaguely. Strange voices answered. 'Of course, my dear.' But Leila felt the girls didn't really see her. They were looking towards the men. Why didn't the men begin? What were they waiting for? There they stood, smoothing their gloves, patting their glossy hair and smiling among themselves. Then, quite suddenly, as if they had only just made up their minds that that was what they had to do, the men came gliding over the parquet.[2] There was a joyful flutter among the girls. A tall, fair man flew up to Meg, seized her programme, scribbled something; Meg passed him on to Leila. 'May I have the pleasure?' He

2. Wooden floor inlaid with geometric patterns.

ducked and smiled. There came a dark man wearing an eyeglass, then cousin Laurie with a friend, and Laura with a little freckled fellow whose tie was crooked. Then quite an old man—fat, with a big bald patch on his head—took her programme and murmured, 'Let me see, let me see!' And he was a long time comparing his programme, which looked black with names, with hers. It seemed to give him so much trouble that Leila was ashamed. 'Oh, please don't bother,' she said eagerly. But instead of replying the fat man wrote something, glanced at her again. 'Do I remember this bright little face?' he said softly. 'Is it known to me of yore?' At that moment the band began playing; the fat man disappeared. He was tossed away on a great wave of music that came flying over the gleaming floor, breaking the groups up into couples, scattering them, sending them spinning. . . .

Leila had learned to dance at boarding school. Every Saturday afternoon the boarders were hurried off to a little corrugated iron mission hall where Miss Eccles (of London) held her 'select' classes. But the difference between that dusty-smelling hall—with calico texts on the walls, the poor terrified little woman in a brown velvet toque with rabbit's ears thumping the cold piano, Miss Eccles poking the girls' feet with her long white wand—and this was so tremendous that Leila was sure if her partner didn't come and she had to listen to that marvellous music and to watch the others sliding, gliding over the golden floor, she would die at least, or faint, or lift her arms and fly out of one of those dark windows that showed the stars.

'Ours, I think—' Some one bowed, smiled, and offered her his arm; she hadn't to die after all. Some one's hand pressed her waist, and she floated away like a flower that is tossed into a pool.

'Quite a good floor, isn't it?' drawled a faint voice close to her ear.

'I think it's most beautifully slippery,' said Leila.

'Pardon!' The faint voice sounded surprised. Leila said it again. And there was a tiny pause before the voice echoed, 'Oh, quite!' and she was swung round again.

He steered so beautifully. That was the great difference between dancing with girls and men, Leila decided. Girls banged into each other, and stamped on each other's feet; the girl who was gentleman always clutched you so.

The azaleas were separate flowers no longer; they were pink and white flags streaming by.

'Were you at the Bells' last week?' the voice came again. It sounded tired. Leila wondered whether she ought to ask him if he would like to stop.

'No, this is my first dance,' said she.

Her partner gave a little gasping laugh. 'Oh, I say,' he protested.

'Yes, it is really the first dance I've ever been to.' Leila was most fervent. It was such a relief to be able to tell somebody. 'You see, I've lived in the country all my life up till now. . . .'

At that moment the music stopped, and they went to sit on two chairs against the wall. Leila tucked her pink satin feet under and fanned herself, while she blissfully watched the other couples passing and disappearing through the swing doors.

'Enjoying yourself, Leila?' asked Jose, nodding her golden head.

Laura passed and gave her the faintest little wink; it made Leila wonder for a moment whether she was quite grown up after all. Certainly her partner did not say very much. He coughed, tucked his handkerchief away, pulled down his waistcoat, took a minute thread off his sleeve. But it didn't matter. Almost immediately the band started, and her second partner seemed to spring from the ceiling.

'Floor's not bad,' said the new voice. Did one always begin with the floor? And then, 'Were you at the Neaves' on Tuesday?' And again Leila explained. Perhaps it was a little strange that her partners were not more interested. For it was thrilling. Her first ball! She was only at the beginning of everything. It seemed to her that she had never known what the night was like before. Up till now it had been dark, silent, beautiful very often—oh, yes—but mournful somehow. Solemn. And now it would never be like that again—it had opened dazzling bright.

'Care for an ice?' said her partner. And they went through the swing doors, down the passage, to the supper room. Her cheeks burned, she was fearfully thirsty. How sweet the ices looked on little glass plates, and how cold the frosted spoon was, iced too! And when they came back to the hall there was the fat man waiting for her by the door. It gave her quite a shock again to see how old he was; he ought to have been on the stage with the fathers and mothers. And when Leila compared him with her other partners he looked shabby. His waistcoat was creased, there was a button off his glove, his coat looked as if it was dusty with French chalk.[3]

'Come along, little lady,' said the fat man. He scarcely troubled to clasp her, and they moved away so gently, it was more like walking than dancing. But he said not a word about the floor. 'Your first dance, isn't it?' he murmured.

'How *did* you know?'

'Ah,' said the fat man, 'that's what it is to be old!' He wheezed faintly as he steered her past an awkward couple. 'You see, I've been doing this kind of thing for the last thirty years.'

'Thirty years?' cried Leila. Twelve years before she was born!

3. Chalk sprinkled on dance floors to assist gliding.

'It hardly bears thinking about, does it?' said the fat man gloomily. Leila looked at his bald head, and she felt quite sorry for him.

'I think it's marvellous to be still going on,' she said kindly.

'Kind little lady,' said the fat man, and he pressed her a little closer, and hummed a bar of the waltz. 'Of course,' he said, 'you can't hope to last anything like as long as that. No-o,' said the fat man, 'long before that you'll be sitting up there on the stage, looking on, in your nice black velvet. And these pretty arms will have turned into little short fat ones, and you'll beat time with such a different kind of fan—a black bony one.' The fat man seemed to shudder. 'And you'll smile away like the poor old dears up there, and point to your daughter, and tell the elderly lady next to you how some dreadful man tried to kiss her at the club ball. And your heart will ache, ache'—the fat man squeezed her closer still, as if he really was sorry for that poor heart—because no one wants to kiss you now. And you'll say how unpleasant these polished floors are to walk on, how dangerous they are. Eh, Mademoiselle Twinkletoes?' said the fat man softly.

Leila gave a light little laugh, but she did not feel like laughing. Was it—could it all be true? It sounded terribly true. Was this first ball only the beginning of her last ball after all? At that the music seemed to change; it sounded sad, sad; it rose upon a great sigh. Oh, how quickly things changed! Why didn't happiness last for ever? For ever wasn't a bit too long.

'I want to stop,' she said in a breathless voice. The fat man led her to the door.

'No,' she said, 'I won't go outside. I won't sit down. I'll just stand here, thank you.' She leaned against the wall, tapping with her foot, pulling up her gloves and trying to smile. But deep inside her a little girl threw her pinafore over her head and sobbed. Why had he spoiled it all?

'I say, you know,' said the fat man, 'you mustn't take me seriously, little lady.'

'As if I should!' said Leila, tossing her small dark head and sucking her underlip. . . .

Again the couples paraded. The swing doors opened and shut. Now new music was given out by the bandmaster. But Leila didn't want to dance any more. She wanted to be home, or sitting on the verandah listening to those baby owls. When she looked through the dark windows at the stars, they had long beams like wings. . . .

But presently a soft, melting, ravishing tune began, and a young man with curly hair bowed before her. She would have to dance, out of politeness, until she could find Meg. Very stiffly she walked into the middle; very haughtily she put her hand on his sleeve. But in one minute, in one turn, her feet glided, glided. The lights, the azaleas, the dresses, the pink faces, the velvet chairs, all became one beautiful flying wheel. And when her next partner bumped her into the fat man and he said, 'Par*don*,' she smiled at him more radiantly than ever. She didn't even recognize him again.

Marriage à la Mode (1921)†

On his way to the station William remembered with a fresh pang of disappointment that he was taking nothing down to the kiddies. Poor little chaps! It was hard lines on them. Their first words always were as they ran to greet him, 'What have you got for me, daddy?' and he had nothing. He would have to buy them some sweets at the station. But that was what he had done for the past four Saturdays; their faces had fallen last time when they saw the same old boxes produced again.

And Paddy had said, 'I had red ribbing on mine *bee*-fore!'

And Johnny had said, 'It's always pink on mine. I hate pink.'

But what was William to do? The affair wasn't so easily settled. In the old days, of course, he would have taken a taxi off to a decent toyshop and chosen them something in five minutes. But nowadays they had Russian toys, French toys, Serbian toys—toys from God knows where. It was over a year since Isabel had scrapped the old donkeys and engines and so on because they were so 'dreadfully sentimental' and 'so appallingly bad for the babies' sense of form.'

'It's so important,' the new Isabel had explained, 'that they should like the right things from the very beginning. It saves so much time later on. Really, if the poor pets have to spend their infant years staring at these horrors, one can imagine them growing up and asking to be taken to the Royal Academy.'[1]

And she spoke as though a visit to the Royal Academy was certain immediate death to anyone. . . .

'Well, I don't know,' said William slowly. 'When I was their age I used to go to bed hugging an old towel with a knot in it.'

The new Isabel looked at him, her eyes narrowed, her lips apart.

'*Dear* William! I'm sure you did!' She laughed in the new way.

Sweets it would have to be, however, thought William gloomily, fishing in his pocket for change for the taxi-man. And he saw the

† Published in the *Sphere* (31 December 1921) and collected in *The Garden Party and Other Stories* (1922). The title means "Fashionable Marriage."

1. An institution established in London in the eighteenth century to cultivate the visual arts and to display exhibitions. By Mansfield's time its taste was regarded by artists and critics as outmoded.

kiddies handing the boxes round—they were awfully generous little chaps—while Isabel's precious friends didn't hesitate to help themselves. . . .

What about fruit? William hovered before a stall just inside the station. What about a melon each? Would they have to share that, too? Or a pineapple for Pad, and a melon for Johnny? Isabel's friends could hardly go sneaking up to the nursery at the children's meal-times. All the same, as he bought the melon William had a horrible vision of one of Isabel's young poets lapping up a slice, for some reason, behind the nursery door.

With his two very awkward parcels he strode off to his train. The platform was crowded, the train was in. Doors banged open and shut. There came such a loud hissing from the engine that people looked dazed as they scurried to and fro. William made straight for a first-class smoker, stowed away his suit-case and parcels, and taking a huge wad of papers out of his inner pocket, he flung down in the corner and began to read.

'Our client moreover is positive. . . . We are inclined to reconsider . . . in the event of—' Ah, that was better. William pressed back his flattened hair and stretched his legs across the carriage floor. The familiar dull gnawing in his breast quietened down. 'With regard to our decision—' He took out a blue pencil and scored a paragraph slowly.

Two men came in, stepped across him, and made for the farther corner. A young fellow swung his golf clubs into the rack and sat down opposite. The train gave a gentle lurch, they were off. William glanced up and saw the hot, bright station slipping away. A red-faced girl raced along by the carriages, there was something strained and almost desperate in the way she waved and called. 'Hysterical!' thought William dully. Then a greasy, black-faced workman at the end of the platform grinned at the passing train. And William thought, 'A filthy life!' and went back to his papers.

When he looked up again there were fields, and beasts standing for shelter under the dark trees. A wide river, with naked children splashing in the shallows, glided into sight and was gone again. The sky shone pale, and one bird drifted high like a dark fleck in a jewel.

'We have examined our client's correspondence files. . . .' The last sentence he had read echoed in his mind. 'We have examined. . . .' William hung on to that sentence, but it was no good; it snapped in the middle, and the fields, the sky, the sailing bird, the water, all said, 'Isabel'. The same thing happened every Saturday afternoon. When he was on his way to meet Isabel there began those countless imaginary meetings. She was at the station, standing just a little apart from everybody else; she was sitting in the open taxi outside; she was at the garden gate; walking across the parched grass; at the door, or just inside the hall.

And her clear, light voice said, 'It's William,' or 'Hillo, William!' or 'So William has come!' He touched her cool hand, her cool cheek.

The exquisite freshness of Isabel! When he had been a little boy, it was his delight to run into the garden after a shower of rain and shake the rose-bush over him. Isabel was that rose-bush, petal-soft, sparkling and cool. And he was still that little boy. But there was no running into the garden now, no laughing and shaking. The dull, persistent gnawing in his breast started again. He drew up his legs, tossed the papers aside, and shut his eyes.

'What is it, Isabel? What is it?' he said tenderly. They were in their bedroom in the new house. Isabel sat on a painted stool before the dressing-table that was strewn with little black and green boxes.

'What is what, William?' And she bent forward, and her fine light hair fell over her cheeks.

'Ah, you know!' He stood in the middle of the strange room and he felt a stranger. At that Isabel wheeled round quickly and faced him.

'Oh, William!' she cried imploringly, and she held up the hairbrush. 'Please! Please don't be so dreadfully stuffy and—tragic. You're always saying or looking or hinting that I've changed. Just because I've got to know really congenial people, and go about more, and am frightfully keen on—on everything, you behave as though I'd—' Isabel tossed back her hair and laughed—'killed our love or something. It's so awfully absurd'—she bit her lip—'and it's so maddening, William. Even this new house and the servants you grudge me.'

'Isabel!'

'Yes, yes, it's true in a way,' said Isabel quickly. 'You think they are another bad sign. Oh, I know you do. I feel it,' she said softly, 'every time you come up the stairs. But we couldn't have gone on living in that other poky little hole, William. Be practical, at least! Why, there wasn't enough room for the babies even.'

No, it was true. Every evening when he came back from chambers it was to find the babies with Isabel in the back drawing-room. They were having rides on the leopard skin thrown over the sofa back, or they were playing shops with Isabel's desk for a counter, or Pad was sitting on the hearthrug rowing away for dear life with a little brass fire-shovel, while Johnny shot at pirates with the tongs. Every evening they each had a pick-a-back up the narrow stairs to their fat old Nanny.

Yes, he supposed it was a poky little house. A little white house with blue curtains and a window-box full of petunias. William met their friends at the door with 'Seen our petunias? Pretty terrific for London, don't you think?'

But the imbecile thing, the absolutely extraordinary thing was that he hadn't the slightest idea that Isabel wasn't as happy as he. God, what blindness! He hadn't the remotest notion in those days that she really hated that inconvenient little house, that she thought the fat Nanny was ruining the babies, that she was desperately lonely, pining for new people and new music and pictures and so on. If they hadn't gone to that studio party at Moira Morrison's—if Moira Morrison hadn't said as they were leaving, 'I'm going to rescue your wife, selfish man. She's like an exquisite little Titania'[2]—if Isabel hadn't gone with Moira to Paris—if—if. . . .

The train stopped at another station. Bettingford. Good heavens! They'd be there in ten minutes. William stuffed the papers back into his pockets; the young man opposite had long since disappeared. Now the other two got out. The late afternoon sun shone on women in cotton frocks and little sunburnt, barefoot children. It blazed on a silky yellow flower with coarse leaves which sprawled over a bank of rock. The air ruffling through the window smelled of the sea. Had Isabel the same crowd with her this week-end, wondered William?

And he remembered the holidays they used to have, the four of them, with a little farm girl, Rose, to look after the babies. Isabel wore a jersey and her hair in a plait; she looked about fourteen. Lord! how his nose used to peel! And the amount they ate, and the amount they slept in that immense feather bed with their feet locked together. . . . William couldn't help a grim smile as he thought of Isabel's horror if she knew the full extent of his sentimentality.

'Hillo, William!' She was at the station after all, standing just as he had imagined, apart from the others, and—William's heart leapt—she was alone.

'Hullo, Isabel!' William stared. He thought she looked so beautiful that he had to say something, 'You look very cool.'

'Do I?' said Isabel. 'I don't feel very cool. Come along, your horrid old train is late. The taxi's outside.' She put her hand lightly on his arm as they passed the ticket collector. 'We've all come to meet you,' she said. 'But we've left Bobby Kane at the sweet shop, to be called for.'

'Oh!' said William. It was all he could say for the moment.

There in the glare waited the taxi, with Bill Hunt and Dennis

2. The Queen of the Fairies in Shakespeare's *A Midsummer Night's Dream*.

Green sprawling on one side, their hats tilted over their faces, while on the other, Moira Morrison, in a bonnet like a huge strawberry, jumped up and down.

'No ice! No ice! No ice!' she shouted gaily.

And Dennis chimed in from under his hat. '*Only* to be had from the fishmonger's.'

And Bill Hunt, emerging, added, 'With *whole* fish in it.'

'Oh, what a bore!' wailed Isabel. And she explained to William how they had been chasing round the town for ice while she waited for him. 'Simply everything is running down the steep cliffs into the sea, beginning with the butter.'

'We shall have to anoint ourselves with the butter,' said Dennis. 'May thy head, William, lack not ointment.'[3]

'Look here,' said William, 'how are we going to sit? I'd better get up by the driver.'

'No, Bobby Kane's by the driver,' said Isabel. 'You're to sit between Moira and me.' The taxi started. 'What have you got in those mysterious parcels?'

'De-cap-it-ated heads!' said Bill Hunt, shuddering beneath his hat.

'Oh, fruit!' Isabel sounded very pleased. 'Wise William! A melon and a pineapple. How too nice!'

'No, wait a bit,' said William, smiling. But he really was anxious. 'I brought them down for the kiddies.'

'Oh, my dear!' Isabel laughed, and slipped her hand through his arm. 'They'd be rolling in agonies if they were to eat them. No'—she patted his hand—'you must bring them something next time. I refuse to part with my pineapple.'

'Cruel Isabel! Do let me smell it!' said Moira. She flung her arms across William appealingly. 'Oh!' The strawberry bonnet fell forward: she sounded quite faint.

'A Lady in Love with a Pineapple,' said Dennis, as the taxi drew up before a little shop with a striped blind. Out came Bobby Kane, his arms full of little packets.

'I do hope they'll be good. I've chosen them because of the colours. There are some round things which really look too divine. And just look at this nougat,' he cried ecstatically, 'just look at it! It's a perfect little ballet!'

But at that moment the shopman appeared. 'Oh, I forgot. They're none of them paid for,' said Bobby, looking frightened. Isabel gave the shopman a note, and Bobby was radiant again. 'Hullo, William! I'm sitting by the driver.' And bare-headed, all in white, with his sleeves rolled up to the shoulders, he leapt into his place. 'Avanti!'[4] he cried. . . .

3. "Let thy garments be always white, and let thy head lack no ointment" (Eccl. 9:8).
4. Forward! [Italian].

After tea the others went off to bathe, while William stayed and made his peace with the kiddies. But Johnny and Paddy were asleep, the rose-red glow had paled, bats were flying, and still the bathers had not returned. As William wandered downstairs, the maid crossed the hall carrying a lamp. He followed her into the sitting-room. It was a long room, coloured yellow. On the wall opposite William some one had painted a young man, over life-size, with very wobbly legs, offering a wide-eyed daisy to a young woman who had one very short arm and one very long, thin one. Over the chairs and sofa there hung strips of black material, covered with big splashes like broken eggs, and everywhere one looked there seemed to be an ash-tray full of cigarette ends. William sat down in one of the arm-chairs. Nowadays, when one felt with one hand down the sides, it wasn't to come upon a sheep with three legs or a cow that had lost one horn, or a very fat dove out of the Noah's Ark. One fished up yet another little paper-covered book of smudged-looking poems. . . . He thought of the wad of papers in his pocket, but he was too hungry and tired to read. The door was open; sounds came from the kitchen. The servants were talking as if they were alone in the house. Suddenly there came a loud screech of laughter and an equally loud 'Sh!' They had remembered him. William got up and went through the french windows into the garden, and as he stood there in the shadow he heard the bathers coming up the sandy road; their voices rang through the quiet.

'I think it's up to Moira to use her little arts and wiles.'

A tragic moan from Moira.

'We ought to have a gramophone for the week-ends that played "The Maid of the Mountains".'[5]

'Oh no! Oh no!' cried Isabel's voice. 'That's not fair to William. Be nice to him, my children! He's only staying until tomorrow evening.'

'Leave him to me,' cried Bobby Kane. 'I'm awfully good at looking after people.'

The gate swung open and shut. William moved on the terrace; they had seen him. 'Hallo, William!' And Bobby Kane, flapping his towel, began to leap and pirouette on the parched lawn. 'Pity you didn't come, William. The water was divine. And we all went to a little pub afterwards and had sloe gin.'

The others had reached the house. 'I say, Isabel,' called Bobby, 'would you like me to wear my Nijinsky[6] dress to-night?'

'No,' said Isabel, 'nobody's going to dress. We're all starving.

5. *The Maid of the Mountains* (1918), a light opera by Harold Fraser-Simpson.
6. Vaslav Nijinsky (1890–1950), Russian ballet dancer and choreographer, particularly popular at the period when this story was set.

William's starving, too. Come along, *mes amis*, let's begin with sardines.'

'I've found the sardines,' said Moira, and she ran into the hall, holding a box high in the air.

'A Lady with a Box of Sardines,' said Dennis gravely.

'Well, William, and how's London?' asked Bill Hunt, drawing the cork out of a bottle of whisky.

'Oh, London's not much changed,' answered William.

'Good old London,' said Bobby, very hearty, spearing a sardine.

But a moment later William was forgotten. Moira Morrison began wondering what colour one's legs really were under water.

'Mine are the palest, palest mushroom colour.'

Bill and Dennis ate enormously. And Isabel filled glasses, and changed plates, and found matches, smiling blissfully. At one moment she said, 'I do wish, Bill, you'd paint it.'

'Paint what?' said Billy loudly, stuffing his mouth with bread.

'Us,' said Isabel, 'round the table. It would be so fascinating in twenty years' time.'

Bill screwed up his eyes and chewed. 'Light's wrong,' he said rudely, 'far too much yellow'; and went on eating. And that seemed to charm Isabel, too.

But after supper they were all so tired they could do nothing but yawn until it was late enough to go to bed. . . .

It was not until William was waiting for his taxi the next afternoon that he found himself alone with Isabel. When he brought his suit-case down into the hall, Isabel left the others and went over to him. She stooped down and picked up the suit-case. 'What a weight!' she said, and she gave a little awkward laugh. 'Let me carry it! To the gate.'

'No, why should you?' said William. 'Of course not. Give it to me.'

'Oh, please do let me,' said Isabel. 'I want to, really.' They walked together silently. William felt there was nothing to say now.

'There,' said Isabel triumphantly, setting the suit-case down, and she looked anxiously along the sandy road. 'I hardly seem to have seen you this time,' she said breathlessly. 'It's so short, isn't it? I feel you've only just come. Next time—' The taxi came into sight. 'I hope they look after you properly in London. I'm so sorry the babies have been out all day, but Miss Neil had arranged it. They'll hate missing you. Poor William, going back to London.' The taxi turned. 'Good-bye!' She gave him a little hurried kiss; she was gone.

Fields, trees, hedges streamed by. They shook through the empty, blind-looking little town, ground up the steep pull to the station.

The train was in. William made straight for a first-class smoker, flung back into the corner, but this time he let the papers alone. He folded his arms against the dull, persistent gnawing, and began in his mind to write a letter to Isabel.

The post was late as usual. They sat outside the house in long chairs under coloured parasols. Only Bobby Kane lay on the turf at Isabel's feet. It was dull, stifling; the day drooped like a flag.

'Do you think there will be Mondays in Heaven?' asked Bobby childishly.

And Dennis murmured, 'Heaven will be one long Monday.'

But Isabel couldn't help wondering what had happened to the salmon they had for supper last night. She had meant to have fish mayonnaise for lunch and now. . . .

Moira was asleep. Sleeping was her latest discovery. 'It's *so* wonderful. One simply shuts one's eyes, that's all. It's *so* delicious.'

When the old ruddy postman came beating along the sandy road on his tricycle one felt the handle-bars ought to have been oars.

Bill Hunt put down his book. 'Letters,' he said complacently, and they all waited. But, heartless postman—O malignant world! There was only one, a fat one for Isabel. Not even a paper.

'And mine's only from William,' said Isabel mournfully.

'From William—already?'

'He's sending you back your marriage lines[7] as a gentle reminder.'

'Does everybody have marriage lines? I thought they were only for servants.'

'Pages and pages! Look at her! A Lady reading a Letter,' said Dennis.

My darling, precious Isabel. Pages and pages there were. As Isabel read on her feeling of astonishment changed to a stifled feeling. What on earth had induced William. . . ? How extraordinary it was. . . . What could have made him . . . ? She felt confused, more and more excited, even frightened. It was just like William. Was it? It was absurd, of course, it must be absurd, ridiculous. 'Ha, ha, ha! Oh dear!' What was she to do? Isabel flung back in her chair and laughed till she couldn't stop laughing.

'Do, do tell us,' said the others. 'You must tell us.'

'I'm longing to,' gurgled Isabel. She sat up, gathered the letter, and waved it at them. 'Gather round,' she said. 'Listen, it's too marvellous. A love-letter!'

'A love-letter! But how divine!' *Darling, precious Isabel.* But she had hardly begun before their laughter interrupted her.

'Go on, Isabel, it's perfect.'

7. Marriage certificate.

'It's the most marvellous find.'

'Oh, do go on, Isabel!'

God forbid, my darling, that I should be a drag on your happiness.

'Oh! oh! oh!'

'Sh! sh! sh!'

And Isabel went on. When she reached the end they were hysterical: Bobby rolled on the turf and almost sobbed.

'You must let me have it just as it is, entire, for my new book,' said Dennis firmly. 'I shall give it a whole chapter.'

'Oh, Isabel,' moaned Moira, 'that wonderful bit about holding you in his arms!'

'I always thought those letters in divorce cases were made up. But they pale before this.'

'Let me hold it. Let me read it, mine own self,' said Bobby Kane.

But, to their surprise, Isabel crushed the letter in her hand. She was laughing no longer. She glanced quickly at them all; she looked exhausted. 'No, not just now. Not just now,' she stammered.

And before they could recover she had run into the house, through the hall, up the stairs into her bedroom. Down she sat on the side of the bed. 'How vile, odious, abominable, vulgar,' muttered Isabel. She pressed her eyes with her knuckles and rocked to and fro. And again she saw them, but not four, more like forty, laughing, sneering, jeering, stretching out their hands while she read them William's letter. Oh, what a loathsome thing to have done. How could she have done it! *God forbid, my darling, that I should be a drag on your happiness.* William! Isabel pressed her face into the pillow. But she felt that even the grave bedroom knew her for what she was, shallow, tinkling, vain. . . .

Presently from the garden below there came voices.

'Isabel, we're all going for a bathe. Do come!'

'Come, thou wife of William!'

'Call her once before you go, call once yet!'[8]

Isabel sat up. Now was the moment, now she must decide. Would she go with them, or stay here and write to William. Which, which should it be? 'I must make up my mind.' Oh, but how could there be any question? Of course she would stay here and write.

'Titania!' piped Moira.

'Isa-bel?'

No, it was too difficult. 'I'll—I'll go with them, and write to William later. Some other time. Later. Not now. But I shall *certainly* write,' thought Isabel hurriedly.

And, laughing in the new way, she ran down the stairs.

8. Call her once before you go,
Call once yet!
—Matthew Arnold, "The Forsaken Merman," 1849, lines 10–11.

At the Bay (1921)†

I

Very early morning. The sun was not yet risen, and the whole of Crescent Bay was hidden under a white sea-mist. The big bush-covered hills at the back were smothered. You could not see where they ended and the paddocks and bungalows began. The sandy road was gone and the paddocks and bungalows the other side of it; there were no white dunes covered with reddish grass beyond them; there was nothing to mark which was beach and where was the sea. A heavy dew had fallen. The grass was blue. Big drops hung on the bushes and just did not fall; the silvery, fluffy toi-toi[1] was limp on its long stalks, and all the marigolds and the pinks in the bungalow gardens were bowed to the earth with wetness. Drenched were the cold fuchsias, round pearls of dew lay on the flat nasturtium leaves. It looked as though the sea had beaten up softly in the darkness, as though one immense wave had come rippling, rippling—how far? Perhaps if you had waked up in the middle of the night you might have seen a big fish flicking in at the window and gone again. . . .

Ah-Aah! sounded the sleepy sea. And from the bush there came the sound of little streams flowing, quickly, lightly, slipping between the smooth stones, gushing into ferny basins and out again; and there was the splashing of big drops on large leaves, and something else—what was it?—a faint stirring and shaking, the snapping of a twig and then such silence that it seemed some one was listening.

Round the corner of Crescent Bay, between the piled-up masses of broken rock, a flock of sheep came pattering. They were huddled together, a small, tossing, woolly mass, and their thin, stick-like legs trotted along quickly as if the cold and the quiet had frightened them. Behind them an old sheep-dog, his soaking paws covered with sand, ran along with his nose to the ground, but carelessly, as if thinking of something else. And then in the rocky gateway the shepherd himself appeared. He was a lean, upright old man, in a frieze coat that was covered with a web of tiny drops, velvet trousers tied under the knee, and a wide-awake with a folded blue handkerchief round the brim. One hand was crammed into his belt, the other grasped a beautifully smooth yellow stick. And as he walked, taking his time, he kept up a very soft light whistling, an airy, far-away fluting that sounded mournful and tender. The old dog cut an ancient caper or two and then drew up sharp, ashamed

† Written in the second half of 1921, published in the *London Mercury* (January 1922), and then collected in *The Garden Party and Other Stories* (1922).

1. A coarse, flax-like grass with tall silvery plumes.

of his levity, and walked a few dignified paces by his master's side. The sheep ran forward in little pattering rushes; they began to bleat, and ghostly flocks and herds answered them from under the sea. 'Baa! Baaa!' For a time they seemed to be always on the same piece of ground. There ahead was stretched the sandy road with shallow puddles, the same soaking bushes showed on either side and the same shadowy palings. Then something immense came into view; an enormous shock-haired giant with his arms stretched out. It was the big gum-tree outside Mrs Stubbs's shop, and as they passed by there was a strong whiff of eucalyptus. And now big spots of light gleamed in the mist. The shepherd stopped whistling; he rubbed his red nose and wet beard on his wet sleeve and, screwing up his eyes, glanced in the direction of the sea. The sun was rising. It was marvellous how quickly the mist thinned, sped away, dissolved from the shallow plain, rolled up from the bush and was gone as if in a hurry to escape; big twists and curls jostled and shouldered each other as the silvery beams broadened. The far-away sky—a bright, pure blue—was reflected in the puddles, and the drops, swimming along the telegraph wires, flashed into points of light. Now the leaping, glittering sea was so bright it made one's eyes ache to look at it. The shepherd drew a pipe, the bowl as small as an acorn, out of his breast pocket, fumbled for a chunk of speckled tobacco, pared off a few shavings and stuffed the bowl. He was a grave, fine-looking old man. As he lit up and the blue smoke wreathed his head, the dog, watching, looked proud of him.

'Baa! Baaa!' The sheep spread out into a fan. They were just clear of the summer colony before the first sleeper turned over and lifted a drowsy head; their cry sounded in the dreams of little children . . . who lifted their arms to drag down, to cuddle the darling little woolly lambs of sleep. Then the first inhabitant appeared; it was the Burnells' cat Florrie, sitting on the gatepost, far too early as usual, looking for their milk-girl. When she saw the old sheep-dog she sprang up quickly, arched her back, drew in her tabby head, and seemed to give a little fastidious shiver. 'Ugh! What a coarse, revolting creature!' said Florrie. But the old sheepdog, not looking up, waggled past, flinging out his legs from side to side. Only one of his ears twitched to prove that he saw, and thought her a silly young female.

The breeze of morning lifted in the bush and the smell of leaves and wet black earth mingled with the sharp smell of the sea. Myriads of birds were singing. A goldfinch flew over the shepherd's head and, perching on the tiptop of a spray, it turned to the sun, ruffling its small breast feathers. And now they had passed the fisherman's hut, passed the charred-looking little *whare* where Leila the milk-girl lived with her old Gran. The sheep strayed over a yellow swamp and Wag, the sheep-dog, padded after, rounded them up and headed them for the steeper, narrower rocky pass that led out of Crescent Bay and towards Daylight Cove. 'Baa! Baaa!' Faint the cry came as they rocked along the fast-drying road. The shepherd put away his pipe, dropping it into his breast-pocket so that the little bowl hung over. And straightway the soft airy whistling began again. Wag ran out along a ledge of rock after something that smelled, and ran back again disgusted. Then pushing, nudging, hurrying, the sheep rounded the bend and the shepherd followed after out of sight.

II

A few moments later the back door of one of the bungalows opened, and a figure in a broad-striped bathing suit flung down the paddock, cleared the stile, rushed through the tussock grass into the hollow, staggered up the sandy hillock, and raced for dear life over the big porous stones, over the cold, wet pebbles, on to the hard sand that gleamed like oil. Splish-Splosh! Splish-Splosh! The water bubbled round his legs as Stanley Burnell waded out exulting. First man in as usual! He'd beaten them all again. And he swooped down to souse his head and neck.

'Hail, brother! All hail, Thou Mighty One!' A velvety bass voice came booming over the water.

Great Scott! Damnation take it! Stanley lifted up to see a dark head bobbing far out and an arm lifted. It was Jonathan Trout—there before him! 'Glorious morning!' sang the voice.

'Yes, very fine!' said Stanley briefly. Why the dickens didn't the fellow stick to his part of the sea? Why should he come barging over to this exact spot? Stanley gave a kick, a lunge and struck out, swimming overarm. But Jonathan was a match for him. Up he came, his black hair sleek on his forehead, his short beard sleek.

'I had an extraordinary dream last night!' he shouted.

What was the matter with the man? This mania for conversation irritated Stanley beyond words. And it was always the same—always some piffle about a dream he'd had, or some cranky idea he'd got hold of, or some rot he'd been reading. Stanley turned over on his back and kicked with his legs till he was a living waterspout. But even then. . . . 'I dreamed I was hanging over a terrifically high cliff, shouting to some one below.' You would be! thought Stanley. He could stick no more of it. He stopped splashing. 'Look here, Trout,' he said, 'I'm in rather a hurry this morning.'

'You're WHAT?' Jonathan was so surprised—or pretended to be—that he sank under the water, then reappeared again blowing.

'All I mean is,' said Stanley, 'I've no time to—to—to fool about. I want to get this over. I'm in a hurry. I've work to do this morning—see?'

Jonathan was gone before Stanley had finished. 'Pass, friend!' said the bass voice gently, and he slid away through the water with scarcely a ripple. . . . But curse the fellow! He'd ruined Stanley's bathe. What an unpractical idiot the man was! Stanley struck out to sea again, and then as quickly swam in again, and away he rushed up the beach. He felt cheated.

Jonathan stayed a little longer in the water. He floated, gently moving his hands like fins, and letting the sea rock his long, skinny body. It was curious, but in spite of everything he was fond of Stanley Burnell. True, he had a fiendish desire to tease him sometimes, to poke fun at him, but at bottom he was sorry for the fellow. There was something pathetic in his determination to make a job of everything. You couldn't help feeling he'd be caught out one day, and then what an almighty cropper he'd come! At that moment an immense wave lifted Jonathan, rode past him, and broke along the beach with a joyful sound. What a beauty! And now there came another. That was the way to live—carelessly, recklessly, spending oneself. He got on to his feet and began to wade towards the shore, pressing his toes into the firm, wrinkled sand. To take things easy, not to fight against the ebb and flow of life, but to give way to it—that was what was needed. It was this tension that was all wrong. To live—to live! And the perfect morning, so fresh and fair, basking in the light, as though laughing at its own beauty, seemed to whisper, 'Why not?'

But now he was out of the water Jonathan turned blue with cold. He ached all over; it was as though some one was wringing the blood out of him. And stalking up the beach, shivering, all his muscles tight, he too felt his bathe was spoilt. He'd stayed in too long.

III

Beryl was alone in the living-room when Stanley appeared, wearing a blue serge suit, a stiff collar and a spotted tie. He looked almost uncannily clean and brushed; he was going to town for the day. Dropping into his chair, he pulled out his watch and put it beside his plate.

'I've just got twenty-five minutes,' he said. 'You might go and see if the porridge is ready, Beryl?'

'Mother's just gone for it,' said Beryl. She sat down at the table and poured out his tea.

'Thanks!' Stanley took a sip. 'Hallo!' he said in an astonished voice, 'you've forgotten the sugar.'

'Oh, sorry!' But even then Beryl didn't help him; she pushed the basin across. What did this mean? As Stanley helped himself his blue eyes widened; they seemed to quiver. He shot a quick glance at his sister-in-law and leaned back.

'Nothing wrong, is there?' he asked carelessly, fingering his collar.

Beryl's head was bent; she turned her plate in her fingers.

'Nothing,' said her light voice. Then she too looked up, and smiled at Stanley. 'Why should there be?'

'O-oh! No reason at all as far as I know. I thought you seemed rather—'

At that moment the door opened and the three little girls appeared, each carrying a porridge plate. They were dressed alike in blue jerseys and knickers; their brown legs were bare, and each had her hair plaited and pinned up in what was called a horse's tail. Behind them came Mrs Fairfield with the tray.

'Carefully, children,' she warned. But they were taking the very greatest care. They loved being allowed to carry things. 'Have you said good morning to your father?'

'Yes, grandma.' They settled themselves on the bench opposite Stanley and Beryl.

'Good morning, Stanley!' Old Mrs Fairfield gave him his plate.

'Morning, mother! How's the boy?'

'Splendid! He only woke up once last night. What a perfect morning!' The old woman paused, her hand on the loaf of bread, to gaze out of the open door into the garden. The sea sounded. Through the wide-open window streamed the sun on to the yellow varnished walls and bare floor. Everything on the table flashed and glittered. In the middle there was an old salad bowl filled with yellow and red nasturtiums. She smiled, and a look of deep content shone in her eyes.

'You might *cut* me a slice of that bread, mother,' said Stanley. 'I've only twelve and a half minutes before the coach passes. Has anyone given my shoes to the servant girl?'

'Yes, they're ready for you.' Mrs Fairfield was quite unruffled.

'Oh, Kezia! Why are you such a messy child!' cried Beryl despairingly.

'Me, Aunt Beryl?' Kezia stared at her. What had she done now? She had only dug a river down the middle of her porridge, filled it, and was eating the banks away. But she did that every single morning, and no one had said a word up till now.

'Why can't you eat your food properly like Isabel and Lottie?' How unfair grownups are!

'But Lottie always makes a floating island, don't you, Lottie?'

'I don't,' said Isabel smartly. 'I just sprinkle mine with sugar and put on the milk and finish it. Only babies play with their food.'

Stanley pushed back his chair and got up.

'Would you get me those shoes, mother? And, Beryl, if you've finished, I wish you'd cut down to the gate and stop the coach. Run in to your mother, Isabel, and ask her where my bowler hat's been put. Wait a minute—have you children been playing with my stick?'

'No, father!'

'But I put it here,' Stanley began to bluster. 'I remember distinctly putting it in this corner. Now, who's had it? There's no time to lose. Look sharp! The stick's got to be found.'

Even Alice, the servant-girl, was drawn into the chase. 'You haven't been using it to poke the kitchen fire with by any chance?'

Stanley dashed into the bedroom where Linda was lying. 'Most extraordinary thing. I can't keep a single possession to myself. They've made away with my stick, now!'

'Stick, dear? What stick?' Linda's vagueness on these occasions could not be real, Stanley decided. Would nobody sympathize with him?

'Coach! Coach, Stanley!' Beryl's voice cried from the gate.

Stanley waved his arm to Linda. 'No time to say good-bye!' he cried. And he meant that as a punishment to her.

He snatched his bowler hat, dashed out of the house, and swung down the garden path. Yes, the coach was there waiting, and Beryl, leaning over the open gate, was laughing up at somebody or other just as if nothing had happened. The heartlessness of women! The way they took it for granted it was your job to slave away for them while they didn't even take the trouble to see that your walking-stick wasn't lost. Kelly trailed his whip across the horses.

'Good-bye, Stanley,' called Beryl, sweetly and gaily. It was easy enough to say good-bye! And there she stood, idle, shading her eyes with her hand. The worst of it was Stanley had to shout good-bye too, for the sake of appearances. Then he saw her turn, give a little skip and run back to the house. She was glad to be rid of him!

Yes, she was thankful. Into the living-room she ran and called 'He's gone!' Linda cried from her room: 'Beryl! Has Stanley gone?' Old Mrs Fairfield appeared, carrying the boy in his little flannel coatee.

'Gone?'

'Gone!'

Oh, the relief, the difference it made to have the man out of the house. Their very voices were changed as they called to one another; they sounded warm and loving and as if they shared a secret. Beryl went over to the table. 'Have another cup of tea, mother. It's still hot.' She wanted, somehow, to celebrate the fact that they could do what they liked now. There was no man to disturb them; the whole perfect day was theirs.

'No, thank you, child,' said old Mrs Fairfield, but the way at that moment she tossed the boy up and said 'a-goos-a-goos-a-ga!' to him meant that she felt the same. The little girls ran into the paddock like chickens let out of a coop.

Even Alice, the servant-girl, washing up the dishes in the kitchen, caught the infection and used the precious tank water in a perfectly reckless fashion.

'Oh, these men!' said she, and she plunged the teapot into the bowl and held it under the water even after it had stopped bubbling, as if it too was a man and drowning was too good for them.

IV

'Wait for me, Isa-bel! Kezia, wait for me!'

There was poor little Lottie, left behind again, because she found it so fearfully hard to get over the stile by herself. When she stood on the first step her knees began to wobble; she grasped the post. Then you had to put one leg over. But which leg? She never could decide. And when she did finally put one leg over with a sort of stamp of despair—then the feeling was awful. She was half in the paddock still and half in the tussock grass. She clutched the post desperately and lifted up her voice. 'Wait for me!'

'No, don't you wait for her, Kezia!' said Isabel. 'She's such a little silly. She's always making a fuss. Come on!' And she tugged Kezia's jersey. 'You can use my bucket if you come with me,' she said kindly. 'It's bigger than yours.' But Kezia couldn't leave Lottie all by herself. She ran back to her. By this time Lottie was very red in the face and breathing heavily.

'Here, put your other foot over,' said Kezia.

'Where?'

Lottie looked down at Kezia as if from a mountain height.

'Here where my hand is.' Kezia patted the place.

'Oh, *there* do you mean?' Lottie gave a deep sigh and put the second foot over.

'Now—sort of turn round and sit down and slide,' said Kezia.

'But there's nothing to sit down *on*, Kezia,' said Lottie.

She managed it at last, and once it was over she shook herself and began to beam.

'I'm getting better at climbing over stiles, aren't I, Kezia?'

Lottie's was a very hopeful nature.

The pink and the blue sunbonnet followed Isabel's bright red sunbonnet up that sliding, slipping hill. At the top they paused to decide where to go and to have a good stare at who was there already. Seen from behind, standing against the skyline, gesticulating largely with their spades, they looked like minute puzzled explorers.

The whole family of Samuel Josephs was there already with their lady-help, who sat on a camp-stool and kept order with a whistle that she wore tied round her neck, and a small cane with which she directed operations. The Samuel Josephs never played by themselves or managed their own game. If they did, it ended in the boys pouring water down the girls' necks or the girls trying to put little black crabs into the boys' pockets. So Mrs S. J. and the poor lady-help drew up what she called a 'brogramme' every morning to keep them 'abused and out of bischief'. It was all competitions or races or round games. Everything began with a piercing blast of the lady-help's whistle and ended with another. There were even prizes—large, rather dirty paper parcels which the lady-help with a sour little smile drew out of a bulging string kit. The Samuel Josephs fought fearfully for the prizes and cheated and pinched one another's arms—they were all expert pinchers. The only time the Burnell children ever played with them Kezia had got a prize, and when she undid three bits of paper she found a very small rusty button-hook. She couldn't understand why they made such a fuss. . . .

But they never played with the Samuel Josephs now or even went to their parties. The Samuel Josephs were always giving children's parties at the Bay and there was always the same food. A big wash-hand basin of very brown fruit-salad, buns cut into four and a washhand jug full of something the lady-help called 'Limmonadear'.[2] And you went away in the evening with half the frill torn off your frock or something spilled all down the front of your open-work pinafore, leaving the Samuel Josephs leaping like savages on their lawn. No. They were too awful.

On the other side of the beach, close down to the water, two little boys, their knickers rolled up, twinkled like spiders. One was digging, the other pattered in and out of the water, filling a small bucket. They were the Trout boys, Pip and Rags. But Pip was so busy digging and Rags was so busy helping that they didn't see their little cousins until they were quite close.

'Look!' said Pip. 'Look what I've discovered.' And he showed them an old, wet, squashed-looking boot. The three little girls stared.

'Whatever are you going to do with it?' asked Kezia.

'Keep it, of course!' Pip was very scornful. 'It's a find—see?'

Yes, Kezia saw that. All the same. . . .

'There's lots of things buried in the sand,' explained Pip. 'They get chucked up from wrecks. Treasure. Why—you might find—'

'But why does Rags have to keep on pouring water in?' asked Lottie.

'Oh, that's to moisten it,' said Pip, 'to make the work a bit easier. Keep it up, Rags.'

2. Lemonade.

And good little Rags ran up and down, pouring in the water that turned brown like cocoa.

'Here, shall I show you what I found yesterday?' said Pip mysteriously, and he stuck his spade into the sand. 'Promise not to tell.'

They promised.

'Say, cross my heart straight dinkum.'

The little girls said it.

Pip took something out of his pocket, rubbed it a long time on the front of his jersey, then breathed on it and rubbed it again.

'Now turn round!' he ordered.

They turned round.

'All look the same way! Keep still! Now!'

And his hand opened; he held up to the light something that flashed, that winked, that was a most lovely green.

'It's a nemeral,' said Pip solemnly.

'Is it really, Pip?' Even Isabel was impressed.

The lovely green thing seemed to dance in Pip's fingers. Aunt Beryl had a nemeral in a ring, but it was a very small one. This one was as big as a star and far more beautiful.

V

As the morning lengthened whole parties appeared over the sand-hills and came down on the beach to bathe. It was understood that at eleven o'clock the women and children of the summer colony had the sea to themselves. First the women undressed, pulled on their bathing dresses and covered their heads in hideous caps like sponge bags; then the children were unbuttoned. The beach was strewn with little heaps of clothes and shoes; the big summer hats, with stones on them to keep them from blowing away, looked like immense shells. It was strange that even the sea seemed to sound differently when all those leaping, laughing figures ran into the waves. Old Mrs Fairfield, in a lilac cotton dress and a black hat tied under the chin, gathered her little brood and got them ready. The little Trout boys whipped their shirts over their heads, and away the five sped, while their grandma sat with one hand in her knitting-bag ready to draw out the ball of wool when she was satisfied they were safely in.

The firm compact little girls were not half so brave as the tender, delicate-looking little boys. Pip and Rags, shivering, crouching down, slapping the water, never hesitated. But Isabel, who could swim twelve strokes, and Kezia, who could nearly swim eight, only followed on the strict understanding they were not to be splashed. As for Lottie, she didn't follow at all. She liked to be left to go in her own way, please. And that way was to sit down at the edge of the water, her legs straight, her knees pressed together, and to make vague motions with her arms as if she expected to be wafted out to sea. But when a bigger wave than usual, an old whiskery one, came lolloping along in her direction, she scrambled to her feet with a face of horror and flew up the beach again.

'Here, mother, keep those for me, will you?'

Two rings and a thin gold chain were dropped into Mrs Fairfield's lap.

'Yes, dear. But aren't you going to bathe here?'

'No-o,' Beryl drawled. She sounded vague. 'I'm undressing farther along. I'm going to bathe with Mrs Harry Kember.'

'Very well.' But Mrs Fairfield's lips set. She disapproved of Mrs Harry Kember. Beryl knew it.

Poor old mother, she smiled as she skimmed over the stones. Poor old mother! Old! Oh, what joy, what bliss it was to be young. . . .

'You look very pleased,' said Mrs Harry Kember. She sat hunched up on the stones, her arms round her knees, smoking.

'It's such a lovely day,' said Beryl, smiling down at her.

'Oh, my *dear*!' Mrs Harry Kember's voice sounded as though she knew better than that. But then her voice always sounded as though she knew something more about you than you did yourself. She was a long, strange-looking woman with narrow hands and feet. Her face, too, was long and narrow and exhausted-looking; even her fair curled fringe looked burnt out and withered. She was the only woman at the Bay who smoked, and she smoked incessantly, keeping the cigarette between her lips while she talked, and only taking it out when the ash was so long you could not understand why it did not fall. When she was not playing bridge—she played bridge every day of her life—she spent her time lying in the full glare of the sun. She could stand any amount of it; she never had enough. All the same, it did not seem to warm her. Parched, withered, cold, she lay stretched on the stones like a piece of tossed-up driftwood. The women at the Bay thought she was very, very fast. Her lack of vanity, her slang, the way she treated men as though she was one of them, and the fact that she didn't care twopence about her house and called the servant Gladys 'Glad-eyes', was disgraceful. Standing on the veranda steps Mrs Kember would call in her indifferent, tired voice, 'I say, Glad-eyes, you might heave me a handkerchief if I've got one, will you?' And Glad-eyes, a red bow in her hair instead of a cap, and white shoes, came running with an impudent smile. It was an absolute scandal! True, she had no children, and her husband. . . . Here the voices were always raised; they became fervent. How can he have married her? How can he, how can he? It must have been money, of course, but even then!

Mrs Kember's husband was at least ten years younger than she was, and so incredibly handsome that he looked like a mask or a most perfect illustration in an American novel rather than a man. Black hair, dark blue eyes, red lips, a slow sleepy smile, a fine tennis player, a perfect dancer, and with it all a mystery. Harry Kember was like a man walking in his sleep. Men couldn't stand him, they couldn't get a word out of the chap; he ignored his wife just as she ignored him. How did he live? Of course there were stories, but such stories! They simply couldn't be told. The women he'd been seen with, the places he'd been seen in . . . but nothing was ever certain, nothing definite. Some of the women at the Bay privately thought he'd commit a murder one day. Yes, even while they talked to Mrs Kember and took in the awful concoction she was wearing, they saw her, stretched as she lay on the beach; but cold, bloody, and still with a cigarette stuck in the corner of her mouth.

Mrs Kember rose, yawned, unsnapped her belt buckle, and tugged at the tape of her blouse. And Beryl stepped out of her skirt and shed her jersey, and stood up in her short white petticoat, and her camisole with ribbon bows on the shoulders.

'Mercy on us,' said Mrs Harry Kember, 'what a little beauty you are!'

'Don't!' said Beryl softly; but, drawing off one stocking and then the other, she felt a little beauty.

'My dear—why not?' said Mrs Harry Kember, stamping on her own petticoat. Really—her underclothes! A pair of blue cotton knickers and a linen bodice that reminded one somehow of a pillow-case. . . . 'And you don't wear stays, do you?' She touched Beryl's waist, and Beryl sprang away with a small affected cry. Then 'Never!' she said firmly.

'Lucky little creature,' sighed Mrs Kember, unfastening her own.

Beryl turned her back and began the complicated movements of some one who is trying to take off her clothes and to pull on her bathing-dress all at one and the same time.

'Oh, my dear—don't mind me,' said Mrs Harry Kember. 'Why be shy? I shan't eat you. I shan't be shocked like those other ninnies.' And she gave her strange neighing laugh and grimaced at the other women.

But Beryl was shy. She never undressed in front of anybody. Was that silly? Mrs Harry Kember made her feel it was silly, even something to be ashamed of. Why be shy indeed! She glanced quickly at her friend standing so boldly in her torn chemise and lighting a fresh cigarette; and a quick, bold, evil feeling started up in her breast. Laughing recklessly, she drew on the limp, sandy-feeling bathing-dress that was not quite dry and fastened the twisted buttons.

'That's better,' said Mrs Harry Kember. They began to go down the beach together. 'Really, it's a sin for you to wear clothes, my dear. Somebody's got to tell you some day.'

The water was quite warm. It was that marvellous transparent blue, flecked with silver, but the sand at the bottom looked gold; when you kicked with your toes there rose a little puff of gold-dust. Now the waves just reached her breast. Beryl stood, her arms outstretched, gazing out, and as each wave came she gave the slightest little jump, so that it seemed it was the wave which lifted her so gently.

'I believe in pretty girls having a good time,' said Mrs Harry Kember. 'Why not? Don't you make a mistake, my dear. Enjoy yourself.' And suddenly she turned turtle, disappeared, and swam away quickly, quickly, like a rat. Then she flicked round and began swimming back. She was going to say something else. Beryl felt that she was being poisoned by this cold woman, but she longed to hear. But oh, how strange, how horrible! As Mrs Harry Kember came up close she looked, in her black waterproof bathing-cap, with her sleepy face lifted above the water, just her chin touching, like a horrible caricature of her husband.

VI

In a steamer chair, under a manuka[3] tree that grew in the middle of the front grass patch, Linda Burnell dreamed the morning away. She did nothing. She looked up at the dark, close, dry leaves of the manuka, at the chinks of blue between, and now and again a tiny yellowish flower dropped on her. Pretty—yes, if you held one of those flowers on the palm of your hand and looked at it closely, it was an exquisite small thing. Each pale yellow petal shone as if each was the careful work of a loving hand. The tiny tongue in the centre gave it the shape of a bell. And when you turned it over the outside was a deep bronze colour. But as soon as they flowered, they fell and were scattered. You brushed them off your frock as you talked; the horrid little things got caught in one's hair. Why, then, flower at all? Who takes the trouble—or the joy—to make all these things that are wasted, wasted. . . . It was uncanny.

On the grass beside her, lying between two pillows, was the boy. Sound asleep he lay, his head turned away from his mother. His fine dark hair looked more like a shadow than like real hair, but his ear was a bright, deep coral. Linda clasped her hands above her head and crossed her feet. It was very pleasant to know that all these bungalows were empty, that everybody was down on the

3. A common bush with small delicate flowers.

beach, out of sight, out of hearing. She had the garden to herself; she was alone.

Dazzling white the picotees[4] shone; the golden-eyed marigolds glittered; the nasturtiums wreathed the veranda poles in green and gold flame. If only one had time to look at these flowers long enough, time to get over the sense of novelty and strangeness, time to know them! But as soon as one paused to part the petals, to discover the under-side of the leaf, along came Life and one was swept away. And lying in her cane chair, Linda felt so light; she felt like a leaf. Along came Life like a wind and she was seized and shaken; she had to go. Oh dear, would it always be so? Was there no escape?

. . . Now she sat on the veranda of their Tasmanian home, leaning against her father's knee. And he promised, 'As soon as you and I are old enough, Linny, we'll cut off somewhere, we'll escape. Two boys together. I have a fancy I'd like to sail up a river in China.' Linda saw that river, very wide, covered with little rafts and boats. She saw the yellow hats of the boatmen and she heard their high, thin voices as they called. . . .

'Yes, papa.'

But just then a very broad young man with bright ginger hair walked slowly past their house, and slowly, solemnly even, uncovered. Linda's father pulled her ear teasingly, in the way he had.

'Linny's beau,' he whispered.

'Oh, papa, fancy being married to Stanley Burnell!'

Well, she was married to him. And what was more she loved him. Not the Stanley whom every one saw, not the everyday one; but a timid, sensitive, innocent Stanley who knelt down every night to say his prayers, and who longed to be good. Stanley was simple. If he believed in people—as he believed in her, for instance—it was with his whole heart. He could not be disloyal; he could not tell a lie. And how terribly he suffered if he thought anyone—she—was not being dead straight, dead sincere with him! 'This is too subtle for me!' He flung out the words, but his open quivering, distraught look was like the look of a trapped beast.

But the trouble was—here Linda felt almost inclined to laugh, though Heaven knows it was no laughing matter—she saw *her* Stanley so seldom. There were glimpses, moments, breathing spaces of calm, but all the rest of the time it was like living in a house that couldn't be cured of the habit of catching on fire, on a ship that got wrecked every day. And it was always Stanley who was in the thick of the danger. Her whole time was spent in rescuing him, and restoring him, and calming him down, and listening to his

4. A type of flower.

story. And what was left of her time was spent in the dread of having children.

Linda frowned; she sat up quickly in her steamer chair and clasped her ankles. Yes, that was her real grudge against life; that was what she could not understand. That was the question she asked and asked, and listened in vain for the answer. It was all very well to say it was the common lot of women to bear children. It wasn't true. She, for one, could prove that wrong. She was broken, made weak, her courage was gone, through child-bearing. And what made it doubly hard to bear was, she did not love her children. It was useless pretending. Even if she had had the strength she never would have nursed and played with the little girls. No, it was as though a cold breath had chilled her through and through on each of those awful journeys; she had no warmth left to give them. As to the boy—well, thank Heaven, mother had taken him; he was mother's, or Beryl's, or anybody's who wanted him. She had hardly held him in her arms. She was so indifferent about him that as he lay there. . . . Linda glanced down.

The boy had turned over. He lay facing her, and he was no longer asleep. His dark-blue, baby eyes were open; he looked as though he was peeping at his mother. And suddenly his face dimpled; it broke into a wide, toothless smile, a perfect beam, no less.

'I'm here!' that happy smile seemed to say. 'Why don't you like me?'

There was something so quaint, so unexpected about that smile that Linda smiled herself. But she checked herself and said to the boy coldly, 'I don't like babies.'

'Don't like babies?' The boy couldn't believe her. 'Don't like *me*?' He waved his arms foolishly at his mother.

Linda dropped off her chair on to the grass.

'Why do you keep on smiling?' she said severely. 'If you knew what I was thinking about, you wouldn't.'

But he only squeezed up his eyes, slyly, and rolled his head on the pillow. He didn't believe a word she said.

'We know all about that!' smiled the boy.

Linda was so astonished at the confidence of this little creature. . . . Ah no, be sincere. That was not what she felt; it was something far different, it was something so new, so. . . . The tears danced in her eyes; she breathed in a small whisper to the boy, 'Hallo, my funny!'

But by now the boy had forgotten his mother. He was serious again. Something pink, something soft waved in front of him. He made a grab at it and it immediately disappeared. But when he lay back, another, like the first, appeared. This time he determined to catch it. He made a tremendous effort and rolled right over.

VII

The tide was out; the beach was deserted; lazily flopped the warm sea. The sun beat down, beat down hot and fiery on the fine sand, baking the grey and blue and black and white-veined pebbles. It sucked up the little drop of water that lay in the hollow of the curved shells; it bleached the pink convolvulus[5] that threaded through and through the sand-hills. Nothing seemed to move but the small sand-hoppers. Pit-pit-pit! They were never still.

Over there on the weed-hung rocks that looked at low tide like shaggy beasts come down to the water to drink, the sunlight seemed to spin like a silver coin dropped into each of the small rock pools. They danced, they quivered, and minute ripples laved the porous shores. Looking down, bending over, each pool was like a lake with pink and blue houses clustered on the shores; and oh! the vast mountainous country behind those houses—the ravines, the passes, the dangerous creeks and fearful tracks that led to the water's edge. Underneath waved the sea-forest—pink thread-like trees, velvet anemones, and orange berry-spotted weeds. Now a stone on the bottom moved, rocked, and there was a glimpse of a black feeler; now a thread-like creature wavered by and was lost. Something was happening to the pink waving trees; they were changing to a cold moonlight blue. And now there sounded the faintest 'plop'. Who made that sound? What was going on down there? And how strong, how damp the seaweed smelt in the hot sun. . . .

The green blinds were drawn in the bungalows of the summer colony. Over the verandas, prone on the paddock, flung over the fences, there were exhausted-looking bathing-dresses and rough striped towels. Each back window seemed to have a pair of sand-shoes on the sill and some lumps of rock or a bucket or a collection of pawa shells. The bush quivered in a haze of heat; the sandy road was empty except for the Trouts' dog Snooker, who lay stretched in the very middle of it. His blue eye was turned up, his legs stuck out stiffly, and he gave an occasional desperate-sounding puff, as much as to say he had decided to make an end of it and was only waiting for some kind cart to come along.

'What are you looking at, my grandma? Why do you keep stopping and sort of staring at the wall?'

Kezia and her grandmother were taking their siesta together. The little girl, wearing only her short drawers and her under-bodice, her arms and legs bare, lay on one of the puffed-up pillows of her grandma's bed, and the old woman, in a white ruffled dressing-gown, sat in a rocker at the window, with a long piece of pink knit-

5. A twining and trailing plant.

ting in her lap. This room that they shared, like the other rooms of the bungalow, was of light varnished wood and the floor was bare. The furniture was of the shabbiest, the simplest. The dressing-table for instance, was a packing-case in a sprigged muslin petticoat, and the mirror above was very strange; it was as though a little piece of forked lightning was imprisoned in it. On the table there stood a jar of sea-pinks, pressed so tightly together they looked more like a velvet pincushion, and a special shell which Kezia had given her grandma for a pin-tray, and another even more special which she had thought would make a very nice place for a watch to curl up in.

'Tell me, grandma,' said Kezia.

The old woman sighed, whipped the wool twice round her thumb, and drew the bone needle through. She was casting on.

'I was thinking of your Uncle William, darling,' she said quietly.

'My Australian Uncle William?' said Kezia. She had another.

'Yes, of course.'

'The one I never saw?'

'That was the one.'

'Well, what happened to him?' Kezia knew perfectly well, but she wanted to be told again.

'He went to the mines, and he got a sunstroke there and died,' said old Mrs Fairfield.

Kezia blinked and considered the picture again. . . . A little man fallen over like a tin soldier by the side of a big black hole.

'Does it make you sad to think about him, grandma?' She hated her grandma to be sad.

It was the old woman's turn to consider. Did it make her sad? To look back, back. To stare down the years, as Kezia had seen her doing. To look after *them* as a woman does, long after *they* were out of sight. Did it make her sad? No, life was like that.

'No, Kezia.'

'But why?' asked Kezia. She lifted one bare arm and began to draw things in the air. 'Why did Uncle William have to die? He wasn't old.'

Mrs Fairfield began counting the stitches in threes. 'It just happened,' she said in an absorbed voice.

'Does everybody have to die?' asked Kezia.

'Everybody!'

'Me?' Kezia sounded fearfully incredulous.

'Some day, my darling.'

'But, grandma.' Kezia waved her left leg and waggled the toes. They felt sandy. 'What if I just won't?'

The old woman sighed again and drew a long thread from the ball.

'We're not asked, Kezia,' she said sadly. 'It happens to all of us sooner or later.'

Kezia lay still thinking this over. She didn't want to die. It meant she would have to leave here, leave everywhere, for ever, leave—leave her grandma. She rolled over quickly.

'Grandma,' she said in a startled voice.

'What, my pet!'

'*You're* not to die.' Kezia was very decided.

'Ah, Kezia'—her grandma looked up and smiled and shook her head—'don't let's talk about it.'

'But you're not to. You couldn't leave me. You couldn't not be there.' This was awful. 'Promise me you won't ever do it, grandma,' pleaded Kezia.

The old woman went on knitting.

'Promise me! Say never!'

But still her grandma was silent.

Kezia rolled off the bed; she couldn't bear it any longer, and lightly she leapt on to her grandma's knees, clasped her hands round the old woman's throat and began kissing her, under the chin, behind the ear, and blowing down her neck.

'Say never . . . say never . . . say never—' She gasped between the kisses. And then she began, very softly and lightly, to tickle her grandma.

'Kezia!' The old woman dropped her knitting. She swung back in the rocker. She began to tickle Kezia. 'Say never, say never, say never,' gurgled Kezia, while they lay there laughing in each other's arms. 'Come, that's enough, my squirrel! That's enough, my wild pony!' said old Mrs Fairfield, setting her cap straight. 'Pick up my knitting.'

Both of them had forgotten what the 'never' was about.

VIII

The sun was still full on the garden when the back door of the Burnells' shut with a bang, and a very gay figure walked down the path to the gate. It was Alice, the servant-girl, dressed for her afternoon out. She wore a white cotton dress with such large red spots on it, and so many that they made you shudder, white shoes and a leghorn[6] turned up under the brim with poppies. Of course she wore gloves, white ones, stained at the fastenings with iron-mould, and in one hand she carried a very dashed-looking sunshade which she referred to as her *perishall*.

Beryl, sitting in the window, fanning her freshly washed hair, thought she had never seen such a guy. If Alice had only blacked

6. A straw hat.

her face with a piece of cork before she started out, the picture would have been complete. And where did a girl like that go to in a place like this? The heart-shaped Fijian fan beat scornfully at that lovely bright mane. She supposed Alice had picked up some horrible common larrikin[7] and they'd go off into the bush together. Pity to make herself so conspicuous; they'd have hard work to hide with Alice in that rig-out.

But no, Beryl was unfair. Alice was going to tea with Mrs Stubbs, who'd sent her an 'invite' by the little boy who called for orders. She had taken ever such a liking to Mrs Stubbs ever since the first time she went to the shop to get something for her mosquitoes.

'Dear heart!' Mrs Stubbs had clapped her hand to her side. 'I never seen anyone so eaten. You might have been attacked by canningbals.'

Alice did wish there'd been a bit of life on the road though. Made her feel so queer, having nobody behind her. Made her feel all weak in the spine. She couldn't believe that some one wasn't watching her. And yet it was silly to turn round; it gave you away. She pulled up her gloves, hummed to herself and said to the distant gum-tree, 'Shan't be long now.' But that was hardly company.

Mrs Stubbs's shop was perched on a little hillock just off the road. It had two big windows for eyes, a broad veranda for a hat, and the sign on the roof, scrawled MRS. STUBBS'S, was like a little card stuck rakishly in the hat crown.

On the veranda there hung a long string of bathing-dresses, clinging together as though they'd just been rescued from the sea rather than waiting to go in, and beside them there hung a cluster of sand-shoes so extraordinarily mixed that to get at one pair you had to tear apart and forcibly separate at least fifty. Even then it was the rarest thing to find the left that belonged to the right. So many people had lost patience and gone off with one shoe that fitted and one that was a little too big. . . . Mrs Stubbs prided herself on keeping something of everything. The two windows, arranged in the form of precarious pyramids, were crammed so tight, piled so high, that it seemed only a conjuror could prevent them from toppling over. In the left-hand corner of one window, glued to the pane by four gelatine lozenges, there was—and there had been from time immemorial—a notice.

LOST! HANSOME GOLE BROOCH
SOLID GOLD
ON OR NEAR BEACH
REWARD OFFERED

7. A street rowdy, a young lout.

Alice pressed open the door. The bell jangled, the red serge curtains parted, and Mrs Stubbs appeared. With her broad smile and the long bacon knife in her hand, she looked like a friendly brigand. Alice was welcomed so warmly that she found it quite difficult to keep up her 'manners'. They consisted of persistent little coughs and hems, pulls at her gloves, tweaks at her skirt, and a curious difficulty in seeing what was set before her or understanding what was said.

Tea was laid on the parlour table—ham, sardines, a whole pound of butter, and such a large johnny cake that it looked like an advertisement for somebody's baking-powder. But the Primus[8] stove roared so loudly that it was useless to try to talk above it. Alice sat down on the edge of a basket-chair while Mrs Stubbs pumped the stove still higher. Suddenly Mrs Stubbs whipped the cushion off a chair and disclosed a large brown-paper parcel.

'I've just had some new photers taken, my dear,' she shouted cheerfully to Alice. 'Tell me what you think of them.'

In a very dainty, refined way Alice wet her finger and put the tissue back from the first one. Life! How many there were! There were three dozzing at least. And she held hers up to the light.

Mrs Stubbs sat in an arm-chair, leaning very much to one side. There was a look of mild astonishment on her large face, and well there might be. For though the arm-chair stood on a carpet, to the left of it, miraculously skirting the carpet-border, there was a dashing water-fall. On her right stood a Grecian pillar with a giant fern-tree on either side of it, and in the background towered a gaunt mountain, pale with snow.

'It is a nice style, isn't it?' shouted Mrs Stubbs; and Alice had just screamed 'Sweetly' when the roaring of the Primus stove died down, fizzled out, ceased, and she said 'Pretty' in a silence that was frightening.

'Draw up your chair, my dear,' said Mrs Stubbs, beginning to pour out. 'Yes,' she said thoughtfully, as she handed the tea, 'but I don't care about the size. I'm having an enlargemint. All very well for Christmas cards, but I never was the one for small photers myself. You get no comfort out of them. To say the truth, I find them dis'eartening.'

Alice quite saw what she meant.

'Size,' said Mrs Stubbs. 'Give me size. That was what my poor dear husband was always saying. He couldn't stand anything small. Gave him the creeps. And, strange as it may seem, my dear'—here Mrs Stubbs creaked and seemed to expand herself at the memory—'it was dropsy that carried him off at the larst. Many's the time they

8. A brand of portable cooking stove.

drawn one and a half pints from 'im at the 'ospital. . . . It seemed like a judgmint.'

Alice burned to know exactly what it was that was drawn from him. She ventured, 'I suppose it was water.'

But Mrs Stubbs fixed Alice with her eyes and replied meaningly, 'It was *liquid*, my dear.'

Liquid! Alice jumped away from the word like a cat and came back to it, nosing and wary.

'That's 'im!' said Mrs Stubbs, and she pointed dramatically to the life-size head and shoulders of a burly man with a dead white rose in the button-hole of his coat that made you think of a curl of cold mutting fat. Just below, in silver letters on a red cardboard ground, were the words, 'Be not afraid, it is I.'[9]

'It's ever such a fine face,' said Alice faintly.

The pale-blue bow on the top of Mrs Stubb's fair frizzy hair quivered. She arched her plump neck. What a neck she had! It was bright pink where it began and then it changed to warm apricot, and that faded to the colour of a brown egg and then to a deep creamy.

'All the same, my dear,' she said surprisingly, 'freedom's best!' Her soft, fat chuckle sounded like a purr. 'Freedom's best,' said Mrs Stubbs again.

Freedom! Alice gave a loud, silly little titter. She felt awkward. Her mind flew back to her own kitching. Ever so queer! She wanted to be back in it again.

IX

A strange company assembled in the Burnells' washhouse after tea. Round the table there sat a bull, a rooster, a donkey that kept forgetting it was a donkey, a sheep and a bee. The washhouse was the perfect place for such a meeting because they could make as much noise as they liked, and nobody ever interrupted. It was a small tin shed standing apart from the bungalow. Against the wall there was a deep trough and in the corner a copper with a basket of clothes-pegs on top of it. The little window, spun over with cobwebs, had a piece of candle and a mouse-trap on the dusty sill. There were clothes-lines criss-crossed overhead and, hanging from a peg on the wall, a very big, a huge, rusty horseshoe. The table was in the middle with a form at either side.

'You can't be a bee, Kezia. A bee's not an animal. It's a ninseck.'

'Oh, but I do want to be a bee frightfully,' wailed Kezia. . . . A tiny bee, all yellow-furry, with striped legs. She drew her legs up under her and leaned over the table. She felt she was a bee.

9. Matt. 14:27.

'A ninseck must be an animal,' she said stoutly. 'It makes a noise. It's not like a fish.'

'I'm a bull, I'm a bull!' cried Pip. And he gave such a tremendous bellow—how did he make that noise?—that Lottie looked quite alarmed.

'I'll be a sheep,' said little Rags. 'A whole lot of sheep went past this morning.'

'How do you know?'

'Dad heard them. Baa!' He sounded like the little lamb that trots behind and seems to wait to be carried.

'Cock-a-doodle-do!' shrilled Isabel. With her red cheeks and bright eyes she looked like a rooster.

'What'll I be?' Lottie asked everybody, and she sat there smiling, waiting for them to decide for her. It had to be an easy one.

'Be a donkey, Lottie.' It was Kezia's suggestion. 'Hee-haw! You can't forget that.'

'Hee-haw!' said Lottie solemnly. 'When do I have to say it?'

'I'll explain, I'll explain,' said the bull. It was he who had the cards. He waved them round his head. 'All be quiet! All listen!' And he waited for them. 'Look here, Lottie.' He turned up a card. 'It's got two spots on it—see? Now, if you put that card in the middle and somebody else has one with two spots as well, you say "Hee-haw," and the card's yours.'

'Mine?' Lottie was round-eyed. 'To keep?'

'No, silly. Just for the game, see? Just while we're playing.' The bull was very cross with her.

'Oh, Lottie, you *are* a little silly,' said the proud rooster.

Lottie looked at both of them. Then she hung her head; her lip quivered. 'I don't not want to play,' she whispered. The others glanced at one another like conspirators. All of them knew what that meant. She would go away and be discovered somewhere standing with her pinny thrown over her head, in a corner, or against a wall, or even behind a chair.

'Yes, you *do*, Lottie. It's quite easy,' said Kezia.

And Isabel, repentant, said exactly like a grown-up, 'Watch *me*, Lottie, and you'll soon learn.'

'Cheer up, Lot,' said Pip. 'There, I know what I'll do. I'll give you the first one. It's mine, really, but I'll give it to you. Here you are.' And he slammed the card down in front of Lottie.

Lottie revived at that. But now she was in another difficulty. 'I haven't got a hanky,' she said; 'I want one badly, too.'

'Here, Lottie, you can use mine.' Rags dipped into his sailor blouse and brought up a very wet-looking one, knotted together. 'Be very careful,' he warned her. 'Only use that corner. Don't undo it. I've got a little starfish inside I'm going to try and tame.'

'Oh, come on, you girls,' said the bull. 'And mind—you're not to look at your cards. You've got to keep your hands under the table till I say "Go." '

Smack went the cards round the table. They tried with all their might to see, but Pip was too quick for them. It was very exciting, sitting there in the washhouse; it was all they could do not to burst into a little chorus of animals before Pip had finished dealing.

'Now, Lottie, you begin.'

Timidly Lottie stretched out a hand, took the top card off her pack, had a good look at it—it was plain she was counting the spots—and put it down.

'No, Lottie, you can't do that. You mustn't look first. You must turn it the other way over.'

'But then everybody will see it the same time as me,' said Lottie.

The game proceeded. Mooe-ooo-er! The bull was terrible. He charged over the table and seemed to eat the cards up.

Bss-ss! said the bee.

Cock-a-doodle-do! Isabel stood up in her excitement and moved her elbows like wings.

Baa! Little Rags put down the King of Diamonds and Lottie put down the one they called the King of Spain. She had hardly any cards left.

'Why don't you call out, Lottie?'

'I've forgotten what I am,' said the donkey woefully.

'Well, change! Be a dog instead! Bow-wow!'

'Oh yes. That's *much* easier.' Lottie smiled again. But when she and Kezia both had a one Kezia waited on purpose. The others made signs to Lottie and pointed. Lottie turned very red; she looked bewildered, and at last she said, 'Hee-haw! Ke-zia.'

'Ss! Wait a minute!' They were in the very thick of it when the bull stopped them, holding up his hand. 'What's that? What's that noise?'

'What noise? What do you mean?' asked the rooster.

'Ss! Shut up! Listen!' They were mouse-still. 'I thought I heard a—a sort of knocking,' said the bull.

'What was it like?' asked the sheep faintly.

No answer.

The bee gave a shudder. 'Whatever did we shut the door for?' she said softly. Oh, why, why had they shut the door?

While they were playing, the day had faded; the gorgeous sunset had blazed and died. And now the quick dark came racing over the sea, over the sand-hills, up the paddock. You were frightened to look in the corners of the washhouse, and yet you had to look with all your might. And somewhere, far away, grandma was lighting a lamp. The blinds were being pulled down; the kitchen fire leapt in the tins on the mantelpiece.

'It would be awful now,' said the bull, 'if a spider was to fall from the ceiling on to the table, wouldn't it?'

'Spiders don't fall from ceilings.'

'Yes, they do. Our Min told us she'd seen a spider as big as a saucer, with long hairs on it like a gooseberry.'

Quickly all the little heads were jerked up; all the little bodies drew together, pressed together.

'Why doesn't somebody come and call us?' cried the rooster.

Oh, those grown-ups, laughing and snug, sitting in the lamp-light, drinking out of cups! They'd forgotten about them. No, not really forgotten. That was what their smile meant. They had decided to leave them there all by themselves.

Suddenly Lottie gave such a piercing scream that all of them jumped off the forms, all of them screamed too. 'A face—a face looking!' shrieked Lottie.

It was true, it was real. Pressed against the window was a pale face, black eyes, a black beard.

'Grandma! Mother! Somebody!'

But they had not got to the door, tumbling over one another, before it opened for Uncle Jonathan. He had come to take the little boys home.

X

He had meant to be there before, but in the front garden he had come upon Linda walking up and down the grass, stopping to pick off a dead pink or give a top-heavy carnation something to lean against, or to take a deep breath of something, and then walking on again, with her little air of remoteness. Over her white frock she wore a yellow, pink-fringed shawl from the Chinaman's shop.

'Hallo, Jonathan!' called Linda. And Jonathan whipped off his shabby panama, pressed it against his breast, dropped on one knee, and kissed Linda's hand.

'Greeting, my Fair One! Greeting, my Celestial Peach Blossom!' boomed the bass voice gently. 'Where are the other noble dames?'

'Beryl's out playing bridge and mother's giving the boy his bath. . . . Have you come to borrow something?'

The Trouts were for ever running out of things and sending across to the Burnells' at the last moment.

But Jonathan only answered, 'A little love, a little kindness;' and he walked by his sister-in-law's side.

Linda dropped into Beryl's hammock under the manuka tree, and Jonathan stretched himself on the grass beside her, pulled a long stalk and began chewing it. They knew each other well. The voices of children cried from the other gardens. A fisherman's light cart shook along the sandy road, and from far away they heard a dog barking; it was muffled as though the dog had its head in a sack. If you listened you could just hear the soft swish of the sea at full tide sweeping the pebbles. The sun was sinking.

'And so you go back to the office on Monday, do you, Jonathan?' asked Linda.

'On Monday the cage door opens and clangs to upon the victim for another eleven months and a week,' answered Jonathan.

Linda swung a little. 'It must be awful,' she said slowly.

'Would ye have me laugh, my fair sister? Would ye have me weep?'

Linda was so accustomed to Jonathan's way of talking that she paid no attention to it.

'I suppose,' she said vaguely, 'one gets used to it. One gets used to anything.'

'Does one? Hum!' The 'Hum' was so deep it seemed to boom from underneath the ground. 'I wonder how it's done,' brooded Jonathan; 'I've never managed it.'

Looking at him as he lay there, Linda thought again how attractive he was. It was strange to think that he was only an ordinary clerk, that Stanley earned twice as much money as he. What was the matter with Jonathan? He had no ambition; she supposed that was it. And yet one felt he was gifted, exceptional. He was passionately fond of music; every spare penny he had went on books. He was always full of new ideas, schemes, plans. But nothing came of it all. The new fire blazed in Jonathan; you almost heard it roaring softly as he explained, described and dilated on the new thing; but a moment later it had fallen in and there was nothing but ashes, and Jonathan went about with a look like hunger in his black eyes. At these times he exaggerated his absurd manner of speaking, and he sang in church—he was the leader of the choir—with such fearful dramatic intensity that the meanest hymn put on an unholy splendour.

'It seems to me just as imbecile, just as infernal, to have to go to the office on Monday,' said Jonathan, 'as it always has done and always will do. To spend all the best years of one's life sitting on a stool from nine to five, scratching in somebody's ledger! It's a queer use to make of one's . . . one and only life, isn't it? Or do I fondly dream?' He rolled over on the grass and looked up at Linda. 'Tell me, what is the difference between my life and that of an ordinary prisoner. The only difference I can see is that I put myself in jail and nobody's ever going to let me out. That's a more intolerable situation than the other. For if I'd been—pushed in, against my will—kicking, even—once the door was locked, or at any rate in five years or so, I might have accepted the fact and begun to take an interest in the flight of flies or counting the warder's steps along the passage with particular attention to variations of tread and so on. But as it is, I'm like an insect that's flown into a room of its own accord. I dash against the walls, dash against the windows, flop against the ceiling, do everything on God's earth, in fact, except fly out again. And all the while I'm thinking, like that moth, or that butterfly, or whatever it is, "The shortness of life! The shortness of life!" I've only one night or one day, and there's this vast dangerous garden, waiting out there, undiscovered, unexplored.'

'But, if you feel like that, why—' began Linda quickly.

'*Ah!*' cried Jonathan. And that 'Ah!' was somehow almost exultant. 'There you have me. Why? Why indeed? There's the maddening, mysterious question. Why don't I fly out again? There's the window or the door or whatever it was I came in by. It's not hopelessly shut—is it? Why don't I find it and be off? Answer me that, little sister.' But he gave her no time to answer.

'I'm exactly like that insect again. For some reason'—Jonathan paused between the words—'it's not allowed, it's forbidden, it's against the insect law, to stop banging and flopping and crawling up the pane even for an instant. Why don't I leave the office? Why don't I seriously consider, this moment, for instance, what it is that prevents me leaving? It's not as though I'm tremendously tied. I've two boys to provide for, but, after all, they're boys. I could cut off to sea, or get a job up-country, or—' Suddenly he smiled at Linda and said in a changed voice, as if he were confiding a secret, 'Weak . . . weak. No stamina. No anchor. No guiding principle, let us call it.' But then the dark velvety voice rolled out:

Would ye hear the story
How it unfolds itself . . .

and they were silent.

The sun had set. In the western sky there were great masses of crushed-up rose-coloured clouds. Broad beams of light shone through the clouds and beyond them as if they would cover the whole sky. Overhead the blue faded; it turned a pale gold, and the bush outlined against it gleamed dark and brilliant like metal. Sometimes when those beams of light show in the sky they are very awful. They remind you that up there sits Jehovah, the jealous God, the Almighty, Whose eye is upon you, ever watchful, never weary. You remember that at His coming the whole earth will shake into one ruined graveyard; the cold, bright angels will drive you this way and that, and there will be no time to explain what could be explained so simply. . . . But to-night it seemed to Linda there was something infinitely joyful and loving in those silver beams. And now no sound came from the sea. It breathed softly as if it would draw that tender, joyful beauty into its own bosom.

'It's all wrong, it's all wrong,' came the shadowy voice of Jonathan. 'It's not the scene, it's not the setting for . . . three stools, three desks, three inkpots and a wire blind.'

Linda knew that he would never change, but she said, 'Is it too late, even now?'

'I'm old—I'm old,' intoned Jonathan. He bent towards her, he passed his hand over his head. 'Look!' His black hair was speckled all over with silver, like the breast plumage of a black fowl.

Linda was surprised. She had no idea that he was grey. And yet, as he stood up beside her and sighed and stretched, she saw him, for the first time, not resolute, not gallant, not careless, but touched already with age. He looked very tall on the darkening grass, and the thought crossed her mind, 'He is like a weed.'

Jonathan stooped again and kissed her fingers.

'Heaven reward thy sweet patience, lady mine,' he murmured. 'I must go seek those heirs to my fame and fortune. . . .' He was gone.

XI

Light shone in the windows of the bungalow. Two square patches of gold fell upon the pinks and the peaked marigolds. Florrie, the cat, came out on to the veranda, and sat on the top step, her white paws close together, her tail curled round. She looked content, as though she had been waiting for this moment all day.

'Thank goodness, it's getting late,' said Florrie. 'Thank goodness, the long day is over.' Her greengage[1] eyes opened.

Presently there sounded the rumble of the coach, the crack of Kelly's whip. It came near enough for one to hear the voices of the men from town, talking loudly together. It stopped at the Burnells' gate.

Stanley was half-way up the path before he saw Linda. 'Is that you, darling?'

'Yes, Stanley.'

He leapt across the flower-bed and seized her in his arms. She was enfolded in that familiar, eager, strong embrace.

'Forgive me, darling, forgive me,' stammered Stanley, and he put his hand under her chin and lifted her face to him.

'Forgive you?' smiled Linda. 'But whatever for?'

'Good God! You can't have forgotten,' cried Stanley Burnell. 'I've thought of nothing else all day. I've had the hell of a day. I made up my mind to dash out and telegraph, and then I thought the wire mightn't reach you before I did. I've been in tortures, Linda.'

1. That is, greenish, like the small plum.

'But, Stanley,' said Linda, 'what must I forgive you for?'

'Linda!'—Stanley was very hurt—'didn't you realize—you must have realized—I went away without saying good-bye to you this morning? I can't imagine how I can have done such a thing. My confounded temper, of course. But—well'—and he sighed and took her in his arms again—'I've suffered for it enough to-day.'

'What's that you've got in your hand?' asked Linda. 'New gloves? Let me see.'

'Oh, just a cheap pair of wash-leather ones,' said Stanley humbly. 'I noticed Bell was wearing some in the coach this morning, so, as I was passing the shop, I dashed in and got myself a pair. What are you smiling at? You don't think it was wrong of me, do you?'

'On the *con*-trary, darling,' said Linda, 'I think it was most sensible.'

She pulled one of the large, pale gloves on her own fingers and looked at her hand, turning it this way and that. She was still smiling.

Stanley wanted to say, 'I was thinking of you the whole time I bought them.' It was true, but for some reason he couldn't say it. 'Let's go in,' said he.

XII

Why does one feel so different at night? Why is it so exciting to be awake when everybody else is asleep? Late—it is very late! And yet every moment you feel more and more wakeful, as though you were slowly, almost with every breath, waking up into a new, wonderful, far more thrilling and exciting world than the daylight one. And what is this queer sensation that you're a conspirator? Lightly, stealthily you move about your room. You take something off the dressing-table and put it down again without a sound. And everything, even the bed-post, knows you, responds, shares your secret. . . .

You're not very fond of your room by day. You never think about it. You're in and out, the door opens and slams, the cupboard creaks. You sit down on the side of your bed, change your shoes and dash out again. A dive down to the glass, two pins in your hair, powder your nose and off again. But now—it's suddenly dear to you. It's a darling little funny room. It's yours. Oh, what a joy it is to own things! Mine—my own!

'My very own for ever?'

'Yes.' Their lips met.

No, of course, that had nothing to do with it. That was all nonsense and rubbish. But, in spite of herself, Beryl saw so plainly two people standing in the middle of her room. Her arms were round his neck; he held her. And now he whispered, 'My beauty, my little beauty!' She jumped off her bed, ran over to the window and kneeled on the window-seat, with her elbows on the sill. But the beautiful night, the garden, every bush, every leaf, even the white palings, even the stars, were conspirators too. So bright was the moon that the flowers were bright as by day; the shadow of the nasturtiums, exquisite lily-like leaves and wide-open flowers, lay across the silvery veranda. The manuka tree, bent by the southerly winds, was like a bird on one leg stretching out a wing.

But when Beryl looked at the bush, it seemed to her the bush was sad.

'We are dumb trees, reaching up in the night, imploring we know not what,' said the sorrowful bush.

It is true when you are by yourself and you think about life, it is always sad. All that excitement and so on has a way of suddenly leaving you, and it's as though, in the silence, somebody called your name, and you heard your name for the first time. 'Beryl!'

'Yes, I'm here. I'm Beryl. Who wants me?'

'Beryl!'

'Let me come.'

It is lonely living by oneself. Of course, there are relations, friends, heaps of them; but that's not what she means. She wants some one who will find the Beryl they none of them know, who will expect her to be that Beryl always. She wants a lover.

'Take me away from all these other people, my love. Let us go far away. Let us live our life, all new, all ours, from the very beginning. Let us make our fire. Let us sit down to eat together. Let us have long talks at night.'

And the thought was almost, 'Save me, my love. Save me!'

. . . 'Oh, go on! Don't be a prude, my dear. You enjoy yourself while you're young. That's my advice.' And a high rush of silly laughter joined Mrs Harry Kember's loud, indifferent neigh.

You see, it's so frightfully difficult when you've nobody. You're so at the mercy of things. You can't just be rude. And you've always this horror of seeming inexperienced and stuffy like the other ninnies at the Bay. And—and it's fascinating to know you've power over people. Yes, that is fascinating. . . .

Oh why, oh why doesn't 'he' come soon?

If I go on living here, thought Beryl, anything may happen to me.

'But how do you know he is coming at all?' mocked a small voice within her.

But Beryl dismissed it. She couldn't be left. Other people, perhaps, but not she. It wasn't possible to think that Beryl Fairfield never married, that lovely fascinating girl.

'Do you remember Beryl Fairfield?'

'Remember her! As if I could forget her! It was one summer at the Bay that I saw her. She was standing on the beach in a blue'—no, pink—'muslin frock, holding on a big cream'—no, black—'straw hat. But it's years ago now.'

'She's as lovely as ever, more so if anything.'

Beryl smiled, bit her lip, and gazed over the garden. As she gazed, she saw somebody, a man, leave the road, step along the paddock beside their palings as if he was coming straight towards her. Her heart beat. Who was it? Who could it be? It couldn't be a burglar, certainly not a burglar, for he was smoking and he strolled lightly. Beryl's heart leapt; it seemed to turn right over, and then to stop. She recognized him.

'Good evening, Miss Beryl,' said the voice softly.

'Good evening.'

'Won't you come for a little walk?' it drawled.

Come for a walk—at that time of night! 'I couldn't. Everybody's in bed. Everybody's asleep.'

'Oh,' said the voice lightly, and a whiff of sweet smoke reached her. 'What does everybody matter? Do come! It's such a fine night. There's not a soul about.'

Beryl shook her head. But already something stirred in her, something reared its head.

The voice said, 'Frightened?' It mocked, 'Poor little girl!'

'Not in the least,' said she. As she spoke that weak thing within her seemed to uncoil, to grow suddenly tremendously strong; she longed to go!

And just as if this was quite understood by the other, the voice said, gently and softly, but finally, 'Come along!'

Beryl stepped over her low window, crossed the veranda, ran down the grass to the gate. He was there before her.

'That's right,' breathed the voice, and it teased, 'You're not frightened, are you? You're not frightened?'

She was; now she was here she was terrified, and it seemed to her everything was different. The moonlight stared and glittered; the shadows were like bars of iron. Her hand was taken.

'Not in the least,' she said lightly. 'Why should I be?'

Her hand was pulled gently, tugged. She held back.

'No, I'm not coming any farther,' said Beryl.

'Oh, rot!' Harry Kember didn't believe her. 'Come along! We'll just go as far as that fuchsia bush. Come along!'

The fuchsia bush was tall. It fell over the fence in a shower. There was a little pit of darkness beneath.

'No, really, I don't want to,' said Beryl.

For a moment Harry Kember didn't answer. Then he came close

to her, turned to her, smiled and said quickly, 'Don't be silly! Don't be silly!'

His smile was something she'd never seen before. Was he drunk? That bright, blind, terrifying smile froze her with horror. What was she doing? How had she got here? The stern garden asked her as the gate pushed open, and quick as a cat Harry Kember came through and snatched her to him.

'Cold little devil! Cold little devil!' said the hateful voice.

But Beryl was strong. She slipped, ducked, wrenched free.

'You are vile, vile,' said she.

'Then why in God's name did you come?' stammered Harry Kember.

Nobody answered him.

XIII[2]

A cloud, small, serene, floated across the moon. In that moment of darkness the sea sounded deep, troubled. Then the cloud sailed away, and the sound of the sea was a vague murmur, as though it waked out of a dark dream. All was still.

The Voyage (1921)†

The Picton boat[1] was due to leave at half-past eleven. It was a beautiful night, mild, starry, only when they got out of the cab and started to walk down the Old Wharf that jutted out into the harbour, a faint wind blowing off the water ruffled under Fenella's hat, and she put up her hand to keep it on. It was dark on the Old Wharf, very dark; the wool sheds, the cattle trucks, the cranes standing up so high, the little squat railway engine, all seemed carved out of solid darkness. Here and there on a rounded woodpile, that was like the stalk of a huge black mushroom, there hung a lantern, but it seemed afraid to unfurl its timid, quivering light in all that blackness; it burned softly, as if for itself.

Fenella's father pushed on with quick, nervous strides. Beside him her grandma bustled along in her crackling black ulster; they went so fast that she had now and again to give an undignified little skip to keep up with them. As well as her luggage strapped into a neat sausage, Fenella carried clasped to her her grandma's

2. Although the story is usually printed in twelve sections, Mansfield made the last paragraph into a section of its own in the American edition of *The Garden Party and Other Stories* (New York: Alfred A. Knopf, 1922).

† Published in the *Sphere* (24 December 1921) and collected in *The Garden Party and Other Stories* (1922).

1. The overnight boat from Wellington to Picton, a small port at the top of the South Island of New Zealand.

umbrella, and the handle, which was a swan's head, kept giving her shoulder a sharp little peck as if it too wanted her to hurry. . . . Men, their caps pulled down, their collars turned up, swung by; a few women all muffled scurried along; and one tiny boy, only his little black arms and legs showing out of a white woolly shawl, was jerked along angrily between his father and mother; he looked like a baby fly that had fallen into the cream.

Then suddenly, so suddenly that Fenella and her grandma both leapt, there sounded from behind the largest wool shed, that had a trail of smoke hanging over it, *Mia-oo-oo-O-O!*

'First whistle,' said her father briefly, and at that moment they came in sight of the Picton boat. Lying beside the dark wharf, all strung, all beaded with round golden lights, the Picton boat looked as if she was more ready to sail among stars than out into the cold sea. People pressed along the gangway. First went her grandma, then her father, then Fenella. There was a high step down on to the deck, and an old sailor in a jersey standing by gave her his dry, hard hand. They were there; they stepped out of the way of the hurrying people, and standing under a little iron stairway that led to the upper deck they began to say good-bye.

'There, mother, there's your luggage!' said Fenella's father, giving grandma another strapped-up sausage.

'Thank you, Frank.'

'And you've got your cabin tickets safe?'

'Yes, dear.'

'And your other tickets?'

Grandma felt for them inside her glove and showed him the tips.

'That's right.'

He sounded stern, but Fenella, eagerly watching him, saw that he looked tired and sad. *Mia-oo-oo-O-O!* The second whistle blared just above their heads, and a voice like a cry shouted, 'Any more for the gangway?'

'You'll give my love to father,' Fenella saw her father's lips say. And her grandma, very agitated, answered. 'Of course I will, dear. Go now. You'll be left. Go now, Frank. Go now.'

'It's all right, mother. I've got another three minutes.' To her surprise Fenella saw her father take off his hat. He clasped grandma in his arms and pressed her to him. 'God bless you, mother!' she heard him say.

And grandma put her hand, with the black thread glove that was worn through on her ring finger, against his cheek, and she sobbed, 'God bless you, my own brave son!'

This was so awful that Fenella quickly turned her back on them, swallowed once, twice, and frowned terribly at a little green star on a mast head. But she had to turn round again; her father was going.

'Good-bye, Fenella. Be a good girl.' His cold, wet moustache brushed her cheek. But Fenella caught hold of the lapels of his coat.

'How long am I going to stay?' she whispered anxiously. He wouldn't look at her. He shook her off gently, and gently said, 'We'll see about that. Here! Where's your hand?' He pressed something into her palm. 'Here's a shilling in case you should need it.'

A shilling! She must be going away for ever! 'Father!' cried Fenella. But he was gone. He was the last off the ship. The sailors put their shoulders to the gangway. A huge coil of dark rope went flying through the air and fell 'thump' on the wharf. A bell rang; a whistle shrilled. Silently the dark wharf began to slip, to slide, to edge away from them. Now there was a rush of water between. Fenella strained to see with all her might. 'Was that father turning round?'—or waving?—or standing alone?—or walking off by himself? The strip of water grew broader, darker. Now the Picton boat began to swing round steady, pointing out to sea. It was no good looking any longer. There was nothing to be seen but a few lights, the face of the town clock hanging in the air, and more lights, little patches of them, on the dark hills.

The freshening wind tugged at Fenella's skirts; she went back to her grandma. To her relief grandma seemed no longer sad. She had put the two sausages of luggage one on top of the other, and she was sitting on them, her hands folded, her head a little on one side. There was an intent, bright look on her face. Then Fenella saw that her lips were moving and guessed that she was praying. But the old woman gave her a bright nod as if to say the prayer was nearly over. She unclasped her hands, sighed, clasped them again, bent forward, and at last gave herself a soft shake.

'And now, child,' she said fingering the bow of her bonnet-strings, 'I think we ought to see about our cabins. Keep close to me, and mind you don't slip.'

'Yes, grandma!'

'And be careful the umbrellas aren't caught in the stair rail. I saw a beautiful umbrella broken in half like that on my way over.'

'Yes, grandma.'

Dark figures of men lounged against the rails. In the glow of their pipes a nose shone out, or the peak of a cap, or a pair of surprised-looking eyebrows. Fenella glanced up. High in the air, a little figure, his hands thrust in his short jacket pockets, stood staring out to sea. The ship rocked ever so little, and she thought the stars rocked too. And now a pale steward in a linen coat, holding a tray high in the palm of his hand, stepped out of a lighted doorway and skimmed past them. They went through that doorway. Carefully over the high brass-bound step on to the rubber mat and then down such a terribly steep flight of stairs that grandma had to put both feet on each step, and Fenella clutched the clammy brass rail and forgot all about the swan-necked umbrella.

At the bottom grandma stopped; Fenella was rather afraid she was going to pray again. But no, it was only to get out the cabin tickets. They were in the saloon. It was glaring bright and stifling; the air smelled of paint and burnt chop-bones and indiarubber. Fenella wished her grandma would go on, but the old woman was not to be hurried. An immense basket of ham sandwiches caught her eye. She went up to them and touched the top one delicately with her finger.

'How much are the sandwiches?' she asked.

'Tuppence!' bawled a rude steward, slamming down a knife and fork.

Grandma could hardly believe it.

'Twopence *each*?' she asked.

'That's right,' said the steward, and he winked at his companion.

Grandma made a small, astonished face. Then she whispered primly to Fenella. 'What wickedness!' And they sailed out at the further door and along a passage that had cabins on either side. Such a very nice stewardess came to meet them. She was dressed all in blue, and her collar and cuffs were fastened with large brass buttons. She seemed to know grandma well.

'Well, Mrs Crane,' said she, unlocking their washstand. 'We've got you back again. It's not often you give yourself a cabin.'

'No,' said grandma. 'But this time my dear son's thoughtfulness—'

'I hope—' began the stewardess. Then she turned round and took a long mournful look at grandma's blackness and at Fenella's black coat and skirt, black blouse, and hat with a crêpe rose.

Grandma nodded. 'It was God's will,' said she.

The stewardess shut her lips and, taking a deep breath, she seemed to expand.

'What I always say is,' she said, as though it was her own discovery, 'sooner or later each of us has to go, and that's a certingty.' She paused. 'Now, can I bring you anything, Mrs Crane? A cup of tea? I know it's no good offering you a little something to keep the cold out.'

Grandma shook her head. 'Nothing, thank you. We've got a few wine biscuits, and Fenella has a very nice banana.'

'Then I'll give you a look later on,' said the stewardess, and she went out, shutting the door.

What a very small cabin it was! It was like being shut up in a box with grandma. The dark round eye above the washstand gleamed at them dully. Fenella felt shy. She stood against the door, still clasping her luggage and the umbrella. Were they going to get undressed in here? Already her grandma had taken off her bonnet, and, rolling up the strings, she fixed each with a pin to the lining before she hung the bonnet up. Her white hair shone like silk; the little bun at the back was covered with a black net. Fenella hardly ever saw her grandma with her head uncovered; she looked strange.

'I shall put on the woollen fascinator[2] your dear mother crocheted for me,' said grandma, and, unstrapping the sausage, she took it out and wound it round her head; the fringe of grey bobbles danced at her eyebrows as she smiled tenderly and mournfully at Fenella. Then she undid her bodice, and something under that, and something else underneath that. Then there seemed a short, sharp tussle, and grandma flushed faintly. Snip! Snap! She had undone her stays. She breathed a sigh of relief, and sitting on the plush couch, she slowly and carefully pulled off her elastic-sided boots and stood them side by side.

By the time Fenella had taken off her coat and skirt and put on her flannel dressing-gown grandma was quite ready.

'Must I take off my boots, grandma? They're lace.'

Grandma gave them a moment's deep consideration. 'You'd feel a great deal more comfortable if you did, child,' said she. She kissed Fenella. 'Don't forget to say your prayers. Our dear Lord is with us when we are at sea even more than when we are on dry land. And because I am an experienced traveller,' said grandma briskly, 'I shall take the upper berth.'

'But, grandma, however will you get up there?'

Three little spider-like steps were all Fenella saw. The old woman gave a small silent laugh before she mounted them nimbly, and she peered over the high bunk at the astonished Fenella.

'You didn't think your grandma could do that, did you?' said she. And as she sank back Fenella heard her light laugh again.

The hard square of brown soap would not lather, and the water in the bottle was like a kind of blue jelly. How hard it was, too, to turn down those stiff sheets; you simply had to tear your way in. If everything had been different, Fenella might have got the giggles. . . . At last she was inside, and while she lay there panting, there sounded from above a long, soft whispering, as though some one was gently, gently rustling among tissue paper to find something. It was grandma saying her prayers. . . .

A long time passed. Then the stewardess came in; she trod softly and leaned her hand on grandma's bunk.

'We're just entering the Straits,'[3] she said.

'Oh!'

2. A head shawl.
3. Cook Strait, the narrow and often turbulent sea between the North and South Islands.

'It's a fine night, but we're rather empty. We may pitch a little.'

And indeed at that moment the Picton boat rose and rose and hung in the air just long enough to give a shiver before she swung down again, and there was the sound of heavy water slapping against her sides. Fenella remembered she had left that swan-necked umbrella standing up on the little couch. If it fell over, would it break? But grandma remembered too, at the same time.

'I wonder if you'd mind, stewardess, laying down my umbrella,' she whispered.

'Not at all, Mrs Crane.' And the stewardess, coming back to grandma breathed, 'Your little granddaughter's in such a beautiful sleep.'

'God be praised for that!' said grandma.

'Poor little motherless mite!' said the stewardess. And grandma was still telling the stewardess all about what happened when Fenella fell asleep.

But she hadn't been asleep long enough to dream before she woke up again to see something waving in the air above her head. What was it? What could it be? It was a small grey foot. Now another joined it. They seemed to be feeling about for something; there came a sigh.

'I'm awake, grandma,' said Fenella.

'Oh, dear, am I near the ladder?' asked grandma. 'I thought it was this end.'

'No, grandma, it's the other. I'll put your foot on it. Are we there?' asked Fenella.

'In the harbour,' said grandma. 'We must get up, child. You'd better have a biscuit to steady yourself before you move.'

But Fenella had hopped out of her bunk. The lamp was still burning, but night was over, and it was cold. Peering through that round eye, she could see far off some rocks. Now they were scattered over with foam; now a gull flipped by; and now there came a long piece of real land.

'It's land, grandma,' said Fenella, wonderingly, as though they had been at sea for weeks together. She hugged herself; she stood on one leg and rubbed it with the toes of the other foot; she was trembling. Oh, it had all been so sad lately. Was it going to change? But all her grandma said was, 'Make haste, child. I should leave your nice banana for the stewardess as you haven't eaten it.' And Fenella put on her black clothes again, and a button sprang off one of her gloves and rolled to where she couldn't reach it. They went up on deck.

But if it had been cold in the cabin, on deck it was like ice. The sun was not up yet, but the stars were dim, and the cold pale sky was the same colour as the cold pale sea. On the land a white mist rose and fell. Now they could see quite plainly dark bush. Even the shapes of the umbrella ferns showed, and those strange silvery withered trees that are like skeletons. . . . Now they could see the landing-stage and some little houses, pale too, clustered together, like shells on the lid of a box. The other passengers tramped up and down, but more slowly than they had the night before, and they looked gloomy.

And now the landing-stage came out to meet them. Slowly it swam towards the Picton boat, and a man holding a coil of rope, and a cart with a small drooping horse and another man sitting on the step, came too.

'It's Mr Penreddy, Fenella, come for us,' said grandma. She sounded pleased. Her white waxen cheeks were blue with cold, her chin trembled, and she had to keep wiping her eyes and her little pink nose.

'You've got my—'

'Yes, grandma.' Fenella showed it to her.

The rope came flying through the air, and 'smack' it fell on to the deck. The gangway was lowered. Again Fenella followed her grandma on to the wharf over to the little cart, and a moment later they were bowling away. The hooves of the little horse drummed over the wooden piles, then sank softly into the sandy road. Not a soul was to be seen; there was not even a feather of smoke. The mist rose and fell, and the sea still sounded asleep as slowly it turned on the beach.

'I seen Mr Crane yestiddy,' said Mr Penreddy. 'He looked himself then. Missus knocked him up a batch of scones last week.'

And now the little horse pulled up before one of the shell-like houses. They got down. Fenella put her hand on the gate, and the big, trembling dew-drops soaked through her glove-tips. Up a little path of round white pebbles they went, with drenched sleeping flowers on either side. Grandma's delicate white picotees were so heavy with dew that they were fallen, but their sweet smell was part of the cold morning. The blinds were down in the little house; they mounted the steps on to the verandah. A pair of old bluchers[4] was on one side of the door, and a large red watering-can on the other.

'Tut! tut! Your grandpa,' said grandma. She turned the handle. Not a sound. She called, 'Walter!' And immediately a deep voice that sounded half stifled called back, 'Is that you, Mary?'

'Wait, dear,' said grandma. 'Go in there.' She pushed Fenella gently into a small dusky sitting-room.

On the table a white cat, that had been folded up like a camel, rose, stretched itself, yawned, and then sprang on to the tips of its

4. Leather half-boots.

toes. Fenella buried one cold little hand in the white, warm fur, and smiled timidly while she stroked and listened to grandma's gentle voice and the rolling tones of grandpa.

A door creaked. 'Come in, dear.' The old woman beckoned, Fenella followed. There, lying to one side of an immense bed, lay grandpa. Just his head with a white tuft, and his rosy face and long silver beard showed over the quilt. He was like a very old wide-awake bird.

'Well, my girl!' said grandpa. 'Give us a kiss!' Fenella kissed him. 'Ugh!' said grandpa. 'Her little nose is as cold as a button. What's that she's holding? Her grandma's umbrella?'

Fenella smiled again, and crooked the swan neck over the bed-rail. Above the bed there was a big text in a deep-black frame:——

Lost! One Golden Hour
Set with Sixty Diamond Minutes.
NO *Reward Is Offered*
For It Is GONE FOR EVER!

'Yer grandma painted that,' said grandpa. And he ruffled his white tuft and looked at Fenella so merrily she almost thought he winked at her.

The Garden Party (1921)†

And after all the weather was ideal. They could not have had a more perfect day for a garden party if they had ordered it. Windless, warm, the sky without a cloud. Only the blue was veiled with a haze of light gold, as it is sometimes in early summer. The gardener had been up since dawn, mowing the lawns and sweeping them, until the grass and the dark flat rosettes where the daisy plants had been seemed to shine. As for the roses, you could not help feeling they understood that roses are the only flowers that impress people at garden parties; the only flowers that everybody is certain of knowing. Hundreds, yes, literally hundreds, had come out in a single night; the green bushes bowed down as though they had been visited by archangels.

Breakfast was not yet over before the men came to put up the marquee.

'Where do you want the marquee put, mother?'

'My dear child, it's no use asking me. I'm determined to leave

† Written in November 1921 and published as the title story in *The Garden Party and Other Stories* (1922). As Antony Alpers noted in *The Stories of Katherine Mansfield* (1984), p. 572, the names of Meg, Jose, and Laurie appear to have been borrowed from Louisa May Alcott's *Little Women* (1868).

everything to you children this year. Forget I am your mother. Treat me as an honoured guest.'

But Meg could not possibly go and supervise the men. She had washed her hair before breakfast, and she sat drinking her coffee in a green turban, with a dark wet curl stamped on each cheek. Jose, the butterfly, always came down in a silk petticoat and a kimono jacket.

'You'll have to go, Laura, you're the artistic one.'

Away Laura flew, still holding her piece of bread-and-butter. It's so delicious to have an excuse for eating out of doors, and besides, she loved having to arrange things; she always felt she could do it so much better than anybody else.

Four men in their shirt-sleeves stood grouped together on the garden path. They carried staves covered with rolls of canvas, and they had big tool-bags slung on their backs. They looked impressive. Laura wished now that she was not holding that piece of bread-and-butter, but there was nowhere to put it, and she couldn't possibly throw it away. She blushed and tried to look severe and even a little bit short-sighted as she came up to them.

'Good morning,' she said, copying her mother's voice. But that sounded so fearfully affected that she was ashamed, and stammered like a little girl, 'Oh—er—have you come—is it about the marquee?'

'That's right, miss,' said the tallest of the men, a lanky, freckled fellow, and he shifted his tool-bag, knocked back his straw hat and smiled down at her. 'That's about it.'

His smile was so easy, so friendly, that Laura recovered. What nice eyes he had, small, but such a dark blue! And now she looked at the others, they were smiling too. 'Cheer up, we won't bite,' their smile seemed to say. How very nice workmen were! And what a beautiful morning! She mustn't mention the morning; she must be business-like. The marquee.

'Well, what about the lily-lawn? Would that do?'

And she pointed to the lily-lawn with the hand that didn't hold the bread-and-butter. They turned, they stared in the direction. A little fat chap thrust out his under-lip, and the tall fellow frowned.

'I don't fancy it,' said he. 'Not conspicuous enough. You see, with a thing like a marquee,' and he turned to Laura in his easy way, 'you want to put it somewhere where it'll give you a bang slap in the eye, if you follow me.'

Laura's upbringing made her wonder for a moment whether it was quite respectful of a workman to talk to her of bangs slap in the eye. But she did quite follow him.

'A corner of the tennis-court,' she suggested. 'But the band's going to be in one corner.'

'H'm, going to have a band, are you?' said another of the workmen. He was pale. He had a haggard look as his dark eyes scanned the tennis-court. What was he thinking?

'Only a very small band,' said Laura gently. Perhaps he wouldn't mind so much if the band was quite small. But the tall fellow interrupted.

'Look here, miss, that's the place. Against those trees. Over there. That'll do fine.'

Against the karakas.[1] Then the karaka-trees would be hidden. And they were so lovely, with their broad, gleaming leaves, and their clusters of yellow fruit. They were like trees you imagined growing on a desert island, proud, solitary, lifting their leaves and fruits to the sun in a kind of silent splendour. Must they be hidden by a marquee?

They must. Already the men had shouldered their staves and were making for the place. Only the tall fellow was left. He bent down, pinched a sprig of lavender, put his thumb and forefinger to his nose and snuffed up the smell. When Laura saw the gesture she forgot all about the karakas in her wonder at him caring for things like that—caring for the smell of lavender. How many men that she knew would have done such a thing. Oh, how extraordinarily nice workmen were, she thought. Why couldn't she have workmen for friends rather than the silly boys she danced with and who came to Sunday night supper? She would get on much better with men like these.

It's all the fault, she decided, as the tall fellow drew something on the back of an envelope, something that was to be looped up or left to hang, of these absurd class distinctions. Well, for her part, she didn't feel them. Not a bit, not an atom. . . . And now there came the chock-chock of wooden hammers. Some one whistled, some one sang out, 'Are you right there, matey?' 'Matey!' The friendliness of it, the—the—Just to prove how happy she was, just to show the tall fellow how at home she felt, and how she despised stupid conventions, Laura took a big bite of her bread-and-butter as she stared at the little drawing. She felt just like a work-girl.

'Laura, Laura, where are you? Telephone, Laura!' a voice cried from the house.

'Coming!' Away she skimmed, over the lawn, up the path, up the steps, across the veranda, and into the porch. In the hall her father and Laurie were brushing their hats ready to go to the office.

'I say, Laura,' said Laurie very fast, 'you might just give a squiz at my coat before this afternoon. See if it wants pressing.'

'I will,' said she. Suddenly she couldn't stop herself. She ran at Laurie and gave him a small, quick squeeze. 'Oh, I do love parties, don't you?' gasped Laura.

1. A tree with glossy dark leaves and large orange-yellow berries.

'Ra-ther,' said Laurie's warm, boyish voice, and he squeezed his sister too, and gave her a gentle push. 'Dash off to the telephone, old girl.'

The telephone. 'Yes, yes; oh yes. Kitty? Good morning, dear. Come to lunch? Do, dear. Delighted of course. It will only be a very scratch meal—just the sandwich crusts and broken meringue-shells and what's left over. Yes, isn't it a perfect morning? Your white? Oh, I certainly should. One moment—hold the line. Mother's calling.' And Laura sat back. 'What, mother? Can't hear.'

Mrs Sheridan's voice floated down the stairs. 'Tell her to wear that sweet hat she had on last Sunday.'

'Mother says you're to wear that *sweet* hat you had on last Sunday. Good. One o'clock. Bye-bye.'

Laura put back the receiver, flung her arms over her head, took a deep breath, stretched and let them fall. 'Huh,' she sighed, and the moment after the sigh she sat up quickly. She was still, listening. All the doors in the house seemed to be open. The house was alive with soft, quick steps and running voices. The green baize door that led to the kitchen regions swung open and shut with a muffled thud. And now there came a long, chuckling absurd sound. It was the heavy piano being moved on its stiff castors. But the air! If you stopped to notice, was the air always like this? Little faint winds were playing chase in at the tops of the windows, out at the doors. And there were two tiny spots of sun, one on the inkpot, one on a silver photograph frame, playing too. Darling little spots. Especially the one on the inkpot lid. It was quite warm. A warm little silver star. She could have kissed it.

The front door bell pealed, and there sounded the rustle of Sadie's print skirt on the stairs. A man's voice murmured; Sadie answered, careless, 'I'm sure I don't know. Wait. I'll ask Mrs Sheridan.'

'What is it, Sadie?' Laura came into the hall.

'It's the florist, Miss Laura.'

It was, indeed. There, just inside the door, stood a wide, shallow tray full of pots of pink lilies. No other kind. Nothing but lilies—canna lilies, big pink flowers, wide open, radiant, almost frighteningly alive on bright crimson stems.

'O-oh, Sadie!' said Laura, and the sound was like a little moan. She crouched down as if to warm herself at that blaze of lilies; she felt they were in her fingers, on her lips, growing in her breast.

'It's some mistake,' she said faintly. 'Nobody ever ordered so many. Sadie, go and find mother.'

But at that moment Mrs Sheridan joined them.

'It's quite right,' she said calmly. 'Yes, I ordered them. Aren't they lovely?' She pressed Laura's arm. 'I was passing the shop yesterday, and I saw them in the window. And I suddenly thought for once in my life I shall have enough canna lilies. The garden party will be a good excuse.'

'But I thought you said you didn't mean to interfere,' said Laura. Sadie had gone. The florist's man was still outside at his van. She put her arm round her mother's neck and gently, very gently, she bit her mother's ear.

'My darling child, you wouldn't like a logical mother, would you? Don't do that. Here's the man.'

He carried more lilies still, another whole tray.

'Bank them up, just inside the door, on both sides of the porch, please,' said Mrs Sheridan. 'Don't you agree, Laura?'

'Oh, I *do*, mother.'

In the drawing-room Meg, Jose and good little Hans had at last succeeded in moving the piano.

'Now, if we put this chesterfield against the wall and move everything out of the room except the chairs, don't you think?'

'Quite.'

'Hans, move these tables into the smoking-room, and bring a sweeper to take these marks off the carpet and—one moment, Hans—' Jose loved giving orders to the servants, and they loved obeying her. She always made them feel they were taking part in some drama. 'Tell mother and Miss Laura to come here at once.'

'Very good, Miss Jose.'

She turned to Meg. 'I want to hear what the piano sounds like, just in case I'm asked to sing this afternoon. Let's try over "This Life is Weary".'

Pom! Ta-ta-ta *Tee*-ta! The piano burst out so passionately that Jose's face changed. She clasped her hands. She looked mournfully and enigmatically at her mother and Laura as they came in.

This Life is *Wee*-ary,
A Tear—a Sigh.
A Love that *Chan*-ges,
This Life is *Wee*-ary,
A Tear—a Sigh.
A Love that *Chan*-ges,
And then . . . Good-bye!

But at the word 'Good-bye', and although the piano sounded more desperate than ever, her face broke into a brilliant, dreadfully unsympathetic smile.

'Aren't I in good voice, mummy?' she beamed.

This Life is *Wee*-ary,
Hope comes to Die.
A Dream—a *Wa*-kening.

But now Sadie interrupted them. 'What is it, Sadie?'

'If you please, m'm, cook says have you got the flags for the sandwiches?'

'The flags for the sandwiches, Sadie?' echoed Mrs Sheridan dreamily. And the children knew by her face that she hadn't got them. 'Let me see.' And she said to Sadie firmly, 'Tell cook I'll let her have them in ten minutes.'

Sadie went.

'Now, Laura,' said her mother quickly, 'come with me into the smoking-room. I've got the names somewhere on the back of an envelope. You'll have to write them out for me. Meg, go upstairs this minute and take that wet thing off your head. Jose, run and finish dressing this instant. Do you hear me, children, or shall I have to tell your father when he comes home to-night? And—and, Jose, pacify cook if you do go into the kitchen, will you? I'm terrified of her this morning.'

The envelope was found at last behind the dining-room clock, though how it had got there Mrs Sheridan could not imagine.

'One of you children must have stolen it out of my bag, because I remember vividly—cream-cheese and lemon-curd. Have you done that?'

'Yes.'

'Egg and—' Mrs Sheridan held the envelope away from her. 'It looks like mice. It can't be mice, can it?'

'Olive, pet,' said Laura, looking over her shoulder.

'Yes, of course, olive. What a horrible combination it sounds. Egg and olive.'

They were finished at last, and Laura took them off to the kitchen. She found Jose there pacifying the cook, who did not look at all terrifying.

'I have never seen such exquisite sandwiches,' said Jose's rapturous voice. 'How many kinds did you say there were, cook? Fifteen?'

'Fifteen, Miss Jose.'

'Well, cook, I congratulate you.'

Cook swept up crusts with the long sandwich knife, and smiled broadly.

'Godber's has come,' announced Sadie, issuing out of the pantry. She had seen the man pass the window.

That meant the cream puffs had come. Godber's were famous for their cream puffs. Nobody ever thought of making them at home.

'Bring them in and put them on the table, my girl,' ordered cook.

Sadie brought them in and went back to the door. Of course Laura and Jose were far too grown-up to really care about such things. All the same, they couldn't help agreeing that the puffs looked very attractive. Very. Cook began arranging them, shaking off the extra icing sugar.

'Don't they carry one back to all one's parties?' said Laura.

'I suppose they do,' said practical Jose, who never liked to be carried back. 'They look beautifully light and feathery, I must say.'

'Have one each, my dears,' said cook in her comfortable voice. 'Yer ma won't know.'

Oh, impossible. Fancy cream puffs so soon after breakfast. The very idea made one shudder. All the same, two minutes later Jose and Laura were licking their fingers with that absorbed inward look that only comes from whipped cream.

'Let's go into the garden, out by the back way,' suggested Laura. 'I want to see how the men are getting on with the marquee. They're such awfully nice men.'

But the back door was blocked by cook, Sadie, Godber's man and Hans.

Something had happened.

'Tuk-tuk-tuk,' clucked cook like an agitated hen. Sadie had her hand clapped to her cheek as though she had toothache. Hans's face was screwed up in the effort to understand. Only Godber's man seemed to be enjoying himself; it was his story.

'What's the matter? What's happened?'

'There's been a horrible accident,' said cook. 'A man killed.'

'A man killed! Where? How? When?'

But Godber's man wasn't going to have his story snatched from under his very nose.

'Know those little cottages just below here, miss?' Know them? Of course, she knew them. 'Well, there's a young chap living there, name of Scott, a carter. His horse shied at a traction-engine, corner of Hawke Street this morning, and he was thrown out on the back of his head. Killed.'

'Dead!' Laura stared at Godber's man.

'Dead when they picked him up,' said Godber's man with relish. 'They were taking the body home as I come up here.' And he said to the cook, 'He's left a wife and five little ones.'

'Jose, come here.' Laura caught hold of her sister's sleeve and dragged her through the kitchen to the other side of the green baize door. There she paused and leaned against it. 'Jose!' she said, horrified, 'however are we going to stop everything?'

'Stop everything, Laura!' cried Jose in astonishment. 'What do you mean?'

'Stop the garden party, of course.' Why did Jose pretend?

But Jose was still more amazed. 'Stop the garden party? My dear Laura, don't be so absurd. Of course we can't do anything of the kind. Nobody expects us to. Don't be so extravagant.'

'But we can't possibly have a garden party with a man dead just outside the front gate.'

That really was extravagant, for the little cottages were in a lane to themselves at the very bottom of a steep rise that led up to the house. A broad road ran between. True, they were far too near. They were the greatest possible eyesore, and they had no right to be in that neighbourhood at all. They were little mean dwellings painted a chocolate brown. In the garden patches there was nothing but cabbage stalks, sick hens and tomato cans. The very smoke coming out of their chimneys was poverty-stricken. Little rags and shreds of smoke, so unlike the great silvery plumes that uncurled from the Sheridans' chimneys. Washerwomen lived in the lane and sweeps and a cobbler, and a man whose house-front was studded all over with minute bird-cages. Children swarmed. When the Sheridans were little they were forbidden to set foot there because of the revolting language and of what they might catch. But since they were grown up, Laura and Laurie on their prowls sometimes walked through. It was disgusting and sordid. They came out with a shudder. But still one must go everywhere; one must see everything. So through they went.

'And just think of what the band would sound like to that poor woman,' said Laura.

'Oh, Laura!' Jose began to be seriously annoyed. 'If you're going to stop a band playing every time some one has an accident, you'll lead a very strenuous life. I'm every bit as sorry about it as you. I feel just as sympathetic.' Her eyes hardened. She looked at her sister just as she used to when they were little and fighting together. 'You won't bring a drunken workman back to life by being sentimental,' she said softly.

'Drunk! Who said he was drunk?' Laura turned furiously on Jose. She said just as they had used to say on those occasions, 'I'm going straight up to tell mother.'

'Do, dear,' cooed Jose.

'Mother, can I come into your room?' Laura turned the big glass door-knob.

'Of course, child. Why, what's the matter? What's given you such a colour?' And Mrs Sheridan turned round from her dressing-table. She was trying on a new hat.

'Mother, a man's been killed,' began Laura.

'*Not* in the garden?' interrupted her mother.

'No, no!'

'Oh, what a fright you gave me!' Mrs Sheridan sighed with relief, and took off the big hat and held it on her knees.

'But listen, mother,' said Laura. Breathless, half-choking, she told the dreadful story. 'Of course, we can't have our party, can we?' she pleaded. 'The band and everybody arriving. They'd hear us, mother; they're nearly neighbours!'

To Laura's astonishment her mother behaved just like Jose; it was harder to bear because she seemed amused. She refused to take Laura seriously.

'But, my dear child, use your common sense. It's only by accident we've heard of it. If some one had died there normally—and I can't understand how they keep alive in those poky little holes—we should still be having our party, shouldn't we?'

Laura had to say 'yes' to that, but she felt it was all wrong. She sat down on her mother's sofa and pinched the cushion frill.

'Mother, isn't it really terribly heartless of us?' she asked.

'Darling!' Mrs Sheridan got up and came over to her, carrying the hat. Before Laura could stop her she had popped it on. 'My child!' said her mother, 'the hat is yours. It's made for you. It's much too young for me. I have never seen you look such a picture. Look at yourself!' And she held up her hand-mirror.

'But, mother,' Laura began again. She couldn't look at herself; she turned aside.

This time Mrs Sheridan lost patience just as Jose had done.

'You are being very absurd, Laura,' she said coldly. 'People like that don't expect sacrifices from us. And it's not very sympathetic to spoil everybody's enjoyment as you're doing now.'

'I don't understand,' said Laura, and she walked quickly out of the room into her own bedroom. There, quite by chance, the first thing she saw was this charming girl in the mirror, in her black hat trimmed with gold daisies, and a long black velvet ribbon. Never had she imagined she could look like that. Is mother right? she thought. And now she hoped her mother was right. Am I being extravagant? Perhaps it was extravagant. Just for a moment she had another glimpse of that poor woman and those little children, and the body being carried into the house. But it all seemed blurred, unreal, like a picture in the newspaper. I'll remember it again after the party's over, she decided. And somehow that seemed quite the best plan. . . .

Lunch was over by half-past one. By half-past two they were all ready for the fray. The green-coated band had arrived and was established in a corner of the tennis-court.

'My dear!' trilled Kitty Maitland, 'aren't they too like frogs for words? You ought to have arranged them round the pond with the conductor in the middle on a leaf.'

Laurie arrived and hailed them on his way to dress. At the sight of him Laura remembered the accident again. She wanted to tell him. If Laurie agreed with the others, then it was bound to be all right. And she followed him into the hall.

'Laurie!'

'Hallo!' He was half-way upstairs, but when he turned round and saw Laura he suddenly puffed out his cheeks and goggled his eyes at her. 'My word, Laura! You do look stunning,' said Laurie. 'What an absolutely topping hat!'

Laura said faintly 'Is it?' and smiled up at Laurie, and didn't tell him after all.

Soon after that people began coming in streams. The band struck up; the hired waiters ran from the house to the marquee. Wherever you looked there were couples strolling, bending to the flowers, greeting, moving on over the lawn. They were like bright birds that had alighted in the Sheridans' garden for this one afternoon, on their way to—where? Ah, what happiness it is to be with people who all are happy, to press hands, press cheeks, smile into eyes.

'Darling Laura, how well you look!'

'What a becoming hat, child!'

'Laura, you look quite Spanish. I've never seen you look so striking.'

And Laura, glowing, answered softly, 'Have you had tea? Won't you have an ice? The passion-fruit ices really are rather special.' She ran to her father and begged him. 'Daddy darling, can't the band have something to drink?'

And the perfect afternoon slowly ripened, slowly faded, slowly its petals closed.

'Never a more delightful garden party. . . .' 'The greatest success. . . .' 'Quite the most. . . .'

Laura helped her mother with the good-byes. They stood side by side in the porch till it was all over.

'All over, all over, thank heaven,' said Mrs Sheridan. 'Round up the others, Laura. Let's go and have some fresh coffee. I'm exhausted. Yes, it's been very successful. But oh, these parties, these parties! Why will you children insist on giving parties!' And they all of them sat down in the deserted marquee.

'Have a sandwich, daddy dear. I wrote the flag.'

'Thanks.' Mr Sheridan took a bite and the sandwich was gone. He took another. 'I suppose you didn't hear of a beastly accident that happened to-day?' he said.

'My dear,' said Mrs Sheridan, holding up her hand, 'we did. It nearly ruined the party. Laura insisted we should put it off.'

'Oh, mother!' Laura didn't want to be teased about it.

'It was a horrible affair all the same,' said Mr Sheridan. 'The chap was married too. Lived just below in the lane, and leaves a wife and half a dozen kiddies, so they say.'

An awkward little silence fell. Mrs Sheridan fidgeted with her cup. Really, it was very tactless of father. . . .

Suddenly she looked up. There on the table were all those sandwiches, cakes, puffs, all un-eaten, all going to be wasted. She had one of her brilliant ideas.

'I know,' she said. 'Let's make up a basket. Let's send that poor creature some of this perfectly good food. At any rate, it will be the greatest treat for the children. Don't you agree? And she's sure to have neighbours calling in and so on. What a point to have it all ready prepared. Laura!' She jumped up. 'Get me the big basket out of the stairs cupboard.'

'But, mother, do you really think it's a good idea?' said Laura.

Again, how curious, she seemed to be different from them all. To take scraps from their party. Would the poor woman really like that?

'Of course! What's the matter with you to-day? An hour or two ago you were insisting on us being sympathetic, and now—'

Oh well! Laura ran for the basket. It was filled, it was heaped by her mother.

'Take it yourself, darling,' said she. 'Run down just as you are. No, wait, take the arum lilies too. People of that class are so impressed by arum lilies.'

'The stems will ruin her lace frock,' said practical Jose.

So they would. Just in time. 'Only the basket, then. And, Laura!'—her mother followed her out of the marquee—'don't on any account—

'What mother?'

No, better not put such ideas into the child's head! 'Nothing! Run along.'

It was just growing dusky as Laura shut their garden gates. A big dog ran by like a shadow. The road gleamed white, and down below in the hollow the little cottages were in deep shade. How quiet it seemed after the afternoon. Here she was going down the hill to somewhere where a man lay dead, and she couldn't realize it. Why couldn't she? She stopped a minute. And it seemed to her that kisses, voices, tinkling spoons, laughter, the smell of crushed grass were somehow inside her. She had no room for anything else. How strange! She looked up at the pale sky, and all she thought was, 'Yes, it was the most successful party.'

Now the broad road was crossed. The lane began, smoky and dark. Women in shawls and men's tweed caps hurried by. Men hung over the palings; the children played in the doorways. A low hum came from the mean little cottages. In some of them there was a flicker of light, and a shadow, crab-like, moved across the window. Laura bent her head and hurried on. She wished now she had put on a coat. How her frock shone! And the big hat with the velvet streamer—if only it was another hat! Were the people looking at her? They must be. It was a mistake to have come; she knew all along it was a mistake. Should she go back even now?

No, too late. This was the house. It must be. A dark knot of people stood outside. Beside the gate an old, old woman with a crutch sat in a chair, watching. She had her feet on a newspaper. The voices stopped as Laura drew near. The group parted. It was as though she was expected, as though they had known she was coming here.

Laura was terribly nervous. Tossing the velvet ribbon over her shoulder, she said to a woman standing by, 'Is this Mrs Scott's house?' and the woman, smiling queerly, said, 'It is, my lass.'

Oh, to be away from this! She actually said, 'Help me, God,' as she walked up the tiny path and knocked. To be away from those staring eyes, or to be covered up in anything, one of those women's shawls even. I'll just leave the basket and go, she decided. I shan't even wait for it to be emptied.

Then the door opened. A little woman in black showed in the gloom.

Laura said, 'Are you Mrs Scott?' But to her horror the woman answered, 'Walk in, please, miss,' and she was shut in the passage.

'No,' said Laura, 'I don't want to come in. I only want to leave this basket. Mother sent—'

The little woman in the gloomy passage seemed not to have heard her. 'Step this way, please, miss,' she said in an oily voice, and Laura followed her.

She found herself in a wretched little low kitchen, lighted by a smoky lamp. There was a woman sitting before the fire.

'Em,' said the little creature who had let her in. 'Em! It's a young lady.' She turned to Laura. She said meaningly, 'I'm 'er sister, miss. You'll excuse 'er, won't you?'

'Oh, but of course!' said Laura. 'Please, please don't disturb her. I—I only want to leave—

But at that moment the woman at the fire turned round. Her face, puffed up, red, with swollen eyes and swollen lips, looked terrible. She seemed as though she couldn't understand why Laura was there. What did it mean? Why was this stranger standing in the kitchen with a basket? What was it all about? And the poor face puckered up again.

'All right, my dear,' said the other. 'I'll thenk the young lady.'

And again she began, 'You'll excuse her, miss, I'm sure,' and her face, swollen too, tried an oily smile.

Laura only wanted to get out, to get away. She was back in the passage. The door opened. She walked straight through into the bedroom where the dead man was lying.

'You'd like a look at 'im, wouldn't you?' said Em's sister, and she brushed past Laura over to the bed. 'Don't be afraid, my lass,'—and now her voice sounded fond and sly, and fondly she drew down the sheet—' 'e looks a picture. There's nothing to show. Come along, my dear.'

Laura came.

There lay a young man, fast asleep—sleeping so soundly, so deeply, that he was far, far away from them both. Oh, so remote, so peaceful. He was dreaming. Never wake him up again. His head was sunk in the pillow, his eyes were closed; they were blind under the closed eyelids. He was given up to his dream. What did garden parties and baskets and lace frocks matter to him? He was far from all those things. He was wonderful, beautiful. While they were laughing and while the band was playing, this marvel had come to the lane. Happy . . . happy. . . . All is well, said that sleeping face. This is just as it should be. I am content.

But all the same you had to cry, and she couldn't go out of the room without saying something to him. Laura gave a loud childish sob.

'Forgive my hat,' she said.

And this time she didn't wait for Em's sister. She found her way out of the door, down the path, past all those dark people. At the corner of the lane she met Laurie.

He stepped out of the shadow. 'Is that you, Laura?'

'Yes.'

'Mother was getting anxious. Was it all right?'

'Yes, quite. Oh, Laurie!' She took his arm, she pressed up against him.

'I say, you're not crying, are you?' asked her brother.

Laura shook her head. She was.

Laurie put his arm round her shoulder. 'Don't cry,' he said in his warm, loving voice. 'Was it awful?'

'No,' sobbed Laura. 'It was simply marvellous. But, Laurie—' She stopped, she looked at her brother. 'Isn't life,' she stammered, 'isn't life—' But what life was she couldn't explain. No matter. He quite understood.

'*Isn't* it, darling?' said Laurie.

The Doll's House (1921)†

When dear old Mrs Hay went back to town after staying with the Burnells she sent the children a doll's house. It was so big that the

† Written at the end of 1921, published in the *Athenaeum* (4 February 1922), and collected in *The Doves' Nest and Other Stories* (1923).

carter and Pat carried it into the courtyard, and there it stayed, propped up on two wooden boxes beside the feed-room door. No harm could come to it; it was summer. And perhaps the smell of paint would have gone off by the time it had to be taken in. For, really, the smell of paint coming from that doll's house ('Sweet of old Mrs Hay, of course; most sweet and generous!')—but the smell of paint was quite enough to make anyone seriously ill, in Aunt Beryl's opinion. Even before the sacking was taken off. And when it was. . . .

There stood the doll's house, a dark, oily, spinach green, picked out with bright yellow. Its two solid little chimneys, glued on to the roof, were painted red and white, and the door, gleaming with yellow varnish, was like a little slab of toffee. Four windows, real windows, were divided into panes by a broad streak of green. There was actually a tiny porch, too, painted yellow, with big lumps of congealed paint hanging along the edge.

But perfect, perfect little house! Who could possibly mind the smell? It was part of the joy, part of the newness.

'Open it quickly, someone!'

The hook at the side was stuck fast. Pat prised it open with his penknife, and the whole house-front swung back, and—there you were, gazing at one and the same moment into the drawing-room and dining-room, the kitchen and two bedrooms. That is the way for a house to open! Why don't all houses open like that? How much more exciting than peering through the slit of a door into a mean little hall with a hatstand and two umbrellas! That is—isn't it?—what you long to know about a house when you put your hand on the knocker. Perhaps it is the way God opens houses at dead of night when He is taking a quiet turn with an angel. . . .

'O-oh!' The Burnell children sounded as though they were in despair. It was too marvellous; it was too much for them. They had never seen anything like it in their lives. All the rooms were papered. There were pictures on the walls, painted on the paper, with gold frames complete. Red carpet covered all the floors except the kitchen; red plush chairs in the drawing-room, green in the dining-room; tables, beds with real bedclothes, a cradle, a stove, a dresser with tiny plates and one big jug. But what Kezia liked more than anything, what she liked frightfully, was the lamp. It stood in the middle of the dining-room table, an exquisite little amber lamp with a white globe. It was even filled all ready for lighting, though of course you couldn't light it. But there was something inside that looked like oil and that moved when you shook it.

The father and mother dolls, who sprawled very stiff as though they had fainted in the drawing-room, and their two little children asleep upstairs, were really too big for the doll's house. They didn't look as though they belonged. But the lamp was perfect. It seemed to smile at Kezia, to say, 'I live here.' The lamp was real.

The Burnell children could hardly walk to school fast enough the next morning. They burned to tell everybody, to describe, too—well—to boast about their doll's house before the school-bell rang.

'I'm to tell,' said Isabel, 'because I'm the eldest. And you two can join in after. But I'm to tell first.'

There was nothing to answer. Isabel was bossy, but she was always right, and Lottie and Kezia knew too well the powers that went with being eldest. They brushed through the thick buttercups at the road edge and said nothing.

'And I'm to choose who's to come and see it first. Mother said I might.'

For it had been arranged that while the doll's house stood in the courtyard they might ask the girls at school, two at a time, to come and look. Not to stay to tea, of course, or to come traipsing through the house. But just to stand quietly in the courtyard while Isabel pointed out the beauties, and Lottie and Kezia looked pleased. . . .

But hurry as they might, by the time they had reached the tarred palings of the boys' playground the bell had begun to jangle. They only just had time to whip off their hats and fall into line before the roll was called. Never mind. Isabel tried to make up for it by looking very important and mysterious and by whispering behind her hand to the girls near her, 'Got something to tell you at playtime.'

Playtime came and Isabel was surrounded. The girls of her class nearly fought to put their arms round her, to walk away with her, to beam flatteringly, to be her special friend. She held quite a court under the huge pine trees at the side of the playground. Nudging, giggling together, the little girls pressed up close. And the only two who stayed outside the ring were the two who were always outside, the little Kelveys. They knew better than to come anywhere near the Burnells.

For the fact was, the school the Burnell children went to was not at all the kind of place their parents would have chosen if there had been any choice. But there was none. It was the only school for miles. And the consequence was all the children of the neighbourhood, the Judge's little girls, the doctor's daughters, the storekeeper's children, the milkman's, were forced to mix together. Not to speak of there being an equal number of rude, rough little boys as well. But the line had to be drawn somewhere. It was drawn at the Kelveys. Many of the children, including the Burnells, were not allowed even to speak to them. They walked past the Kelveys with their heads in the air, and as they set the fashion in all matters of behaviour, the Kelveys were shunned by everybody. Even the teacher had a special voice for them, and a special smile for the other children when Lil Kelvey came up to her desk with a bunch of dreadfully common-looking flowers.

They were the daughters of a spry, hard-working little washerwoman, who went about from house to house by the day. This was awful enough. But where was Mr Kelvey? Nobody knew for certain. But everybody said he was in prison. So they were the daughters of a washerwoman and a jailbird. Very nice company for other people's children! And they looked it. Why Mrs Kelvey made them so conspicuous was hard to understand. The truth was they were dressed in 'bits' given to her by the people for whom she worked. Lil, for instance, who was a stout, plain child, with big freckles, came to school in a dress made from a green art-serge table-cloth of the Burnells', with red plush sleeves from the Logans' curtains. Her hat, perched on top of her high forehead, was a grown-up woman's hat, once the property of Miss Lecky, the postmistress. It was turned up at the back and trimmed with a large scarlet quill. What a little guy she looked! It was impossible not to laugh. And her little sister, our Else, wore a long white dress, rather like a nightgown, and a pair of little boy's boots. But whatever our Else wore she would have looked strange. She was a tiny wishbone of a child, with cropped hair and enormous solemn eyes—a little white owl. Nobody had ever seen her smile; she scarcely ever spoke. She went through life holding on to Lil, with a piece of Lil's skirt screwed up in her hand. Where Lil went, our Else followed. In the playground, on the road going to and from school, there was Lil marching in front and our Else holding on behind. Only when she wanted anything, or when she was out of breath, our Else gave Lil a tug, a twitch, and Lil stopped and turned round. The Kelveys never failed to understand each other.

Now they hovered at the edge; you couldn't stop them listening. When the little girls turned round and sneered, Lil, as usual, gave her silly shamefaced smile, but our Else only looked.

And Isabel's voice, so very proud, went on telling. The carpet made a great sensation, but so did the beds with real bedclothes, and the stove with an oven door.

When she finished Kezia broke in. 'You've forgotten the lamp, Isabel.'

'Oh, yes,' said Isabel, 'and there's a teeny little lamp, all made of yellow glass, with a white globe that stands on the dining-room table. You couldn't tell it from a real one.'

'The lamp's best of all,' cried Kezia. She thought Isabel wasn't making half enough of the little lamp. But nobody paid any attention. Isabel was choosing the two who were to come back with them that afternoon and see it. She chose Emmie Cole and Lena Logan. But when the others knew they were all to have a chance, they couldn't be nice enough to Isabel. One by one they put their arms round Isabel's waist and walked her off. They had something to whisper to her, a secret. 'Isabel's *my* friend.'

Only the little Kelveys moved away forgotten; there was nothing more for them to hear.

Days passed, and as more children saw the doll's house, the fame of it spread. It became the one subject, the rage. The one question was, 'Have you seen Burnells' doll's house? Oh, ain't it lovely!' 'Haven't you seen it? Oh, I say!'

Even the dinner hour was given up to talking about it. The little girls sat under the pines eating their thick mutton sandwiches and big slabs of johnny cake spread with butter. While always, as near as they could get, sat the Kelveys, our Else holding on to Lil, listening too, while they chewed their jam sandwiches out of a newspaper soaked with large red blobs. . . .

'Mother,' said Kezia, 'can't I ask the Kelveys just once?'

'Certainly not, Kezia.'

'But why not?'

'Run away, Kezia; you know quite well why not.'

At last everybody had seen it except them. On that day the subject rather flagged. It was the dinner hour. The children stood together under the pine trees, and suddenly, as they looked at the Kelveys eating out of their paper, always by themselves, always listening, they wanted to be horrid to them. Emmie Cole started the whisper.

'Lil Kelvey's going to be a servant when she grows up.'

'O-oh, how awful!' said Isabel Burnell, and she made eyes at Emmie.

Emmie swallowed in a very meaning way and nodded to Isabel as she'd seen her mother do on those occasions.

'It's true—it's true—it's true,' she said.

Then Lena Logan's little eyes snapped. 'Shall I ask her?' she whispered.

'Bet you don't,' said Jessie May.

'Pooh, I'm not frightened,' said Lena. Suddenly she gave a little squeal and danced in front of the other girls. 'Watch! Watch me! Watch me now!' said Lena. And sliding, gliding, dragging one foot, giggling behind her hand, Lena went over to the Kelveys.

Lil looked up from her dinner. She wrapped the rest quickly away. Our Else stopped chewing. What was coming now?

'Is it true you're going to be a servant when you grow up, Lil Kelvey?' shrilled Lena.

Dead silence. But instead of answering, Lil only gave her silly shamefaced smile. She didn't seem to mind the question at all. What a sell for Lena! The girls began to titter.

Lena couldn't stand that. She put her hands on her hips; she shot forward. 'Yah, yer father's in prison!' she hissed, spitefully.

This was such a marvellous thing to have said that the little girls rushed away in a body, deeply, deeply excited, wild with joy. Someone found a long rope, and they began skipping. And never did they skip so high, run in and out so fast, or do such daring things as on that morning.

In the afternoon Pat called for the Burnell children with the buggy and they drove home. There were visitors. Isabel and Lottie, who liked visitors, went upstairs to change their pinafores. But Kezia thieved out at the back. Nobody was about; she began to swing on the big white gates of the courtyard. Presently, looking along the road, she saw two little dots. They grew bigger, they were coming towards her. Now she could see that one was in front and one close behind. Now she could see that they were the Kelveys. Kezia stopped swinging. She slipped off the gate as if she was going to run away. Then she hesitated. The Kelveys came nearer, and beside them walked their shadows, very long, stretching right across the road with their heads in the buttercups. Kezia clambered back on the gate; she had made up her mind; she swung out.

'Hullo,' she said to the passing Kelveys.

They were so astounded that they stopped. Lil gave her silly smile. Our Else stared.

'You can come and see our doll's house if you want to,' said Kezia, and she dragged one toe on the ground. But at that Lil turned red and shook her head quickly.

'Why not?' asked Kezia.

Lil gasped, then she said, 'Your ma told our ma you wasn't to speak to us.'

'Oh, well,' said Kezia. She didn't know what to reply. 'It doesn't matter. You can come and see our doll's house all the same. Come on. Nobody's looking.'

But Lil shook her head still harder.

'Don't you want to?' asked Kezia.

Suddenly there was a twitch, a tug at Lil's skirt. She turned round. Our Else was looking at her with big imploring eyes; she was frowning; she wanted to go. For a moment Lil looked at our Else very doubtfully. But then our Else twitched her skirt again. She started forward. Kezia led the way. Like two little stray cats they followed across the courtyard to where the doll's house stood.

'There it is,' said Kezia.

There was a pause. Lil breathed loudly, almost snorted; our Else was still as a stone.

'I'll open it for you,' said Kezia kindly. She undid the hook and they looked inside.

'There's the drawing-room and the dining-room, and that's the—'

'Kezia!'

Oh, what a start they gave!

'Kezia!'

It was Aunt Beryl's voice. They turned round. At the back door stood Aunt Beryl, staring as if she couldn't believe what she saw.

'How dare you ask the little Kelveys into the courtyard?' said her cold, furious voice. 'You know as well as I do you're not allowed to talk to them. Run away, children, run away at once. And don't come back again,' said Aunt Beryl. And she stepped into the yard and shooed them out as if they were chickens.

'Off you go immediately!' she called, cold and proud.

They did not need telling twice. Burning with shame, shrinking together, Lil huddling along like her mother, our Else dazed, somehow they crossed the big courtyard and squeezed through the white gate.

'Wicked, disobedient little girl!' said Aunt Beryl bitterly to Kezia, and she slammed the doll's house to.

The afternoon had been awful. A letter had come from Willie Brent, a terrifying, threatening letter, saying if she did not meet him that evening in Pulman's Bush, he'd come to the front door and ask the reason why! But now that she had frightened those little rats of Kelveys and given Kezia a good scolding, her heart felt lighter. That ghastly pressure was gone. She went back to the house humming.

When the Kelveys were well out of sight of Burnells', they sat down to rest on a big red drainpipe by the side of the road. Lil's cheeks were still burning; she took off the hat with the quill and held it on her knee. Dreamily they looked over the hay paddocks, past the creek, to the group of wattles where Logans' cows stood waiting to be milked. What were their thoughts?

Presently our Else nudged up close to her sister. By now she had forgotten the cross lady. She put out a finger and stroked her sister's quill; she smiled her rare smile.

'I seen the little lamp,' she said, softly.

Then both were silent once more.

The Fly (1922)†

'Y' are very snug in here,' piped old Mr Woodifield, and he peered out of the great, green leather armchair by his friend the boss's

† Published in the *Athenaeum* (18 March 1922) and collected in *The Doves' Nest and Other Stories* (1923).

desk as a baby peers out of its pram. His talk was over; it was time for him to be off. But he did not want to go. Since he had retired, since his . . . stroke, the wife and the girls kept him boxed up in the house every day of the week except Tuesday. On Tuesday he was dressed and brushed and allowed to cut back to the City for the day. Though what he did there the wife and girls couldn't imagine. Made a nuisance of himself to his friends, they supposed. . . . Well, perhaps so. All the same, we cling to our last pleasures as the tree clings to its last leaves. So there sat old Woodifield, smoking a cigar and staring almost greedily at the boss, who rolled in his office chair, stout, rosy, five years older than he, and still going strong, still at the helm. It did one good to see him.

Wistfully, admiringly, the old voice added, 'It's snug in here—upon my word!'

'Yes, it's comfortable enough,' agreed the boss, and he flipped the *Financial Times* with a paper-knife. As a matter of fact he was proud of his room; he liked to have it admired, especially by old Woodifield. It gave him a feeling of deep, solid satisfaction to be planted there in the midst of it in full view of that frail old figure in the muffler.

'I've had it done up lately,' he explained, as he had explained for the past—how many?—weeks. 'New carpet,' and he pointed to the bright red carpet with a pattern of large white rings. 'New furniture,' and he nodded towards the massive bookcase and the table with legs like twisted treacle. 'Electric heating!' He waved almost exultantly towards the five transparent, pearly sausages glowing so softly in the tilted copper pan.

But he did not draw old Woodifield's attention to the photograph over the table of a grave-looking boy in uniform standing in one of those spectral photographers' parks with photographers' storm-clouds behind him. It was not new. It had been there for over six years.[1]

'There was something I wanted to tell you,' said old Woodifield, and his eyes grew dim remembering. 'Now what was it? I had it in my mind when I started out this morning.' His hands began to tremble, and patches of red showed above his beard.

Poor old chap, he's on his last pins, thought the boss. And, feeling kindly, he winked at the old man, and said jokingly, 'I tell you what. I've got a little drop of something here that'll do you good before you go out into the cold again. It's beautiful stuff. It wouldn't hurt a child.' He took a key off his watch-chain, unlocked a cupboard below his desk, and drew forth a dark, squat bottle. 'That's

1. Mansfield's younger brother, Leslie (Chummie), had been killed in Flanders in October 1915, six years before this story was written.

the medicine,' said he. 'And the man from whom I got it told me on the strict Q.T.[2] it came from the cellars at Windsor Cassel.'[3]

Old Woodifield's mouth fell open at the sight. He couldn't have looked more surprised if the boss had produced a rabbit.

'It's whisky, ain't it?' he piped, feebly.

The boss turned the bottle and lovingly showed him the label. Whisky it was.

'D'you know,' said he, peering up at the boss wonderingly, 'they won't let me touch it at home.' And he looked as though he was going to cry.

'Ah, that's where we know a bit more than the ladies,' cried the boss, swooping across for two tumblers that stood on the table with the water-bottle, and pouring a generous finger into each. 'Drink it down. It'll do you good. And don't put any water with it. It's sacrilege to tamper with stuff like this. Ah!' He tossed off his, pulled out his handkerchief, hastily wiped his moustaches, and cocked an eye at old Woodifield, who was rolling his in his chaps.[4]

The old man swallowed, was silent a moment, and then said faintly, 'It's nutty!'

But it warmed him; it crept into his chill old brain—he remembered.

'That was it,' he said, heaving himself out of his chair. 'I thought you'd like to know. The girls were in Belgium last week having a look at poor Reggie's grave, and they happened to come across your boy's. They're quite near each other, it seems.'

Old Woodifield paused, but the boss made no reply. Only a quiver in his eyelids showed that he heard.

'The girls were delighted with the way the place is kept,' piped the old voice. 'Beautifully looked after. Couldn't be better if they were at home. You've not been across, have yet?'

'No, no!' For various reasons the boss had not been across.

'There's miles of it,' quavered old Woodifield, 'and it's all as neat as a garden. Flowers growing on all the graves. Nice broad paths.' It was plain from his voice how much he liked a nice broad path.

The pause came again. Then the old man brightened wonderfully.

'D'you know what the hotel made the girls pay for a pot of jam?' he piped. 'Ten francs! Robbery, I call it. It was a little pot, so Gertrude says, no bigger than a half-crown. And she hadn't taken more than a spoonful when they charged her ten francs. Gertrude brought the pot away with her to teach 'em a lesson. Quite right, too; it's trading on our feelings. They think because we're over

2. On the quiet, secretly.
3. Windsor Castle, a royal residence near London.
4. Cheeks.

there having a look round we're ready to pay anything. That's what it is.' And he turned towards the door.

'Quite right, quite right!' cried the boss, though what was quite right he hadn't the least idea. He came round by his desk, followed the shuffling footsteps to the door, and saw the old fellow out. Woodifield was gone.

For a long moment the boss stayed, staring at nothing, while the grey-haired office messenger, watching him, dodged in and out of his cubby hole like a dog that expects to be taken for a run. Then: 'I'll see nobody for half an hour, Macey,' said the boss. 'Understand? Nobody at all.'

'Very good, sir.'

The door shut, the firm heavy steps recrossed the bright carpet, the fat body plumped down in the spring chair, and leaning forward, the boss covered his face with his hands. He wanted, he intended, he had arranged to weep. . . .

It had been a terrible shock to him when old Woodifield sprang that remark upon him about the boy's grave. It was exactly as though the earth had opened and he had seen the boy lying there with Woodifield's girls staring down at him. For it was strange. Although over six years had passed away, the boss never thought of the boy except as lying unchanged, unblemished in his uniform, asleep for ever. 'My son!' groaned the boss. But no tears came yet. In the past, in the first months and even years after the boy's death, he had only to say those words to be overcome by such grief that nothing short of a violent fit of weeping could relieve him. Time, he had declared then, he had told everybody, could make no difference. Other men perhaps might recover, might live their loss down, but not he. How was it possible? His boy was an only son. Ever since his birth the boss had worked at building up this business for him; it had no other meaning if it was not for the boy. Life itself had come to have no other meaning. How on earth could he have slaved, denied himself, kept going all those years without the promise for ever before him of the boy's stepping into his shoes and carrying on where he left off?

And that promise had been so near being fulfilled. The boy had been in the office learning the ropes for a year before the war. Every morning they had started off together; they had come back by the same train. And what congratulations he had received as the boy's father! No wonder; he had taken to it marvellously. As to his popularity with the staff, every man jack of them down to old Macey couldn't make enough of the boy. And he wasn't in the least spoilt. No, he was just his bright, natural self, with the right word for everybody, with that boyish look and his habit of saying, 'Simply splendid.'

But all that was over and done with as though it never had been. The day had come when Macey had handed him the telegram that brought the whole place crashing about his head. 'Deeply regret to inform you. . . .' And he had left the office a broken man, with his life in ruins.

Six years ago, six years. . . . How quickly time passed! It might have happened yesterday. The boss took his hands from his face; he was puzzled. Something seemed to be wrong with him. He wasn't feeling as he wanted to feel. He decided to get up and have a look at the boy's photograph. But it wasn't a favourite photograph of his; the expression was unnatural. It was cold, even stern-looking. The boy had never looked like that.

At that moment the boss noticed that a fly had fallen into his broad inkpot, and was trying feebly but desperately to clamber out again. Help! help! said those struggling legs. But the sides of the inkpot were wet and slippery; it fell back again and began to swim. The boss took up a pen, picked the fly out of the ink, and shook it on to a piece of blotting-paper. For a fraction of a second it lay still on the dark patch that oozed round it. Then the front legs waved, took hold, and, pulling its small, sodden body up it began the immense task of cleaning the ink from its wings. Over and under, over and under, went a leg along a wing, as the stone goes over and under the scythe. Then there was a pause, while the fly, seeming to stand on the tips of its toes, tried to expand first one wing and then the other. It succeeded at last, and, sitting down, it began, like a minute cat, to clean its face. Now one could imagine that the little front legs rubbed against each other lightly, joyfully. The horrible danger was over; it had escaped; it was ready for life again.

But just then the boss had an idea. He plunged his pen back into the ink, leaned his thick wrist on the blotting paper, and as the fly tried its wings down came a great heavy blot. What would it make of that? What indeed! The little beggar seemed absolutely cowed, stunned, and afraid to move because of what would happen next. But then, as if painfully, it dragged itself forward. The front legs waved, caught hold, and, more slowly this time, the task began from the beginning.

He's a plucky little devil, thought the boss, and he felt a real admiration for the fly's courage. That was the way to tackle things; that was the right spirit. Never say die; it was only a question of. . . . But the fly had again finished its laborious task, and the boss had just time to refill his pen, to shake fair and square on the new-cleaned body yet another dark drop. What about it this time? A painful moment of suspense followed. But behold, the front legs were again waving; the boss felt a rush of relief. He leaned over the fly and said to it tenderly, 'You artful little b . . . .' And he actually had the brilliant notion of breathing on it to help the drying process. All the same, there was something timid and weak about its efforts now, and the boss decided that this time should be the last, as he dipped the pen deep into the inkpot.

It was. The last blot fell on the soaked blotting-paper, and the draggled fly lay in it and did not stir. The back legs were stuck to the body; the front legs were not to be seen.

'Come on,' said the boss. 'Look sharp!' And he stirred it with his pen—in vain. Nothing happened or was likely to happen. The fly was dead.

The boss lifted the corpse on the end of the paper-knife and flung it into the waste-paper basket. But such a grinding feeling of wretchedness seized him that he felt positively frightened. He started forward and pressed the bell for Macey.

'Bring me some fresh blotting-paper,' he said, sternly, 'and look sharp about it.' And while the old dog padded away he fell to wondering what it was he had been thinking about before. What was it? It was. . . . He took out his handkerchief and passed it inside his collar. For the life of him he could not remember.

The Canary (1922)†

. . . You see that big nail to the right of the front door? I can scarcely look at it even now and yet I could not bear to take it out. I should like to think it was there always even after my time. I sometimes hear the next people saying, 'There must have been a cage hanging from there.' And it comforts me. I feel he is not quite forgotten.

. . . You cannot imagine how wonderfully he sang. It was not like the singing of other canaries. And that isn't just my fancy. Often, from the window I used to see people stop at the gate to listen, or they would lean over the fence by the mock-orange for quite a long time—carried away. I suppose it sounds absurd to you—it wouldn't if you had heard him—but it really seemed to me he sang whole songs, with a beginning and an end to them.

For instance, when I'd finished the house in the afternoon, and changed my blouse and brought my sewing on to the verandah here, he used to hop, hop, hop from one perch to the other, tap against the bars as if to attract my attention, sip a little water, just as a professional singer might, and then break into a song so exquisite that I had to put my needle down to listen to him. I can't

† Mansfield's last story, "The Canary" was written in July 1922 and first published in *The Doves' Nest and Other Stories* (1923).

describe it; I wish I could. But it was always the same, every afternoon, and I felt that I understood every note of it.

. . . I loved him. How I loved him! Perhaps it does not matter so very much what it is one loves in this world. But love something one must! Of course there was always my little house and the garden, but for some reason they were never enough. Flowers respond wonderfully, but they don't sympathise. Then I loved the evening star. Does that sound ridiculous? I used to go into the backyard, after sunset, and wait for it until it shone above the dark gum tree. I used to whisper, 'There you are, my darling.' And just in that first moment it seemed to be shining for me alone. It seemed to understand this . . . something which is like longing, and yet it is not longing. Or regret—it is more like regret. And yet regret for what? I have much to be thankful for!

. . . But after he came into my life I forgot the evening star; I did not need it any more. But it was strange. When the Chinaman who came to the door with birds to sell held him up in his tiny cage, and instead of fluttering, fluttering, like the poor little goldfinches, he gave a faint, small chirp, I found myself saying, just as I had said to the star over the gum tree, 'There you are, my darling.' From that moment he was mine!

. . . It surprises even me now to remember how he and I shared each other's lives. The moment I came down in the morning and took the cloth off his cage he greeted me with a drowsy little note. I knew it meant 'Missus! Missus!' Then I hung him on the nail outside while I got my three young men their breakfasts, and I never brought him in, to do his cage, until we had the house to ourselves again. Then, when the washing-up was done, it was quite a little entertainment. I spread a newspaper over a corner of the table and when I put the cage on it he used to beat with his wings, despairingly, as if he didn't know what was coming. 'You're a regular little actor,' I used to scold him. I scraped the tray, dusted it with fresh sand, filled his seed and water tins, tucked a piece of chickweed and half a chili between the bars. And I am perfectly certain he understood and appreciated every item of this little performance. You see by nature he was exquisitely neat. There was never a speck on his perch. And you'd only to see him enjoy his bath to realise he had a real small passion for cleanliness. His bath was put in last. And the moment it was in he positively leapt into it. First he fluttered one wing, then the other, then he ducked his head and dabbled his breast feathers. Drops of water were scattered all over the kitchen, but still he would not get out. I used to say to him, 'Now that's quite enough. You're only showing off.' And at last out he hopped and standing on one leg he began to peck himself dry. Finally he gave a shake, a flick, a twitter and he lifted his throat—Oh,

I can hardly bear to recall it. I was always cleaning the knives by then. And it almost seemed to me the knives sang too, as I rubbed them bright on the board.

. . . Company, you see, that was what he was. Perfect company. If you have lived alone you will realise how precious that is. Of course there were my three young men who came in to supper every evening, and sometimes they stayed in the dining-room afterwards reading the paper. But I could not expect them to be interested in the little things that made my day. Why should they be? I was nothing to them. In fact, I overheard them one evening talking about me on the stairs as 'the Scarecrow'. No matter. It doesn't matter. Not in the least. I quite understand. They are young. Why should I mind? But I remember feeling so especially thankful that I was not quite alone that evening. I told him, after they had gone. I said 'Do you know what they call Missus?' And he put his head on one side and looked at me with his little bright eye until I could not help laughing. It seemed to amuse him.

. . . Have you kept birds? If you haven't, all this must sound, perhaps, exaggerated. People have the idea that birds are heartless, cold little creatures, not like dogs or cats. My washerwoman used to say every Monday when she wondered why I didn't keep 'a nice fox terrier', 'There's no comfort, Miss, in a canary.' Untrue! Dreadfully untrue! I remember one night. I had had a very awful dream—dreams can be terribly cruel—even after I had woken up I could not get over it. So I put on my dressing-gown and came down to the kitchen for a glass of water. It was a winter night and raining hard. I suppose I was half asleep still, but through the kitchen window, that hadn't a blind, it seemed to me the dark was staring in, spying. And suddenly I felt it was unbearable that I had no one to whom I could say 'I've had such a dreadful dream,' or—'Hide me from the dark.' I even covered my face for a minute. And then there came a little 'Sweet! Sweet!' His cage was on the table, and the cloth had slipped so that a chink of light shone through. 'Sweet! Sweet!' said the darling little fellow again, softly, as much as to say, 'I'm here, Missus. I'm here!' That was so beautifully comforting that I nearly cried.

. . . And now he's gone. I shall never have another bird, another pet of any kind. How could I? When I found him, lying on his back, with his eye dim and his claws wrung, when I realised that never again should I hear my darling sing, something seemed to die in me. My breast felt hollow, as if it was his cage. I shall get over it. Of course. I must. One can get over anything in time. And people always say I have a cheerful disposition. They are quite right. I thank God I have.

. . . All the same, without being morbid, or giving way to—to memories and so on, I must confess that there does seem to me something sad in life. It is hard to say what it is. I don't mean the sorrow that we all know, like illness and poverty and death. No, it is something different. It is there, deep down, deep down, part of one, like one's breathing. However hard I work and tire myself I have only to stop to know it is there, waiting. I often wonder if everybody feels the same. One can never know. But isn't it extraordinary that under his sweet, joyful little singing it was just this—sadness?—Ah, what is it?—that I heard.

Katherine Mansfield

FROM HER LETTERS

To Sylvia Payne[1]†

30 Manchester Street[2] W. [London]
24. iv. 06

* * *

A great change has come into my life since I saw you last. Father is greatly opposed to my wish to be a professional 'cellist or to take up the 'cello to any great extent—so my hope for a musical career is absolutely gone. It was a fearful disappointment—I could not tell you what I have felt like—and do now when I think of it—but I suppose it is no earthly use warring with the Inevitable—so in the future I shall give *all* my time to writing. There are great opportunities for a girl in New Zealand—she has so much time and quiet—and we have an ideal little "cottage by the sea"[3] where I mean to spend a good deal of my time. Do you *love* solitude as I do—especially if I am in a writing mood—and will you do so—too. Write, I mean, in the Future. I feel sure that you would be splendidly successful—

I am so keen upon all women having a *definite* future—are not you? The idea of sitting still and waiting for a husband is absolutely revolting—and it really is the attitude of a great many girls. Do you know I have read none of the books that you mentioned. Is not that shocking—but—Sylvia—you know that little "Harold Brown" shop in Wimpole Shop [*for* Street]—I picked up a small collection of poems entitled "The Silver Net" by Louis Vintras[4]—and I liked some of them immensely. The atmosphere is so *intense*. He seems to me to belong to that school which flourished just a few years ago—but which now has not a single representative—a kind of impressionist literature school. Don't think that I even approve of them—but they interest me—Dowson—Sherard—School.[5] It rather made me smile to read of you wishing you could create your fate—O, how many times I have felt just the same. I just long for power

† Reprinted by permission of Oxford University Press. The letters to the end of 1921 are from *The Collected Letters of Katherine Mansfield*, edited by Vincent O'Sullivan and Margaret Scott, vol. 1, 1903–1917 (1984), pp. 18–19, 84, 87–88, 124, 167–68, 177, 287–88, 330–31; vol. 2, 1918–19 (1987), pp. 54–55, 169; Volume Three, 1919–20 (1993); vol. 4, 1920–1921 (1996), pp. 75, 97, 118–19, 278, 323–24, 333. The letters for 1922 are from *Katherine Mansfield Selected Letters*, edited by Vincent O'Sullivan, 1989, pp. 248, 249–50, 257–59.) All notes are the Editor's.

1. Sylvia Payne was Mansfield's cousin; they attended Queen's College, Harley Street, London, at the same time.
2. Mansfield and her sisters were staying at Fripps Hotel during a school vacation.
3. At Downes Point, Days Bay, across the harbor from Wellington city.
4. Louis Vintras, *The Silver Net* (1903).
5. The poet and fiction writer Ernest Dowson (1867–1900) died at the home of novelist and critic Robert Harborough Sherard (1861–1943), but they did not form any kind of "school." Mansfield uses the word "impressionist" to suggest intensity, vividness, and emotional color.

over circumstances—& always feel as though I could do such a great deal more good than is done—& give such a lot of pleasure—aber[6]———————

* * * I am enjoying this Hotel life. There is a kind of feeling of irresponsibility about it that is fascinating. Would you not like to try *all* sorts of lives—one is so very small—but that is the satisfaction of writing—one can impersonate so many people—

Au revoir—dear friend.

* * *

Your friend
K.

To Garnet Trowell[1]

[Beauchamp Lodge[2]
Warwick Crescent, London.
2 November 1908]

* * *

* * * I have a strange ambition—I've had it for years—and now, suddenly here it is revived—in a different way—and coming hammering at my door—It is to write—and recite what I write—in a very fine way—you know what I mean. Do you know exactly what I mean. Revolutionise and revive the art of elocution———take it to its proper plane—Nothing offends me so much as the conventional reciter—stiff—affected—awkward—but there is another side to it—the side of *art*. A darkened stage—a great—high backed oak chair—flowers—shaded lights—a low table filled with curious books—and to wear a simple, beautifully coloured dress—You see what I mean. Then to study *tone* effects in the voice—never rely on gesture—though gesture is another art and should be linked irrevocably with it—and express in the voice and face and atmosphere all that you say. *Tone* should be my secret—each word a variety of tone—————I remember once hearing a Danish woman with a violinist at the Eolian Hall give a recital[3] but it was conventional & not on these lines—Even then it was fine—Well, I should like to do this—and this is in my power because I know I possess the power of holding people. I would like to be the Maud

6. But [German].
1. Garnet Trowell (1889–1947) was the son of Mansfield's cello teacher in Wellington. After studying in Brussels, he became a violinist with an opera company in England. He and Mansfield became lovers in 1908. His parents forced their separation. He was the father of the child she miscarried the next year in Bavaria.
2. When Mansfield returned from Wellington to London in August 1908, she stayed for some months at Beauchamp Lodge, a girls' hostel near Paddington Railway Station.
3. No Danish woman performed in this way. Mansfield may have been thinking of a dramatic recital by Blanche Theeman at the Aeolian Hall in June 1906.

Allen[4] of this Art—what do you think. Write me about this—will you? You see—I could then write just what I felt would suit me—and could popularise my work—and also I feel there's a big opening for something sensational and new in this direction- - - - -

* * *

To Garnet Trowell

44 Keynham Terrace H. M.[1] Dockyard Devonport.
[8 November 1908]

Since writing to you yesterday—a great deal seems to have happened—that is always the case- - - - -Yesterday afternoon I saw the launching of a great battle-ship—one of the most splendid, impressive sights possible, I think. There were thousands of people—from the ultra smart to the poorest workmen and their wives—all gathered together—And the ship was held in place by iron girders and supports. She towered above everybody. On a flag enveloped platform—Mrs Asquith[2]—a very large section of the Naval world—and a chaplain and choir assembled. We were all you see down below. It was a brilliant day, but a fierce wind rushed down and about. The crowd was silent, while the choir & sailors sang a hymn. You see the dramatic effect—it caught me. Strange visions of the victories and defeats—death—storms—their voices seemed crying in the wind. And all the builders of the ships—the rough men who had toiled at her—stood silently on her deck, waiting for the moment to come- - -And all the time we heard inside the ship a terrible—knocking—they were breaking down the supports, but it seemed to me almost symbolical as tho' the great heart of the creature pulsated—And suddenly a silence so tremendous that the very wind seemed to cease—then a sharp, wrenching sound, and all the great bulk of her swept down its inclined plank into the sun—and the sky was full of gold—into the sea—which waited for her. The crowd cheered, screamed—the men on board, their rough faces—their windblown hair—cheered back—In front of me an old woman and a young girl—the little old woman, whose grand uncle had been in the fighting Temeraire[3]—trembled & shook and cried—but the girl—her flushed face lifted—was laughing, and I seemed to read in her tense, young body, anticipation, realisation—comprends tu? . . .[4]

4. Maud Allen (1883–1956), a Canadian dancer and actress who attempted to revive Greek classical dance.

1. Mansfield was staying with friends near His Majesty's Naval Dockyard at Devonport, where she saw the launching of the battleship *Collingwood*.
2. Margot Asquith, the wife of the British prime minister Herbert Asquith.
3. A famous battleship in the British fleet during the Napoleonic Wars.
4. You understand?

Oh, Garnet, why is it we so love the strong emotions? I think because they give us such a keen sense of *Life*—a violent belief in our Existence. One thing I cannot bear and that is the mediocre—I like always to have a great grip of Life, so that I intensify the so-called small things—so that truly everything is significant. In Winter—to look out over a silent garden—I like first, to get that sense of loneliness, so [*for*? that] simplicity of barrenness—and *then* always—I like to be able to see the flowers pushing their way up through the brown earth. It is the superficial attitude which kills Art, always. Give Life a little attention, a little enthusiasm—and "Fair Exchange is no robbery", she says, & heaps out arms with treasures. Why, it is the same with Love. The more you give me, the more I feel that you enrich my nature so I can give you more.

* * *

To John Middleton Murry[1]

["The Gables," Cholesbury.
19 May 1913]

Dear Jack.

I've nursed the epilogue to no purpose.[2] Every time I pick it up and hear "you'll keep it to six," I *cant* cut it. To my knowledge there aren't any superfluous words: I mean every line of it. I don't "just ramble on" you know, but this thing happened to just fit 6½ pages—you cant cut it without making an ugly mess somewhere. Im a powerful stickler for form in this style of work. I hate the sort of licence that English people give themselves-–to spread over and flop and roll about. I feel as fastidious as though I wrote with acid. All of which will seem, I suppose unconvincing and exaggeration. I can only express my sincerest distress (which I do truly feel) and send you the epilogue back. If you & Wilfred[3] feel more qualified for the job-–oh, do by all means—But I'd rather it wasn't there at all than sitting in the Blue Review with a broken nose and one ear as though it had jumped into an editorial dog fight. It's a queer day, with flickers of sun. The epilogue has worried me no end—and I can still hear—tossing about—the aftermath of that thunder.* * *

* * *

1. John Middleton Murry (1889–1957), journalist and scholar, was the editor of the literary journal *Rhythm* when Mansfield met him in 1911. They became lovers the next year and were married in 1919. A large part of Mansfield's extensive correspondence was written to Murry during the periods she was obliged to spend abroad because of ill health.
2. Mansfield contributed an "Epilogue," which in fact was a short story, to each number of the *Blue Review* which Murry was then editing. She is referring here to "Epilogue II," which she had written for the June 1913 issue, and which was later published as "Violet" in *Something Childish But Very Natural* (1924).
3. The poet W. W. Gibson (1878–1962) was Murry's assistant editor.

To John Middleton Murry

[13 Quai aux Fleurs Paris.
25 March 1915]

* * *

I had a great day yesterday. The Muses descended in a ring like the angels on the Botticelli Nativity[1] roof—or so it seemed to "humble" little Tig and I fell into the open arms of my first novel.[2] I have finished a huge chunk but I shall have to copy it on thin paper for you. I expect you will think I am a dotty when you read it—but—tell me what you think—won't you? Its queer stuff. Its the spring makes me write like this. Yesterday I had a fair wallow in it and then I shut up shop & went for a long walk along the quai—very far. It was dusk when I started—but dark when I got home. The lights came out as I walked—& the boats danced by. Leaning over the bridge I suddenly discovered that one of those boats was exactly what I want my novel to be—Not big, almost 'grotesque' in shape I mean perhaps *heavy*––with people rather dark and seen strangely as they move in the sharp light and shadow and I want bright shivering lights in it and the sound of water. (This, my lad, by way of uplift) But I *think* the novel will be alright. Of course it is not what you could call serious—but then I cant be just at this time of year & Ive always felt a spring novel would be lovely to write.

* * *

To John Middleton Murry

[13 Quai aux Fleurs Paris
7 May 1915]

Whose fault is it that we are so isolated—that we have no real life—that everything apart from writing and reading is "felt" to be a waste of time.

I walked on today and came to a garden behind Notre Dame.[1] The pink and white flowering trees were so lovely that I sat down on a bench. In the middle of the garden there was a grass plot and a marble basin. Sparrows taking their baths turned the basin into a fountain and pigeons walked through the velvety grass pluming their feathers. Every bench and every chair was occupied by a mother or a nurse or a grandfather and little staggering babies with

1. *The Mystic Nativity* by Sandro Botticelli is in the National Gallery, London.
2. Mansfield began *The Aloe*, which she refers to here as her first novel. Two years later she refashioned it as her long story "Prelude," which opened her first collection, *Bliss and Other Stories*, 1920. Tig: one of the many nicknames Mansfield used for Murry.
1. The twelfth-century cathedral in the center of Paris.

spades and buckets made mud pies or filled their buckets with fallen chestnut flowers or threw their grandfathers caps on to the forbidden grass plot. And then there came a chinese nurse trailing 2 babies. Oh, she was a funny little thing in her green trousers and black tunic, a small turban clamped to her head. She sat down with her darning and she kept up a long bird like chatter all the time, blinking at the children and running the darning needle through her turban. But after I had watched a long time I realised I was in the middle of a dream. Why haven't I got a real "home", a real life—Why haven't I got a chinese nurse with green trousers and two babies who rush at me and clasp my knees—Im not a girl—Im a woman. I *want* things. Shall I ever have them? To write all the morning and then to get lunch over quickly and to write again in the afternoon & have supper and *one* cigarette together and then to be alone again until bed-time—and all this love and joy that fights for outlet—and all this life drying up, like milk, in an old breast. Oh, I want life—I want friends and people and a house. I want to give and to spend (the P.O.[2] savings bank apart, darling.)

To Bertrand Russell[1]

[3 Gower Street, Bloomsbury, London.
17 December 1916]

I meant to write to you immediately after you left me on Friday night to say how sorry I was to have been such cold comfort and so useless to lift even ever so little the cloud of your fatigue. For a long time I sat before the fire after you had gone feeling that your good-bye had been quite final—was it? And I did not explain myself as I wished to—I left unsaid so much that perhaps you were misled. Its true that my desire is to bring all that I see and feel into harmony with that rare 'vision' of life of which we spoke, and that if I do not achieve this I shall feel that my life has been a fault at last, and its my God terribly true that I dont see the means yet—I don't in the least know definitely *how* to live. But its equally true that life never bores me. It is such strange delight to observe people and to try to understand them, to walk over the mountains and into the valleys of the world, and fields and road and to move on rivers and seas, to arrive late at night in strange cities or to come into little harbours just at pink dawn when its cold with a high wind blowing somewhere *up* in the air, to push through the heavy door into little cafés

2. Post Office.
1. Bertrand Russell (1872–1970), eminent philosopher, mathematician, radical activist, and author, was a Fellow of Trinity College, Cambridge, and an influential voice in British public affairs. For a time he was much fascinated by Mansfield.

and to watch the pattern people make among tables & bottles and glasses, to watch women when they are off their guard, and to get them to talk then, to smell flowers and leaves and fruit and grass—all this—and all this is nothing—for there is so much more. When I am overcome by one of the fits of despair all this is ashes—and so intolerably bitter that I feel it never can be sweet again—But it is—To air oneself among these things, to seek them, to explore them and then to go apart and detach oneself from them—and to write—after the ferment has quite subsided— — — —

After all youll cry me very vague & dismiss me perhaps as a woman with an ill regulated mind . . But—

Goodnight

Katherine.

To Dorothy Brett[1]

[141 A Church Street Chelsea, London.
11 October 1917]

My dear Brett,

It is a cold sharp day—I can see the sun flying in the sky like a faint far-away flag—My Japanese doll has gone into boots for the winter and the studio smells of quinces. I have to write all day with my feet in the fringe of the fire—and Oh Alas! it is sad to think that I shall be warm in front and cold behind from now until next June. It seems to me so extraordinarily right that you should be painting Still Lives just now. What can one do, faced with this wonderful tumble of round bright fruits, but gather them and play with them—and *become them*, as it were. When I pass the apple stalls I cannot help stopping and staring until I feel that I, myself, am changing into an apple, too—and that at any moment I may produce an apple, miraculously, out of my own being like the conjuror produces the egg. When you paint apples do you feel that your breasts and your knees become apples, too? Or do you think this the greatest nonsense. I don't. I am *sure* it is not. When I write about ducks I swear that I am a white duck with a round eye, floating in a pond fringed with yellow blobs and taking an occasional dart at the other duck with the round eye, which floats upside down beneath me. In fact this whole process of becoming the duck (what Lawrence[2] would, perhaps, call this "consummation with the

1. The Honorable Dorothy Brett (1883–1977) was an art student when she and Mansfield met in 1915. They remained close friends until Mansfield's death.
2. D. H. Lawrence (1885–1930), novelist and poet, was at this time friendly with both Mansfield and Brett.

duck or the apple") is so thrilling that I can hardly breathe, only to think about it. For although that is as far as most people can get, it is really only the 'prelude'. There follows the moment when you are *more* duck, *more* apple or *more* Natasha[3] than any of these objects could ever possibly be, and so you *create* them anew. * * * But that is why I believe in technique, too (you asked me if I did.) I do, just because I don't see how art is going to make that divine *spring* into the bounding outlines of things if it hasn't passed through the process of trying to *become* these things before recreating them.

* * *

I threw my darling to the wolves[4] and they ate it and served me up so much praise in such a golden bowl that I couldn't help feeling gratified. I did not think they would like it at all and I am still astounded that they do. What form is it? you ask. Ah, Brett, its so difficult to say. As far as I know its more or less my own invention. And how have I shaped it? This is about as much as I can say about it. You know, if the truth were known I have a perfect passion for the island where I was born. * * * Well, in the early morning there I always remember feeling that this little island has dipped back into the dark blue sea during the night only to rise again at beam of day, all hung with bright spangles and glittering drops—(When you ran over the dewy grass you positively felt that your feet tasted salt.) I tried to catch that moment—with something of its sparkle and its flavour. And just as on those mornings white milky mists rise and uncover some beauty, then smother it again and then again disclose it. I tried to lift that mist from my people and let them be seen and then to hide them again. . . It so difficult to describe all this and it sounds perhaps overambitious and vain. But I don't feel anything but intensely a longing to serve my subject as well as I can—But the unspeakable thrill of this art business. What is there to compare! And what more can one desire. Its not a case of keeping the home fire burning for me. Its a case of keeping the home fire down to a respectable blaze and little enough. If you don't come and see me soon there'll be nothing but a little heap of ash and two crossed pens upon it.

* * *

3. Natasha Rostov, heroine of Tolstoy's epic novel *War and Peace* (1863–69).
4. *Prelude* was first published by the novelist and essayist Virginia Woolf (1882–1941) and her husband Leonard Woolf (1880–1969) on their private press, The Hogarth Press, in 1918.

To John Middleton Murry

[Hotel Beau Rivage Bandol, France.
February 3rd 1918.]

* * *

I really feel I *ought* to send you some boughs and songs, for never was there a place more suited, but to tell you the truth I am pretty well absorbed in what I am writing & walk the bloody countryside with a 2d <envelope> note book shutting out les amandiers.[1] But I don't want to discuss it in case it dont come off . . . . .

Ive two 'kick offs' in the writing game. *One* is joy—real joy—the thing that made me write when we lived at Pauline,[2] and that sort of writing I could only do in just that state of being in some perfectly blissful way *at peace*. Then something delicate and lovely seems to open before my eyes, like a flower without thought of a frost or a cold breath—knowing that all about it is warm and tender and 'steady'. And *that* I try, ever so humbly to express.

The other 'kick off' is my old original one, and (had I not known love) it would have been my all. Not hate or destruction (both are beneath contempt as real motives) but an *extremely* deep sense of hopelessness—of everything doomed to disaster—almost wilfully, stupidly—like the almond tree and 'pas de nougat pour le noël'[3]— There! as I took out a cigarette paper I got it exactly—*a cry against corruption* that is *absolutely* the nail on the head. Not a protest—a *cry*, and I mean corruption in the widest sense of the word, of course—

I am at present fully launched, right out in the deep sea with this second state. I may not be able to 'make my passage'—I may have to put back & have another try, thats why I don't want to talk about it—& have breath for so little more than a hail. But I must say the boat feels to be driving along the deep water as though it smelt port—(no darling, better say 'harbour' or youll think I am rushing into a public house)

After lunch.

My Boge,[4]

I have just read your Tuesday note, written after *another* raid.[5] You sound awfully tired, darling and awfully disenchanted. You are overworking . . . its too plain. * * *

1. The almond trees.
2. The Villa Pauline, Bandol, in the South of France, where Mansfield and Murry had lived for three and a half months from December 1915.
3. "No nougat for Christmas," a line Mansfield remembers from a song by the French poet and naturalist Jean-Henri Fabre (1823–1915).
4. Another nickname for Murry.
5. There had been a German air raid on the outskirts of London on the night of 29 January 1918.

Yes I agree with you—blow the old war. It is a toss up whether it dont get every one of us before its done. Except for the first warm days here when I really did seem to almost forget it its never out of my mind & everything is poisoned by it. Its *here in* me the whole time, eating me away—and I am simply terrified by it—Its at the root of my homesickness & anxiety & panic—I think. It took being alone here and unable to work to make me fully fully *accept* it. But now I don't think that even you would beat me.[6] I have got the pull of you in a way because I am working but I solemnly assure [you] that every moment away from my work is MISERY. And the human contact—just the pass the time away chat distracts you—& that of course I dont have at all. I miss it very much. Birds & flowers and dreaming seas dont do it. Being a biped—I must have a two legged person to *talk* to—You cant imagine how I feel that I walk alone in a sort of black glittering case like a beetle————

To Dorothy Brett

[47 Redcliffe Road, Fulham, London.
12 May 1918]

* * *

I saw Virginia[1] on Thursday. She was very nice. She's the only one of them that I shall ever see but she *does* take the writing business seriously and she *is* honest about it and thrilled by it. One cant ask more. My poor dear Prelude is still piping away in their little cage and not out yet. I read some pages of it & scarcely knew it again. It all seems so once upon a time. But I am having some notices printed and they say it will be ready by June. And won't the "Intellectuals" just hate it. They'll think its a New Primer for Infant Readers. Let 'em.

* * *

To John Middleton Murry

[Villa Isola Bella, Menton, France.
18 October 1920]

* * *

I return De la Mare's[1] letter. I long to hear of your time with him. Its very queer; he haunts me here—not a persistent or substantial ghost but as one who shares my (our) joy in the *silent world*. Joy is

6. That is, in his pessimism regarding the war.
1. This was the period of closest friendship between Virginia Woolf and Mansfield.
1. Walter De la Mare (1873–1956), a poet and short-story writer Mansfield admired.

not the word: I only used it because it conveys a stillness—a remoteness—because there is a faraway sound in it.

You know, darling, I have felt very often lately as though the silence had some meaning beyond these signs these intimations. Isn't it possible that if one yielded there is a whole world into which one is received? It is so near and yet I am conscious that I hold back from giving myself up to it. What is this something mysterious that waits—that beckons?

And then suffering—bodily suffering such as Ive known for three years. It has changed forever everything—even the *appearance* of the world is not the same—there is something added. *Everything has its shadow.* Is it right to resist such suffering? Do you know I feel it has been an immense privilege. Yes, in spite of all. How blind we little creatures are! Darling, its only the fairy tales we *really* live by. If we set out upon a journey the more wonderful the treasure the greater the temptations and perils to be overcome. And if someone rebels and says Life isn't good enough on those terms one can only say: 'It *is*'. Dont misunderstand me. I don't mean a "thorn in the flesh,[2] my dear"—its a million times more mysterious. It has taken me three years to understand this—to come to see this. We resist—we are terribly frightened. The little boat enters the dark fearful gulf and our only cry is to escape—"put me on land again". But its useless. Nobody listens. The shadowy figure rows on. One ought to sit still and uncover ones eyes.

I believe the greatest failing of all is *to be frightened*. Perfect Love casteth out Fear.[3] When I look back on my life all my mistakes have been because I was afraid . . . Was that why I had to look on death. Would nothing less cure me? You know, one can't help wondering, sometimes . . . No, not a personal God or any such nonsense. Much more likely—the soul's desperate choice . . .

Am I right in thinking that you too have been ridden by Fear (of quite a different kind). And now its gone from you—and you are whole. I feel that only now you have *all* your strength—a kind of *release*.

* * *

2. "There was given to me a thorn in the flesh . . . lest I should be exalted above measure." 2 Cor. 12:7.
3. John 4:18.

To John Middleton Murry

[Villa Isola Bella, Menton, France.]
3 November 1920.

* * *

Here it is under my hand—finished—another story about as long as The Man Without a Temperament[1]—praps longer. Its called *The Stranger.*[2] Its a "New Zealand" story. My depression has gone, Boge, so it was just this. And now its here—thank God—& the fire burns and its warm and tho the wind is howling—it can howl. What a QUEER business writing is. I don't know. I dont believe other people are ever as foolishly excited as I am while Im working. How could they be? Writers would have to live in trees. Ive *been* this man *been* this woman. Ive stood for hours on the Auckland Wharf. Ive been out in the stream waiting to be berthed. Ive been a seagull hovering at the stern and a hotel porter whistling through his teeth. It isn't as though one sits and watches the spectacle. That would be thrilling enough, God knows. But one IS the spectacle for the time. If one remained oneself all the time like some writers can it would be a bit less exhausting. Its a lightning change affair, tho. But what does it matter. Ill keep this story for you to read at Xmas.

To John Middleton Murry

[Villa Isola Bella, Menton, France.
23 November 1920]

* * *

About the punctuation in The Stranger. Thank you, Bogey. No, my dash isn't quite a feminine dash (certainly when I was young it was). But it was intentional in that story. I was trying to do away with the three dots. They have been so abused by female & male writers that I fight shy of them—*much* tho' I need them. The truth is—punctuation is infernally difficult. If I had time Id like to write an open letter to the A.[1] on the subject. Its boundaries need to be enlarged. But I wont go into it now. Ill try however to remember *commas*. Its a fascinating subject, ça, one that Id like to talk over with you. If only there was time to write all one wants to write. There seems less & less time. * * *

* * *

1. A story Mansfield had written in January 1920 and published in *Art and Letters*, Spring 1920.
2. Published in the *London Mercury*, January 1921.
1. The *Athenaeum*, a weekly literary journal that Murry edited.

And about Poison.[2] I could write about that for pages. But Ill try & condense what Ive got to say. The story is told by (evidently) a worldly, rather cynical (not wholly cynical) man *against* himself (but not altogether) when he was so absurdly young. You know how young by his idea of what woman is. She has been up till now only the *vision*, only she who passes. You realise that? And here he has put *all* his passion into this Beatrice. Its *promiscuous love* not understood as such by him, perfectly understood as such by her. But you realise the vie de luxe they are living—the very table, sweets, liqueurs, lilies, pearls. And you realise? she expects a letter from someone calling her away? *Fully* expects it? which accounts for her farewell & her declaration. And when it doesn't come even her *commonness* peeps out—the newspaper touch of such a woman. She can't disguise her chagrin. She gives herself away . . . He of course laughs at it now, & laughs at her. Take what he says about her 'sense of order' & the crocodile. But he also regrets the self who dead privately would have been young enough to have actually wanted to *Marry* such a woman. But I meant it to be light—tossed off, & yet through it—oh—subtly—the lament for youthful belief. These are the rapid confessions one receives sometimes from a glove or a cigarette or a hat. I suppose I haven't brought it off in 'Poison'. It wanted a light, light hand—and then with that newspaper a sudden . . . let me see *lowering* of it all—just what happens in promiscuous love after passion. A glimpse of staleness. And the story is told by the man who gives himself away & hides his traces at the same moment.

* * *

To Dorothy Brett

[Chalet des Sapins, Montana-sur-Sierre, Switzerland.
12 September 1921]

The Cezanne[1] book, Miss, you won't get back until you send a policeman or an urgent request for it. It is fascinating, & you can't think how one enjoys such a book on our mountain tops. He is awfully sympathetic to me. I am absolutely uneducated about painting. I can only look at it as a writer, but it seems to me the real thing. Its what one is aiming at. One of his men gave me quite a shock. He is the *spit* of a man Ive just written about—one Jonathan Trout.[2] To the life. I wish I could cut him out & put him in my

2. A story Mansfield had just written, but which was not published until her posthumous collection, *Something Childish and Other Stories*, 1924.
1. Paul Cézanne (1839–1906), French painter.
2. A character, based on an uncle, who appears in "At the Bay."

book. Ive finished my new book. Finished last night at 10.30. Laid down the pen after writing 'Thanks be to God'. I wish there was a God, I am longing to (1) praise him (2) thank him. The title is *At The Bay*. Thats the name of the very long story in it, a continuation of 'Prelude'. Its about 60 pages. Ive been at it all last night. My precious children have sat in here playing cards.[3] Ive wandered about all sorts of places—in and out. I hope it is good. It is as good as I can do and all my heart and soul is in it—every single bit. Oh God, I hope it gives pleasure to someone . . . It is so strange to bring the dead to life again. Theres my grandmother, back in her chair with her pink knitting, there stalks my uncle over the grass. I feel as I write "you are not dead, my darlings. All is remembered. I bow down to you. I efface myself so that you may live again through me in your richness and beauty." And one feels *possessed*. And then the peace where it all happens. I have tried to make it as familiar to 'you' as it is to me. You know the marigolds? You know those pools in the rocks? You know the mousetrap on the wash house window sill? And, too, one tries to go deep—to speak to the secret self we all have—to acknowledge that. I mustn't say any more about it.

* * *

To Dorothy Brett

Chalet des Sapins, Montana-sur-Sierre [Switzerland]
11. XI. 1921

* * *

* * * Tchekhov[1] *said* over and over again, he protested, he begged, that he had no problem. In fact you know he thought it was his weakness as an artist. It worried him but he always said the same. No problem. And, when you come to think of it what was Chaucer's[2] problem or Shakespeare's? The 'problem' is the invention of the 19th century. The artist takes a *long look* at Life. He says softly, "So this is what Life is, is it?" And he proceeds to express that. All the rest he leaves. * * *

* * *

3. In section IX of "At the Bay" the children play cards together until terrified by a face at the window.
1. Anton Chekhov (1860–1904), the Russian playwright and short story writer with whom Mansfield felt a strong affinity.
2. Geoffrey Chaucer (1345–1400), English poet and author of *The Canterbury Tales*.

To William Gerhardi[1]

Chalet des Sapins Montana-sur-Sierre Switzerland.
21. xi. 1921

* * *

You know—if I may speak in confidence—I shall not be 'fashionable' long. They will find me out; they will be disgusted; they will shiver in dismay. I like such awfully unfashionable things—and people—I like sitting on doorsteps, & talking to the old woman who brings quinces, & going for picnics in a jolting little waggon, and listening to the kind of music they play in public gardens on warm evenings, and talking to captains of shabby little steamers, and in fact, to all kinds of people in all kinds of places. But what a fatal sentence to begin. It goes on for ever. In fact one could spend a whole life finishing it.

But you see I am not a high brow. Sunday lunches and very intricate conversations on Sex and that 'fatigue' which is so essential and that awful 'brightness' which is even more essential—these things I flee from. I'm in love with life—terribly. Such a confession is enough to waft Bliss out of the Union . . .[2]

* * *

To Dorothy Brett

Chalet des Sapins Montana-sur-Sierre Switzerland.
[5 December 1921]

* * *

Wasn't that Van Gogh shown at the Goupil ten years ago?[1] Yellow flowers—brimming with sun in a pot? I wonder if it is the same. That picture seemed to reveal something that I hadn't realised before I saw it. It lived with me afterwards. It still does—that & another of a sea captain in a flat cap. They taught me something about writing, which was queer—a kind of freedom—or rather, a shaking free. When one has been working for a long stretch one begins to narrow ones vision a bit, to fine things down too much. And its only when something else breaks through, a picture, or something seen out of doors that one realises it. It is—literally—years since I have been to a picture show. I can *smell* them as I write.

* * *

1. William Gerhardie (1895–1977), an English novelist brought up in St. Petersburg, Russia, and an expert in Russian affairs, was then a student at Oxford. Soon after this he added a final "e" to his surname.
2. The library of the Oxford Union.
1. Mansfield had seen "Sunflowers" by the Dutch artist Vincent van Gogh at the Grafton Galleries (not the Goupil) in London in 1912.

To Dorothy Brett

[Victoria Palace Hotel, Paris.
26 February 1922]

* * *

I think my story for you will be about Canaries.[1] The large cage opposite has fascinated me completely. I think & think about them—their feelings, their *dreams*, the life they led before they were caught, the difference between the two little pale fluffy ones who were born in captivity & their grandfather & grandfather who knew the South American forests and have seen the immense perfumed sea . . . Words cannot express the beauty of that high shrill little song rising out of the very stones. It seems one cannot escape Beauty—it is everywhere.

I must end this letter. I have just finished a queer story called *The Fly* about a fly that fell into an ink pot and a Bank Manager. I think it will come out in The Nation.[2] The trouble with writing is that one seethes with stories. One ought to write one a day at least—but it is so tiring. *When* I am well I shall still live always far away in distant spots where one can work and look undisturbed. No more literary society for me *ever*. * * *

* * *

To William Gerhardi

[Victoria Palace Hotel, Paris]
March 13, 1922

I've been wanting to say—how strange, how delightful it is you should feel as you do about *The Voyage*.[1] No one has mentioned it to me but Middleton Murry. But when I wrote that little story I felt that I was on that very boat, going down those stairs, smelling the smell of the saloon. And when the stewardess came in and said, 'We're rather empty, we may pitch a little,' I can't believe that my sofa did not pitch. And one moment I had a little bun of silk-white hair and a bonnet and the next I was Fenella hugging the swan neck umbrella. It was so vivid—terribly vivid—especially as they drove away and heard the sea as it slowly turned on the beach. Why—I don't know. It wasn't a memory of a real experience. It was a kind of *possession*. I might have remained the grandma for ever af-

1. "The Canary," Mansfield's last story, which she wrote in July 1922, was published in her posthumous volume, *The Doves' Nest and Other Stories*, London, Constable, 1923.
2. "The Fly" was published in the *Athenaeum*, 18 March 1922. From early 1921 the *Athenaeum* was amalgamated with another journal, the *Nation*, and was known by both names.

1. The story was first published in *The Garden Party and Other Stories*, in early 1922.

ter if the wind had changed that moment. And that would have been a little embarrassing for Middleton Murry . . . But don't you feel that when you write? I think one always feels it, only sometimes it is a great deal more definite.

* * *

And yes, that is what I tried to convey in *The Garden Party*. The diversity of life and how we try to fit in everything, Death included. That is bewildering for a person of Laura's age. She feels things ought to happen differently. First one and then another. But life isn't like that. We haven't the ordering of it. Laura says, 'But all these things must not happen at once.' And Life answers, 'Why not? How are they divided from each other.' And they *do* all happen, it is inevitable. And it seems to me there is beauty in that inevitability.

* * *

To Sarah Gertrude Millin

[Victoria Palace Hotel, Paris]
March. [1922]

Dear Mrs Sarah Gertrude Millin[1]

Your letter makes me want to begin mine with 'Do write again. Don't let this be your last letter. If ever you feel inclined for a talk with a fellow-writer summon me.' I cannot tell you how glad I am to hear from you, how interested I am to know about your work. * * *

Now I am walking through the third page of your letter. Yes I do think it is 'desolate' not to know another writer. One has a longing to talk about writing sometimes, to talk things over, to exchange impressions, to find out how other people work—what they find difficult, what they really aim at expressing—countless things like that. But there's another side to it. Let me tell you my experience. I am a 'Colonial'. I was born in New Zealand, I came to Europe to 'complete my education' and when my parents thought that tremendous task was over I went back to New Zealand. I hated it. It seemed to me a small petty world; I longed for 'my' kind of people and larger interests and so on. And after a struggle I did get out of the nest finally and came to London, at eighteen, *never* to return, said my disgusted heart. Since then Ive lived in England, France, Italy, Bavaria. Ive known literary society in plenty. But for the last four–five years I have been ill and have lived either in the S. of France or in a remote little chalet in Switzerland—always remote,

1. Sarah Gertrude Millin (1889–1968), a South African author whose novel, *The Dark River*, Mansfield reviewed in the *Athenaeum*, 20 February 1921. (See Katherine Mansfield, *Novels and Novelists*, London, Constable, 1930, pp. 55–59.)

always cut off, seeing hardly anybody, for months seeing really nobody except my husband and our servant and the cat and 'the people who come to the back door'. Its only in those years Ive really been able to work and always my thoughts and feelings go back to New Zealand—rediscovering it, finding beauty in it, re-living it. Its about my Aunt Fan who lived up the road I really want to write, and the man who sold goldfinches, and about a wet night on the wharf, and Tarana Street in the Spring. Really, I am sure it does a writer no good to be transplanted—it does harm. One reaps the glittering top of the field but there are no sheaves to bind. And there's something, disintegrating, false, *agitating* in that literary life. Its petty and stupid like a fashion. I think the only way to live as a writer is to draw upon one's real *familiar* life—to find the treasure in that as Olive Schreiner[2] did. Our secret life, the life we return to over and over again, the 'do you remember' life is always the past. And the curious thing is that if we describe this which seems to us so intensely personal, other people take it to themselves and understand it as if it were their own.

Does this sound as though Im dogmatising? I don't mean to be. But if you knew the numbers of writers who have begun full of promise and who have succumbed to London! My husband and I are determined never to live in cities, always to live 'remote'—to have our own life—where making jam and discovering a new bird and sitting on the stairs and growing the flowers we like best is—are—just as important as a new book. If one lives in literary society (I dont know why it *is* so but it is) it means giving up one's peace of mind, one's leisure—the best of life.

But Im writing as if to beg you to unpack your trunk, as if you were on the very point of leaving South Africa tomorrow. And that's absurd. But I am so awfully glad you have Africa to draw upon.

I am writing this letter in Paris where we are staying at [*i.e.* till] May. I am trying a new Xray treatment which is supposed to be very good for lungs. Its early spring, weather very lovely and gentle, the chestnut trees in bud, the hawthorn coming into flower in the Luxembourg Gardens.[3] I can't go out, except to the clinic once a week but my husband is a very faithful messenger. He reports on it all for me, and goes to the Luxembourg Gardens every afternoon. We work hard—we are both very busy—and read a great deal. And both of us are longing to be back in the country. If this treatment succeeds at all we'll be gone in May. But its hard to write in a hotel. I

2. Olive Schreiner (1855–1920) left her native South Africa for England in 1881 and under the name of "Ralph Iron" published her most famous novel, *The Story of an African Farm*, in 1883.
3. While undergoing the treatment for her lungs, which proved medically useless, Mansfield lived close to the extensive Gardens.

can only do short things and think out long stories. Do you have anemones in South Africa. I have a big bowl of such beauties in this room. I should like to put them into my letter, especially the blue ones and a very lovely pearly white kind—

It is late—I must end this letter. Thank you again for yours. I warmly press your hand—

Katherine Mansfield.

CRITICISM

REBECCA WEST

The Garden Party†

* * *

One result of the conquest of prose by the logic of poetry is that many writers who would in any past age have written verse are now just as pleased to say what they want to in prose; and Katherine Mansfield is one of these. There is at the end of "At the Bay" something that in any other age would have been a lyric, where the young girl, dreaming desperately of love in her moonlit room, hears a call from the wood beyond the garden that sends her, still half dreaming, out into the moonlight to answer it; where she encounters such an unpleasing substitute as the world often offers to such dreamers, from which only her young strength rescues her, but afterwards it does not seem to matter, in spite of the ugliness, in spite of the disappointment, because there are still the clouds and the moon in the sky, and the deep sound of the sea. How one admires Miss Mansfield for conceiving that moment, as well as for insisting on working under conditions that make it possible for her to conceive such beauty. For "At the Bay" is a continuation of "Prelude", that section of a work of genius which was the best thing in *Bliss*. In other words, Miss Mansfield is writing a novel, but it is coming to her slowly. There is, after all, no reason why creation in art should take only an infinitesimal fraction of the time that is taken by creation in life. Abandonment to the leisurely rhythm of her own imagination, and refusal to conform to the common custom and finish her book in a year's session, has enabled her to bring her inventions right over the threshold of art. They are extraordinarily solid; they have lived so long in her mind that she knows all about them and can ransack them for the difficult, rare, essential points. Thus she produces such attenuated yet powerful sketches as the scene in the garden, when Linda thinks of her husband with love and disgust and fatigue and at the same time is forced by the personality of her new baby, to whom she thought she was indifferent, to recognise that she loves it. And to deal with those visions born of her deliberations she brings a technique that has been sharpened on the products of her swifter and more immediate work. Her choice of the incident that will completely and economically prove her point is astonishing, and only not invariable because she is oc-

† From the *New Statesman* 18 March 1922: 678. Reprinted by permission of the *New Statesman*.

casionally betrayed into excessive use of her power of grotesque invention. (There is a passage in "The Daughters of the Late Colonel" which has strayed out of *Charley's Aunt*.)[1] For instance, "Marriage à la Mode" with its picture of the ordinary but loving and fine-natured husband and his silly little wife, who turns from him to a rabble of sponging sham poets and painters, might very easily have appeared as the lesser tragedy of the shattering of an illusion. It might quite well have appeared that Isabel was a minx who was showing her quality, and that William was only losing what he had never had when he noticed it. But with extraordinary ingenuity Miss Mansfield invents an incident which convinces one that this is the greater tragedy of the shattering of a beautiful reality, that before her debauchment by this greedy, chattering horde she had been the miracle of kindness and loveliness that William thought her. "When he had been a little boy, it was his delight to run into the garden after a shower of rain and shake the rose-bush over him. Isabel was that rosebush, petal-soft, sparkling, and cool." To exhibit the drama of her decline, Miss Mansfield shows Isabel on the lawn among her horrid friends, receiving a desperate love-letter from William, who has returned to town after a week-end, during which he has not succeeded in being alone with her. One measures the extent of her ruin when she reads it aloud to them: "God forbid, my darling, that I should be a drag on your happiness." But one measures from what heights she has fallen when she suddenly runs from the giggling circle of her friends and runs to her own room and throws herself down on the bed. "But she felt that even the grave bed-room knew her for what she was, shallow, tinkling, vain. . . ." It is an excellent invention, though not more dazzling, perhaps, than the monologue at the end of the book in which "The Lady's Maid" artlessly betrays herself the predestined victim of the predatory egotist, or the curious study of spiritual jealousy and the hostility of a gross man for grim uncomfortable things in "The Stranger".

One of the results of Miss Mansfield's poetic temperament is that beauty is the general condition of her story. Most of her tales are laid in the glowing setting of the sub-tropics: "Marriage à la Mode" is acted in a midsummer countryside: even the miserable "Miss Brill" sits in a pleasant springtide day. Even in the lamentable "Life of Ma Parker" there is a kind of sensuous beauty in the description of the love of the old charwoman for her grandson. The mind takes pleasure in merely moving in such an atmosphere, apart from the meanings it may find there. That is where the writer who is a poet like Miss Mansfield scores over a writer who is not a poet.

1. A popular English farce by Brandon Thomas, first produced in 1892 [*Editor*].

CONRAD AIKEN

The Short Story as Colour†

Miss Katherine Mansfield's *Bliss*, a volume of short stories published a year or so ago, attracted, and deserved, a great deal of attention. It was at once recognized that Miss Mansfield was a short-story writer of unique sensibility—sensibility in the modern, not in the pre-Victorian sense[1]—and exquisite deftness. If her stories suggested the influence of Chekhov, notably in their repeated use of what might be termed the completeness and charm of the incomplete, the suggestion was fleeting and unimportant: method is, after all, not a copyrightable affair, and all we have the right to ask of the borrower of a method is that he shall not permit it to cloud his own personality, or to supplant it. In the case of Miss Mansfield there could be no question of this. If one thing was arresting in her work, it was the evidence, luminous, colourful, and resonant everywhere, of a tactilism extraordinarily acute and individual. One was inclined to question, even, whether this perpetual coruscation, this amazing sensitiveness to rhythms and sounds and almost shuddering awareness of texture, was not symptomatic of a sort of febrility which would, sooner or later, impose on Miss Mansfield's work its very definite limitations; limitations already quite clearly implied. "Exquisite! yes—this song of sensibility," one might then have commented "this poetry of the eyes, the ears and hands a little feverish; but is it, ultimately, quite enough?"

It depends, of course, on what one means by enough. Clearly, this sort of febrility, clairvoyant and clairaudient, *is* enough, if one wants, in one's fiction, only and always an ecstatic awareness. How admirably such a tone adapts itself to the case of, say, a neurotic young woman, Miss Mansfield has several times triumphantly demonstrated—notably in "The Man Without a Temperament". It lends itself superbly, too, to description of the adolescent—what could possibly be better, more brilliant, than the portrait of "The Young Girl" in Miss Mansfield's new collection of stories? Equally applicable is it, again, to descriptions of children, whose minds may be said to exist wholly in their five senses—no contemporary writer has given glimpses of the bright, disintegrated, peripheral consciousness of the child as exquisitely true as those Miss Mansfield

† From the *Freeman* 21 June 1922: 357. Reprinted in *Collected Criticism*, Notes are the Editor's.

1. One modern meaning of sensibility is an exceptional openness to sense impression. Its earlier meaning emphasized both a highly developed taste in matters of art and a capacity for refined emotion.

gives us in "Sun and Moon"[2] or portions of "Prelude". But it is precisely here that one reaches a suspicion that if Miss Mansfield does these things beautifully it is because in these things she is freest to speak her own language; that her choice of these things is a dictated choice; and that her failure to step often out of this small charmed circle, and her relative failure when she does step out, are failures that we should quite expect.

What we get at is the fact that Miss Mansfield goes to the short story as the lyric poet goes to poetry—Miss Mansfield's short story is, in essence, an essentially "subjective" thing, far more subjective than one is accustomed to expect a short story to be. Of course the distinction between subjective and objective is relative. One may reasonably claim that Chekhov's short stories are "subjective" also, that they represent in the case of Chekhov a psychic compulsion just as unaccountable and uncontrollable as that indicated by Miss Mansfield's "Garden Party". That is perfectly true, and it compels us to see that the difference between the so-called subjective method in art, and the so-called objective method, is at bottom nothing whatever but a difference in range. Chekhov's range was enormous. He was as tremendously "rooted" in life, perhaps, as Shakespeare. His sensibilities, and therefore his curiosity, were not merely of one sort, but led him everywhere, gave him joy, pain, understanding everywhere, were both sensitive and tough. The world of consciousness (and of subconsciousness) with which he was thus by experience gradually endowed, and the language of associations which he spoke, were not merely intensely individual (independent of the literary) but, by comparison with the language of associations of the average writer, infinitely various. This is what leads us to think of Chekhov as a superlatively "objective" artist, and it is the reverse of this that leads us to think of Miss Mansfield as—just as superlatively?—a "subjective" artist. For Miss Mansfield's sensibilities, if clearly individual, are remarkably limited, and the language of associations which she speaks is, if brilliant, extremely small. The awareness, the personality of the larger artist is an infinitely more divisible, and therefore infinitely less recognizable thing; but the personality of the smaller artist is recognizable everywhere.

Thus, in Miss Mansfield's short stories, as in the poems of a lyric poet, it is always Miss Mansfield's voice that we hear, it is always Miss Mansfield that we see. How it is that limitations of this sort impose themselves on an artist, in childhood or infancy, we leave psychology to discover. Why did Miss Mansfield's extraordinary sensibilities find, as it were, so little to feed on? That is the ques-

2. A story in *Bliss and Other Stories* not included in this Norton Critical Edition.

tion we must ask, whether or not we answer it. Did she lack the requisite "toughness"? At all events, her awareness is a very special and limited sort of awareness; the circle of her consciousness is small and bright, and we soon know its outermost limits. Miss Mansfield's new book confirms our speculations in this regard. If one makes the reservation that "Prelude" in the earlier book is the best thing she has written, then one can say that the second volume is just as good as the first. But the limitations are here again, and now seem more striking. We are not so easily deceived a second time, and we perceive too clearly that it is all a beautiful, an exquisite, a diabolically clever masquerade, with the protean Miss Mansfield taking now the part of Beryl, now that of "The Young Girl", now that of both "Daughters of the Late Colonel", now that of Miss Brill; * * * though she seldom attempts the masculine; and shining out beautifully, with not even the pretence of a mask, as Kezia. Yes, these people are all Miss Mansfield, all speak with her voice, think as she thinks, are rapidly, ecstatically aware, as she is aware, share her gestures and her genius; and represent, in short, not so many people or lives, but so many projections of Miss Mansfield's mind and personality into other people's bodies and houses. How exciting to disguise oneself, for a morning, as Ma Parker, or, for an afternoon, as the singing teacher! And Miss Mansfield's dexterity in the matter is extraordinary. She almost completely deceives us, and even when she has ceased to deceive she continues to delight.

The secret of this legerdemain is simply in Miss Mansfield's mastery of local colour, of twinkling circumstance, of the inflection of the moment. It is the song of a sensibility ecstatically aware of the surfaces of life. Her people are not real people, in the sense of being individual, of appearing to have, as Chekhov's characters have, whole lives, apart from the particular story, which the author does not touch on; but they give the illusion of reality; first, because Miss Mansfield endows them all with her own supersensitive and febrile (and perhaps sentimental) awareness, and, second (which follows from the first) because, therefore, the small circumstances of mood and scene are thus given to us with the feverish vividness of objects seen under lightning. Miss Mansfield puts a kitchen before us with her mention of the gritty soap in the sink; she desolates us, when, describing the bare floors of an abandoned house, she notes the carpet-tacks with their shreds of wool. She sees everything, sees miraculously, feels textures where the less sensitive would see only a smooth surface, hears rhythms and intonations where others would only note the persistence and dullness of a sound. Yes, it is the scene, the scene as apprehended by the hungriest of sensibilities, that Miss Mansfield above all gives us. Must we content ourselves with this? For if Miss Mansfield has little skill at characterization—substituting for "character" a combination of vivid externalities and vivid mood—one must also observe that even in "mood" her range is very small. In a sense the mood *is* the scene—it is the eternal responsiveness to scene. Whether the particular state of mind to be presented is gay or melancholy, bitter or resigned, capricious or saturnine, whimsical or cruel, hardly seems to matter. For the psychological process by which her people are gay or melancholy, bitter or resigned, is always, for Miss Mansfield, the same; the content may change but never the *tempo*. Everything is staccato and exclamatory, everything is intense, even grief is somehow sibilant. If one may use a metaphor which will not bear close psychological scrutiny, but nevertheless conveys one's impression, one may say that Miss Mansfield, instead of submerging herself in her characters, submerges her characters in herself. They come up shining, certainly, and peacock-hued; they burn and glisten in the bright air, shed fine plumes of flame; but they are all just so many Mansfields.

Well, this sort of vividness is something to be profoundly thankful for. The short story created in this manner approaches the poetic in proportion as its theme is largely and emotionally significant, and the colour thereby patternized. When the theme is slight, the story tends to become merely a triumph of colourism. In "Prelude", and in one or two other instances, Miss Mansfield has given us poetry; but mere cleverness—cleverness to the point of brilliance—too often betrays her into giving us a colourism which, for all its vividness and verisimilitude, is comparatively empty. The delight that many of these stories afford on the first reading is intense: it wanes a little on the second, and we notice the cleverness—fatal sign! And on the third reading—but is there a third? One can not dine on the iridescent.

T. S. ELIOT

[The Feminine Voice]†

* * *

* * * In Miss Mansfield's story a wife is disillusioned about her relations with her husband; in the others a husband is disillusioned about his relations with his wife. Miss Mansfield's story—it is one of her best known—is brief, poignant and in the best sense, slight.

† From *After Strange Gods* (London: Faber and Faber, 1934), pp. 85–86. Reprinted by permission of the publisher.

* * * In *Bliss*, I should say, the moral implication is negligible: the centre of interest is the wife's feeling, first of ecstatic happiness, and then at the moment of revelation. We are given neither comment nor suggestion of any moral issue of good and evil, and within the setting this is quite right. The story is limited to this sudden change of feeling, and the moral and social ramifications are outside of the terms of reference. As the material is limited in this way—and indeed our satisfaction recognises the skill with which the author has handled perfectly the *minimum* material—it is what I believe would be called feminine. * * *

KATHERINE ANNE PORTER

[Life into Art]†

* * *

Life, love, beauty, pain, acceptance, response, these are great words and they should mean something, and their meaning depends upon their exact application and reference. Whose life? What kind of love? What sort of beauty? And so on. It was this kind of explicitness that Katherine Mansfield possessed and was able to use, when she was at her best and strongest. She was magnificent in her objective view of things, her real sensitiveness to climate, mental or physical, her genuinely first-rate equipment in the matter of the five senses, and my guess, based on the evidence of her stories, is that she by no means accepted everything, either abstractly or in detail, and that whatever her vague love of something called Life may have been, there was as much to hate as to love in her individual living. Mistakenly she fought in herself those very elements that combined to form her virtue: a certain grim, quiet ruthlessness of judgment, an unsparing and sometimes cruel eye, a natural malicious wit, an intelligent humor; and beyond all she had a burning, indignant heart that was capable of great compassion. Read "The Woman at the Store," * * * read "The Fly," and then read "Millie," or "The Life of Ma Parker." With fine objectivity she bares a moment of experience, real experience, in the life of some one human being; she states no belief, gives no motives, airs no theories, but simply presents to the reader a situation, a place, and a character, and there it is; and the emotional content is present as implicitly as the germ is in the grain of wheat.

Katherine Mansfield has a reputation for an almost finicking delicacy. She was delicate as a surgeon's scalpel is delicate. Her choice

† From "The Art of Katherine Mansfield," *Nation* 145 (23 October 1937): 435.

of words was sure, a matter of good judgment and a good ear. Delicate? Read * * * the seduction of Miss Moss in "Pictures." "An Indiscreet Journey" is a story of a young pair of lovers, set with the delicacy of sober knowledge against the desolate and brutalized scene of, not war, but a small village where there has been fighting, and the soldiers in the place are young Frenchmen, and the inn is "really a barn, set out with dilapidated tables and chairs." There are a few stories which she fails to bring off, quite, and these because she falls dangerously near to triviality or a sentimental wistfulness, of which she had more than a streak in certain moments. But these are few, and far outweighed by her best stories, which are many. Her celebrated "Prelude" and "At the Bay," "The Doll's House," "The Daughters of the Late Colonel" keep their freshness and curious timelessness. Here is not her view of life but her many views of many kinds of lives, and there is no sign of even a tacit acquiescence in these sufferings, these conflicts, these evils deep-rooted in human nature. * * *

* * *

V. S. PRITCHETT

[Who Are These People?]†

* * *

Regret is strengthened when we compare her stories with Chekhov's, under whose influence much of her work was done. After him, she concentrated on the "moment of truth" rather than on plot or even character in her stories; more precisely she sought to isolate the cry of ecstasy or the cry of fear or loneliness in her people. (It is untrue, incidentally, that her stories have no plots; this is true only of her imitators who disastrously misread her work and lacked her talent as a story-teller.) But in Chekhov we find an indispensable element which is strong in his writing and weak in hers: the sense of a country, a place; the sense of the unseen characters, the anonymous people, what we may call "the others," from which the people of his stories are taken. Katherine Mansfield's *At the Bay* is one of the minor masterpieces of our language—but who are these people, who are their neighbours, what is the world they belong to? We can scarcely guess. Too self-sufficiently, they drop out of the sky and fill the little canvas. There is no silent character in the background. True, there is the mystery of life and death, suggested by the grandmother's memories of her dead son. But in a

† From "Books in General," review of *The Collected Stories of Katherine Mansfield, New Statesman* 2 February 1946: 87. Reprinted by permission of the *New Statesman*.

story like Chekhov's *The Steppe*[1] there is something else besides the mystery of life and death: Russia, the condition of Russia, is the silent character, always haunting us. And this is so true of the bulk of Chekhov's work, that one is led to an important conclusion about what is called "the plotless" short story: this kind of story depends upon its power to suggest things more mysterious or more powerful than itself. There are gaps and silences in the "plotless" short story: fatally limiting, if we do not detect in those silences the murmur of a containing society of other human beings. Katherine Mansfield's own rootlessness, her fretful attempts to break down her isolation from her country, by purifying and isolating herself, made her the kind of writer who draws in her horns. It is significant that she criticised Virginia Woolf for being a "deliberate" writer.

All the same, it is idle to blame (or to praise) writers for limitations which may be due to their position in society or their time. We have the virtues of our shortcomings; and good writing is the fruit of a struggle with total disadvantages. Out of the impossible comes the best. When we take Katherine Mansfield's stories as they are, we see what original and sometimes superlative use she made of herself. Rootless, isolated, puritan, catty, repentantly over-fond? She made stories as clear as glass. Isolated, she seeks to describe how people feel and think when they are alone. Can one find a more precise portrait of a play-acting, adolescent girl than Beryl in *At the Bay*, a more terrifying notion of what it may be like to be a cynical woman of a certain age than Mrs. Harry Kember in the same story:

* * *

We see through all these people, one by one, as they will never see through themselves. And Stanley Burnell, the back-slapping, go-getting business man with his awful energy and his hopelessly egotistical remorse, provides another light on the desire for isolation. It is Romantic—life-wish as well as death-wish: his morning bathe is ruined because his neighbour has got into the Pacific Ocean before him. The Pacific has been spoiled. It is like being beaten on the customer's doorstep by your competitor. Katherine Mansfield may have rejected an enormous amount of material; but she did get that key character, the business man, into her doll's house.

It is a truism—but one so neglected by writers of short stories that one must repeat it—that the telling of stories, plot or no plot, depends upon the writer's use of surprise. In the "plotless" story, one must move from one unexpected word, image or sentence, to the next, even less expected, and all must be effortless, limpid, quick. In this sparkling quality Katherine Mansfield excelled when

1. A story of Chekhov's published in 1888 [*Editor*].

she was at her best—and I would put *Prelude*, *At the Bay*, *The Daughters of the Late Colonel*, *The Woman at the Store*, *Pictures*, *The Garden Party*, and *The Little Governess* in this class—and here she added something to the technique of story writing. I am thinking of the grace with which she drops dramatically back into the past or slides into the thoughts and daydreams of her characters. Her writing changes its landscapes as noiselessly as they are changed in our minds and with the alacrity of Nature. The young girl acting her imaginary life before the mirror, then catching herself at it, repenting, vowing she will never do such a thing again, beginning to act once more in the middle of her remorse, and then going down to the drawing-room to pose without knowing it—all those subtle changes which another writer would analyse, argue or edge with a moral, glance and flutter with the freedom of a bird passing through sunlight and shadow. The vulgar daydreams, the poor thoughts of Miss Moss, who can't get a job, and who becomes a prostitute, are just as adroitly caught. Every sentence astonishes.

* * *

Katherine Mansfield liquefied the short story. She destroyed many of its formal conventions. She cut out the introductions, the ways and means which are simply barriers. She cut across country, following a line which must have seemed erratic to her early readers, but which is really the direct line. Her early sketches, *In a German Pension*, which are very uneven, though not all as poor as she thought them, show how much of this quickness she owed to listening to people talk. She learned that one or two lines of talk can displace whole paragraphs of description or narrative argument. And she learned, too, how a spoken sentence may start the speaker's own mind on to things absurdly, poetically, strangely at variance with what he or she has said. She caught lives as they dissolved and formed again, and made her stories, very often, about the disparate selves which were set free in the process.

Scratchy and arch, slick and gossipy, mimsy, Katherine Mansfield's manner often was; but the revived art of writing short stories has not, on the whole, drawn the most useful conclusions from her work. Her sensibility, her waywardness were not transferable; but her economy, the boldness of her comic gift, her speed, her dramatic changes of the point of interest, her power to dissolve and reassemble character and situation by a few lines, or to excite by an image, are things that might have been studied more closely. Twenty years after her death it is too soon to define her place, for the sound of our early reading of her work still bewilders and dulls our ear; I fancy her tone will recover some of its early hardness and integrity as time goes on; and I am sure that she is one of those key writers who in their generation mark a new point of departure.

ELIZABETH BOWEN

"A Living Writer"†

If Katherine Mansfield were living, she would this year be sixty-eight. Is this fact out of accord with our idea of her? Sometimes it may be that an early death so fixes our image of a person that we cannot envisage them any older. Youth comes to seem an attribute of the personality—in the case of a beautiful woman or romantic artist, both of which Katherine Mansfield was, this happens particularly often. Yet in the case of Katherine Mansfield it seems particularly wrong. For one thing, we lose much and deny her something if we altogether banish her in imagination from the place she could have had in our own time. For another, she had no desire whatever to be 'spared' life or anything further it could bring. Useless as it is to lament her going, let us not forget she would have stayed if she could, and fought to do so with savage courage.

True, she could not have gone on as she was, she was far too ill. To restore health, at the stage her illness had reached, would have taken a miracle—she sought one. Could that have been granted, a fresh start, one can think of few people more fitted than Katherine Mansfield to have aged without decline, ignominy or fear. One can picture her at sunset, but not in twilight. Born with good nerve, she had learned comprehensive courage, and in a hard school. In spite of setback after setback, she was already on her own way towards equilibrium. Her spirit was of the kind which does not die down. Her beauty even, was of the enduring kind, hardy and resolute in cast as it was mysterious in atmosphere—nor need one imagine her without the peculiar personal magic she emanated: a magic still so much part of her legend. Already she was 'old' in imagination—up to any age would she not have been young in temperament?

She was drawn to old people, seeing them as victors. They stood to her for vision, and for the patience she so impatiently longed to have. (She was aware, of course, also of ancient monsters.) Is it too much to say that she envied old age, and the more so as her own hopes of attaining it grew slender? But one does not waste desire on the unlikely: her real need was pressing, and grew obsessive—she needed time, time in which to achieve a body of work. By now, she would have had thirty-four years more. Enough? I suspect that in the extreme of her desperation she would have been content to compound for ten. There is never enough of the time a writer

† From the *Cornhill Magazine*, no. 1010 (Winter 1956–57): 120–30. All notes are the Editor's.

wants—but hers was cut so short, one is aghast. The more one sees the fulfilment in her work, the more one is awed by its stretching promise. The perfectedness of the major pieces sets up anguish that there could not be more of them. Equally, I may say that a fellow writer cannot but look on Katherine Mansfield's work as interrupted, hardly more than suspended, momentarily waiting to be gone on with. Page after page gives off the feeling of being still warm from the touch, fresh from the pen. Where is she—our missing contemporary?

'Katherine Mansfield's death, by coming so early, left her work still at the experimentary stage.' This could be said—but would it be true? To me, such a verdict would be misleading, for two reasons. First, her writing already *had* touched perfection a recognisable number of times; second, she would have been bound to go on experimenting up to the end, however late that had come. One cannot imagine her settling down to any one fixed concept of the short story—her art was, by its very nature, tentative, responsive, exploratory. There are no signs that she was casting about to find a formula: a formula would, in fact, have been what she fled from. Her sense of the possibilities of the story was bounded by no hard-and-fast horizons: she grasped that it is imperative for the writer to expand his range, never contrast his method. Perception and language could not be kept too fresh, too alert, too fluid. Each story entailed a beginning right from the start, each brought unknown demands, new risks, unforeseeable developments. Often, she worked by trial-and-error.

So, ever on the move, she has left with us no 'typical' Katherine Mansfield story to anatomise. Concentrated afresh, each time, upon expression, she did not envisage 'technique' in the abstract. As it reached her, each idea for a story had inherent within it its own shape: there could be for it no other. That shape, it was for her to perceive, then outline—she thought (we learn from letters and journal) far more of perception than of construction. The story is there, but she has yet to come at it. One has the impression of a water-diviner, pacing, halting, awaiting the twitch of the hazel twig. Also, to judge from her writings about her writing, there were times when Katherine Mansfield believed a story to have a volition of its own—she seems to stand back, watching it take form. Yet this could not happen apart from her: the story drew on her steadily, into itself.

Yet all of her pieces, it seems clear, did not originate in the same order. Not in all cases was there the premonitory stirring of an idea: sometimes the external picture came to her first. She found herself seized upon by a scene, an isolated incident or a face which, something told her, must have meaning, though she had yet to divine what the meaning was. Appearances in themselves could touch alight her creative power. It is then that we see her moving into the story, from its visual periphery to its heart, recognising the 'why' as she penetrates. (It could seem that her great scenic New Zealand stories came into being by this process.) Her failures, as she uncompromisingly saw them, together with her host of abandoned fragments, give evidence of the state of mind she voices in anguished letters or journal entries—the sensation of having lost her way. She could finish a story by sheer craftsmanship; but only, later, to turn against the results.

Able and fine as was her intelligence, it was not upon that that she depended; intuitive knowing, vision, had to be the thing. She was a writer with whom there could be no secondary substitute for genius: genius was vision. One might speak of her as having a burning gaze. But she faced this trouble—vision at full intensity is not by nature able to be sustained; it is all but bound to be intermittent. And for Katherine Mansfield those intermittences set up an aesthetic disability, a bad, an antipathetic working condition. Under such a condition, her work abounded, and well she knew it, in perils peculiar to itself. She dreaded sagging of tension, slackening of grip, flaws in interior continuity, numbness, and, most of all, a sort of synthetic quality which could creep in. She speaks of one bad day's work as 'scrappy and dreamy'. Dreaminess meant for her, dilution.

Subjects, to be ideal for Katherine Mansfield, had first to attract, then hold, her power called vision. There occurred a false dawn, or false start, when a subject deceived her as to its possibilities—there were those which failed her, I feel, rather than she them. We must consider later which kind or what range of subject stood by her best, and why this may have been so. There was not a subject which did not tax her—raising, apart from anything else, exacting problems of treatment, focus and angle. Her work was a succession of attempts to do what was only just not impossible. There is danger that in speaking of 'attempts' one should call to mind those which have not succeeded: one forgets the no less attempt which is merged in victory. Katherine Mansfield's masterpiece stories cover their tracks; they have an air of serene inevitability, almost a touch of the miraculous. (But for the artist, remember, there are no miracles.) Her consummate achievements soar, like so many peaks, out of the foothills of her working life—spaced out, some nearer together in time than others. One asks oneself why the artist, requited thus, could not have been lastingly reassured, and how it could have happened that, after each trough of frustration, anxiety, dereliction should have awaited her once again?

The truth was, she implacably cut the cord between herself and any completed story. She admits, in the journal: 'It took me nearly a month to "recover" from "At the Bay". I made at least three false starts. But I could not get away from the sound of the sea, and Beryl fanning her hair at the window. These things would not *die* down.'[1] She must not look back, she must press forward. She had not time to form a consistent attitude to any one finished story: each stood to her as a milestone passed, not as a destination arrived at. Let us say, she reacted to success (if in Katherine Mansfield's eyes there were such a thing) as others react to failure—there seemed to be nothing left but to try again.

To be compelled to experiment is one thing, to be in love with experiment quite another. Of love for experiment for its own sake, Katherine Mansfield shows not a sign. Conscious artist, she carries none of the marks of the self-consciously 'experimentary' writer. Nothing in her approach to people or nature is revolutionary; her story-telling is, on its own plane, not much less straightforward than Jane Austen's.[2] She uses no literary shock tactics. The singular beauty of her language consists, partly, in its hardly seeming to *be* language, so glass-transparent is it to her meaning. Words had but one appeal for her, that of speakingness. (In her journal we find, noted, 'The *panting* of a saw.')[3] She was to evolve from noun, verb, adjective, a marvellous sensory notation hitherto undreamed of outside poetry; nonetheless she stayed subject to prose discipline. And her style, when the story-context requires, can be curt, decisive, factual, abrupt. It is a style generated by subject and tuned to mood—so flexible as to be hardly *a* style at all. One would recognise a passage from Katherine Mansfield not by the manner but by the content. There are no eccentricities.

Katherine Mansfield was not a rebel, she was an innovator. Born into the English traditions of prose narrative, she neither turned against these nor broke with them—simply, she passed beyond them. And now tradition, extending, has followed her. Had she not written, written as she did, one form of art might be still in infancy. One cannot attribute to Katherine Mansfield the entire growth, in our century, of the short story. Its developments have been speedy, inspired, various; it continues branching in a hundred directions, many of which show her influence not at all. What she did supply was an immense impetus—also, did she not first see in the short story the ideal reflector of modern day? We owe to her the prosperity of the 'free' story: she untrammelled it from conventions and,

1. *Journal of Katherine Mansfield*, ed. J. Middleton Murry (London: Constable, 1962), p. 267.
2. Jane Austen (1775–1817), English novelist.
3. *Journal*, p. 261.

still more, gained for it a prestige till then unthought of. How much ground Katherine Mansfield broke for her successors may not be realised. Her imagination kindled unlikely matter; she was to alter for good and all our idea of what goes to make a story.

She could have been a writer of more than one kind. Alternations went on throughout her working life. In her letters appears a brusque, formidable, masculine streak, which we must not overlook in the stories. Her art has backbone. Her objectiveness, her quick sharp observations, her adept presentations—are these taken into account enough? Scenically, how keen is her eye for the telling detail! The street, quayside, café, shop interior, teatime terrace or public garden stand concretely forward into life. She is well documented. Her liking for activity, for the crowd at play, for people going about their work, her close interest in process and occupation, give an extra vitality to stories. Admire the evening Chinamen in "Ole Underwood", or Alice, the servant in "At the Bay", taking tea with Mrs. Stubbs of the local store.

She engraves a scene all the more deeply when it is (as few of her scenes are not) contributory to a mood or crisis. Here, at the opening of "The Voyage", are the awarenesses of a little girl going away with her grandmother after her mother's death:

> The Picton boat was due to leave at half-past eleven. It was a beautiful night, mild, starry, only when they got out of the cab and started to walk down the Old Wharf that jutted out into the harbour, a faint wind blowing off the water ruffled under Fenella's hat, and she had to put up a hand to keep it on. It was dark on the Old Wharf, very dark; the wool sheds, the cattle trucks, the cranes standing up so high, the little squat railway engine, all seemed carved out of solid darkness. Here and there on a rounded woodpile, that was like the stalk of a huge black mushroom, there hung a lantern, but it seemed afraid to unfurl its timid quivering light in all that blackness; it burned softly, as if for itself.

Fancifulness, fantastic metaphor, play more part in her London (as opposed to New Zealand) scene-setting. Less seems taken for granted. "The Wrong House"[4] furnishes one example. Here, in a residential backwater, an unloved old woman looks out of a window:

> It was a bitter autumn day; the wind ran in the street like a thin dog; the houses opposite looked as though they had been cut out with a pair of ugly steel scissors and pasted on to the grey paper sky. There was not a soul to be seen.

4. An unfinished story included in the posthumous *Something Childish and Other Stories*, 1924.

This factual firmness of Katherine Mansfield's provides a ballast, or antidote, to her other side—the high-strung susceptibility, the all but hallucinatory floatingness. Nothing is more isolated, more claustrophobic than the dreamfastness of a solitary person—no one knew the dangers better than she. Yet rooted among those dangers was her genius: totally disinfected, wholly adjusted, could she have written as she did? Perhaps there is no such thing as 'pure' imagination—all air must be breathed in, and some is tainting. Now and then the emotional level of her writing drops: a whimsical, petulant little-girlishness disfigures a few of the lesser pieces. And some others (how she disliked these) are febrile, or show a transferred self-pity. She could not always keep up the guard.

Katherine Mansfield was saved, it seems to me, by two things—her inveterate watchfulness as an artist, and a certain sturdiness in her nature which the English at their least friendly might call 'colonial.' She had much to stand out against. She was in danger of being driven, twice over, into herself—by exile to begin with, then by illness. In London she lived, as strangers are wont to do, in a largely self-fabricated world.

She lived, indeed, exactly the sort of life she had left New Zealand in hopes of finding. Writers and intellectuals surrounded her—some merely tempestuous, some destructive. She accustomed herself to love on a razor's edge. Other factors made for deep insecurity. She and her husband were agitatingly and endlessly short of money; for reasons even other than that they seemed doomed to uproot themselves from home after home. As intelligenzia they were apt to be preyed upon by the intelligenzia-seeking sub–*beau monde*[5]—types she was to stigmatise in "Bliss" and again in "Marriage à la Mode". Amid the etherealities of Bloomsbury she was more than half hostile, a dark-eyed tramp. For times together, there was difficulty as to the placing of her stories; individually, their reception was uncertain; no full recognition came till she published the volume *Bliss*. In England she moved, one gets the impression, among nothing but intimates or strangers—of family, familiar *old* friends, neighbours, girlhood contemporaries, there were none. Habits, associations were lacking also: here was a background without depth, thwarting to a woman's love of the normal. From this parched soil sprang the London stories.

To a degree it was better, or always began by being better, in the South of France. She felt a release among Mediterranean people; and the Midi[6] light reminded her of New Zealand's. It was at Bandol, late in 1915, that she began "The Aloe", original version of "Prelude", and thereby crossed a threshold. At Bandol was suffered

5. Fashionable society.
6. The South of France.

the agony out of which the story had to be born. She had retreated to Bandol to be alone with loss: her brother Chummie, over with the army from New Zealand, had been killed fighting in France. His last leave, before going to the front, had been spent with Katherine in London. That same month, late at night in her sea-facing French hotel room, she wrote in her journal:

> The present and future mean nothing to me. I am no longer 'curious' about people; I do not wish to go anywhere; and the only possible value that anything can have for me is that it should put me in mind of something that happened or was when we were alive.
>
> 'Do you remember, Katie?' I hear his voice in the trees and flowers, in scents and light and shadow. Have people, apart from these far-away people, ever existed for me? Or have they always failed me and faded because I denied them reality? Supposing I were to die as I sit at this table, playing with my Indian paper-knife, what would be the difference? No difference. Then why don't I commit suicide? Because I feel I have a duty to perform to the lovely time when we were both alive. I want to write about it, and he wanted me to. We talked it over in my little top room in London. I said: I will just put on the front page: To my brother, Leslie Heron Beauchamp. Very well, it shall be done.[7]

That winter, though she had other maladies, tuberculosis had not declared itself. When it did, South of France winters became enforced. War continued, the wind whistled, *volets*[8] clattered, the Mediterranean Sea turned to black iron. She burned, shivered, coughed, could not bear herself, wrote, wrote, wrote. 1919–20 brought the Italian nightmare, Ospedaletti.[9] These weeks, months, in cut-price hotels, ramshackle villas, were exile twice over, exile with doubled force. One man's letters from London were the lifeline, and letters did not invariably come. Who can measure the power of that insatiable longing we call homesickness? Home, now she was torn from it, became hers in London. She thought of the yellow table, the Dresden shepherdess, the kitten Wingley—growing up without her. Loneliness, burning its way into Katherine Mansfield, leaves its indelible mark upon her art.

She wrote the august, peaceful New Zealand stories. They would be miracles of memory if one considered them memories at all—more, they are what she foresaw them as: a re-living. And, spiritually as in art, they were her solution. Within them fuse the two

7. *Journal*, pp. 89–90.
8. Shutters.
9. In her belief that its climate would assist her declining health, Mansfield spent from September 1919 to the end of January 1920 at Ospedaletti on the Italian Riviera.

Katherine Mansfields: the sturdy soul and the visionary are one. The day-to-day receives the full charge of poetry.

> And now one and now another of the windows leaped into light. Someone was walking through the empty rooms carrying a lamp. From a window downstairs the light of a fire flickered. A strange beautiful excitement seemed to stream from the house in quivering ripples.

This is the child Kezia's first, late-night sight of the Burnells' new home. Katherine Mansfield the artist is also home-coming.

F. W. BATESON AND B. SHAHEVITCH

"The Fly": A Critical Exercise†

"The Fly" is probably the shortest *good* short story in modern English. Its two thousand words therefore permit, indeed encourage, the kind of close analysis that has been so successful in our time with lyric poetry but that is impossibly cumbrous or misleadingly incomplete when applied to the novel or the *conte*. The object of this exercise is to demonstrate that, granted the difference of *genres*, exactly the same critical procedure is in order for realistic fiction as for a poem. "The Fly" was written in February 1922 and was included later that year in *The Garden Party and Other Stories*.

"The Fly" assumes in its readers a readiness to accept and respond to two parallel series of symbolic conventions: (1) those constituting the English language as it was spoken and written in the first quarter of the twentieth century, (ii) those constituting the realistic narrative in prose of the same period. That this story is written in modern English is immediately apparent, and the initial display of irrelevant descriptive detail is an equally clear signal to the critical reader that the narrative *genre* to be employed here is realism. Why *Woodifield* (dozens of other surnames would have done just as well)? Why a *green* armchair (rather than light brown, purple, dark brown, etc.)? Why the cut back to the City on *Tuesdays* (rather than Mondays, Wednesdays, Thursdays or Fridays)?

That the critical reader does not in fact ask such questions is because of his familiarity already with the realistic formula. The particular suspension of disbelief that realism demands is an acquiescence in the author's limited omniscience provided his external setting 'looks' historically authentic. The reader must be able

† From *Essays in Criticism* January 1962: 39–53. Reprinted by permission of Oxford University Press. All notes are the Editor's.

to say, 'On the evidence provided, which seems adequate, this series of events could have taken place in real life as I know it.'

It follows that to look for allegorical symbols in "The Fly" is to accuse Katherine Mansfield of a breach of her chosen convention. Specifically "The Fly" is not a beast-fable, like Blake's poem[1] with the same title in "Songs of Experience". In this story the confrontation of the boss with the fly is only subjectively anthropomorphic. It is the boss who attributes human courage—and the human necessity to suffer pain under torture—to the fly. The boss's corrupt imagination has blown this up into the semblance of a human being, but objectively, as the reader knows, the fly is just an ordinary house-fly. * * * It is certainly tempting to relate the story to Katherine Mansfield's tuberculosis and to her dislike of her father, who was a New Zealand banker. But such elements are of the nature of 'sources'. No doubt without them the story could not have been begun, but they are not *inside* the story. The realistic convention is resistant both to abstractions and to strict autobiography. The story must appear to tell itself; it must be the sort of concrete human situation that might have happened just so. And once the reader begins to detect the intrusion of abstract concepts or moral attitudes, such as the hatred of war, or alternatively of obviously autobiographical episodes, his confidence in the writer's omniscience will be weakened. An unnecessary strain is being put on the realistic suspension of disbelief.

The irrelevance of allegorical interpretations in this case can be clarified by contrasting the proverb, an even shorter narrative *genre*, with the realistic short story. The concrete details in a proverb are all functional. Nobody wants to know what kind of stone it is that gathers no moss, or that is thrown by the inhabitants of glasshouses. The exact size, colour, weight and shape of the respective stones are irrelevant, because a proverb demands immediate implicit conceptualisation ('Restlessness is unprofitable', 'Guilty parties should not accuse others of guilt'); it is in fact allegory in capsule form. But in a realistic short story the particularity is a large part of the meaning. Suppress Mr. Woodifield's name, the colour of the armchair, the day of the week allotted to his City visits, and the convention collapses. They are indispensable signals from author to reader; they also assume a common interest and confidence in the concrete detail of the phenomenal world. * * *

But "The Fly" is something more than narrative imbedded in slice-of-life realism. Some sort of general statement about modern life is implicit in it. How has Katherine Mansfield managed to evade the limitations of the realistic convention? How can a value-

1. William Blake, "The Fly," in *Songs of Experience*, 1794.

judgement emerge at all from what appears to be a temporal sequence of particularities? These are the essential questions the critic must ask.

One answer, an important critical one, is that the medium of a narrative sequence is language, and that it is always possible to exploit the generality inherent in both vocabulary and grammar so that a value-judgement emerges. This is just what Katherine Mansfield does, but discreetly, tactfully. A simple linguistic device is to use descriptive epithets to hint at a generalisation. Thus at the beginning of "The Fly" the boss is 'stout' and 'rosy'. In combination with the 'snug' office to which Woodifield pays a tribute twice in the first two paragraphs, the epithets produce an impression of luxuriant good health, of self-indulgence perhaps, though at this stage in the story the indulgence is not apparently censured in any overt way. Later, in the mounting tension of the passage when the boss, having sent Woodifield on his way, returns to the office, he treads with 'firm heavy steps'. These, especially in contrast to Woodifield's 'shuffling footsteps', loom rather ominously. The boss who 'plumps' down in the springchair is no longer merely stout, he has become 'fat'. Still later, when he suddenly 'has an idea' and plunges his pen into the ink, before we quite know what he is up to we get a premonition of it as he leans his 'thick' wrist on the blotting paper. The harmless stout and rosy figure has turned out to be physically coarse, even brutal.

Similarly we get an inkling of the boss's character from the colouring of the verbs long before we are introduced to the decisive situation. When he is still 'stout and rosy', he 'rolls' in his chair. Soon he 'flips' his *Financial Times*—a slightly arrogant gesture. By this time he is 'planted' there, 'in full view of that frail old figure', and the adjective qualifying his satisfaction is 'solid'. Later on we suddenly see him 'swooping' across for two tumblers ('Coming down with the rush of a bird of prey . . . making a sudden attack', *Oxford Dictionary*).

The adjectives and verbs serve to 'place' Woodifield too, who never speaks but 'pipes' (three times) or 'quavers'. He does not look, he 'peers'. The wife and girls keep him 'boxed up' in his home. On Tuesdays, he did not dress but *was* 'dressed and brushed' and then 'allowed' to go to town—all images reinforcing the smile in which he is originally introduced, that of a baby in a pram.

But the crucial linguistic device in "The Fly" is the protagonist's anonymity. He is always referred to as 'the boss', twenty-five times to be precise, or approximately once every eighty words. The word is etymologically an Americanism (adopted from the Dutch *baas* = master in the beginning of the nineteenth century), which passed into British English about the middle of that century and had certainly lost all its foreignness by 1922. The dictionary meaning then as now is 'a master, a business manager, anyone who has a right to give orders'. The word has still an unpleasantly vulgar connotation, which is perhaps heightened by its use in U.S. political jargon, where 'boss' means the 'dictator of a party organisation'. Used with a capital it turns into a particular, not a general, word, in fact, from a common noun into a proper noun, thus making the connotation depend on what we know of the person so named. Thus 'Boss' may often have a kindly ring. But in "The Fly" Katherine Mansfield persists in spelling the word with a minuscule, that is, as a common noun, at the same time refusing to alternate it with any synonym or other appellation. She even refuses to let us know what the boss's actual name is. 'Mr. Woodifield', 'Gertrude', 'Woodifield', 'Macey', but the hero's names (and his son's) are resolutely excluded. Katherine Mansfield cannot, of course, altogether prevent the process by which a common noun becomes a proper noun, but she does her best to keep in the reader's mind the more general significance of the word. Each time we read it, the general somewhat repugnant idea of the term is again imprinted in our consciousness, even after it has almost become a proper name. The boss, clear-cut individual as he is in the realistic narrative, is *nominally* an allegorical figure simply by virtue of the word's insistent repetition.

The other linguistic device deserves notice. This is Katherine Mansfield's habit here of allowing direct description to merge into reported speech. Here are a few examples: 'His talk was over; it was time for him to be off. But he did not want to go. Since he had retired. . . .' Up to this point the description is in straightforward narrative prose, but in 'since his . . . stroke' the short break which the three dots denote—so expressive of the reluctance of a sick man to call his complaint by its frightening real name—turns author's statement into semi-direct speech. The reluctance is now Woodifield's, not the narrator's.

A few lines later an inversion occurs. 'Though what he did there, the wife and girls couldn't imagine' may still be taken as objective statement with emphasis causing the object-clause to be put first. But the following clause, 'Make a nuisance of himself they supposed' has the full effect of direct speech. Again the object-clause is given first, but the main clause does not seem to be the author speaking; it is as if between concealed quotation marks, a comment really spoken in the first person instead of the apparent third person.

A little later the boss's 'he explained, as he had explained for the past—how many?—weeks' seems to be another bit of direct speech that is masquerading as narrative statement. In a story within the realistic convention the author is supposed to know all about how often one of the characters did this or that. The slight uncertainty here, the momentary ignorance—perhaps only half genuine—belongs to everyday speech. The boss, not the author, is speaking.

Again in 'How on earth could he have slaved, denied himself, kept going all those years without the promise, for ever before him, of the boy's stepping into his shoes and carrying on where he left off?' the complete sentence in the form of a question is not introduced by any main clause, nor is it in quotation marks. But can it in fact be anything but a question asked by the boss himself?

This mixing of direct statement with indirect or concealed dialogue is used all through the story—by interpolating exclamation in otherwise regular narrative, by putting complete sentences in the form of questions not introduced by main clauses yet impossible to be taken otherwise than as questions asked by the characters, by breaks in the line, and by inversions of a colloquial nature. The result is that we have very little regular narrative. Instead, in a frame of thin lines of this quasi-narrative, which could almost be spoken by a chorus, we have the effect of drama. In this setting the repeated recurrence of the two words 'the boss' has the impersonality of a stage-direction, a datum, as it were, outside the narrative. It reiterates so as to become an alternative title to the story: "The Fly [Boss]: a Short Story".

The point at which a linguistic device, either of vocabulary ('the boss') or syntax (the indirect speech), becomes a rhetorical figure should not be detectable in realistic fiction. The reader has suspended his disbelief on condition that the naturalistic particularities are maintained, as they certainly are in "The Fly". What could be more reassuringly particular than the story's penultimate sentence? 'He took out his handkerchief and passed it inside his collar.' But in some of the devices here analysed language has unquestionably become rhetoric. The repetition of *any* phrase or construction will give it, if repeated often enough, a new semantic dimension. A similar process occurs if some parallelism establishes itself between the separate episodes in a narrative or drama. Gradually an unstated generality superimposes itself on the sequence of particulars. A narrative pattern emerges.

The most memorable episode in "The Fly" begins when the boss, having completed the rescue operations from the inkpot, conceives his 'idea'. This is the story's *peripeteia*,[2] the point of dramatic reversal in the reader's attitude to the protagonist. We began with a distinct liking for him. Woodifield was expected by his family to make a nuisance of himself to his old friends on the Tuesday excursions into the City; and in general, from the specimen provided us of his

2. Sudden change, or reversal in fortune. (Greek)

conversational powers, their gloomy anticipations seem likely to be fulfilled. But the boss's reaction is different. The boss is genuinely delighted to see Woodifield, and he produces his best whisky to entertain him, 'feeling kindly', as the narrator (apparently it *is* the narrator) informs us. At this early point in "The Fly" the tone is light and almost comic: the bars in the electric heater are compared to sausages, and Woodifield couldn't have been more surprised, when the whisky bottle appears, 'if the boss had produced a rabbit'. This boss—in spite of his descriptive label—cannot be taken very tragically because of the disarming atmosphere of cordiality in which we make his acquaintance. Moreover his son has been killed in the war (of 1914–18), and we are naturally sorry for him. It is true some disturbing elements in the boss's character already contradict the generally good impression he creates. Some of the pleasure he takes in Woodifield's company seems to derive from the contrast he cannot help drawing between his own excellent health and the younger man's frail condition. And the ritual of immediately available tears in his son's memory, if pathetic, is also distasteful. But these reservations—the list could be extended—do not affect our general liking for him and sympathy with him until he turns his experimental attention on to the fly.

As the three blobs of ink fall the reader's attitude changes from considerable sympathy to total antipathy. The admiration the boss professes to feel for the fly's determination is no doubt real, but it does not prevent him from proceeding with his appalling 'idea'. The horrifying thing is that this admiration makes the experiment all the more entrancing for him. As flies to wanton boys are we to the gods, they kill us for their sport.[3] If the victim did not show some spirit, the gods would lose half their sport. (A half-consciousness of Gloucester's dictum is no doubt expected in the reader.)

In the light we now possess of the boss's other nature we can see how ambiguous the boss's earlier words and actions were. From this moment therefore the story takes on a two-way pattern. It is read as mere 'story', so that we can discover what comes next, but with each step forward a mental step is also taken back into earlier more or less parallel episodes, and so we correct our first impressions in the light of the new information. A dual element reveals itself at this point in the boss's relations with both Woodifield and his son. The tenderness with the one or admiration for the other is not to be denied, but it is a sadistic tenderness, unconscious of course, but almost that of an executioner for his victim. Woodifield was not allowed whisky at home, and the boss must have known that drink-

3. "As flies to wanton boys, are we to the gods. / They kill us for their sport." Shakespeare, *King Lear*, 4.1.36–37. The lines are spoken by the blinded Gloucester.

ing it might precipitate a second stroke. But the 'generous finger' is enthusiastically provided. The son was no doubt genuinely loved and mourned, but the son's death provided the boss with a splendid opportunity to demonstrate his superiority to other bereaved parents, like the Woodifields. *His* tears were Niobean;[4] hence the shock of aggrieved disappointment when they finally dry up.

A second *peripeteia* presents itself, there, at the fly's death. The grinding and frightening feeling of wretchedness is not what either the boss or the reader had expected. This emotional reversal in the boss creates a new reversal in the reader's attitude to him. Had the boss perhaps glimpsed, briefly and startlingly, the abyss of moral nihilism into which he had unconsciously descended? Katherine Mansfield leaves the question unanswered, almost unasked. * * * But the framework of parallel episodes that has built itself up in the reader's mind forces us to half-formulate some ghost of a conceptual conclusion. What *had* the boss been thinking about before the fly entered his life? 'For the life of him he could not remember'. And so the reader dismisses him, finally, with some contempt. Early in the story we had quite liked the boss, then we had discovered that we detested him, and now we can merely despise him. The boss's final gesture with the handkerchief, which he passes inside his stiff collar to cool and dry the hot sticky skin, 'places' him with superb economy and precision. The intensity of the battle the mighty boss has waged with the minute fly has left him physically exhausted, mere weak brutal oblivious flesh.

In terms of plot, then, though there is dramatic progress (shifts in the reader's sympathies, a mounting intensity, a transition from the near-comic to the near-tragic), there is also dramatic repetition. The episodes combine similitude with dissimilitude in a kind of extended metaphor. If the Woodifield episode is called Act I, the re-enactment of the son's death Act II, and the murder of the fly Act III, then the parallelism works out as follows:

(i) in each of the three acts the boss holds the centre of the stage, and the three subsidiary characters' dramatic function is to throw light on him as the protagonist;

(ii) in Act I Woodifield's feebleness illumines the boss's image of himself as a man of affairs, in Act II it is the boss's image of himself as father that is illumined, in Act III the image is of the boss as animal-lover;

(iii) in each act the boss's image of his own altruism is found to be contradicted by his actions;

(iv) the cumulative effect of the parallelisms is to super-

4. Niobe, in Greek mythology, whose boasting about her children provoked the gods into destroying them.

impose on the boss's image of himself in Act I the self-images of Acts II and III, but the image of the hospitable man of the world is blurred by that of the proud heart-broken father and the cheerer-on of flies in difficulties (the images do not cohere);

(v) contrasting with this blur is the clear-cut outline that emerges from the superimpositions of the essential boss as he really is all the time—an ordinary decent human being irretrievably demoralised by the power that corrupts.

A final critical corollary remains to be drawn. Katherine Mansfield's realism has begun with a tactful introduction of the story's setting. The reader, encouraged by the apparent authenticity of the details, tends unconsciously to identify himself with the *dramatis personae*, as though they were being presented by living actors in a West End theatre. They—that is, Katherine Mansfield's accounts of her characters—accept identification. Under the make-up and the costume a living heart is beating, but it is the actor's heart—in the case of a realistic short story, the reader's heart—not the *persona*'s. The authenticity is confirmed, re-created, guaranteed, by the reader. But the judgement that he passes on these impersonations of his, who are technically the characters of the story, is the author's contribution, not the reader's, because the reader is not aware that a moral attitude is gradually forming itself within his consciousness. The test of the good short story is therefore the degree of the reader's surprise when he discovers in himself the judgements that have been forced upon him. But the surprise has also to be followed by conviction. This is what the particular words and the particular word-orders *must* mean; this is what the significance of the dramatic episodes in their sequence of parallelisms *must* add up to.

It will be remembered that Dr. Johnson's discussion of poetic wit proposed a similar criterion: a good poem is 'at once natural and new', because what it is saying, 'though not obvious, . . . is acknowledge to be just'.[5]

FRANK O'CONNOR

An Author in Search of a Subject†

Katherine Mansfield is for me something unusual in the history of the short story. She was a woman of brilliance, perhaps of genius;

5. Samuel Johnson, "Abraham Cowley," *Lives of the Poets* (1779), in *Johnson Prose and Poetry* (London: Rupert Hart-Davis, 1957), p. 798.

† From *The Lonely Voice: A Study of the Short Story* (London: Macmillan, 1963), pp. 128–42. Reprinted by permission of Palgrave Macmillan. All notes are the Editor's.

she chose the short story as her own particular form and handled it with considerable skill, and yet for most of the time she wrote stories that I read and forget, read and forget. My experience of stories by real storytellers, even when the stories are not first-rate, is that they leave a deep impression on me. It may not be a total impression; it may not even be an accurate one, but it is usually deep and permanent. I remember it in the way in which I remember poetry. I do not remember Katherine Mansfield's stories in that way. She wrote a little group of stories about her native country, New Zealand, which are recognized as masterpieces and probably are masterpieces, but I find myself forgetting even these and rediscovering them as though they were the work of a new writer.

It may be that for me and people of my own generation her work has been obscured by her legend, as the work of Rupert Brooke[1] has been, and the work is always considerably dimmer than the legend. The story of the dedicated doomed artist, the creature of flame married to a dull unimaginative man persists; persists so strongly, indeed, that one has to keep on reminding oneself that the story is largely the creation of the dull unimaginative man himself. Most of us who were young when the *Journal* was published took an immediate dislike to John Middleton Murry,[2] and I suspect that some of the scornful obituaries that appeared after his death were the work of men who had taken the legend of Katherine Mansfield too seriously. Meanwhile, Murry, a man with an inordinate capacity for punishment, continued to publish letters of hers that seemed to show him in a still worse light.

Obviously there was some truth in the legend since Murry himself believed it, and since the mark left on one's imagination by the *Journal* and letters remains; and yet I get the impression that in the editing of the book he was unfair to himself and far, far too fair to his wife. There must have been another side to her which has not yet emerged from the memoirs of the time. Friends of Murry and hers have told me that they seemed less interested in each other than in the copy they supplied to each other—a likely enough weakness in two young writers who were both in love with literature, though one wouldn't gather it from what either has written. Francis Carco,[3] after his flirtation with Katherine, portrayed her as a rapacious copyhound, while in "Je ne parle pas français" she caricatured him as a pimp. Childish, spiteful, vulgar if you like, but something that has been carefully edited out of the legend. One

1. Rupert Brooke (1887–1915), an English poet who died in Greece during World War One and became for many a figure of romantic patriotism.
2. As Middleton Murry continued to publish volumes of his wife's letters and papers after Mansfield's death, he was thought by many to be both sentimental and exploitative.
3. Francis Carco, the French novelist with whom Mansfield had a brief affair in 1915, which she wrote of in "An Indiscreet Journey."

might even say that by creating the legend Murry did his wife's reputation more harm than good, for by failing to describe, much less emphasize, the shoddy element in her character, he suppressed the real miracle of her development as an artist.

* * *

There is one quality that is missing in almost everything that Katherine Mansfield wrote—even her New Zealand stories—and that is heart. Where heart should be we usually find sentimentality, the quality that seems to go with a brassy exterior, and nowhere more than with that of an "emancipated" woman. In literature sentimentality always means falsity, for whether or not one can perceive the lie, one is always aware of being in the presence of a lie.

"Je ne parle pas français" is a good example. It is generally accepted as a free description of Katherine Mansfield's first meeting with Francis Carco, and Carco himself admits the resemblance. It describes a sensitive, dreamy girl brought on an illicit honeymoon to Paris by a Mother's Boy who, because he does not wish to hurt Momma, abandons her there to the care of his pimp friend—drawn from Carco—though the pimp friend, finding no use for her, abandons her as well.

A touching little story, and if one could read it "straight," as I am told such stories should be read, one's sympathy would go out to the heroine, every one of whose glances and tears is lovingly observed. But how can one read it straight? The first question I ask myself is how this angelic creature ever became the mistress of anybody, let alone of such a monster of egotism as her lover. Is it that she was completely innocent? But if so, why doesn't she do what any innocent girl with money in her pocket would do on discovering that she has been abandoned in a strange city by a man she had trusted and go home on the next train? Not perhaps back to her parents but at least to some old friend? Has she no home? No friend? None of the essential questions a short story should answer is answered here, and in fact, when I read the story "straight," knowing nothing of the author's life, I merely felt it was completely unconvincing.

Knowing what I do now, I do not find it much more satisfactory. Was Murry, to whom Katherine Mansfield submitted it first, supposed to read it "straight"? "But I hope you'll see (of course you will)," she wrote to him, "that I'm not writing with a sting."[4] Apparently he did not see. Indeed, being a very sensitive man, he may even have wondered at the insensitiveness of a woman who could send such a story for his approval.

But even more than by the element of falsity in these stories I am

4. *Collected Letters,* vol. 2, p. 56.

put off by the feeling that they were all written in exile. I do not mean by this merely that they were written by a New Zealander about Germany, England, and France, three countries any one of which would be sufficient to keep a storyteller occupied for several lifetimes. I mean that there is no real indication of a submerged population, a population which is not by its very nature in need of a coherent voice. To Katherine Mansfield as to Dickens the lower classes are merely people who say "perishall" when they mean "parasol" and "certingty" when they mean "certainty." Reading the stories all through again I experienced the same shock I experienced thirty years ago when I came on "The Life of Ma Parker" and I found myself saying, "Ah, so this is what was missing! So this is what short stories are really about!"

Like much of Katherine Mansfield's work, this story is influenced directly by Chekhov. * * * "The Life of Ma Parker" is imitated from an equally famous story, "Misery,"[5] in which an old cab driver who has lost his son tries to tell his grief to his customers and finally goes down to the stable and tells it to his old nag. Ma Parker, too, having lost her little grandson, is full of her grief, but when she tries to tell her employer about it he merely says, "I hope the funeral was a—success."

And at this point I always stop reading to think, "Now *there* is a mistake that Chekhov wouldn't have made!" and I do not need to go on to the point at which Ma Parker's employer rebukes her for throwing out a teaspoon of cocoa he had left in a tin. Chekhov knew that it is not heartlessness that breaks the heart of the lonely, and it is not Ma Parker's employer who is being coarse but Katherine Mansfield. It is not the only example in her work of a story being spoiled by her assertiveness.

At the same time the story is impressive because Ma Parker is a genuine member of a submerged population, not so much because she is old and poor, which is largely irrelevant, as because, like Chekhov's teachers and priests, she has no one else to speak for her.

It is generally agreed that the principal change in Katherine Mansfield's work occurs after the death of her brother, Chummie, in the First World War. It seems to have been her first contact with real personal grief, and her reaction was violent, even immoderate. "First, my darling, I've got things to do for both of us, and then I will come as quickly as I can," she writes in her *Journal*.[6] What the things were she revealed when she asked herself why she did not commit suicide. "I have a duty to perform to the lovely time when

5. A Chekhov story published in 1885.
6. *Journal*, p. 86.

we were both alive. I want to write about it, and he wanted me to. We talked it over in my little top room in London. I said: I will just put on the front page: To my brother, Leslie Heron Beauchamp. Very well: it shall be done."[7]

Of course, it is all girlishly overdramatic in the Katherine Mansfield way, but that is no reflection on its sincerity. After all, it was done, and done splendidly.

She had always been fond of her brother, though to my mind—still speaking in the part of devil's advocate—this is scarcely sufficient to explain the violence of her grief, which sent a normally affectionate husband like Murry home from the South of France, ashamed of himself for thinking of a dead boy as a rival. Once more, I begin to wonder whether the assertive, masculine streak in her had not made her jealous of her brother. There is nothing abnormal about that: it is possible for a woman to love a brother dearly and yet be jealous of the advantages which he seems to possess; and of course, the jealousy cannot survive death, for once the superiority, real or imaginary, is removed, and the beloved brother is merely a name on a tombstone, the struggling will has no obstacles to contend with and the place of jealousy tends to be taken by guilt—by the feeling that one had grudged the brother such little advantages as he possessed, even by the fantasy that one had caused his death. All this is well within the field of ordinary human experience; it is the immoderacy of the reaction in Katherine Mansfield that puzzles me.

I feel sure that something of the sort is necessary to explain the extraordinary change that took place in her character and work—above all in her work, for here the change does not seem to be a normal development of her talent at all but a complete reversal of it. In fact, it is much more like the result of a religious crisis than of an artistic one, and, like the result of a lot of other religious crises, it leaves the critic watchful and unsatisfied. "Did he give up the drink too soon?" is a question we must all have had to ask ourselves from time to time in connection with our friends. For Katherine Mansfield, the woman, the crisis was to end in the dreary charlatanism of Fontainebleau[8] and become the keystone of her legend, but from the point of view of Katherine Mansfield, the writer, that gesture seems immoderate, heroic, and absolutely unnecessary. No one need point out to me that this viewpoint is lim-

7. *Journal*, p. 90.
8. Toward the end of 1922, Mansfield went for what turned out to be the last months of her life to live at Fontainebleau, near Paris, where the teacher and philosopher George Gurdjieff (1872–1949) had established the Institute for the Harmonious Development of Man. Gurdjieff and his followers were considered by some to promote a fraudulent mysticism. In defense of his dealings with Mansfield see James Moore, *Gurdjieff and Mansfield* (London: Routledge and Kegan Paul, 1980).

ited, and that it is not for a critic of literature to say what act of heroism is or is not necessary, but he must do it just the same if he is to be true to his own standards.

It seems to me that Katherine Mansfield's tragedy is, from the inside, the tragedy that Chekhov never tired of observing from the outside—the tragedy of the false personality. That clever, assertive, masculine woman was a mistake from beginning to end, and toward the close of her life she recognized it herself. Writing of herself, characteristically in the third person, she said, "She had led, ever since she can remember, a very typically false life."[9] This is my complaint of John Murry's legend: because he loved Katherine Mansfield he gave no indication of the false personality, and so blotted the true and moving story of the brassy little shopgirl of literature who made herself into a great writer. * * *

The conflict between the false personality and the ideal one is very clear in some of the stories, and nowhere more than in the second book in which the two personalities stand side by side in "Je ne parle pas français" and "Prelude." The false personality, determined largely by the will, dominates the former story; an ideal alternative personality—*not* the true one because that never emerged fully—determined by a complete surrender of the will, dominates the latter. As a result of the conflict in her, Katherine Mansfield's reply to the activity imposed on her by her own overdeveloped will is an antithesis—pure contemplation.

For obvious reasons she identified this contemplativeness with that of Chekhov, the least contemplative writer who ever lived, but her misunderstanding of the great artist with whom she identified herself was a necessary part of her development.

> How *perfect* the world is, with its worms and hooks and ova, how incredibly perfect. There is the sky and the sea and the shape of a lily, and there is all this other as well. The balance how perfect! (Salut, Tchehov!) I would not have the one without the other.[1]

One can imagine the embarrassed cough with which Chekhov would have greeted that girlish effusiveness. His contemplativeness, the contemplativeness of a doctor who must resign himself to the death of a patient he has worked himself to death trying to save, was a very different affair from Katherine Mansfield's, and if, as a wise man he resigned himself, it was never because he had not suffered as a fool.

In one story, "The Garden Party," Katherine Mansfield tries to blend the two personalities, and her failure is even more interesting

9. *Journal*, p. 330.
1. *Journal*, p. 168.

than the success of stories like "Prelude," where one personality is held in abeyance. Apparently, part of her assertiveness came from her resentment of the aimless life of the moneyed young lady in the provincial society of New Zealand, and during the religious crisis, part of her penance has to be the complete, uncritical acceptance of it. In the story the Sheridans' garden party is haunted by the accidental death of a carter who lives at their gate. Young Laura does not want the garden party to take place; she tries to talk her family out of it but *is* constantly frustrated and diverted, even by her beloved brother Laurie.

> "My word, Laura! You do look stunning," said Laurie. "What an absolutely topping hat!"
>
> Laura said faintly, "Is it?" and smiled up at Laurie, and didn't tell him after all.

In the evening, at her mother's suggestion, Laura goes to the carter's cottage with a basket of leftovers from the party. It is true she has her doubts—"Would the poor woman really like that?"—but she manages to overcome them with no great difficulty. For one reader at least, the effect that Katherine Mansfield has been trying to achieve is totally destroyed. The moment she moves from her ideal world, "with its worms and hooks and ova," into a real world where the critical faculty wakes, she ruins everything by her own insensitiveness. It is exactly the same mistake that she makes in "The Life of Ma Parker." Any incidental poetry there may be in bands, marquees, pastries, and hats—and there is plenty—is dissipated in the sheer grossness of those who enjoy them. The Duc de Guermantes, determined not to hear of the death of an old friend in order not to spoil his party, at least knows what is expected of him. Nothing, one feels, can be expected of the Sheridans.

That is why in the best of the New Zealand stories there is no contact with the real world at all. In his excellent life of Katherine Mansfield, Mr. Antony Alpers quotes a brilliant passage by V. S. Pritchett, contrasting the absence of a real country from "At the Bay" with the flavor of old Russia in Chekhov's "The Steppe," but when Mr. Alpers replies that this quality is absent from Katherine Mansfield's story because it is absent from New Zealand he misses Mr. Pritchett's point entirely. The real reply to Mr. Pritchett—which he probably knows better than anybody—is that to introduce a real country into "At the Bay" would be to introduce history, and with history would come judgment, will, and criticism. The real world of these stories is not New Zealand but childhood, and they are written in a complete hypnotic suspension of the critical faculties.

This is clearest in the episode in "Prelude" in which Pat, the Irish gardener, decapitates a duck to amuse the children and the headless body instantly makes a dash for the duck pond. It would be almost impossible for any other writer to describe this scene without horrifying us; clearly it horrified the critical and fastidious Katherine Mansfield since it haunted her through the years, but she permits the little girl, Kezia, only one small shudder.

> "Watch it!" shouted Pat. He put down the body and it began to waddle—with only a long spurt of blood where the head had been; it began to pad away without a sound towards the steep bank that led to the stream. . . . That was the crowning wonder.
>
> "Do you see that? Do you see that?" yelled Pip. He ran among the little girls rugging at their pinafores.
>
> "It's like a little engine. It's like a funny little railway engine," squealed Isabel.
>
> But Kezia suddenly rushed at Pat and flung her arms round his legs and butted her head as hard as she could against his knees.
>
> "Put head back! Put head back!" she screamed.

For me this is one of the most remarkable scenes in modern literature, for though I have often accused myself of morbid fastidiousness, of a pathological dislike of what is obscene and cruel, I can read it almost as though it were the most delightful incident in a delightful day. No naturalist has ever been able to affect me like this, and I suspect that the reason is that Katherine Mansfield is not observing the scene but contemplating it. This is the Garden of Eden before shame or guilt came into the world. It is also precisely what I mean when I say that the crisis in Katherine Mansfield was religious rather than literary.

These extraordinary stories are Katherine Mansfield's masterpieces and in their own way comparable with Proust's[2] breakthrough into the subconscious world. But one must ask oneself why they *are* masterpieces and afterward whether they represent a literary discovery that she might have developed and exploited as Proust developed and exploited his own discovery. They are masterpieces because they are an act of atonement to her brother for whatever wrong she felt she had done him, an attempt at bringing him back to life so that he and she might live forever in the world she had created for them both. They set out to do something that had never been done before and to do it in a manner that had never been used before, a manner that has something in common with that of the fairy tale.

For instance, to have described the world of childhood through the mind of any of the children would have made this the child's

2. Marcel Proust (1871–1922), French novelist.

own particular world, subject to time and error, and so the only observer is an angelic one for whom the ideas of good and evil, right and wrong, do not exist. Not only does the narrative switch effortlessly from one character to another, but as in a fairy tale speechless things talk like anyone else. Florrie, the cat in "At the Bay," says, "Thank goodness, it's getting late. Thank goodness, the long day is over"; the infant says, "Don't like babies? Don't like *me*?" and the bush says "We are dumb trees, reaching up in the night, imploring we know not what"; while Beryl's imaginary voices, which describe how wonderful she looked one summer at the bay, are not more unreal—or real—than those of Linda Burnell and her husband.

These stories are conscious, deliberate acts of magic, as though a writer were to go into the room where his beloved lay dead and try to repeat the miracle of Lazarus. In this way they can be linked with the work of other writers like Joyce[3] and Proust, who in their different, more worldly ways were also attempting a magical approach to literature by trying to make the printed page not a description of something that had happened but a substitute for what had happened, an episode as it might appear in the eyes of God—an act of pure creation.

Whether Katherine Mansfield could ever have exploited her own breakthrough into magic is another matter; and here, I think, we are getting closer to the discomfort of V. S. Pritcher before "At the Bay" and my own before that whole group of stories because they continue to fade from my mind, no matter how often I reread them.

Are they really works of art that could have given rise to other works of art and followed the law of their own being? Or are they in fact an outward representation of an act of deliberate martyrdom—the self-destruction of Fontainebleau, which was intended to destroy the false personality Katherine Mansfield had built up for herself. If they represent the former, then the old Katherine would have had to come back in however purified a form. She could never have escaped entirely into a magical version of her childhood and would have had to deal with her own sordid love affairs, her dishonesties, her cruelties. There are tantalizing hints of how this might have happened, for in "The Young Girl" and "The Daughters of the Late Colonel" I seem to see a development of her sense of humor without her coarseness:

But death came too soon, and at the end we can only fall back on the legend that her husband created for her and which has placed her forever among "the inheritors of unfulfilled renown."[4]

3. James Joyce (1882–1941), Irish short-story writer and novelist. Arguably he and Proust are the two most significant fiction writers of the twentieth century.
4. Percy Bysshe Shelley, *Adonais* (1821), XLV, l. 1.

CLARE HANSON AND ANDREW GURR

["The Daughters of the Late Colonel"]†

'The Daughters of the Late Colonel' was written in Menton on 13 December 1920. Ida Baker was present, ministering, and records the occasion:

> I remember the night she finished *The Daughters of the Late Colonel*, that gentle caricature of her cousin Sylvia Payne and me, which she wrote in about three or four hours with hardly a break or correction. 'It's finished! It's finished!' she called. 'Celebration with tea!'[1]

In February 1922, after a year of splendid creativity had followed, she could still call it one of her favourites. To William Gerhardi she wrote,

> The only story that satisfies me to any extent is the one you understand so well, *The Daughters of the Late Col.*, and parts of *Je ne parle pas.*[2]

What she seems to have had in mind when she recorded that opinion was its technical brilliance rather than its subject matter. In a letter to Richard Murry, written only a few weeks after the story was put on paper, she told him,

> I have written a huge long story of a rather new kind. It's the outcome of the *Prelude* method—it just unfolds and opens—But I hope it's an advance on *Prelude*. In fact, I know it's that because the technique is stronger.[3]

Her own affection for the story carries weight. It is technically one of the most sophisticated stories she wrote, and she knew how very much more than Ida's 'gentle caricature' her technique made it.

The style she adopts is interior monologue externalised by the use of the third person, which allows continual shifts of focus, from the Daughters in concert, to their separate trains of thought, and into the author's own discreetly distancing comments. In the opening of the final section, for instance, the interior perspective is chiefly Josephine's, but it modulates from inside to outside, never quite detaching itself from Josephine while permitting only the

† From *Katherine Mansfield* (London: Macmillan, 1981), pp. 87–94. Reprinted by permission of Palgrave Macmillan.

1. Ida Baker, *Katherine Mansfield: The Memories of L. M.* (London: Michael Joseph, 1971), p. 153.
2. *The Letters of Katherine Mansfield*, ed. John Middleton Murry (London: Constable, 1928), vol. 2, p. 185.
3. Ibid., p. 87.

faintest subjective bias to the outside happenings, the barrel-organ, the sunlight, and finally the music again.

> But at that moment in the street below a barrel-organ struck up. Josephine and Constantia sprang to their feet together.
>
> 'Run, Con,' said Josephine. 'Run quickly. There's sixpence on the—'
>
> Then they remembered. It didn't matter. They would never have to stop the organ-grinder again. Never again would she and Constantia be told to make that monkey take his noise somewhere else. Never would sound that loud, strange bellow when father thought they were not hurrying enough. The organ-grinder might play there all day and the stick would not thump.
>
> *It never will thump again,*
> *It never will thump again,*
>
> played the barrel-organ.
>
> What was Constantia thinking? She had such a strange smile, she looked different. She couldn't be going to cry.
>
> 'Jug, Jug,' said Constantia softly, pressing her hands together. 'Do you know what day it is? It's Saturday. It's a week today, a whole week.'
>
> *A week since father died,*
> *A week since father died,*
>
> cried the barrel-organ. And Josephine, too, forgot to be practical and sensible; she smiled faintly, strangely. On the Indian carpet there fell a square of sunlight, pale red; it came and went and came—and stayed, deepened—until it shone almost golden.
>
> 'The sun's out,' said Josephine, as though it really mattered.
>
> A perfect fountain of bubbling notes shook from the barrel organ, round, bright notes, carelessly scattered.

Even the Colonel is present here, in the phrase 'make that monkey take his noise somewhere else'. The author slips in with 'And Josephine, too, forgot', but the adjectives which follow are rather Josephine's than the author's, her conscious pose, so that we are immediately back inside her. When the sunshine penetrates the room we hear Josephine's thought, 'as though it really mattered', at the same time as we hear the author hinting at a judgement and at the conclusion of the story. The sunshine matters, and yet it will signal no real change. Every word here is luminous with implication.

Structurally, too, it is a sophistication of the *Prelude* method. It 'unfolds' like *Prelude* through twelve sections or scenes, but with an even more functional appropriateness than the earlier story. Like *Prelude* each section develops by a seemingly random association of ideas from its predecessor, but more functionally because the randomness directly imitates the random thought-processes of the Daughters. Section III shifts into Section IV, for instance, via the memory of father opening only the one distinctly glaring eye before he died, into the difficulty which the memory of that sight created when the vicar conventionally enquired whether the Colonel's end had been peaceful.

> It had made it very awkward for them when Mr Farolles, of St John's, called the same afternoon.
>
> 'The end was quite peaceful, I trust?' were the first words he said as he glided towards them through the dark drawing-room.
>
> 'Quite,' said Josephine faintly. They both hung their heads. Both of them felt certain that eye wasn't at all a peaceful eye.

The inconsequential sequence covers, by the end, all the revelatory incidents which have followed the Colonel's death. Their inconsequentiality accurately reflects the waywardness of the Daughters' thinking and the way events impinge on them from unforeseeable directions.

The structure of the twelve scenes, however, is anything but inconsequential. It falls into two halves, the second six scenes repeating the pattern of the first six exactly. Nurse Andrews dominates the second and third scenes of the first half, while Cyril dominates the second and third scenes of the second half. Mr Farolles confronts the Daughters in the fourth scene of the first half, and they try to confront Kate in the fourth scene of the second half. The fifth scene of the first half is entirely Josephine's, while the fifth scene of the second half is entirely Constantia's. Both opening scenes in each half show them together, with a brief separate thought from each of them, and both of the concluding scenes, the sixth and the twelfth, begin with the two of them considered jointly and then alternately. The sixth gives us Jug and Con together, then Jug alone, then Con alone, and finally Jug. The twelfth gives us Jug and Con together, followed by Jug alone, then Con, then Jug, then Con, and ends with the two of them together again. This hidden organisation of the seemingly inconsequential is in its way an accurate image of Katherine Mansfield's presentation of the sisters. The wayward surface appearance of their actions, like the ripples of wind on water, conceals a powerful current which sweeps them directly on to their fate, the remainder of their timorous and sunless existence.

The effect of the wayward scenes is of course cumulative. The first half, which deals with the events of the week following the Colonel's death, is like a door slowly opening. The second, which is chiefly set at the end of the week, sees it close again. The first half has an ascending scale of victimisers, from Nurse Andrews, through Kate to the Colonel himself, the prime mover of the victimisations. It ends in the sixth section with Constantia's triumphant assertion of the freedom to be weak.

> 'Why shouldn't we be weak for once in our lives, Jug? It's quite excusable. Let's be weak—be weak, Jug. It's much nicer to be weak than to be strong.'
>
> And then she did one of those amazingly bold things that she'd done about twice before in their lives; she marched over to the wardrobe, turned the key, and took it out of the lock. Took it out of the lock and held it up to Josephine, showing Josephine by her extraordinary smile that she knew what she'd done, she'd risked deliberately father being in there among his overcoats.

The second half brings in the different perspective of Cyril, the nephew equally intimidated by the Colonel and by his Daughters. Cyril's aunts in their auntishness hint at some of the Colonel's legacies, while at the same time making a contrast with the temporary nature of the embarrassment that Cyril suffers in front of the Colonel. Cyril's eagerness to escape makes the feminist point about the Daughters being caught in the Colonel's trap, in preparation for the full recognition of the trap which emerges via the problem of Kate in the final scene of the story.

Kate with her noise and her insistence on decisions ('Fried or boiled?') is the Colonel's most malign legacy. To dismiss her, to make that decision, would mean the Daughters rejecting all the inheritance of their old maid roles. Kate's 'bouncing' is like the Colonel's stick-thumping, or Nurse Andrews with her clock-watching, or the barrel-organ's music bursting out, manifestations of energy which they have come to associate with terror. The Colonel's noise-making instrument, his thumping stick, is also an emblem of his helplessness, but the Daughters have inherited too much terror to know that. They live in continual fear of things bursting out of confined spaces—including the Colonel himself out of his cupboards and drawers—and so cannot see the confined space in which they too are trapped as anything but a protection.

The trap, the predetermined fate of the Daughters, is suggested through Katherine Mansfield's stock symbol of life, the sun. Josephine, the more 'practical and sensible' of the sisters, is sun and Constantia is moon. In the final scene the sun intrudes its light on their consideration of the new pattern offered them by life now that the Colonel is dead.

> The sunlight pressed through the windows, thieved its way in, flashed its light over the furniture and the photographs. Josephine watched it. When it came to mother's photograph,

> the enlargement over the piano, it lingered as though puzzled to find so little remained of mother, except the ear-rings shaped like tiny pagodas and a black feather boa.

Josephine thinks over their past life and its fragile cargo of lost opportunities.

> . . . And that was all. The rest had been looking after father, and at the same time keeping out of father's way. But now? But now? The thieving sun touched Josephine gently. She lifted her face. She was drawn over to the window by gentle beams . . .

Attention then turns to moon-like Constantia and her even more vague sense of deprivation. They turn to one another with the same question, and with the same inabilities:

> They stopped; they waited for each other.
> 'Go on Con,' said Josephine.
> 'No, no, Jug; after you,' said Constantia.
>
> A pause. Then Constantia said faintly, 'I can't say what I was going to say, Jug, because I've forgotten what it was . . . that I was going to say.'
>
> Josephine was silent for a moment. She stared at a big cloud where the sun had been. Then she replied shortly, 'I've forgotten too.'

Constantia's amazing boldness has gone, and she dare not follow her train of thought. Josephine has to follow down the same cul-de-sac. They cannot face the outflow of energy that would mean their release from confinement. This is the point to which their week of adjustment has taken them, and it is the end of their adjustment. The rest of their lives is predetermined. The sun, weirdly foreshadowed by the one eye glaring from the dying Colonel's purple face, has followed the ogre to his grave.

> Oh, what a difference it would have made, what a difference to their memory of him, how much easier to tell people about it, if he had only opened both! But no—one eye only. It glared at them a moment and then . . . went out.

The Daughters' clouds are grey, not purple, but their sun expires in the same way. They are the Colonel's too-late Daughters.

In a letter to Gerhardi of June 1921 Katherine Mansfield registered her distress at the callow way in which the story had been read. She did acknowledge that the response it calls for is a difficult feat of balance. 'While I was writing it,' she told Gerhardi,

> I lived for it but when it was finished, I confess I hoped very much that my readers would understand what I was trying to express. But very few did. They thought it was 'cruel'; they

> thought I was 'sneering' at Jug and Constantia; or they thought it was 'drab'. And in the last paragraph I was 'poking fun at the poor old things.'[4]

The response must be as deliberately exact as the story. The balancing act is needed because the pathos so precisely matches the comedy, and the comic old maids are helpless in their everlasting trap. Out of the comedy and framed by the trap emerges the beauty of which they can know nothing, except for the door which momentarily opens to Constantia on her announcement that 'It's much nicer to be weak than to be strong.' The letter to Gerhardi continues:

> It's almost terrifying to be so misunderstood, There was a moment when I first had 'the idea' when I saw the two sisters as *amusing*; but the moment I looked deeper (let me be quite frank) I bowed down to the beauty that was hidden in their lives and to discover that was all my desire . . . All was meant, of course, to lead up to that last paragraph, when my two flowerless ones turned with that timid gesture, to the sun. 'Perhaps *now* . . .' And after that, it seemed to me, they died as surely as Father was dead . . .

If we have to see Carco in Raoul Duquette and Murry in Robert Salesby, we should also register in Constantia the tribute to Ida Baker, in whose company the story was set down, as a comparably scrupulous portrait with an incomparably more far-reaching frame of reference. Duquette is a portrait of a poseur, Robert Salesby a man castrated by a highly specific trap. The trap the Daughters are in is deeper, more basic, in a social perspective which reaches far beyond the bounds of their capacity to recognise it. And the telling of their story, that supremely delicate feat of balance and subtly allusive images, fully justifies the accolade David Daiches[5] gave it, as a landmark in the history of the short story.

CLAIRE TOMALIN

[Dreams and Danger]†

* * *

The pattern of Katherine Mansfield's life is both pathetic and almost ludicrously retributive: for every rash, false or wild thing she

4. Ibid., p. 20.
5. David Daiches, *New Literary Values* (Edinburgh: Oliver and Boyd, 1936), p. 105.

† From "Introduction," *Katherine Mansfield Short Stories*, ed. Claire Tomalin (London: Everyman's Library, 1983), pp. xiv–xxii. Reprinted by permission of The Orion Publishing Group. Tomalin is also the author of an important biography, *Katherine Mansfield: A Secret Life* (London: Viking, 1987). All notes are the Editor's.

did she suffered a heavy punishment of the kind a Victorian novelist might have inflicted on an erring heroine. But the moral climate of her stories has nothing to do with sinful subplots and retribution, although it has to do with danger and vulnerability and the deadening of the spirit. The stories, published first in the *New Age*[1] were very consciously of a new age. Up-to-dateness was their distinctive mark, in their themes, their tone and their technique. Mansfield worked out for herself the modernist creed that a story can be coherent without a plot that moves from A to B to C, her point of departure being simply the idea of inhabiting other selves than her own. 'Would you not like to try all sorts of lives—one is so very small—but that is the satisfaction of writing—one can impersonate so many people'[2] she wrote in a letter to a cousin when she was only seventeen. She practised a little as a *diseuse*[3] in her Westbourne Park hostel days[4] and had ambitions towards the stage; some of her early pieces are written in the form of dramatic sketches. To inhabit a character you must watch and listen with preternatural acuteness, snatching up scraps of speech and behaviour that come your way and using them to suggest a whole world. And this is what she learnt to do, using whatever scraps of her past and present that she could.

The earlier stories * * * are the work of an angry young woman, acutely alive to the problems and plights of women in a world in which power of all kinds lay with men, and mocking of the pomposity of the established male and the complicity of many women with it. * * * Indeed, the twin themes of women crushed by male power and women subverting that power are rarely absent from her stories, although they are often present by implication rather than directly. Her first story, 'The Tiredness of Rosabel', was written at the height of the suffragette movement's activities; but stories are not necessarily mirrors of political movements, and Katherine was never a suffragette; in fact she ran laughing from the intensities of the only meeting she attended in London, not because she was out of sympathy with its general aims, but because she could not confine her vision of life to those terms. Rosabel looks at first glance like a simple rendering of the consciousness of a girl working in a hat shop; but there is more to it than that.

The story follows Rosabel home to her lodgings after her day's work and shows her daydreams of luxury, inspired by the young woman who has bought a hat from her, and the young woman's escort, who has murmured a word of flattery to Rosabel during the

1. An English socialist weekly, in which Mansfield published many of her early stories.
2. *Collected Letters*, vol. 1, p. 19.
3. Fortune-teller, entertainer.
4. When Mansfield returned to London from Wellington in 1908, she first stayed at a student hostel near Paddington Station.

transaction. Rosabel is a girl who buys violets rather than a proper evening meal, who despises the advertisements in the bus and the cheap romance being read by another girl, and who laughs at the memory of her stupid customers; but the banality of her own imagination is not glossed over. She sustains herself in a bleak life—picking her way through the mud of the London streets endlessly, not having enough to eat, living in an uncomfortable and lonely room—with dreams. And here the story bites, for the dreams that sustain Rosabel also make her vulnerable since, it is implied, the only escape from the humiliating realities of her life lies through the admiration of the sort of men who accompany young ladies into the shop where she works, and spare her an appraising glance. No harm is done in the story but to Rosabel's imagination, which has in any case been given nothing else to turn to but thin fantasy; it is not terrifying, like the end of 'The Little Governess', where the heroine is brought to the brink of the pit, but neither is it a simple, tender-hearted tale.

The relationship between dreams and danger appears again in 'Frau Brechenmacher Attends a Wedding'. The name of the heroine and some of the physical details are taken from Bad Wörishofen[5], but the story is about something much more general: about the bullying of a young woman, and about the echo it draws from the mind of the older woman called on to observe it. The bitterness of Frau Brechenmacher lies in the contrast between the emotions that are supposed to be aroused by a wedding and the actual occasion under observation, which is one of gross maltreatment. A simple young unmarried mother is being married off to a man she does not like; the woman who observes it, a good solid wife and mother of five, finds herself remembering more than she really cares to about her own wedding. (When one reflects that Katherine herself had, at the time of writing, been recently rejected by her own solid, bourgeois mother[6] of five, 'Frau Brechenmacher' speaks volumes for her power to abstract herself from personal experience.)

The thread of Mansfield's own experience runs through most of her stories, and yet very few of them are autobiographical in a strict sense, and her 'German' stories are not necessarily about Germany at all. 'Frau Brechenmacher' is a cry against the stupidity and brutality of men and the women who support their arrangements, through sentimentality or weakness; it is is written with feminist rage, and is clearly protective towards its matronly heroine, showing how her complicity in the degrading wedding celebrations has come about

5. In Bavaria, Germany, where Mansfield lived for several months in 1909.
6. Annie Beauchamp, provoked by Mansfield's one-day marriage in March 1909 and suspecting a lesbian relationship as well, sailed to England, accompanied her daughter to Germany, then returned to New Zealand, where she cut Katherine out of her will.

through the way in which she too had been made a victim. * * *

'The Swing of the Pendulum', while it takes up the themes of vulnerable women and brutal men, is really remarkable for something else again. It is a study in self-knowledge; the observer of the satirical early stories (such as 'Bains Turcs', a cheerful, savage blast against prurience) turns her sardonic eye on herself to devastating effect. The scene is, as in Rosabel, a single room high up in a house where the heroine has taken lodgings. She is penniless, alone, waiting for her lover to arrive (clearly Katherine is drawing on the year 1909 when she wandered in Europe). The landlady is mistrustful and abusive, as a landlady of that period would be towards a young woman with no visible means of support. The girl's self-dramatization is one theme: her rapidly and comically changing spectrum of feelings about the landlady, about the absent lover Casimir, about the other man who arrives, about the room, the weather, her plight. The other theme is the way in which she deals with her situation in practice. She has a series of encounters. The first is a spirited one with the landlady, the second a straightforward one with an unexpected and unknown caller. Then, in an interlude, she recreates this man and his possibilities in her imagination; she will get something out of him, he is a glamorous and worldly creature who will help her, and so on. Summoning him back, she finds of course that he does not treat her at all as she hoped, but as a prostitute. For a moment she is in real danger; there is a sexual struggle from which she saves herself only by biting through his glove to his hand so that she hurts and frightens him in turn. He leaves. And then instantly her thoughts fly to Casimir who—the reader knows—is going to be little more support than the visitor. For all her resourcefulness and courage, she cannot resist the idea that some man will smooth her path. It is a vital and intelligent piece of writing, physically vivid and unsettling in its clear-sighted account of its high-spirited and appallingly vulnerable heroine.

* * *

It is this same cool reporter's eye that makes 'An Indiscreet Journey' so interesting, because in this case she is observing nothing less than the 1914–18 war in action, not in its heroics or horror even, but in the casualness, the muddle and confusion of the French army just behind the lines in 1915, the brief look at the weedy soldier with the bandage newly removed from his eyes who cannot control their watering as he sits in a café. Madame behind the till comments on his disgustingness:

> '*Mais vous savez, c'est un peu dégoûtant, ça,*[7] she said severely.
> '*Ah, oui, Madame,*' answered the soldiers, watching her bent

7. "But you know, it's a little disgusting, that."

head and pretty hands, as she arranged for the hundredth time a frill of lace on her lifted bosom.

This story is directly drawn from her own experience, when she made a visit to her lover Francis Carco while he was serving at Gray, near Dijon, on the Saône. The foolhardy journey into the war zone was carried out in a spirit of reckless adventurousness; Katherine had wanted an erotic adventure and fancied herself in love. By the time she came to write, her feelings for Carco had been brushed aside; he became the 'little corporal' with curly lashes, the least significant feature of the story. Almost banishing the personal and romantic, Mansfield has drawn instead a picture of the interaction of civilian and military life in which irreverence for the great theme of war and insistence on detail captures a vanished moment of history. There are not many war stories by women; this is a little classic.

KATE FULLBROOK

[Freedom and Confinement]†

* * *

'The Tiredness of Rosabel' marks the start of Katherine Mansfield's mature writing. Although it was composed in 1908 it was not published until 1924 in the posthumous volume, *Something Childish*, which included many of Katherine Mansfield's previously uncollected early stories. The subject is a crucial one for feminist writers—the contrast between the material conditions and the dream life of a working girl. In the story, Katherine Mansfield works the same ground as that in Henry James's fine *nouvelle*[1] of 1898, *In the Cage*, uncovering the fantasies that support and make tolerable the otherwise crushing conditions of exploitation which entrap the girl. Katherine Mansfield stresses the connection between the economic function of her tired Rosabel, a milliner at the end of a long day, and her daydreams which pathetically uphold the whole sexual and social structure that degrades her.

The story begins with an account of Rosabel's return from the shop to her sad fourth-floor room. The girl, for all the expendable anonymity of her position in society, has a hunger for beauty for which she pays heavily—she buys a bunch of violets in spite of only being left with enough money for a meagre tea. As she drags

† From *Katherine Mansfield* (Brighton: The Harvester Press, 1986), pp. 36–38, 96–102.

1. Long short story. Henry James (1843–1916), American novelist who spent most of his adult life in England or on the Continent.

through London on her way home, the city is presented in two series of images, both representing the girl's perceptions. The first series stresses crowding, ugliness and dirt, and is summed up by a description of Rosabel's wet feet, and her skirt and petticoat's coating of 'black greasy mud'. The other is a function of the girl's consciousness too, which oscillates between her unhealthy lack of basic material needs (her first daydream is of food: 'roast duck and green peas, chestnut stuffing, pudding with brandy sauce') and her lack of excitement, pleasure and beauty. Rosabel's mind provides her with what is palpably not there to satisfy her in the physical world. She interprets the scene she sees through the steamed windows of a crowded bus as magical: everything seem 'blurred and misty, but light striking on the panes turned their dullness to opal and silver, and the jewellers' shops seen through this, were fairy palaces.' What is important here is Rosabel's consciousness as she infuses the wet city with the glamour that satisfies her craving for something other than the life she actually leads.

Katherine Mansfield picks up the symbol of the violets and meshes it with a typical incident in the milliner's working day for the central daydream of the story. The handsome, rich young couple that Rosabel has waited on during the day becomes a starting-point for her tired, slightly feverish fantasies. She imagines herself changing places with the rich woman; the handsome young man brings her masses of Parma violets, feeds her luxuriously, keeps her warm, dry, loves her, marries her. Katherine Mansfield inserts a brilliantly placed aside into the daydream at the moment of sexual surrender—'(The real Rosabel, the girl crouched on the floor in the dark, laughed aloud and put her hand up to her hot mouth).' Having drawn her emotional sustenance from her dream, Rosabel pulls her grimy quilt around her neck and goes to sleep, waking only to smile as she shivers in the 'grey light' of dawn in the 'dull room'.

The intersection of the daydream's comforts with Rosabel's real needs makes the fantasy more than a condescending excursion into the clichés of 'silver-spoon' romance, though the fact that Katherine Mansfield used these clichés to populate her character's mind is itself as much her comment on the power of entrenched imaginative forms to control the contents of consciousness as it is an attack on the final cruelty of such images as drugs for the minds of oppressed women. The young Katherine Mansfield recognised the *function* of trash romance for women (whose elements have not significantly changed), which invites dreams of being the perfect beneficiaries of the sexual system that in fact victimises them. Rosabel is part of a complex social system in which she works and suffers so that rich women may catch their rich men. But there are other impulses revealed as well. Rosabel's need for beauty in her life is as real to her as her need for food. The crudities of her day-dream are the semi-conscious expression of needs that are reflected in buying the violets and in her vision of the opalescent city for which there is no outlet for her except in dreams. The discontinuity between what Rosabel 'knows' at one level and what she 'dreams of' on another level of her consciousness is, as much as the wet clothes and lack of food, part of the reason for the fever, the slight hysteria that the narrator implies is the representative state of the trapped working girl, 'the girl crouched on the floor in the dark'. The inaccessibility of the meaning of the story, with its two disparate sets of images that only the reader can pull together, to the consciousness of the central character forms a crucial aspect of the story's meaning. It marks Katherine Mansfield's engagement from the first with experimental narration as part of her commitment to speak truly of the lives of women.

* * *

In talking about sexual response herself, Katherine Mansfield works closely to the conventions of obliqueness that characterised nineteenth-century fiction—conventions of metaphor and symbolic suggestion that point to the inextricability of body and mind in desire, rather than adopting the twentieth-century 'empirical' conventions that represent sexual activity as a collision of bodies—mechanical and unproblematic occasions for the manufacture of 'natural', physiological pleasure. * * * This does not mean that Katherine Mansfield was not interested in the subject, she would scarcely belong to this century if she were not. But the *kind* of account she gives of desire works in a different direction to that of most other modernist writers.

'Bliss' takes account of the impact of socially dictated patterns which structure the individual's conception of what should legitimately satisfy desire, and enacts the wonder and distress that follows from an awakening to the insufficiency of those definitions. Katherine Mansfield sees desire as diffuse and unpredictable, and in the story shows her awareness of the fine mesh of social definition that is supposed to contain, express and control the desires of an advanced, western woman.

It is because of this social theme that 'Bliss' is crowded with people, in this case members of a smart London arty set, the kind of sophisticated social group that Katherine Mansfield often pilloried. The bantering cleverness of her satire of the set—Mrs Norman Knight, with her coat patterned with monkeys, plays crudely for shock value; Eddie Warren enthuses about a line in the latest poem in the latest review: ' "Why Must it Always be Tomato Soup?" '—

gives a representation in the narrative of the pretensions it mocks. The group is wrapped in conventions, though it takes itself to be frightfully liberated and knowing.

Liberation and knowledge are exactly what are in question for Bertha Young, the thirty-year-old hostess of the party that takes place in the story and whose consciousness is reflected in the writing. As far as she consciously knows, she has everything she has been told she could want:

> She was young. Harry and she were as much in love as ever, and they got on splendidly and were really good pals. She had an adorable baby. They didn't have to worry about money. They had this absolutely satisfactory house and garden. And friends—modern thrilling friends, writers and painters and poets and people keen on social questions—just the kind of friends they wanted. And then there were books, and there was music, and she had found a wonderful little dressmaker, and they were going abroad in the summer and their new cook made the most superb omelettes . . .

As she consciously rifles through her assets, Bertha tries hard to find the item that will 'prove' to herself she is happy. The barely suppressible waves of emotion that Bertha identifies as 'bliss' at the opening of the story are really signs of the hysteria that threatens to overcome her and that negates her conviction of well-being. She feels that this 'bliss', despite her modern 'freedom', is something she must hide:

> Oh, is there no way you can express it without being 'drunk and disorderly?' How idiotic civilisation is! Why be given a body if you have to keep it shut up in a case like a rare, rare fiddle?

The story makes it clear that Bertha is caught between two 'civilised' conventions of female desire—the convention that outlaws women's physicality as taboo and unnatural, and, on the other hand, the alternative 'modern' convention that speaks endlessly of desire, defining it and channelling it into patterns that may not accord with individual experience. Even though Bertha's life is supposedly so free, it is, in fact, arranged so that she is restrained from physical contacts of all kinds, though the *talk* about such satisfactions is endless. The result is that the physical contacts she does make electrify her.

Katherine Mansfield deploys various emblems of female sexuality through the story and shows Bertha responding to them. Arranging bowls of fruit becomes such a sensuous activity that Bertha can hardly control herself. Being allowed to feed her baby, who is really 'mothered' by a nurse, pushes her again to the brink of hysteria. As much in control of the imagery as in 'Prelude', Katherine Mansfield provides the analogues to the danger of sensuous response that so torments Bertha in images of the 'wild' life of the animals and plants that persist in their elemental forms in the city. Even in Bertha's bright modern world, in which consciousness is supposed to have banished secrets, there is her garden, full of its own life in the dusk of her psyche:

> At the far end, against the wall, there was a tall, slender pear tree in the fullest, richest bloom; it stood perfect, as though becalmed against the jade-green sky. Bertha couldn't help feeling, even from this distance, that it had not a single bud or faded petal. Down below, in the garden beds, the red and yellow tulips, heavy with flowers, seemed to lean upon the dusk. A grey cat, dragging its belly, crept across the lawn, and a black one, its shadow, trailed after. The sight of them, so intent and quick, gave Bertha a curious shudder.

Bertha attempts a 'modern' reaction to the scene. ' "What a creepy thing cats are!" she stammered.' The garden, with its flaming Blakean pear tree, heavy Rubensesque tulips and Lawrencian cats, is redolent with sexual suggestion for Bertha, who only unconsciously registers her response to the scene. The image is well chosen. The walled garden itself has been a classic image for unawakened female sexuality since the Middle Ages: here it works as a feature of Bertha's ordinary landscape that suddenly explodes into meaning for her. Katherine Mansfield makes all these associations work in this metaphorical garden of the unawakened woman. The paradox is that Bertha's 'fast' set bases its swagger on its freedom regarding sexual matters. Bertha's acquiescence to these mores is, then, radically fraudulent, though she does not know this. Everything she is is based on a lack of knowledge.

Bertha dresses for her party in the colours of her garden, the bridal colours of white and green of the pear tree and the sky. If Bertha is dressed as a bride, her most interesting guest, Pearl Fulton, is dressed in the silvery, pearly colours of the moon, echoing primitive connections between the moon and full female sexuality.[2] While the dinner guests jabber on (' "Isn't she very *liée* with Michael Oat?" "The man who wrote *Love in False Teeth*?" '), Bertha feels herself in sudden, wordless intimacy with Pearl who surveys the scene indirectly through 'heavy eyelids'. Her bedroom eyes and bedroom manner work powerfully on Bertha who is pulled toward her. Again the 'bliss' returns and Bertha looks for a sign that Pearl

2. See Cherry Hankin, *Katherine Mansfield and Her Confessional Stories* (London: Macmillan, 1983) pp. 144–45.

has also felt the disturbing link between them. Bertha tries to account for her feelings: 'I believe this does happen very, very rarely between women. Never between men,' she thinks while looking again for a sign from the first adult object of her newly awakened but misunderstood desire. Pearl gives the sign. She asks to see Bertha's garden.

> 'Have you a garden?' said the cool, sleepy voice.
>
> This was so exquisite on her part that all Bertha could do was to obey. She crossed the room, pulled the curtains apart, and opened those long windows.
>
> 'There!' she breathed.
>
> And the two women stood side by side looking at the slender flowering tree. Although it was so still it seemed, like the flame of a candle, to stretch up, to point, to quiver in the bright air, to grow taller and taller as they gazed—almost to touch the rim of the round, silver moon.
>
> How long did they stand there? Both, as it were, caught in that circle of unearthly light, understanding each other perfectly, creatures of another world, and wondering what they were to do in this one with all this blissful treasure that burned in their bosoms, and dropped, in silver flowers, from their hair and hands.

Or so Bertha interprets their communion. The reader, of course, is meant to see things differently. While Bertha dramatically reveals the garden of her sexual potential in triumph to a creature who has finally become the focus for her crystallised desire in a way that Bertha herself does not understand, she does not know that she is standing with a woman who is already emblematically identified with the full moon high above the garden, and already in her own communion with the phallic implications of the pear tree which Bertha disregards, but which are also a part of its significance. Symbolically, both women are bathed in the light of the moon of female sexuality, but Pearl already *is* the moon; Bertha is merely the guardian of a garden, hidden behind windows and curtains, stunned by the moon's light.

Bertha's free-flowing sexual response moves from Pearl to her own husband. For the first time she desires him. As she takes cognisance of this amazing new sensation, she identifies the source of the 'bliss' she has been fighting back. And as she looks around to take possession of him when the guests leave, she sees him kissing Pearl. They are lovers. She understands that she has discovered her sexuality only in time to see its first two objects already in full possession of the pleasure she is only on the threshold of knowing. Bertha is left alone, on the edge of an abyss, her bliss turned to dismay, and with the pear tree, bisexual emblem of her just discovered sexual need, 'as lovely as ever and as full of flower and as still.'

The ending is one of absolute and bleak exclusion; the outlets for Bertha's belated sexual flowering are suddenly blocked; a possibility is left senseless and dead in her hands. Katherine Mansfield's simultaneous control of a Jazz Age story as characteristic of the period as F. Scott Fitzgerald's,[3] and of a deep structure drawing on a pattern of images that effortlessly shapes the story demonstrates the power of her late technique. The symbols are selected and placed with great tact and evocativeness, suggesting their multiple meanings without ever insisting on them. (For example, Pearl is associated with the moon but also with the grey cat dragging its belly through Bertha's walled garden, her sexuality seen as both utterly transcendent and utterly sordid. At the same time the moon and the cat are both functions of Bertha's unconscious, overdetermined in their meaning by her heightened emotional state.) But the most telling aspect of the story is the ending, with Bertha pushed from the chatter of her self-consciously modern, sophisticated life into the internal crisis whose source she has just discovered and whose cure was theoretically within her reach until the moment she was ready to grasp it.

The double structure of symbol and social critique provides two axes along which Katherine Mansfield can make her observations about the cultural base of women's psychology. Modern assumptions about sex are indirectly shown to be ill-suited to understanding the waywardness and unpredictability of individual response. The 'advanced' notions of the 'Bliss' clique are as useless as the more traditional orthodoxy operative in most of the other stories. The ethical undertones of the story are still more complex. 'Bliss' not only raises difficult questions about loyalties inside and outside of marriage and that place that sexuality holds within it, but also about the kind of freedom enacted as self-serving practice. Betrayed by both male and female, and part of a set that would not recognise Pearl and Harry's affair as betrayal at all, Bertha's distress must be masked by the hypocrisy of a social posture of openness. Superficial poses of freedom lead here to inauthenticity as surely as surfaces of repression do. The group still closes ranks against the outsider. Bertha is a victim of a psychological game she had no conscious idea she was playing.

* * *

3. F. Scott Fitzgerald (1896–1940), American novelist and short story writer. One of his books, *Tales of the Jazz Age*, 1922, gave the descriptive phrase to the decade that followed World War One.

SYDNEY JANET KAPLAN

[Sex, Danger, Freedom]†

* * * "Prelude" [is] an awakening into female sexuality. It is also a rejection of male modes, and this strategy is apparent in its all-over structure: its multiplicity, its fluidity, its lack of a central climax, and its many moments of encoded sexual pleasure. What makes "Prelude" so revolutionary as a narrative is its implicit statement that the construction of gender should be the motivating center of the text. The technical innovations are devices to reveal this process of reproduction. Reproduction in several forms dominates the text: in terms of procreation—Linda's pregnancy, the blossoming of the aloe; re-production of gender roles in the games of the children and in Kezia's questioning about sexual differences; and the re-production of bourgeois family life in the interactions of the family members as they respond to the pressures of their "roles." This reproduction assumes the continued dominance of the patriarchal society—the dominance of Stanley as businessman, rule-maker, center of authority—and it occurs in a world of upward mobility—"fleets of aloes," more children, more property. And it relies on the proficiency of the matriarchal center in Mrs. Fairfield: her managing, bringing order, situating the process of reproduction within an aesthetically satisfying and efficient home. But "Prelude" also reveals that a counter-process of resistance and rebellion is always at work within these dynamics. Linda's resistance counters Stanley's demands, but ineffectively. Hers is primarily a negative force: passive resistance. The imaginative powers necessary for active rebellion are not brought into force. She fantasizes escape but cannot envision what shape it should take. Yet the imaginative powers, the talents she will never develop, are also in her daughter Kezia, who shares so many of her mother's internal responses: fears of rushing animals, a sense of things coming alive through a force that Kezia calls "It" and Linda, "THEY."

Three modes of female sexual response are suggested in this story: First, Linda's initial attraction to sexuality (the baby bird in her dream), revulsion when the bird swells, and fear when it turns into a human baby; second, Beryl's fantasies of romance, centered in self-love, narcissism, and envy, a body-consciousness purely visual—specular. The third response is that of Kezia, the child not yet completely gendered, who longs for her grandmother's arms, to

† From *Katherine Mansfield and the Origins of Modernist Fiction* (Ithaca and London: Cornell University Press, 1991), pp. 114–22.

be stroked and to stroke, to experience the tactile pleasures. She is still polymorphous, responsive to a whole range of stimuli. But she already fears any that might overpower her. Her sexuality requires mutuality, not assault.

* * *

In "Prelude" we are presented with multiple viewpoints, nearly all those of female characters. Only the short sections from the point of view of the father, Stanley Burnell, allow for the intrusion of the masculine. His consciousness works as counterpoint in a minor key. It strikes me that the story is structured like a female organism (which invariably contains some subordinated masculine characteristics). In working on this story, nearly a decade before Woolf's *Mrs. Dalloway*, Mansfield was already attempting a spatial rendering of a few days in the inner lives of her characters (she was even closer to Woolf's technique in revealing several minds living through *one* day in the later story about the Burnells, "At the Bay").

Remarkable as it is as a piece of experimental fiction, "Prelude" is even more immediately accessible to us as an exploration of feminine consciousness. Within the story Mansfield grapples with her own relationships with the members of her family—mother, father, grandmother, aunt, sisters. It is her most directly autobiographical story, but she discovers a way of exploring these relationships without centering them in the mind of a fictional alter ego. Although the child, Kezia, is a re-creation of the author herself, Kezia's consciousness is but one focus of attention in the story. Mansfield establishes connections, psychic connections that link all of the female characters. The overriding theme of the story is female sexual identity. Linda Burnell, Kezia's mother, strains against her given role and does not want to be a mother. She avoids her children and dreads the sexuality that might lead to the birth of yet another one. She thinks of her husband with a mixture of affection and revulsion: "For all her love and respect and admiration she hated him. And how tender he always was after times like those, how submissive, how thoughtful. . . . There were all her feelings for him, sharp and defined, one as true as the other. And there was this other, this hatred, just as real as the rest."

Linda's ambivalence toward her role is one possible direction for female sexual identity which Mansfield explores in this story. Linda's unmarried sister Beryl represents another. Her outlet is fantasy; she imagines a lover while she gazes at herself in the mirror for self-gratification. And yet another direction is embodied in the grandmother, who represents the earlier, more traditional generation and totally accepts her role. She gives Kezia the affection she craves and is always generous, practical, hard-working, and sensitive to everyone's feelings. Kezia adores her grandmother, but

Mansfield makes us see that Kezia shares more deeply the fearsome personal isolation and acute imagination of the mother she does not really know very well than the placid, assured rootedness of the grandmother she hugs, strokes, and calls her "Indian brave."

Early in the story Kezia asks the storeman the difference between a ram and a sheep, expressing the central question of her awakening consciousness. The storeman, embarrassed, typically avoids the truth by saying, "well, a ram has horns and runs for you." But Kezia intuitively knows what he means:

> "I don't want to see it frightfully," she said. "I hate rushing animals like dogs and parrots. I often dream that animals rush at me—even camels—and while they are rushing, their heads swell e-enormous."

Kezia's language here is nearly identical to her mother's later in the story when she alludes to her husband with:

> If only he wouldn't jump at her so, and bark so loudly, and watch her with such eager, loving eyes. He was too strong for her; she had always hated things that rush at her, from a child.

Such similar thought patterns establish a psychic connection between mother and daughter deeper than the external aloofness of their behavior with each other. "Prelude" is filled with points of connection like this one: images repeated in new contexts, phrases echoed or parodied by different characters, daydreams merging into waking reality.

"Prelude" breaks the form of the *bildungsroman* but is a narrative of *bildung* nonetheless. The spatial organization suggests simultaneity, but the typical linear pattern of individual development is rather spread out among the female characters, who tend to represent the central consciousness at various stages of her life: early childhood, late adolescence, young motherhood, and old age. The child, aunt, mother, and grandmother embody the female life cycle. But the inevitability of the continuation of conventional female roles seems implicit in this structuring. The only opening is for Kezia, the child yet unformed, but already containing within herself the inner structure to be unfolded.

* * *

Not long before Katherine Mansfield began to write the first chapters of *The Aloe* (spring 1915), she completed a story similarly innovative in technique: "The Little Governess." If *The Aloe* seems a response to memories of childhood, questions of engendering, and women's relations with one another, "The Little Governess" seems a response to women's victimization, isolation, and lack of support for one another. "The Little Governess" serves as a reminder of the difficulties Mansfield faced as a woman alone, traveling abroad, difficulties that competed for attention with her attempts to write her retrospective probings of a family-centered, less alienated environment.

"The Little Governess" belongs with the "realistic" rather than "aesthetic" strand of Mansfield's thematic concerns as a writer of fiction; it focuses on the vulnerability of women in a world dominated by male power. As I discussed in relation to Mansfield's difficulties with the *bildungsroman*, this subject is bound to the female line of influence, the tradition of women's writing which is enmeshed in a conflict of competing fictional conventions. "The Little Governess" follows a line of development in Mansfield's work originating with "Juliet" (1906–1907)[1] and "The Tiredness of Rosabel" (1908) and continuing in some of the stories in her first published collection, *In a German Pension* (1911). But "The Little Governess" is more sophisticated in both technique and psychology than these. * * * Ian Gordon dates Mansfield's "new method" of writing fiction to "The Little Governess," although he sees the earlier version of "Prelude" as the place where "she finally broke through to a new structure and a new technique."[2] The story is centered in the protagonist's perceptions and holds the reader tightly within her misconceptions of reality. However, by situating this young female protagonist in an alien environment, alone, without the traditionally supportive interactions of female community, Mansfield exposes women's vulnerability in the world of men. Aside from the kind stewardess in the "Ladies Cabin" on the evening boat, who serves as a watchful, maternal figure, with "a long piece of knitting on her lap," no women protect the governess on her journey to Bavaria. Like Kezia in "Prelude," fearful of things "rushing" at her, "the little governess" fears "a stamping of feet and men's voices." Men are again intruders in Mansfield's fictional world: they are loud; they push their way in; they rush at you.

The old man on the train seems in counterpoint to *** the grandmother whose protective arms symbolized maternal love for Kezia. Kindly, sentimental, on the surface the old man appears capable of providing a masculine form of sympathy complementary to that of Mrs. Fairfield. Sylvia Berkman, writing in 1951, believed that Mansfield had shifted her attitude in this story "from that of the early German stories with their fierce antagonism against the male, for although the little governess is set upon by a philandering old gentleman, we are given to see clearly that her own ignorance

1. An early story, unpublished until the *Turnbull Library Record* 3.1 (March 1970): 7–28 [*Editor*].
2. Ian A. Gordon, ed., *Undiscovered Country: The New Zealand Stories of Katherine Mansfield* (London: Longman, 1974), p. xix.

and unworldliness largely bring about her discomfiture."[3] Feminist theory helps us interpret Mansfield's response in a different way. In fact, she is even more antagonistic against the male here than she was in many of the earlier stories. For by now, she appears to understand that the victimization of women by men is systemic and that "blaming the victim"—as Berkman's reading tends to do by suggesting that the little governess brings on her own catastrophe—merely ignores the methods that patriarchal ideology sets in place to condition the dependency of women. The "ignorance and unworldliness" that Berkman describes are the end result of that conditioning, which sets women up to fail. The little governess is not merely an emblem of woman as victim, but a representation of ideology's construction of woman as a *target* for victimization. Engendering, therefore, is as much a theme of this story as it is of "Prelude."

Treated to an education compiled of warnings, women are punished when they assert themselves beyond those strictures, when they seek freedom and adventure. The story begins with exactly such warnings. "Don't go out of the carriage . . . *be sure* to lock the lavatory door," the young woman is cautioned at the Governess Bureau; "it's better to mistrust people at first rather than trust them." Her fear makes her tight, miserly, sure she is being taken advantage of. She refuses to give the porter his rightful tip, angers him, and "trembling with terror she screwed herself tight, tight, and put out an icy hand and took the money—stowed it away in her hand." She catches sight of herself in a mirror and sees that her face is white, her eyes round: " 'But it's all over now' she said to the mirror face, feeling in some way that it was more frightened than she." The mirror face is "more frightened"; it is separate from the governess herself. (This kind of dissociation of mind and body recurs with frequency in the thought patterns of Mansfield's women characters; it is notable in "Prelude" when Beryl holds a discussion with her own mirror face.)

Her rudeness to the porter disregarded, the little governess settles into a false security on the train: "She looked out from her safe corner, frightened no longer but proud that she had not given that franc. 'I can look after myself—of course I can.' " But she fears the young men in the compartment next door, whose "singing gave her a queer little tremble in her stomach," and is relieved when an old man arrives to share her compartment.

Mansfield gives us the mixed point of view of a narrator who sees only part of the truth—almost with the naiveté of the young woman

3. Sylvia Berkman, *Katherine Mansfield: A Critical Study* (New Haven: Yale University Press, 1951), p. 80.

herself. But the imagery reveals more than the governess can understand about herself:

> How kindly the old man in the corner watched her bare little hand turning over the . . . pages, watched her lips moving as she pronounced the long words to herself, rested upon her hair that fairly blazed under the light. Alas! how tragic for a little governess to possess hair that made one think of tangerines and marigolds, of apricots and tortoise-shell cats and champagne! Perhaps that was what the old man was thinking as he gazed and gazed, and that not even the dark ugly clothes could disguise her soft beauty. Perhaps the flush that licked his cheeks and lips was a flush of rage that anyone so young and tender should have to travel alone and unprotected through the night. Who knows he was not murmuring in his sentimental German fashion: *"Ja, est is eine Tragodie!"*

In whose mind are these thoughts formulated? Would the little governess have described herself with such sensuous imagery? Would she have moved her gaze from hand to lips to hair? At this moment there is no mirror available to capture her self-admiration, her pleasure in narcissistic self-objectification. As a matter of fact, her pleasure is increased by the mirror's absence and the accompanying freedom to indulge her powers of imagination, which provoke her drastic misreading of the old man's gestures. This seeming pleasure, however, is the sign of how deeply she is entrapped in what Luce Irigaray calls the "dominant scopic economy."[4] She must become the object of desire for the other, the passive recipient of the other's lust. Ignorant of the nature of female sexuality, which Irigaray believes "takes pleasure more from touching than from looking," she distorts it and projects it into the innocent-seeming, grandfatherly gaze of the stranger. In a sense she transports herself into a creature looking *through* the old man's eyes, as the following description of the young woman's response to the old man's gift of fresh strawberries suggests: "They were so big and juicy she had to take two bites to them—the juice ran all down her fingers—and it was while she munched the berries that she first thought of the old man as a grandfather."

So the association made first by the narrator, who only surmises (for we never actually penetrate the mind of the old man), is made explicit as the governess eats and the old man tells her that it has been twenty years since he "was brave enough to eat strawberries." * * * The charged sexuality of this encounter may be unconsciously perceived by the young woman who misplaces its meaning. The old man asks: "Are they good? . . . As good as they look?" The

4. Luce Irigaray, *This Sex Which Is Not One* (Ithaca: Cornell University Press, 1985), p. 26.

governess really *wants* pleasure, life, excitement, and gives in to these desires as she relaxes her guard. For after all, she *loves* the strawberries. And after she agrees to the old man's invitation, "the little governess gave herself up to the excitement of being really abroad, to looking out and reading the foreign advertisement signs, to being told about the places they came to—having her attention and enjoyment looked after by the charming old grandfather." By giving "herself up" to the agency of the old man, she loses her own. The sentence poses her in dependency: "being told about," "having her attention . . . looked after." Consequently, her pleasured passivity is destroyed by the old man's attempted sexual assault. After running away from his apartment, she boards a tram and carries with her an image, a physical one, of "a world full of old men with twitching knees." In a flamboyant metonymic transposition, Mansfield describes a woman on the tram who notices the upset young woman and says to her companion, "She has been to the dentist." The substitution of body parts could not be more appropriately euphemized: the governess has been assaulted in either case. Once again, in Mansfield's fiction, sexuality is dangerous, and a woman becomes a coconspirator in her own destruction when she incorporates the ideology of her oppressor into her sense of identity.[5]

I have no doubt that the technical advance of "The Little Governess"—noticeable in its sophisticated and intricate interplay between a diffused narrative voice and a character's stream of consciousness, and also in its skillful yet unobtrusive handling of sexual symbolism—is a function of Mansfield's struggle to discover narrative techniques to convey the contradictions and ambiguities of women's encounters with the world at large. She needed to find a method flexible enough to incorporate both a character's self-division and her self-deception, both her impulses toward freedom and her conditioned responses of self-denial.

PAMELA DUNBAR

[Violence and Power in Mansfield Stories]†

* * *

'Millie' * * * investigates what becomes of femaleness and female identity in the outback—this time through an investigation of

5. In an earlier story, "Millie," Mansfield shows a woman joining in the bloodlust of men who try to capture a young fugitive to whom she has been sympathetically—and sexually—attracted.

† From *Radical Mansfield: Double Discourse in Katherine Mansfield's Short Stories* (London: Macmillan, 1997), pp. 54–57, 100–104. Reprinted by permission of Palgrave Macmillan. All notes are the Editor's.

the emotional trajectory of the heroine, a farmer's wife, through a day in which she is left alone at home while her husband joins in the hunt for a young Englishman presumed to have murdered a neighbour.

After seeing the husband off, Millie retreats to their bedroom and gazes at herself in the fly-specked mirror. Her gaze explores, not her physical image but her state of mind—the way she is feeling. However, her consciousness, like Underwood's,[1] is unreflective, and leaves her unenlightened: 'She didn't know what was the matter with herself that afternoon. She could have a good cry—just for nothing—and then change her blouse and have a cup of tea'.

Next her attention is caught by a couple of pictures on the walls. One is a print of a Windsor Castle (*sic*) garden party, with emerald lawns and oak trees and gracious gentlemen and ladies in the foreground, and the head of Queen Victoria superimposed; the other, a photograph of Millie herself and her husband Sid on their wedding day. Here the background is a distinctively New Zealand one (though it is just as opposed to the burning landscape of the story's opening as to that of the garden party): 'behind them were some fern trees and a waterfall, and Mount Cook in the distance, covered with snow.'

Taken together, the pictures offer a clue to Millie's predicament. For, like a similar pair of pictures in the home of the Woman at the Store, they indicate the cultural and social gulf between New Zealand and the far-off country from which its settlers derive their origins, and which in those days they called home. There is also a marked contrast between the ceremonial 'showpiece' occasions rendered with painstaking realism in the pictures, and the emotions which the tale conveys—raw, unstable, unreasoning, unpredictable. Millie the colonial even doubts the veracity of the garden party print: ' "I wonder if it really looked like that." '

When she eventually finds a young man lying prostrate in the yard outside, her earlier feeling of unease switches abruptly to one of rage. But as she gazes intently at him she discovers what she had been unable to find in her own mirror—a figure of vulnerable and suffering, humanity. She feels his heart then offers him brandy and water. As she comforts him she experiences another change in mood—this time to tenderness. The change is rendered as a painful and unaccustomed, insemination:

> A strange dreadful feeling gripped Millie Evans' bosom—some seed that had never flourished there, unfolded and struck deep roots and burst into painful leaf. 'Are yer coming round? Feeling all right again?'

1. The old man and murderer in "Ole Underwood."

Millie's new-found tenderness comes about because of the stranger's youthfulness and childlike helplessness, but it is also the result of her own frustrated urge towards motherhood. This has already been highlighted—significantly, just before she sensed the presence of the young man in her yard:

> 'I wunner why we never had no kids. . . .' She shrugged her shoulders—gave it up. 'Well, *I've* never missed them. I wouldn't be surprised if Sid had, though. He's softer than me.'

When it eventually dawns on her that her visitor is the 'English johnny' who is wanted for murder she at first determines to stand by him. Yet late that night, when he is heard trying to make his escape and the hunting-party charges after him, her mood again switches—this time from protectiveness to the primitive elation of pursuit:

> at the sight of Harrison in the distance, and the three men hot after, a strange mad joy smothered everything else. She rushed into the road—she laughed and shrieked and danced in the dust, jigging the lantern. 'A—ah!! Arter 'im, Sid! A—a—a—h! Ketch him, Willie. Go it! Go it! A—ah, Sid! Shoot 'im down. Shoot 'im!'

With her night-dress flicking her legs—goading her on as it were—and shrieking a wild call of encouragement, Millie ends the tale as she began it ('My word! when they caught that young man! Well, you couldn't be sorry for a young fellow like that'—by supporting the hunting-down of Harrison. Except that now her support is fuelled by the dark elation of repressed feelings and the hunting instinct.

Her final shrieks of exhilaration have as little to do with the impartiality of justice as her earlier vows in support of Harrison. And even the notion of retributive justice, an ideal though a harsh one, is broken against the force (and gleefulness) of the characters' determination to pursue.

The fact that the fugitive is a citizen of old England as well as a suspected murderer makes the tale at another level an exposition of colonial/metropolitan oppositions and tensions. The alienation of Millie from her adoptive land has already been indicated in her unexplained childlessness—a condition which stands against the typically large pioneering family of history, but which for Mansfield is evidence of her heroine's alienation. Translated to a strange land she is unable either to bond with it or to commit herself to it—something the birth of a child might have implied.

It is moreover an *English* 'child' who awakens Millie's maternal feelings—a child of the nationality any son or daughter of hers, would have had if she or her parents or grandparents had remained 'at home' in England, and thus a further indication of her displacement.

But if a future in the adoptive country is to be entertained at all then any sentimental feeling for 'home' on the part of the settlers—represented in this tale by Millie's feelings for the Englishman—must be hunted down, and ruthlessly exterminated: hence her final, dramatic resort to bloodlust. Fundamentally she, like Ole Underwood, is in pursuit of her own 'weakness'.

In 'Millie' Mansfield shows how conventional primness operates even—perhaps especially—in the colonial world to repress the primitive and the instinctual. At the same time she demonstrates the strength of these urges. Both Millie's late-flowering tender impulses and her zeal for pursuit stem partly from her childlessness. They are also linked to the frigidity of her relations with her husband. Sexual inhibition is implied in a scatter of small details—the presence of the snow-covered Mount Cook in their wedding photograph and perhaps also the image of Queen Victoria, signifier of an age of sexual restraint, in the garden-party print; Millie's 'tight screw' of hair; the spark of interest she shows in the suggestively named Willie Cox ('Not a bad young fellow, Willie Cox, but a bit too free and easy for her taste'). These frustrations combine with the isolation and the masculine ethos of the colonial outback to drive Millie into apeing male behaviour—at the same time as she is seen to be playing out her most instinctual responses as a woman.

Nowhere of course does the story confirm the fugitive's guilt in the number that his pursuers—self-appointed agents of summary justice—accuse him of: he has been convicted only by their settler animosity. In essence it is Millie and her friends who are the would-be murderers, their bloodthirsty behaviour which is under scrutiny; not his.

The colonial tales, then, reveal the complex psychological play which comes about as the settler struggles both to adapt to the new land and to develop a new psychology with which to confront it. The most significant aspect of this attempt has, in the intensely macho colonial world, to do with the debate between the sexes—or between gendered aspects of the personality. These tales are disturbing pieces which deal in discord and displacement, but also in disintegration: the conventional colonial tale of the physical struggle for survival has become in Mansfield's hands one for the survival of the reasoning and reasonable self—one in which even the prior existence of that self has been called into question.

Particularly intriguing is the case of Ole Underwood. * * * He is the one who is closest to disintegration—his inability to handle language and through this to re/construct his identity and his world indicate this. But he also serves as a counter-figure to later, Romantic and somewhat sentimentalised yarns by male New Zealand writers about what has become known as the 'man alone' type—the gruff but essentially goodhearted loner who ventures into the bush, endures, returns unscathed. Mansfield's rendering of the type exposes a darker truth—that of an incoherent and deranged figure whose eruption into the social arena, the town, triggers his final crackup.

* * * Mansfield also re-visions the genre of the colonial tale itself, inscribing into it a role for woman and the feminine principle and investing its bluff, blunt, action-oriented hero with a disturbed psychology. At the same time she makes use of the tales' strong narrative line and mystery elements to render what had often in her earlier works been unacknowledged material, as an integrated part of the text.

* * *

Two later stories, 'A Dill Pickle' (1917) and 'Psychology' (1919?), both published by 'Mansfield in her second collection, *Bliss*, also investigate the element of power in sexual relationships. Here, however, the issue is the socially sanctioned one of mental control, and there is a corresponding emphasis on psychological complexity.

'Psychology' is the more interesting of the two. It records a meeting between two lovers who * * * are a fashionably 'modern' couple, both writers, who attempt to live up to the rationalist ideal of a love-relationship based on 'pure' friendship.

The story deals in the gap between the couple's tranquil Platonist ideal[2] and their disturbingly passionate and complex feelings for each other. Though issues like domination, exploitation and passion are brushed aside by Mansfield's lovers, a deep-seated attachment to them remains, unsettling both their behaviour and their image of themselves.

The extent to which they are self-deceived is indicated in the ambivalence and inconsistency of their assertions. Here, for instance, is the woman rhapsodising to herself about the nature of their relationship:

> the special thrilling quality of their friendship was in their complete surrender. Like two open cities in the midst of some vast plain their two minds lay open to each other. And it wasn't as if he rode into hers like a conqueror, armed to the eyebrows and seeing nothing but a gay silken flutter—nor did she enter his like a queen walking soft on petals. No, they were eager, serious travellers, absorbed in understanding what was to be seen and discovering what was hidden—making the most of

2. A "platonic" friendship is one that is intense but not sexual, a meaning derived from an interpretation of the Greek philosopher Plato (c. 427–348 B.C.E.).

> this extraordinary absolute chance which made it possible for him to be utterly truthful to her and for her to be utterly sincere with him.

The image of the lovers' minds as 'two open cities in the midst of some vast plain' clearly conveys the aloofness and aridity of 'rational' friendship; and though rejected, the old romantic stereotypes (man as conqueror, woman as 'a queen walking on soft petals') remain seductive: what is more, they even suggest a solution to the lovers' dilemma—that of *mutual* conquest.

Later on, the man describes how he is entranced by the bust of a sleeping boy he has admired in the woman's studio:

> 'Often when I am away from here I revisit it in spirit—wander about among your red chairs, stare at the bowl of fruit on the black table—and just touch, very lightly, that marvel of a sleeping boy's head.'
>
> He looked at it as he spoke. It stood on the corner of the mantelpiece; the head to one side down-drooping, the lips parted, as though in sleep the little boy listened to some sweet sound. . . .
>
> 'I love that little boy,' he murmured. And then they both were silent.

The man's admission of an attachment to the statue—a hint either of homosexuality or of a devotion to high aestheticism, or most likely, in a shaft at Bloomsbury,[3] both—suggests deeper feelings. But these are again suppressed in the name of Platonic friendship.

Then the man, speaking with what sets itself up as the voice of propriety but which may well be a submission to more irrational or more complex feelings, abruptly declares his intention to leave.

The woman is deeply hurt by this apparent rejection. But then an adoring friend—an 'elderly virgin'—makes a chance call, offering a bunch of violets and a boost to her confidence. Having no deep emotional commitment the heroine finds it easy in this case both to demonstrate affection and to retain control. Moreover the meeting leads to her writing a warmly conciliatory letter to her lover: by increasing her—the woman lover's—self-esteem the 'elderly virgin' has enabled her to take the initiative with her man. In other words, the complexities of the relationship are not limited to the couple's own behaviour: an apparently uninvolved a third party—presumably based on Mansfield's friend Ida Constance Baker—has also had a critical effect.

The connection between the two episodes is signalled in the fact

3. An area in central London associated with the writers and intellectuals who lived there in the first half of the twentieth century. Mansfield satirized Bloomsbury in "Bliss" and "Marriage à la Mode."

that the heroine addresses both man and woman in the same way: ' "Good night, my friend. Come again soon." ' More importantly, there is also a link-passage—a scene that invades the heroine's consciousness as the man is taking his leave of her, and which returns as the 'elderly virgin' offers her gift:

> For a moment she did not take the violets. But while she stood just inside, holding the door, a strange thing happened. . . . Again she saw the beautiful fall of the steps, the dark garden ringed with glittering ivy, the willows, the big bright sky. Again she felt the silence that was like a question. But this time she did not hesitate. She moved forward. Very softly and gently, as though fearful of making a ripple in that boundless pool of quiet, she put her arms round her friend.

The setting itself however, another Eden scene with its references to a fall and a dark garden, to (poison) ivy and a (weeping) willow—the Book of Genesis was mentioned earlier in the sketch—does not augur well for the future course of the lovers' relationship. An earlier description of their misunderstandings has already made ironical reference to the labours of Adam and Eve:

> 'What a spectacle we have made of ourselves,' thought she. And she saw him laboriously—oh, laboriously—laying out the grounds and herself running after, putting here a tree and there a flowery shrub and here a handful of glittering fish in a pool. They were silent this time from sheer dismay.

And the pool-image recalls the description of the statue:

> That silence could be contained in the circle of warm, delightful fire and lamplight. How many times hadn't they flung something into it just for the fun of watching the ripples break on the easy shores. But into this unfamiliar pool the head of the little boy sleeping his timeless sleep dropped—and the ripples flowed away, away—boundlessly far—into deep glittering darkness.

Here the striking thing is how the 'circle of warm, delightful fire and lamplight' modulates into the depth-image of the pool—an analogue for the shift from the conscious to the unconscious mind; from the light of perception to the dark springs of action.

In an earlier conversation the lovers had touched upon the then avant-garde subject of 'psycho-analysis'—the only direct indication in any of Mansfield's writings that she was aware of Freud's work. The man praises the habit amongst his generation of writers of 'going into its symptoms—making an exhaustive study of them—tracking them down—trying to get at the root of the trouble,' on the ground that it is 'just wise enough to know that it is sick and to realise that [this is] its only chance of recovery.' The woman declares herself against such a view. But in a letter written at the story's end—that is, after her meeting with the 'elderly virgin' has transformed her attitude towards her lover—she seems to cede to his point of view: ' "I have been thinking over our talk about the psychological novel . . . it really is intensely interesting. . . ." '

The story does indeed underline the way in which the mind's depths work against its conscious intentions—something which the then revolutionary practice of 'psycho-analysis' was intended to reveal. The rational relationship to which the hero and heroine aspire is represented as a living lie—hindering access to disturbing but deeper and more 'genuine' feelings, and in contrast to one of its stated objectives forcing the woman to make all the concessions. (In a touch of black comedy—which draws again on the sex-food analogy—the man observes that he looks on food as something just 'to be devoured': when asked if that shocks her the woman replies, ' "To the bone." ') The story's real joke is that the subject of the would-be rationalist lovers' one item of intellectual discussion concerns recent insights into the mind's irrationality.

VINCENT O'SULLIVAN

[The New Zealand Stories]†

Kathleen Mansfield Beauchamp was born into a family, and a country, constantly checking themselves in a mirror. So much of their reality had to do with how 'Britain' was reflected in their values and assumptions, with how they gave back, at times in aggressive miniature, features defined on the other side of the world.

If, like the youngish, kindly, and mildly pompous Harold Beauchamp, you had made a fist of commerce through hard work and acumen, were infused with public zeal, and had a sharp eye for the main chance, then you knew very well that you played an important role in the vast enterprise of Empire. Didn't Wellington like to call itself 'the Empire city'? Weren't you part and parcel of what Joseph Chamberlain[1] had called, mid-way through the 1890s, the greatest governing race the world had ever seen? If you had four daughters and only one son—well, you still gave the girls the best, which meant, to top it off, the polish of a ladies' college in London. And although the paradox

† From "Introduction," *The New Zealand Stories of Katherine Mansfield*, ed. Vincent O'Sullivan (Melbourne: Oxford University Press, 1997), pp. 1–14. Reprinted by permission of Oxford University Press. Notes have been revised for this Norton Critical Edition.

1. Joseph Chamberlain (1836–1914), a prominent English politician who strongly promoted the British Empire.

might never have struck you, the further you lived from the imperial centre, the more you deserved a share of its fruits; the more loyalty you had to 'Home', the more you believed yourself a New Zealander. But if your cleverest daughter was inclined to size you up with a beady intelligence, and was volatile to a fault, then the verities could be in for a challenge. It was a challenge, in one form or another, that defined her writing for the next twenty-five years, under a name she preferred to take from her maternal grandmother.

The early stories * * * show something of the same imitative drive that was the mark of her city and her class, yet the pull towards what was local and at hand. 'About Pat', written as a schoolgirl in London, is a simple enough anecdote from life in distant Karori.[2] Her early 'prose poems', as she saw them, surfaced from her immersion in *fin-de-siècle* fashions, and were written once she was back in Wellington at the end of her teens.

The first Mansfield stories to attract wider attention were the ones she wrote soon after the months she spent in Bavaria, during her pregnancy in 1909. Collected as *In a German Pension* in 1911, they are mostly blunt satiric lunges at the provoking targets of foreignness, love, and social conventions. As with much of her later work, the best of them take their force from quick dashes of mood, the swerve from calm, and perhaps suppression, to moments in which rage or unexpected truth buckle the surface of apparent normality. * * *

Commentary on Mansfield seldom picks up on just how much of her writing is primarily satirical. Of the stories set in England or Europe—more than half of what she wrote—at least two-thirds of those are satiric in intent or form. And within those again, the greater part of the satire is directed at the exacting, deceptive and self-deceiving intricacies of sexual exchange. 'Europe', if constructed from Mansfield's fiction, is above all the site of sexual complexity, a complexity that rings the changes on naivety, ethnic resonances, the obsessiveness inseparable from emotional rapport. Many of the stories move within the perspective of 'adventure', a synonym perhaps for the constantly fluid sense of the outsider. As the novelist Elizabeth Bowen put it, 'Amid the etherealities of Bloomsbury she was more than half hostile, a dark-eyed tramp'.[3] So much in those stories derives from alert, imposed detachment. It is a position particularly congenial to the satirist, even as it implies that ease or intimacy are hardly at her command. Yet satire is a mode of reinforcing oneself, a protection on the principle of the pre-emptive strike. To focus from the margins can also be a partic-

2. A sketch included in *The New Zealand Stories*, pp. 15–18.
3. See Bowen, p. 350.

ularly fruitful procedure for a temperament that demands an almost photographic fixing of momentary patterns, a declared affinity with impressionism.[4]

> It is such strange delight to observe people and to try to understand them, to arrive late at night in strange cities or to come into little harbours just at pink of dawn when it's cold with a high wind blowing somewhere *up* in the air, to push through the heavy door into little cafés and to watch the pattern people make among tables & bottles and glasses, to watch women when they are off their guard . . . To air oneself among these things, to seek them out, to explore them and then to go apart and detach oneself from them—and to write—after the ferment has subsided.[5]

This, it seems, was the particular gift of isolation, the habitual condition of those *femmes seules*[6] who appear in so much of her fiction. To be so 'ecstatically aware' of the surface of things, in her friend Conrad Aiken's words, her mastery of 'twinkling circumstance',[7] helped to bring such conviction to her edgy, febrile young women, to her adolescents and children, for that too was how they received the world. Mansfield herself knew the limitations of this vivid alertness. In a review in 1919, she remarked how 'It is not enough to be comforted with colours, to finger bright shawls, to watch the fireworks, to wonder what those strange men are shouting down at the wharves . . . our curiosity is roused as to what lies beneath these strange rich surfaces.[8]

How, then, do her New Zealand stories relate to those set on the other side of the world? Stories in which there was far less call for satiric defence, for defensive attack; where she does not need to articulate so pressingly that '*cry against corruption*'[9] which she claimed was one of her compelling reasons for writing, and which is there, in one form or another, in practically everything set in London or on the Continent.

* * *

With a touch of staged moroseness, Mansfield once imagined herself as 'the little colonial' being shouted at for 'pretending this is her garden . . . She is a stranger—an alien'.[1] She did not always be-

4. A style of painting and writing that emphasised immediacy and attempts to catch "the moment."
5. *The Collected Letters of Katherine Mansfield*, ed. Vincent O'Sullivan and Margaret Scott, (Oxford: Clarendon Press), vol. 1, 1984, pp. 287–88.
6. Single women.
7. See Aiken, p. 339.
8. "Glancing Light," a review of *Java Head* by Joseph Hergesheimer, *Athenaeum* (13 June 1919), collected in Katherine Mansfield, *Novels and Novelists*, 1930, p. 40.
9. *Collected Letters*, vol. 2, p. 54.
1. *Journal*, p. 157.

lieve that, nor worry about it for long. But Elizabeth Bowen's remark is pertinent: 'In London she lived, as strangers are wont to do, in a largely self-fabricated world.'[2] Many of her stories are delicate calibrations on quite what belonging does mean.

The New Zealand fiction is a different matter. It might now seem odd that the most impressive of her early stories set in her own country were written to meet the editorial agenda of *Rhythm*, a magazine established by the young John Middleton Murry. Determined to be Modern above all else, the journal was committed to challenging convention, and carried the slogan it took from the Irish playwright, J. M. Synge: 'Before art can be human again it must learn to be brutal.'[3]

What Mansfield provided in answer to that call has variously been dismissed as untypical of her work, or taken to suggest that she might have become a predominantly regionalist writer. In a sense her *Rhythm* stories come out of the blue. They go far beyond the backblock sketches and colonial yarns that preceded them in New Zealand writing, and there is nothing to make one think she drew on her Australian contemporary, Henry Lawson.[4] The probing rawness as much as the melodramatic psychology of 'The Woman at the Store' and 'Millie' seem vividly her own. Yet when she turned to middle-class Wellington in 'The Wind Blows' a few years later, she moved not only closer to home but also towards a quite different conception of narrative. In the form she now devised, with its deft switches in time levels, the merging of mood and image in ways more usually found in poetry, the discarding of anything like conventional plot, she attempts something much further from what was usually meant by the short story. When Mansfield reviewed Jane Mander's *Story of a New Zealand River* in 1920, she took her compatriot to task for leaning too hard on English models, for not trusting herself more to those 'moments when we catch a bewilderingly vivid glimpse of what she really felt and knew about the small settlement of people'. At such moments, 'her characters move quickly, almost violently'. The new material of colonial fiction, she insists, must find its own form, 'the new sketch, the new story'.[5]

Within weeks of 'The Wind Blows', the death of her brother in Belgium directed Mansfield even more towards 'recollections of my own country. . . . But all must be told with a sense of mystery, a radiance, an afterglow. . . . Almost certainly in a kind of special

2. See Bowen, p. 350.
3. J. M. Synge (1871–1909), Irish playwright. For a fuller discussion see Antony Alpers, *The Life of Katherine Mansfield* (London: Penguin Books, 1982), p. 134.
4. Henry Lawson (1867–1922), Australian short-story writer who wrote vivid and original stories of colonial life.
5. "First Novels," *Athenaeum*, 9 July 1920, collected in *Novels and Novelists*, pp. 217–20.

prose'.[6] That dual prompting to commemorate, and to find a new aesthetic form, now define Mansfield as both a Modernist and as a specifically New Zealand writer. First in *Prelude* in 1917, then in 'At the Bay' four years later, she hit on the narrative form she was after when she spoke of that 'kind of special prose'. As she wrote to a painter friend about the first of these stories, 'As far as I know it's more or less my own invention'. As she thinks back to Wellington,

> I always remember feeling that this little island had dipped back into the dark blue sea during the night only to rise again at beam of day, all hung with bright spangles and glittering drops . . . I tried to catch that moment—with something of its sparkle and its flavour. And just as on those mornings white milky mists rise and uncover some beauty, then smother it again and then again disclose it, I tried to lift that mist from my people and let them be seen and then to hide them again.[7]

In arriving at what was 'more or less my own invention', Mansfield had learned from her interest in film. In those two long stories as much as in cinema, narrative proceeds not in linear completeness but in setting its images, its discrete episodes, in relation to each other, one scene cutting against another in mid action. Mansfield was writing of a painting, but might well have been describing each single section of these stories, when she described 'the sudden arrest, poise, *moment captured* . . . in a flowing shade and sunlight world'.[8] Both *Prelude* and 'At the Bay' are written in sections whose apparent randomness works towards the overarching revelation of one family. Its members are seen in their public and private roles, in their shared identity, and their diverse fragmentary selves. In 'At the Bay' we are shown not just a single day, although that is what the movement from dawn to night suggests. But that one day is part too of a process of life, a rhythmic fragment of a much larger rhythm. Through apparently trivial incidents, we have seen the cycle of women's lives from childhood to old age, and something of a male cycle as well.

* * *

There are times when the reading of Mansfield in her own country has meant fairly persistent simplifying. The almost innate belief in most New Zealanders that theirs is a classless community, that the social hierarchies of an older world, if not quite shucked off, are certainly less constraining, has perhaps led to odd distortions. 'The Garden Party', understandably a classroom favourite, is usually read as a story about growing up, one in which there might in-

6. *Journal*, pp. 93–94.
7. *Collected Letters*, vol. 1, p. 331.
8. *Collected Letters*, vol. 4, p. 354.

deed be an element of social criticism, but where most of all we see a 17-year-old girl face the impenetrable reality of death and mature before its disturbing wonder. The story is read too in terms of its lingering colonial charm, a further and older glimpse, under another name, of the engaging Kezia, her conventional sisters, delicate Mother again drifting off in the background, Father still footing the bills. We tend to assume that because Mansfield clearly enjoyed writing her Wellington stories, because 'the memory game' (as she called it) was a consoling recovery of a kind, then there is an implied approval of a family so evidently similar to her own. The text defies such an easy assumption. Unless we are swamped by a particular biographical wash, the narrative will not allow us to regard the Sheridans as other than pampered, conventional, smugly riddled with the certainties of a class for whom the rest of society exists in a tributary role. Laura's early amazement at a workman's delighting in the scent of lavender is merely a novice's version of her mother's fully fledged snobbery, her self-sustaining remark that 'People like that don't expect sacrifices from us', as one side of Tinakori Road looks across at the other. 'The very smoke out of their chimneys was poverty-stricken. Little rags and shreds of smoke, so unlike the great silvery plumes that uncurled from the Sheridans' chimneys.'

If Laura's sensitivity is read as the story's commanding focus, then surely such politically insistent images are to be taken up and modified by the teenager's growing wisdom. For doesn't the girl from the big house come to realise that such otherness as poverty, and such total otherness as death, assume their place in a finer, more encompassing view of life? That to see the workingman's corpse, so peaceful and handsome, takes her quite beyond her sisters who did not cross the road with the garden party's leftovers? After all, hadn't she been unable to realise, even a few hours before, that death was actually *there*? 'Why couldn't she [realise]? She stopped a minute. And it seemed to her that kisses, voices, tinkling spoons, laughter, the smell of crushed grass, were somehow inside her. She had no room for anything else.'

Against the reality and gaiety of her own afternoon, poverty at close quarters is suitably melodramatic. It smells, it talks funny, it stares, it is obsequious, it is stagily 'lighted by a smoky lamp'. But the dead man atones for all this, as it were. He is 'wonderful, beautiful . . . All is well, said that sleeping face'. The point, of course, is that all seems well *because* the man is dead. The fact of his total absence means that quite rightly she might think, 'What did garden parties matter to him? He was far from all those things', just as his working-class reality is no longer a trouble to her. Everything, for the moment, is transcended—Laura's own earlier sense of guilt, the nastiness of the poor, that intimation that there was 'no room in her' for anything beyond the privileges of her class.

But the story does not stop there. Laura hurries back past 'all those dark people', cherishing her *frisson*, her vision of death-as-provided-by-a-handsome-workingman, to a brother who asks, as she herself might have asked a few minutes before, 'Was it awful?' When she can only stammer, 'Isn't life . . . isn't life?' he 'quite understood'. Which he did not, in the least. He has no idea what she is speaking of, how a man's death has been aesthetically transformed to her moment of vague, comforting enlightenment. 'This is just as it should be, I am content', she had supposed the dead man, with his five young fatherless children and his new widow, as conveying to her. The experience is deeply, egotistically, about Laura and nothing else. But the workman's corpse sustains it, a final service from poor to rich, the final appropriation by the wealthy from the impoverished.

Yet for all that, one does take Laura's experience as instructive and enlightening. Hers is a genuine moment of fulfilment, even as it does not alter in the least the limiting rigidity of her class. The reader is directed to acknowledge both. The play of one against the other is where the pathos of the story lies.

This dimension in Mansfield's fiction, this sharp and particular scoring of social demarcations, like the psychological ploys through which one class engages with another, is more usually picked up in the English stories than in the New Zealand ones. But in both there are few narratives that do not trace out the exercise of authority, and at least the opportunities for happiness, along economic lines. This underwrites other aspects of the stories. Whether Mansfield depicts the sexual manoeuvres that corral single women, or the experiences of the solitary and the bereft, the economic framing of her characters almost always is apparent. The events of a story are primarily the consequence of that.

'The Doll's House', that equally celebrated story Mansfield wrote just after 'The Garden Party', extends her critique of the New Zealand middle class and its rather smudged carbon copy of how the English do things. Again, here is a story that usually is admired for its 'sympathy' with the way Kezia eludes the starchy social postures of her family and, even more, for that final image of 'our Else', daughter of a washerwoman and a convict, delighting in the little lamp she was never meant to see. It has become an iconic moment in Mansfield fiction, the child sitting in her ecstasy of achieved desire, which 'the world' has conspired to deny her. The impact of that final image, the narrative's pace as it draws towards the diminishment of anything but the light of Else's illumination, has perhaps prevented our taking the story for what it also does. After the Kelveys are driven off by Aunt Beryl who so 'frightened those little rats', the outcast sisters, rodent-like still, huddle together on a drainpipe. Earlier in the story, when one of the schoolchildren had bawled out in front of the playground that the Kelveys' father was in prison, the rest of the children 'rushed away in a body, deeply, deeply excited, wild with joy'. The language, the veering and welter of emotional release, is close to that scene in *Prelude* when Pat the handyman beheads the duck and the children move from fear to hysterical delight. In 'The Doll's House' it is again the excitement of the kill, but as well as that, it is the social ritual of the scapegoat, a stoning of the pests. And set against this malevolence, the tiny defiant flare of what an individual cannot be deprived of. In her own country, the reading of Mansfield has been so loaded with a kind of cosiness, an assumed final endorsement on her part not just of her family but also the *kind* of family her fiction returns to, that her hard clarity in depicting its limitations is often obscured.

It is true that her family stories were a considered attempt to propose a particular kind of love, 'warm, vivid, intimate—not "made up"—not *self conscious*',[9] and to carry the enchantment that memory and distance gave her childhood. They were also, in the last years of her life, predominant among the stories where she achieved those 'new moulds for our new thoughts & feelings'[1] that a post-war, modern consciousness demanded. It is the richness of those stories that they do precisely that, as they offer a critique of her own country, her own social *milieu*; that they convey expansive family warmth so convincingly, even as the ferocity of individual drives is tempered by the roles community sets in place.

The insincerity Aunt Beryl detects in herself in both *Prelude* and 'At the Bay', her tacking between a troubled questing self and a fabricated display, is the status of settler society writ small. One remembers the fractious teenage Mansfield saying after her trip to the Ureweras, 'Give me the tourist and the Maori but nothing in-between',[2] That 'in-between', however, is where her New Zealand fiction is placed, while her characters shuttle between performance and authentic selves. This is a process, should one care to trace it out, in Mansfield's own considered observations of herself. Her 'shedding false selves' was a deeply personal challenge. It was as much a pressing factor in the society in which she was raised, where values tended to accrue about the colonial 'fault-line', as one might call it, with its sense of regretted severance and persistent

9. *Collected Letters*, vol. 4, p. 242.
1. *Collected Letters*, vol. 3, p. 82.
2. *The Urewera Notebook*, ed. Ian A. Gordon (Auckland: Oxford University Press, 1978), p. 61.

mimicry, and yet an insistence on local worth, on achieved difference.

The stories in this collection demand that we read them with an eye to both. At the gentler end of the spectrum, Kezia winningly refuses to think or behave quite as siblings or parents would expect, while her mother's fey sexual revolt takes her no further than a dreamy, enfolding egotism. At the other end of that spectrum, an unbalanced child—the incipient artist?—draws the forbidden pictures that give the family away; a pakeha[3] child must be rescued from the encompassing attraction and threat of Maori *aroha*,[4] the poor are savaged in an implacable class war. Even in the best known anthology pieces, where the fiction moves in the warm tidal affection that family evokes, there are those other currents as well. In their sublimated violence and incipient rebellion, their drift of sexual recklessness, there move the refined filaments of that 'bloodiness and guts' the editor of *Rhythm* asked for and drew from Mansfield in her early local stories. And so often, in the shaping of individual experience, there is a presence like that of the warning fat man in 'Her First Ball', his shadow for the moment put aside in 'the beautiful flying wheel of the dance'. Yet that very word *wheel* tells us that his time will come again.

These hovering intimations are not so much ranged against the patterned ringing immediacy of the fiction as set in counterpoint. Each is given its due, while it is the living moment, always, which for the space of the story at least wins out. Yet this alertness to what threatens, to what troubles the borders, helps to place the stories so firmly as historical occasions, to define their period and place; at the same time as their first attraction is somewhere else, in their total freshness within the genre of the short story, in their accomplishment as art.

This is the first time Katherine Mansfield's stories about her own country have been brought together in the order in which she wrote them.[5] To take them in sequence and as a group defines, rather more acutely than we might have thought, how emphases fall differently than in her other fiction. Certainly it presents, with a more insistent local accent, her quest for that 'new story' she believed was called for to put forward a new world.

3. European New Zealander. [Maori]
4. Affectionate regard, love. [Maori]
5. Referring to *The New Zealand Stories of Katherine Mansfield*.

W. H. NEW

[Form and Value in "Je Ne Parle Pas Français"]†

"Je ne parle pas français"—her most desolating critique of both the French and the English * * * (she reads the French as parasitic and the English as dull)—is a scarcely oblique attack on the New Caledonia–born writer Francis Carco (with whom Mansfield had a short-lived affair in 1915), and it is a self-declared "cry against corruption,"[1] but it also uses two (at least two) interrelated lovers' triangles to tell a formal story about the paradigms of power. The first triangle involves the jaded French narrator, Raoul Duquette, his English friend (or quondam[2] friend) Dick Harmon, and Dick's English "bride" (though it turns out they have never formally married) Mouse. The second involves Dick, Mouse, and Dick's mother (to whom Dick belongs more than he belongs to Mouse and for whom he abandons Mouse in Paris), which establishes the primary story that Raoul recalls. Whether or not there are more triangles depends on how one reads the detail of the text: Mouse, Raoul, and Raoul's admiration of himself might constitute a third triangle; Raoul, the Madame of the cafe where he works as a pimp, and the sequence of women for whom he claims to have been a gigolo might constitute a fourth; Raoul, Dick, and their sexual ambivalence might constitute a fifth; and so on.

The number here matters less than the recognition of the triangular pattern, one that is conventionally associated with a corrupted love; the overlay of triangles reiterates the force of Raoul's ego in these several relationships (his name, Duquette, perhaps implies both *questeur* and *quêteur*, both questor and collector/beggar)—all else and all others in the story are in his eyes subservient to their relevance to him. Relevance, moreover, is something Raoul implicitly equates with their degree of usability; as gigolo he "services" others, he does not love them, and he manipulates the world whenever he can so that it services him. Women supply him with money; Dick is useful to him first as a potential aid to his would-be career as a writer, but later just serves as entertainment, a toy to be played with and discarded; the Madame (whom he imagines in bed, in the long-suppressed original ending of the story, * * * and whom he rejects because he thinks her skin will "disgustingly" have moles like "mushrooms,") tolerates his presence in her

† From *Reading Mansfield and Metaphors of Form* (Montreal and London: McGill-Queen's University Press, 1999), pp. 93–99. Reprinted by permission of the publisher. Notes are the Editor's.

1. *Collected Letters*, vol. 3, p. 54.
2. Former. [Latin]

café; and Mouse is a problem, for she is a woman he once sought to exploit but whom he has abandoned at the moment he thought he had achieved power over her, only to discover that her stubborn independence has proved somehow stronger than circumstance and that in present memory she still dislocates his life. All else he puts aside: "I have made it a rule of my life never to regret and never to look back. Regret is an appalling waste of energy, and no one who intends to be a writer can afford to indulge in it. You can't get it into shape; you can't build on it; it's only good for wallowing in." But recurrently he remembers the African laundress who kissed him as a child, and recurrently he remembers Mouse. In looking back, moreover, he is forced to try to justify a life that has long mistaken power for cleverness and recognition for value. Mansfield's story, reconstructing Raoul's, exposes the extent of his self-delusion; but it also reveals to the reader, by means of its form, a kind of closet dialogue about the relation between language and authority.

The mushroom image that closes the story does much more than describe the Madame's skin or Raoul's fungoid imagination; it works self-reflexively to epitomize Raoul's entire life—that of a parasite. Language does not take him out of himself; it merely displays his limitations. Even as a writer, that is, he cannot stretch; he sees his published books as "triumphs," but the titles tell a different story—"*False Coins, Wrong Doors, Left Umbrellas*"—and when he three times refers to one of his works simperingly, with false humility, as "my little book," the construction of his words has to be read as carefully as the words themselves. For Raoul uses words for their effect more than for their meaning: he makes "a pretty mouth" at Dick; he sends him a copy of his book "with a carefully cordial inscription." Words such as "true," "simple," "perfectly," "purely," and his most recurrent adjective, "charming," he uses as techniques of ingratiation rather than as statements of fact. The adjective "little," however, he uses on other occasions as though it were natural speech, as though it were denotatively neutral. He opens with a reference to the "little café" in which he sits; he refers to "little things, like gloves and powder boxes and a manicure set," which he's been given by "little prostitutes and kept women" and "even advanced modern literary ladies." "I am little," he says of himself; he has hands, a woman tells him, "for making fine little pastries"; he says that Dick drinks from a "little glass"; he observes that Mouse has "a little face more like a drawing than a real face" and that her eyebrows look like "two little feathers"; and at the end of the story he says " 'Good-night, my little cat' " to a "fattish old prostitute" and fantasizes about promising a young virgin to a "dirty old gallant" in these words: " 'But I've got the little girl for you, mon vieux. So little. . . .' "

Raoul tarnishes the world, just by being in it. The effect of repeating the word "little" is to diminish whomever or whatever is being talked about and to transform person, place, and thing alike into objects. That he and his books should appear "naturally" in this list reveals Mansfield's control over irony: she writes the story so that Raoul, in the act of using words, will undermine the self-serving image of himself that his choice of words ostensibly concocts. The word "little" reveals his contempt for women, and his language further suggests that his clear contempt for others derives from his underlying contempt for himself. One woman is called Mouse, another a "little cat," a third a "tall charming creature" with a large "balcony"; his concierge is dismissed as "the old spider"; and Mouse, dressed in "grey fur," is said to be "tame." If they are not things, then women are merely animals in his lexicon. But he is not free from animal behaviour himself; he is a "Parisian fox-terrier," and Mouse and Dick are his "prey." When, then, he also avers, "I confess, without my clothes I am rather charming. Plump, almost like a girl . . . I am like a little woman in a café," and later, "I felt as a woman must feel," the text is enacting two separate lexical dramas: one suggests the relation between Raoul's contempt for himself (in that he identifies with a class of person he also expresses contempt for) and his inadequate grasp of masculinity; the other suggests the disparity between his version of womanhood and the reality of femaleness (which Mansfield makes clear is nothing like Raoul's notion). Because, to Raoul's eyes, appearance and reality are one, he seeds illusions; but he is no poet, and his language serves more than anything else to demonstrate that he prefers contrivance over substance.

In his own room he can make the two equate; he sees himself in the mirror in the third person: "from top to toe, drawing on his soft grey gloves. He was looking the part; he was the part." For the reader, the word "grey," however, links Raoul both with the ineffectual Mouse that Raoul describes and with the "grey, flat-footed and withered" waiter he depicts in Madame's café. Raoul's words, in consequence, come not only to *convey* his hypocrisy but also to *stand for* his emptiness. For Raoul, that is, *formal appearance* is the quintessence of effect; for Mansfield, *literary form* is at once the medium of communication and the paradigm of character.

To read this story further for its formal paradigms is to see that Raoul tries on a succession of verbal paradigms as if each were a suit of clothes, to see what reaction it invites. In his first conversation with Dick, for example, when he talks about "the tendency of the modern novel, the need of a new form," he keeps throwing "in a card that seemed to have nothing to do with the game, just to see how he'd take it." He defines Dick's neutral replies as "charming," though Mansfield's elliptical portrayal more satirically suggests that English Dick is just preoccupied with his own uncertainties, somnolent and dull. But Raoul sees first of all whatever he would like to see, whatever flatters his own ego. Standing before a mirror, he asks his own reflection, "How can one look the part and not be the part? Or be the part and not look it? Isn't looking—being? Or being—looking? . . . This seemed to me extraordinarily profound at the time, and quite new. But I confess that something did whisper: . . . 'You—literary? You look as though you've taken down a bet on a racecourse!' But I didn't listen."

Other techniques multiply as the story progresses. Raoul tries out description as a literary technique; he tries out anecdotes; he devises meaningless similes (likening "pink blotting-paper" to "the tongue of a little dead kitten, which I've never felt" and going on to admit that, while "rolling [this] . . . soft phrase round my mind," he is taking in "girls' names and dirty jokes" and anything else within earshot). He repeats the words to songs and reads letters that others have written; he sentimentalizes; he insults; he employs "comme il faut" formulas, uses tourist-brochure clichés, and mimics the language of customs officials; he poses apparently shamelessly ("I was Agony, Agony, Agony,"), and draws hopelessly inadequate analogies; he interprets photographs, with only relative perspicacity; he digresses; he refers to himself calculatedly as One, He, and I; he even tries out the question-and-answer technique, as though to introduce a gruff reality into the monologue he performs before the reader:

> Query: Why am I so bitter against Life? And why do I see her as a rag-picker on the American cinema, shuffling along wrapped in a filthy shawl with her old claws crooked over a stick?
>
> Answer: The direct result of the American cinema acting upon a weak mind.

The convention is rhetorical, both literally and metaphorically. That he should characterize life as an old woman accords with the rest of his behaviour; so is the fact that he then dismisses this recognition as a joke. But the cinematic allusion is no textual accident. It reinforces his dependence on appearance and the degree to which he accepts the glibly conventional as a working truth.

His first portrait of Madame indicates how much he reads the world according to his own limitations and generalizes his own inadequacies into absolutes of human behaviour:

> Madame is thin and dark, too, with white cheeks and white hands. In certain lights she looks quite transparent, shining out of her black shawl with an extraordinary effect. When she

> is not serving she sits on a stool with her face turned, always, to the window. Her dark-ringed eyes search among and follow after the people passing, but not as if she was looking for somebody. Perhaps, fifteen years ago, she was; but now the pose has become a habit.

The absolutes (always, black and white) run up against the relative words (quite, perhaps, and the implied grey that turns up in subsequent glimpses of the waiter, Mouse, and himself); the word "habit" suggests clothing as well as behaviour (Raoul wears a "grey felt hat," as well as grey gloves); "pose" and "effect" are the criteria that govern his own system of values. Raoul projects himself upon the world, makes his language the norm, even if by doing so he destroys others.

"Je ne parle pas français" is this story's title. It is Mouse's phrase—she is the foreigner whom love and circumstance abandon abroad here; and what Raoul calls her "stupid, stale little phrase" is precisely the stimulus that compels him to remember her. It also reveals another dimension of this story of power politics. Raoul pretends that his memory of Mouse tells a narrative of love and loss, not of Dick's love for Mouse and the intrusion of the powerful mother but of Raoul's discovery of true love at last in the lost relationship he never himself took up with Mouse. ("If you think what I've written is merely superficial and impudent and cheap you're wrong," he says. "I'll admit it does sound so, but then it is not all. If it were, how could I have experienced what I did when I read that stale little phrase written in green ink, in the writing-pad? That proves there's more in me and that I really am important, doesn't it?") The question marks tell a different story. They tell of the uncertainty that has begot the attitudinizing in the first place: his statements reek of self-justification; they do not hint of love. The memory as it is gradually re-enacted reveals a Raoul with mercenary designs on Mouse more than one with sensitivity to others' feelings, whereas the memory as it is reconstructed in Raoul's mind further testifies to his capacity for corrupting truth.

The words "Je ne parle pas français" declare a vulnerability. If Raoul is moved at all by the way the phrase invites him into the past, it is not because Mouse's innocence sways him—she is "not Madame" in more ways than one, and he makes use of her isolation—but because the phrase so acutely functions as a metaphor for his own vulnerability, the insecurity he hides in pretentious effects. The difference is that Mouse is other people's victim, the (as it were, colonial) woman induced (without language) abroad; he is a victim of himself, a (Parisian, male) victim of (and in) the language he claims to be his own. That he should hide from the inadequacy of his own language simply perpetuates his weakness; that the story should reveal both the inadequacies and the effects of language form, however, illustrates the complexity of Mansfield's narrative practice.

The opening sentences of the story make clear how Raoul's words work. At once they declare (lexically) his faith in the efficacy of form to hide desolate truths and they reveal (structurally) his denial of the truths he does not wish to recognize. The passage is studded with contrivances:

> I do not know why I have such a fancy for this little café. It's dirty and sad, sad. It's not as if it had anything to distinguish it from a hundred others—it hasn't; or as if the same strange types came here every day, whom one could watch from one's corner and recognise and more or less (with a strong accent on the less) get the hang of.
>
> But pray don't imagine that those brackets are a confession of my humility before the mystery of the human soul. Not at all; I don't believe in the human soul. I never have.

The number of negatives (do not know, not as if, don't, not at all, don't, never) signals a deep-seated denial of anything wrong, a refusal to admit to failure. The shift in person (from "I" to "one" and back again) suggests the slippery nature of his sense of identity. The adjectives (dirty, sad) hint that there might be a correlative link between himself and the café. The brackets (so self-consciously acknowledged) describe the process of digression that characterizes his subsequent narrative. The habits of his verbal practice, that is, equate with his habits of attitude and expectation. He speaks the world that he wants to be believed; he denies the world that might change him. As a result, he lives (like those whom he in turn victimizes) only in parentheses. He constructs similes to shape reality because he lives only in likeness, never in fact. His world, the story's opening tropes make clear, is a world of "as if," from which his denials, digressions, and formulaic utterances will not let him escape. When he later says "(I've been there)," the visual appearance of the parentheses is as important to the story as the particular referent of the adverb. The identity is contained—in the orthography as well as in the memory, the place, the verbal form.

To understand corruption, the story argues, it is necessary to recognize it; and to recognize corruption, it is necessary to pierce the false articulateness behind which it hides. Mansfield manages to make Raoul Duquette at once unappealing and understandable, which is not to praise him. But the story is not simply a character study. "Je ne parle pas français" uses language in order to expose language, constructs a form (the recalled memory, which shapes the whole story as an extended "as if") that will also function metaphorically—as an embodiment, here, of the menace of pretence. To recognize that power without value can be attractive and that value without power can be debilitating is, in other words, a concrete challenge to language as well as an abstract problem in morality. And "Je ne parle pas français" is not alone in probing this issue. The value of language is one of the most pervasive motifs in Mansfield's writing, and questioning the consequences of language can be one of the most unsettling results of examining her formal practice. "Value," always, is a quality the margins redefine. While by no means inconsequential, therefore, any reading of her stories that confines itself to plots, historical antecedents, biographical implications, and insights into individual behaviour is limited. Reading the stories also for their formal design asks about convention and conventional paradigms of power, about alternatives and the artistry of alternatives, and about the systems of value that conventions and alternatives separately enshrine.

ANGELA SMITH

[Writing the Secret Self]†

* * *

During the war, Mansfield became intensely aware of her own mortality, and of the dark side to her physical pleasures: in February 1918 she bounded into bed, coughed, and began to spit blood. Diagnosed as suffering from tuberculosis, probably caused by gonococcal infection, she considered entering a sanatorium but decided against it because it would interfere with her writing, though from 1919 she had to spend the winter months in the Mediterranean or Switzerland as her health could not withstand a British winter. In a letter that contains a brilliant analysis of her own fiction she explains to Murry how she responds to post-war writing:

> I cant imagine how after the war these men can pick up the old threads as tho' it had never been. Speaking to *you* Id say we have died and live again. How can that be the same life? It doesn't mean that Life is the less precious of [*sic*] that the 'common things of light and day'[1] are gone. They are not gone, they are intensified, they are illumined. Now we know ourselves for what we are. In a way its a tragic knowledge. Its as though, even while we live again we face death. But *through*

† From "Introduction," *Katherine Mansfield Selected Stories* (Oxford: Oxford University Press, 2002), pp. xx–xxv, xxxi–xxxii. Reprinted by permission of Oxford University Press.

1. "And fade into the light of common day," William Wordsworth, "Ode: Intimations of Immortality," 1807, I. 77 [*Editor*].

> *Life*: thats the point. We see death in life as we see death in a flower that is fresh unfolded.

She uses the shorthand of the literary language she and Murry shared when she says that her consciousness of death is of 'deserts of vast eternity', taken from Andrew Marvell's poem 'To His Coy Mistress'[2] and referring to the long inactivity of the grave. Then she compares her own method with Murry's very explicit fiction:

> But the difference between you and me is (perhaps Im wrong) I couldn't tell anybody *bang out* about those deserts. They are my secret. I might write about a boy eating strawberries or a woman combing her hair on a windy morning & that is the only way I can ever mention them. But they *must* be there. Nothing less will do.[3]

Mansfield's creative energy from 1918 until her death from tuberculosis in January 1923, at the age of 34, focused on finding a form for her fiction that would 'speak to the secret self we all have—to acknowledge that',[4] never explicitly. Characteristically this involves a moment of disruption, when the world as a character believes it to be is disturbed by a darker vision, as it is when Kezia confronts the possibility that her grandmother will die or when Miss Brill's sense of living as being part of a theatrical company is jarred by a young girl's perception of her. There is never any intervention or commentary by the narrator of the stories, no telling *bang out*, and the moment passes, but its significance for the consciousness that experiences it is not in doubt.

* * *

The secret self is not, of course, only concerned with disappointment or death. One aspect of Mansfield's mature fiction that becomes increasingly subtle is her control of comedy. Her early stories are overtly satirical; as she wrote to Murry: 'Ive two "kick offs" in the writing game. *One* is joy—real joy . . . The other "kick off" is my old original one . . . *a cry against corruption*.'[5] The second kick off was initially expressed through parodies in the *New Age*, in the stories she wrote for the magazine that were collected and published as *In a German Pension*, and eventually through the sophisticated satire of such stories as '*Je ne parle pas français*', in which the macabre vision of the narrator constructs his favourite Parisian café as a haunt for the vampiric undead, for instance the waiter:

2. "But at my back I always hear / Time's wingèd chariot hurrying near: / And yonder all before us lie / Deserts of vast Eternity." Andrew Marvell, "To His Coy Mistress," 1681, II. 21–24 [*Editor*].
3. *Collected Letters*, vol. 3, pp. 97–98.
4. *Collected Letters*, vol. 4, p. 278.
5. *Collected Letters*, vol. 2, p. 54.

> He is grey, flat-footed and withered, with long, brittle nails that set your nerves on edge while he scrapes up your two sous. When he is not smearing over the table or flicking at a dead fly or two, he stands with one hand on the back of a chair, in his far too long apron, and over his other arm the three-cornered dip of dirty napkin, waiting to be photographed in connection with some wretched murder. 'Interior of Café where Body was Found.' You've seen him hundreds of times.

Mansfield's comedy pivots on disruption, here the disjunction between the common view of the hygiene desirable in cafés and the grisly spectacle offered by the ghoulish waiter. The comedy that stems from joy, on the other hand, reveals a sympathetic pleasure in idiosyncrasy, for instance at the timidity of the two sisters in 'The Daughters of the Late Colonel'. Their genteel vicar asks if they would like a consolatory 'little Communion', and the narrative perspective enacts the sisters' response:

> But the idea of a little Communion terrified them. What! In the drawing-room by themselves—with no—no altar or anything! The piano would be much too high, thought Constantia, and Mr Farolles could not possibly lean over it with the chalice. And Kate would be sure to come bursting in and interrupt them, thought Josephine. And supposing the bell rang in the middle? It might be somebody important—about their mourning. Would they get up reverently and go out, or would they have to wait . . . in torture?

Here the disruption stems from the sisters' own sense that there is a place for everything: religion belongs in church and would be embarrassing if it invaded the drawing-room. Their conservatism is not mocked, but is part of a subtle revelation of their suppressed secret selves which come out of the shadows fleetingly, and temporarily, at the end of the story. The harsh comedy of '*Je ne parle pas français*', however, gives the reader an insight into the secret self of the narrator, Duquette, the gigolo and pimp who poses as a writer. Comedy pervades Mansfield's stories as it does her personal writing; not long before her death she wrote in her notebook: 'the sense of humour I have found true of every single occasion of my life'.[6] * * * Her wit flickered even over her own death: 'I told poor old L.M. [Ida Baker] yesterday that after I died to PROVE there was no immortality I would send her a coffin worm in a matchbox. She was gravely puzzled.'[7]

Roger Fry defines the Modernism of the Post-Impressionists in a way that also applies to Mansfield's fiction: 'They do not seek to im-

6. *The Katherine Mansfield Notebooks*, vol. 2, ed. Margaret Scott (Wellington: Lincoln University Press and Daphne Brasell Associates), p. 329.
7. *Collected Letters*, vol. 4, p. 100.

itate form, but to create form; not to imitate life, but to find an equivalent for life'.[8] His stress is on their avoidance of realism and of imitating life, creating in their art an experience for the viewer or reader that is like living, that gives the readers a charge that is an event in their lives, not a mirror of reality. Mansfield's friend Virginia Woolf, who was also a close friend and biographer of Roger Fry, shared Mansfield's dissatisfaction with conventional realism in fiction, and expressed her frustration with it in a review essay which Mansfield admired, written in 1919, and called 'Modern Fiction' when it appeared in *The Common Reader*. In it Woolf attacks her contemporaries, not the great nineteenth-century realists, and says that writers like Arnold Bennett and John Galsworthy[9] fill their novels with details about contexts and clothes but 'Life escapes'. She then asks the reader to think what it is like to inhabit 'an ordinary mind on an ordinary day':

> The mind receives a myriad impressions—trivial, fantastic, evanescent, or engraved with the sharpness of steel. From all sides they come, an incessant shower of innumerable atoms; and as they fall, as they shape themselves into the life of Monday or Tuesday, the accent falls differently from of old; the moment of importance came not here but there . . . Let us record the atoms as they fall upon the mind in the order in which they fall, let us trace the pattern, however disconnected and incoherent in appearance, which each sight or incident scores upon the consciousness. Let us not take it for granted that life exists more fully in what is commonly thought big than in what is commonly thought small.[1]

What this implies is that something small, such as a moment in a shop, might be more vivid to us than something more apparently significant, like an election or a battle; human consciousness does not respond according to an existing hierarchy of events. Similarly, our experience of an ordinary day will bring conflicting sensations; there is not a necessary order of significance. The seeing mind, and therefore the memory, do not notice every item of dress worn by companions; they will, for instance, register how a shirt enhances the colour of the wearer's eyes but not notice or remember what kind of shoes accompany it. Woolf requires a pared-down fiction, a simplified line that records the atoms as they fall and makes the ordinary life of Monday different from Tuesday.

In Mansfield's fiction the various kinds of disruption that signify disturbance are not as obvious formally as they are either in the

8. Roger Fry, *Vision and Design* (Harmondsworth: Penguin, 1937), p. 195.
9. Arnold Bennett (1867–1931), John Galsworthy (1867–1933), English novelists [*Editor*].
1. Virginia Woolf, *The Common Reader* (London: Hogarth Press, 1962), vol. 1, pp. 189–90.

fragmented *Waste Land*, or in the strange juxtaposition of the various parts of *To the Lighthouse*.[2] None the less the pared-down line is there, requiring an observant reader who is not seduced by nostalgia into thinking that stories like 'The Garden Party' celebrate the lost colonial world of Mansfield's childhood. Pound's definition of Imagism, that the artist seeks out luminous detail without commenting on it,[3] resembles what Mansfield writes after the war about ordinary things being intensified and illumined. She rejects realism: 'Art is not an attempt to reconcile existence with his [the artist's] vision: it is an attempt to create his own world in this world. That which suggests the subject to the artist is the unlikeness of it to what we accept as reality. We single out, we bring into the light, we put up higher.[4] Mansfield's stories focus on luminous details which resonate within the story and gain significance in the reader's mind in retrospect because they elude definition. The aloe in 'Prelude', the pear tree in 'Bliss', the little lamp in 'The Doll's House', the swan-headed umbrella in 'The Voyage', the signet ring in 'The Man Without a Temperament', the fur necklet in 'Miss Brill' are all brought into the light, but the light flickers as the object is seen from different angles, and no two readers interpret it in the same way. This nebulous but haunting symbolism has affinities with Woolf's rather than with D. H. Lawrence's writing practice. When Roger Fry first read *To the Lighthouse* he wrote to the author asking what the lighthouse symbolized. She replied tartly:

> I meant *nothing* by The Lighthouse. One has to have a central line down the middle of the book to hold the design together. I saw that all sorts of feelings would accrue to this, but I refused to think them out, and trusted that people would make it the deposit for their own emotions—which they have done, one thinking it means one thing another another. I can't manage Symbolism except in this vague, generalised way. Whether its right or wrong I don't know, but directly I'm told what a thing means, it becomes hateful to me.[5]

There must be the question put, as Mansfield said to Woolf of Chekhov's stories;[6] both Woolf and Mansfield invite the reader to speculate about the luminous details in their fiction, but their texts resist definitive readings as Chekhov's do. For both writers it is the de-

2. T. S. Eliot, *The Waste Land*, 1922; Virginia Woolf, *To the Lighthouse*, 1927 [*Editor*].
3. Ezra Pound (1885–1972), American poet and critic. In the *New Age* 7 December 1911: 130, Pound wrote, "the artist seeks out the luminous detail and presents it. He does not comment." [*Editor*].
4. *The Katherine Mansfield Notebooks*, vol. 2, p. 267.
5. *The Letters of Virginia Woolf*, ed. Nigel Nicholson and Joanne Troutmann (London: Chatto & Windus, 1980–83), vol. 3, p. 385.
6. *Collected Letters*, vol. 2, p. 320 [*Editor*].

sign of the novel or story which is crucial rather than plot or character.

Mansfield enacts in their form the disruption that is often the oblique focus of the stories. They frequently open abruptly, plunging readers into a situation about which they know nothing, * * * their urgency intensified by the use of the present tense. Even more disconcertingly, stories sometimes begin apparently in the middle of a sentence, with a conjunction, as if the reader is coming in on a conversation. * * * Beneath the sharply observed detail and the shimmering grace of the prose there is constant pressure on readers to be more alert to the nuances of what they encounter. 'The Daughters of the Late Colonel' is one of what are sometimes called the 'twelve-cell' stories, meaning that the parts are organically connected, 'multi-cellular like living tissue'.[7] A logical reader might expect the separate parts to shift in time, or to focus on different characters, and the openings to the sections seem to indicate this. The second part begins 'Another thing which complicated matters', but there is no indication of what the first thing was. Sections begin 'But, after all', 'Well, at any rate', 'But at that moment', as if the reader is inhabiting the sisters' fuzzy debate that is never articulated. The sister's inability to name what has happened is implied in the first sentence: 'The week after was one of the busiest weeks of their lives'. After what? 'On the morning—well, on the last morning' is as close as we get to an answer, though we understand that the event is the death of the colonel. The title implies the daughters' subordination, as they are seen exclusively in relation to their father; they may be unable to think clearly because they are overcome with grief, but the comic disjunctions in the story hint at something else. * * *

* * *

* * * Mansfield herself, in some of her plans for volumes of her stories, thought of alternating New Zealand and European stories though she did not carry this out. Though the stories set in Europe often focus on lonely, displaced women, many of the New Zealand stories give a different twist to a similar theme, in that their characters suddenly feel themselves to be in danger where they thought they were safest, in the supposedly known world of home. The moment of insecurity and terror is caught in sharply defined clarity, often through an object which gains symbolic significance such as Laura's hat, Linda's wallpaper, the window of the washhouse, or the aloe.

Disruption is as characteristic of Mansfield's European stories as

7. See Ian Gordon, ed., *Undiscovered Country: The New Zealand Stories of Katherine Mansfield* (London: Longman, 1974), p. xix.

of her New Zealand ones. The opening paragraph of 'The Man Without a Temperament' enacts through the rhythm of its sentences the action of its protagonist: 'He pursed his lips—he might have been going to whistle—but he did not whistle—only turned the ring—turned the ring on his pink, freshly washed hands'. The reader hears, rhythmically, the ring being turned through the punctuation of the passage; part of the pared-down quality of Mansfield's prose is the crafting of the lines. She said of rhythm: 'In Miss Brill I chose not only the length of every sentence, but even the sound of every sentence—I chose the rise and fall of every paragraph to fit her . . . After Id written it I read it aloud—numbers of times—just as one would *play over* a musical composition.'[8] The man's consciousness is never revealed by his speech, but by unexplained disjunctions in the text that are signalled by an ellipsis and a line space:

> On the hedges on the other side of the road there were grapes small as berries, growing wild, growing among the stones. He leaned against a wall, filled his pipe, put a match to it. . . .
>
> Leaned across a gate, turned up the collar of his mackintosh. It was going to rain. It didn't matter, he was prepared for it. You didn't expect anything else in November. He looked over the bare field.

The reader experiences the disruption, and realizes that the man who is dutifully caring for his invalid wife is in-between, in that he is imagining himself to be far from the Provençal countryside, and at home in England; if he were portrayed only through his speech and behaviour he could seem a conventionally patriarchal figure. A portfolio of pictures of him emerges from the story apart from the privileged insight into his consciousness: some guests see him as an ox rather than a man, some are contemptuous of him, to the staff he is autocratic, to his wife he is 'bread and wine', to three little local girls he seems a potential child molester. The question about him is posed but not answered by the story; its final line, with its 'penetrating, punning bitterness',[9] is ' "Rot!" he whispers'. He may be dismissing her anxieties as he tucks her in, he may be longing for her to decay, he may be describing how he feels about his own situation; the reader can only speculate. The story is sharply etched but not tidily wrapped up with a narrative twist that provides a conclusive ending.

The man is aware of the stranger within, but represses his yearning for that otherness and mimics a model husband, Mansfield's

8. *Collected Letters*, vol. 4, p. 165.
9. *Collected Letters*, vol. 3, p. xi.

youthful experience of the empire city's mimicry of the metropolitan centre, and of its repression of guilt, prepared her to recognize the potential of experimental Modernism for her own fiction: she quickly registered how she could adapt a Fauvist[1] aesthetic to her writing, by paring down her stories to luminous detail and cogent design in order to put a question. * * *

ANGELA SMITH

[Capture and Imagination]†

* * * 'How Pearl Button was kidnapped' was written in 1910 and published in *Rhythm* in 1912 under the pseudonym Lili Heron; 'The Doll's House' was first published in the *Athenaeum* in 1922. In both stories the protagonist, a little girl, swings on the gate; both children are transgressive, in that they want either to get out of the world for which the gate is a demarcation line, or to admit outsiders to the well-regulated inside world. In the early story the alternatives are posed quite simply but surprisingly for the period. What makes it interesting is that the perspective is the child's, and she does not categorize as an adult would. The expectations raised by the title are not fulfilled; there is no tension in the story, the reader is not invited to hope that the child will be rescued, but it is not either a narrative of the 'Off with the wraggle-taggle gypsies' kind. The title gives an adult perspective on the events, but since the child enjoys the adventure, she does not perceive what happens as kidnapping.

Pearl Button thinks of her home as 'the House of Boxes'. The phrase is never explained, but the reader gains some clues as to what it means: when Pearl is asked where her mother is, she replies that she is in the kitchen 'ironing-because-its-Tuesday'. She is frightened by the beach but there 'were some little houses down close to the sea, with wood fences round them and gardens inside. They comforted her'. A constraining boundary, with nature under control, is what she is familiar with. Eventually she asks the women who have 'kidnapped' her: 'Haven't you got any Houses of Boxes? . . . Don't you all live in a row? Don't the men go to offices? Aren't there any nasty things?' When she is frightened she craves for the familiar order of bourgeois life, but increasingly she enjoys disorder: eating a peach and letting the juice run over her clothes and

1. From "fauve," a word for "wild beast," used of an emotionally charged style of painting at the beginning of the twentieth century that used strong, non-naturalistic colors [*Editor*].

† From *Katherine Mansfield: A Literary Life* (London: Palgrave, 2000), pp. 40–45. Reprinted by permission of Palgrave Macmillan.

being kissed and cuddled by the two maternal women. The reader gradually realizes who the kidnappers are, but since race does not matter to Pearl she does not perceive it. The men wear 'feather mats round their shoulders', one of the women is wearing a tiki, a greenstone amulet, and they live and travel in community groups; Pearl sees their difference but not that they are Maoris. The pivotal moment in the story comes when they reach the sea; Pearl is terrified of it but the Maoris coax her into it. * * * At the moment that she begins to paddle she is released into a wider life, in which she can express herself spontaneously; the text's short sentences enact the infant consciousness, using objects, like a cup, which she is familiar with from the House of Boxes, modulating into a narratorial voice with the observation of the child's thin arms:

> She paddled in the shallow water. It was warm. She made a cup of her hands and caught some of it. But it stopped being blue in her hands. She was so excited that she rushed over to her woman and flung her little thin arms round the woman's neck, hugging her, kissing . . .

At this point the transience of the natural world, which excites her with its novelty by changing colour as she looks at it, is replaced by much more substantial 'Little men in blue coats—little blue men' who have come 'to carry her back to the House of Boxes'. Her perception, and so the reader's, is that the prison-house is closing on her again, and that the uniformed men are jailers rather than liberators. * * *

The doll's house in the second story has in some ways the same connotations as the House of Boxes. The children's excitement when the doll's house arrives seems depressingly incestuous. They appear, in gazing at the verisimilitude of the house, to be looking in at their own lives, especially when they see the 'father and mother dolls, who sprawled very stiff as though they had fainted in the drawing-room'. The reader has already been given a sense of the stiffness of the adults in the supercilious and falsely effusive tone of the opening paragraph: 'For, really, the smell of paint coming from that doll's house ("Sweet of old Mrs Hay, of course: most sweet and generous!")—but the smell of paint was quite enough to make anyone seriously ill'. Mansfield's mimicry is in evidence here; it is obvious where the many exaggerated stresses must fall. But one child perceives what the others do not notice, 'an exquisite little amber lamp' which 'seemed to smile at Kezia, to say, "I live here" '. This is the side of domestic life that counters the sprawling dolls; there is snobbery in the house but there is also light and warmth. In other stories about the Burnells the lamp is a signifier of understanding between women and girls: Kezia's grandmother in 'Prelude' asks her if she can ' "trust you to carry the lamp?" "Yes, my granma." The old woman bent down and gave the bright breathing thing into her hands'.

The fact that Kezia's sisters have not noticed the lamp indicates their priorities. They identify with the sneer evident in Aunt Beryl's attitude to old Mrs Hay, and their particular victims are the two little Kelvey girls:

> They were the daughters of a spry, hard-working little washerwoman, who went about from house to house by the day. This was awful enough. But where was Mr Kelvey? Nobody knew for certain. But everybody said he was in prison. So they were the daughters of a washerwoman and a gaolbird. Very nice company for other people's children!

The mimicry is subtle here, beginning with a mildly sympathetic description of Mrs Kelvey, if Mrs she be, a possibility too shocking to contemplate, though it is an underlying question. The passage then shifts its narrative perspective to local gossip, showing how snobbish guesses quickly become accepted until the false logic culminates in the justification for ostracizing the little Kelveys; it is done with deft concision. The evocation of our Else is even more concise; she is 'a tiny wishbone of a child', a visual description which also conveys Else's yearning. Her name suggests that she is doomed to be the other, the someone else, of polite society. After the little Kelveys have been publicly humiliated in the playground, the other children experience a quasi-sexual pleasure in it: 'the little girls rushed away in a body, deeply, deeply excited, wild with joy'. Their pleasure resembles Beryl's, at the end of the story, when, having been intimidated by a lover, 'she had frightened those little rats of Kelveys and given Kezia a good scolding'. This releases her tension: 'That ghastly pressure was gone. She went back to the house humming'. The implication is that social and sexual scoring are closely aligned.

When the Burnell children return home from school after the playground episode, Kezia's two sisters, 'who liked visitors', enter the house but Kezia stays outside, on the gate, between the family and the Kelveys. Her potential for transgression is implied in the use of 'thieved':

> But Kezia thieved out at the back. Nobody was about; she began to swing on the big white gates of the courtyard . . . Kezia stopped swinging. She slipped off the gate as if she was going to run away. Then she hesitated. The Kelveys came nearer, and beside them walked their shadows, very long, stretching right

> across the road with their heads in the buttercups. Kezia clambered back on the gate; she had made up her mind; she swung out.

Kezia is tempted to avoid the encounter but is prevented by the Kelvey's shadows, as if she recognizes in them the shadowy version of themselves that always accompanies the two little girls: the malicious gossip about their parents and background. When Kezia swings out she is opening both the doll's house and her own world to the two dispossessed children, though she remains in control, as her sisters did when their visitors came in groups of two to see the doll's house. Bourgeois life continues to be a spectacle to be admired and envied, but Else notices what Kezia likes best. When she and her sister have been routed by Beryl, she rests beside her sister, stroking the quill on her sister's hat, and says 'I seen the little lamp'. The lamp, as in 'Prelude', seems to represent a perception and domestic warmth that women and girls can, but do not necessarily, share. The final isolated line of the story implies that the momentary rapport cannot affect social barriers for Lil and Else: 'Then both were silent once more'.

'How Pearl Button was Kidnapped' was written at the beginning of Mansfield's professional life; * * * Pearl's temporary escape from the House of Boxes leads the reader into a recognition of Maori entrapment. The narrative prioritizes Pearl's predicament as it uses her perspective, but the unanswered question about what happens to the Maori kidnappers remains. Neither is there any indication of why they take the child; the narrative method reveals the pakeha assumption that the settler's interests are paramount, and it enacts the taint of the pioneer in its apparent indifference to the fate of the Maoris. 'The Doll's House' was one of the last stories Mansfield wrote. * * * Its child on the gate is a much more complex mixture of responses and initiatives than Pearl Button; the narrative method has 'that strange, perpetual weaving and unweaving' of the self that Pater[1] describes. Its construction of a colonial situation is ambivalent. The colony has been tainted by the social hierarchies of the metropolitan centre, but the lamp remains as a bond between Kezia and her apparent other, Else. Mansfield's encounter with European art and writing enables her to hone her technique and realize that 'a young country is a real heritage, though it takes one time to recognise it. But New Zealand is in my very bones.'[2]

1. Walter Pater, "Conclusion" to *The Renaissance: Studies in Art and Poetry*, 1873 (London: Macmillan, 1910), p. 236 [*Editor*].
2. *The Letters of Katherine Mansfield* (1928), vol. 2, p. 199.

LINDA GRANT

[The German Stories]†

A young woman sits in the garden of a German pension in the first decade of the last century trying to write a poem. Dissatisfied with her imagery she eavesdrops on a pair of lovers (a student from Bonn and the sister of a baroness), hoping she will hear something she can filch. The student, she understands, must do his utmost to woo the high-born lady: 'He had hitherto relied upon three scars and a ribbon to produce an effect, but the sister of a baroness demanded more than these.' The young poetess has high hopes. A pair of hands, she hears, is like 'white lilies lying on the pool of your black dress.' This sounds promising. Next, the prospect of a kiss is raised, but must be dismissed: ' ". . . you know I am suffering from severe nasal catarrh, and I dare not risk giving it to you. Sixteen times last night did I count myself sneezing. And three different handkerchiefs." ' Even worse, over the page we find a case of mistaken identity: the lady in question is the baroness' dressmaker.

Katherine Mansfield's was one of the first modern voices. She breezes over to Europe from her birthplace, New Zealand, and lets fresh air into rooms from which the aroma rises of camphor, tea, sausage, dusty flowers, stale eau de Cologne. The stories that follow under the title *In a German Pension* were the first she published, in 1911. She wrote them while recuperating in Germany, apparently after a miscarriage and a short, violent marriage. Some are first-person satirical studies of her fellow-guests in a boarding house, others walk through the town and into the bedrooms of the houses, eavesdropping on childbirth, an attempted rape, a child smothering another child. Stifled lives, close, overheated rooms. What would chill them was the coming war. In Mansfield's stories the Germans and the English bicker over their cultural superiority. The correct method of making a pot of tea provokes a row that threatens to boil over.

Mansfield was funny, as her contemporaries D. H. Lawrence and Virginia Woolf were not: in 'Frau Fischer' the narrator is forced to invent a seafaring husband to avoid the enquiries of her fellow-guests about her personal situation; her creation becomes so fanciful that the more she embroiders, the more her credulous enquirer believes her: 'This husband that I had created for the benefit of Frau Fischer became in her hands so substantial a figure that I could no longer see myself sitting on a rock with seaweed in my

† From "Foreword," *In a German Pension* (London: Hesperus, 2003), pp. vii–x.

hair, awaiting that phantom ship for which all women love to suppose they hunger. Rather I saw myself pushing a perambulator up the gangway and counting up the missing buttons on my husband's uniform jacket . . . I decided to wreck my virgin conception and send him down somewhere off Cape Horn.'

She seems to specialise in found speech, * * * and records it with a young woman's glee, and I'm reminded of Jane Austen, but the narrator's precarious position in this world makes her more like the Jean Rhys[1] who wrote of women who sit in a room waiting for a cheque from a lover so they can buy a dress to enable them to go to a restaurant and find another lover. Between marriage and prostitution there are limited opportunities for those without a trust fund. Mansfield's stories are full of these women of the early years of the century, teetering between domination by their menfolk and the first tentative steps towards independence. In 'The Advanced Lady' a woman in a white gown and her hair loose * * * amazes the fellow-guests with the announcement that she is writing a book: ' "Yes, it is a novel—upon the Modern Woman. For this seems to me the woman's hour." ' It was and it wasn't. Mansfield was writing during the suffragette period. If women could not even vote what hope was there for personal liberation? Her female characters are, in turns, vapid, vain, pompous, timid, but above all bourgeois. Suffering occurs behind closed doors, out of sight, as sexually ignorant new wives submit in terror to the brutal advances of bridegrooms, and a mother gives birth in an upstairs room while below her husband has a neurotic moment and imagines he has suffered.

Who and what is a woman to be? asks Viola in 'The Swing of the Pendulum'. Sitting in her room in the German pension, without the money for the rent, she weighs her options. Her suitor, Casimir, and his future promise as a dull, serious and unsuccessful husband? Independence? Doesn't want it; she feels herself to have been born for 'ease and any amount of nursing in the lap of luxury'. The life of a great courtesan? She doesn't know how to go about it. Then a knock at the door, an attractive stranger, 'he looked as though he could order a magnificent dinner . . . How hungry she had been for the nearness of someone like that—who knew nothing at all about her—and made no demands—but just lived.' There are hungers and there are appetites. The stranger finds a woman alone in a room, flirtatious, unprotected, and 'slipped one arm round her body, and drew her towards him—like a bar of iron across her back—that arm.'

In a later short story ('Bliss', published after the war), Mansfield

1. Jean Rhys (1890–1979), novelist and short-story writer best known for *Wide Sargasso Sea* (1966), which tells the history of Bertha Mason, previously known to readers only as the mad, incarcerated wife in Charlotte Brontë's *Jane Eyre* (1847) [*Editor*].

would ask: 'What can you do if you are thirty and, turning the corner of your own street, you are overcome, suddenly, by a feeling of bliss—absolute bliss!—as though you'd suddenly swallowed a bright piece of that late afternoon sun and it burned in your bosom, sending out a little shower of sparks into every particle, into every finger and toe? . . .'

The girl in the pension longed for bliss; she was offered sauerkraut or rape. The assault on both was to be Mansfield's (too short) life's work.

Selected Bibliography

• indicates works included or excerpted in this Norton Critical Edition.

WORKS BY KATHERINE MANSFIELD

In A German Pension. London, 1911.

Bliss and Other Stories. London, 1920.

The Garden Party and Other Stories. London, 1922.

The Doves' Nest and Other Stories, edited by J. Middleton Murry. London, 1923.

Something Childish and Other Stories, edited by J. Middleton Murry. London, 1924.

The Stories of Katherine Mansfield, edited by Antony Alpers. Oxford, 1984.

The Letters of Katherine Mansfield, 2 vols., edited by J. Middleton Murry. London, 1928.

Novels and Novelists, edited by John Middleton Murry. London, 1930.

Katherine Mansfield's Letters to John Middleton Murry 1913–1922, edited by J. Middleton Murry. London, 1951.

Journal of Katherine Mansfield, edited by J. Middleton Murry. London, 1954.

The Urewera Notebook, edited by Ian A. Gordon. Auckland, 1978.

The Collected Letters of Katherine Mansfield, edited by Vincent O'Sullivan and Margaret Scott. Oxford, vol. 1, 1984; vol. 2, 1987; vol. 3, 1993; vol. 4, 1996.

Katherine Mansfield Selected Letters, edited by Vincent O'Sullivan. Oxford, 1989.

The Katherine Mansfield Notebooks, edited by Margaret Scott. Wellington, 1997; Minneapolis, 2002.

BOOKS

Alpers, Antony. *The Life of Katherine Mansfield*. London, 1982.

Berkman, Sylvia. *Katherine Mansfield: A Critical Study*. New Haven, 1951.

Boddy, Gill. *Katherine Mansfield: The Woman and the Writer*. Harmondsworth, 1988.

Burgan, Mary. *Illness, Gender, and Writing*. London, 1994.

Daly, Saralyn R. *Katherine Mansfield*. New York, 1965.

• Dunbar, Pamela. *Radical Mansfield: Double Discourse in Katherine Mansfield's Short Stories*. London, 1997.

• Eliot, T. S. *After Strange Gods*. London, 1934.

• Fullbrook, Kate. *Katherine Mansfield*. Brighton, 1986.

Gordon, Ian A. *Katherine Mansfield*. London, 1954.

• Hanson, Clare, and Andrew Gurr. *Katherine Mansfield*. London, 1981.

Hollington, Michael. *Selected Stories* [readings of]. Paris, 1997.

• Kaplan, Sydney Janet. *Katherine Mansfield and the Origins of Modernist Fiction*. Ithaca and London, 1991.

Kirkpatrick, B. J. *A Bibliography of Katherine Mansfield*. Oxford, 1989.

Kobler, J. F. *Katherine Mansfield: A Study of the Short Fiction*. Boston, 1990.

Margalaner, Marvin. *The Fiction of Katherine Mansfield*. Carbondale, 1971.

Meyers, Jeffrey. *Katherine Mansfield, A Biography*. London, 1978.

Michel, Paulette, and Michel Depuis, eds. *The Fine Instrument*. Aarhus, Denmark, 1989. (A collection of perceptive critical essays.)

Murray, Heather. *Double Lives: Women in the Stories of Katherine Mansfield*. Dunedin, 1990.

• New, W. H. *Reading Mansfield and Metaphors of Form*. Montreal and London, 1999.

• O'Connor, Frank. *The Lonely Voice: A Study of the Short Story*. London, 1963.

Pilditch, Jan, ed. *The Critical Response to Katherine Mansfield*. Westport, 1996.

Robinson, Roger, ed. *Katherine Mansfield: In From the Margin*. Baton Rouge, 1994. (An important collection of centennial essays.)

Smith, Angela. *Katherine Mansfield and Virginia Woolf: A Public of Two*. Oxford, 1999.
• ———. *Katherine Mansfield: A Literary Life*. London, 2000.
Tomalin, Claire. *Katherine Mansfield: A Secret Life*. London, 1987.
Van Gunsteren, Julia. *Katherine Mansfield and Literary Impressionism*. Atlanta, 1990.
Woods, Joanna. *Katerina, the Russian World of Katherine Mansfield*. Auckland, 2001.

ARTICLES

• Aiken, Conrad. Review of *Bliss*, by Katherine Mansfield. *Freeman*, 21 June 1922, 357.
• Bateson, F. W., and B. Shahevitch. "Katherine Mansfield's 'The Fly': A Critical Exercise." *Essays in Criticism* (Jan. 1962): 39–53.
Blodgett, Harriet. "The Invisible Self: Reappraising Katherine Mansfield's Women." *New Renaissance* 5.3 (Fall 1983): 104–12.
• Bowen, Elizabeth. "A Living Writer." *Cornhill Magazine* 1010 (Winter 1956–57): 120–30.
Brophy, Bridget. "Katherine Mansfield." In *Don't Never Forget*. London, pp. 256–57.
Carter, Angela. "The Life of Katherine Mansfield." In *Nothing Sacred*. London, 1982, pp. 158–61.
Daiches, David. "Katherine Mansfield and the Search for Truth." *The Novel and the Modern World*. Chicago, 1939, pp. 65–79.
Garver, L. "The Political Katherine Mansfield." *MODERNISM/modernity* 8 (2001): 225–43.
• Grant, Linda. "Foreword." In *In a German Pension*. London, 2003.
Kaplan, Sydney Janet. "Katherine Mansfield's 'Passion for Technique.'" In *Women's Language and Style*, edited by Douglas Butturff and Edmund L. Epstein. Akron, 1978, pp. 119–31.
Meisel, P. "What the Reader Knows, or The French One." In *Katherine Mansfield: In From the Margin*. edited by Roger Robinson. Baton Rouge, 1994, pp. 112–18.
Mitchell, J. Lawrence. "Katherine Mansfield and the Aesthetic Object." In *Journal of New Zealand Literature* 22 (2004): 31–54.
Neaman, Judith. "Allusion, Image, and Associative Pattern: The Answers in Mansfield's 'Bliss.'" *Twentieth Century Literature* 32.2 (Summer 1986): 242–54.
Orr, Bridget. "Reading with the Taint of the Pioneer: Katherine Mansfield and Settler Criticism." *Landfall* 43–44 (December 1989): 447–61.
• O'Sullivan, Vincent. "Introduction." In *The New Zealand Stories of Katherine Mansfield*, edited by Vincent O'Sullivan. Melbourne, 1997, 1–14.
Parkin-Gounelas, Ruth. "Katherine Mansfield Reading Other Women: The Personality of the Text." In *In From the Margin*, edited by Roger Robinson. Baton Rouge, 1994, pp. 36–52.
• Porter, Katherine Anne. "The Art of Katherine Mansfield." *Nation* 145 (23 Oct. 1937): 435.
• Pritchett, V. S. Review of *The Collected Stories of Katherine Mansfield*. *New Statesman*, 2 Feb. 1946, 87.
Sandley, Sarah. "The Middle of the Note: Katherine Mansfield's 'Glimpses.'" In *In From the Margin*, edited by Roger Robinson. Baton Rouge, 1994, pp. 70–89.
• Smith Angela. "Introduction." In *Katherine Mansfield Selected Stories*, edited by Angela Smith. Oxford, 2002.
Stead, C. K. "Katherine Mansfield and the Art of Fiction." *The New Review* 4 (September 1977): 27–36.
• Tomalin, Claire. "Introduction." In *Katherine Mansfield Short Stories*, edited by Claire Tomalin. London, 1983.
• West, Rebecca. Review of *The Garden Party*, by Katherine Mansfield. *New Statesman*, 18 March 1922, 678.
Williams, Mark. "Mansfield in Maoriland: Biculturalism, Agency and Misreading." In *Modernism and Empire*, edited by H. J. Booth and H. Rigby. Manchester, 2000, pp. 249–74.
Zinman, Toby Silverman. "The Snail Under the Leaf: Katherine Mansfield's Imagery." *Modern Fiction Studies* 24 (1978–79): 457–64.